STAR FALLS

THE COMPLETE SERIES

www.chellebliss.com

CHELLE BLISS

USA TODAY BESTSELLING AUTHOR

Publisher © Chelle Bliss 2023 & 2024
Edited by Lisa A. Hollett
Proofread by Read By Rose & Shelley Carlton
Cover Design © Chelle Bliss

www.chellebliss.com
CHELLE BLISS
USA TODAY BESTSELLING AUTHOR

never too SOON

www.chellebliss.com

CHELLE BLISS

USA TODAY BESTSELLING AUTHOR

CHAPTER ONE

I cannot start my day without an extra-large cup of coffee. And on days like today, the only coffee that will do is the stuff made by my sister-in-law, Chloe, at the bookstore next to my tattoo shop.

I crash through the door of the bookstore, expecting to see my brother's wife behind the counter, looking nerdy and precious as she always does in her cargo pants and boots. Instead, I'm smacked with a sight I wish I could unsee.

Tucked into the back pockets of Chloe's tan cargo pants are my brother's hands, and his face is nuzzled into the crook of her neck.

"Shit, Franco." I halfway cover my eyes, keeping a space between two fingers to see, and stalk to the counter. "It's too early for that."

My brother lifts his face from Chloe's neck, his eyes looking love-drunk and his lips looking disgustingly puffy.

I groan again and wave a hand in front of me. "Don't you both have jobs to do instead of groping each other?"

Franco snorts and smooths back his hair. The bastard has the nerve to look smug when I'm the one whose eyeballs are forever sullied.

"Did you see the sign on the door?" He jerks a thumb toward the

3

entrance that I just burst through. "Store emergency. The plumbing is all jacked up. Carpet's wet. The whole nine. Chloe had to close for the day while she waits for a plumber."

Chloe looks at me with a sweet grin. "We're closed to the public, Gracie, but I figured you'd come in for your coffee. That's why I left the door unlocked. You're right on time. I have it ready and waiting."

"I'm going to come behind that counter and smooch your face off. I love you so much right now," I say on a sigh.

Instead, I blow Chloe a kiss and watch as she adjusts her clothes while she runs back into the small kitchen to pour my coffee.

I slap my brother on the shoulder, then rest my elbows on the front counter. "You two are gross. Isn't that shit supposed to end after you get married?"

Franco ruffles my hair. "Jealous much?"

I smack him a second time. He's a jerk.

"So, what the hell happened to the plumbing?"

Franco frowns. "Don't know. Chloe doesn't think it happened here, though. I took a peek when I shut off the water. Might be a building-wide problem. Tree roots breaking the sewer line or maybe one of the other tenants clogged the drains. You guys okay next door?"

I shake my head. "I haven't opened the shop yet. I came here first." This news makes a sucky morning even suckier. "Fuck," I sigh and rake a hand through my hair.

Franco lifts a brow at me. "You're extra salty today. You okay?"

But my eldest brother's right. On top of my normal snark, today, I've got anxiety practically oozing from my pores.

What's going on with me is something I haven't shared with anyone yet. I'm definitely not ready for that at this hour.

Franco has always been the most helicopter brother of the three male Bianchis, but this... If any one of them found out what was going on with me, I'd never hear the end of it.

"Earth to Gracie." Franco cocks his head, studying my face as though he can read my mind.

Thank God that's not a thing. I'd never have a moment's peace if my mother or brothers could see inside my head.

"Just need my coffee," I say dismissively. "I didn't sleep well last night."

"Me either. I was up half the night with Violet." Franco leans across the counter and taps my nose with a finger. "You want to come to our place for dinner tonight? You got plans?"

I shrug. "I'm working until seven. We'll see how I feel. If I can't keep my eyes open, it's better if I go home after work than come over. Or else I might end up sleeping on your couch."

Franco stares at me with a puzzled look on his face, but then Chloe comes back with an extra-large cup of coffee in each hand.

"You looked like you could use a double today," she says sweetly.

I take the cups, lean close, and smooch her on the cheek. "You're the best, sis."

Her face lights up when I call her that. She's loved it since I did it the first time.

I'm juggling the two paper cups when it hits me that someone is missing from the bookstore. "Where's the dog?" I call over my shoulder.

Franco gives Chloe a kiss on the cheek in an annoyingly long goodbye and then walks around the counter. "In my truck," he says. "That's why I'm here. When Chloe got here and discovered the mess, we figured it'd be safer to keep the dog away from the plumber and whatnot. I'm taking her back with me to the shop."

The lightbulb goes on in my brain, despite my lack of caffeine. Now his being at the bookstore in the middle of the day makes perfect sense.

He yanks open the door for me so I don't spill my coffees.

"Give her ear scratches for me," I call after Franco before glancing over my shoulder again. "Thanks, Chloe."

I only have to walk about ten paces to get to the place I work. The Body Shop is the only tattoo shop in Star Falls. It just so happens to have the same name as the only strip club in the county, which has been the source of a lot of jokes over the years. Especially

5

during the short time my brother Vito was married to a dancer with the stage name "Exotic," aka Michelle.

My parents were far from thrilled when I decided to apprentice at a tattoo shop, but I know better than to judge people by what they do for a living, what they drive… All that crap doesn't mean jack shit. Sometimes the choices we make are…the best we can do. Being an adult is damn tough.

I have good parents. I come from an amazing family. But we never had a lot. My brother Vito and I both still live at home, and it's not just because my dad's cooking is to freaking die for. I could go home whenever I wanted a meal. Big Sunday dinners are a requirement for all the Bianchi kids. And now Chloe, too.

I lived alone for a short time and learned a lot of lessons very quickly. I don't like to think too much about that time, but there are days—like today—when all I can think about is what's coming up next. The next doctor's appointment. The next test. The next call to my insurance company about co-pays and approvals.

That's why I didn't give a shit if my brother married a stripper. Michelle was cool, and I think she actually loved my brother. Most people have something about them that you can like if you just give them a chance. Bookseller, stripper… Who cares.

Underneath it all, our hearts are what matter.

I have walked literally two steps from the bookshop, lost deep in my thoughts, when I see a man peering through the still-dark windows of The Body Shop.

"Hey, there. Excuse me. Hi?" I call out as I approach the guy. I look him over, trying to assess why he's looking in the window of a store that's obviously closed.

"Oh, hey. Hello." When he turns around, my stomach does that little flippy thing it does every time I see someone with muscles and a wide, sincere smile.

Ughhhhh.

The man is big and, like, rugby-player muscular. Totally yummy.

I know. I've dated athletes. And with all the bodies my hands have worked on over the years, I can tell gym muscles from muscles that can do miraculous things.

I can see this man has a body that is put through a vigorous regimen.

His thighs are crazy muscled. He's wearing shorts but not suburban dad shorts. These are the shorts of a guy who just rolled off a field someplace after scoring a last-second, game-winning goal. One knee has the etched-looking, well-healed scars from some kind of orthopedic repair. And his arms... He's wearing nothing sexy, just a plain soft blue tee, but the thing must be made of the world's finest cotton. It's stretched over defined pecs that would normally make my mouth water.

But God, those arms...*drool.*

I have to stop myself before I turn into an idiotic puddle of goo. This guy is not *just* my type; he's every stupid stereotype I've ever fallen for in the past.

And, oh, how I've been burned.

As I take him in, he's looking back at me like he's not sure whose turn it is to talk, but if it's his, he might owe me an apology even if he doesn't know why.

"Do you...work here?" he asks, looking from my cups to the shop.

"Sure do," I say. "Here." I thrust both cups of coffee toward him and fumble in my giant silver studded purse for my keys. "You look smart enough to handle this, but just be careful. These are hot," I remind him.

I normally juggle two cups just fine, but if he's a weirdo or a criminal, keeping his hands busy while I open the store feels a lot safer than me having my hands full.

Although the day is clear and sunny, and one scream would no doubt bring Chloe and half of downtown Star Falls running, I refuse to consider that maybe, just maybe, I'm not opposed to the hunky athlete carrying my coffee.

He takes both cups, his lips slightly parted and a confused look on his face.

Wicked cute, this one.

A tangle of brown curls held back from a slightly tanned forehead with a touch of gel. A nice tight shave up the back of his neck. But I stop giving him the once-over and unlock The Body Shop.

Once I return the jangle of keys on my glittery lanyard back to the bottomless pit of my purse, I twist the tablet on the front counter, punch in the security code, and turn up the lights.

"Wow," the guy says, following me in. He scans the cool-gray wallpaper with subtle gold-foil roses, the mid-century-style oak furniture, and the pops of green from a few thriving potted plants. "This is not what I expected of a tattoo shop."

My words come out along with a ferocious glare before I can stop them. "What did you expect? Sweat-stained couches and cracked poster frames with sheets of generic flash? We don't cater to frat boys here." Before he can answer, I give him a look and hold up a finger. "I need to check something. You can set those on the counter."

I walk through a bifold door, planning to secure my purse at my station, when I feel a slosh of water under my boot.

"Fuck. No," I groan. Ahead of me, the floor surrounding the six tattoo stations is flooded. Water at least an inch deep in spots pools around the bays. The floor back here is easy-to-clean strip flooring in a natural honey shade that complements the classic and calming decor. And it's freaking soaked.

My curses echo through the store, and in a heartbeat, I hear the guy from up front push open the bifold door.

"Are you okay?" he asks.

I throw him a dirty look. He's still holding the cups of coffee, but now his sneakers are soaking up who knows what this is.

He looks down at his feet, then back at me, then looks at the cups in his hands.

"Get back," I tell him, careful not to slip as I step through the water. I wave at him to go back up front.

Thankfully, the lobby floor is still dry.

My customer's expensive-looking sneakers squeak as he sets the coffees on the counter. "Do you know where the water shutoff is? I might be able to help."

But I'm too busy digging in my purse for my cell phone to think

straight. "I'm calling the building owner," I tell him, panic edging my voice.

"Can I look?" he asks, nodding toward the back room.

I shrug as I pull up the contact for the management company.

The second the voice mail picks up, I start hollering about water flooding the store. I drop as many colorful adjectives and curse words as I possibly can before hanging up.

I dig through my purse for the keys and lock the front door so no one else can walk in on this mess.

When I head into the back room, Mr. Rugby is on his hands and knees. He has taken a pair of black nitrile gloves from someone's station. He's wearing them on his hands as he blots up the water from the floor with a stack of our black shop towels.

"Oh my God," I gasp. "What are you doing?"

He's looking calm, cool, and very confident for a guy who's probably soaked to his ankles in sewage.

He gives me the thumbs-up with a very wet black glove and does this half-push-up, half-lunge-like move to get from his knees to his feet.

"Shit," he grumbles, and I hear his knee audibly pop as he stands. "Should've taken that a little slower."

"You shouldn't have done any of this," I wave my hand at his cleanup efforts, "at all. You could get sick from crawling around in dirty water."

I'm starting to straight-up panic. Our equipment is sterile. Our workplace meticulously cleaned. We book tattoos by appointment only, and we have more than sufficient time to keep The Body Shop to the highest standards.

Now, the whole place has had a shit wash and has to be sanitized.

I crumple down into the chair at my station, the bottom of my boots submerged in the water. "Holy fuck," I gasp. The reality of the situation is fully hitting me now.

"The news isn't that bad," my knight in shining nitrile gloves says.

He bounces on his squeaky shoes, all smiles and reassurances.

He's got the energy of a golden retriever and the deep brown eyes of a heartthrob.

"I think you have an issue with your water inlet valve," he says. "Come look."

I arch a brow at him and shake my head. "What in the fuck is that?"

"Come on," he urges. "I promise. This isn't sewage water or anything like that. If it were, you'd definitely smell it. I'm pretty sure you have an issue with the washing machine. I'll show you."

I throw him a look because if he's planning to murder me or pull anything dodgy, I want him to know I'm not going down without a fight. But I take my life in my hands because we do, after all, have security cameras and follow him to the back of the store. We have two bathrooms—one we reserve for customers and one marked *Employees Only*.

The employee bathroom is huge. At the back is a washer and dryer where we clean and dry the shop towels right here on the premises.

"I shut off the water to the toilets and sinks in both bathrooms, but I'm pretty sure that valve back here is the problem." He's pointing at the colored handles and twisty knobs with hoses installed in the wall behind the washing machine and dryer. I'm sure he thinks I understand, but my mind is a mess.

The shop is flooded.

We have a schedule full of appointments today. Clients who might already be waiting at the front door.

It might be our fault that the bookshop flooded.

Shit.

Or it might be some other tenant's fault, which means there will be arguments with the property owner, cleanup, and a whole lot of headaches we don't need.

And worst of all, I haven't even had my coffee yet.

"So, you'll definitely need a plumber," he finishes, as I realize I haven't been listening to any of what he explained. "But I think this is just tap water. Not sewage. A couple of towels and a mop, you'll be back in business."

I know there is no way this could be that easy, but somehow his cheerfulness makes it hard to keep frowning. "You drink coffee?" I ask.

He looks at me curiously.

"Cream and sugar?"

When he gives the cutest little nod, looking so adorably trusting, I head to the front of the shop, grab one of my extra-larges, and walk back to where he's standing. I offer one to my hero and drop down in my chair. "Have a seat," I say. "And drink up. You deserve it."

CHAPTER TWO

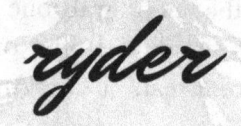

The spitfire flailing her arms while she tells the owner of the building about the flooding has me biting back a grin.

But I shouldn't even be here. I don't know what drove me to stop in front of a tattoo shop, of all places, today.

Well, that's not true. I know why I came here, and I know why I came *today*.

But I never once imagined that I'd actually go inside. Being dragged in and force-fed coffee by a woman with raven-black hair is the last thing I imagined when I decided to get a tattoo.

"No," the woman snaps into the phone. She's finished a full cup of coffee and seems to be calming. "Echo wasn't on the schedule until three today, when I am scheduled for my first client. I'm here alone right now." She looks at me as she says that but then raises a dramatic brow. "Not alone-alone," she corrects. "The customer who shut off the water is here."

She paces the lobby until she finishes her conversation.

"All right. All right. I know, I know. I will. Bye." Finally, she hangs up the phone and jams the device into the rear pocket of shredded black jeans, then she turns those startling gray eyes on me.

"So," she says, "I've got to close the shop. This is going to take some time to clean and investigate. I need to call my appointments and get things canceled. It's going to be a clusterfuck in here."

I understand without her saying it. She's asking me to leave. I take another sip of the coffee and nod. "Understood," I say. I start walking to the door, but the squeak of my drenched shoes is so loud, I begin to laugh.

"Your shoes." She scurries around the counter and grabs my arm.

I look down at her, at the softness of her skin on mine. Heat pools in my gut as she quickly pulls her hand away.

"I...uh. I should replace your shoes," she says, her words tumbling out in a rush. "I'm so sorry. They got ruined just because you were trying to do a good thing."

I shake my head. "Nah. Not a problem. Both these shoes and I have been through much worse. They'll dry." I lift the cup in mock salute. "Consider us even. Really good coffee. Best I've had in Star Falls yet."

She smiles, and the action softens her considerably.

She's got jet-black hair that doesn't look dyed. It's glossy and cut in long layers that frame her face. She's wearing a loose-fitting tank top with a skull made out of roses on it and a tighter tank underneath. It's hard not to notice the cleavage that seems to want to be anywhere but hidden. Her arms and the backs of her hands are covered in tattoos. She looks and sounds scary as hell, but up close, when she smiles, she's pure sugar.

"My brother's wife," she explains, hooking a thumb over her shoulder. "Next door. They make the best coffee in town. And peanut butter crisps. But you got to get there early because they sell out fast."

I nod in thanks. "I'm an early riser," I tell her, not sure why I'm offering so much personal information to a total stranger. "I'll have to try them someday."

I give her a smile, but something stops me from grabbing the door handle. I should go. I mean, I *should* just leave. What I came here for is something I definitely don't need. Hell, I'm not even sure I want a tattoo. But I'm here now and have a few more hours to myself. I can afford to linger. Even if it is just to talk to a beautiful woman for a couple more minutes.

It's been so long...

And with this woman, it feels easy. Way too easy.

The way she's looking at me feels like she's thinking about saying more too. With just a lift of one of those perfectly shaped brows, she's expressive and thoughtful. I'd always know where I stood with a woman like this, and that feeling intrigues me.

"Did you have an appointment?" she asks, sounding both a little confused and a little suspicious.

"No," I admit. "No appointment."

"But you came here for a tattoo?" she presses.

Her gaze skating over my body is as sensuous as a caress. My skin heats under her appraisal.

"Yeah..." I laugh awkwardly. "I did want a tattoo. I still do, maybe? I thought I'd come in, look at a few pictures, get ignored by some hipster at the front desk, and feel ashamed enough of myself to never think about getting a tattoo again."

"Why would you be ashamed?" she asks again with that brow.

I consider her question, and I debate being honest. I'd actually prepared an answer just in case anyone did ask me what I was doing here. It felt better having something prepared so I wouldn't be surprised into giving anyone the whole truth. At least, not before I am ready.

I hold up my arms, the last dregs of the coffee sloshing in the cup I'm still holding. "I'm a virgin," I admit. "Blank canvas. Clean slate. I have no clue what I'm doing."

She softens even more, and if it's possible, she grows even more gorgeous. Her eyes are an inviting gray, like the soothing, welcoming gray of the wallpaper. She has heavy wings of eyeliner that accentuate the shape of her eyes and the stark black peaks of her brows. She's beautiful and unlike anyone I've ever known.

"Does anybody?" she asks. Her words are serious, and somehow the sincerity in them makes my heart rate speed up.

There was a time when I thought I had all the answers. A time

when every moment of my life was scheduled and full and happy and safe.

Until it wasn't and nothing made any sense.

I know I'm not the only one who's lost a hell of a lot at far too young an age. But every battle is different. And what I've learned over the last couple of years is that no playbook can prepare you for every possibility. Foul balls, penalties, injuries, and illness...

All of that is the chaos of life.

The cost of being alive.

I'm guessing by her reaction that this woman's bright colors mask a darkness underneath. No, scratch that. It's not darkness. There's wisdom behind those gray eyes. Maybe the same kind of weariness that I recognize in myself.

"You got that right," I say, shaking my head. "One day you think you're going to get your first tattoo, and the next thing you know, the only new colors in your life are the water stains on your sneakers."

Her mouth falls open, and both brows get moving. I hold up a hand before she can insist on replacing my trainers again. "Kidding," I tell her. "Humor. It's a coping mechanism. No harm done."

I take a step closer to the door.

She smiles then. Her teeth are white, her lips full and perfectly painted on with dark red lipstick.

I've never kissed anyone who wore lipstick like that.

Even on our wedding day, Elizabeth went for the natural look. She was always beautiful in my eyes.

My life is no longer that of a happily married man, father, and coach.

I'm a widower.

A struggling single dad.

And I'm about to start a new job in a new town miles from my old support system.

Miles from the memories.

This place is supposed to be my new horizon.

But I'm in a tattoo shop, holding an empty coffee cup, and my feet are soaking wet.

Hardly the bright new start I expected when I moved here. Something I thought Elizabeth would want for me as much as I want it for myself.

The tattoo artist has her eyes narrowed and her chin lifted. Her plush lips are pressed together as if she's trying to figure out what to say next. I spare her the effort.

"Best of luck with your plumbing. And thanks again for the coffee." I reach to open the door, but she's locked the dead bolt from inside.

She has the keys around her neck, the tangle of brass and silver dangling between her breasts as she leans past me, selects the right key, and unlocks the door.

As she steps back, I smell her hair and the sweet fragrance of coffee as she exhales. I don't know what I expected a tattoo artist to smell like, but the scent that fills my nose is soft and gentle. Like I'm in a luxury spa or a salon. Elizabeth never used fancy products in her hair. Nothing that could drag me in, seduce me, and envelop me in a soft cloud that promised to carry me away from everything real and hard.

"Hi, hey." A very tall, curvy redhead with a distinctive retro-looking haircut comes hustling up the block on open toe wedge heels. She's exactly the sort of woman you'd expect to see at a tattoo shop. "Are you a customer? I'm sorry I was running late."

I nod. "Right place, wrong time. I'm just heading out. I think things are under control in there."

"Thank you," she says. "Did Gracie get your number? Can we reschedule you? If you decide to get a tattoo, I'll work out a discount with whatever artist you choose."

I commit her name to memory. *Gracie.*

I would have loved an excuse to give her my number, but I'm not even sure I want a tattoo. What I would love is the chance to see her again, though.

"You have a lot going on. I'll stop back sometime when the shop's open. Thanks for the offer."

"Romy, I called the building..." Gracie starts talking with the woman. They close and lock the door behind me, and I stand on the street outside, fighting the urge to look behind me.

I shove aside the thought, spot a trash bin, and toss the empty coffee cup inside. I check the time on my phone and stalk toward my SUV.

This afternoon was a nice distraction. I discovered a great coffee place, explored something on my bucket list, and killed a few hours while my kids spent their first day at their new daycare. Now it's time to put Gracie out of my mind and get back to reality.

Bright Start Daycare Center is anything but. When I arrive at 2:30, a half an hour early for afternoon pickup, I hear my daughter Cora's distinctive wail from the parking lot. I haul ass to the front door of the red brick building, careful not to slide inside my still-wet sneakers.

"Miss Thompson?" I holler into the security camera mounted over the front door. "It's Ryder Cooper."

A frazzled-looking college-aged girl unlocks the door and waves me in. "Hi, Mr. Cooper," she says, wiping loose strands of hair back into her messy ponytail. "Cora hasn't had the best day."

"I hear." I try not to take out my frustrations on this kid because she's just an aide. She doesn't own the most highly recommended daycare center in Star Falls. Miss Thompson does, and that's the woman I want to see. *After* I see my children. "Where is she?"

The girl whose name I remember is Kellyn or Kelly, something wonky that starts with Kell… Or is it Keel? Anyway, the girl nods and motions for me to follow her down the large central hallway.

As we pass each room, I see exactly what I'd expect in a daycare of this size. Kids and aides in various states of play. Some are eating snacks from colorful fabric lunch boxes; some are sleeping. A few of the older children color at small desks.

I see my son Luke's favorite blue-striped shirt as he hunches over a desk. He's by himself, not coloring, not reading…doing nothing. He's five years old and is taking the move to Star Falls as well as can be expected. He seemed excited to start day care, and both of our brief visits went well.

I figured the first full day I left the kids here would be tough, but not like this.

My heart tightens at the sight of my sweet, talkative son alone, seemingly looking at his hands. I can see two aides supervising the Beetles, which is the nickname given to this room. I'll find out why he seems so sad once I know Cora is all right.

My attention goes back to Kell-whatever.

"How long has she been screaming?" I ask loudly, hoping my voice isn't drowned out by the squeak of my shoes on the floor.

She looks back at me with a grimace. "Um, I think she's been pretty upset since lunch."

I check my phone. "Isn't lunch at 11:30?"

She nods. "Yeah. But Miss Thompson thought she'd settle down."

I rub my face hard, working the stubble on my face between my fingertips while I try to control my emotions. My three-year-old child has been a hysterical mess for hours, and no one's called me? I square my shoulders and ready myself for confrontation.

I'm used to managing an entire football field full of rowdy teenagers. I can handle messy.

What I cannot handle is my baby crying. And clearly, Miss Thompson can't either.

When the aide reaches Miss Thompson's office, she taps lightly on the door. I can see Miss Thompson on her knees on the floor, patiently shaking a stuffed animal at Cora, while my daughter stands facing a wall with a window that overlooks the parking lot.

Cora's little hands are spread against the drywall, and I can hear through the door the hysterical shuddering of her breaths as she calls for me on every painful exhale.

"Move," I demand and pull open the door of Miss Thompson's office. "Sweetheart, I'm here. Daddy's here." I swoop down and pick up my daughter before she can even turn around. She immediately drops her head against my shoulder, snot and tears wetting my T-shirt.

She's babbling inconsolably.

I just stand there, rocking lightly in place, patting her back and her soft, dark hair. "Shh," I urge. "It's okay, sweetheart. Daddy's here." While I cuddle my daughter, I glare at Miss Thompson. She looks shocked and a little annoyed.

"Mr. Cooper," she says, scrambling to her feet. She's young, probably just a few years out of college, and yet she's the executive director of this place.

When I interviewed with her before I enrolled my children here, she seemed to understand my situation. Now I am painfully aware that whether she understands my situation and whether she can handle my children are two very different things.

With the hand stroking Cora's back, I wave at the teacher to stop talking. "My children haven't been in anyone's care but family," I grit out. "We discussed at length what they've been through. What we've all been through."

Miss Thompson looks annoyed and yet also a little embarrassed. "Of course, I understand," she says, talking way too fast and way too loudly. I feel Cora jump in my arms at her tone. "Both Cora and Luke have been doing just fine."

"Just fine?" I echo. This is nothing close to fine. "My daughter has been in hysterics since lunchtime? What the hell happened?"

"I'll have to ask you to watch your language," Miss Thompson says primly.

I find my eyebrow lifting up in outrage. "I will speak however I want to speak around my own children," I say. "I'd like a refund for the balance of my deposit," I tell her. "I'm pulling my kids out of here." I turn on my very wet heel and squeak my way down the hallway.

"Mr. Cooper," Miss Thompson calls, trailing after me as I head for Luke's classroom. "Please wait. This is against our safety protocols."

That has my anger boiling over. I turn to her with a glare that I hope is nearly as lethal as it feels. "Safety protocols? You have the nerve to throw safety in my face when you let my child sit in hysterics for how long now? Three hours?"

Miss Thompson firms her lips. "She saw Luke when the classrooms passed by each other over lunch," she explains. "She wanted her brother, but you know, as I explained, we do not allow children to play with children outside of their assigned age pods. It's a safety consideration."

I grip my daughter with both hands. Cora is completely quiet now, her snuffle-snorts absorbed by my shoulder as her tears ease. "You think keeping a three-year-old away from her brother when she's been through what these kids have been through…" I shake my head and turn away. "So you, what? Took her out of the classroom so she could be punished by screaming in your office with you?"

"It's policy, Mr. Cooper," she shouts in a shrill tone. "You were provided a copy of our policies when you enrolled your children."

I don't even bother to lower my voice or turn back to her as I shout, "Your policies are bullshit, lady!"

I turn the knob on the Beetles room and don't bother going in.

"Luke," I yell. "Come on, kiddo. We're going home."

The classroom aides look at me with their mouths open, but my son is already grabbing his backpack.

Shit.

I forgot about that. I'll need to get Cora's. But then I realize Luke's got both his and his sister's.

I bend down to greet him. "Hey, buddy." I clap a hand on his tiny shoulder and pull him to my waist. "How'd you get your sister's backpack?"

Luke looks near tears, and he doesn't answer right away. His lips tremble, and a tiny dribble of spit bubbles on his lower lip.

I shake my head, calming myself down so I can reassure him. When he gets nervous or stressed, he struggles to speak. It's something I've had checked out, and the pediatricians and child therapists have all assured me it's nothing more than an anxiety reaction. He talks up a damn storm when he's happy or angry. But when he's stressed or nervous, it's like he bottles up everything inside and he cannot get his words out. Like father, like son in that respect.

I push past the question.

It doesn't matter now.

I just want to get my kids out of here.

"It doesn't matter. You did great, okay? I'm proud of you for looking out for Cora."

He has their empty backpacks in his hands. Since they only brought their lunches and snacks, there's nothing left to tie us to this place. I let Luke hold on to the backpacks while I keep Cora in my arms, and together, we head for the front door. The small family that's been through so much, going through one more disappointment together.

"Mail me a refund, or I'll dispute the charges with my bank," I call behind me. "My kids aren't coming back."

CHAPTER THREE

The small plumbing problem that forced Chloe's bookstore to close is *not* a small problem for my tattoo shop. As it turns out, The Body Shop needs time to dry out. That means remediation and remodeling. And all of that means the shop is closed and I'm losing income.

Thankfully, Chloe was able to tear up her carpet, dry out the bookstore, and bring in one of my brother's firefighter friends who does floors on the side to lay down some nice new strip flooring pretty quickly, and they were able to reopen in time for the weekend.

The last thing I want to do is sit home and stew, so around noon, I roll into downtown Star Falls, desperate for coffee and hoping against hope that I'm not too late for a peanut butter crisp.

I park my car on the street, because contractor trucks are taking up all the employee spots behind The Body Shop, and fumble through the contents of my purse for loose change. I'm about to give up the hunt and stick my debit card into the meters when a reminder alert goes off on my phone.

"Ugh." I groan and almost drop the precious two quarters I just touched among the numerous tubes of ChapStick, used tissues, and crumpled receipts at the bottom of my bag. "As if I needed a reminder."

The day the shop flooded, I was supposed to call and schedule a doctor's appointment. In all honesty, I'm completely in denial that I need to make this call. Hell, I'm in denial that I need to go back to the doctor. The call is like that tiny first step on a path leading right into a nightmare. If I don't make the call, I don't have to take the step. Or so I keep telling myself.

But something inside me knows I need to get the stinkin' test. It's not a life-and-death health situation. I'm fine, mostly. I just...my stomach tightens even thinking about the mess that started last year. The incredibly hot but short-lived fling. The missed period. The calls and texts that went ignored until the last one. The one that broke my heart into a million pieces until, just a few weeks later, I lost the pregnancy.

Tears sting my eyes as I think about the hours I spent alone in my apartment, wondering if I should just call my mom and tell her everything, but decided against it.

In the year since all that went down, my doctor has begged me to come in for testing to see about future complications or even the viability of another pregnancy.

Part of me wants to sort it out. To know the truth so I can face it and move on with my life. That centered, determined part of me keeps the reminder to call the damn office and schedule the tests active on my phone.

The stronger part of me, though, keeps hitting snooze.

Day after day.

Hitting pause on that alarm makes me feel better and worse at the same time. I know the problem doesn't go away just because I ignore it. But it kind of does, you know?

I see a parking enforcement car pull up the block, so I'm forced to get out of the car before Marianne or Gordon, whoever's on duty today, gives me a ticket.

I snooze the notification on the touch screen and toss the phone back in my purse. I climb out of the car, feed the meter my two measly quarters, and squint into the beautiful sunshine to see how many minutes I've got. Fifty cents won't buy me much time, but it'll be more than enough to get my caffeine and cookies.

The bookstore is crowded with shoppers lingering with coffees in their hands and market bags over their shoulders. The store is warm and cozy, and the new flooring, a faux-wood laminate, looks surprisingly real and inviting.

I breathe in the familiar scent of fresh coffee and paper, my new favorite combination and fixation.

Paper flowers made from donated used books decorate the walls. There are comfy-looking chairs with well-loved pillows just begging to be rocked in. On the large-screen television mounted on the wall, the state poet laureate is reading from her latest book, her beautiful words scrolling by in bold captions.

I notice that the table display set up near the television looks nicely picked over. Meaning the shoppers have noticed the poet and bought her books. Chloe is so, so damn clever. Such a smart businesswoman. She's turned her aunt's failing café into a thriving, homey place.

I drop my purse at my feet and lean my elbows on the counter with a dramatic sigh.

"Extra-large?" Chloe's eyes sparkle as she takes my order.

"Heck yeah, and Chloe, please," I say, "tell me you're not sold out of peanut butter crisps yet."

The luster of her smile dulls a bit as she nibbles on the corner of her lower lip. "Oh Gracie, I sold out. The kids' event…" She waves her hand toward the gathering.

I shake my head. Just my luck, but hell, I can't really be mad. "Next time," I say. "I'll get here *before* story hour."

"Text me in the morning, and I'll set one aside for my favorite sister-in-law."

"I'm your only sister-in-law."

Chloe laughs, waving me off before she walks away.

As she heads to the back to make my coffee, the woman reading in the middle of the circle motions me over.

Carol Miles is one of my mother's best and oldest friends. And by oldest, I mean Ma and her crew of ladies have been tight since, like, high school.

Carol recently separated from her husband, Earl, who owns the shop where my brother Franco works as a mechanic.

Small-town life is something else.

You can't sneeze without someone you know sending their blessings your way.

Carol is standing holding a colorful book, but by the looks of it, story hour just ended. Most of the parents and kids are wandering past the folding chairs toward the waist-high kid-friendly bookshelves. A brand-new lightbulb-shaped area rug rests on the new flooring, and a sign hand-lettered by Chloe reads, "Great Ideas Start with Play."

I steer clear of the kids' section and anything kid-related these days. And while I'm not exactly triggered being around kids, I still sort of go out of my way not to hang with them. There are times when seeing a baby clutching its mother's shoulder in line at the grocery store will bring me to tears. It's not a good look when I'm in line with people I don't know, but here at the bookstore... No, thanks.

I grab my purse and head over to greet Carol. I tiptoe between the folding chairs and lean forward to kiss both her cheeks.

"Gracie. You're a sight for sore eyes," she says a little too loudly. "Your mother told me about the water damage at the shop."

"Thankfully, it's not that bad. The building owner wants to make sure we have all the permits and inspections in order before we reopen. Won't be long now," I assure her.

I live with my parents. Every night since the store closed, I've had to listen to my parents' worries about my finances. The last thing I need is one of my surrogate moms piling on the concern.

"Well, you know you can come help Bev at the shelter. She's always looking for volunteers."

Chloe approaches us with my coffee in her hands but looks rushed. "I have a customer at the register," she says. "Be right back to chat."

I ignore the way Carol is looking at me and get back to the

matter at hand. "With all the fosters Ma brings home, our house is already like a shelter," I remind her.

"Ummm...Excuse me?"

We both lower our eyes to a little boy, maybe five or six years old, who is looking up at Carol. "Can you help me find a copy of the book you read for story hour? My dad can't find it."

The boy is pointing toward the shelves, when a muscled wall of a man ambles between the rows. I see a familiar set of broad shoulders and a sultry, warm smile.

"Coffee?" he calls out. "Is that you?"

I chuckle that he's not talking about my coffee. He's calling *me* Coffee.

"Hello, Kicks." The nickname rolls off my tongue and surprises me. It feels a little intimate, but I don't know his name, so I decide to just shake it off. I jerk a thumb toward the counter, trying not to spill my coffee. "Hate to break the news to you, but they sold out of peanut butter crisps."

"Guilty," he admits, giving me a full-teeth, panty-melting grin. I don't have time to react to the feelings his body and smile are giving me because he bends and scoops up a little girl who links her arms around his neck. "I think Cora and I here devoured every last crumb that Chloe gave us." He nods toward the front counter. "I'm on a first-name basis with the owner now. But I never did get your name."

As she looks from me to the stranger, Carol's cheeks are the same flaming magenta as her lip color. I can already tell she's on fire watching me chat up a hot stranger, but I hope she has the sense to realize this is not one of those matchmaker moments my ma's friends are so fond of orchestrating.

This man is a possible customer of the Body Shop and, by the looks of it, very, very attached.

"I'm Grace," I tell him. "But everyone calls me Gracie."

"Gracie, you haven't met Coach Cooper yet?" Carol hands the book she was holding to the little boy. "Allow me to properly introduce you."

Coach Cooper sets the little girl in his arms on her feet and extends a hand to me. "We sort of met but skipped the names part. I'm Ryder Cooper."

Stupidly sexy name for a stupidly sexy, attached, unavailable, I-can't-have-him man. But this is good. If I can't have him, I can't make any mistakes. I take his hand in mine and squeeze. "I'm Grace Bianchi."

"Gracie is a tremendously talented artist. She owns The Body Shop next door." Carol is oozing motherly charm and the kind of classic lack of subtlety that's practically a requirement for entry into my ma's lady friend group. "And Coach Cooper was just hired by Star Falls High..." She wrinkles her nose at him. "Remind me what you're teaching?"

"I am a coach, but I'm not coaching this year," he supplies. "Not officially." He trails off, and his pretty eyes gather shadows. "This will be my first year back at work after some time off, so I'm keeping my schedule as flexible as I can until these knuckleheads are in school full time."

He releases my hand and scoops the little girl back into his arm. "This is Cora," he says, his voice sweeter than Chloe's peanut butter crisps. "And my son, Luke. Can you two say hi?"

Cora is biting her lower lip and staring at me with eyes as sweet as her father's. Her cheeks are full, and she's got those tiny, perfect baby teeth.

"Hi, Cora," I say.

"Hi," Luke says. He's holding the book Carol gave him in one hand, and he gives me a tentative smile. He looks at his dad with a grave expression. "Dad..."

Ryder lowers himself, groaning audibly as his knee pops. He tightens his hold on his daughter as he rests first one knee then the other on the brand-new flooring. "What is it, buddy?"

Luke ducks his head but never takes his eyes off me. He mumbles something in his dad's ear, and Ryder chuckles. "You can ask her, buddy. Go ahead."

The little boy looks at me with eyes that look nothing like his father's. He must get those from his mom. He looks scared and his lips open like he wants to say something, but he just stands close to his dad, fisting the corner of Ryder's short-sleeved shirt.

I'm no baby whisperer, but I figure the best way to talk to anyone is to get on their level. I kneel on the floor and set my coffee and my big purse on the floor by my knees.

"Let me guess," I say, giving the kiddo my brightest smile. "Are you wondering about the pictures on my arms?"

Luke looks at his dad and then back at me with a tiny nod.

"I knew it." I clap my hands softly. "Okay, look here." I point with my right hand to the figures on my left arm. "Do you like animals?"

Little Luke nods, fully caught up in the moment. Even little Cora is watching, following where my finger is pointing.

"What does this look like to you?" I ask, tapping the colorful design on the top of my left forearm.

"A rabbit," Luke blurts out, looking very proud of himself. "Two rabbits?"

I nod. "You're right. A mama and a papa rabbit." I figure that is a safe place to start, but then Luke steps closer to his dad.

"We don't have a mama anymore," he says. "Only my dad."

A fist tightens around my heart, and I flick a look at Ryder. There's something unreadable in his face, not grief or sadness, but something more resigned and weary. If these kids don't have a mama, I've probably trod on tender ground, but I figure the best way to smooth over the moment is to just keep going.

"Look here. Do you know what this is?" I angle my arm awkwardly but give the little boy a view of the inside of my left bicep.

"It's definitely a squirrel," Luke says confidently.

I nod. "Yep. And do you know why I have a squirrel and bunnies on my arm?"

Luke's eyes go wide. "No. Why?"

I can't help laughing then, and I point to my shoulder. "This is a tree," I explain, my fingers trailing over the intricate green leaves and branches. My entire left arm is covered shoulder to wrist with a woodland scene. I go back to the bunnies. "These two represent my

28

parents..." I catch myself and don't say mama and papa again, just in case that hits a nerve. "And the squirrel represents my middle brother, Vito." I cup my hand to my mouth and lower my voice as though I don't want Vito to hear.

"He's always running around and eating everybody else's snacks," I explain.

Luke starts cracking up, and even little Cora chuckles. There's, of course, more meaning behind the animals I chose for my siblings, but I think this is plenty of information for now. I point out the owl that stands for my older brother.

"Because he's a really bossy know-it-all," I say, and I'm rewarded with yet another round of laughter when I roll my eyes. I save the best for last.

"And this..." I point to a frog wearing a crown that covers the entire top of my left wrist. The jaunty expression is made even more hilarious by the flippered foot that rests on the cap of a bright red-and-white polka-dotted mushroom. "This little guy represents my brother Benito. He thinks he's the king of the family." I lean closer to Luke and whisper loudly, "Benny's kind of a pain in the butt."

Luke now seems completely relaxed. He even leans forward and touches the crown on Benny's little frog head. "Did you draw all that?" he asks.

I shake my head. "I didn't draw it myself. I came up with all the ideas and had a very talented friend draw these. And look." I rub my fingers vigorously against my skin. "It doesn't come off. The colors are there forever."

Most kids who've never seen tattoos this detailed or this up close ask the same things. Does it wash off? Did you use markers? Why is it forever? I've become pretty good at predicting the questions, but then little Luke asks one that throws me.

"What about you?" He cocks his head and inspects the furled leaves and long, lush green grass that fill up the spaces between the animals that represent my family. "There are no more animals, so what happened to you?"

Ryder's voice is warm and invades me like a sudden ray of sunshine breaking through a storm. "Look, buddy. She's the tree."

Without touching me, he points to the front part of my shoulder, where a face has been carefully designed to blend in with the leaves. It's an elegant profile, but the dark brow that's been inked to look like part of a leaf's texture and the distinctive lips and nose are clearly mine.

"It's a family tree," Ryder says, a note of such deep respect in his voice that I feel raw. I'm used to people asking about my tattoos, complimenting them, even. But his appreciation seems so much more profound.

I nod, surprised at the sudden emotions clogging my chest. I stand up and smooth my hair, trying to calm my heart. I don't know why it's racing.

Or why the hell this man with his shoulders and his sneakers and his mama-less kids has my tummy in knots. But this feels like the right time to end this conversation. "Now you know all about my art," I say, trying to sound more cheerful than I feel.

Carol has been quietly watching the whole exchange like we're an episode of her favorite reality show.

I lift a brow at her, trying not to feel annoyed because I know if this man is single, the very next call she'll make will be to my mother. The unofficial Star Falls matchmaking circle doesn't need much to start spinning out of control. My ma and her friends have gotten their panties twisted over a whole lot less than a harmless chat between me and a guy who's new to town.

This means it's definitely time for me to go.

CHAPTER FOUR

It's one thing to have a single tattoo that has some kind of personal meaning, but it's an entirely different story to permanently ink a family portrait of sorts onto your body.

I didn't look closely at her tattoos the other day, but now that I know what her left arm means, I want to know everything about this woman. She must be close to her family, and she clearly has a sense of humor. But more than that, she has depth.

I've caught glimpses of her other designs, and while she didn't walk my son through the images on her right arm, she has a whole sleeve there too that now has me incredibly curious.

I want to ask more, to say anything to stop her from walking away.

"Daddy, your tummy is talking." Cora takes my face in both hands and looks right into my eyes. "We didn't eat lunch yet."

I feel something sticky that I wish I could identify smearing from Cora's hands onto my face.

Gracie is doing that awkward thing where she's rocking on her heels, trying to slip away.

"Daddy, I'm hungry too." Cora's looking like she's about to burst into tears, so I have about two seconds to redirect her before she has a full-on meltdown.

"I'm sooooo hungry," I moan dramatically, amping up the silliness to keep my baby girl happy. "And Cora is sooooo hungry. Let's ask Luke. What about you, little man?"

Luke nods and echoes our enthusiasm as he rubs his belly. "Soooooo hungry."

"All right, let's find a place to eat lunch." I turn my attention to Carol, the lady who read the book at story hour. I specifically avoid looking at Gracie, who is still standing with us, watching the weirdo lengths that I will go to when I'm trying to calm my kids down with one of those perfect brows lifted high on her forehead. "Ms. Carol, it was great meeting you. Kids, can you thank Ms. Carol for the fantastic story?"

While my kids mumble thank-yous, Carol is squinting and opening and closing her mouth until, finally, she blurts out, "Benito's."

"Excuse me?"

"Gracie, why don't you take them to Benito's?" Carol rushes on.

Grace huffs an odd sigh and slings her big purse farther back over her shoulder. "Carol, I don't know if..."

"Is that a lunch place?" I ask, holding up a hand. "I don't want to impose. We're always in the mood for a drive-through food."

"Drive-through," Carol practically screams. "Coach, you're new to Star Falls. Have you eaten at Benito's Italian restaurant yet?" She peers down at Luke with a giant magenta smile that is so sincere it melts my heart.

This is what I expected of small-town living. One part meddlesome, one part enthusiastic, but completely backed by good intentions.

"Do you like pasta?" Carol asks the question like she's asking kids if they want a meal of cookies—breathless and filled with wonder.

Luke's eyes go huge, and I have to stifle a groan. Carol has said the magic word. All Luke ever wants to eat is pasta. I've probably gained ten pounds in carb weight since...well, since I've been cooking solo for these kids. "Pasta is my favorite." Luke is beaming. "With red sauce," he adds. "But I also love mac and cheese."

He's not showing any signs of shyness or anxiety. What the therapists have told me is to let my son lead the way. When he wants to talk, encourage it, but don't make a huge deal out of it. The fact that he's at ease in the bookstore, talking to these complete strangers, reassures me that the drama of the daycare hasn't set him back too much, if at all. Even if I would be fine with a cold sandwich or a kiddie meal, if Star Falls has a pasta place, I'm thrilled to take a recommendation.

"So, buddy, does that mean you want to try a new place for lunch?" I ask him.

"Please, Dad. Can we?" Luke grabs my free hand and swings it, and I crumple inside.

I'd move into Benito's and eat three pasta meals a day if it kept my son feeling happy and balanced. I look to Carol for reassurance. "Is it family-friendly?" I ask. "Cora still needs a booster seat."

Carol barks a laugh so sharp that Cora flinches in my arms. "Is it family-friendly?" she cackles.

Grace holds up a tattooed finger. "All you need to know about Benito's is right here." She points to the jaunty frog prince on her arm. "My brother owns the restaurant. I happen to know that the place is exceptionally family-friendly. If you want, I'll call ahead and let him know to give you a nice table on the terrace."

I'm about to tell her that's not necessary when Carol intervenes.

"Gracie, why don't you take Coach Cooper to lunch? He's new to town. He needs friends. You can be…his friend…"

The look on Grace's face almost has me bursting out laughing. She's huffing her cheeks and glaring, looking mortified and angry, and it's the sweetest and yet sexiest combination imaginable.

I brace for the full eyebrow fury, but to my surprise, she sighs and turns to me. "I don't know if your kids really want me crashing their lunch," she says. "But I didn't get a peanut butter crisp for breakfast, so I could eat."

"You eat cookies for breakfast?" Luke picks up on that

33

immediately, and I'm about to set him straight, when Grace tries to walk back her misstep.

"No way," she tells him, bending slightly. "My...uh, dentist would freak out if I ate cookies for breakfast. But sometimes I skip breakfast, so I kind of think of the cookie as a lunch appetizer."

"A lunch appetizer..." I chuckle under my breath. Before the woman gives my kids any ideas about how to skirt the few rules I do enforce around mealtime, I go back to her question. "Luke, Cora, should we invite Grace to join us for lunch today and go to Benito's for pasta? Or would you rather have drive-through food in the car? Your choice."

I know my kids and I'm sure what Luke's going to say, but I figure Grace will feel more at ease hearing it from them.

"Pasta," Luke says, nodding. "And Grace. Please, Dad."

Cora tightens her arms around my neck and starts whining. "I'm thirsty, Daddy."

"That's close enough to a unanimous vote for me," I say, meeting Grace's eyes. "If you don't mind playing tour guide through the culinary wonders of Star Falls, that is."

"Dad, what is a..." Luke's about to press me for a definition of culinary, but Grace is chuckling and nodding her head.

"I'm in," she confirms.

"I'll explain culinary in the car," I tell Luke. "It's a fancy word that means food." I slip my phone from my pocket, juggling Cora, and hand Grace the device. "Do you mind putting the address in my GPS app? I'm still learning my way around town."

She takes my phone and types in the address and then reaches to hand it back to me. After a moment's hesitation, she says, "Should I..." She looks down at the touchscreen. "Should I put my number in? Just in case you get lost or we get separated?"

My pulse thunders, and I can't explain the sudden lightness in my chest. She's offering me her number? Maybe it is only because she thinks I'm a distracted dad, but whatever her reasons, I don't hesitate to agree.

"That'd be great," I say, trying to downplay the rush of excitement that twists my belly.

It occurs to me then that it would be really rude if I didn't invite Carol to join us since, after all, it was her idea. "Miss Carol," I say, nodding at her, "are you a pasta fan? I'd hate to leave you out of this lunch adventure. Can you join us?"

The woman leaves no doubt about her intentions when she vigorously shakes her head. "Oh no," she says. "No, no, you two go. I've got to get home to make lunch for Earl." Her eyes gleam, and she vigorously waves both hands at us like she's shooing us on our way. "Enjoy, now. Gracie, make sure you call me later!"

Carol scurries off, leaving me alone with a very annoyed-looking Grace. But as soon as our eyes meet, she softens. "You'll get used to them," she says. "Small-town people are the best kind of people, but they will get all up in your business."

Before we're able to head out, Cora says, "Daddy, I have to go potty."

I don't have time to respond before Luke starts complaining. "Dad, I want pasta."

I take the situation in hand before things devolve.

"Okay, kids, listen up." I use my coach voice, trying to remember that I'm in a bookstore where people are reading and shopping. "First," I say loudly, "we find Cora a potty. Then, lunch. Everybody got it? We have a plan, right? Are we cool?"

Luke nods, and Cora wriggles in my arms, which means I need to find a restroom before both Cora and I need a change of clothes.

I turn to Grace. "We're going to be a few minutes. Meet you there?"

She nods. "Bathroom's right there." She points to a partially open door toward the back of the store.

I gather up my kids and give her a last look of thanks. I don't know what else to say because even though she's meeting us at the restaurant, walking away feels like I'm leaving something important behind.

By the time everyone has gone potty, me included, and I've made it to my truck, belted everyone in, and gotten settled, it's probably been a solid half hour. Wherever Grace is, she's probably impatient and questioning whether we bailed.

Once I'm secure in the truck, I pull out my phone and start the mapping app so I know how to get to Benito's. Before I pull out of my parking spot, I search my contacts for Grace. I'm a little nervous when I can't find anything under Grace. I start at the letter A and scan quickly through the list, hoping she didn't change her mind and decide to bail. Then I see it.

A new contact, one I've never created. But the name she entered isn't Grace. It's Coffee.

I pull up the contact, check the GPS for a travel estimate, and type out a quick message.

Coffee, Kicks' crew is on the way. ETA seven minutes.

I hit send and have a response back before I even put the car in reverse. It's a whole message in just emojis—a little coffee cup, a sneaker, two baby faces, and a thumbs-up.

I chuckle and pull out of my parking spot, not at all surprised that a tattoo artist communicates with art. I can't help but think of all the delicious dirty texts someone like her might send, but then I stop myself.

This isn't a date. This is a meal. A kindness done by a woman who was harassed into joining me for lunch.

Grace isn't interested in me. She doesn't even know me, and I don't know her. The woman needs to eat, and how could she refuse Carol's none-too-subtle matchmaking? I'm sure she has no interest in a single father of two. I can't believe I'm even wondering if she might.

As I travel the blissfully traffic-free roads of Star Falls, I let my mind wander to what kind of person a tattoo artist might want to date.

I can't explain the way Grace's boldness, her directness, and her colors draw me in, but as I park the truck in the parking lot of Benito's, I'm feeling excited. I'm looking forward to walking into that restaurant and seeing her dark locks and her expressive face.

I take a deep breath and turn to face the kids. "Who's hungry?" I bellow.

"Me!" Luke shouts back.

"Let me hear you, Cora. Are you hungry?"

"Hungry," she echoes.

A rush of emotion fills my chest. These are my kids. My family. Little people whose lives and hearts I'm responsible for, and yet I've taken them away from both sets of grandparents to start over in a small town. Away from the memories. Away from the only house they ever lived in. Away from the only place that connects them to memories of their mom.

As I unbuckle their seat belts and hold their hands to cross the lot, I say a prayer to Elizabeth to look out for us. To help me do right by our babies.

As if in answer, a bird swoops low as a flock plays some kind of game of bird tag, I duck my head to avoid being hit.

"Whoa." Luke points to the sky. "Dad, that was crazy. Those birds are playing!"

"I don't know if birds play, bud, but they were close, that's for sure. I'm just glad I didn't get bird poop in my hair. Anyone want to check?"

Cora squeals and says, "Ewww, poop in your hair."

I pick her up and remind her of all the poop of hers I've cleaned over the years. I've got my daughter in my arms and Luke holding my hand when I look up and see a set of serious black brows staring at me through the plate glass window that faces the parking lot.

She's here. She really did wait.

As I approach the front, I can see that Benito's is a really cute place. Lush plants and colorful flowers bloom in real planters outside. The chairs out front look like a ragtag assortment of real lawn chairs someone's grandmother might have at a summer cottage.

The vibe is inviting and warm. It's exactly the kind of family-style place where I'd expect to get an amazing meal in a relaxed environment.

My hands are full, so Grace pushes open the door for us.

"Thank you, Coffee," I say, nudging Luke to go on inside.

"You're welcome, Kicks. Glad you made it." She steps aside while I carry Cora indoors.

The inside of Benito's is even more inviting than the outside. I smell garlic and bread and tomato sauce, and a happy buzz of chatter rises from the full tables.

Grace leads me to the hostess stand where a woman who must be close to eighty is adjusting a pair of reading glasses on a beaded chain around her neck. Her stylish ear-length bob is pure white, which makes a sharp contrast to the shocking red lipstick she wears. She's got thin brows that arch deep and fake nails that are ornamented with something sparkly on top.

Gracie goes behind the hostess stand and loops an arm around the woman's shoulder. She plants a loud smooch on the hostess's cheek. "Rita, these are my lunch dates."

The woman lets her glasses flop from her hand to her chest. She looks from me to Cora, back to me, then to Gracie before clasping her hands together in front of her chest.

"Get out of here," she crows.

That's literally the last thing I expect this cute old lady to say, but before I can react, she comes bustling around the hostess stand, headed right for me.

She holds out both hands, and I'm not sure if I should hold them, kiss them, or hand over my baby. I opt to take one hand awkwardly and shake it.

"I'm Ryder Cooper, ma'am," I say.

"Ma'am." The hostess looks back at Grace and crows. "The manners on this one! I like him. Kind eyes, Gracie, and a hell of a body." She looks back at me and shrugs. "Pardon my language in front of the kiddos." She points to Cora and then Luke. "Rita just said a bad word, but you two didn't hear a thing. Am I right?"

Cora giggles and buries her face in my shoulder.

I decide to redirect before this conversation gets out of control. "Cora, Luke, can you say hello to Ms. Rita?"

While the kids chat up Ms. Rita, Grace grabs two large, plastic-coated menus and two paper kids' menus, along with two cups of crayons. She holds up the cups and lifts her brows as if asking whether the kids can have them, and I nod.

"All right, Rita, we've got to get these kids some food." Grace sets a hand on the hostess's shoulder and holds up the menus, grabbing an extra kids' menu to draw on. "I'll seat us," she offers. "I marked out table twenty on the terrace."

"I'll have that cute college boy bring over a booster seat," Rita says. "Have a great date, you two."

"It's not... Oh, never mind." Grace shakes her head and looks me in the eye. "I guess I did call you all my lunch dates."

"I don't mind that at all," I say, a lot more growl in my voice than I intend.

Grace looks at me and flushes a bit, but then heads off through the crowded restaurant, leading us to a terrace.

A young kid dressed in black jeans and a white button-down shirt carries a booster seat in one hand and looks from Grace to me like he's completely lost about what to do with it.

Grace thanks him and points to where she wants the seat, and then she waits while I settle Cora and help Luke into a chair. I start to pull out the chair between the two kids and then stop.

"Is this okay?" I ask. "I feel like I should pull your chair out for you."

She grabs the back of the wooden chair and drags it across the smooth wood flooring.

"No...I mean, yes. This is great. I'll sit here. It's not really a date," she clarifies. "I mean, not that you'd have to do the chair thing even if it were."

She drops into the chair, and I sit. And then it's just the four of us.

Two strangers across the table from one another with my kids. At her brother's restaurant. It freaks me out even to think it, but this feels familiar. Easy. Almost too easy. Like family.

I'm not sure I believe in signs, but I'll take all of this as an omen of good things to come.

CHAPTER FIVE

grace

The second we sit down, I set a kids' menu and a paper cup filled with crayons in front of Cora. Ryder takes one of the menus and the second cup, then holds up an extra menu.

"Did you want this?" he asks, grinning wide.

I can't help the massive, goofy smile that takes over my face. "Yeah," I tell him, then turn to Cora. "Can I borrow a few crayons from you? I promise to share."

Cora is a seriously cute kid. She's got light brown curly hair that just reaches her chin. She has a perfect set of baby teeth, and when she smiles, every one of them is on full display.

"Here," she says, holding the whole cup out to me. Her hand shakes a little, and I take the cup gently so the whole mess of colors doesn't spill on the floor.

"Thank you." I look over the rounded, dull points and scowl. "This sucks." I flick a look at Ryder. "Pardon my language." I make a mental note to watch what I say around the kids. It's been a while since I've been around kids this age. Probably since I babysat in the neighborhood for cash in high school. I don't see the need to censor myself normally, but with kids, I should probably set a little bit of an example.

I hold up a red with an unacceptably flat tip. It's like somebody dropped and snapped the end off and then tried to chew their way through the crayon. I grimace and stick the thing back in the cup. "We need a crayon sharpener or something. Hang on."

I turn around to dig in the purse on the back of my chair and turn back at Ryder's sexy chuckle. "What?"

"If you have a crayon sharpener in that purse, I might just have to marry you."

If the words surprise me, they look like they shock him.

"Inappropriate. I'm sorry. I'm going to stuff my face with bread and look at the menu," he says before I have a chance to say anything.

I twist my lips into a grin and grab the phone from my purse. I punch in a text message, and a few moments later, Rita comes walking toward the table with two brand-new boxes of crayons in her hands.

"Let me see those," she says, peering down the end of her nose.

I hand her a cup of crayons and shake my head. "You tell my brother if I have to come in here and sharpen the crayons, I'm charging him my hourly rate plus."

Rita cackles. "You do that, Gracie." She takes the cup from me and the second one from Luke, and then leaves us with two brand-new, unopened boxes.

I crack open a pack and breathe the familiar, waxy scent. I pull out a soft shade of salmon pink and admire the sharp tip. "Hmm," I sigh. "Now that's bliss. Nothing beats a brand-new crayon." I return the pink to the box and hand it to Cora.

While she dumps every single color onto the table in front of her, I tuck her chair closer to the end of the table and bend over to grab two strays that have fallen to the floor.

Then I lift up the kids' menu in front of me. "Luke," I call out. "See this?"

I point to a piece of pasta drawn in a cartoon style, complete with a bow tie, big eyes, and a happy smile.

Little Luke nods.

"I drew the whole thing," I tell him proudly. "Look here." I point to a tiny squiggle in the lower right corner of the menu. "That's my name. Grace Bianchi."

Luke's wide eyes would be adorable, but the way his mouth drops as though I just told him I could fly makes me positively glow.

"No way." He grabs the menu and looks at every piece of food and every character I've made. "You drew this?"

I nod proudly. "My brother asked me to design the kids' menu, so that's what I did. Take a look."

Ryder holds one end of the menu and reads the food choices out loud to Luke. "Cora," he says. "They have grilled cheese. Do you want grilled cheese or pasta?"

"Grilled cheese," she says without looking up. Her little head is bent over, and she's dutifully coloring the eyes on Mr. Mostaccioli red.

"I respect your bold colors," I tell her, tapping my finger on the menu.

Just then, a different college-aged kid comes by with two tall plastic glasses of ice water for Ryder and me.

"Hi, Grace," he says. "Can I bring drinks for the kids?"

"Do you have anything kid-safe?" Ryder asks. "I left my little one's sippy cup in the car."

"Dad, it's not a sippy cup. Cora isn't a baby." Luke sounds annoyed in a very protective older brother way. He reminds me of Franco when we were young, and it melts away a layer of ice I hadn't even realized was frozen around my heart.

"Right. Sorry, buddy." Ryder ruffles the boy's hair and then orders organic apple juice pouches and one glass of water for the kids to share.

"I know what I'm having," I say, borrowing a crayon from Cora. "Do you want a recommendation?"

Ryder nods. "If it's good enough for the sister of the chef, yeah. Please."

I flip open the adult menu and point. "The wood-fired pizzas are the best you'll ever eat." I bring my fingertips together and blow a kiss. "Mmmm. So good. But my favorite dish is the ravioli."

I'm looking Ryder right in the eyes when he says, "I trust you."

There's a moment when we stare each other down, and neither one of us looks away.

I hear Luke scribbling on his menu and Cora peeling the wrapper from a crayon she just snapped in half. But I can't look away from Ryder. His beautiful eyes. His sexy grin. And the way he stares at me as though he very much likes what he sees.

He runs a hand through his hair and blinks. I think he's going to look away, but he doesn't. We stare and stare, my heartbeat thundering in my chest and a buzz of excitement competing with the hunger pangs in my belly.

He's hot. He's exactly my type. But he's a *dad*.

I give in and let him win, snapping my gaze away and focusing on my kiddie menu. I use the black crayon I borrowed from Cora to sketch two whimsical birds in flight.

Todd returns with the juice, and Ryder places the orders for the kids—grilled cheese for Cora and pasta with meatballs for Luke.

"I'll have the ravioli," Ryder says.

I glance up and give him an approving nod, but it's like his eyes never left my face. His stare is intense, and there's something real that passes between us. Something charged and exciting.

Nope, I think. *Absolutely not.*

"Make that two," I tell Todd, then immediately busy myself drawing.

The man is hot, yes. But he's got two kids. He's new to Star Falls. And *because* he's exactly the type I normally am attracted to, he's bound to be a mess.

Even as I think the words, I am not sure I want to believe them. He's an attentive dad. He seems to know his kids really well and to be a really hands-on father. Maybe he's a total user or a cheat. I run through the list of every shitty thing every well-built, athletic, clean-cut guy I've ever dated has done. This Ryder guy… I mean, damn. Even his name is sexy.

He's no different from any of them, I remind myself, pressing the wax even harder into the menu paper.

He wants one thing from a woman.

And when he gets it, he'll be gone.

I know how this would go if I gave in to the flirtatious little dance we seem to have going on. I'd have sex with him. It'd be great because, look at him. I mean, my mouth has been watering since long before we came to the restaurant. We'd have a few weeks of fun, and the minute I started to get attached, the excuses would start.

They are all the same. Guys like Ryder. Men in general.

I have three brothers. I know the best that men can be, and I know they are self-righteous, immature, selfish, and every other shitty thing on the planet. Too bad this one is so incredibly freaking hot.

I focus on finishing the birds and sipping my ice water, until Ryder finally says something.

"Wait…are you drawing those birds? The two from outside?" He's staring across the table, peering at my work.

"Yeah."

"I swear they were trying to attack me when we got out of the car." Ryder reaches a hand across the table. "Can I see that?"

I hand him my menu and then lean over to inspect Cora's work. "I love that," I tell her, pointing to the flaming-pink hair on the Lady Meatball. "You know what I like to do? Can I show you something?"

Cora nods, and I reach over and open my hand for a crayon. "Give me any two colors," I say, "doesn't matter which ones."

Cora hands me turquoise and orange. I nod appreciatively. "These are going to go really well together. Look."

I pick the tube-shaped character made out of ziti. She hasn't colored it all in yet, so I use the turquoise to make gently curved lines that follow the shape of the ziti's body. Then I make small round polka dots with the orange. "Another color," I say, holding my palm up for more.

Cora hands me green and pink, and I color in around the orange circles with the pink, then draw large flares spiraling out from the pasta body in green.

"See?" I say, handing her back the paper. "You don't just have to fill in the lines. You can make anything your mind can imagine. Patterns inside the lines, emphasis outside. You can add anything. You just need a little inspiration and a few colors."

"What's inspiration?" Luke asks. He's busy drawing a railroad track on the bottom of his menu.

"That right there." I jab my finger in the air excitedly. "Look at that. I would never have thought to put a train with pasta people, but how cool is that? You were *inspired* by an idea to do something different."

Luke blushes and hands me his menu. "Will you inspire something on mine?"

I smirk and take his menu. "Only if you inspire something on mine."

Ryder is still looking at the birds I drew. I made two very classic, old-school tattoo-style swallows. Not at all the birds from the parking lot, but it doesn't matter if they are exactly what I saw. These are, I guess, inspired by the doves or whatever they were flying in tandem.

Ryder stares at my artwork, a little tightness around his lips. "Your birds are really, really stunning," he says. "I might have to come back for a tattoo after all."

"What?" Luke gasps and stares at his dad with wonder. "You'd get a tattoo, Dad? All over your arm?"

Ryder holds up a hand and shakes his head. "We'll see. I was just complimenting Grace's skill."

The kids and I color in silence until I hear something that stops my heart in my chest.

"Gracie?"

"Oh God." I literally drop the crayon and cover my face with both hands. "Brace yourself," I mutter.

"Sorry?" Ryder looks confused, but before I can explain, I leap out of my seat.

Rita is leading none other than my mother and her friend Bev over to our table.

"Lookie here." Rita looks incredibly proud of herself, and under normal circumstances, I'd be thrilled to run into my mom on a random outing. But seeing her like this is literally my worst nightmare. I'm going to have to do a lot of damage control.

"Hey, Ma," I say, clasping her in a hug and kissing both cheeks.

When I move on from my mom and kiss Bev, I can see my mom's face is so damn red, it nearly matches her store-bought hair color.

Then before my mom can say anything embarrassing, I turn to Ryder. "Ryder, this is…"

But I'm way, way too late to stop the embarrassment train. It's like Luke's picture, except my mom is the conductor and she is revving the engine and aiming right for Ryder.

"I'm Lucia Bianchi," Ma says, holding out her hand to Ryder. "I'm so sorry. I had no idea Gracie was on a date."

"Ma," I snap. "It's not a date. Ryder's new to town, and…" I sigh and clamp my lips together. I could be reciting the nuclear codes from memory, and my mother would be completely oblivious. She only has eyes for the man she thinks her daughter is on a date with.

Ryder takes my mother's hand, but then she draws him in for a huge hug.

If the hug bothers Ryder, he definitely doesn't show it. He hugs her back and seems like an old pro at making mom small talk. He introduces the kids one at a time, having them say their names and how old they are.

"Luke, you're five years old. Such a beautiful boy, you are." Lucia coos over his gorgeous kids just like she coos over everything. Enthusiasm overload. It's actually really cute, and Luke seems happy with the attention, at least.

"I'm almost six," Luke clarifies. "I'm in first grade."

"Will be," Ryder corrects. "Luke starts Star Falls Elementary in a couple weeks."

"We have very good public schools here in Star Falls." Then Ma turns her attention to Cora. "And who are you, sweetheart?" Ma bends over, her necklace dangling like a tiny sparkly windchime.

Cora points to it but doesn't touch it. "I like your necklace," she says in the sweetest, shyest toddler voice ever.

My mother full-on flushes, and I swear, if she could have done it without getting arrested, she would have scooped Cora up and taken her home.

"You know my Gracie is an artist," Ma says proudly.

Luke looks confused. "You're her mom?"

"Yes, I am. Gracie is my youngest, but she's all grown up now. I have three sons as well, but Grace is my only girl. My baby." My mom lights up, and for a minute, I feel the pride and love she feels for me.

My mom introduces the kids to one of her best friends, Bev, who runs the local animal shelter, and then drops the bomb I should have known was coming.

"So, what brings you to town, Ryder? Did you and your wife relocate for work?"

I want to slap my forehead at the brutally obvious question, but Ryder's answer deflates my anger before it can even gather steam.

"I'm a widower," he says simply. "We lost her not long after Cora was born. I took some time off to raise the kids, but now that they are a little older, we're making a fresh start. I'll be teaching part time at Star Falls High this fall, with plans to ease into coaching when I can put Cora in all-day kindergarten."

That information lands hard. Ma's affection can feel like a spotlight—harsh and direct sometimes—but if you see it for what she intends it to be, it's just pure. Like sunshine she can't contain. It pours out of her and spills onto anyone who cares to listen. Beside Luke and Cora, who are growing up without their mother, Lucia's purity, her passion for her kids, suddenly feels like a blessing I've taken for granted.

I look Ryder over curiously. I didn't know he was a widower, but how would I? I know virtually nothing about him, so anything I might have assumed about his life is just my attempt to put together a story to keep myself safe.

I have such a terrible track record with men. I'm questioning every look and every word that have passed between us. Is he a lonely single dad looking for love? A hookup? A mama for these little kids?

Aw, hell no. I promised after what happened last year, I would not—I repeat, *not*—rush into anything. Not sex. Not a relationship. Not even a date. That's not what this is, and if he had any confusion about that whatsoever, I'll set his ass straight.

For her part, my mom doesn't miss a beat. She clutches a hand to her chest and shakes her head. "I'm so sorry for your loss," she says, genuine tears sparkling in her eyes. She lowers her voice and steps closer to Ryder. "No one should experience something like that so young." She looks at Cora and Luke, and again, I'm thankful Ma doesn't pick up both kids and march them to her house.

If she had her way, she'd probably stuff them with treats and love and play surrogate grandma for as long as Ryder would allow it.

But instead, she firms her lips and reaches up a hand to cup Ryder's cheek.

He looks stunned at first, because who wouldn't?

Can you cut it with the touching, Ma? She and I are really going to have to have a talk later about boundaries.

But he looks at me, and I shrug and shake my head like I'm washing my hands of the ticker tape parade that is Lucia. He seems to relax, though, and sort of leans in as if giving her permission to manhandle him.

"Ryder—and this goes for you and your children—any friend of Gracie's is *family*," she says emphatically. "Anything you need— babysitters, recommendations for doctors, homemade dinners—you call me. You come to any one of us."

She motions with her free hand toward Bev. "Any of us, you hear? That's what small-town living means. All for one, and one for all. Isn't that what they say? In fact, Gracie—" she turns to me with a glare "—why haven't you invited Ryder over for dinner yet?"

I don't even bother trying to explain myself. When Ma goes on a rant, there's nothing that can stop her. Maybe my dad, but not always. So, I just sigh and watch while Ma practically inducts Ryder into the Bianchi family. She's a one-woman welcome wagon.

He looks overwhelmed and a little flustered, but seeing him listen to my mom, his stubbled cheek in her hand, is strangely satisfying. He seems like he's actually listening to her, which is endearing. Sweet. He's got a grateful smile and the faintest hint of a blush reddening his cheeks.

I'm honestly a little jealous it's so easy for Ma to touch the guy.

She releases his face, and I expect him to brush her off or

politely decline all of her offers, but to my absolute shock, he accepts.

"We'd love a little help," he says. "I actually just pulled my kids out of Miss Thompson's daycare, and I haven't made much progress finding alternative arrangements. If you had any suggest—"

Ma cuts him off with a dramatic hand gesture at her friend Bev. "What did I tell you? Did I not tell you?"

Ma shakes her head, moving her body so much with the gesture that her jangly bracelets clang together as she moves. "That woman is a mess. I know Kelly's mother and that whole family... Nothing but drama."

"Ma." I butt in, putting a stop to small-town gossip. "Kelly runs a fine place. If it didn't work out for Ryder, it didn't work out."

"Miss Thompson's name is Kelly? I thought her summer aide was Kelly?" Ryder looks even more confused.

Thankfully, Todd is coming our way with a tray heavily loaded with food.

"Ma, our food's coming," I say, lifting my brows to dismiss her. "We can continue this another time."

"Oh, all right. All right, I'll leave you to your meal." She grips Ryder's arm and gives it a visible squeeze. "We'll talk later, sweetie. Grace will give you the details about dinner. Enjoy your date."

She gives him such a bright smile that I don't even have the heart to correct her. The fact that he's a widower doesn't make this a date. It wasn't a date before I knew he didn't have an ex-wife hanging around. For all I know, he has a girlfriend or a side squeeze. And on top of it, if he's a widower, the man is a full-time dad.

But correcting her won't discourage my mother. Not now that she's got the idea in her head. I'm going to be hearing about this not-a-date date later. I'm damned sure of that.

Ryder grins at my mom, and it's like the temperature on the already hot terrace goes up ten degrees. He's so sincere. So sweet. And yet there's nothing sweet about the way he looks at me after he calls out, "Nice to meet you, Mrs. Bianchi." His toothy smile and those chocolate-brown eyes look me over in a way that's positively brazen.

Ma tuts for a minute about him calling her Lucia before Bev has to physically take Ma by the elbow and end the world's longest goodbye. By the time poor Todd has managed to get our plates on the table, I'm glaring with my entire face.

"Goodbye, Ma," I warn.

"My Benny's the best chef in Star Falls. Enjoy."

Ma teeters off on her heels, but they aren't going far. Rita seats Lucia and Bev at a table literally ten feet away.

Great.

"You're not from a small town?" I ask.

I watch while Ryder comes around to cut Cora's grilled cheese triangles into four smaller triangles. He squirts a little line of ketchup on the plate for her to dip her fries and then two small dollops to make a smiley face out of ketchup.

She laughs and says, "I'm going to eat the eyes first."

"Savage," Ryder teases, then kisses his daughter on the hair. Once he sits, he looks directly at me and answers my question. "We moved from Columbus," he explains. "We had a condo downtown. City folk through and through."

I nod, lifting a brow and sighing. "Well, good luck. It may take some getting used to, living in a place like Star Falls. The people are the best you'll ever know, but..." I motion my hand back toward my mom. "They will get right up in your business. And I mean, right up in there."

Ryder laughs and rubs his chin as if remembering my mom grabbing his face. "I haven't been grandma-bombed in a while," he says. "I can't say I minded one bit."

I unroll the paper napkin from around my silverware. "Grandma-bomb," I repeat, unable to shake the warmth that fills my chest. He's so...sweet. "Just don't go giving her any encouragement, or she'll order wedding invitations and start looking at venues."

Ryder's grinning, but he has no idea how serious I am. My mother's mission is to make sure her kids are happy, and that includes being happily partnered. If she didn't spend so much time volunteering and hanging out with her lady friends, marrying off

Benny, Vito, and me—now that Franco has Chloe—would be her full-time job.

"So, what do you think, bud?" Ryder nods at Luke, who hasn't said a word since his lunch was delivered.

"This is the best ever," Luke says through a very full mouth. "Like, my new favorite, Dad."

"That's good, but try to chew and swallow before you talk next time." Ryder smiles, making even the correction seem loving. Then he looks at me, a fork poised over his plate. "So, this smells amazing."

I spear a single ravioli and smile. "Tastes even better."

Cora drops a fry on the front of her shirt and leaves a massive ketchup streak on the pale pink top she's wearing. She picks up the fry from where it fell between her legs and sticks it back into her mouth.

"Oh," I say, a little grossed out, a little impressed. "Should I get, like, a wet wipe or something?" I ask, pointing to the stain.

Ryder shakes his head. "Did anybody really eat if there's no visible proof on the front of at least one shirt?"

I chuckle and watch Ryder. He widens his eyes, chews, then rubs his face with a hand. "That might literally be the best thing I've ever eaten in my life," he says. "What's in it?"

I nod, then take a bite of my own, letting the meatball mixture inside the ravioli linger on my tongue. "Spinach, pork, beef, and three types of cheese. Super freakin' good, right?"

Ryder watches as I eat, licking the remnants of sauce from my lips. "Super freakin' amazing," he agrees.

Within a few seconds of our finishing eating, my brother hustles up to the table wearing a long-sleeved double-breasted chef's jacket embroidered with his name.

"Hey, Gracie. I didn't know you were coming for lunch. You should've texted." He leans over and kisses my cheek, then extends a hand to Ryder. "Nice to meet you, man. I'm Benito Bianchi."

Ryder introduces himself, standing and pumping Benny's hand vigorously. "Pleasure to meet you. I was just telling your sister this may be the best thing I've ever eaten."

Benny's grin is sly, and he points at me. "Get your phone and record that," he says. "I want bragging rights with Pops."

I shove my brother away. "Your ego's big enough. Let us eat before your personality ruins the meal." I stick out my tongue at him playfully, which makes both Luke and Cora laugh.

"Hey." Benny points at the kids. "Can I send over a little something for after the meal? Any dietary no-no's here?"

My brother has owned a family-style restaurant long enough to be a master at discreetly asking if he can send over some dessert for the kids. No faster way to annoy a customer than to offer something the parents don't want or don't allow.

"Anything's fine," Ryder says. "Thanks again, man. Absolutely delicious."

Before he leaves, Benny bends down and stage-whispers in a voice so loud, I'm sure the whole terrace hears him. "Enjoy your lunch *date*, little sis."

I shake my head, mindful of the fact that if I smack him, I'm setting a bad example for Luke and Cora.

I'm just about to take a sip of water when I feel a hot set of eyes boring into me. I peek over at my mom, and she waves like a child, all giddy and big smiles.

I groan and drop my face into my hand. "Welcome to Star Falls."

CHAPTER SIX

ryder

After I tuck the kids into bed for the night, I settle in front of the TV and fall asleep. I don't mean to, but it's a habit I can't seem to break. Every morning I set my alarm, so I have at least an hour before either of them wakes up. It may seem like a small thing, but getting a first cup of coffee and a shower with minimal interruptions is a major indulgence.

Not that I don't love having little kids. I love those two more than anything in the world. I wouldn't change a thing about being Luke and Cora's dad. Except, of course, being a single parent. Doing this without a partner. My wife. Their mother. Complete shitshow.

The time flickers across the screen, reminding me in black-and-white that it's nearly nine. I massage the crick out of my neck before checking Cora on the baby monitor. She's far too old to need it anymore, but I set it up after we moved to Star Falls while she got used to a new room.

I think it made us both feel better at first. I'll wean us off the device in a few weeks, but for now, I can peek in on her and be confident that she's safely asleep in her big-girl bed. And she can feel good knowing that the room is new, the house is new, but she only needs to open her eyes and look at the little camera to know Daddy's right there. Like I always have been. And always will be.

I roll my shoulders and debate what to do. It's too late to start a movie, but I really don't have the energy to throw in laundry or unload the dishwasher. I grab my phone and figure I'll check the sports scores on some of the apps I follow, when I see I have three missed texts.

One's from Elizabeth's mom:

Send more pics of the kids when you have time, Ryder. Tell them Grandma loves them.

Back home, Elizabeth's parents lived in a suburb of Columbus and would watch the kids every once in a while to give me a break. I knew leaving the circle of friends and what little family we had close by would be an adjustment, but Rebecca and Daniel were surprisingly supportive of this move. As much as they love their grandkids, Rebecca is managing partner of a law firm and has no plans to retire. Daniel's a senior vice president at a place he's worked at since he graduated college after serving in the Air Force.

Neither one of them is the kind of grandparent to spend hands-on time with the kids. And that's not a bad thing. To be honest, it's made moving away easier. There was so little left back in Columbus to hold on to.

I sigh and make a note to send Grandma Rebecca some of the pics of the kids getting settled in Star Falls. Her message came in around seven when I was putting the kids to bed, so she probably knew better than to expect a text back tonight.

The next message is from my buddy Austin, the one good thing I miss from Columbus.

What'd I tell ya, bro. You see the news about Goodwin?

Austin is single and will most definitely be up at this hour. It's Saturday night, so he's probably not sitting at home on his phone, but I drop him a message back anyway.

Missed the news. What about Goodwin?

Austin is a sports fanatic. He's one of the guys who was never good enough to play past high school. But he's got a mind for stats.

Austin was the one friend who stayed close after Elizabeth died.

After I reply to Austin, I read the third text I missed. It's the oldest one, the one that arrived sometime between when I gave the kids baths and brushed their teeth. I hardly register the name of the sender when I open the message and see a load of emojis.

Sorry about my family today. They're a lot, but they mean well.

Gracie's message is followed by an angry face emoji, a sweary face, and then at least five mind-blowing emojis.

My pulse quickens, and I drop back down on the couch. What are the odds she's even home right now? A woman like that's probably on a date or out with friends. The same things I'd probably be doing if I were single.

I debate for a bit whether I should text her back. What should I say? It means something that she texted me first, right? Could she be interested?

Rather than question myself anymore, I pull up her message and reply back.

Your family was great. Lunch was great. Now I know about the best coffee and the best lunch in Star Falls. What other best of's am I missing out on?

I hesitate before hitting send. Does that sound too flirty? Too forward? I don't want to sound like a dick who's asking her to keep playing tour guide.

"Fuck." I delete it and start over.

Your family is great. Lunch was great. You are great.

"Oh, sweet fuck, no. I can't send that."

Delete. Delete.

I get up off the couch and start pacing, annoyed with myself that I'm literally breaking into a cold sweat over a stupid basic text.

Loved meeting your family. Thanks for the "best of" tour of Star Falls. Any chance you can hook me up with the best sneaker store in town?

Nope, nope, nope. The sneaker thing is done and dusted. Time to put the tired joke in the bin. I delete the whole thing and nearly toss my phone on the floor. But then, I get an idea. I punch out the message, then read it over:

Your family seems great. I'm planning on eating at least five meals a week at Benito's. But next time, I'm bringing a crayon sharpener. I don't think I'll have as much pull with the hostess if you're not with me.

I think that one over a bit, then add an emoji of a crayon, which I swear I had no idea was even an option before I looked for it.

As I click send, even my hands are starting to sweat. I feel like a kid who can't believe his crush is actually texting him.

Before I can stress myself out further, I get a reply:

ravioli, peanut butter crisps, crayon emojis. Life-changing week.

I chuckle and wish I could see her face. Maybe I should call her. Is that weird? Would she answer? Instead, I go the neutral route.

Was your mom serious about helping me find childcare?

I click send before I can second-guess myself. But the moment the text leaves my drafts, I know it was the wrong thing to say.

"Shit. I went right into dad mode."

I rub my eyebrows and mumble, "Way to shut things down fast, asshole."

Was my mom serious? You might want to leave a spare key under the mat for her. That way, she doesn't have to bother you when she drops by unannounced to meddle in your business.

That message has no emoijs in it, but she follows it up with a second text of a girl with dark hair shrugging and another one of a yellow face laughing.

I start to feel the tiniest glimmer of relief, and I say so.

Very cool. I could use a meddling mom-type in my life. Especially if that means I'm free to let you take me out again.

I click send and wait, watching my phone for a reply, but nothing comes. *Annnnd shit.* What I thought was clever and flirty was probably just…not.

I'd ask her out in a hot second. I don't know how I'd get time alone with her without some sort of childcare, but Grace is gorgeous and funny. She seems so at ease with my kids. I don't know if a woman like her would have any interest in me, let alone any man with kids, but I don't have long to fixate on my worries. My phone rings a second later.

"Hey, I know it's late. You got dad stuff to do?" Her voice is sultry and quiet, like maybe she's lying in bed.

"No, uh, no," I stammer, jumping up from the couch and pacing the living room again. "Kids are sound asleep, and I did all the dad stuff."

"Good." I can hear rustling as she adjusts the phone. "I'm watching a movie in bed. Thought it would be easier to talk. You have a lot to learn about living in a small town." She chuckles, and I walk to the kitchen to pour myself something to drink.

"Enlighten me," I say, holding the phone with one hand. "And if you hear that in the background, I swear I'm pouring a glass of water. I did not take you into the bathroom with me."

She laughs, a loud, surprisingly sweet sound that sends chills down my spine. "I have three brothers," she says. "Not much would surprise me. But I might be a little less inclined to go on that date with you if you took me to piss on our first phone call."

"Ah," I say, grabbing the glass and heading back to the couch. "So, a date isn't totally off the table."

She groans. "Keep this up, and my mom's going to have us married off by Christmas. She loves to meddle in her kids' lives, in case you couldn't tell."

"I can appreciate a mom like that," I say. The words come out a lot quieter than I intended, and Grace grows serious.

"I'm sorry," she says. "I feel like I need to say that. You lost your wife. The mother of your kids. And they are so, so little. I'm close to my entire family, even if sometimes they feel way too damn close. It just feels weird to not talk about what you've been through. Is it weird for you?"

"With you, no. Can I be completely honest?"

"No, lie to me, Ryder." Gracie snorts, and I picture one of those brows putting me in my place. "Seriously," she says, growing more somber. "Tell me anything. You don't know me, but I'm a very trustworthy person. Even though Star Falls is practically fueled by gossip, I prefer to keep private shit private."

There's something else in her voice when she says that. Almost a note of sadness. I'm sure she's been on the receiving end of small-town talk at some point. She's probably speaking from experience.

"Well, I'm probably making the buildup a lot more serious than it needs to be," I say. "I have dated a little bit since Elizabeth passed, but I didn't tell any of those women that I was a widower."

"What?" she squawks, and I hear rustling sounds like she's sitting up in bed. "So, what did you do? Like, make up crazy stories when they asked?"

I laugh. "Nothing quite that exciting. It's not like I told them she ran off to join the circus or anything like that."

"Who even does that?" she challenges. "Nobody joins the circus anymore. Aren't they, like, unethical? You need to come up with a better story. Really make them wonder."

I laugh again. "I'm shit at this."

I realize that makes me sound insecure, and I try to backpedal fast. Fuck, I'm not cool. I tell myself to calm down. She's just a woman. A beautiful, tattooed, spunky woman who called me. I just have to talk to her.

"Most of the time, when it came up, it was enough to say that we weren't together anymore, and I had full custody of my kids. Most women were either turned off or turned on by that."

"Yup. Exploding ovaries," she murmurs. "It's a real thing. A hot guy with two cute kids. I can just see the dating profile bio."

I can't let that one go. After I put visions of me next to Keanu Reeves in her head, I'm soaring at the compliment. "Hot guy?" I grin and push ahead before she can answer and break my heart. I don't think I want to hear it if she really wasn't flirting with me. "So, what about you? Ever try the online thing?"

I'm more than curious about her life. I want to ask everything. I want to know it all.

"I tried the online thing when I was younger," she says.

"Younger. How old are you?" I ask.

"Thirty-one," she says. "I tried a couple apps in my twenties, but every single guy either wanted a free tattoo or thought someone who looked like me just wanted to hook up."

"Damn," I say, trying to lighten the mood. She sounds pissed, and I can't say I blame her. "Well, since I am not even sure I want a tattoo and I have no hope of bringing you into my bed unless you mind sharing it with a pile of plush toys, I think you're safe with me."

The words come out so fast, but I regret them even faster.

"So, if you don't want a tattoo, why did you come in the shop?"

"It's funny," I admit. "I've always wanted a tattoo, but I just never knew exactly what I wanted. Which is completely the opposite of who I am. I'm a coach by training, a teacher. I'm a rules guy. I like to know the rules of the game and then play by them. I color in the lines. I don't usually second-guess myself."

Except when it comes to beautiful women who feel totally out of my league.

"Wait. Did it drive you crazy today when I drew all over the menu? I color inside the lines when it matters, but if I'm playing? The whole world is my canvas."

My heart catches in my chest when she says that. That's something I already feel about her. Her freedom. Her passion. Her immediate honesty and sincerity that can feel almost brash. She's a big personality whom I could get swept up in and love every second of the ride.

"Your creativity is amazing," I tell her. "But I don't mean that in a 'hook me up with a free tattoo' kind of way. I loved that you showed Cora she didn't just have to color in the lines. That kind of freedom is inspiring. It's not something that comes naturally to me."

She's quiet, and I can't tell if what I've said is a good thing or a bad thing.

"So, if you weren't sure you wanted a tattoo, why again did you come into The Body Shop?" she asks.

I sigh. "New town, fresh start... I don't know. I've never actually been in a tattoo shop. I thought I'd go inside, check it out, and get the whole idea out of my system for good. I sort of did want one, I just...I don't know."

She laughs. "Oh, Ryder. That's rarely how it works. Tattoos are like snacks. You can never eat just one. Once you have a taste, it's an addiction."

"Addiction?" I echo. "That sounds dangerous."

"Fuck no," she says. "We only have so much skin, and most people only have so much money and time to devote. If you find a good artist, they won't let you get shit ink. Once you see something that is so beautiful and meaningful that it inspires you every time you look at it… I don't know. Plain skin just feels incomplete."

I can't imagine a woman like her ever feeling incomplete. I lean back against the couch and flick a look at the baby monitor to see Cora still sound asleep. I tug a blanket over my legs and settle in. "So, tell me about it. What do you like about what you do?"

"Well, I can't speak for all artists. There are a lot of trace jockeys out there who will put a French fry and burgers on the chest of a drunk kid for the right price. But most of us are artists. The body is just the canvas, you know? Each person is so unique, and each piece tells some kind of story. When I ink someone, I want to know the vision my client has. Not just for the one piece I'm doing, but any future pieces they think they might get. I ask about their plans, because if someone has a lot of real estate to cover and they put a giant turtle with googly eyes on their calf, that's going to be hard to fit into a bigger piece or even cover up later. I like to know the story behind why my clients want their design, so that if the piece won't work exactly the way they think it will, I can suggest options that maybe tell the story even better."

I'm intrigued by that and really curious. "So, your arm, for example. Did you have the whole design planned when you started it?"

She barks a harsh laugh. "Oh hell, no. I learned by screwing stuff up. I had a bunch of janky shit I let my friends do when we were learning. The tree is a cover-up that I designed once I got established."

"It's beautiful," I tell her. "It suits you."

She's really quiet when I say that, and I hope I haven't misstepped.

"I think you're beautiful. And I promise that's not just my way of getting free tattoo advice."

She giggles, and it's that sultry, sexy voice with a note of sweetness in it that reaches through the phone and grips my heart in a fist.

"Are you flirting with me, Ryder? You really don't have to try too hard. My mother's friends are probably firing up the matchmaking bat signal right now. You don't know the power of a small-town mom when she thinks she's found someone for her kid."

"Your mom didn't find me," I clarify. "We found each other."

That seems to take the conversation in a more serious direction than I intended, but I don't care. I'm interested in this woman. She texted me first. And I know all too well that life is unpredictable and short. It'll tear your fucking heart out and leave you with nothing left. It's up to us to fill up the spaces in our soul, so that when the tough times happen, we aren't alone.

"Gracie," I say, "I'm a single dad. A widower. I have some baggage, to put it mildly. But I would love to take you to breakfast tomorrow. Well, my kids and I would like to take you to breakfast. As soon as I can find someone I trust to help with Cora and Luke, I'd like to take you on a real date."

She's quiet again, and I wait. Maybe I pushed too far. Maybe I'm too forward. But I'd rather know now and focus on being her friend if that's all she's up for. This is exactly what I wanted, running off to Star Falls. Someplace different. New friends. People who might truly care about me and my kids. People in my life who don't just want me to send pictures of the kids they can look at from far away.

The work of starting over didn't just happen the day after we lost Elizabeth. I have to work to rebuild a life for myself and my kids every minute of every day.

I need a partner who will be there day in and day out to live the reality with me. Maybe it won't be the first gorgeous woman I set eyes on in this town, but hell if Gracie isn't a start.

Is it crazy to already be thinking about the happy ending? Yeah, it is.

Do I give a single fuck? Absolutely not.

I'll never know what a better life might look like if I don't color outside the lines once in a while. So, I ask again.

"Meet us for breakfast until I can ask you on a proper date?"

"I don't get it," she says, a smirk I can clearly hear coming through the phone. "I thought we'd already had a real date? Are you saying lunch at Benito's didn't count?"

I laugh, but she's saying yes. She's going to meet me.

We're doing this.

"I want pancakes smothered in syrup," I tell her. "Crisp bacon. Coffee as close to the bookstore's as we can find at a sit-down place."

She tells me about a couple diners and sit-down places, and we finally settle on Eddi's Eatery.

"It's in a strip mall, but if you like breakfasts, there's no better place. The food is fantastic and fast. Eddi with two D's and one I. You want me to punch the address into your GPS?" she offers, her voice a sensual tease.

"Are you offering to come over and do that now?" I growl, finally feeling the flirtation between us flowing again.

"If you leave a key under the mat for my mom, I might just take it first," she says.

We chat for a few minutes about what time to meet. By the time we hang up, I have half an erection and a whole-ass smile on my face.

It may be a family date, but I've got a date with Grace Bianchi.

CHAPTER SEVEN

Breakfast with Ryder and the kids is nothing like our lunch yesterday. To start, Cora is an irritable mess from the moment Ryder stumbles through the parking lot with her in his arms.

"Bad night's sleep," he explains, his cheeks flushed. "Might be a rocky breakfast."

While we wait to be called for a table, Ryder paces the parking lot, doing his best to distract Cora. I keep track of Luke, talking to him about the bees that buzz around the potted lavender plants and asking about his favorite breakfast food.

All the while, I trade flirtatious smiles and longing looks with Ryder. Even though I am excited to see him, and he seems really glad to be here, it is hard to maintain our vibe from last night while he is bouncing a fussy three-year-old in his arms.

When we finally are seated at a booth, the waitress forgets to bring us a booster seat. When we finally flag her down to remind her, she says they are all out of them, so Cora ends up sitting in Ryder's lap.

The final shoe drops when an entire tray stacked with dirty dishes falls to the floor in an ear-splitting crash near our table. That sends Cora into a meltdown-level crying fit, thereby putting a glorious end to what has already been a difficult breakfast.

I shove the last bite of my Belgian waffle into my mouth while Ryder stares at what remains of his three-egg scramble.

"I'm sorry. We'd better go." Ryder picks up Cora and motions for me to meet him at the cashier. We reach the front counter, where a line of people are impatiently waiting to pay. He hands me his wallet.

"Can you pull out the red one? That's my debit card."

I don't even bother arguing with him over who is going to pay the bill. He has more than enough on his hands at the moment. I take the card and, when it's our turn, hand it over.

After the completely bored-looking woman rings up our order, I grab Ryder's debit card back and scribble his signature.

"Thanks," he says, his face tight.

"No problem," I reassure him, wishing I could be more help as I put his card back in his wallet.

I follow Ryder to his truck, not sure if he'll want my help getting the kids settled. I don't really know what to do. The entire morning has been off. And not just because the kids were fussy. I think, honestly, part of what's off is me.

I am interested in this guy. I like the patient way he talks to his daughter, the way he seems as helpless as I feel to ease her discomfort. He never once yelled or snapped. He is upbeat, positive, and involved. Nothing like the men I've known. Nothing like the last man who couldn't even be bothered to text me back even after everything that happened between us.

There's no doubt I'm starting to like Ryder already. But that just makes me feel all the worse. I don't know where or how I could fit into his life. The kids are a lot. I'm a lot. I am sure all of that combined will be too much for him. I've been too much for so many people, and those were people who weren't trying to raise two little ones alone.

Out in the crowded parking lot, I pull my sunglasses from my bag and give him a small wave as I turn to head toward my car.

"Gracie," Ryder calls, his voice finally sounding strained. "Can you wait a second?"

His cheeks are bright red from the heat and the exertion of juggling the kids. But his eyes search my face with a look so hopeful, it breaks my heart.

"Yeah. Do you want a hand?"

He shakes his head. "Just give me a sec."

I shift my weight from one foot to the other and fan the summer air, heavy with humidity.

Once he's fastened Cora and Luke into their child safety seats, Ryder pulls out his phone and plays a loud video. Some cartoon I've never heard of with a catchy beat on the device, which he hands to Luke. Then he leaves both rear doors open to keep the air flowing into the car.

Then he turns to me, reaches for my hand, and steps close to me.

"I am so sorry," he says. "This is nothing like what I'd hoped today would be. I want to make this up to you, Grace," he says. "I probably should have canceled this morning, but I really…"

He stops and leans closer. I can smell the heat mixing with the faint fragrance of his cologne.

"I just really wanted to see you," he says, his chocolate-brown eyes meeting mine. "I'm sorry if that was selfish."

I smile and shake my head, gripping his hand tighter. "It's fine," I say.

But to be honest, I'm not sure what more to say. Getting close to a guy like this is complicated, and not just because he has kids. Because he's everything I want. Because he has everything I've ever wanted.

Seeing what I want and getting it are two entirely different things. Just feeling how much this man draws me in makes me all the more certain I need to pull away before one of us gets hurt.

I stroke the light dusting of hair on his knuckles with one hand. "I hope Cora feels better," I say. "Is there anything I can do?"

"Gracie." Ryder's voice saying my name feels as intimate as a kiss. As caring. As insistent. It's like he can read the doubts as if they are written all over my face. "You don't have to *do* anything. I just want time with you. Time to get to know you. But if this is too much..." His grasp loosens on my hands, but instinctively I hold him tighter. "It doesn't make you a bad person." He waves toward the car, where the music from the video fills the air. "This isn't for everybody. I get that."

"It's not too much," I assure him, but I'm lying. "It's not about you or the kids. I just...I don't know what to do here. I'm not sure I fit or how to help."

"You fit because I want you to fit," he says, his eyes narrowing and his lips parting. "Come to dinner tonight. My place. We can watch a movie and talk after I get the kids to bed."

I shake my head. "I can't. I have dinner at my parents' tonight."

Ryder looks down at our hands. He laces his fingers through mine. "Do you want to see me again?" His voice is low, rocky. "Ever?"

I don't answer right away, even though I know that I do. I wish I didn't. I wish I could stop myself from leaning into something that I know can only lead to heartache.

I try to talk myself out of this. I hardly know him. Now is the time to shut things down. Walk away and chalk this up to a funny chance encounter. I clamp my lips shut, try to stop the words from coming out. And I almost do it. I almost release his hands, head straight to my car, and leave all this behind.

But then he lifts his eyes to mine. He grins, and it's the cutest, sweetest, most endearing look he gives me as he mouths the words. "Please, Grace. Give me one more chance."

The gesture steals the air from my lungs. My eyes flutter closed, and all I feel is a rush of desire, of longing, flooding my limbs. He is sexy, sweet, powerful, and gentle all at once. I wish I were strong enough to run right now, but I'm not. I can't.

"Can I come by after dinner?" I blurt. "It's not that I don't want to be around the kids. If they're still up, we can all hang out together. But..."

He curls a hand under my chin, lowers his lips to my ear, and whispers, "Of course."

He lightly nuzzles my hair with his nose. A moment that passes so fast, the only way I'm sure it's happened is the racing of my heart that remains when he steps away.

"I'm going to try to salvage the day," he says. "Naps for everyone." He gives me a smile and then leans into the back seat to retrieve his phone from Luke.

"Say goodbye to Grace, kids," he calls out.

"Bye," Cora pouts, looking like she's about to start wailing again. Poor thing.

Luke waves vigorously while Ryder taps away at his phone, and then he slides into the driver's seat. He hasn't even turned on the car when my phone buzzes with an incoming text.

I dig through my bag, swipe the touchscreen, and grin. I have a text from Ryder. It's his street address with an emoji of a house and a little clock with the message, *can't wait.*

They pull away, and I get into my car. I roll down the windows to let in some fresh air, then grip the steering wheel while I lower my head to rest on my outstretched arms.

This is either going to be the start of something amazing—or my most epic heartbreak yet.

"Yo, sis. How's the boyfriend?"

By the time Benny makes an appearance at my parents', the rest of us are already seated at the table. Chloe and Franco are next to each other on one side. Vito and I sit on the other with our chairs pulled close to each other so there's room for Benny.

"Shut your stupid face," I tell him. "We're all waiting to eat."

"Gracie." My dad peers at me over the rim of his new eyeglasses. He scrubs a hand through his long waves of gray hair and shakes his head. "Your brother's face *is* stupid," he says, giving me a smirk. "That's not what I'm upset about. But what is this about a boyfriend? Why am I always the last to know?"

I shake my head and mutter, "I don't have a boyfriend, Dad. It's nothing. Can we drop it?"

"Pass the wine," Vito says. "And spill the details on this non-boyfriend boyfriend."

"Could we please talk about something else?" I grumble, grabbing the bottle of wine and pouring myself just a couple of sips since I'm planning to go to Ryder's after, and I want to be clearheaded. Not only for the drive, but for the time we'll spend together.

"When is The Body Shop going to open?" Franco asks.

I shrug my response.

"Honey, you know if you need something to do until you get the shop back open, we can always use a helping hand at the shelter." Ma sets a huge salad on the table and rests a hand on my shoulder. "Now, let's talk about the real news of the week. Doesn't your father look dashing in his new glasses?"

My pops groans, and my brothers start teasing him. Chloe stares adoringly at Franco, and I'm just relieved that everyone is consumed with catching up and digging in.

Before long, Benito is on his feet, kissing cheeks, and rushing back to the restaurant. "Love you all. Great meal, Ma and Pops."

Once Benny leaves, Vito's next, making his excuses and heading downstairs to bed.

"I think your brother is depressed," Mom says in a hushed voice.

"Vito?" Dad looks concerned. "He'll be fine. Don't worry about him so much."

There have been some problems at the firehouse this year, and Vito's hours have been cut way back. He's applied to other stations, but for now, he's basically working part time. Not at all the career path he'd planned for when he went into firefighting.

Franco and Chloe help clear the dishes from the table, and I follow them into the kitchen.

"I'll do these," I tell them. "You two go relax or go do whatever lovebird stuff you all do. Go for a sunset ride or something."

My brother is a mechanic and treasures his motorcycles. The one he rode here tonight he restored with his own hands not long after he and Chloe moved in together.

Franco gives me a look. "You sure? You never volunteer for dishwashing duty."

"You're such a liar." I swat him with a dish towel and kiss Chloe on the cheek. "Go. Love you both."

Once they're gone, I lose myself in washing the dishes, but quickly, my mind drifts to Ryder, and then goes even further back.

I start to think about Levi.

Leviticus Olson. The worst mistake I ever made. The last guy I dated. It's been over a year since we broke up... God, if you can even call it that. We didn't even really date—at least not as far as he's concerned. A fling, a hookup—that's what it really was. A couple weeks-long flirtation that ended in a colossal ghosting.

I wonder if Ryder's ever ghosted anyone. If he'd do what Levi did. My cheeks burn with shame at the memories. Just thinking about it is enough to send me back to my room to swear off men forever.

"Sweetheart?" I feel Ma's hand on my shoulder, and I sigh.

"I got this. Go have a drink in the yard with Pops. It's a beautiful night."

"I know it's a beautiful night." Ma strokes my hair with a hand, scratching her nails lightly against my back. "I want to spend time with my baby girl. Is that okay?"

I nod and turn on the faucet, letting hot water wash away the suds I've made. "Yeah," I say softly. "Of course, it's okay."

Ma stands beside me and takes a towel. She dries the glass dish and sets it on the counter. I can smell her distinctive perfume, and I'm overcome with emotion.

This is my world.

My mother.

My home.

I can't imagine what life is like for Cora and Luke. Not having a mother. Not having a big family always around.

Yes, sometimes we're all way too close for comfort. But I've been so loved my entire life. I've never gone a day without talking to my mom, texting her a hundred times even though we live under the same roof. I can't imagine a life where I didn't have Lucia Bianchi as my North Star. Can't imagine never knowing her as a person, as an adult with a personality and interests and plans.

"You've been awfully quiet tonight." My mom clangs a cabinet door that's loose on its hinge as she puts away the dry dish. She curses under her breath, a mom-style curse. "Shiitake mushrooms. I've asked Vito ten times to repair that door. You'd think the man could find the time to squirt a little lube on it and find a screwdriver or something. Sometimes I don't know about that brother of yours."

"They're all idiots," I say.

"Yes," Ma laughs, "but they're our idiots."

It's an inside joke we've shared since I was a teenager, the youngest of four and the only girl.

We keep washing dishes until they're all done and the sun streaks pink through the kitchen window.

"Lucia!" Dad shouts from the living room. "Should I turn off the air? It's supposed to cool down tonight."

My mom lifts a brow and shouts back. "Your call, babe!" Then she turns to me and kisses me on the cheek. She grows serious and pets my hair. I close my eyes and savor her soothing touch.

"You know you can talk to me about anything, right? Anything, Gracie."

I swallow back the guilt and the shame. Maybe now is the time. Get this off my chest. Explain what really happened and what might happen next.

"I... Ma, I..."

"Lucia. Grab the wine and come outside. This sunset's going to be gorgeous."

My mom doesn't seem to want to leave me. It's like she senses I'm close to opening up. She cups my cheek with a hand. "You want to come watch the sunset?" she asks. "I bought new citronella candles. Maybe we won't get eaten alive by mosquitos this time."

I shake my head. "I'm good, Mom. I'm going to run out for a bit."

She looks like she's going to ask where I'm going, but then she stops herself. She looks me square in the eyes and just smiles. "I love you, sweet girl. And I'm proud of you. You know that, right?"

I wrap my arms around my mom and hold her close.

I do know. I know I'm loved. I know I matter. I have always been able to rely on the strength of my family. Why, then, is it so hard to forgive myself for what happened?

CHAPTER EIGHT

Luke is playing with his toy train inside the bathroom as I hunch over the tub, giving Cora a bath.

"Dad, your phone." He grabs my phone, holding it out to me as he sits down on the toilet lid.

I'm on my knees on a folded-over bath towel, trying to wash Cora's hair without getting the suds in her eyes.

"Okay, bud," I say. "I'll check it in one second."

I smooth Cora's hair into a pile on top of her head and lean my face close to hers. "Listen, baby," I say, "you've got a pile of teeny tiny baby chipmunks wrapped up in your hair. If you hold very, very still, they won't fall into the water. Can you hold your head level so they don't get wet?"

This is one of Cora's favorite games. If she's in the mood to play, I've got about ninety seconds before she forgets and starts moving around so much the shampoo bubbles drip into her face.

"Munk?" she squeals, because chipmunks is a word she hasn't quite mastered yet.

"Yes, now hold still." I wipe my hands on the bath towel and check the message. It's from Gracie.

*You really did leave a key under the mat! But I'm not letting myself in...
That seems forward, even for me.*

A smile spreads across my face as I quickly punch in a reply.

*I'm elbows-deep in bathwater. You'll be doing me a favor if you let yourself
in. Grab something to drink, make yourself at home. I'll be down ASAP.*

I set the phone on the bathroom vanity and grab the cup I've
used to rinse Cora's hair since she was an infant.

While she covers her eyes with her hands, I rinse out the
shampoo, miraculously not getting any in her eyes.

I make quick work of getting her out of the tub, getting her into
her pajamas, and brushing her hair.

Our bedtime routine after the bath usually takes a solid half
hour, but with Grace downstairs, I need to give her a heads-up about
story time and our usual routine.

I race down the stairs, finding Grace standing in front of the
bookshelf behind the couch, thumbing through a photo album. It's
marked Memories, and she's smiling as she flips the pages.

"Hey," I say. "Sorry I took so long." I'm so excited to see her, I
hardly register what I look like. The front of my T-shirt is soaked,
and the knees of my threadbare gray sweatpants are too.

She looks up at me, then looks me over from head to toe.

I walk up to her and shake my head. She's wearing a sleeveless
black tank top that's all flowy and low-cut, exposing a sensual bit of
cleavage. Tonight, she has on pink jeans that would look positively
girly if they weren't intentionally shredded and frayed. She's
barefoot, her black wedge sandals resting by the front door. Her hair
is loose and soft, the black wings of liner around her eyes in stark
contrast to the rest of her face which looks dewy and clean. No bold
makeup, no lipstick. Just her.

"You look stunning. I'm so glad I dressed up just for you," I say,
trying to make a joke out of how seriously inadequate I feel next
to her.

"Are you fucking with me?" She gives me a grimace. "You make
loungewear look stupid good."

"Is that a good thing?" I hesitate a minute, but then I open my
arms, and she comes in for a hug.

She lifts up on her toes and whispers against my ear. "That's a very good thing," she says.

I growl a little and hold her close but then quickly release her. "Bedtime normally takes a while," I say. "Can you give me maybe thirty minutes? Make yourself at home. Dig through my drawers, eat my food..."

She pats her belly. "I ate with my parents, remember? But I will stalk your paperwork. Make copies of your social security number. Stuff like that."

"Excellent," I say, not caring what she does, as long as she stays. "Every strong relationship starts with identity theft or some other felony."

"Is identity theft a felony?" she asks, lifting a brow. "I might be in more trouble than I thought."

I chuckle and motion toward the kitchen. "I have wine and beer if you want an adult beverage. Raid the cabinets for glassware. Only the butterfly and kitten cups are off-limits. Those are just for me. I don't share well."

She twists her lips into a smirk and waves me off. "Go on, then. I have snooping to do."

I dash back up the stairs and start with Cora. I read her a book, answer at least ten unnecessary questions, turn on her white noise machine, and check the monitor camera before I give her a bunch of kisses. Luke is wide awake and playing on the floor of his room when I get to him.

"Bud," I say, clapping my hands. "Bedtime, sleepyhead."

"I'm not tired." He looks at me and then yawns a long, drawn-out, dramatic yawn.

"Really?" I ask. "I had no idea you weren't tired."

I pick him up and sling him over my shoulder, making sure I've anchored my weight on my good knee.

Luke giggles, and I check the time on my phone. Twenty minutes. Grace has been alone downstairs for about twenty minutes.

"Buddy," I tell him. "Tonight, we need to pick a short book, or you can ask me five questions."

"Five?" he echoes and rubs his chin like he's seriously weighing his options. "How about ten?"

I shake my head. "It's too late. We have a big day tomorrow. We need to find a new daycare for you two chuckleheads." I ruffle his hair. "Dad's got a job to go to, and unless you're old enough to babysit yourself and your sister..."

Luke sighs loudly. "Five questions."

After giving him answers to five questions I never would've thought of in a million years, I turn the tables on him.

"Buddy," I tell Luke, tapping him on the nose. "I have a question for you now. Would you like to join a class? What would you like to do for fun with other kids? Soccer or gymnastics?"

Luke opens his eyes wide. "Anything?" he asks.

I nod.

"Can we go to a pool?" He asks it so immediately and so completely that my heart twists. Swimming in the pool at the condo where Elizabeth and I lived was just about the only thing Elizabeth could do with Luke when he was little.

"Do you remember swimming with your mom?" I ask.

He nods. "I loved splashing. I don't really remember Mom, though."

"You know what does remember her?" I tap his chest. "Your heart. She's always there, buddy, even when your brain is filled with so many new things you don't think you remember her." I stroke his hair and kiss his forehead. "Get a good night's sleep, and I promise, I will find a pool tomorrow."

I turn on the night-light, flip off the wall switch, and dash down the hall to my bedroom. I peel off the damp sweats and T-shirt, throw on my most comfortable jeans and a short-sleeved button-down shirt. Not a job interview kind of button-down, but what I hope looks like a date shirt, a comfy blue chambray. Then I head into my bathroom, roll on a refresh of deodorant, brush my teeth, and spritz the tiniest bit of cologne.

When I get to the living room, Grace is sitting on my couch. Her feet are curled up beneath her. She has poured two small glasses of red wine and two glasses of ice water. Both are on the coffee table. She's thumbing through another album of photos.

"I feel like I need to give you some kind of award for most patient woman alive. You waited forty minutes for me. I'm so sorry."

"Don't apologize. You're worth the wait." She pats the couch next to her and lifts one of those dark brows at me.

I sit beside her, not sure how close I should get, but wanting to be so much closer than this. Now that she's here, in my space, it's like I can't see anything else.

I am fascinated by her bare lips, the sharp ridges I want to run my tongue over on her top lip and feel each peak. I drag my eyes away from her lips and look down, but even the tops of her feet are tattooed. I could look at this woman forever and never grow bored.

"I am so glad you're here," I tell her. "I'm so glad you stayed."

She cocks her chin at me, her full lips twisting into a grin. "I'm glad to be here. Now I have questions." She scoots closer to me. She points to the wineglasses. "The bottle was open and fresh, so I assume you drink red?"

I nod. "I'm not a big drinker, so anything is fine. The water is perfect, but I won't let the wine go to waste either."

"Good." She lines herself up beside me so our thighs touch. She has two photo albums and opens one to a page she's clearly looked at a couple of times. "Who's this?" she asks.

"My wife's mother, Rebecca. You can tell by the scowl she's a lawyer."

Grace laughs and points to a woman in a wheelchair. "And this?"

"My sister, Allison," I explain. "Cora is named after her. My sister Allison is also a lawyer, oddly enough, but she has no connection to my wife's mom."

"I'm glad I decided against stealing your identity while I waited for you," she says. "Too many lawyerly types in the family."

I laugh. "You won't get Allison to come after you. She's a high-powered LA entertainment attorney. She does weird stuff. Intellectual property, contracts, stuff like that. And she hates leaving the West Coast. She insists, even though we were born and raised in Ohio, that she's allergic to rain."

"Can I ask about the wheelchair?" she asks. "I mean, I guess I just did. I don't want to be insensitive, though."

"Nah, nah. It's fine. Allison would prefer people just ask and be open about their questions. It's like when people stare at your tattoos. I'm sure you'd rather them just say something than look at you funny and leave you both feeling weird."

"True," she says. "True."

"Allison was hit while she was crossing a street on foot. She was in college at the time, and so was the driver. The kid who hit her didn't have insurance on the car, and his parents had nothing. No money, no assets. Allison had always wanted to be a lawyer, so after she got through the recovery and rehab, she picked up right where she left off and went on to become the Elle Woods she always wanted to be."

Grace smiles. "That's awesome. Are you two close?" She asks the question gently.

I shake my head. "Allison has always been super independent, even before the accident. She is my half-sister. My mom married three times but only had two kids. We have different dads, and there's an eight-year age gap between us. She's a super-supportive older sister, but..." I shrug. "We lead very different lives. I became a high school teacher and stayed close to home. She doesn't visit often, but we video chat once a month so she can see my kids."

"I can't imagine not being close to my family," she says. She flips to another page in the photo album. "I still live at home with my parents and one of my brothers. I moved out for a short time but ended up deciding to come back."

She grows quiet, and I wonder what happened to make her move home. She looks like she's about to open up, so I wait and let her share what she wants. But then she pivots.

"My family is huge," she says. "Cousins and second cousins. My parents both come from big families, so reunions and weddings and stuff are jam-packed with people."

I lean back against the couch and loop my arm over the back of the cushions.

Grace looks up at me and gives me that brow. "Are you trying to cozy up to me, Ryder? Are you making a move?"

I am sure I blush eight shades of red. "I've been dying to touch you since you came through that door."

Grace gives a hilarious little huff and scoots closer to me, tucking herself under my arm. "I'll allow it," she says playfully. "So where are your parents now? And your wife's parents? Did you move to Star Falls alone?" She looks up at me and shrugs. "Sorry if I sound like a journalist. I just want to know your story. All the details."

"Okay," I say. "I was born in a little house outside of Columbus…" I'm teasing her. I'm not really going to tell her my life story from the beginning, but as I talk, I stroke the ends of her hair. My arm is over her shoulder so I can easily reach the soft strands. When I touch her, she presses her head back against my arm and breathes deeply. I smell lavender and something sharper, but I don't know what it is. "Grace," I murmur, lowering my face to her ear. "You smell freakin' amazing."

She rests a hand on my knee and squeezes. "So do you," she says. "Good enough to eat." She tips her head against my chest and stabs a finger against the photo album. "Stories first. Making out later."

"Making out?" I echo. "Will there be making out?"

"I think I'm owed, don't you?" She lifts her face to mine, her full lips pursed into a smirk.

"Do we have to wait?" I lower my face to hers and press a kiss against her forehead.

She looks at me, and her eyes sparkle. "Ryder," she breathes. "If I start kissing you now, I won't want to talk anymore."

I swallow and lift my head after taking one long, delicious breath. Her hair, if it's even possible, smells even better up close. I stroke the silky strands between my fingers but then pull away, trying to put maybe an inch of distance between us. Even though I really don't want to.

I groan. "All right," I tell her, scooting away just a bit. "You want my life story, you'll get it. But before you leave tonight…"

Since I've shifted my weight, her hand moves from my knee, but she manages to reach the muscles of my left thigh. "Keep going. Before I leave tonight, what?"

Her touch is gentle but firm. She kneads the tight muscles of my leg with a knowing hand.

"You were saying?" she teases.

Oh fuck. This is worse. I may not be touching her, but her hand on me... The blood floods my dick, leaving my mouth speechless and my brain completely empty.

"I'm, um... I was born..."

"That's Elizabeth?" Gracie traces the shape of my wife's hair with a fingernail.

"Yes," I breathe, feeling the familiar ache in my chest.

"She looks happy here." Gracie points to the one picture that sticks a stake in my heart every time I see it.

"Oh, she was," I say cryptically.

It's way too fucking soon to talk about Owen. My wife's ex-boyfriend. The guy she loved. The man she should have married instead of me. Yeah, I have a picture of her dancing with him at our wedding. I've compared the smile on her face as she whirled on the dance floor with him, arms wide, laughing, to the ones she took with me a billion times over the last few years.

I cannot believe I missed all the signs. They were there even on what should have been the happiest day of our lives. With me, she looked stiff. Like she was being forced to pose with a composed smile. With him? Well, the picture Gracie is studying says it all. Elizabeth was free, silly, alive. I didn't make her feel that. Another man did. Even on our wedding day.

As if picking up on the change in me, Gracie scoots a little closer, closing the gap I just tried to put between us.

"Let's close the album," she says quietly. "I feel like living in the moment."

I happily slam the album shut and move it aside. "I can get behind that. What kind of living would you like to do in this moment?"

She reaches a hand toward my chin and scratches her nails

against the stubble that's growing in. "I'm thinking this is a perfect place to have a first kiss, Ryder. What do you think?"

I don't have to think. I turn on the couch and take her face in both my hands. I breathe her in as she snakes her hands up my arms, shoulders, and laces them behind my neck. I want to bury my fingers into her hair and get lost in the soft, warm layers. Caress her neck, her ears, her chin with my lips, exploring every sensitive inch of skin.

But she's the one who kisses me first. Her lips are so soft, so gentle as they press against mine. She seems as eager to taste me as I am to explore her. She holds my chin in her hand and nuzzles my stubble with her nose. Then I feel the slightest flick as she teases my lower lip with her tongue.

I'm twisting toward her, feeling as awkward as a kid on a first date trying to hold her, feel her, get as close to her as I can while we're side by side on the couch.

I let her take the lead as long as I can, allowing her to set the pace. She devours my skin with small, hot kisses. My cheeks, my chin, my neck. When she finally presses her lips to mine, I can hardly slow my body's response. I claim her lips with mine, giving in to the surge of electricity that draws my buzzing limbs to her.

She makes tiny purring noises with every gasp of breath. She is as colorful and sweet and delicious and erotic as I imagined. When I open my eyes, I see the wings of her eyeliner, her perfect brows, the inky blue images on her tattooed fingers as they hold my face.

I slam my eyes shut and give over to the moment. No more thinking. No more looking. All I want to do is feel her. Feel the heat of her mouth when I open mine and taste her. She does not disappoint. Our tongues tangle in a nearly frantic bid for control.

I'm breathless and hard as a goddamn baseball bat when she shoves me back against the couch and climbs into my lap, then pulls my face close. If this were a movie, this would be about the time when Luke would come down the stairs or Cora would start crying on the monitor. But my kids are sound asleep, and Gracie is moving my hand from her hip to her breast.

I moan through our kiss, and her breath hitches. I'm sure she feels the raging erection between us, and I realize there's just no good way for this to end. I can't take her upstairs. I won't. I haven't done that with anyone since Elizabeth died. I'm a father. And as much as I feel like tearing the tank from her shoulders and tasting every inch of her skin, that kind of thing just can't happen spontaneously.

I'm sure she senses my hesitation. She eases her mouth from mine and pulls back, looking into my eyes. She's even more gorgeous now. Her face is flushed, and her lips parted. The perfect, silky hair is mussed from my hands weaving through it. Her lids are half closed, but even through the erotic haze that consumes both of us, I can tell she's looking at me with concern.

"Hey," she says. "Too much? Everything okay?"

"Too okay," I grumble. I look down at my lap and slide my hands out from under her hair. "You are fucking amazing, Gracie. I just want to be able to enjoy you without worrying a kid's going to come down the stairs."

"You're right. We're responsible adults. We can control our… urges, right?"

"Totally. Urge control. Got it." Even as I say the words, I'm pulling her in. Tasting her again because now I know she's going to leave. I practically asked her to, but I want her to know it's not what I want to do. It's what I need to do. "Nope," I whisper. "You undo me. I'm powerless. You're everything I want, Gracie, and fuck. You're right here for the taking. I want you."

She's trembling as our kisses soften and ease from hungry and hard to gentle.

"I want you too," she whispers.

But wanting and having are two different things.

Reluctantly, we disengage, Gracie pulling herself from my lap and standing to smooth her clothes.

"Well," she says brightly, tugging her top back into place. "This was fun. We'll have to do it again as soon as possible."

"Yeah?" I ask. "You want that?"

Instead of answering, she pulls me close for a sweet, soft kiss.

"Yeah, I want that." She reaches out a hand and tugs me to

standing, then nestles against my chest and hugs me. "But if I keep kissing you tonight, I can't be responsible for what happens. And I know tonight isn't the night for anything more. So, I'm going to say goodnight. Until next time."

I hold her firmly against me, breathing in her hair. I try to memorize the scent of her so I can hold it even when she's not with me. When I finally let her go, she looks into my face, and we grin like idiots. Like teenagers. This was fun. This was good. No drama. No games. Gracie is the real deal. More real than anything I've known.

She turns away but laces her fingers through mine. She leads me to the door, where she slips on her sandals and grabs her purse.

"Leave that key under the mat, Ryder." She gives me a grin full of promise, then I watch as she walks to her car. She starts it up, waves goodbye, and drives off into the night.

It's by far the best first date I've ever had. And it feels like the start of forever.

CHAPTER NINE

"Babe, you posted for the shop last night? I could fucking kiss you."

Romy drops a small white paper bag on my station. "I noticed it had been a few days." She winks at me before scurrying to her station.

"If what I think is in that bag is in that bag, I'm going to kiss your face," I say, unwrapping a peanut butter crisp. I don't know how the hell she snagged one, but it smells fresh so I'm not going to ask.

"She's a suck-up," Toni, another amazing artist at my shop, says before she sticks a finger in her mouth like she's going to gag herself.

"You could learn a thing or two from her," I say, pulling the cookie from the bag and pretending to eat it right in front of her. We're actually not allowed to eat at our stations, but Toni gets the point.

She blows me a kiss because even though we diss each other constantly, we love each other to bits. Staff comes and goes in this business, but Toni has been here since the beginning. We have each other's backs when it comes to just about any drama that comes up in the shop.

Toni sees everything in life as a fight. She tends to see the negative, and I get that's just how some people are wired. But she won't offer anything, ever. Not to take out the trash, not to cover the phones. One of her favorite lines is "Not part of my job description," and while I can't help but agree with her at times, that attitude is the only thing that ever really causes us to clash.

If she cares about the cookie Romy brought me, she doesn't really linger on it. Toni asks about my schedule for the day, and we bitch for a few minutes about how the last weeks of summer have passed way too fast and all we've been able to do was play catch-up.

Since The Body Shop reopened, every day has been absolutely chaotic. While our shop was closed for cleaning, our clients were anxious to get back on our schedule to get their tattoos done. Every chair has been full, and most days, Echo is so busy answering phones that the rest of us have to chip in and do things that normally aren't our jobs, which has made Toni frazzled and bitchy, which has me playing the mediator more than I'd like to.

And it seems as if, with every spare second I have, my thoughts can only go to one place.

Ryder.

We've been having phone dates every night since I went to his house. I've been craving more of those fucking kisses ever since I got a taste. I knew he was attractive. I mean, one look at his sculpted thighs and shoulders...and then those chocolate-brown eyes that would melt any woman who isn't made of stone. I'm sure we look like total opposites together, but somehow, the way he felt under my lap, the touch of his hands in my hair... God, the taste of him. We fit like we are made for each other.

Since our make-out session at his place, things have definitely progressed. We haven't even gone on a first date yet—not a real one at least—but our attraction is off the freakin' charts.

But I'm brought back to reality when my phone buzzes, and I check the caller ID.

My gut turns over when I see who it is. My doctor's office. I debate actually answering it. Running outside so I can have a few minutes of privacy and deal with whatever this is. But the stronger part of me, the part that wants no distractions before I start inking someone's body, wins.

I let it go to voice mail. I'm not dealing with it. Not today. I've got clients back-to-back, a backlog of designs to catch up on. Email and voice mail and... Yeah, I know. They're all excuses. The trivia and bullshit of everyday life that I'm putting ahead of my health. I know that's exactly what I'm doing.

I shut off the ringer, grab my purse and phone, and go into the bathroom. I close the door and splash water on my face. My heart is racing, and I feel overwhelming guilt and fear.

This is so stupid. I scold myself.

It's my doctor, not a bill collector.

My doctor wants what's best for me, and it's not like they are in the business of stalking patients. But no matter how I try to console myself, I lean my hands on the cool porcelain, fighting tears.

Whatever it is, it's already there, I remind myself.

But the reassuring words do nothing to calm the flutters in my stomach. The tears that have been threatening to spill out finally do. I don't fight it. I just sit on the toilet and let them flow. If I'd fought them, I'd end up feeling even worse and just making myself sick. And I need to be clearheaded and calm to work.

I let myself fall apart for a few minutes, yelling internally at myself.

Why am I so afraid of not being able to have kids? I'm thirty-one. I have a great life, a great job. It's not like my life couldn't be complete without them. I could adopt... I could...end up with a man who already has kids.

That kind of thinking is dangerous, and I know it. I've only known Ryder for a couple of weeks.

I spin the roll of toilet paper and wad some two-ply up in my hands. Blot my eyes, blow my nose, then flush.

"Yo, Gracie, you almost done in there? I got to shit." Toni's voice carries through the closed door.

"Are you serious right now?" I bark. "I'm in here. Go crap in the other bathroom."

I'm half certain Toni's being nosy. It's probably because she cares. But still, I'm pissed that whatever I need to do in the bathroom is interrupted. It's nobody's business, and we have two stalls for a reason.

"Don't you have a client?" she calls through the door. "Sis, you got to come out eventually."

I wait until I hear her walking away to blow my nose again and wash my hands. Then I look in the mirror, and it's obvious I'm not going to be able to hide that I was crying. Toni caught me looking just like this in this exact same place a dozen times after everything that happened with Levi last year.

Same year, different problem.

Or maybe it's the same problem. Me not facing up to what really needs to be done. Me jumping in too fast with a guy and getting my heart obliterated in the inevitable fall.

I grab some makeup and decide I have to load it up. My face will be puffy and red for at least an hour, and the last thing a client wants to see is an emo artist. I reline my eyes and add some mascara, then blink fast as the tears threaten to undo everything I just touched up.

Why the fuck am I so emotional about something, when I don't even know what's at stake?

I paint on a perfect dark red lip, dab a little concealer under my eyes, wash my hands again, and shake out my hair.

I've got this. I've fucking got this.

No matter what it is, I have been through the hardest parts already. I'm sure of it. Or maybe that's what I'm afraid of. That what I've been through already nearly broke me. And maybe what's ahead is going to feel even worse.

But today is not a day to doomscroll through my memories. I have work to do. A job I love. And reasons to walk through the shop with a smile on my face. Even if it takes a mountain of makeup to cover up my tears.

When I finally leave the bathroom, Toni is at her station, talking to a customer who's already in the chair. She throws me a look, but I ignore her and head straight for Echo, who's waving at me through the peekaboo window in the door. I head toward her and yank open the door to see her shifting from one high-gloss Doc Marten boot to the other.

"What's up?" I ask, hoping I don't look as bad as I suddenly feel.

Echo shrugs. She digs through a purse that looks like a brown grocery sack behind the counter and then points to three familiar faces standing on the sidewalk outside. "Somebody's here to see you." She frowns. "Says he doesn't have an appointment."

"I'll be right back," I say to Echo and then push through the glass door.

Ryder is standing on the sidewalk. Luke is holding Cora's hand, while Ryder holds two cups of coffee, one in each hand. Pinched between two fingers is a small white paper bag.

"Good morning," he says. "You look beautiful."

"Dad, it's not morning," Luke scolds.

"You're right about that, buddy." He's talking to Luke, but his eyes… God, his eyes. Ryder looks at me like he wants to devour me. He licks his lips, and a grin so seductive crosses his face every inch of my body tingles. The memory of what I did to myself while thinking of him last night rushes back to me, and I know I'm blushing hard.

"Good morning and good afternoon," I say, dragging my eyes from Ryder and bending down to greet the kids. "What are you all up to today?"

"Last Friday of summer vacation," Ryder says. "Monday, Luke starts first grade."

"Wow." I give Luke a smile. "Are you excited? All my brothers and I went to Star Falls Elementary. Do you know who your teacher is yet?"

Luke nods. "Mrs. Lee."

"No way." I clap my hands. "Mrs. Lee is the best. She must be about a hundred years old now. Both Benny and I had Mrs. Lee for first grade. You're going to love her."

Ryder's watching my every move with a look so dirty, I feel like even the kids are going to pick up on the heat between us.

I turn my attention to Cora. "And what about you, sweetie? What are you going to do while Luke is in school?"

I already know the answer to this because Ryder and I have been talking about it all week, but I want to hear if she's excited. I can tell by the pout on her little face that she's not.

"I have to go to the new babysitter," Cora says, grimacing.

"Well," I say lightly, flicking a glance up at Ryder, "I hope she's fantastic. I'm sure you're going to have so much fun."

"We brought you something." Ryder holds out a coffee cup and the paper bag.

"If this is what I think it is," I say, trying not to think about the cookie I already have at my station. This is definitely a two peanut butter crisp day. "I'm going to have to find a way to thank you."

"That's what I'm hoping for," Ryder teases. "I can admit when I have ulterior motives."

"Dad, what's an—"

"I'll explain it to you later, buddy," Ryder says, cutting Luke off.

I smirk at him, take the bag and the coffee, and lean close enough that I can murmur, "I can't wait to show my appreciation."

He chuckles, a low rumble in his chest. "I had another reason for wanting to visit you today," he says.

I raise a brow at that and grin. "Hmm? There's more?" I'd tease him and maybe even risk a discreet kiss on the cheek just so I could smell him, but a really attractive young guy, probably in his mid-twenties, walks up to the sidewalk, pointing at me.

He looks from me to Ryder. "Hey. Are you Gracie? I recognize you from the website."

I take a step back from Ryder and squint into the sun.

I nod at the guy.

"I'm a couple minutes early. I thought maybe we could go over a few last-minute changes to the design."

"Sure thing," I tell him. I motion toward the door. "Check in with Echo at the counter. I'll be right in."

I turn back to Ryder, whose sexy grin is gone. "That's your tattoo client?" he asks.

I laugh at his ridiculousness.

"Try not to fall for any of your clients until I get a chance to woo you," Ryder says. I listen for any real note of jealousy, but I don't detect any, which brings a grin back to my lips.

"Woo me?" I shake my head. "You're lucky I only fall for almost-clients. Not ones I actually work on," I say, meeting his eyes.

Well, at least that's the rule now since the last client I worked on and then slept with ended in absolute disaster.

He sucks in a breath and smiles, his teeth so pretty that I wish I could feel them against my skin.

I look back at the shop. "I'd better get to work."

"Have a great day, Gracie," he says.

We stand there on the sidewalk, and I don't know what we should do, but it's clear we're both debating something. A hug? A kiss?

But then Ryder looks down at his kids and gives me a look that promises *soon*.

I sigh, knowing this is how it has to be.

CHAPTER TEN

ryder

Now that we're three weeks into the school year, the entire Cooper clan seems to be settling into a routine. Luke loves first grade. His teacher, Mrs. Lee, has more than lived up to the hype. She is patient and sweet, and when Luke is too overwhelmed to say much, she spends extra time making sure he participates.

I've been swapping emails with her and am pleased to learn he's now raising his hand and seems to have no hesitation to speak when called on. He even has a little group of friends he plays with every day on the playground. I'm just relieved he seems happy. Well-adjusted. I'm not sure I can say the same for me.

Cora, on the other hand, is clearly not loving her daycare situation. I've considered bailing half a dozen times on the woman who offered to help. She's great, but Cora has just been... I don't know.

Maybe it's a toddler thing or a separation anxiety issue that's new since I've never left her with anyone. Every morning when I drop Luke off at school, we wave goodbye to her brother. I turn on some happy kid music and hope we can avoid the waterworks, but by the time I'm turning up the block toward the babysitter's house, the tears start.

She doesn't usually throw big tantrums, but when she does, it kills me. The fat tears, the trembling lip. Every day I have to leave her to go to work, I question all my choices.

Did I make a mistake not getting babysitters for my kids earlier? When they were young enough to adapt easily to new people.

Am I wrong to be back at work now?

Maybe it is too soon.

And to be honest, teaching isn't the thrill it always has been for me. Yeah, it's only a couple weeks into the year and everything is new for me too, but that's never been an issue. I meet people easily. I get along with everybody. Sports form immediate bonds, so whether I'm coaching or teaching, I find my place and fill my role, and the pieces just fall into place effortlessly.

At least, they used to.

It's nothing specific about Star Falls High. Nice people, engaged educators. The usual teacher drama. An assistant principal who seems to hate kids but expects them to find his weird, trying-too-hard sense of humor funny. You know, the typical stuff.

As much as Star Falls is starting to feel like home, teaching doesn't feel like the fit it once did. And that scares me.

Financially, I could take another year off work. But I feel like I've spent the last three years delaying the inevitable.

But I don't know if what I'm going through is normal transition anxiety or a real sign that I'm not the same man I was before.

Obviously, Elizabeth is gone. The transition back to something that feels normal was always going to hurt. I just wish I felt more confident that I'm doing it the right way. That the life I'm building is the life I still want. I never imagined I'd be doing all of this alone.

Except, I don't feel completely alone.

Whatever this is with Gracie, it's growing day by day. She's the first woman I've ever spent this much time just getting to know. It's been two months since I soaked my sneakers at The Body Shop, and we haven't shared more than a few angsty, rushed kisses.

If I never solve my childcare situation, we'll pass into the "old married couple" phase of sexless companionship before we ever get to the good stuff.

As I pull into the teachers' lot at the high school, it's between bells. Thousands of kids are switching classes, and a few who know me call out greetings as we pass in the hall.

"Hey, Coach Cooper." A group of freshmen boys tumbles over one another roughly.

"Hey, we're walking in the halls, right, guys? We're walking." I can't help but remind them that they can be friendly with me, but I'm still here to keep order and enforce the rules.

"Morning, Coach Coop." The nickname is followed by a chorus of giggles that I am sure comes from some of the sophomore girls whose class I subbed in last week.

I give them a neutral nod and a stern, "Good morning. Have a great day." I learned my first year of teaching that, as a young guy who some might call good-looking, making sure I don't encourage crushes or inappropriate attachments in my students starts with setting an example.

Friendly but not too friendly.

Firm but not mean.

Boundaries are everything, and that rule has kept my work life clean and my personal life clear.

Well, at least as far as my own behavior is concerned.

I hit the teacher's lounge and review my schedule for the day. For as long as I'm only part time, I'm on permanent sub duty, filling in where needed.

That means during the hours I'm on the clock, I can be dragged into any class where a teacher needs a sub. When there are no classes to sub, I pitch in and help the PE staff, which mostly means I help move and sort equipment and spend a lot of time in the athletic gym talking with the coaches.

The plan is for me to start coaching full time next fall and teach my own classes, but I'm starting to have my doubts about whether I can do it.

Before I was a single dad, my school and my athletes were my everything. I got up early, my head swimming with ideas and inspiration. Conditioning plans and drills excited me. I watched hours of game footage and practice tapes and rehearsed the pep talks I'd give the kids before games.

Now, I'm a full-time coach in a job that never ends. It's not that I don't still love sports, but whenever I think about throwing my whole heart and soul into anything new, I feel exhausted. Drained. It's not just doing this without a partner, although that's definitely part of it.

Moving to Star Falls was supposed to jump-start my return to reality, but I realize now that the change of scenery has only made me question myself and everything I've chosen even more deeply.

As I'm reviewing the instructions left for me by the teacher who's out sick, I feel a buzz from my phone.

Finally coming up for some air. I have tomorrow completely off. No clients, no sketching. I can literally unplug and maybe drag my favorite high school teacher away for a lunch break. Is that a thing? Can you get away for a few minutes tomorrow?

Gracie's first real day off since The Body Shop flooded and she wants to spend it with me.

Heat travels through my belly as I think about what we could do with a few unsupervised hours during the day. Before I reply, I check my schedule for tomorrow. I'm scheduled to teach PE and to cover a study hall for a teacher with a planned absence.

Fuck.

After dropping Cora off at day care, I make it to school by nine. Even with a part-time schedule, I have to work enough hours per week to be eligible for union benefits and everything else. I just can't leave campus for a lunch break that easily.

I hate to have to tell her no. I don't want to tell her no. But, yet again, fate doesn't seem to want to make anything easy.

That night, after I put the kids to bed, I text Gracie to see if she's up for a video chat. She replies right away.

Just home from work and about to shower. Can you give me fifteen mins? I'll be quick. I don't want to keep you up too late, Coach.

She follows up the message with a little shower emoji and a

winky face. I send her back a thumbs-up and then settle back into bed with a bottle of water as I scroll through some job listings, feeling a little lost and a lot frustrated.

If I leave teaching, I have no clue what else I would do. I must lose track of time because before I realize how long I've been scrolling, Gracie calls.

I pick up on the first ring.

"Hey," I say, letting the first real smile take over my face.

She immediately looks serious. "You okay? You look tired or mad. Tell me what this is I'm seeing." She motions at the screen.

"Yeah," I chuckle. "Annoying thoughts in my head. I'm a lot better now, though. How are you? I'm really sorry I can't meet you tomorrow."

She lifts a brow at me and gives me that skeptical look I love so much. "You're deflecting," she accuses. "No deflecting. What's going on?"

I sigh. "I feel like I've lost interest in teaching," I admit. "It's all I've been trained to do, but somehow, it's different now. It's not like before."

"Before," she says gently. "Before you lost your wife?"

I don't want her to think this is all about Elizabeth because, really, it's not. "Sort of," I explain. "Before we had kids, mostly. Now, the idea of spending all day every day taking care of someone else's kids…even as a job…" I rub my face and groan. "I don't know. I'm not making any sense. I'm rambling."

"You do make sense," she says. She adjusts her camera view, and I can see she's wearing a T-shirt with the sleeves cut off and the collar cut to be much wider. The thin fabric slips off her shoulders and past her collarbone. She must see where my eyes are because she points a finger at me. "Hey, eyes up here, sexy."

"Busted," I say. "Sorry. But in my defense, have you seen yourself?"

She grins and rolls her shoulders back, so her cleavage is even more pronounced.

"You don't play fair."

"How about this?" she says. "You talk for three whole minutes about what's going on, no deflecting, no excuses, and I'll reward you."

A wicked grin claims my lips. "What's my reward?" My dick is already semi-hard just imagining what she wants to share.

"It depends on how you do." She lifts her brows and nods at me. "So, talk. Timer starts now."

I sigh but agree. If I ever want to face what I'm really feeling, I've got to admit it to myself.

"When Elizabeth passed, she left behind some money," I explain. "Not a lot. She had some life insurance from her job, and her parents had taken out a policy when she was a kid. We had some savings too, which I lived off until I sold our condo and moved here."

"Why did you leave Columbus?" she asks, adjusting herself into a more comfortable position on her bed. "I mean, wouldn't it have been easier to stay close to your friends and your in-laws?"

I cover my mouth and yawn. "Sorry," I say, "not the company." I debate how much to tell her. I've never explained what happened with Elizabeth. Is there ever really a good time? "I, uh, got into a little trouble after Elizabeth passed."

She quirks up one of those brows, and I smile even though what I'm about to share is far from funny. "So, you're a felon?" she teases. "All that identity theft talk wasn't just jokes?"

I shake my head. "Nothing that white-collar," I admit. "The story is long, but I'll make it short. Elizabeth got pregnant with Luke while she was on a break from her forever on-again, off-again boyfriend. I didn't know it at the time, but I was the rebound guy. And I knocked her up. We'd been dating about eight months, and she said she really wanted to try to make things work with me."

I'm not able to hold back my sadness. It still makes me feel like shit, even now. "Elizabeth thought I was the whole package, you know? A teacher, stable job. A better father figure than the other guy, Owen, would have been." I laugh, a bitter, grating sound. "I didn't realize when we got married that she was still completely hung up on Owen. She wanted the dream, but she wanted it with the guy she loved, and that man was not me."

Gracie moves the phone closer to her face. She looks tearful, and her lips are parted. "Ryder, I'm so sorry. I can't imagine you being anyone's second choice."

When she says that, real anger flushes my cheeks. "Thank you. That means a lot."

I wave a hand in front of my face, trying to force the feelings to keep moving. I have a little more to get out, and I'd rather do it and not fall to pieces sharing it.

"Spoiler alert. Having Luke didn't save our marriage." I shake my head and can't resist a sad smile. "We were in the process of separating when Elizabeth got pregnant again. That's right...Oops number two."

Gracie's lips are pressed firmly together like she's biting back tears, so I try to lighten the mood.

"Potent swimmers," I say. "I should maybe double or even triple bag in the future."

Maybe my joke is in poor taste because Gracie pales and doesn't look at all like she thinks it's funny.

"I'm sorry," I tell her. "This is a shitty thing to joke about." I groan. "I'm a mess, Gracie. My life is a mess. I wouldn't blame you if you cut and run now. I really hope you don't," I say, meaning every single word, "but now's probably the time. I'm getting... attached to you."

She's quiet for a moment and just looks at me through the video feed. "I'm waiting for the felony part? So, did you get carted off to jail for stealing boxes of condoms because you couldn't afford to double-bag it?"

I chuckle. "Right. That's where the story gets good. Both of Elizabeth's pregnancies were smooth, and of course, once we found out she was expecting again, we hit pause on getting separated. But as soon as Cora was born, Elizabeth developed a heart condition that I guess is very rare. She was sleeping while the kids were napping and went into heart failure. Didn't know the signs, and she passed. Here's where it gets even uglier."

I sniff hard and brace myself for what I have to share. "It turns out that her ex-boyfriend had a key to our place. He was supposed to come to the condo to see her that day, and when she didn't answer his calls or come to the door, he let himself in. My wife's former lover is the one who found her dead in our bed."

Gracie must drop her phone because I see a flurry of movement, and then the camera is facing the ceiling. "For fuck's sake. No fucking way." I hear her shouting, and then a wild swath of color covers the camera before she's holding the phone upright again. "Ryder," she breathes. "I don't even know what to say."

I nod. "It's okay. It's a lot, I know. So anyway, Owen called the ambulance but did not bother calling me. The hospital called me when they pronounced her dead."

The story gets a little ridiculous from there.

The fucking mess of calling Elizabeth's parents.

"When I laid eyes on Owen at the hospital, I tried to tackle him. I planned on beating his face in, but I ended up twisting my knee, falling to the floor, and going to the hospital myself for an X-ray. Didn't even land a punch."

She's quiet now. I can almost see her mind working a million miles a minute.

"Gracie," I grit out. "It's okay if this is a lot. It's been a lot for me. My life has been full of disappointments and missteps. I left Columbus for a fresh start, but yeah. This is all a fucking lot. I know." I wish I could tip her chin, look into her eyes, and reassure her with a touch. Hold her close.

Instead, I bring the phone farther from my face so she can't see the tightness of my smile as I fight an unexpected wave of emotion.

"I don't feel like it's a lot," she says quietly. "It's life. If your shit's heavy, well, mine is too. I get it. Thank you for sharing all of this. I just wish I could hold you. Hug you. Let you know that none of this changes what I think about you. Except the Owen part. I really hope you beat his ass eventually."

I chuckle and shake my head. "By the time reality set in, I was too worried about raising a newborn and a toddler on my own to deal with assault charges. Besides, if I really did beat the asshole to a pulp, I could have lost my teaching license. Back then I just...I was just reacting. I felt so deceived. Like my whole life had been a lie.

And then there were these two kids… They were the only things that kept me tethered to reality. I don't know what I would have done without them. Everything was a mess and I wanted to blame Owen, but in the end…it wouldn't have changed anything."

Gracie sits upright and holds the phone a little closer to her face. I can see a gravity in her eyes that melts me. "Ryder, I really want to see you. A conversation this heavy shouldn't happen over the phone."

"You want this?" I ask, not sure I can believe what I'm hearing. "After everything I've shared, you're not running for the hills?"

"If you'd let me," she says, her voice thick, "I'd come to your place. Right now. Tonight."

"I want that," I tell her. "I don't care if it's late or if it's strange. I want to see you."

She gets out of bed and steadies the phone on something with the camera facing her. "You're not streaming this over the internet, are you?" she teases.

"Of course I am," I say. "I want the entire universe to know about my sordid past."

While I watch, she wiggles out of her sleep shorts and gifts me a nice view of her bare ass. My dick takes notice, and I clench my fists, groaning at the sight. She's even more gorgeous and far more toned than I've seen under those shredded jeans.

She pulls on a pair of comfy-looking sweatpants and drags a cardigan over her sleep shirt. Then she looks into the camera. "Are we doing this?" she asks and I nod. "See you in fifteen minutes?"

I lean forward and stare into her stunning gray eyes. "The key is under the mat."

CHAPTER ELEVEN

When I get to Ryder's, he's standing in the open front door. I'm wearing a pair of trashy sweats and a cardigan over my T-shirt without even a bra to keep the girls from bouncing, but I don't care. I practically run up the driveway and launch myself into his arms.

We don't speak.

He just holds me, fists the back of my hair, and presses my head to his heart. I can feel its steady beat through the soft fabric.

I hold him as tightly as I've wanted to for the last two months. Through every flirty text, every video chat, every longing look we traded over a table, a child, or a coffee… It all comes together in this moment.

The front door is still wide open when he lowers his face to mine. He claims my lips with his in a first tentative kiss. Just a taste. A touch that sends my body into overdrive and my heart into outer space. I reach my fingers to the back of his neck and gently scratch my way through his hair. Our mouths open, and we deepen the kiss, his tongue dipping past my lips to explore me.

He tastes fucking divine. Better than I'd remembered and more addictive than a peanut butter crisp. Our mouths fit together perfectly, and we kiss and taste and grope until finally he pulls back, gasping for air.

"Come in. Please." His words are as ragged as his breathing. I follow him inside, and he locks the door, then looks a little shy. "Upstairs? Downstairs? I don't know what comes next."

I take his hand and lead him to the couch. There is a large afghan and enough throw pillows to make this the perfect place to do what I came here to do. Hold him. Be with him.

I have no intention of fucking him, and I practically say it out loud, so my body is forced to pay attention. I want him. That kiss was more than enough to show me that our first kiss wasn't a fluke. We have the heat. But it's way too soon to dance with this kind of fire.

He's got some potent swimmers, and I have unresolved fertility issues. There's no reason to make things harder than they have to be. Sex is off the table, but that's not what I came here for anyway. Despite how tempting he looks in his thin, form-fitting sleep sweats and ultra-soft tee. Despite how my body feels like it's finally waking up after a long, uncomfortable sleep.

I don't say a word as I settle into the cushions and strip off my cardigan. I toss it over the back of the couch and pat my chest. "Here." I murmur just the one word and he complies.

He climbs onto the couch and angles his legs so they intertwine with mine. He curls onto his side and rests his face between my throat and collarbone. We lace fingers and tighten our hands together.

"So, all I had to do was spill my trauma in your lap to get you alone?" He whispers the words against my thin top, and I untangle my fingers from his and stroke his hair.

I don't want to speak. We've done nothing but talk for months now. The flirting and the banter have been great, but if you want to really know someone, you need to spend time in their space.

Sharing the quiet.

Sharing peace.

I run my fingers through his hair and scratch lightly against his head.

"This is torture," he whispers. "Having you here like this. But the best kind. Don't stop, okay? Can you stay with me, Gracie?"

I feel his hard cock pressing against my thigh, but I say nothing and only nod.

I hear the white noise machine that must be running in Cora's room. I close my eyes and inhale the rich scent of Ryder's hair, the clean shampoo and soap smell of him refreshing and real. This is a place that feels good. It feels like home. I can't imagine a man like this ghosting me. I can't imagine anything beyond resting my head against the pillows and staying here until the sun comes up.

After just a few minutes, I feel his body relax and his breathing grows even. I close my eyes and let my head fall back against the throw pillows. I'm more comfortable than I think I've ever felt in my life.

I feel safe.

Accepted.

Wanted.

Loved.

And I let those feelings wash over me while I cover our legs with the afghan, until I, too, fall fast asleep.

The incessant buzzing of my phone in my purse wakes me. I try to open my eyes, but they are sealed shut. I grumble and then realize I can't move.

Ryder is fast asleep, not in the same position he was when we crashed, but he's still beside me, our bodies curled together like nestled spoons.

I can tell by the faint light seeping in through the windows that it's early. And if someone is calling or texting me at this hour, it's serious.

I reluctantly slip from Ryder's arms and untangle myself from the blankets before scrambling toward the front door where I left my purse.

With one eye half closed, I fumble for my phone and check the messages. There are six in all, each in escalating urgency. I read them from oldest to newest.

Gracie, honey, I came up to say goodnight and saw you weren't in bed and your car was gone. Text me when you're home so I know you're safe.

Gracie, honey, it's well after midnight. I'm not sure if you're out or if I should call the police. Your father's convinced me to wait until morning, but please, baby, call me when you see this.

Gracie, this is your mother. Are you safe? Honey, please... Call me when you get this. Lucia.

I don't bother reading the last two from this morning. I pick up the phone and dial home. Ma answers on the first ring.

"Oh my God, sweetheart."

"Ma." I cut her off, talking softly. "I'm so sorry. I came over to Ryder's and fell asleep on the couch. I should have left you a text or something. I didn't expect to stay the whole night."

"Honey," Ma says, "I have been sick with worry. Do you know how much I love you? You've been so quiet and so off since last year. I didn't know what to think, what to do." She pauses and sucks in a breath. "Will you be home later today?"

"Yeah. I'll be home in a bit."

"I did call the police and tried to make a report. They told me you were an adult and I'd have to wait a ridiculous number of days before I could file a missing persons report."

"Ma, for real? You did not."

"I did. I'm sorry. You've been so distant, and you've been so stressed with the stuff going on at the shop..."

"Ma, I'm so sorry," I say seriously. "Can you get some rest? I'm off work today. Maybe we can spend the day together. After you take a good nap."

She's sniffling, and I hear a lot of racket, which probably means she's trying to hold the phone to her ear while she fumbles around for tissues.

"Yeah, honey, of course. I'm supposed to help Bev at the shelter today, and then Carol and I were going to meet Sassy for lunch. It's her day off from Benito's, and..."

"Okay, Ma, we'll talk when I get home."

"I love you, Gracie," Ma says.

"I love you," I say on a whisper.

When I end the call, Ryder is standing in the doorway of the kitchen, looking concerned. "Everything all right?"

"I'm a fucking idiot. I didn't tell my parents I was leaving last night. My mom went in to say goodnight and apparently spent the whole night thinking I'd run away from home or been kidnapped."

Ryder's smile is small and stiff. "You're a little old to be kidnapped, but I get it." He looks at me with worry in his face. "Why would she think you ran away from home?"

Now that he's opened up to me, I should tell him everything. But I'm not ready to. Not yet.

I have some unfinished business that I need to handle first. And I want to handle it on my own. The last thing I want is my mother or a boyfriend or anyone coming in to save the day. I don't want to be like Ryder's ex. I still can't believe that woman hid so much from the man she was supposed to share everything with.

And then there's Levi, the hotshot athlete whose star shines so bright, he thinks he is untouchable.

I'm a woman with flaws and faults. But before I share everything with Ryder, I want to bring him a story that may not have a happy ending, but a story where I'm my own hero.

I lift my face from his chest and loop my arms around his waist. I meet his eyes. "I haven't exactly been honest with my mom about things going on in my life lately." That's true; it's just not the entire truth. "There's more I want to share with you when we have time to talk, but I should get home and clear the air with her." I take him by the hand and lead him back to the couch. We sit side by side and hold hands in silence. "You know," I say quietly, "I'd like to date you, Ryder. Get to really know you. See if there is as much between us as I think there might be."

He tightens his grip on my fingers. "Hell yes. I'm in. If you're not already scared away, you're…" He grows quiet, and I bite back a smile.

Slow and steady. That's how this relationship has been. No flare, no wildfire. But the strongest things are forged over time, so maybe…just maybe.

"Would you consider letting my parents babysit Luke and Cora so we can go on a real date?" I throw out the suggestion that I've been sitting on for a while now.

It means bringing Ryder into the Bianchi universe, but after this morning, that cat is out of the bag for good. I don't want him to feel pressured, though. "You can bring them to my parents' house if you'd be comfortable with them there. Or I can ask my mom if she'll come here. This isn't just me trying to get you alone. I mean, it is. But the kids' safety comes first. Ahead of my dirtier needs."

Ryder's massive smile dims just a bit. "I appreciate the suggestion. I do. I just don't know how the kids would feel about that," he says. "They're adjusting to a lot of new people all at once. I'd be willing to try, I just…"

I shake my head and tighten my hold on his hands. "Say no more. I get it." The tears sting my nose and eyes again. "Look at what just happened with my mom and I'm old. Your babies are your heart and your soul. I get that. I will never push something that won't be in their best interests. If you say it's a no-go, that's that."

"Thank you for understanding. You're incredible. You don't know how few women would feel the way you do."

I shrug. "Good. Less competition for all of this." I motion my hand from his head to the waistband of those wrecked sweats. "And I really want all of this."

He chuckles and loops an arm around my shoulder, pulling me close. "Why don't you invite us over to meet your parents? I know it's not the normal way these things are done, but if we meet them and the kids are okay, we'll see where it goes."

I wrap my arms around his waist and breathe him in. I close my eyes and nod against the softness of his shirt. Beneath his shirt is warm, solid muscle. That steady heartbeat.

"I like the sound of seeing where it goes."

CHAPTER TWELVE

When I let myself in the front door, Ma is upstairs, and Dad is drinking coffee and reading the paper.

"Morning, sweetheart." He greets me with a kiss and not a word of warning or worry. "Coffee?"

I chuckle to myself. Leave it to Pops to act like everything is completely normal, even though I'm sure Ma kept him up all night freaking out.

I've already decided today is going to be a day of hard things. "I'd love some," I say. "Do you mind if I listen to a voice message with you? Not like with you, with you, but. Like, while we sit here?"

My dad looks at me over the stylish tortoiseshell rims of his glasses. "Not at all. Do what you got to do." He pours me a full cup of coffee and sets the mug and a spoon in front of me at the dining room table.

I punch in the voice mail code and listen to the message from my doctor.

"Hi, Grace. This is Anna from Dr. Calder's office. It's time to book your annual exam, but there's a note in the file that the doctor wanted to schedule a hysterosalpingogram. We can't book them on the same day, but when you call back to schedule your annual, just have them pull the chart and schedule both appointments. There are some activity restrictions before the test, so you'll need to schedule based on your cycle and will need to avoid vaginal intercourse. We'll tell you more when you call to set the appointment. Thanks, Grace."

Well, that's exactly what I expected. Not better, but certainly no worse. It's time to schedule the tests. And time to face whatever the results mean.

I delete the message and take a sip of coffee.

"Everything all right, kiddo?" My pops looks at me over those glasses, and I'm overcome with love for him. I can just imagine Ryder someday sitting with Cora as she faces hard things. I believe he'll be even more involved and loving than my dad has been, which is saying a lot. My dad, even before he retired, was involved, passionate, and supportive.

It hits me then how hard it must be for Ryder to have to put his own desire for adult time, time with me, even, so far down the list of everyone else's needs.

I've only ever had to take care of myself. Pitch in with the dogs. Pick up some slack if Ma or Pops is sick. I've had such an easy life. I realize how much harder I could work. How much harder other people have it. It's a humbling realization to think through. It's gut-wrenching to look at my dad and see a glimpse into Ryder's reality.

I get up from my chair and bend over to hug my father. "Yeah, I'm okay," I say quietly. "I'm so sorry I worried you guys last night."

Just then, my mom comes down the stairs still wearing her nightgown. Her feet are in fuzzy slippers, and her auburn hair is sticking up every which way.

"Baby," she says, coming into the kitchen. "You're home."

I pull my mother into my arms, and we hug each other hard.

My dad watches the two of us, sipping his coffee and sneaking peeks at his newspaper. "Should I go?" he asks.

"No, please," I tell him. "I want to talk to both of you." I take a seat at the table and slug back some coffee. "Is now a good time?"

"I've got no place to be." My dad's grin lightens the mood. "I'm retired, kiddo. I'm permanently off the clock."

Ma nods and heads toward the kitchen to pour some coffee. "I'm not due at the shelter until ten," she says. "But I'll call out if you need me here, honey."

"No, Ma, this won't take long." I definitely don't want my mom messing up her day any more than it already is because of me. I wait until the three of us are sitting at the table with refilled coffee mugs to start talking.

"I have some things to tell you," I say, "and it's stuff I probably should have told you last year. But I haven't been dealing with any of it well."

My mom's face is drained of color, so I rush on.

"I'm fine, first of all," I say. "Nothing really bad happened, I just, well… What happened was very hard, but I'm okay. I will be."

I explain how the short fling I had with the pro football player ended suddenly. He apparently grew up nearby but went to private schools, so I never knew who he was until he came into the shop for a tattoo.

"He was here for a family wedding, I think," I explain. "We hit it off, hooked up a couple times, and then that was it. He left town." I shake my head, feeling embarrassment and shame heat my cheeks.

"He didn't say goodbye, and it's not like I thought we had any great romance or anything. We used protection," I rush on, having a hard time believing that I'm thirty-one years old and sharing the details of my sex life with my parents. But this is the truth. This is my truth, and if I am going to face what happened, that means facing all of it. "He was the only guy I'd been with in a while, and I don't know what happened. The condom broke or tore. I missed my period after he left town. I took a test, and it came back positive."

I have to pause when Ma gasps and covers her mouth. "You were pregnant, Gracie?"

I nod, tears stinging my eyes. "I was so shocked and afraid. I didn't know what to do. I called and texted, but Levi didn't reply. Not once. That felt shitty enough. I figured he didn't believe me or thought I was just some…I don't know. But then I…"

This is where I lose my words. I haven't said this out loud to anyone.

"I miscarried," I blurt out. "It was early. I texted Levi to let him know what happened." I grow bitter then, the irony and the rage and the emotions I've bottled up for so long coming out in a rush. "I didn't want him thinking I was some dumb-ass chick trying to shake him down for money. I told him I'd lost the baby and he'd never be hearing from me again."

Mom wipes her eyes, and Pops hands her the paper napkin he's been using as a coaster for his mug.

"The asshole finally responded to that text." I remember it like it was yesterday. I pull out my phone and let his words speak for themselves.

This number's not in my contacts. Who's this?

My mom's hands shake as she passes my phone to my father. He reads the words and pounds a fist on the table. "What the hell does that mean? Was he fucking around with you, Gracie?"

I shrug. "That means after I texted that I was pregnant, he probably deleted my number from his phone. He didn't block me," I explain. "Which means he could still get calls and texts from me. He was sending a message that I meant nothing to him. That what happened to me was my problem and I mean nothing to him."

"That son of a bitch." Now my father's furious. "What do we do? Do we call his agent? Call the team? What do we do?"

"Mario." Ma's voice is sharp. "Let Gracie finish. We're not going to tweet about this and get the boy in trouble unless Gracie tells us that's what she wants."

I hold back a chuckle because I am damned sure my parents don't know what tweeting is.

"There's a little more," I say, and I firm my lips and just get on with it. "With everything that happened, my gynecologist did an ultrasound. She thinks there may be some issues going on. Nothing like cancer, so don't panic. But she wants to see if something might prevent me carrying a pregnancy to term in the future."

"Oh, sweetheart." My mom is gripping her coffee cup in two shaking hands. "What can we do? What do you need?"

I shrug. "Well, that's why I wanted to talk to you. I moved home last year because I couldn't face this alone, but I wasn't ready to deal with it at all. I haven't scheduled the tests yet. But I want to now."

"We'll drive you. We'll be in the room with you. Anything you need, Gracie. We will hold your hand through it all. Anything you need." My father's voice cracks, and his eyes shimmer with tears. "And if you can't have kids, you can't have kids. Kids aren't all they are cracked up to be."

"Mario," my mother cries out, but something about the sincerity in Dad's voice has me cracking up.

"Pops…" I laugh so hard my stomach starts to hurt. "Nice one."

My dad looks confused, like he didn't realize he made a joke, and he shrugs. "Well, I'm serious. You kids mean the world to me, but life isn't about just getting married and popping out babies."

Dad gets up from the chair and stands in front of me. "Gracie, you're an artist. You're passionate. You're the most powerful, beautiful woman. Your life has value and meaning, no matter what. Stay here forever and adopt a hundred more shelter pets. I don't care. We love you, kiddo." He squeezes my hands and looks at my mom. "The real question is who do I got to pay to crack the kneecaps of this son of a bitch?"

"Mario, stop." My mom stands up and drags her chair close to me. She cups my face in her hands. "We're not going to hurt that man. Unless you want us to."

I shake my head, knowing full well my parents are only half kidding. They'd probably wage war for me if I asked them to. And I love them for it. But Levi Olson is a selfish prick. Karma will find its way to him. My only job is to take care of myself.

"I want to forget about him and focus on me. On healing." I face my mom. "But I do have a favor to ask."

CHAPTER THIRTEEN

ryder

I'm stirring powdered cheese and milk into cooked macaroni noodles with one hand and flipping chicken breasts in a pan so they don't burn when my phone rings. Austin never calls, so I pick up the phone on the first ring.

"Hey, man. I'm cooking dinner. You're on speaker."

I can see Cora and Luke playing together while I cook, which warms my heart. Luke doesn't always have the patience to show his sister his trains, but since he's started school, he's learned a whole new way of dealing with other kids. Sometimes I love what I see, like now, when he's clearly demonstrating how to be patient with others. And then other times, he calls his sister a fuckface, and I have to write a carefully worded email to Mrs. Lee, asking who the hell is saying fuckface in the first grade… Yeah. The changes in my son don't always make me proud.

Parenthood, man. It's a trip.

"Ryder!" Austin sounds peppy and breathless, so basically the same as always. His consistency is one of the things I love most about him. "S'all good, brother. Hey, I'm calling for a quick favor. You got time this weekend?"

"Depends. Time for what?" I say honestly. "I kept the kids in swimming lessons, so we're busy tomorrow morning. You need me to come home? I could probably drive up after swim on Saturday."

I make sure the burner is off under the dinosaur-shaped mac and cheese and focus on not burning the chicken. My mind is already spinning. A trip to Columbus could be great. Maybe Gracie would be able to come? Ah, fuck. She works almost every Saturday, so probably not. Maybe we could go up on Sunday? She's always off on Sunday when the shop's closed.

"No, man. Nothing like that. I'm thinking about driving to you. You got a couch I can sleep on if I invite myself to Star Falls for the weekend?"

"Are you serious? Hell yeah, man. When you thinking?"

This is a surprise. Austin's always watching sports, managing games, or writing about them when he's not working his nine-to-five. For him to take a drive out to see us? I wonder what's going on to bring him out to Star Falls.

"You okay, man? Anything serious going on?"

"Serious, yeah, but not bad or anything." He sounds happy, so maybe he's met someone? News like that would hardly justify a trip out here, but he sounds even better than his usual happy self, if that's possible. "I'm not sick or anything. I just wanted to hang with you and talk. See my best friend's kids before they forget what I look like."

It's only been three months since we moved to Star Falls, but fuck, it feels like a lifetime since we left Columbus.

"Just come. You're welcome anytime. I legit mean it. This is a safe small town. I'll leave the key under the mat, and you just come whenever and let yourself in."

"Key under the mat?" Austin blows out a loud, long breath and laughs. "That is a whole world away from Columbus. But why do you need to leave a key out? You got somebody you're seeing?"

His question is a fair one, but I don't know how to answer it. "I mean, maybe? Sort of. I met someone, but…" I pierce the chicken with a cooking thermometer and watch the numbers rise. "We haven't even been on a real date yet. The childcare situation is all screwed up here. I'm interested, but so far, it's been tables for four on all our dates."

Satisfied that the chicken is done, I pull the frozen broccoli out of the freezer and let the chicken rest while I toss the whole bag into a pot of boiling water.

"Man, that sucks. Well, that settles it. I'm taking tomorrow afternoon off work. I'll be out to your place before dinner, and we can hang. Is there someplace I can take the kids Saturday night? Give you a date night while I'm in town?"

I can't believe he just offered to watch the kids. Give me a night alone with Grace? I pick up the phone and take it off speaker. "You'd do that?" I ask.

Austin has known my kids since the moment they were born, and he's my best friend. Even though it's been three months since they've seen him, I'm sure they won't miss a beat. Even if he just stays in the house with them once I put them to bed, there's no one on earth I'd trust my kids with more than Austin.

Austin chuckles. "Fuck yeah, bro. Are you kidding? I'm coming to town to ask for some help, so I'm fully prepared to return the favor."

Help? I'm curious what Austin could possibly need help with. The guy is a perpetual motion machine and is the most driven man I know. He knows I've got my hands more than full right now, so if he's coming to see me, it's gotta be serious.

"All right," I say. "I'll see you Friday."

We end the call, and I drain the broccoli. Luke isn't gonna be happy, but I plan on introducing him to honey mustard tonight to see if that makes the greens go down a little easier.

"Luke," I call. "Take your sister and wash your hands. Dinner is ready."

Then I pick up the phone and text Grace.

I have some sort of news. If you're free this weekend, I might be able to take you on an actual date Saturday night. I still want to meet your parents, tho. Video chat later?

Since it's only five o'clock, I doubt she's free to answer, but I'm grinning ear to ear when I see a little red *100* emoji come back in response.

Luke is not at all a fan of honey mustard, but we get through dinner, toothbrushing, baths, and our bedtime ritual without any major meltdowns or disasters. By 7:55, when both kids are sound asleep and I've started a load of laundry, I text Gracie.

Call whenever you're free, gorgeous.

I add a fire heart emoji, because what the fuck. I have feelings for her. And in the last two days since she slept in my arms on my couch, all I can think about is holding her again. My body's on fire for her, and my heart is already burning with something that wants to engulf me.

She surprises me by video calling instead of replying. I lean back against my pillow and start the chat.

"Hey. That was quick. How was your day?"

"Good. Good. My last client was a no-show, which was even better," she tells me. "I caught up on some stuff that I've been putting off."

"That's gotta feel good," I say.

She nods, and I can see she's got a marker or pen stuck behind her ear.

"Were you drawing?" I point to my ear. "Marker?"

She pulls it from between the strands of her hair and laughs. "Yeah. Just fucking around. Not client stuff. Something just for me."

"Can I see sometime?" I ask. "I mean, if it's not too personal or anything."

She blinks a few times, and I feel like maybe it was personal. Maybe I touched a nerve. But she nods. "Yeah. I'd love to share it sometime."

"So…" I run a hand through my hair and pivot to the good news. "Gracie Bianchi, can I please…take you…on a date this Saturday night?"

She grins and nods. "Fuck yes. What about the kids? Do you have a sitter?"

I tell her my best buddy, who's like an uncle to the kids, is crashing with me for the weekend.

She claps her hands and rubs them together. "Holy shit. What should we do? What do you want to do? My mind is racing!" Then she grows serious. "It's Saturday, though, so I might work until like nine. I have a client at six who will definitely be there for about three hours."

I shake my head. "Doesn't matter. I'll take one hour alone with you if that's all I can get." I'm definitely disappointed that she has to work so late on the one night I can wrangle a sitter, but I look on the bright side. Austin will be here, and maybe I can convince him to wake up with the kids and feed them breakfast. If I can sleep in until even eight, I'll be able to spend a couple hours with Gracie. And that's a couple hours more than we've had in months.

She smiles. "What should I wear? What do you want to do? We could hit my brother's for a late dinner?"

I hold up a hand. "Can I plan it? Do you trust me? I have something in mind, but I want it to be a surprise."

Gracie frowns. "I fucking hate surprises." But then she softens. "But for you, yeah. I'm willing to go with it."

"I'll take willing to go with it. But note to self, no surprise parties for Grace in the future."

She laughs and shakes her head. "Will I get to meet your friend while he's here? It'll be cool to meet someone close to you instead of you always being smothered by Bianchis."

"Yeah, absolutely. Maybe we can stop by The Body Shop on Saturday between appointments. Just drop off peanut butter crisps and run."

"Are you trying to make me fall in love with you?" She lifts a brow at me, but she's grinning.

"Stop trying to ruin the surprise," I say. "I've got this master plan, and yeah, if you're madly in love with me by the end of it, then..." I shrug.

She looks straight into the camera and murmurs, "I can't believe we're going to be alone. Like real grown-ups."

"Real grown-ups, indeed," I joke. "Did you smooth things over with your mom?"

We chat a bit about that until I yawn. "Sorry," I say. "This rock-and-roll lifestyle is wearing me out."

"I still have a crick in my neck from sleeping on your couch the other night," she says. "But it was worth it."

"I think I still have a case of maddening blue balls from the other night," I tell her. "*Totally* worth it. In fact, if you want to wear that same sleep tee and no bra on Saturday..."

She lowers the phone so I get a quick view of her chest. "Already wearing that," she says. "My favorite sleepwear."

I groan. "Gracie," I say on a rough whisper. I see the outline of her nipples through the tee. "The things I want to do to you."

"The things I want you to do to me," she purrs. "Want a sample?"

I swallow hard against the sudden dryness in my throat. Is she serious? Now? On live video?

I think of all the things that could happen and all the things that could go wrong. My Wi-Fi network is private. My kids are in bed, and a quick look at the monitor confirms that Cora is sound asleep. I'm sure by this time Luke is completely conked out, but I decide to lock my bedroom door just in case.

"I'm gonna kid-proof my room," I tell her. "Hold, please."

I jump out of bed, and the boner I'm already sporting makes it that much tougher to hustle to the door. But I manage to turn the lock with the phone still in my hand. I carefully angle the camera to show her exactly the effect her invitation has on me.

"I'd say that's a yes to the sample you're offering." I practically growl the words.

She smiles then holds up a finger for me to wait. I hear rustling and get an extreme close-up of her tee while she adjusts the camera. It looks like she's resting it against something. "Aw, fuck, hold on a sec," she says.

While she figures out how to prop up her phone, I settle back against the pillows and adjust my cock in my sweats. I wonder if I should strip them off but then think that's too much. I don't know what she has planned, so I just let my dick chafe the inside of my sweats and wait. My heart is thundering and my palms are damp with excitement when I see the lights dim in Gracie's room.

"Ambience," I say softly. "Nice."

She chuckles and then climbs back into bed. "Good view?" she asks.

"The best," I confirm. "Gracie…" I don't know what to say. It seems like we've been dating for months, and yet we've never been alone for more than a couch snuggle. She is gorgeous and sexy, and I don't know that I can pretend anymore that I don't want to go all in. That I don't want all of her. I don't care if it's hard. I don't care if it's not a "normal" way to date. Was it normal to marry a woman who wasn't over her ex? Was it normal for her to have a second kid with me, even though she'd planned on leaving? Has any of my so-called perfect life been anything close to what other people would consider normal?

"Yeah?" she prods. But I lose my words entirely while I watch her circle the fullness of her breast with her fingertips. The tip grows hard, and she tugs at a nipple through the thin fabric of her tee. "You were saying?"

"Nope. I wasn't saying a goddamn thing," I growl. I narrow my eyes and watch as she holds the weight of her ample breast between her hands. With her phone propped up, she can use both hands to touch herself.

"I'm open to suggestions," she says, flicking a glance into the camera.

"Skin." I practically beg the single word, unable to form complete thoughts. "I wanna see."

She lifts one of those perfect, dramatic, dark brows and puckers her lips like she's going to blow me a kiss. Then her hands disappear from view. One second later, the entire top lifts, and she rests the loose hem on top of her cleavage. I drink in the sight of her exposed breasts like a man dying of thirst.

"Holy fuck," I gasp. "You're even more perfect than I imagined."

"You imagined this?" she asks with a smirk.

"Only every night, morning, and probably every second shower since I met you." I can't be cool. I don't even try. I want Gracie, and the sight of her baring herself to me fills me with an urgency I can't wait to release. I want to taste the coppery peaks, suck those hard buds deep into my mouth and nibble them until she cries out my name.

She's smiling as she lowers her chin to watch herself as she twists the erect tips between her fingers.

"Do you like that?" I pant. "Tell me what makes you wet."

"You," she says. "Imagining you doing this to me."

"More," I say. "Tell me everything. Show me everything."

She cups the fullness of her breasts together and squeezes them. "Can you imagine yourself here?" she asks. She holds her tits tightly together with one hand, then licks her index finger and slides it down the line of her cleavage until it disappears.

Holy fuck. To slide myself between those tits, slippery from oil or lube or my come... I lower a hand to my cock and pant. "Fuck yes. Right there. Show me," I demand.

She nods and twists a little, giving me a perfect sideways view of her breasts. They are full, more than a handful in size, and they bounce when she opens a bedside drawer. She pulls out a black satin bag and a small bottle of lube.

She looks into the camera with heat glazing over her expression. She licks her lips and pulls open the drawstrings on the bag. "Do you want this?" she asks. "Do you want to see what I want you to do to me?"

I nod, speechless.

She pulls out a sleek black dildo that looks space-age in its design. The body of the thing isn't shaped like a realistic cock, but it has a handle, which I assume gives it a good grip for her to use on herself. I jam a hand down the front of my sweats and watch.

The cap on the bottle of lube makes a little clicking noise as she opens it and dribbles a generous amount over the shaft of the dildo.

I groan and stroke myself in time with the long, sensual strokes she uses to work the lube over the toy. When it's slippery, she leans back against her pillows and then licks just the tip of the toy with her tongue.

My eyes want to close. I want to smash my head back against the bed and jerk myself until I release, but I can't tear my eyes away from her.

She uses her left hand to cup the underside of her breasts together, creating the perfect valley to thrust into. Holding the dildo in her right hand, she slides it between her tits, slowly moving the toy back and forth.

My hips jerk reflexively. The blood races through my limbs, and I swear to fuck, if I didn't have two kids asleep in bed right now—two kids whose safety I value above my own life—I'd be in the car on my way to her now. I'd throw her against the bed and grab the toy from her hands and take its place.

"Faster," I coax, gripping my painfully hard erection.

She does, moaning lightly as the toy slips from between her slick breasts. She thrusts faster, making her tits move as the toy disappears between the perfect flesh. She pauses and pulls the dildo out and rubs the wet tip against her nipples. Her eyes flutter closed, and I can tell by the flush that climbs across her chest that she's aroused.

I have lube of my own, but it's hidden out of kid-reaching heights in an upper cabinet in my bathroom. I normally have time to prepare to use it, but now I need it and I am not about to leave the show to get it. I do, however, keep hand lotion at the bedside as a backup. I reach for a pump of it and fill my palm.

"What are you doing out of my view?" she purrs. "Show me?"

I hesitate for only a second. I'm a teacher and a dad, and showing my cock on camera to anyone—even someone I trust as much as I trust Gracie—makes me a little nervous. She picks up on my hesitation and smiles.

"It's okay. You can just tell me. Feel like taking off your shirt so I'm not the only one topless?"

I nod. "I just squirted in my hand," I tell her. "Lotion, that is."

"Tell me more," she urges.

I stick my hand down the front of my sweats and wipe the lotion across my shaft. Then, with nearly dry hands, I pull my T-shirt over my head.

"I knew it." Her words are low and throaty. A velvet purr and an enticing sigh all at once. "You're a fucking hottie, Ryder Cooper."

I twist my lips into a half smile, but I get right back to touching myself. "You're explosive, Gracie Bianchi. I want to watch you make yourself come. Above the waist is fine, but I want to see your face."

She nods. "Yeah?" Then she takes the toy from between her breasts and bends her legs so her knees are in the view of the camera. Her tits are exposed, and I can only imagine what is happening between those legs. She operates the dildo with one arm, and I watch her tattoos move as she works the toy with one hand and lifts and teases her nipple with the other.

Her lips part, but she manages to keep her eyes open, watching me as I thrust my lotioned-up cock into my fist. I try to keep pace with her. I don't want to miss a thing, but my dick is demanding attention. I grip myself but fight the need to tug faster, harder, until her breathing turns from panting to an all-out gasp.

"*Ryder.*" She grits out my name and then closes her eyes, slams her head back against the pillows, and spreads her knees even wider. She shudders silently, her tits bouncing lightly with the tremors that rock her body. I can't stop myself from coming, and with a few fast, furious jerks, I spill my whole load right into my palm.

I gasp but keep my eyes open, watching every second of her release.

I wipe my hand on my wadded-up shirt and wait until she opens her eyes to make a sound.

"I've never watched anyone titty-fuck a dildo before," I say, awe in my tone. "It might just be my new favorite foreplay."

"Just you wait," she says. "I've been pining for you for months now. I've got lots of creative ways to work out the frustration."

We talk a few more minutes and then blow each other kisses and say goodnight. By the time I end the video call, I'm happy. Satisfied. I feel complete here in Star Falls in a way I never felt back in Columbus. I'm sure of it now. I'm falling head over fucking sneakers for Gracie Bianchi.

CHAPTER FOURTEEN

gracie

No matter how many times or ways I look at the calendar, there's no changing the timing. I called my doctor the same morning I told my parents what happened.

The catch?

My test is on Tuesday. Three days *after* my first real date with Ryder.

The karmic joke's on me, because I can't have sex that close to the test.

But God do I want him. Really, really want him.

I smile as I get ready for work. This is, without a doubt, the strangest relationship I've ever been in. But it's also the most exciting. The most hilarious. Ryder can crack me up with a single emoji. And I know I've done the same for him. I'm just amazed at the way I feel. This feels real and right, even if it's far from normal.

Once I'm dressed, I head over to the small drafting table I have in my room and look over the pages. I've been putting the finishing touches on a special project I've been working on the last few weeks.

A few weeks ago, Luke and I got into a conversation about trains. He knows a lot about them, in kind of a nerdy, adorable way. Especially for a first grader. It's obvious his dad has either read him a lot of books or answered a lot of questions about trains, so I started looking for a train coloring book or kids' encyclopedia on trains, but I couldn't find anything.

I don't normally draw technical pieces. Pistons and machinery I usually leave to my colleagues, but I've been practicing drawing trains so I can maybe put together a custom coloring book or something for Christmas.

I know, I know. It's only been a few months that I've even known Ryder. Thinking about giving his kids holiday gifts is maybe a stretch. But these kinds of gifts take time. I'd rather practice making trains now and toss the whole ream of paper into the bin than wake up on Christmas morning wishing I'd spent the time when I could sneak a few minutes here and there.

Once I'm dressed and ready, I pass my brother Vito in the hallway.

"You leaving?" he asks.

"No, idiot. I just got home. I'm going to bed." I smack him before he has the chance to smack me and run down the stairs.

"Real mature, Gracie," he shouts, but he's laughing and I'm laughing.

Brothers. They never get any better, just older.

My pops is at the dining room table with his glasses in his hand, reading. I head over to kiss him goodbye, but the look on his face stops me.

"Dad?" I say. "Everything okay?"

He shrugs. "I don't know, bella. You tell me." He hands me the sports section of the newspaper.

"Just tell me," I say, anxiety starting to pool in my belly.

"That asshole," he spits, shaking his phone in the air like he wants to toss it. "That Levi Olson kid."

I taste bile in my throat and grimace. "What? What is it? Is he dead or something?"

"I only wish. He deserves no less for what he did to my daughter."

"All right, Pops. Thanks, but out with it. I need to go to work."

My pops walks over to me. He puts his hands on my shoulders

and looks me square in the eye. "Something big happened. I don't know what, the news isn't saying. All I know is the team made a statement this morning that Olson's been cut. He's done. And his publicist followed the statement up with this."

My dad puts on his glasses and reads from his phone: "Levi Olson has officially terminated his position on the Cleveland Cyclones. This separation is mutual and was made with the understanding that Levi could return to play in the league and on the team at any point in the future if an agreement were to be reached. There are allegations that may be made in the media, and we urge the fans not to be distracted by unsubstantiated rumors. Levi consulted with the coaching staff, his teammates, and league officials prior to reaching this life-changing decision. His personal health and well-being come first, and he will spend the next few months away from the field to focus on himself. We'd ask that the privacy of Levi and his family be respected during this time."

I'm shocked, and it must show on my face. "What the fuck happened?" I ask.

My dad shrugs. "I've been searching every news feed I can find. I don't know what he did, but it had to be bad. The league wouldn't cut him loose mid-season unless it was a conduct violation. That or maybe drugs?"

This isn't great news for him. Whatever it is, something like that could end his career. While I should be dancing on cloud nine and popping champagne, this doesn't feel like cause to celebrate.

Someone else's downfall doesn't make me feel better about myself. I was probably just another casualty of a man whose life was already showing signs of falling apart. I wouldn't have known that, of course, until it was too late.

"Well, I'm not happy for him. Even if karma did come calling quick. Shitty situation. Thanks for telling me, though, Dad."

"Gracie," he says. "There's one more thing. There're a few stories reporting that the asshat's coming back to Star Falls. Tail between his legs kind of shit."

"What? Why the hell would he come back here?" I knew he had family here, but…a guy with his money and connections, shouldn't he go to rehab out in Malibu or disappear abroad for a couple months?

Pops shrugs. "All I know is if I run into him, I'll take a mallet to his knees, Gracie. So help me God, I will."

I pull my pops into a hug. "Thank you," I murmur. "But, Pops. You didn't work at the steel mill for all those years to spend your retirement behind bars."

"I'm an old man. How long they going to give me?" he asks. "Ten years? I'd do ten years for you, Gracie. I'd do a lifetime if it meant getting even with the shit-stain that hurt my little girl."

I chuckle at that. "It looks like karma took care of the shit-stain for us, Dad." I kiss him on the cheek and check the time. "I got to roll. Thanks for letting me know. Does Ma know?"

He nods. "I had her run into town to set up a bail fund."

I give him a single-brow scolding, and he laughs. "Kidding. I texted her the story. She told me to tell you before you heard it on the news."

I doubt that's the kind of news that would ever reach me in my day-to-day life, but I appreciate their looking out for me. I kiss my dad goodbye and head to work, ready to put Levi Olson and the shame of my past in the grave forever.

Well, if I'd thought I could live in Star Falls even five minutes without the whole town buzzing about it, I was seriously mistaken.

The second I unlock the door to The Body Shop, Toni is coming in on my heels. "Bitch, did you hear about that hottie you inked last year?" She's wearing the most obscenely tight leopard-print leggings with a hot-pink top and an armload of jelly bracelets. She's wearing sunglasses, but the second she takes them off, she starts eyeballing me with this curious look on her face. "You know who I'm talking about, right?"

I glare at her. "No," I say.

This is exactly why I didn't tell anyone when it happened.

"We never hooked up," I lie to her, confirming the story I told everyone last year. "We had drinks, traded a few texts, and he was back to his real life."

"Maybe he wants another tattoo," she says. "If he comes back in, he fair game?"

I grimace, not entirely sure what she means. "Like, you want him as a client? Go for it. I could not care less."

I turn away from her and greet Echo, who pushes through the door looking rather plain. She's wearing a long-sleeved black shirt, a pair of black pants, and her face is free of makeup.

"What happened to you?" Toni demands, leaning on the counter while Echo punches into the app on the tablet. "You look like normal."

Echo rolls her eyes. "Job interview," she says, sounding incredibly grumpy about it.

"What?" I ask. "Why?"

Echo grabs a giant purse shaped like an old-school metal lunch box, complete with metal clasp and plastic handle. "I'm looking for something else part time. Wish me luck finding anything where I can dress the way I want."

She storms to the back, where I assume she plans to change her clothes, leaving Toni and me behind.

"She's a strange bird," Toni says.

"There's only one Echo."

"You know what I'd be doing if I were you?" Toni asks, getting back to a juicier topic and forgetting all about Echo. "I'd be reaching out to that hottie football player, and I'd try to get him out for a date. Maybe he'll spill some dirt about why he got fired. That's a story worth big money to the media. You know what I'm saying?"

"What the fuck, Toni? You want to go seduce some loser and sell his story to the press, go for it. I don't want anything to do with that shady shit."

Toni clucks her tongue and heads toward the back. "That's a mistake, babe," she says. "Look, we're not like those people. He's rich, and he's fucking over other people with his money and his position in life. Having people fuck you back just comes with the territory. I wouldn't hesitate to sell a dick pic, a story... Shit. If there was enough money in it, I don't know there's much aside from illegal shit that I wouldn't do."

There's no arguing with Toni. I'm not even going to try to change her mind. She's entitled to her views.

I'm suddenly exhausted. I check the tablet and see my client for two is confirmed. He's a regular, and he just wants a small addition to a piece I did for him two summers ago. Should take me no more than three hours, including sketching and placing the stencil.

I am relieved in some ways. Glenn is a great guy. Older man, not too chatty. Easy to talk to if I'm in the mood, but able to be quiet and let me work once I'm in the flow. It's a small gift from the universe that I'll take today because the last thing I want is to hear any more about Levi Olson.

CHAPTER FIFTEEN

ryder

I walk into my rental house to find my buddy Austin, sleeves rolled to his elbows, feet on the coffee table, furiously typing on his laptop.

"Uncle Austin," I say as we walk through the door.

Austin jumps up from the couch, immediately closing the lid on his laptop. "Would you look at this." He opens his arms and bends down to greet Cora and Luke. "Who are these kids? They're so big."

Cora throws herself into Austin's arms, which breaks my heart. We looked at pictures of him last night so I was sure she hadn't forgotten him and wouldn't be scared. She rests her head on his shoulder, and he kisses her hair while he rocks her in a giant hug.

Then he sets her down and extends a hand to Luke. "Hey, little man. Do we shake hands now or what?"

Luke chuckles, but I can see he's a little more nervous than Cora was. He doesn't say anything but sort of leans close to Austin, who wraps him in his arms. "It's been a minute, man. It's okay if you kind of forgot me."

But then, Austin sniffles. He steps away from Luke and covers his face with his hand. He dramatically flops to the floor, pretending to be hurt. "You don't remember your favorite uncle. It's okay, guys. I'm not hurt."

125

Luke flops onto the floor and hugs Austin, reassuring him, "I remember. I remember."

As much as I doubt I'll try the same technique to get Luke past his speaking anxiety, I'm impressed at how effective it is.

Once everyone is standing and the hugs are done, I send the kids to the bathroom to wash their hands so I can give Austin a hug of my own.

"Hey, man. Amazing to see you." I clap him hard, and he hugs me back before motioning his arms around the place. "Cute house, adorable neighborhood. I can see why you left the city. This is a whole change of pace."

I nod. "Star Falls is starting to feel like home. You want to go out for dinner? Gracie's brother owns the best Italian restaurant here in town."

"Gracie?" He cocks his chin and grins at me. "Is that her name? Tell me all about her. And yeah, I'm down for Italian. Luke still love pasta?"

"More than anything," I confirm. "I should call and see if we need a reservation."

When the kids come back to the living room, I empty their backpacks and send them upstairs to play so Austin and I can talk.

"Fifteen minutes," I tell Luke. "Watch your sister for fifteen minutes. I'm going to try to get us a reservation at Benito's. You feel like going out for pasta?"

"Is Gracie going to come?" he asks.

Austin shoots me a look that says everything.

"Nah, bud. Gracie's working tonight. But we'll see her this weekend, I'm sure. I want her to meet Uncle Austin. Go on now. Fifteen minutes."

Once the kids are upstairs, Austin drops onto the couch. "I see the kids like her. What's she do?"

"You're not going to believe this," I say, kicking off my shoes. "She's a fucking artist. A tattoo artist. She's amazing. Creative, colorful. Bold. I just... She's incredible. She really is something."

Austin is quiet for a second. "I'm happy for you, Ryder," he says.

He walks to the kitchen, where pictures colored and signed by Cora, Luke, and Gracie decorate the refrigerator. "This is her?" he asks, pointing to the menu from Benito's enhanced by the pair of swallows she drew at lunch three months ago.

I nod. "That's her."

Austin whistles. "That's talent." He picks up a small note that has a train sketched on it. A handmade card crafted from textured paper with a small, highly stylized image of a boy riding a train into Mrs. Lee's classroom. "She did this? For Luke?"

I grin. "Yeah." There are little signs of Gracie's presence in our lives everywhere. "They say opposites attract, but we're not opposites," I tell him.

"Does she want kids? Has she ever been married?"

"No to the marriage thing. I don't know about kids. That's one thing we haven't talked about. It seems like putting the cart before the horse when we haven't even had an overnight date yet."

Austin wanders to the art and looks closer. "You weren't even like this with Elizabeth," he says softly. "Not even when things were good."

"I know." I join him in the kitchen to pour us something to drink. "I'm happy. I like her and...I don't know. Since I have my kids already, I don't feel in a rush to figure out what this is. If it could be forever. It's so different dating women now, you know?"

Austin slaps his hands together and crows out a laugh. "God, remember that one woman? She wanted to meet your kids on the first date?"

"Correction," I tell him. "She wanted my kids to try calling her Mama Colleen on the first date just to see if she could imagine herself being their stepmom someday."

"I don't get women," Austin says.

I know better than to poke that sleeping bear. But still, I'm concerned. "You doing okay?"

Austin still doesn't talk about the one who got away. People do some shady-ass shit, and when you're a trusting, sweet guy with loads of money, you can make some bad choices. Or get tricked into making bad choices. Either way, Austin brought it up, so I feel like it's fair game to at least ask.

"I feel better than I have in a long time," he says excitedly. "Still not dating, but…"

That's probably as much as he'll say on the topic, so I move on. "You want a beer?"

Austin shakes his head. "Just water."

When we sit back down on the couch, Austin's attitude has shifted. He doesn't seem nearly as excited as he did.

"I'm glad you're happy," he says. "So, you think it's serious with Gracie?"

I nod. "Hope so. Think so. But you know, we haven't really dated. I don't know how to date a woman without babysitters and family around. But in time, I hope it all happens for us. That's one of the craziest parts about this. She doesn't push. Never makes me feel guilty. Never puts her needs above the kids, but doesn't act like a martyr about it either. I always know where I stand with her. I'm happy."

"I want that for you. I do."

I'm not sure why the mood in the room has changed, but I want to hear more about what's going on for him. "So, tell me everything. Catch me up. Why the visit? How's your mom? We've got less than fifteen minutes before somebody's going to want Uncle Austin to play trains."

He chuckles and leans back against the couch. "I don't want to burst your Star Falls bubble," he says. "But I came here hoping I could talk you into moving home. Sounds like the girlfriend complicates that."

Move home? I don't know why I'd do that now. If I'd never met Gracie, there'd be nothing other than the great food and quaintness of this small town to keep me here. And that's a lot, but not enough to build a life around.

He's right. Gracie is the reason I feel at home in Star Falls. But still, I'm curious what Austin has in mind.

"Why do you want me to move back?" I ask. "What's going on in Columbus?"

Austin sighs and leans back against the couch. "I'm done with the corporate shit, Ryder. I'm happy with the money, but the work I do every day is just... I don't care anymore. Maybe it's me getting older, but... I've applied for a management spot three times over the last year."

I nod, remembering two of the times he'd tossed his name in the ring. "Well, the first time you were passed over..."

"Right. Because they hired someone outside they'd been trying to recruit away from our biggest competitor for a year. Fine. But these last two times? Ryder, something isn't working for me anymore. My numbers are good, but my heart's not in it. That's basically what they said when they let me know I didn't get either of the last two promotions. I'm good at what I do, just not good enough for a corner office."

I rake a hand through my hair. "That's rough, man. Corporate bullshit. I can't pretend I know anything about it. You need to vent about teachers having affairs with each other, I might be able to help. But this..." I shrug. "I'm sorry. So, what, you're thinking about leaving your job?"

I'm not sure what this has to do with me, or me moving back to Columbus. I can't imagine what he needs that I can help him with.

"Here's where you come in," he says, getting excited. He leans forward and props his hands on his knees. "I want to start a business, Ryder. Something that I'm passionate about. Something that means more to me than just managing people's money."

"Okay. Do you have a business plan? Investors? What do you want to do?"

He gets up and starts pacing the floors. "Yeah, I'm in the final stages now. I want to start a franchise of gyms for kids. But not just gyms. Sports academies. Where do kids go to learn, really learn, how to play sports?"

"School, local teams, park districts. Private camps and stuff." I think of the aquatic center and how few classes they have for kids.

"Exactly," he says, getting excited. "There's no national brand in the space. No company that parents immediately think of when they are looking for a place to send their kids to learn everything. Ice skating, swimming, football, tennis…"

"I see the merit in the idea. I mean, I'd take my kids to a place like that if I could afford it. But if it hasn't been done before, there's got to be a reason why there's no one dominating that space in the market."

Austin's pacing faster, talking almost more quickly than I can believe. "There are three problems facing a brand trying to break into this space." He starts listing things off on his fingers, like real estate and capital and technical details that I'm sure fill out a business plan someplace on that laptop of his.

"My vision is to start small. Come up with a simple, scalable model. I want every kid who goes to T-ball when they're four to grow up in our facilities. Sees his little buddy playing soccer and wants to try it. Little Cora sees her friends bowling, next week she tries bowling. Think instead of Chuck E. Cheese for kids parties, they come to The Gym."

"That's the name?" I ask. "The Gym?"

"The name is still a work in progress, but think about it, Ryder. It has potential, right?"

I nod, thinking through all the ways a business like that could fail. "Are you going to buy or build the facilities?"

"We'll start with whatever we can get quickly. My plan is to bring in food and retail to support all the costs. Imagine a gym with a food court. No more needing to stop for dinner before class or a game. Mom and Dad can eat healthy adult food at any upscale dining place right inside the gym. All under one roof. We'll have childcare facilities and an entire section of the gym dedicated to athletes who need accommodations. Adapted swings, ramps. We'll bring in sponsors who want the good PR for donating gear and supporting the vision. We'll offer packages and scholarships so all kids who want to play can afford to play."

I applaud Austin's initiative, but this sounds like a big dream with very little chance of making it in the real world. "Have you thought this through?" I ask. "You're willing to give up your job to make this happen?"

He nods. "Ryder, I've secured a third of the start-up capital I need to break ground on a location in Columbus. If things go as planned, we'll open the first gym in less than three years. That's if we have to build. If I can rent a space to launch, we could be live in a matter of months."

I shake my head. "I'm impressed, man. Excited. If this is your dream, then I know you'll make it a reality."

"That's where you come in," he says. "Ryder, I came here to ask you to run the business. I'm making so much money at my job right now even just staying in my position, I can afford to pay you and cover health insurance costs for the kids. For the next year or so while I keep working, you can run the business. Be my right hand. In three years, you can be director of coaching. Shit, you can name your title, and I'll throw in a shareholder stake if you want."

I can't believe what I'm hearing. My best friend is offering me a chance to do something I love without the grind of teaching. To move home and work with him on his dream. I'm touched and humbled. Excited and scared.

"There's only one thing..." I tell him. "Gracie."

"That might not be the problem you think it is," he says, a childlike grin lighting up his face. "So, you heard about what happened to Olson today? Levi Olson of the Cyclones?"

I shake my head. "The only drama I'm aware of that happened today is what Aiden, this fuckface in fourth grade, said to Luke at recess."

Austin drops beside me on the couch and claps his hands excitedly. "Levi Olson ran into some kind of trouble and left the Cyclones. Word is he's coming back to Star Falls to lie low for a while. He's probably dying for some good press. We reach out to him, get him on board as a sponsor, and bam. The missing piece we need to fulfill the last of the funding. And maybe we could start in Star Falls, Ryder. Maybe you stay here and don't move to Columbus. Scout a site for a first location right here in Olson's own backyard."

I'm not so sure about that. "Is a guy who was cut from an NFL team the guy you want supporting kids sports? What did he do?"

Austin waves away my fears with a hand. "It's probably some

stupid shit. But a little time away forgives everything. Talent like that won't go to waste. The league knows that. They're probably just trying to apply pressure or get ahead of some PR nightmare before it blows up. Worst-case scenario, if he has to prove that he's ready to go back on the field, there's no better redemption story than spending his time on this while he's here. He doesn't ever have to have contact with kids, Ryder. A couple social media posts, a few photo ops. A little exposure from a guy like that could go a long, long way."

I'm not sure how I feel, but it's impossible not to get swept up in Austin's passion. "I like the idea of staying here in Star Falls and opening a small starter gym first," I say, starting to get into it. "Lower real estate costs, lower taxes. And a wealth distribution not unlike the city. There's upper class and lower, so it could be a good test case for expanding into bigger cities and more locations."

"Exactly," he says. "I was pretty stoked about having you back in Columbus, but I could live with you working out here. I can work remotely from my job once in a while anyway. I'll come out here once a month and work with you, handle anything that needs to be done on-site. And that'll give you time to figure things out with your lady. And if shit goes south, you can move back to Columbus. Or anywhere you want, man. We could go national with this. You want to move to LA to be near your sister—"

"Uh, thanks, but no. I'm allergic to celebrities."

He laughs, and at that point, our fifteen minutes are more than up. Luke and Cora thunder down the stairs, demanding dinner and playtime, respectively. I'm honestly surprised we got so much time to ourselves.

I pick up Cora and make that call to Benito's to see if we can get a table for dinner. While Austin gets on the floor to check out Luke's newest train, he gives me a look. "You'll think about it?"

Like anything that's going to impact the lives of my kids, I need to know everything that's involved, but I admit, I'm more than intrigued. "Yeah. We'll go over the details, and we'll talk more before you go back."

I am pretty sure that this is the last sign I've been looking for. A dream job working for my best friend, doing something in a place I want to be. I want to say yes now, but before I make any future-altering plans, I don't just want to think about it. I want to talk to Gracie.

CHAPTER SIXTEEN

My last client of the night is a sweetie, but it's after nine by the time I peel off my gloves. My plan is to head home and shower and then quickly meet up with Ryder for whatever he has planned. I should be exhausted after a full day of work, but as soon as I grab my purse and keys, I realize it's happening.

My first real date alone with Ryder.

Excitement buzzes through my system while nervous energy has me feeling a little worried. I don't know what he has planned, but this feels big.

Time alone.

A real date.

After a little over three months, we know each other.

The second I'm in my car, I drop him a text.

Leaving work. Home to shower then I'll meet you at your place?

I add a string of fire and hearts, hit send, and head home to shower. Thankfully, my parents are playing cards with friends tonight. They should be out for at least another hour or two.

After I shower, I pick a pair of jeans with a few well-placed shreds in them and a tank top that pops against my skin tone. I wear a slouchy black sweater that falls over one shoulder, revealing the face of the family tree tattoo. I zip into some ankle boots and shake out my hair. Once I drag some product through my hair, I toss it around so the natural waves give it some shape, and I finish my look with eyeliner and a little blush. I leave my lips glossy and check my reflection in the mirror.

I look flushed and happy, but that small worry tightens my belly. What if Ryder really wants to have sex? Expects it? I mean, fuck, I would. If I didn't have this medical test in a few days, I'd pounce on him the second I climbed into his car.

I start to worry that I should have told him sooner...prepared him that I'm having a test and have to abstain. But I don't know if he's going to want to go someplace we can be alone or if he really wants to make this a "date."

When I arrive, I knock softly at the door. Ryder answers within seconds and draws me to his chest in a hug.

"You look stunning," he says into my hair. "God, Gracie."

I hold him close, pressing my face to a long-sleeved black shirt with a green pattern of leaves and vines in it. He's wearing regular blue jeans, and when I breathe him in, he smells divine. Better than I remember. Like fresh laundry and musky cologne and him. It's impossible to describe the way he smells, and I've been up close and personal with a lot of different people. His skin smells like sunshine and dry leaves, an enticing scent to match an enticing man.

He pulls back and takes my hand. "Do you want to meet Austin?"

I nod and follow Ryder into the living room, where a really attractive guy with muscles for days and sandy blond hair reaches out his hand. If a reality show lifeguard and male model produced offspring, that child wouldn't grow up to be as hot as Austin.

"Gracie," he says warmly. "So good to meet you. I can hardly get the kids and Ryder to talk about anything else."

I shake his hand and smile. "Great to meet you too."

"I met your brother Benito last night. Oh my God, that food."

I grin and nod. "He's an asshole, but he can cook."

Ryder grabs a jacket and pockets his keys and wallet. "Anything comes up, just text. You know where we'll be."

135

We head out together, our fingers tightly laced. "So," I murmur, "Austin knows where we're going. Feel like sharing with your date?"

"Quite the opposite," he says, grinning. "Climb in, please."

He holds the passenger door open for me, and I get into a car that is noticeably absent of car seats. I breathe deeply. "It smells like Icy Rain in here," I tease, making up a scent to match the heavy smell of car fragrance. "Car detailed, no car seats... What do you have planned, Mr. Cooper?"

"Well, the car seats are just practical. I put them in Austin's car in case he has any emergencies while we're out. Much faster than waiting for me to get home and move the seats."

He has a point there, but it strikes me then how different his date prep was from mine.

He climbs behind the wheel, and I reach for his arm. "Thank you," I tell him. "For going to all this trouble."

He leans across the seats to kiss me. "None of this is trouble. It's effort. There's a big difference." His lips are soft and sweet on mine. Tasting, lingering, but not probing. The hunger and drive for more isn't there. This is a sweet kiss. Loving and reassuring. "There's no amount of effort I wouldn't go to for you, Gracie."

He settles in his seat and pulls something out of the pocket of his jacket. It's a child's scarf.

"I'm not cold," I say, confused.

Ryder laughs, and the sound is real and loud. "I don't have a sexy kit like yours," he teases. "This was the best blindfold I could find on short notice."

"Blindfold?" I ask, raising an eyebrow.

"Yeah," he says. "You've lived in this town your whole life. If this is the only chance I get to surprise you, it's not going to be much of a surprise if you see exactly where we're headed."

I nod and wrap the scarf around my eyes, then I lean back in my seat. At this hour, I can't imagine what he has planned, but I don't have long to wait. When the car finally stops, he tells me to wait.

"I'll come and open the door."

The night air chills my cheeks when he opens the door and takes my hand. "Blindfold stays on, please."

I chuckle and grip his hand tighter. "Should I be afraid right now?"

He takes both my hands and leads me with his voice and his slow steps less than fifteen paces. I can peek under the scarf and see sidewalk, so I'm not too concerned I'm going to fall, but I don't hear anything that hints at where we are. A club? A restaurant? A mall?

I hear a click and then a door open, after which Ryder helps me over a small threshold and then closes a door behind me. Then he gently turns my head and unties the scarf.

"Okay, now this is going to take a little explaining, so bear with me."

When I open my eyes, I know exactly where we are. We are in a suite at the Star Falls Inn. A gorgeous local bed-and-breakfast. I see things scattered all over the room, but Ryder is excitedly tugging me toward the small desk to our left.

"Okay," he says. "This is speed dating single dad style. But not with, like, different people. With different dates. Date number one..."

On the small desk is a bouquet of flowers. Soft blue hydrangeas mixed with bright orange tiger lilies, white roses, and beautiful leafy greens. "Flowers for our first date," he explains.

Then he hurries me to the next "station." On the hotel dresser, he's collected single-serving size bottles of wine. There is a small plate of tasty-looking seeded crackers, olives, and fruit spread out. "Hold, please." He runs to the mini-fridge and pulls out a tiny cheesecake. "Date number two—drinks and apps, plus dessert."

"Date number three is the big one," he says, a boyish grin on his face. He drags me to the big TV, where he fumbles for a moment before pulling up a rom-com. "The 'come to my place and watch a movie' date."

The last place he brings me is to the bed. Sitting on top of a pristine white duvet is an envelope with my name scribbled on it. "Open it," he says, his voice soft.

I reach across the pillows and grab the envelope. Inside is a piece of plain white paper folded into a card. On the front, Ryder has drawn some absolutely hilarious stick people in four sizes. Two kids, one man, and I assume the stick figure with the long waves of black hair is me. Inside, the card reads,

Tonight is about getting to know you better, nothing more. No pressure. Just great conversation, old movies, and a lot of snacks no little kid is going to steal.
Yours,
Ryder

I put the card back in the envelope and face him. "When did you have time to do all this?"

He chuckles. "Austin's a good friend. He helped and took the kids to the hotel pool while I set all this up earlier."

"You..." I rise up on my toes and touch his cheek. His face is smooth where he's shaved for our date, and I trail my fingers along the supple skin. "You did so much. No one's ever done anything like this for me before."

I want to look back at the flowers and the snacks and the movie queued up and ready to watch, but I can't tear my eyes from his face.

"No one's ever treated me the way you do," he murmurs.

He lifts my face to his and kisses me, long and slow and sweet. I hum and sigh at the ease of it all. We're not rushing. No one to hide from here. Heat pools between my legs, and I know I'm going to struggle with this huge comfy bed and hours of privacy ahead of us.

He pulls his lips from mine just far enough to whisper against my mouth. "We're finally alone."

"Ryder, I..." I swallow, my throat feeling like sandpaper. "I want all of this," I tell him. "Fuck, I want all of you. But I can't. Not tonight."

Ryder looks concerned, his brows knitting together. "Are you okay, Gracie? What's going on?"

I'm not sure I want to tell him everything. How can I open up about my health and not completely obliterate the mood?

"Hey." He loops his arms around my waist, and I rest my back against his front. Our eyes meet in the bathroom mirror. He's smiling and nodding at me. "Whatever it is, I can handle it. You don't feel ready for sex for any reason, it's off the table. I'll shut the door, and we won't come back in here. Unless, I mean, you have to pee or something."

I chuckle and shake my head. It's nice looking at him this way. Seeing us together makes something shift in my chest. I'm seeing us the way the world does. Like a couple. Two people bonded and together. There for each other. Ryder literally has my back right now. And I'm not sure there's ever going to be a good time to tell him everything.

So I watch his face and explain. "I have a gynie appointment Tuesday," I say. "I have to have a test done, so I can't have intercourse until after the test is over. Bad timing," I say sadly. "When I found out we were going to have this date, I thought about rescheduling the test. But they schedule based on my cycle, so…"

"Why would you reschedule? If you need the test, my God, get it done, Gracie." His face is worried, his lips drawn thin. "Is there any chance something is wrong? Is this a routine thing?"

I nod. "There's a chance I won't be able to have kids, or if I can, that it won't be easy. I…"

This is where it gets to be impossible. Do I share everything? On our first official date?

"Gracie," he says, turning me to face him. "Don't worry about telling me. I want to know everything there is to know about you. I don't care about sex tonight or what date this is. I am falling for you. So if it affects you, it matters to me."

I take his hand and lead him to the table by the first date station. I hold his hands and give him the simplest version of the story. "I've only been pregnant once," I tell him. "It was an accident. I hooked up with a guy, and he's totally out of the picture now. Not a part of my life. He ghosted me, actually, and it was a pretty horrific and shameful experience." My face is lowered as I tell him about the miscarriage.

"Holy shit," Ryder says. He gets up from the table and pulls me close in a hug. "First of all, I wanna know the name of this fucking douchebag."

I laugh. "Get in line. My pops has already decided he's willing to spend his retirement years in prison serving time for assault."

"I can't let your dad do it alone," he says, holding me tight. "There are no words, Gracie. What you went through. My God. You're so strong."

He holds me, and a few tears of gratitude wet the front of his shirt. I knew deep down that he would be supportive and understanding. But now...

"Ryder." I lift my face to look at him. "I'm sorry to ruin the mood."

"Stop." He holds a finger to my lips. "Never, ever apologize for being honest with me. I want to know the truth, Gracie. After everything I've been through, I can handle whatever it is that's happening with you. What I can't handle is lies. If you need me to be there when you have the tests, I can try to..."

I shake my head. "No, it's okay. My mom is taking me, and I promise, if I need anything, I'll let you know."

"Are you afraid?" he asks.

I sigh. "Honestly, yeah. But not of the test or pain or anything. I'm afraid what I'll feel like if I know for sure I can't have kids of my own. My family is so big and so close. It'll be weird thinking that this is it. Just me. Living with my parents until I die."

Ryder chuckles. "You know, Gracie, I doubt that you have to live with your parents just because you don't have kids. You can get a place of your own. Or, you know, move in with a boyfriend. Or husband. If someday you were to have one of those."

I nudge him in the ribs. "You think maybe someday I might have one of those, huh? Maybe?"

"I'll make you your own key," he says, his voice thick with emotion. "No hiding it under the mat."

I can't reply to that. Just grab him and hold him tight. I scratch my nails along his back and breathe in the scent of him. There could be a real future with this man. A future where we love each other, and it doesn't matter whether or not the children in our lives came from my body. Together, we could make a new branch on the family tree.

He pulls me toward the bed. "Sit," he says. "I'm gonna get all our stuff together. Let's get this date started."

I kick off my boots and tug off my sweater, then climb onto the bed on top of the covers. Ryder comes back from the bathroom with a hand towel and the massage oil and sets that beside the bed. Then he gathers all the snacks and drinks, toes off his boots, and climbs on the bed beside me.

"So," he says, "your choice, Gracie. Where do we start?"

I point to the massage oil. "Can we use that without…"

He nods. "You don't have to tell me twice. We follow the doctor's rules."

I take the bottle, peel away the plastic safety seal, and flip open the cap. "But there is a whole lot that doesn't break the rules, right?"

"So, so much." His voice is low and heavy with promise. His eyes sparkle, and he nods at the massage oil. "Do you have ideas? Because I am happy to make suggestions…"

"You've done a lot of work on this date already," I tell him. "Let me take over."

I stand up off the bed and strip off my jeans and top. He watches me climb back onto the bed in nothing but a nude-colored lace bra and matching panties. I raise a brow at him and wait. "And?" I insist. "Are those clothes staying on?"

He takes the hint and leaps off the bed. Unzipping his pants, he wriggles out of them, pulls off his socks, then unbuttons his shirt and sets it all on a chair. He thumbs the waistband of his boxer briefs. "Leave these?"

"For now," I say. "On your back, please."

He climbs back into the bed and sits upright, propped against the pillows. I turn down the lights so only the bright image from the TV lights the room.

CHAPTER SEVENTEEN

ryder

By the glowing light coming from the TV, I stare into her beautiful gray eyes.

"I want more of this," I tell her. "More of you."

"How late can we stay?" she purrs seductively.

"You can stay all night if you want," I tell her. "I should get home before the kids wake up. I prepaid for the room, so anything you need, just charge to it and sign my name before you leave."

She smiles at me, and I want this forever.

"Do you think this could be more?" I ask. "I want it all with you, Gracie. I don't care if this is fast. We've known each other over three months. You know my kids. This isn't just…a fling for you, is it?"

She bristles at the word, and I immediately feel like a dick.

"If this is a fling, it'll go down in history as the longest, slowest fling ever."

I laugh and push the hair back from her face. Even with us just lying here facing each other, she's the most perfect thing I've ever seen. "I just…"

It occurs to me that lying in bed half dressed, spilling my heart out is probably the worst time to tell her about Austin's business and the job he offered me. But maybe it's also the best time.

If Grace doesn't feel the same way, like this is more than I expected and everything I want, maybe I should take the opportunity now to go back to Columbus.

Before things go any further.

Before I get my heart broken. Again.

"So, my friend Austin," I start, trying to ease into it. "He came for the weekend to talk to me about a business he wants to start."

"Yeah?" she snuggles deeper under the covers but then looks like she's thinking. "Want some cheesecake?"

"Oh, hell yeah," I say. I forgot we have snacks and treats, but the real treat is watching Gracie walk around in nothing except her sexy underwear to bring everything to the bed.

"Plates," I say, banging my forehead with the heel of my hand. "I knew I forgot something."

"Who needs plates?" she asks, sticking a fork into the creamy delight. She scoops a big hunk of the fresh strawberry swirl. "You got this from Taste, didn't you? Over by the aquatic center?"

I nod. "You know Star Falls."

"It's home," she says. "Always has been. Always will be."

That hits me hard, and I wonder if she would ever be open to moving. To going anyplace else. If what this is could be enough to convince to her leave if I did.

My appetite is starting to die, but I slice a huge bite of cheesecake with the tines of my fork and scoop it up. "Have you ever wanted to live in a big city?"

She lifts one of those perfect brows and licks the last bit of cream from her fork. "No. Everything I love is here."

I nod and look down at my fork. I slip the bite into my mouth and...fuck. I mean, it's freaking good. Everything about Star Falls is better than I expected.

"I always thought kids who grew up in small towns had big-city dreams." I laugh to try to cover my own feelings of anxiety about the topic. "I mean, isn't there a whole genre of movies dedicated to that?"

She matches my humor with a smile so beautiful I want to put aside the dessert and kiss her again. "Yeah, of course. A lot do. But

143

when you have such a big, tight family like I do... I don't know." She's quiet for a minute. "Sometimes I think Vito isn't happy here. His life hasn't turned out the way he planned, and I mean, whose has? That's adulthood. But I wonder if someday we'll wake up and he'll just announce that he's leaving."

I nod. "How would your parents take it? His moving, let's say, really far away. Like my sister in Los Angeles?"

She raspberries a breath through her lips and shakes her head. "No one in my family is the LA type." But then she's quiet for a moment. Really thinking about it. "God, it'd be hard," she admits. "It'd be hardest on my mom and dad. They'd worry every day they couldn't run down the street and check on their kids."

I don't say anything to that, and she finally fills up the silence.

"It does sound a little smothering when I say it out loud."

"No, no," I reassure her. "That's not what I'm getting at. I've been thinking about all this ever since we moved here. I wanted a fresh start, and I am falling hard for Star Falls..."

She leans over and plants a kiss on my shoulder when I say that.

"I just wonder how parents make those decisions. Like if I stay here with Luke and Cora, and then someday they want to leave? Would I give them better opportunities if I moved to, say, New York?"

She widens her eyes. "That's a leap."

"I know. And I'm not saying I've considered it, but..." I decide to get it all out. Put my cards on the table and see how Gracie reads them. "Austin wants to start a business," I tell her. "He asked me to move back to Columbus and run it for him."

"Whoa, whoa. Back up." She doesn't give me the brow, but the look of utter shock on her face makes me feel sick. She looks like she thinks I've betrayed her. "You're thinking about leaving?"

I lean back against the pillow. "No. I mean, I honestly don't know what to do. I want to do the right thing for my kids above everything else. But I'm not enjoying teaching the way I did before. I have been thinking about all the choices I've made. Where I live. Who I keep around me. All of it." I look at her, trying to gauge how she feels, but she is stone silent, her face completely unreadable.

The next words she says cracks a crater in my heart.

"I need a glass of water. Excuse me." She gets up from the bed and walks into the bathroom. Then she returns and climbs back into bed, holding a glass of water.

"Are you okay? Did I do something wrong?"

All of a sudden, there are tears in her eyes. "I just..." She wipes a tear that falls down her cheek, and she shakes her head. "I can't believe you'd leave. I know it's really early, but I'm attached, Ryder. To you. To the kids. I..." She rubs a hand across her face and sniffs hard. "This isn't just a fling to me. I am falling for you."

I reach for her, opening my arms, and she climbs across the bed and cuddles against my chest.

"I feel the same way," I tell her. "Since the day I set eyes on you, I knew there was something about you. I think it was your coffee addiction, your bossiness, and your right eyebrow."

She lifts her face to glare at me. "It's not an addiction. It's a habit I can break if I need to, but come on."

I kiss her forehead. "So, you're not going to deny being bossy and having eyebrows that basically have their own personalities?"

She grimaces but then smiles. "You know me well. And I want to get to know you better, Ryder. I want more of these times. Is that selfish? Am I pressuring you to stay?"

I don't know the answer to that. What I don't want to do is make a mistake because of my feelings for a woman. I've done that. And while my marriage to Elizabeth wasn't what I wanted it to be, I have two kids who are part of my soul now. I can't afford to make the same mistakes again. It's not just me they will affect.

"It's not pressure," I tell her. The light from the TV shifts into sleep mode. The logo of the inn pops up in plain stark-white letters, casting a slightly ghostly glow on our faces. I feel colder and tuck the blankets up to our chests. "You're just being honest with me. That's one of the things I love about you. I always know where I stand."

She nods. "Yeah, but you should be excited about your work. Or at least satisfied with your choice. You shouldn't waste energy wondering what if. So, what's going on with the high school? Is it being part time or is it not coaching yet? Do you think you'd feel the same way if you were teaching back in Columbus?"

"I don't know," I admit. "It's been three years now that I've been away. And coming back to a new school seemed like the right idea. New faces, no old memories to drag me into the past. But nothing about it feels the same as it did before I had kids. I want to work—I mean, fuck, I need to work. I've been off longer than I ever imagined I would be. But the idea of doing something else…the idea of running a business with my best friend is exciting, Gracie."

I tell her about Austin's gym idea, and even though I don't know a lot of details, she agrees it sounds like an amazing opportunity. Something that would be perfect for me. Great for the kids.

"Austin said he'd consider launching here in Star Falls, but I don't know if he meant it. But what if it doesn't work?" I ask. "What if I end up accepting the job, but then I need to move to Columbus in three or six months anyway? It's a ton of risk. I mean, my god. I trust Austin with my kids, but trusting him with my financial future?"

She frowns. "So many start-ups don't make it even when they are well-funded. Having a good idea and great people isn't enough. I didn't have anyone else to consider when I started The Body Shop. If it failed, it wouldn't hurt anyone, except it would sting a little for me."

I nod. I wish it was easier to know I'm doing the right thing. I wish I could just follow my heart and not have to worry about the lives and futures that depend on my making the right choices.

"I can't believe I'm responsible for making a choice this big and there's no clear path," I say. "I mean, following my heart felt a lot simpler when I was in college. Now? How do I look at Luke and Cora and tell them we're moving again? Or in six months if the business fails and I have to…I don't know what, Gracie. It's scary."

She looks into my eyes. "I don't know if I could lose you. And I don't know how to tell you to make this decision. All I can say is every decision I've ever made, I made with my heart. Not my head." She sighs. "And fuck, those haven't all been good. But at least I knew I went with what I wanted, Ryder. If you deny yourself what you think you want, even if you think it's for the good of your kids, don't you think that could lead to resentment someday? Not toward your kids, of course, but toward the world, toward life? I don't know if I could make a good choice if I felt backed into a corner."

"I have options, though," I tell her. "If I take the job with Austin and it doesn't work out, I can probably go back to Columbus and teach there. But then we're right back to where we started. Where do I go and why?"

She nods. "I'm going to make this really simple for you, because what I want is easy. My life is here, Ryder. But there's more to consider than that. You have other people counting on you."

I lift her face to mine and kiss her. She tastes like strawberries and cheesecake, and it's the best damn thing I've ever tasted. I can't imagine leaving her any more than I can imagine letting her down.

"But," she continues, "Columbus isn't that far away. We could do the long-distance thing for a while."

The crater in my heart fills immediately at her words. The fact that she would consider a long-distance relationship means something. This is a woman I can make decisions around. Make decisions with. Most of all, I need to make decisions in my life because she's in it.

"I can't take you from this place," I tell her. "Benito's restaurant. The Body Shop. Your family. Everyone you've known. There's still a chance it could work here in Star Falls. Austin has some ideas."

As we talk about logistics, I start yawning. I'm exhausted and should probably get some sleep before I head home.

"You going to sleep here or leave now?" she asks.

"I'll set an alarm to get home before the kids wake up. Do you want to tell your parents where you are, so we don't have a repeat?"

She shakes her head and tosses the towel aside to curl up with me. "No. They know I'm with you. I told them there is a chance I wouldn't come home until tomorrow."

She snuggles against me, and I stroke her hair, when a thought occurs to me. "Gracie, do you or your brothers know anything about Levi Olson?"

Gracie sits upright, clutching the blanket to her chest. She's glaring at me, a wild, angry look on her face. "What do I know about Levi Olson?"

"Yeah. By the look on your face, I'd say it's nothing good."

She cackles in the darkest way. "Not a damn thing."

"Austin heard he was a hometown boy who's coming back to Star Falls. One of the ideas he brainstormed for keeping me in Star Falls was reaching out to the guy to see if he wants to sponsor or in some way affiliate with the kids gym."

"Levi Olson, sponsoring a kids gym? You've got to be fucking kidding me. That's ripe."

"What happened?" I ask, completely confused by how pissed she seems. "Based on your answer, I'd say you know him, know him. Is he an asshole or something? I told Austin the guy might have some baggage…"

"Baggage," she says, her lips trembling. "I'll tell you what kind of baggage Levi Olson has. And then you tell me if you still want to work with him."

"What did he do to you?"

All the sleepiness of a few minutes ago has disappeared. Now I'm worried.

"If that asshole hurt you…" I say, starting to get worked up.

She blurts out the whole story then. When she's done, when it's over, she hangs her head as she sits on the edge of the bed.

"I can't do this," she says quietly. "It's taken all my strength to put myself out there again. It was hard enough that you have kids, and this is nothing against Luke and Cora, but Ryder, I can't take another heartbreak. I've been working through that, but to have Levi Olson come back to town, and to think of you courting him…"

"I won't," I promise. "I don't care what's at stake for Austin's business. That fucker hurt you, Gracie. The last thing you have to worry about is that I'm going to work with the guy. I don't do business with men who treat women like shit, and I'm guessing you're not the first woman he's done this to. Tell me how to find him. Give me his number. While Austin's in town, we'll pay him a visit."

She looks at me with doubt on her face, but when she sees I'm dead serious, she manages a weak smile. "Dad's got it covered. Ma offered to tweet about it, and Dad wants to take a mallet to his knees."

"Give me a turn with the mallet," I offer.

She sighs and folds her hands in her lap. "Maybe this is a sign, Ryder," she says. "A sign that your future is in Columbus. Maybe we shouldn't be together. What are the odds that—"

"Whoa, whoa, whoa. Back up. You think what that fucker did has anything to do with what's happening between us? The odds that an asshole ballplayer gets canned and comes running home with his tail between his legs to hide out? Pretty high, actually. Our actions always catch up to us, Gracie. Even though, for some people, it takes a while. Look. The fact that the guy is from here is the only reason why you ever met him. If he hadn't been in town for a wedding, would he have ever come through The Body Shop?"

She shakes her head. "Unlikely."

"All right. So that's small-town life. For better or worse, you know everybody, and everybody knows you. The real question is, are you going to be okay when that waste of human flesh comes back to town? Maybe we should *all* move to Columbus."

I'm not sure how's she going to react to that, but I'm surprised when she scoots closer to me. She laces her fingers through mine and squeezes. "I don't want to run from anything," she says. "Look, he didn't hurt me. Not physically. He ghosted me. Bailed on his responsibility. Was a colossal asshole, but not completely surprising. But other than make me feel like shit about myself, he is nothing to me. Not then, and not now. I'll handle it in the future. I don't want to run away from anything ever again."

I raise her hand to my lips. "I won't have anything to do with the gym if Austin insists on working with the guy. There are some good, principled men out there, Gracie. Your father is one. I'm sure your brothers are. I'm one of them too, Gracie."

"Meh," she quips. "I'm not so sure about Benito."

We both crack up, but then I take her face in my hands. "You just made a tough decision a lot easier. I'll tell Austin no. I'll be here for you when that asshole comes back to town. I'll figure out what to do with my career eventually. This matters to me, Gracie—how you feel about what I choose to do with my life. That's what a real relationship looks like."

We kiss again, but the heat isn't there. It's reassuring and loving, but we're both exhausted.

Despite everything we've talked about in this crazy hotel room, I've never felt more at home in my life.

CHAPTER EIGHTEEN

ryder

I'd come to a decision before we parted ways at the hotel early this morning, but I hadn't shared my decision with anyone, including Gracie. Not yet. I wanted to be one hundred percent certain about that decision before I told anyone.

What did I decide? I'd be fucking bananas if I quit my job to join my buddy in a new start-up. No matter how great his vision is… it may amount to nothing. I'm not a single man with no responsibilities. I don't have the luxury of taking risks that very well could affect our happiness and financial means.

Even if I were able to take a huge financial risk, there is Gracie to consider. I've barely touched the woman, but none of that matters. I know her on a different level; I don't think I know any other female in my life in quite the same way.

And in a short amount of time, I've allowed myself to dream of future possibilities. And every single one of them includes Star Falls and Gracie.

My love for coaching and teaching will come back eventually. There's an ebb and flow to everything in life, including work. Once I get accustomed to life in Star Falls and get to know more of the people and kids, that vigor I felt before will return.

The gray cloud of grief that has been over my head for what feels like forever has started to break apart, allowing me to see things in a new light.

My life isn't over.

Gracie has shown me that.

My time for love and happiness hasn't passed.

The world is filled with possibilities.

But every single one of them is in Star Falls.

"I don't want to pressure you, man," Austin says as we stand in the park with the kids, giving them something to do this morning to burn some energy. "If you're out, I do want to start talking to some of our other friends. Maybe start looking at talent recruitment companies to get the best of the best."

I shake my head and give Cora a little boost, and I watch her ladybug-patterned sneakers kick high in the air. "I don't know," I tell him. "The idea is intriguing. I just..." I decide to tell him as little about Levi as I can. "I asked Gracie what she knows about this Olson guy, and..." I shake my head.

Austin moves around to the front of the swings to face me. "What did she say?"

"He sounds like bad news. I don't know what kind of trouble he's in, but if you're fixed on getting a guy like him on board, you're asking for a world of trouble."

Austin looks shocked but nods. "He's out, then. Anything else stopping you?"

"This part's harder," I tell him. "I believe in this vision more than anything, but I don't want you to change your business model because of me and where I live or where I might want to live. I'm falling in love with Gracie, and I want to see where that goes. Enough that I've decided I'm going to stay put in Star Falls. This is your dream, man, and I support it even if I can't be part of it."

Austin kicks the spongy turf beneath the swings with the tip of his running shoe. "I appreciate you doing some digging on that ballplayer," he says. "That could have been a minefield I stepped right into." He looks disappointed but says, "Would you consider maybe being a consultant for the company? You can work from home and maybe come down to Columbus for a weekend when something can't be done online?"

"Really?" I ask, shocked he's still trying to find a way for me to stay part of the business.

"Heck yeah. Most things can be done online now. I really value your input, Ryder, and there's no one else I trust more than you, too. It won't take up much time, and I promise it won't interfere with your current job or life."

"I'm only working part time right now. A teacher is retiring next year, and I'll be getting his position. But I do have the rest of this school year, and my summers are free except for coaching, which includes training and practice for the next season."

"So, Gracie's the real deal, huh? You're staying put for good. You're home?"

"Yeah, she is."

"I'm happy for you, buddy. Really happy for you."

"It's just..." Cora wants off the swing, so I wait to answer the question until both my kids have climbed the ladder to the curly slide. While Luke goes down first and Cora stands at the top waiting for her turn, I explain. "My whole marriage was a lie."

Austin lowers his eyes and nods. "I know, Ryder. I can't imagine..."

I sigh. "I hope you never have to either. Every day, I tried to make things better. I tried to prove I was worth the life I had, even though, deep down, I always knew I'd never be what Elizabeth really wanted. That's the thing about Gracie. I always know what she thinks. Where she stands. I never, ever have to worry that she's giving me some bullshit."

"It's rare to find someone you trust," he says, a bitterness underlying his words. "And even when you do trust someone..."

He doesn't have to finish that thought. I don't know how badly Austin's ex fucked him over, but I know that what I went through with Elizabeth is something he can relate to. The only difference is I ended up having two kids as a permanent reminder that I wasn't enough.

But with Grace, I feel like I am enough. More than enough. I feel like I'm exactly what she wants. We're so different, and yet, we're exactly the same in the ways that matter.

Our families mean everything. Our work is important, but family comes first. Honesty and trust, directness and integrity. I know the hours she puts in helping at the shop that she doesn't get paid for. The time she spends because she wants to make a difference to her employees and her town.

She is what I want, and I believe she wants me. Where we'll be come summer or next spring or two winters from now, I don't know. But I know what we have is worth trying for. Worth putting first. Ahead of Austin's opportunity. Ahead of any lingering doubts, insecurities, or fears that might hold me back.

"She's going to win out if I have to choose," I tell Austin with a grin. "I mean, come on. Look at her. Look at you."

"I'd worry if you didn't pick her," Austin laughs. "So, I'll send text and email updates. If it's urgent or exciting, I'll call, and we'll just play it by ear week to week."

"I'd like that," I tell him. We clap hands and pull each other into a half hug. "So, what's next for you? You going to start dating or just keep your nose deep in sports stats and business plans?"

"Definitely the second," he grits out. I can tell by the tension in his voice that he's not ready to talk.

Thankfully, the kids are.

"Dad!" Luke screams. "Cora ate a piece of gum from the slide. It was just sitting there, and I told her not to touch it, and she ate it anyway."

Austin looks like he's going to be sick, and I raise a brow at him. "Parenthood. Most exciting game you'll ever play." Then I trot over to the slide to find Cora, working her jaw on the old piece of gum. "Did you put something from the slide in your mouth?"

This is one of those moments I'm sure I'll forget in twenty years. I won't care about how many pieces of used gum my kids ate, if they cried through their naps, or whether they ate their broccoli.

"You think you could watch the kids again tonight? I need to talk to Gracie. I'll stay until the kids go down, and then I need two hours, tops."

"Ryder, who are you bullshitting? You'll last maybe five minutes. You'll be there and back in under thirty."

I smack him in the arm. "Don't be an asshole. I'm just going to talk to her."

He smirks. "Sure, man. Whatever you say."

CHAPTER NINETEEN

"Ryder, what are you doing here? Where are the kids?" I look out the shop window, expecting to see the kids outside, but they're not.

Ryder takes a step forward. "You alone?"

I nod. "Just finishing up some paperwork I've been putting off for far too long. What's wrong?"

He shakes his head and smiles. "Nothing's wrong, Gracie. And the kids are with Austin. He splays his palms out across my back as he pulls me closer until our bodies are fully pressed together. "I wanted to talk to you alone. It couldn't wait. I couldn't wait."

My stomach turns, and I brace myself for the news I've been dreading. We've barely had a chance to begin, and he's already going to leave. "Okay," I whisper, trying to keep the tremble out of my voice as I stare into his eyes.

"I can't leave you. I won't leave. The last few months with you have made me feel more alive than I've felt in…well, forever really. Or at least it feels that way. I'm not ready to throw that all away to chase Austin's dream. I want to stay here, in Star Falls, and see where this goes. I'm falling for you harder and faster than I ever thought possible, and I'm not willing to walk away from this for anything, including chasing someone else's dream. I want you. I choose you."

A warmth fills my chest at his words. A sense of calm washes over me. He's staying. He's staying for me. For us. "Really?" I'm dumb struck by his decision.

I haven't had the best track record with men, and I fully expected Ryder to be no different. Heartbreak has always been the story of my life. I figured love wasn't written in my cards, and I was okay with it.

Ryder raises a hand to my face, cradling my cheek in his hand. He gazes into my eyes. "I will always choose you."

His words steal my breath and momentarily stun me. No man has ever said those words to me. No one has ever put me first. No one until now. "I love you, Ryder," I tell him, wanting nothing more than to have him in my life forever.

He smiles as he strokes his thumb back and forth against my cheek. "I love you too, Gracie." As soon as the words are out of my mouth, his lips are on mine.

He snakes his arm around my back, holding me tight until there's no space left between us. The kiss is rough, but his lips are soft.

"I want you," I breathe into his mouth, needing to feel him inside me, wanting to feel him inside me.

"Fuck," he growls against my lips, sending goose bumps scattering across my skin.

The dam of restraint breaks as I move my hands to the bottom of his shirt, pulling it upward. Ryder pulls back, breaking our kiss long enough for me to tear the shirt over his head.

His mouth comes down on mine, and he lifts me in the air, carrying me toward the back of the shop.

"What are you doing?" I ask as I wrap my legs around his middle.

"Privacy," he tells me, kicking open the door to my office and taking me inside.

I don't say another word as he sets my ass down on the desk, and I rip off my top and bra, feeling more impatient than I have in a long time. "Pants," I command as I toss my top and bra at his face, watching them hit his bare chest and fall to the floor.

Ryder smirks as he moves his hands to his zipper before yanking his jeans down to his ankles. The way he stares at me as he does this has my body aching for his touch.

"All the way." I point at his ankles, waving my finger at his pants. "No restraints."

"Baby, off the desk," he tells me, raising an eyebrow before kicking off his pants into a puddle on the floor. "Turn around. Hands on top."

A thrill runs through me at the thought of Ryder taking me from behind and being rough instead of his usual sweet.

I do as I'm told, hopping down from the desk, placing my palms flat on the top, facing away from him, and shaking my ass in an open invitation.

A second later, Ryder's hands are at the waistband of my leggings, ripping them down my legs. But he doesn't take them all the way off. "I prefer you restrained," he whispers in my ear with his front plastered against my bare back.

I shiver, thinking of being tied up and Ryder having his way with me. That isn't what this was, but my mind drifts there as his mouth finds the tender skin of my neck and his hands explore the rise of my hips and swell of my ass.

I drop my head forward and close my eyes, focusing on every sensation as he touches and kisses my body.

This isn't slow. This isn't making love.

This is pure need. Total want.

Ryder's warm lips and soft tongue blaze a trail across my back to my shoulder. I stick out my ass, rubbing it against his hard cock.

"Ryder," I moan.

"What, baby?" he asks against my skin.

"I need you."

He slides his hand across the front of my hip and nestles it between my legs, finding my wetness and my clit. His fingertips are gentle but hit the perfect spot. "You want this?" he purrs against my ear, sending shock waves through my system as his finger circles my clit.

I ache to be stuffed, pounded into by him, as his fingers work their magic, driving me closer to an orgasm. Without my having to beg, Ryder lines up his cock to my opening and pushes inside, filling me completely.

I arch my back, adjusting to the sweet bite of his deliciously large length and girth.

Ryder's arm comes around my middle to palm my breast, while his other hand works my clit in perfect precision.

All thoughts leave my mind as he pounds into me, moving me upward and onto my tiptoes with each thrust. I'm consumed by the way he makes me feel, the pleasure he delivers.

"I love your cunt," he whispers against my ear.

I shudder with pleasure from his words as he drives into me, sending me closer to the edge. I want to spread my legs but can't. The damn leggings on the bottoms of my legs are making it impossible. But instead of struggling, I give in, taking what he's giving me.

"Ryder," I moan again, so close to the edge.

"You want to come, baby?"

"Yes," I answer, my voice hoarser than before.

"How do you want it?"

"Harder," I tell him, pushing my ass backward.

"Fuck my cock, Gracie."

I moan at the thought and do as he commands. I use my palms for leverage, slamming myself against his length, taking him as deep as I can. He works his fingers faster, pressing harder with each passing thrust of my body down his shaft.

As the orgasm starts to build, my pace quickens, trying to push myself over the edge. But I can't quite get there on my own. As if he can read my mind, Ryder flattens his fingers between my legs, swiping his hand back and forth so hard and fast, I can't stop the ecstasy from crashing over me.

My breath ceases as the air escapes my lungs, and my muscles seize from the overwhelming sensation of being pleasured. I slow my pace, wanting to savor the feeling of this moment. Ryder takes over, chasing the same pleasure as he drives me straight into another orgasm that threatens to turn my legs into jelly.

He tightens his arm around my middle, holding me to him and keeping me upright as he moans, cresting and dipping through his pleasure.

The only sounds in the shop are our heaving breathing as we try to right ourselves after something so perfect.

"Fuck," Ryder whispers.

I peer over my shoulder, still bent over the desk. "What?"

"I didn't use a condom." He gives me a pained and apologetic smile.

"It's okay. Doctor said it'll be damn near impossible for me to get pregnant without intervention."

"Damn near isn't zero," he says.

"With my luck, it's zero, Ryder. Don't worry so much."

"Okay," he says, drawing out the word. "But remember, my sperm is no joke, Gracie."

I roll my eyes at the ridiculousness of his statement. Every guy likes to think his sperm is somehow magical and superhuman.

"I think we'll be okay. I have a better chance of hitting the lottery than getting knocked up by you."

CHAPTER TWENTY

Six months later

"Cora, Put down the puppy, sweetheart." Ma holds open her arms to take the Chihuahua who normally snarls at everyone and everything except my ma and me from the little girl.

Cora is wearing a tiara and sparkly pink dress for her fourth birthday party. Something we've spent weeks planning.

At the moment, she has two sets of grandparents hovering over her—Ryder's parents and mine.

Ryder's parents have become really close to my family over the last few months. They drove up and stayed here at the house with my parents over Christmas, and ever since, they have kept in touch. My mother makes it impossible to lose touch unless you actively block her, but Deloris fits into Ma's gang of lady friends so well, I've overheard my parents talking about the Coopers buying a cabin near Star Falls so they can be a lot closer to their grandchildren once they retire.

When Ryder went to Columbus for Thanksgiving, he told Elizabeth's parents he was seeing someone, and they promised to try to make it to Star Falls for Christmas and then New Year's. But time after time, they made excuses not to come.

I can't say that I blame them.

Once Ryder and I started seeing each other, all the pictures he sent them either came from me or had me in them. It was probably very painful seeing someone raising their grandchildren. Someone who replaced their daughter, at least in their eyes.

Spring is in full bloom in Star Falls, and my entire family is in on the birthday celebration.

"Yeah. Yeah. Got it. Okay, thanks, sis. Love you too." Ryder slips his phone into his back pocket and loops a hand over my shoulder. "It's not official, but my sister thinks she's got him."

Austin claps his hands excitedly. "I knew it, man. I knew it. Great job, Allison."

"I'm not Allison," Cora whirls on Austin with a pout. "I'm just Cora."

He bends down to pick her up and spins her in a circle. "I know, sweetheart. I'm talking about your aunt Allison in LA. She connected me to a very famous basketball player, and I am very, very excited."

"I brought dessert. Not that we need it with that cake," Chloe says with Franco and their little girl at her side, and what I can smell is a plate of peanut butter crisps. The second I catch a whiff, I have to turn away.

"Excuse me a sec," I say and run up to my room for some fresh air.

While I'm up there, I grab Cora's birthday gift, which I'd left wrapped on my desk. I have a small gift for Luke too. I hear footsteps on the stairs, and my dad knocks lightly on the door.

"Sweetheart," he calls. "Rebecca and Daniel just pulled up."

"Thanks, Dad." I grab the gift bags and turn to face my father. "Thanks for hosting. I feel so much better doing this here."

Pops pulls me in for a hug. "This will always be your home, sweetheart. I'm just glad we can share it with more people than your idiot brothers." He starts to head downstairs, but I hold back a minute.

"I'll be right there, Pops."

I run my hands along the bedding and my drafting table. All the familiar things that make up my home. I've lived in this room and under this roof almost my entire life. Everything has changed so fast over the last year.

I savor the sounds of the dogs barking and yipping. My brothers chatting. My parents shouting back and forth through it all. And now, adding to the lovable chaos, is Ryder. His beautiful kids. More grandparents and friends. It's the family I always dreamed of. And I am so blessed to have it. And everything else that is to come.

I pop a ginger sweet into my mouth and breathe in through my nose. I've been avoiding peanut butter crisps, but until we make the big announcement, I haven't told anyone. Not even my parents. I've changed my two-cup-a-day habit to one decaf, but thankfully, I've also been working out with Ryder regularly, so Chloe just thinks I'm trying to be more fit.

I stroke my still-flat belly and wonder if everything is okay in there.

My very own little one.

Only Ryder knows I'm pregnant, but he and I plan to share the news when we're all together today.

He was worried how Elizabeth's parents would take it, but I told him this is our news. Our family. And they are part of it.

If they are unhappy, they can tell us.

They can leave.

Or they can do what any reasonable people would do and congratulate Ryder on finally finding happiness.

I hope they are as happy for us as I know everyone else will be.

Ryder and I weren't trying to conceive, but the guy must, indeed, have super swimmers. The very first time we had sex without protection, I missed a period two weeks later.

I've been terrified that something would happen, but at the same time, I know I already have everything I could ever want. If we add to the family with a child now, I will accept it and be grateful. If that doesn't happen, I will accept it and work toward finding peace.

It's all we can do. Do our best.

Push past the fears. Face the hard stuff.

With so much out of my hands, the only thing I can do is lean on the loved ones I have when the going gets rough.

It's all possible with just a few good people at your side. And I have so, so many good people.

The phone in the back pocket of my jeans buzzes with a text. I pull it out and read the message from Ryder.

Baby, if you're up in your bedroom for much longer, I'm going to come up there and…

He follows that up with a string of emojis so filthy, I grab the gifts and head down the stairs. The last thing we need is to ruin his daughter's birthday by getting it on in my bedroom.

When I reach the top of the stairs, Ma is yelling at Vito to put the dogs in the basement. Franco and Chloe are standing together talking to Austin, while Luke and Cora run to greet Rebecca and Daniel, who are just now arriving. Benito is supervising the food with Ma's friends, Bev, Sassy, and Carol, who are on hand to help serve and clean.

Ryder is the only one standing alone. His eyes are fixed on me as I come down the stairs.

I hold the banister and lift a brow at him, curious what he's thinking.

He doesn't rush to the door to meet Rebecca and Daniel. He's waiting for me.

When I reach the bottom, he clasps me in a hug and holds me close. "I love you, Gracie," he murmurs against my hair. "This is more than I ever imagined. I'm so, so happy right now. Are you?" He looks at me with such sincerity and such hope.

"I could not possibly be any happier," I tell him. And it's true.

"Gracie," a slim, beautiful woman dressed in expensive-looking black clothing, her white hair piled high in a soft topknot holds out her hands to me. "Well, it's so very nice to meet you."

"Rebecca," I say, taking her hands. "I'm so glad you're here."

She introduces me to Daniel, her husband, and we hug a little awkwardly, but Daniel seems kind. He has sad eyes, a sort of perpetual grief that hits me like a ton of bricks the moment I meet him. "Gracie, you're even more beautiful in person. Thank you for taking such good care of our grandchildren. All I ever hear about is Gracie this and Gracie that. You are a special woman to love these kids the way you do."

I've seen Elizabeth's parents on video chats before and, of course, in pictures, but as I see them for the first time in person, I can see Cora's eyes in her grandfather. Luke's slightly crooked smile bears a very clear resemblance to Rebecca's mouth. I imagine what doing something like this would be like for my parents. If they lost me and Ryder moved on to someone else. I can't imagine how painful and emotional it must be to meet me, the woman who stands in the place where their daughter should have been.

As soon as the thought hits me, tears start to well in my eyes. Rebecca immediately frowns. "Are you okay? Was it something we said?"

I shake my head. "I'm okay. Can I speak with you alone for a moment?" I look to Ryder and ask him to come with us.

By the time we reach the backyard, away from the ongoing party, I'm a lot calmer and am starting to question whether I'm overreacting.

Ryder puts an arm around my shoulders. "Everything okay?" he asks. I can tell he's concerned and a little confused. "Something happen?"

"No," I tell him. "I just don't think it would be fair to spring the news on Rebecca and Daniel. I'd like to talk to them first if you don't mind."

Ryder bites down on his lower lip but doesn't say anything. He nods at me and then kisses me on the cheek. "I'll leave you three alone."

He crosses the yard to chat up his parents, who are sitting on lawn chairs around my dad's firepit.

Rebecca immediately covers her mouth with her hand. "Gracie, perhaps we were wrong to come." She turns to her husband. "I thought we might just be in the way." She looks at me with such kindness and sadness, I want to take her in my arms and hold her. "We'll make our excuses and drive home if you prefer we not be here. This is your family now, and we're just... I am not sure we belong."

I shake my head, and tears start rolling down my cheeks. I hold up a hand. "Please, no. I'm glad you're here. You absolutely belong. Let me explain." I wipe my face and chuckle. "I'm a little emotional, as you can see. And there's a good reason."

I huddle close to them and lower my voice. "Ryder and I plan to announce to the family today while everyone is together that I'm expecting. Fifteen weeks along. I wasn't entirely sure that I could have kids, and so this is a scary blessing but an exciting one."

Rebecca's eyes shimmer with tears. "You're telling us first?" she asks, looking back at Daniel. "Before your parents? Why?"

I can hardly get the words out, but I finally do. "That's exactly why I want to share this with you first and not spring it on you. I know not everyone likes surprises." I take a deep breath and hope I'm doing the right thing. I'm sure my parents will understand if they ever find out that Rebecca and Daniel had a tiny head start on this information.

"I am so close to my parents. It's hard to explain how close. I mean, I'm over thirty years old and I still live at home because I want to." I chuckle. "That's about to change, of course, but I just cannot imagine the kind of loss you went through. Losing your daughter. I'm sure no matter how much time passes, it never gets easier...just different."

Rebecca sniffs and pulls a tissue from her bag. I rush on before any of us starts in with the waterworks.

"I feel terrified that you're going to think I'm disrespecting your daughter's life. Stepping in and taking her place. I just can't handle the thought that you lost your daughter and now you'll think that you're losing your grandchildren too. I have no intention of ever—"

Rebecca stops me with a shake of her head. "Oh, Gracie. I can see why you're the one for Ryder." She pulls me close and hugs me, patting me gently on the back. When she releases me, she holds my shoulders and looks me in the eye. "We know the things our daughter did while she was married to Ryder. We don't defend it, but we also can't hold her choices against her. All any parent wants is for their child to be happy and safe. While Ryder was good to Elizabeth, he wasn't right for her."

Daniel looks like he's near tears, and that breaks me up all over again.

"Now, listen," Rebecca says, growing stern. "No matter what, all that matters is that we are a family to these children. Luke and Cora will always be our grandchildren. Our flesh and blood. We're not as close as you are with your parents, but we are happy that they will grow up with that kind of love. I am sure if Elizabeth had lived, she would have left Ryder. I'm only hoping that he would have found you, and you would have found him, no matter what."

She holds my face between her hands and pats my cheek. "You have nothing to worry about. We are happy for Ryder, happy for you, and most of all, thrilled that Cora and Luke have you as their new mother. You've been that to them, Gracie. You've been more of a mother than our daughter had the chance to be. Accept that role. Embrace it. That's just how it should be."

She turns to Daniel and swats him playfully. "Now try to act surprised when they announce they're expecting. I don't want to get on Lucia and Mario's bad side."

"I hear Mario likes to threaten people with a mallet," I hear Daniel say as they head back toward the house.

"Only some people, dear. Better not to ask." Rebecca and Daniel lace hands and walk back inside.

Ryder is waiting for me a short distance away. He's standing near the patio doors, just watching me.

"Everything okay?" he asks, coming to meet me.

I look off into the afternoon sun. The day is cool and sunny. A light breeze plays over my hair. While I lace hands with him, we see two hummingbirds swoop down, hover near the hedge that separates our lawn from our neighbors and then fly away.

"Did you see that?" I ask. "Those hummingbirds?"

"Maybe they're a sign," Ryder says, wrapping his arms around my waist. He stands behind me and rests his chin lightly on the top of my head. He kisses my hair. "You sort things out with Rebecca and Daniel?"

I nod, and then I turn and hug him. "Let's go inside. We have a party to host."

Inside, the party is bustling. Luke is playing trains with Franco and Chloe. Austin is talking to Sassy, who is probably trying to figure out what kind of woman he likes so she can set him up.

In the yard, Cora has an absolutely ridiculous number of presents to open. Puzzles, books, clothes, sports equipment, and a brand-new sleeping bag for when she sleeps over at Nana Lucia and Papa Mario's house.

Luke gets plenty of gifts too, including a book about trains from Chloe and Franco.

I give Cora and Luke my presents last. I walk across the grass to Luke and present him with two coloring books, each one hand-drawn by me. They are identical books—one is for his sister, of course—and features pictures of many of the adventures we've shared together. There are pictures of the pasta people from Benito's menu. The kids represented by sharks taking swim lessons at the aquatic center. There are trains and pictures of Luke's school, Cora in the car going to day care. Even pictures of us together.

The last gift I have is for Cora to open. I hand the bag to Ryder for him to give his daughter, but he shakes his head and takes my hand. "Together," he says.

The entire family is hushed and watching while we walk up to Cora. She sits on a chair in the center of all of us, looking elated in her tiara and pretty dress.

"Cora," I say. "Your dad and I got you a present, but it's really something you're going to have to share with the whole family. Luke included."

She doesn't look at all discouraged that she has to share and asks, "What is it?"

I hand her the bag and watch as she pulls out a baby doll wearing a T-shirt that reads, "My big sister loves me."

She holds the doll up to the family, and I smile at Ryder. "Go on," I say. "You tell them."

"We got Cora and Luke a baby brother or sister," he says with a chuckle. "We won't know which for a few more weeks, but sometime in October, you'll have a little sibling."

I'm not at all prepared for the uproar the announcement causes. I should have been ready to be swarmed by crying, laughing, smiling family, but every hug and every well-wish feels like a massive gift they're giving to me. Everyone at the party celebrates with us, but it's not until Cora starts demanding we sing happy birthday and have cake that my parents pull me into a corner of the kitchen.

"Baby," Ma says. She is sobbing, full-body sobs as she pulls me to her chest.

"I'm okay, Ma," I assure. "It's going to be okay."

"I know," she says, stroking my hair. "It's just... you're *my* baby."

My dad joins the hug, and by the time we're all cried out, Carol, Bev, and Sassy stampede into the kitchen to start talking about a baby shower, a gender reveal, where the nursery will be. Ma turns and looks at me.

"That's the other news," I tell my parents. And this is the hardest part of all. "I'm going to move in with Ryder and the kids. He wants to be there in case anything goes wrong, and I'd like some time for Cora and Luke to adjust to me before they have a new brother or sister."

My parents shock me by high-fiving. "One more out of the nest," Pops says.

"Dad," I blurt out, smacking him on the chest. "Seriously."

Ma laughs. "Honey, we've spent the last nine months trying not to hear you through the walls while you 'talk' on the phone. It's about time you two live under one roof. We might finally get some sleep again."

I'm blushing, and Ryder is nearly bent over laughing. Cora comes running in crying because she dropped her cake on the floor, and Ryder picks her up and carries her to the bathroom to wash her face.

"Let the sugar crash begin," he calls out as he leaves.

It's a perfect party.

A perfect day.

And a perfect life.

And this is just the beginning.

CHAPTER TWENTY-ONE

gracie

Six months later

Life changes fast. Quicker than I ever imagined.

A little over a year ago, I thought I'd never have a family of my own. I thought my body had robbed me of the opportunity. And when I met Ryder and fell in love with him and his two kids, I knew they were my family. I had everything I needed. I would think of the kids as my own, even if they didn't come from my womb. By all accounts, I'd be their mother for the rest of their lives.

But as with all things, life had other plans.

"He's so big," Ryder says, walking around the hospital room, rocking Ethan in his arms. "Way bigger than Cora or Luke."

"It's my Italian genes. We do everything bigger."

"He's going to be a rugby player," Ryder says, stealing a glance at me.

I shake my head. "I'm not sending my kid out there on the battlefield. Rugby is vicious. He's going to be a drummer... something artsy."

Ryder laughs, not missing a beat with the rocking motion. "This is not an artsy kid. He's a footballer, babe. Through and through. Trust me."

I roll my eyes, too tired to argue with him about something that won't have a possibility of happening for years. "He's healthy. That's all I care about," I say on a yawn.

Ryder slides onto the bed next to me, and Ethan looks miniature in his giant arms. "He'll be whatever he wants to be."

"Now you're talking, buddy."

"He has your nose."

"Lucky him. He'll grow into it." I smile as I close my eyes, wanting nothing more than a nap.

There's a knock on the door before it swings open, and my parents walk in holding a bunch of balloons, wrapped presents, and a bouquet of flowers. "You awake?" Ma asks in a tone so loud that if I wasn't already, I sure as hell would be now.

"Yeah." I pull myself up in bed to sit up, trying to find the energy to be chatty.

"Come in," Ryder tells them when they don't fully walk into the room.

Ma looks at me for a second before her eyes dip to her newest grandchild. "Look, Mario. He's so little."

Pops smiles with a slow nod. "He's not that little, though, Lucia. He's a big boy. I see sports in his future."

Ryder turns his head toward me and smiles. "See."

"Yeah. Yeah," I mutter, waving the comment away with my hand. "We'll see. Maybe he'll be a tuba player."

My father winces. "Nope. Not him. He's like an Italian god. He's going to be a helluva tackle."

"I was thinking rugby," Ryder tells my dad as they set everything on the end of the bed except the flowers.

My father scrunches his nose. "No money in rugby."

"Sometimes things are bigger than money," Ryder tells my pop, and I know they're about to go ten rounds on if the love of a sport is more important than future earning potential.

Ma pulls out a vase from her purse like it's a normal thing to carry in there. "I brought these for you to brighten your room. It's so dreary in here."

"Thanks, Ma," I tell her, even though I don't plan to stick

around long enough to let the gray walls have any effect on me. "You think of everything."

"How are the kids?" Ryder asks my mom as she fills the vase with water in the small bathroom inside my room.

"They're good. Excited. They barely slept last night. Vito is going to feed them breakfast and get them ready before bringing them over."

"Oh boy," I mumble. "That'll be interesting."

"He can do it. If not, it'll be a great learning experience. The way he plays around, he's lucky he doesn't have a half dozen little ones running around," Pops says as he moves to Ryder's side to get a better look at Ethan. "May I?"

Ryder doesn't hesitate in handing over our son.

My father takes him like a pro, supporting his head and holding him tight against his body. "My beautiful grandson," Pops says with so much pride. "I can't wait to watch you grow up."

Ma places the vase next to me on the small table they keep placing over my bed. "I'm going to spoil that baby rotten."

"Worse than Franco's kid?" I ask, thinking it's impossible.

Ma laughs as she moves the flowers around to make them look prettier. "You haven't seen anything yet."

"Our bank account is already in shock," Pops says, tipping the baby so my mother can see him.

My parents were there when he was born. They cried the moment their eyes landed on his face. I'd never seen them so happy. Not even when Franco's kid was born, but I'd never tell anyone that, especially my brother.

"I've made a decision," Ma announces as she takes the baby from my father's arms without asking. Surprisingly, he gives him over without even missing a beat. "I'm going to give up volunteering."

"Really?" I ask, completely shocked because my mother loves the time she spends in the community. I really think she enjoys the ability to hear the latest gossip from a variety of people.

Ma nods. "I'm going to start watching Franco's little one, and now that Ethan is born, I can watch him too. Cora's welcome to join them at my house each day too, Ryder."

"Ma, no. You don't have to—"

"I know," she says, cutting me off. "But when you're my age, there's nothing more important than family. I want to surround myself with these babies for as long as I possibly can. Before you know it, they'll be going to kindergarten. I want to do it. Let me, Gracie."

"I'm not going back to work for a while, and when I do, it'll be part time."

"Then I'll take the baby part time, along with Cora."

"Are you sure you can handle three kids?" I ask and immediately regret the question.

Ma raises her eyebrow, the same way I do to everyone else when I want to challenge a bullshit statement. "You want to rephrase that?"

"I... Uh..." I shake my head and plaster on a fake smile.

Ma turns her attention to Ryder after a huff. "Are you okay with that, Ryder? Me watching the kids?"

Ryder shrugs. "Not a problem here. Cora will love that. She adores you."

"I adore that little girl too. It's nice to be able to spoil someone who can actually talk back to me."

And oh my God, do the two of them talk. My mom has finally found her soul mate for the gift of gab. The two of them can chatter for hours, bouncing from one topic to another, and none of it makes sense, but that doesn't stop them.

"It's set, then. When you head back to work, the kids will come to our house."

"Pops?" I ask because he hasn't said he's on board with it. "You want this?"

He grabs my hand and gives my fingers a squeeze. "It's been too quiet around the house since you moved out, Gracie. Between your mom and me, we can handle the kids, and it'll allow us to feel young again."

"I am young," Ma says to him.

"You'll always be young in my eyes," he tells her, schmoozing her like he always does.

174

"It'll give us a chance to spoil all the babies without you or Franco making a stink."

"I won't make a stink," I promise her. They spoiled me rotten, and I turned out okay. I expect them to do the same with their grandchildren. It would be weird if they didn't.

"I'm going to set up a little nursery."

My father rubs his forehead, muttering something I can't quite make out under his breath.

"The babies need somewhere to sleep when we watch them," she explains, somehow justifying the obscene amount of money she's about to spend. "You want them to sleep, don't you?"

Dad nods. "Of course, dear."

Ma looks to Ryder. "Does Cora nap?"

Ryder lets out a loud laugh, startling the baby. "I wish."

"Okay. Then we only need a crib."

"Only," Pops whispers.

Ma takes a finger and rubs the baby's cheek to calm him from Ryder's loudness. "Can I take the kids on field trips?"

"I guess," I say, but right now, I'd probably agree to just about anything.

"I promise I'll drive. It's safer that way."

My father grunts. "I drive just fine."

"When you can find your glasses," she teases him. "But I'm not risking the lives of my babies to those wonky orbs inside your head."

"My eyes are not wonky orbs."

Ma rolls her eyes. "Your prescription says otherwise."

Pops swipes his hand through the air before he collapses in the blue pleather chair across from my bed. "Whatever."

"So, I have a nursery to shop for and some field trips to plan." She smiles. "I'm going to show you everything. We're going to have so much fun. Just you wait, Ethan."

"Can I come sometimes?" I ask. "Or are adults not allowed to go on the field trips?"

Ma looks up with her eyes big. "You want to come?"

I raise a shoulder, feeling weirdly left out. "I mean, I like the museum and stuff too."

Ma smiles. "You're always welcome to come. You're my baby too."

And no matter how old I am, I know it's true. I'll always be their baby. Their little girl. After laying eyes on Ethan, I can't imagine the protective feeling that's buried in my gut ever going away.

"How about a family field trip once a month? There's plenty to do around here," Ryder adds because he clearly wants to go too.

"I like that," Ma says. "I'll ask Franco and Chloe if they want to come too. Vito and Benny, though…"

"They won't come. Don't bother," I tell her.

"I'll invite them. Maybe eventually they'll feel like they're missing out on something."

I pull the blanket up over my chest and wiggle my back against the world's most uncomfortable bed. "That'll never happen."

Ma walks around the bed and sits opposite Ryder with Ethan in her arms. "Your uncles are fuddy-duddies."

"Someday they'll settle down," Pops says, but there isn't a person in this room who believes that.

I busy myself with the extra-large water container they left with me, telling me I needed more hydration after labor. Which sounds great in theory, but that also makes me have to pee more than usual, and nothing about that is fun after pushing an abnormally large human out of that general area.

"Maybe your uncle will marry a different stripper this time," Ma says to Ethan. "One who wants to settle down and have a baby."

I choke on the water, and it dribbles down my chin as I quickly wipe it away. "Ma, that's awful."

She shrugs with a shitty smirk. "Well, where's the lie?"

"Lucia, you're rotten sometimes." Pops shakes his head and purses his lips.

"I'm always rotten, Mario. You know this, especially when it comes to my boys. They go where they let their penises take them, and it's never anywhere good."

"Ma, they may change."

"I'll be dead before that happens, Gracie."

"Two out of four isn't bad," Pops adds, trying to help, but Ma isn't having it.

She gives my father a wicked look. "I won't be able to rest until I know all my children are settled and happy."

"They're happy," Pops tells her.

"That they are," I say. "And they'll settle when they find the one person who makes them want to settle down. And if that never happens, if they never get married or have kids, I think Vito and Benny will still find ways to be happy. We all have different ideas of happiness, Ma."

She busies herself with Ethan, cooing over him as he sleeps in her arms. "At least I have you," she says to him. "I have four wonderful grandchildren to fill my life. What more could a woman want?" She stares down at Ethan like the sun rises and sets on his very presence.

Ryder scoots until his back is next to mine. He takes my hand in his as our arms are nestled between us. "Life's good," he says softly as my parents talk to each other about their two sons and their inability to find stable relationships.

"The best," I whisper, wondering if life will ever get better than this moment. I can't imagine it does.

This is the peak. The thing I dreamed about but wasn't sure would ever happen.

A child of my own and two more I love as if they were.

A family of my own.

And a man who loves me.

CHAPTER TWENTY-TWO

"Close your eyes."

Gracie stares up at me with her eyebrow cocked. "What's going on?"

I shake my head as I take her hands in mine. "It's a surprise."

"I hate surprises," she grumbles before finally complying. "If you scare me, I'm going…"

I squeeze her hands. "I'm not going to scare you, love. Let go a little bit and trust me."

She raises her chin, her face soft even if her eyes are sealed shut. "I do trust you."

"Good," I tell her, pulling her forward, careful to make sure she doesn't trip. "We're almost there."

"This is silly, Ryder. I've been to the falls a hundred times."

"Shush."

She jerks her head back but keeps her eyes closed. "Shush? I'll give you shush."

I've spent a month planning this day, working with her mother and our friends to pull this off. I even had her brothers in on it. The hardest part was keeping everyone quiet. There isn't much that happens around here without the entire town knowing every single detail.

We walk past the ice cream shop, standing at the top of the stairway down to the falls, where our closest friends and family are waiting. "Open your eyes, Gracie."

Her eyes flutter open, and a moment passes before she can get them to focus with the bright sun overhead. "What is this?" she asks as she takes a step forward to look over the railing. It takes her a second to spot her entire family waiting at the landing near the water's edge. "Ryder?"

I get down on one knee, doing something I wanted to do a year ago but didn't. Gracie made it clear that she wasn't ready to get married back then. But now we have a child together, we live together, and are married in every sense of the word except one.

Gracie turns slightly, her eyes searching for me before her gaze drops to where I'm kneeling. "Ryder?" she whispers.

"Gracie, I've never loved another person the way I love you. You've brought color back into my world, making every day full of light and life. I can't imagine spending a single day without you by my side. I love you, Gracie. Will you do me the honor of being my wife?"

Tears form in her eyes, and for the briefest of moments, I worry she'll turn me down. Weirder shit has happened to people. Maybe she still isn't ready and I am pushing the envelope with this elaborate plan.

epilogue

RYDER

"I'm proud of you, man," Austin says, adjusting my crooked tie.

I'm a mess. A bigger mess than I was when I married Elizabeth. I was too stupid and naïve back then to be nervous, but everything with Gracie is different.

"Why are you proud?" I ask, narrowing my eyes at my friend.

"You didn't give up. But then again, you never do."

"Quitting has never been an option."

"There he is," Lucia says as she walks over to me with her arms up, ready for a hug.

I welcome her embrace, knowing fighting it never works. Lucia gets her way no matter what, and it's easier and faster to give in.

"There's my new son," she whispers in my ear. "You've made me a very happy woman today. I wasn't sure my Gracie was ever going to get married."

I hug her tightly, knowing everything she does is out of love, and she means every word of welcome into their family. Even before today, I felt like I belonged...almost like I'd always been there. "I'm honored she chose me."

Lucia pulls back and gazes up at me with the softest look. "She knew you were out there somewhere and wasn't willing to settle for anyone else, Ryder. You were worth the wait for all of us."

"You're too sweet, Lucia."

"Mom," she reminds me. "You're married now, which means you're my child too. Please call me Ma at least. Can you do me that small favor and make this old woman happy?" The way she's looking at me makes it impossible for me to say no.

She's been wonderful since the moment I met her. I don't know what I would do without the help she and Mario provide with the kids. They have always been able to fill in to watch them when I don't have anyone else to handle them.

"Yes, Ma."

My words instantly get me another squeeze. "You made me the happiest woman in the world."

"That would be me, Ma." Gracie glides my way, looking like an angel with sunlight behind her. When she gets to my side, she snakes her arm around my back. "I don't know what I did to deserve all this."

Lucia reaches out, placing her hand on Gracie's bare arm. "You deserve the world, sweetheart. Don't ever forget that."

Gracie tips forward and presses her lips to her mother's cheek. "I know, Mama. I love you."

"Love you too," Lucia whispers, smiling at the small, intimate gesture.

"Nonna, Nonna," Cora says, running toward Lucia at full speed, liable to knock her over. She's small but mighty, especially when she's using every bit of her energy and momentum.

But Lucia is prepared, having months of practice handling Cora. "Come here, baby," Lucia says, holding her arms out, leaning forward, and bracing for impact.

Gracie looks up at me with a smile, her eyes bright and filled with possibilities. "I can't wait for Ethan to be that age."

"Don't rush it. He'll be that age in the blink of an eye, followed by a mouthy teenager."

"He's not allowed to get that old."

I brush the backs of my fingers against her cheek. "We can't stop time, no matter how hard we try, but at least I'll have my best friend by my side for the journey."

"There's no one else I'd rather grow old with."

"I hope so. You're stuck with me now, Mrs. Cooper."

Her smile widens. "Today was perfect."

I peer up, looking over the small group of people we've invited to celebrate our wedding day with us as they laugh and enjoy the party. "I wouldn't change a thing."

This is my home.

It's where I belong.

Star Falls isn't just a small town; it's where I'm meant to be.

I have more friends and family than I ever thought possible. Finding peace is nearly impossible, but I'm never lonely anymore. I have an entire army of people to help me raise my kids, when I used to think I had to shoulder the stress alone.

And I have a wife, someone who loves me unconditionally, and I can't wait to see where the future takes us.

I hope you loved Never Too Soon and I can't thank you enough for reading. If you love the Bianchi family, there's more to come in **Never Too Close** - Vito's story.

Please ignore the stated release date of July 2024. It'll release sooner, but I don't have a firm date yet. I can't rush my creativity.

If you want to get the latest updates on my new book releases, join my newsletter at menofinked.com/news

Preorder Your Copy >> **TAP HERE...**
or visit *menofinked.com/ntc*

never too LATE

www.chellebliss.com

CHELLE BLISS

USA TODAY BESTSELLING AUTHOR

CHAPTER ONE

"Frankie, for fuck's sake. Answer your phone." Jack's voice carries through the shop, echoing from deep under the hood of a late nineties town car.

I'm leaning my elbows on the ancient metal shop desk, sorting through a goddamn mountain of paperwork as though the answer to the meaning of the universe is on one of those purchase orders. The even more ancient desk chair creaks under my weight.

"Frankie!" Jack times his shout to the momentary pause before the bass of the song booming through the speakers kicks up to eardrum-splitting.

"Fuck, man, you want me to find that slip or what?" I yell back.

I've got a one-track mind, and I mean that literally.

You want my attention, you get it. All of it.

You want diagnostics run on a fuel pump, the best cup of coffee you ever had, a night of mind-melting orgasms courtesy of my tongue, or even a lost purchase order found—I can do every one of those things exceptionally well. But only one damned thing at a time.

Finding that piece of paper Jack lost in this mess on the desk will take every shred of patience I have left.

And to be honest, I didn't even hear my phone. I can't believe *he* can hear anything over the hair band he has blaring.

I curse under my breath and try to find the slip of paper that my buddy insists is here—somewhere.

If Jack's parents weren't going through some shit, I would have gotten my ass out from behind the desk and back under one of the dozen cars we have waiting for work, telling him to find the goddamn paperwork himself. But Jack's my oldest friend, this is his shop, and without his mom here to keep the books, he's in way over his head.

"Come on, man. Did you find it?" Jack demands.

I want to tell him to find his own needle in this haystack, but instead, I just hold up a hand and flip him the bird while I shove aside papers of all shapes and sizes.

One problem at a time.

I grab my phone and swipe the screen, and I see not one, not two, but three different messages, all from the same sender.

Mom: Frankie, sweetheart, it's your mother. Can you take a quick break and meet me at Latterature? It's urgent but not life-threatening. Love, Ma

Mom: Franco, honey. It's almost lunch. Do your mother a favor and run down to the bookstore. I won't keep you long. It's very, very important. Love you, sweetheart. Ma

Mom: Son, please, now I'm getting worried. You work five minutes away. Are you coming? Love, your mother Lucia

Three separate text messages composed in full sentences. Each one addressed to me. Each one signed by my mother.

No matter how many times I've explained that she doesn't have to sign her texts, it's a habit she'll never break. And just like when we were kids, Ma escalates the urgency of her texts by switching from *Ma* to *your mother*. And worse, her full name.

"J!" I yell over the music, rolling back on the wheelie chair that normally belongs to Carol, Jack's mom. "I got to run out. You want me to bring back lunch?"

Jack isn't listening or didn't hear me, so I head over to the hood of the town car and press the off button on that damn Hello Kitty speaker.

"Yo!" I shout in the sudden silence. "I'm running to Latterature. You want somethin'?"

Jack shakes his head and rolls his eyes. "My mom made me lunch today, man. I'm sorted."

Even though the marriage stuff going down with his parents is rough, I have to give him shit about it. "What, she pack you a Lunchable and a little note?" I tease.

Jack kicks a work boot at my leg, but intentionally misses. "Fuck off." Then he sighs. "She's staying with me this week. She insists on packing me lunches and making dinners. It's her way of thanking me for letting her crash at my place."

I clap a hand on the hood of the car and nod. "All right, man. So, you're set with your ham sando with the crusts cut off. You want a coffee or something while I'm out?"

"Nah." Jack sniffs and gives me half a grin. "Ma packed my camping thermos. She thinks I spend too much money eating out."

I snort-laugh and almost give him shit for that. Almost.

Yeah, we may be grown men in our late thirties, but if Ma makes it, we eat it. Ma says it, we pay attention.

Hell, I'm about to leave work, thanks to three text messages from my ma, so I don't have much room to give him a hard time about being a mama's boy.

"All right," I say instead and nod. "I'll be back."

I take the love of my life, my Harley-Davidson Road King, through town, waving and nodding at the many people I know along the two-mile drive between the shop and downtown Star Falls.

When I finally reach Main Street, I drive all the way to the farthest end of the strip of quaint storefronts and park right outside the bookstore café.

It isn't even noon yet, so I don't bother stopping by The Body Shop, the tattoo parlor next door. It's Tuesday, which means my little sister, Grace, will be opening the shop, but not until one—and that's if she is on time. Gracie is unpredictable, stubborn, and—more than anything—loves her sleep.

As I pull open the door to Latterature, I'm braced for the string of Christmas bells that normally go off like a wind chime caught in

187

a tornado. But today—nothing. No warning bells, no chimes. No customers.

"Ma?" I call out into the store.

It's unusually quiet in the place, and I don't just mean the lack of welcome bells. Given the fact that my ma practically called a three-alarm fire trying to get me over here, I'm not seeing any sign that she's actually in the store.

I wander past the cash register and note a couple people browsing the stacks.

"Hey, Bob." I nod at Bob Horton, who's got his reading glasses at the end of his nose. He's leaning back in a vintage—and by that, I mean old as shit—plush rocking chair, looking over some figures on a clipboard.

"Frankie." He greets me but doesn't bother looking up from his notes. Bob's always been a little off, but he owns the local electronics store. One of the last in a twenty-mile radius that's not owned by a big corporate retailer.

"Workin' or playin', Bob?" I give the old man a half smile and scan the aisles for my mother.

Bob grunts in response.

I'm used to Bob being a man of very few words, and awkward ones when he does talk, so I give him a nod and keep on moving.

The vibe in Latterature is a cross between an elderly aunt's attic and somebody's grandma's kitchen. I can smell the familiar scents of freshly ground coffee, vintage books, and old upholstery as I walk past bookshelves and head toward the back kitchen.

Finally, the familiar scent of hair spray and perfume greets me. Evidence that Ma was here recently, along with her friends.

"Franco. Where have you been? I've been worried sick."

I turn around and look down at Lucia Bianchi. Matriarch of our family and overall force to be reckoned with.

She's short but curvy, and despite turning fifty-nine this past spring, Ma's hair is drugstore auburn, sprayed to within an inch of its life, and perfectly styled around her smiling face.

"Come here." She holds out her manicured hands, her nails perfectly colored and bedazzled with some sparkly looking things on the ends. She pulls my face close and kisses my cheek, then loops her hand through my arm and lowers her voice. "I wish you'd gotten here sooner. What took you so long? My God, son, I was about to get in the car and make sure you weren't crushed under one of those cars or something worse."

"Morbid, Ma, but thanks for the concern." I look around us, but my mom's crew of best friends is nowhere to be found, which is unusual.

Lucia was a stay-at-home mom who never went to work even after we grew up, but by God, she made knowing the ins and outs of her kids' lives more than just her job. It was her passion.

Now that Vito, Benny, Gracie, and I are all in our thirties, Ma makes *everyone's* business her job. And unless she's with my father, she's never far from her crew of best lady friends.

"What's with the urgency? You made it sound like—"

Ma shushes me a little too vigorously and points a red nail toward the lounger where Bob is rocking back and forth. She gives me the universal mom-eyes, half wide and then settling into a frustrated glare, as she huffs, "Come back into the kitchen."

"In the kitchen? Ma, come on, I got to get back to work."

My mother ignores me and takes hold of my arm. All five foot nothing of her pedals off toward the back of the store, dragging me with her.

I would stop and argue the point, but when Lucia Bianchi gets her mind set on something, there is only one person who can stop her and that's my father, Mario.

We push through the door with an ancient, paint-chipped sign that would read *Employees Only* if all the letters were still there, but which now reads, "E p l ees On ."

As soon as we're in the back, Ma starts talking a million miles a second. "Did you see Bob out there? Franco, you've got to get rid of him." My mother's gesturing wildly, her nails like tiny daggers already dripping with Bob Horton's blood.

"Come on, Ma. What's the problem with Bob? He's harmless." As I peer around the room, the rest of Mom's crew rushes toward me, and then I get it.

The gang is all here after all.

They're all just hiding from Bob.

Carol, Jack's mom, who's currently living with him and making him sandwiches and coffee, starts first. She's wearing a low-cut fuchsia top that reveals an expanse of cleavage the likes of which I never want to see on anyone's mom.

She touches my forearm before she starts to speak. "Franco, the man's odd. You know he's odd, and his nephew's odd. The lot of those Hortons are strange. Always have been." As if she remembers that I have history with his niece, she pats my arm. "Not that sweet Celeste, though. Good thing she married and ditched the Horton last name."

I'm just about to roll my eyes and set the ladies straight, when Sassy, who's never been called by her given name of Shirley, slaps a hand against my arm. "Listen to your mother, Frankie."

Sassy waits tables at the only Italian restaurant in town, owned by none other than my cocky, asshole younger brother Benny.

She's like a second mother to us kids, which is why she feels comfortable laying hands on me, especially in front of my own mother.

Hell, all the women in my mom's lady gang are like mothers to me. Although to be fair, Ma is more mother than any one man needs.

"Thank you, Sassy," my mother says, sounding exasperated. "You know what a pain in the ass that man is. Plus, he's..." Ma taps the tips of her long nails together while she thinks of just the right insult.

"He's got *sociopath* vibes," a voice calls from just behind Sassy.

"Bev's right." Sassy moves aside and nudges forward the quietest —which by no definition of the word means quiet—friend of my mother's. Sassy nods vigorously. "You tell him, Bev."

"Ladies, please." I hold up a hand and hold back an impatient sigh before Bev can launch into a spiel about her assessment of Bob's mental state. "You all have known Bob Horton for freakin' ever, and he's..." I have to bite back the words. "All right, he's a little off, but so what? Has he done anything? I just saw him out front, and he seemed harmless enough."

A little grumpy, but if he had the first idea that his anti-fan club was hiding out in the bookstore's café kitchen, I'd have been a grumpy asshole too.

"This isn't about us, Franco." Ma clutches the trio of gold charms that hangs around her neck—an Italian horn, a simple cross, and an engraved heart, a gift from my father for their 25th wedding anniversary. She glares at me and steps away from her three best friends. "This is about Chloe. We can't let that lecherous creep take the girl for the little she's got. She's been through so much already."

"Chloe?" I draw in a long, calming breath and check the time on my phone. "Ma, who the hell is Chloe and what's Bob done to her?"

"Well, nothing yet, but that's why you're here." My mother, on her three-inch heels, marches through the kitchen toward the commercial refrigerator at the back of the room. "Chloe, come meet my son."

Oh, for fuck's sake.

There's another one of them.

Chloe must be the relative who has come up here to take over Latterature since Ann, the previous owner, passed.

Now it's starting to make sense.

My mom's gang just added a plus-one, and I'm being called in to rescue the old lady from what, I have no clue. But I am hoping we're getting close to the point.

"Ma, what could Bob possibly be—" But the words die in my throat.

I squint and blink, expecting my vision to clear at any moment and for a clone of Ann—short, round, and heavily age-spotted—to appear before my eyes.

But that doesn't happen.

What does happen is Sassy, Bev, Carol, and Ma form this mom-circle around me.

I can feel the weight of their meddling looks as Ma coaxes a woman who looks younger than me using a voice better suited to soothing stray puppies and lost kittens at the rescue where she volunteers with Bev.

"Chloe," Ma says, drawing out her name as though it's something precious, "this is my son Franco Bianchi. Franco, this is Chloe Harkin."

The woman in front of me is dressed the opposite of the older women huddled in the kitchen. While the lady gang is a riot of colorful tops, plunging necklines, tight jeans, and artificial nails, Chloe is…simple.

Plain, if you consider she's wearing cargo pants, combat boots, and an oversized striped sweater so big she could probably fit two of her under there and still have room. But there is nothing average about the fire in her green eyes as she looks at me, sucking a plush lower lip into her mouth.

Chloe looks away and tugs nervously on a lock of long auburn hair. "Nice to meet you," she mumbles, her voice as tiny as a mouse.

I wipe my palm on my jeans to make sure I don't have any grease left on it and hold out my hand. "I'm a mechanic," I explain. "Up at Easy Start. Welcome to Star Falls."

Chloe bites down on that lower lip and flicks a look at my mom.

"Go on," Lucia urges. "Franco doesn't bite."

I do, but that's not the kind of information a son shares with his mother.

I hold my hand firm and wait while the timid little thing sniffs, gathers her courage, and then slips her hand in mine.

Chloe gives it a quick pump, then pulls away—like she might actually believe I bite.

"You're related to Ann?" I ask, curious how this slim, pretty redhead shares blood with the lady who for years blended into my mother's friend group in every way.

This woman—or girl—God…I can't tell if she's nineteen or twenty-nine… This Chloe is nothing like Ann.

"This is Ann's niece, Franco," Sassy blurts, but after a cutting glare from my mother, Sassy presses her lips closed.

"Let Chloe talk," Lucia urges, and that's when I know.

This isn't a rescue.

This is a setup.

I inhale deeply though my nose, flaring my nostrils against the overpowering cloud of mom perfumes diluted by something lighter, cleaner. I roll my shoulders and rub my chin where a healthy growth of stubble is already fighting to break through.

I should have known.

I look from Chloe's reddening cheeks to the bright, beaming smiles of every other woman in the room and shake my head.

"Ma," I say, drawing out my syllables so she knows I'm onto her. "It's the middle of my workday. If Bob didn't do something shady, I'm out of here."

Ma's face falls, and I know she's aware that I'm not here to play. "Franco." She sounds almost insulted. "Give me a chance to explain. You just got here. You think Jack can't handle that shop on his own for thirty minutes? Bob's sold Chloe one of those big TVs, and he's charging her—"

"I bought it. He didn't force me." Chloe's voice is soft, but if she's interrupting my mother, she has some kind of spine under that afghan-sized sweater. She gives my mother a pained but sincere smile, the honesty in it breaking something open deep in my chest. "I wanted it, Mrs. Bianchi. I've got some plans to modernize the store."

My mother waves a hand in the air dismissively. "Honey, of course, if you want it, you should buy it. But Bob Horton—"

The sound of a congested throat clearing in the doorway draws every set of eyes in the kitchen.

"Lucia, ladies." Bob Horton wipes his nose along the long sleeve of his blue work shirt, and I can feel my mother bristle beside me. "TV's up and working, Ms. Harkin. I left your copy of the installment agreement on the counter. I don't extend credit. So you miss even one payment, and I'll be back down here to take the set back." He looks at Chloe harshly, and something in my gut tightens as his eyes rake over her.

I don't like the feeling.

"Your aunt was a nice lady," Bob added. "Sorry for your loss. But business is business."

The unpleasant huffing and shifting on heels from each of my mother's friends lets me know exactly how they all feel about Bob, his television, and his warning to Chloe to make the payments for the device on time.

"Thank you, Bob," Sassy says, a sneer in her voice. "You know, the girl's been through so much. You could just leave the paperwork and be done with it."

"It's just business," he repeats in a sort of insulted pout, sniffling loud enough that I almost instinctively look around for a tissue.

Instead, I nod at Chloe. "You good? You wanted this TV?"

Her lower lip is between her teeth when she nods and finally releases it. "Yes, I do. Thank you, Mr. Horton."

She'll learn soon enough that nobody under the age of seventy goes by a title around here. Instead, I nod at Bob and clap him on the shoulder. "I'll walk you out."

I follow the man to the front and notice that in the time it takes me to walk back through the store, Bob's nephew, Tyler, has pulled up and is idling their shitty company pickup beside my bike.

"Hey, Ty." I lift my chin at the kid. "How's the starter? Any better?"

Tyler nods. "Yeah," he grumbles, avoiding eye contact. "Been running fine," he adds, his voice weirdly close to a whisper.

I watch as Bob climbs into the passenger seat, mumbles something to his nephew, and they take off.

When I turn back to Latterature, four old ladies are watching me through the glass. I yank open the door, and I swim through the sea of colorful blouses. "See that?" I ask, gesturing toward the door. "Bob's gone. You can all go on and pick on some other aging electronics salesman."

Bev and Sassy start talking between themselves, while Carol tugs my mom's arm and points to the large television that Bob set up in the reading nook.

It seems like my work here is done, but I feel Chloe's eyes on me. I turn to her and watch as a pretty shade of pink brightens her cheeks.

I don't know if this woman was in on my mother summoning me

over here, but even if she was, she's only in town because she suffered a loss.

"I'm sorry about your aunt," I say sincerely, meaning every word. "She was a great lady. Made my favorite sandwich in all of Star Falls."

Chloe's whole body seems to relax at the mention of her aunt. "Mine too," she says. "Grilled cheese with chicken and bacon. She made it special every time she visited my mom and me."

I cover my belly with both hands and groan in spite of myself. "That's the one. My favorite sandwich. Just don't tell my brother I said that. He's a cocky son of a bitch when it comes to food."

"Franco, maybe you should take Chloe to dinner tonight." Ma has disentangled herself from Carol and has nosed her way between me and the new owner of Latterature. "She's new to town and doesn't know anyone. Take her to your brother's restaurant. You do like Italian food, don't you, dear?"

"Oh no, that's… I mean… Yes, I like Italian, but…" Chloe's stammering, but her eyes are searching my face. An innocent, sweet smile brings light to those green eyes. "You don't have to. I…I'm fine, really. I have so much to do here in the store."

I'm looking her over, the long, luscious locks of auburn hair and that sweet face that somehow doesn't match the dowdy, nerdy clothes she's wearing.

I see just a hint of the curves buried beneath the blanket-like layers, and my fingers suddenly itch to peel them back one by one.

And then I stop myself.

Something about the woman has my body paying attention.

My gut tightens at the way she's biting her bottom lip again, and I wonder if she likes being bitten as much as she seems to like biting.

But my mother's voice is in my ears, loudly demanding that I take Chloe on a date, and I know right there I have to put a stop to the whole thing. If I let myself get set up by my mother once, my entire life will become an episode of *Matchmaking with Lucia and Company*.

"Chloe, no offense, but this—" I motion toward Ma and her lady gang "—is my mother's not-at-all subtle attempt to set her single son up with the new—and I assume single—woman in town." I give Ma a sharp glare.

"She is single," Ma adds. "That was the first thing I asked, son. I'm not trying to wreck a happy home here."

I nod. "Hmm-mm," I mutter. "Thought so." I lean down and plant a kiss on my mother's hair, and she swats me away before fluffing the curls that I flattened back into place. "Ma, I'll talk to you later. Chloe, it was nice meeting you. Enjoy the television." I point at Bev, Sassy, and Carol, all of whom are standing by just waiting, like they'll break out into applause if I agree to take Chloe to dinner. "Ladies." I nod. "I'd appreciate if the next time my ma gets an idea in her head related to my love life, you'll remind her—" I grab the door handle and yank it open "—to butt out."

I hear a chorus of disappointed sighs as one by one the ladies say goodbye.

"We only want what's best for you, Franco."

"Your mother means well, Frankie."

"I told you this wasn't going to work, Lucia. Your son isn't the dating kind."

Isn't the dating kind?

That stops me in my tracks, but if I go back in, I'm only inviting the lot of them to start analyzing my love life. And I've had more than enough time on that topic for one day.

I almost turn back to defend myself, but a frustrated grunt comes out instead, and I decide it's better to leave all this before I start something I really don't want to finish. I tug my sunglasses over my eyes, then climb onto my bike and toss a glare back toward the store since I know every one of them is still standing at the door, watching me pull away.

And curiously enough, so is Chloe.

CHAPTER TWO

chloe

I watch the most gorgeous man I've ever seen kick a thick leg over his bike and ride off into the sunset.

I realize the entire crowd of women is chattering and arguing with one another, while I'm standing here gaping after Lucia's son like a starving puppy.

It's been ages since I had a date, and I don't think any of the guys I've been out with since I broke it off with David compare to the heavily tattooed, muscular man I just met. Not in the looks department—or in the attitude either.

Franco Bianchi.

My skin pebbles just thinking his name, and I nervously bite on my lower lip. There are words for guys like Franco: sexy, powerful, and totally out of my league.

Much as I'm sure Lucia would have been thrilled if her son had taken me out, it would have been nothing more than a pity date. An awkward dinner to appease his mother, and nothing at all to do with me.

I'm as forgettable as yesterday's lunch to a guy like that, and much as Lucia might have good intentions, even thinking about it hurts a little.

I wonder if my thoughts are showing all over my face because Lucia looks like she feels terrible.

"Chloe, I feel like I have to apologize for my son." She's standing in front of me, clutching her necklace. Her face is tight, her lips pressed thin. "Franco is such a good boy. He's not normally so rude and so…"

"Do you blame him, Lucia?" The one called Sassy has a hand on her hip and one perfectly drawn-on eyebrow cocked almost to her hairline. "Franco's a grown man. He doesn't want his mother meddling in his love life."

"Whose side are you on, Sas?" Bev hisses.

My aunt had a very special relationship with Bev, the lady who runs the local animal shelter.

I am only just learning how many amazing relationships my aunt Ann had here in Star Falls. I can now understand why she spent so many years here, running this small bookstore and café, despite the fact that she was losing money hand over fist.

"Why do you need this expensive TV, anyway?"

The sudden silence in the store lets me know I drifted off into my own thoughts again. "I'm sorry." I blink and look from Lucia to Bev, then from Sassy to Carol, before flushing so hard I can feel my cheeks go pink. "I missed the question?"

The ladies all start talking over one another about the television and Franco, but I notice a customer standing near the front door, looking like the crew of women is blocking her way in. I tug open the glass door, and a gorgeous woman with long, glossy black hair and sunglasses over her eyes clomps into the store.

"Ma. What the eff?" She tears the sunglasses away from her face and stares at each woman in turn.

I have no idea which one is her mother, but once I see her eyes, I have a pretty good guess.

She points a heavily tattooed hand at Lucia. "Where you been with the car all morning? You were supposed to drive me to work."

Lucia gasps and looks horrified. "I'm sorry, Gracie. I met the girls down here for an emergency."

"I had to wake up Vito for a ride. Dad drove out to Cleveland just after you left."

"Why on earth did he go to Cleveland without me?" Lucia starts fumbling for her phone, which is encased in a glittery pink protective sleeve. "That man shouldn't be driving until he gets a pair of real glasses. I don't know how he's going to see the signs on the highway."

Gracie grabs the device from her mom and flips a little button. "See, Ma? Your phone was on silent. The entire family could have been calling for help, and you wouldn't have known. Dad must've called five times before he left."

Lucia shakes her head and holds the phone in her hands like it's an explosive device and Grace is the detonation expert who just neutralized the threat. "Oh, son of a gun. I was wondering why I wasn't getting any calls after I texted your brother."

Grace lifts a brow and strikes a dramatic pose.

I'm captivated by her larger-than-life attitude and colorful tattoos.

She jams the sunglasses on top of her head and softens as she looks at each of her mother's friends. "Bev, Sassy, Carol." She kisses each woman on the cheek before turning back to her mother. "Mom, what the hell kind of emergency could you have at a bookstore?"

I squirm a little bit, feeling like I'm drowning in my striped sweater. Next to Grace, who's wearing a shredded concert T-shirt with more holes than fabric, I feel every bit the bookish nerd that I am.

I start to tiptoe backward, hoping to slip unnoticed into the kitchen.

Sassy points a finger at me before I can get away. "That," she says, narrowing her thickly mascaraed eyes at me. "That's the emergency."

Grace looks me over, and it feels like I'm in fifth grade again. I nearly lean against the wall for support under the confident, bold woman's gaze.

Grace squints a little and cocks her head. "Who's this?" she asks, not even addressing her question to me.

Yeah, if I felt invisible before, I feel like a piece of furniture now. "I'm—" I wring my hands together, then awkwardly stick one out toward Grace.

Lucia cuts me off before I can finish introducing myself. "Gracie. This is Ann's niece. I've been talking about her all week, for goodness' sake." Lucia puts a hand on my arm, a thin stack of gold bangle bracelets clicking wildly with the movement. "This is Chloe Harkin."

Grace twists her lips to one side, and a deep dimple marks her cheek. Grace is the kind of girl everyone wanted to be in high school. Cool, pretty, and completely indifferent to what anyone else thinks.

I can already see the family resemblance to her older brother. My heart thumps an excited beat in my chest as I picture Franco's thick waves of hair and piercing eyes. His, though, were blue.

She eyes me curiously, silent for a moment, and then slaps the shredded knee of her black jeans and curses. "I got it now." Instead of shaking my awkwardly outstretched hand, Grace turns to her mom. "This is the girl you were trying to set Frankie up with?"

"Look at her." Lucia crows. "She's a doll. Your brother could use a nice girl like Chloe. Before all the other dogs in this town come sniffing around wanting a shot at the new girl."

I surprise myself by snorting at that. No dogs have ever come sniffing around me. I'm sure Star Falls won't be any different. Not if the women look like Grace, and the men… Well, if the men look like Franco, I may as well put on a habit and turn this bookstore into a convent. I've got as much chance with a guy like that as a nun does.

Sassy puts an end to the conversation by swinging her oversized metallic silver purse over her shoulder. "Gals, I got to run. My boss is a real asshole if I'm late, and I've got to stop home for my uniform."

"Asshole boss." Lucia scowls, but it's clear she's not insulted. "You tell that son of mine to call his mother. Benito hasn't called in days."

"He's sleeping with that new bartender he hired," Grace says with a smirk.

Sassy grumbles. "This week, he is. And last week, it was another one, and next week, it'll be someone else."

Lucia shakes her head, sighing as if the weight of the world rests on her tiny shoulders. "Is it too much to ask that my children settle down and be happy? What is it with all this sexual freedom? When I was young..."

There's a groan from one of the women.

"And that's my cue to go." Sassy air-kisses her friends goodbye and waves at me before breezing out of the store.

Lucia continues, undeterred. "And would it be so much to ask for grandchildren while I'm still healthy enough to enjoy them?" She looks at me, a sadness in her face. "Tomorrow isn't promised to anyone, and I just want grandbabies I can push in their strollers. I don't want them pushing me in mine."

"So, you're Ann's niece?" Grace asks, completely ignoring her mother's pity party as she finally holds out her hand to me.

I nod. "I'm Chloe Harkin. Nice to meet you."

Grace seems to size me up as she takes in my sweater and cargo boots. She releases my hand with a nod. "I work next door at The Body Shop. You'll be seeing a lot of me, as long as you keep making that kick-ass coffee your aunt used to make. I'm literally addicted to her peanut butter crisps too. I'm Gracie, and that one belongs to me." She lifts one of those perfect brows impossibly higher and jerks a thumb toward Lucia.

Of course Gracie works at the town tattoo parlor. If she got any cooler, I might just collapse into a heap of dust on the floor.

"Just so you know," she says, gesturing toward her mother. "My ma's going to try to set you up with her oldest son until you tell her in no uncertain terms to lay the fuck off the matchmaking. Either you tell her, or my brother will."

"I didn't teach my daughter to cuss like a sailor," Lucia says, sounding a little hurt. "And what's so wrong with wanting to see my children happy?"

"Ma, what do you even know about this girl?" Gracie demands.

She waves a hand at me. "Look at her. She might not even be into guys, for all you know. You can't just go around trying to hook up your kids with anything that lives and breathes and hasn't yet slept with Benito." She whips her head, and her long black locks go flying. "You haven't, have you? My brother does get around pretty damn quick."

Lucia makes the sign of the cross over her chest and forehead. "The girl's been here two weeks. Not even your brother moves that fast."

"Yes, he does," they say, and by they, I mean all of them—Bev, Carol, and Gracie.

Lucia purses her lips, reluctantly admitting they are right. "Fine. Maybe I should have asked whether Chloe is attracted to men and whether she's already had relations with my youngest son before I tried to set her up with Franco. I'm just trying to help here."

"Help by not helping," Grace says, then she points a finger at me. "You got any coffee? I'd kill for a shot of caffeine and a peanut butter crisp."

I nod, remembering that I do actually have a business to run, and this place is not just a social club for my aunt's friends. "I'll start a fresh pot," I tell her. "Give me about five minutes."

Grace drops her sunglasses back over her eyes and clomps toward the door. "I'll stop back," she says over her shoulder. "I got to open next door."

I scurry back toward the kitchen, wishing for the millionth time since I set foot in Latterature that my aunt had a peekaboo window in the kitchen.

Before I push past the kitchen door, I hear Lucia call my name. "Chloe, sweetheart. We're leaving."

I hustle back to the front to wish the women goodbye. They hardly seem to notice me. Bev and Lucia are talking about covering shifts at the local animal shelter. Carol is adjusting the top of her blouse, asking if it sends the wrong message for a first date.

"It's coffee with Ray Morris, Carol. What kind of messages do you think that man is going to pick up on from a blouse?" Bev is unzipping a fanny pack that is hanging around her waist and then digging around for her car keys. "Besides," she adds, a heavy note of judgment in her tone. "Aren't you and Earl still married?"

Carol primly adjusts the fuchsia top to cover her cleavage with a bit more modesty. "We're separated," she clarifies. "And it's complicated. These things take time. While Earl is sorting out what he needs, well…in the meantime, I'm sorting out mine."

Bev barks a rough laugh. "For the love of all that's holy, Carol, don't let Ray Morris be the one to scratch your feminine itch. And if he does, please don't tell us about it."

They are all giggling and talking, but as Lucia pulls open the door and holds it for her friends, she cocks her chin and calls out to me. "Chloe, honey. Where're your aunt's welcome bells? You don't want to be in the back and not know if a customer comes in the store!"

I nod and scan the floor and the front counter, but I don't see them. "Bob's nephew took them down when they came to deliver the television." He'd said the constant ringing would be noise we didn't need while they were going in and out. But it looks like he didn't replace them before they left. "I'll find them," I assure her. "Thanks."

She is fussing with a pair of massive sunglasses when she shouts to her friends and trots back into the shop.

"Chloe, you should come to my place for dinner on Sunday." She's breathless and looks excited, like she's just been hit with inspiration. "My husband cooks, and Mario…" She pinches her thumb and fingers together, the tips of her nails clicking lightly, then kisses them and gestures at me with her hand in something that looks like delight. "He's the real cook in the family. Home-cooked Italian food and good company. The whole family will be there… including my Franco." She leans in a little closer and says in a hushed voice, "And don't even think about bringing anything. You're not a guest. You're family."

I give her a weak smile. The thought of sitting down to eat with the bold, outrageous Bianchi family is a lot to take in.

"I'll try to make it," I say vaguely. "I have so much work to do here in the shop."

"It's dinner. You got to eat, and you haven't eaten until you've had my husband's meatballs. You can't say no to Mario's meatballs. Oh, maybe I can get him to make braciole. It's to die for. He'll do it. He'll make it just for you. I'll see you at six sharp, honey."

She doesn't wait for me to respond and hustles down the block toward her ridiculously huge pickup truck. I can see just the top of her auburn-colored hair as she steps up on the running board and climbs behind the steering wheel of the burgundy beast.

I head back inside Latterature. As overwhelmed as I was by the noise and color and chaos of Aunt Ann's friends, somehow, without them here, everything in the shop seems strangely quiet and extremely lonely.

CHAPTER THREE

franco

I roll into my parents' house close to an hour before dinner is served because I know if I'm not there to set the table, Vito will do it and he'll fuck it all up.

Of the four of us Bianchi siblings, two still live at home. Gracie, because even though she's thirty, she's the baby, and Ma and Pops give her absolutely no reason to move from the comforts of her childhood home.

And then there's Vito.

We're eleven months apart and practically went through everything at the same time, and yet we turned out to be two totally different men.

We both like to work with our hands, but that's where the similarities end. Vito's a firefighter, and, to him, mealtime means setting out a stack of plates, a jumble of mismatched silverware, and letting everybody help themselves.

Ma likes things a certain way, and while it may be extra work to pull out the cloth napkins and put the leaf in the dining room table, it makes her happy.

Over the years, we've each fallen into roles in the family.

Gracie is the baby, so she's off the hook, no matter what the issue is. I'm surprised Ma and Pops even make her clear her own plate. She's spoiled fucking rotten and can do no wrong.

Benito, the second youngest, owns an Italian restaurant, but does he lift a finger to help Pops make dinner? Hell no. He can hardly pull himself from his restaurant most weekends for the couple hours it takes to eat and socialize before bolting out the door like he's a CEO and not a chef.

Benny's cocky, annoying, arrogant, and hilarious, but what makes it so frustrating is he's a genuinely good guy. He's got the quickest temper of all of us, but he's driven, generous, and a lot of other good qualities that I'll never admit to his face. He's a brilliant cook, having picked up a ton over the years from our parents and grandparents. But when he comes home, he's all youngest son. The brilliant cook and demanding chef in him take a back seat, and he just lets himself be served and babied. Cocksucker.

And then there's me. The oldest. The one who moved out first—much to my parents' horror—and who is probably the most responsible. I pay attention to my parents and what they need, even if they drive me up a fucking wall sometimes.

They're family.

Wherever they are is my forever home, so even though I don't live under their roof anymore, I show up early enough for table-setting duty.

But today when I arrive, the table's already set. And not only that, the table's set for seven.

There's never an extra place setting.

"Why's it so quiet in here?" I hang my keys on the wall cabinet by the front door Pops built Ma after he retired. I nod at the dining room table, which I can see from the entryway. I kick off my boots and lift my brows at Gracie, who is snuggled down on the leather sectional nibbling the ends of her hair while she watches a football game.

Gracie doesn't bother looking up. "Franco," she mumbles in greeting, her eyes locked on the huge screen that hangs over the fireplace.

206

I drop down onto the couch, annoyingly close to Gracie. A huge, warm lump tucked under a crocheted afghan shifts as I rest my head on my sister's shoulder. "Ladies," I say, greeting my mother's dogs. "Soooo." I bat my eyelashes dramatically. "Watching your man play today?"

"Shut up, heathen." Grace reaches past the dogs to shove me away, but I grab her wrists and hold them tight, locked in an eternal brother-sister wrestling match.

"Come on, Gracie. You can admit you've got a crush on that boy." I release her hands when Venus, the most vicious of my mother's dogs, starts barking. I stand beside the armrest and lean down to kiss the top of Grace's hair. "Serious now. Are you all right?" I ask.

Gracie looks up at me, a moment's softness overtaking her hard glare. "Let it go, all right?" The vulnerability and sorrow in her eyes almost crack my heart in two.

My sister doesn't normally look sad. Her happiness is infectious, and her rage is entertaining. I don't like this other place she's been in lately. This melancholy, withdrawn space. But since she's flipped the switch, I'm not about to drag her back down into something she clearly doesn't want to talk about.

Before I ask anything, she sets her lips in a line and jabs a finger into my chest. "Go change your socks. You stink, and Ma invited some girl over for dinner."

I know for a fact that my feet don't stink, but I lift my leg as far as I can and wiggle my toes at her. "You want to eat my sock? Keep it up."

I drop the jokes and rest my ass on the armrest before Ma sees me and yells at me that I'm going to break the sofa. I stare daggers at the television where the most recent guy who broke my sister's heart is playing defense for the Browns.

This past spring, my sister tattooed a customer, and after she finished, they ended up having some hot and heavy fling.

Turns out he's a major player and not just on the ball field. Gracie's a good girl. Smart, gorgeous. But she's got awful taste in men.

"We could watch the news if you just want to fall into a pit of depression," I remind her, trying to lighten the mood. I tug on the ends of her hair but can't even coax a smile out of her.

She flicks my hand away. "Worry about yourself, Romeo," she says. "Ma's got a bug up her butt to marry you off."

I sigh and quickly yank myself off the arm of the couch as I hear Ma's voice on the phone echoing through the house. "This is going to be some dinner," I mutter and head over to the table to inspect the settings.

Ma must have set it herself, because not only is the fall harvest tablecloth with matching napkins and bronze-colored maple leaf napkin rings already set for seven, I notice little pieces of paper with everyone's name written out on them in my mom's perfect cursive handwriting. I'm not even surprised when I see I've been assigned a seat next to Chloe.

My breath catches a little in my chest as I think about Ann's niece. It's a weird reaction—part resistance and maybe part something else. But I'm not sure what, and I sure as hell don't want to think about that right now.

"What's the bookstore girl doing at family dinner?" I bark out at no one in particular.

Ma shifts immediately from whatever conversation she's having on her cell phone to answering me. "Shh, Franco. I'm on the phone. Go open the wine. It needs to breathe."

I shake my head and wander into the kitchen.

My father is standing at the small butcher block island, a well-worn red apron protecting his navy flannel shirt from splatters. He's got a pair of reading glasses perched on the end of his nose, and he's glaring at a package of breadsticks.

"Son, what does this say?" Without even a hello, Pops shoves the glasses onto the mountain of wavy silver hair that almost perfectly matches mine in thickness and style and scowls. He scrubs a hand over the white bristles on his chin. "It might be time for something stronger than drugstore cheaters."

I take the package from him, then lean in and kiss him on the cheek, taking in his familiar cologne that's fighting for dominance over the massive pot of sauce that's bubbling on the stove.

"Gluten-free rosemary garlic grissini," I tell him, reading the label. "You cutting back on gluten, Pops?"

He lifts his hands in surrender. "So, I grabbed the wrong package. There's going to be enough gluten at the table to smother a hippo. A gluten-free breadstick ain't going to kill anybody." He motions to me with an aged, muscular hand. "Open that, and put them in a basket before your mother sees the package."

I tear open the extremely loud plastic wrapper and sniff the contents. "Mmm." I take one of the grissini and give it a bite. "I don't care what these are or are not made of. They taste damn good," I assure him. "You get these at the specialty market the other day?" I smack my lips and dig in a cabinet for the woven cloth basket Ma likes to serve bread in.

My dad nods. "Probably the last time I'll drive that far until I get my eyes looked at. Don't get old, son. Aging's a bitch, and not the good kind."

"So, go to the eye doctor," I tell him. "It'll get Ma off your back, and then you can drive all over the state looking for cooking stores. It's a pair of glasses. What's the big deal?"

Dad's bent over the stove stirring one pot, checking the contents of the oven, and clicking off the kitchen timer just as it dings. "Yeah, yeah," he says. "I'll go, I'll go. I've been busy. Open the wine, Franco. Two bottles tonight. Your mother invited a guest."

I rummage in the junk drawer for the bottle opener. "About that," I grumble, turning to face my pops. "Why the hell is Ma inviting somebody to dinner?"

My father echoes his favorite catchphrase as he turns to check on the braciole. "What's the big deal? It's one more person."

I can't tell if my father is in on Mom's plans to hook me up with her definition of a "sweet girl," or if he's choosing when and how exactly to battle his wife. An invitation to dinner is one thing. I can grin and be civil, but what Ma doesn't know is a meal with the Bianchis is probably the worst way to entice Chloe to go out with me.

One evening with all of us at the table and the woman will go running back to wherever it is she came from before she moved to Star Falls.

I'm in the dining room uncorking our family's favorite wine when Vito comes tumbling up the basement stairs, a pair of flowery oven mitts on his hands.

"Hey, asshole." I nod at him. "What's for dessert?"

One of the reasons my parents bought this house just after Gracie was born was the second kitchen in the basement.

"What's it smell like, dicknose?" Vito rushes past me, headed for the kitchen.

I shake my head. He never learns. I uncork the second bottle of cab and wait for my dad to yell.

"Vito, where do you think I'm going to find room for the cake to cool up here? Take it back downstairs, and put it on the cooling rack like I told you." My father isn't really mad. More like impatient.

Vito, like I said, ain't nothing like me. He doesn't always think and mostly just runs around like a clueless, curious puppy.

After more than thirty-five years as Mario Bianchi's son, you'd think he'd know not to bring dessert upstairs until some space has been cleared after the meal.

"Shit, yeah. Yeah. Sorry, Pops." Vito comes shuffling back, his bare feet in a pair of open-toe house slippers dragging along the tile floors and a pair of threadbare flannel PJ bottoms sagging at his waist.

"You going to dress for dinner?" I call after him. "Ma invited a guest."

He throws a scowl over his shoulder at me. "A guest? What the fuck?"

"Language, Vito." My mother is still on the phone but manages to hear my brother curse from someplace deep inside the house.

I stifle a grin and set the bottles of wine on the table to breathe. I'm about to head back to the kitchen to help Dad when there's a soft movement against my ankles.

"V!" I shout, bending down to pick up another of Ma's rescues. "One of the cats got out of the basement."

I pick the thing up, and it immediately melts into a vibrating engine of purring as I rub behind its ears. I stalk down the basement stairs, pulling the door closed behind me. "Dumbass, you know to keep the cats locked up down here while Dad's cooking." I set the cat down gently on the cool tile floor of the basement.

Vito is setting the pineapple upside-down cake on the cooling rack on the basement kitchen counter—which he should have done in the first place. "Yeah, yeah, it's fine," he grumbles.

He covers the cake with parchment paper and then grabs a cat toy that looks like a feather at the end of a fishing pole and coaxes the cat back into my old bedroom.

I pull back the paper and sniff the cake. The buttery brown sugar topping is perfectly glazed, locking the bright red maraschino cherries right in the centers of the canned pineapple rings.

It ain't fancy, but it's a taste of home. Of tradition. Of family.

"Go change," I tell him. "You're going to give our mother a heart attack in that getup."

"It's my day off. Just want to be fucking comfy." Vito stomps up the stairs, and I hear him slam the basement door before he clomps through the house.

"Franco!" My mother's shouts echo through the basement.

I check the door to my old bedroom to make sure Fred and Ginger are secure, but Ma's already halfway down the stairs. "Honey, no. Let the cats out." Ma is a blur of tight denim, red hair, and jangling bracelets as she rushes past me.

"Why? I thought you wanted them locked up when Dad's cooking?" I cock my chin and watch as Ma carries one cat and then the other out from my old room.

"I'm fostering a doggie mama, Franco, and the cats make her nervous." Ma checks the water and food dishes and strokes the head of the dog who clearly trusts her. "She's going to be a hard one to give up," my mom says thoughtfully. She does a quick check of each puppy, six in all, and then stands. "She is very gentle but already very protective of me and your father. Isn't she gorgeous, honey? Don't you think you might want a puppy when they're old enough? You live all by yourself in that house…"

"Ma." I shake my head. "You know I'm renting, and I'm not home enough to take care of a puppy." I watch the way the dog tracks my mother's every move, as if she'd haul herself from a nest of puppies to protect Ma if I made the slightest wrong move. "What are they?" I ask.

My mother shrugs. "Hard to say. She came into the shelter pregnant. Time will tell." She loops her arm through mine, and we head upstairs. "Think about it. A puppy would be good for you."

Before I can remind her again why that would *not* be good for me, the doorbell rings.

"Oh, that must be Chloe." Ma hustles the rest of the way upstairs, and I follow, closing the basement door behind me. Dolce and Venus both start barking, and Ma turns her attention to the dogs. "Franco, you get the door."

While Gracie holds Venus in her arms and shushes her, Ma makes sure Dolce gets off the couch without hurting her aging hips.

I have no clue what my mother told Chloe to entice the woman to come for family dinner, so I sigh and brace myself for the inevitable awkwardness.

When I open the door, the only thing that's awkward is the little catch in my throat.

The sun is setting, and somehow the light catches on Chloe's green eyes in a way that takes my breath away.

She looks lost for a moment, shocked or maybe confused that I opened the door and not my mother.

I stare at her without greeting her, licking my lips on instinct as I study her eyes, her hair, the sweet curve of her lips.

She smiles apologetically, ducking her head a little as if she's embarrassed to be here. "Hi, Franco. I'm Chloe. We met the other day at my aunt's café." She says it like a question, as though she doesn't expect me to remember her.

She's standing there holding a plate covered with foil and a small bouquet of flowers. She's wearing something slightly less gigantic than the other day.

"Franco. Let her in." Mom's cry from the living room nudges me into movement.

"Yeah," I say, shaking my head and scowling at the blood that surges through my limbs. I'm thirty-eight, not eighteen. Why the hell does this woman in bag-lady clothes make me feel like a kid? "I remember you," I say gruffly, covering my confusion. "Come in."

She steps past me and stops, her eyes on the floor. "Umm," she mumbles, thrusting the plate in my direction. "Would you mind holding this while I take off my boots?"

I take the plate from her and the flowers. I assume she needs both hands to take off those boots, so I just stand there, like a kid who's never seen a woman's behind before, watching her bend over to unlace the boots.

She leans a hip against the wall to balance herself while she slides her feet from the boots, then she smooths her hair and adjusts the sweater so that, if it were actually possible, it covers even more of her. She tugs it past her waist so it covers the fine curve of her ass, and then she slips her hands deep inside the sleeves.

"I brought my aunt's peanut butter crisp cookies. I hope that's okay?" She's looking at me, studying my chin like there's something stuck there, and very definitely avoiding my eyes.

I self-consciously swipe at my chin with my forearm just in case I have dog hair or something there since I've got her plate of cookies in one hand and the flowers in the other. "Yeah," I say distractedly, "great."

Being reduced to a babbling idiot by a woman's halfway-decent backside sends me into an even fouler mood.

I don't know what it is about Chloe that's turned me stone stupid, but I'm annoyed with myself. I'm even more annoyed with my mother for bringing a non-family member into our dinner, with my brothers for being idiots, and, if I'm reaching, with my sister just because she's been so down and won't let anyone in.

I just want to get through this dinner and get the fuck out of here.

My mother comes to the door to greet Chloe with as much enthusiasm as a one-woman parade. She's cooing and rushing up to us, all excitement and warmth.

Gracie is holding Venus in her arms, and Dolce slowly plods

behind them, her tail slapping the wall as she walks carefully down the hallway on her old dog hips.

"Chloe." Lucia opens her arms and gives me a look. "I told you not to bring anything. You're family."

I can't help rolling my eyes because, no, this woman is not family. But I instantly feel shitty for the impulse.

Chloe has done nothing wrong. Despite the fact that my mother seems hell-bent on fixing me up with any eligible female in Star Falls, I do have two brothers. Vito and Benny aren't half bad. Maybe she'll fall for one of them and I'll be off the hook.

"Did I hear someone say peanut butter crisps?" Gracie holds her body at an awkward angle, keeping snarling little Venus as far away as she can while giving Chloe a one-armed hug. "You're my new favorite person."

"Who is this?" Chloe asks, her voice a nearly breathless whisper. The honey in her voice sends a little pulse from my gut straight to my cock.

I shake my head to clear that shit away. She's whispering at a snarling Chihuahua, but my body is acting like that sweet, low rasp is meant just for me.

"Here," I grunt, thrusting the plate of cookies at my sister.

She raises a sharply angled eyebrow at me but takes the plate. I hear Chloe and Gracie cooing over the dogs, because now, of course, Dulce is sniffing and wagging all over Chloe's legs while Mom's overly loud voice booms introductions to the dogs.

Christ.

Normally, I wouldn't even notice that Ma's rolling out the red carpet for a guest, but something about the whole situation grates on me.

It's as if everyone in the family is conspiring to welcome this girl, and I'm the asshole who just wants a family dinner without the pressure of making small talk with a stranger.

A stranger who my mother seems determined to see me dating, while my body is being a traitor with the way it's reacting to her presence.

I stalk into the dining room in search of a vase for the flowers, but then I think better of it and head toward the kitchen. Dad and some cold water—for the flowers, not for me—will clear me of the shit mood I'm in now.

"Flowers?" Dad asks, pointing to a cabinet.

I grunt. "I know where the vases are." The words come out saltier than I intend, and Mario takes notice.

"What's the matter with you?" he asks. He's yanking off the apron with one hand and turning off the burners with the other. "You look like you spilled your last beer."

I yank open a cabinet and pull out a vase, then jam the small bouquet inside. "Nothing, I'm fine. When do we eat?"

Mario looks me over but doesn't push. "Benito here yet?"

I shake my head. "Course not."

"Your brother is a…" Dad uses a pair of tongs to extract a single strand of pasta from a stockpot of boiling water. He can tell by the way it bends how much longer it needs to cook. "Send him a text, will you? Pasta's on in three minutes, and his ass better be in his chair at the table."

I fill the vase with water and set the thing down in Dad's huge sunny window box over the sink, next to cut herbs in water-filled mason jars.

"Put those on the table," my pops urges, giving me an eyebrow raise that rivals Gracie's. "What's gotten into you in the last five minutes? Is it that girl your mother invited over?"

I take the vase back and scold myself for being so transparent. And for being such a dick. "Nah, I'm fine. Just hungry, and I'm sick of Benny always being late."

"He owns a business," my dad says with a wave of his hand. "But if I'm being honest, it bothers me too. Your brother can be a real pain in the ass."

I'm not sure if my dad's trying to make a joke so I lighten up or if he's serious. Either way, I clap him on the back and head back to the dining room.

While I set the flowers on the table, I tell myself to calm the fuck down. Just because Ma wants to set me up…it doesn't mean anything.

She's tried a million times before, although this is the first time she's ever taken her meddling matchmaking this far.

It's one meal.

I'll be pleasant to Chloe, ignore my mother's heavy-handed hints, eat a delicious meal, and head the fuck out.

In fact, maybe I'll even crash Benito's restaurant tonight and have a cocktail with my brother. He's a dick, but he gives me at least two rounds on the house any time I stop in.

Tonight would be a good night for a gin and tonic and some mindless conversation with the new bartender my brother's banging.

At least no one will be trying to set her up with me.

By the time I get the flowers put down, Chloe and Gracie are settled on the couch, and to my absolute shock, Venus is curled up on Chloe's lap. She looks like she might pounce at any time, but this is the only time I've seen the old dog warm up to anyone who isn't Ma or Grace.

Vito tumbles down the stairs, his wet hair flapping in his face, and interrupts their chatter. Ma introduces him to Chloe, and they all exclaim in a new round of admiration that Chloe has tamed the snarky Venus.

I watch Chloe's face, all shy smiles and self-conscious flushes, as they talk about her like she's not standing right there, and something curls around my heart.

I hate the sensation, something all fluttery and unsettled sinking deep into my chest.

I am actually relieved when I hear the front door open, and my brother Benito starts bellowing.

"I'm here!" Benny shouts and slams the door behind him before kicking off his shoes.

"You were almost late!" my mother shouts back from the living room. "Your father got ten more gray hairs waiting."

"Bullshit." Benito strides into the living room, looks over the group, and leans down to kiss my mother. Noticing Chloe, he adds, "Pardon my language. I didn't realize we had a guest."

Benny kisses our sister and slaps Vito on the back, then extends a hand to Chloe. I can see his body language change immediately, and he straightens his shoulders and lifts his chin.

"I'm Benito," he says. "And you are?"

She takes his hand much more quickly than she took mine the other day, and I have to fight a prickle of white-hot jealousy. Which is absolutely stupid, not to mention unreasonable.

First of all, my brother is a player. He's like this with every woman he meets.

Second, not five minutes ago, I was hoping Chloe *would* show an interest in one of my brothers and take the pressure off me. I should just sit back and enjoy the show.

But now, with Venus in Chloe's arms, Ma batting her eyelashes, and Benny and Vito turning on the charm, I'm not sure what I feel.

Pops comes into the living room and jerks a thumb at me. "Everything's ready," he says, which is my cue to start bringing the food to the table.

We eat family style, so every serving platter and bowl in the house needs to be filled and set out.

"Son," he says to Benny, giving my brother a smooch on the cheek. "One of these times, you could try to come more than ten seconds before we sit." Pops slows, and his voice softens as he approaches Chloe. "And you must be Chloe. Nice to finally meet you, sweetheart. You're all I've heard about for weeks now."

Chloe stands with Venus in her arms and says something I can't fully make out. But I must be staring at her, because as soon as Pops kisses her cheek and adds his surprise to everyone else's that Chloe's managed to tame the beast in Venus, my dad turns to me.

"You okay, son?" He squints at me but then motions with a thumb to my brothers. "One of you help Franco bring out the food."

"I got it," I grunt, realizing I'm the only one who seems pissed off and sour.

Even Gracie seems to warm to Chloe and is more animated and friendly than she is at a normal dinner.

"Franco." I hear disappointment in my mother's voice.

"What is it?" I pause on my way to the kitchen. "I need to help Pops serve."

Ma is glaring at the table where I've rearranged the place settings. She shakes her head but doesn't argue with me.

I pound my way into the kitchen and take a deep breath.

It's one dinner.

Then it'll be over, and I can tell Ma to stop trying to set me up for good.

CHAPTER FOUR

chloe

Family dinner with the Bianchis is…*a lot.*

"So, Chloe…" Lucia is filling my plate with food.

I shift nervously in my seat and fiddle with the buttons on my sweater.

She loads me up with some rolled thing that looks like meat drenched in sauce, forks a pile of noodles so high I'd need a week to eat my way through it, and then uses wooden salad tongs to fill a bowl beside my plate with greens. "How do you take your pasta? Swimming in sauce or lightly coated?"

"Whatever way you want to make it," I tell her.

Mario is pouring me a very full glass of wine. "Do you drink, sweetheart? I should've asked before I started pouring."

"She'll drink if she wants it," Lucia says as she hands me a giant plate of pasta.

I just nod and murmur, "Thank you."

Grace holds up her empty glass for her father to fill more than the half glass he's already poured. "Top it off, Dad. You opened two bottles."

He fills it, and once everyone at the table has wine and a plate

219

full of food, Lucia and Mario take their seats at opposite ends of the table.

"We like to give thanks before we eat." Lucia folds her hands and bows her head.

I notice every head at the table lowers, so I do the same and squeeze my eyes closed. I hope I'm not expected to say anything or hold hands or any of that. I'm not from a religious family, and I don't know any formal prayers.

I'm lost in my thoughts, staring at the steaming heap of food on my plate, when for some reason, I look up. I feel someone watching me, and in spite of the nervousness twisting in my belly, I chance a look at Franco.

It's him.

He's watching me.

Staring at me.

I press my lips in what I hope is a reassuring smile and look away.

"And we're so very thankful for our new friend in Chloe." Lucia finishes her prayer, and around me, everyone lifts their glass of wine.

"*Salud*," Benito says, tapping the rim of his glass to his father's.

Everyone around the table echoes the toast, and I just lift my glass silently and take a sip when everyone else does.

When the meal finally starts, that's when the real awkwardness begins.

"So, Chloe," Lucia starts.

"Ma, for fuck's sake..." Franco has pulled a piece of actual string from the rolled meat on this plate and slices into it with a bang of cutlery against stoneware.

"Franco." It's his father who responds, giving his son a dark look. "We're at the table, son. Language."

Gracie settles back in her chair, a smug look on her face, while Benito grabs the bottle of wine and tops off his glass.

"Would you all just settle down?" Vito, the quietest of the Bianchis, is swirling a forkful of pasta in the air. He looks at me with a warm smile, and I can't help but relax a little.

I look down at my plate piled high with hot, delicious-smelling food.

"Have you ever had braciole before?"

I assume the question is for me. I look up and feel every eye at the table on me. I grab the glass of wine and take a swig, then shake my head. "No, we, uh… No."

Lucia gets all excited at that. "Mario's is the best," she explains, but then she looks at Benito. "No offense, son."

Benito is chewing a mouthful of salad and shrugs.

"It's just beef, dear, rolled into a cute little shape with a filling inside." Lucia is watching me with something so kind and warm on her face, it breaks my heart into little pieces.

She sincerely wants me to eat and like the food. Even if she also sincerely wants me to date her son—and I think by now we all know that isn't going to happen—she's welcoming and warm. She reaches across the table and rubs Vito's arm, urging him to show me how to eat it.

"Ma, stop hovering. You're making *me* nervous. You expect the woman to eat while you're obsessing over every bite?" Gracie is seated next to me, and all three Bianchi sons are across from us on the other side of the table. Gracie takes her braciole in her fork and shows me how to remove the string. "It's just butcher string," she tells me. "Totally sanitary and safe to cook with. It's not like Dad has a sewing kit in the kitchen he uses to wrap up meat with."

I laugh nervously and way too loudly at that, but Mario and Lucia chime in and chuckle. I avoid looking across the table at any of the Bianchi boys and copy what Gracie did, unwrapping the string from the beef.

I don't even need a knife to cut into the thin, tender, rolled strip. I take a bite and widen my eyes, looking from Gracie to Mario. "Holy crap," I gasp as soon as I swallow. "That is…" I'm searching for the right word, while Mario waves a hand at me.

"If you don't care for it, don't eat it." He's trying to be nice, but I'm not.

"No," I say over him, finding my voice. "This is exceptional. I mean, like, the most delicious thing I've ever eaten. It tastes like…"

"Home?" Lucia offers. She sighs and leans back in her chair. "I knew you'd love it. Braciole was your aunt's favorite."

Gracie swirls a forkful of pasta against the inside of a large spoon and cocks her head my direction. "Do you have any brothers or sisters?"

This question gets the whole table's interest. I avoid the stares of the handsome trio across from me and look down at my food.

"You can have half of mine," Benito blurts, laughing at his own joke. "I don't even care which two."

Vito slugs his brother on the shoulder and calls him an asshole, which prompts a whole new round of scolding about language from Lucia and Mario.

"Let her answer," Mario says, shaking his head. "But yeah, if you want one of these knuckleheads, help yourself. You should probably take the one with the smart mouth."

"What did I do?" Gracie blurts before Mario can point to which of his knuckleheads has the smart mouth, and everyone is laughing, even me.

When the giggles calm, I shake my head and answer her. "I don't," I said. "Only child."

They receive that news like I've just said my puppy had been run over by a car, so I can only hope no one asks about my parents.

Alcoholic, abusive dad. Depressed nurse mom… Yeah, I've got all the fun stories when you start to dig for them.

Instead, I decide to turn the tables. "What about you?" I ask, turning to look at Lucia. "Did you and Mario always want a big family?"

Lucia starts talking about how she and Mario are both from big families, but as she speaks, I look down at my plate and spear the last bite of my beef.

I can't help but peek at Franco. He's like the sun, and I'm a seedling just yearning to soak up some of his life-giving strength.

My heart rate speeds up when I see he's watching me, chewing slowly and deliberately, his intense blue eyes locked on me.

Under his hot gaze, I shift uncomfortably in my chair and look away. I hurry to chew my last bite of braciole while Lucia finishes her story.

"After all of that, none of these idiots are mine. They're all adopted."

"You wish," Benito says. "You have no one out there to blame for how we turned out. This is all you and Dad."

The table has turned rowdy and loud, but that's fine with me. No one is asking me any more questions, instead focusing on Benito's restaurant, Vito's job at the fire station, and the latest drama at the animal shelter where Lucia volunteers.

When Gracie gets up to start clearing her plate, I jump up to help, but she stops me with a hand. "Please," she says. "You're our guest." She takes my plate from me, and as I sit back down, I feel it.

I feel him.

Franco's eyes are following my every move. I swallow back my nerves as a little zing of electricity brings my body to life.

My belly is warm and full, but there's a different kind of pleasure when I feel Franco's eyes on me. He looks away when my eyes meet his, and I wipe my clammy hands on my thighs.

The meal was delicious, and the company—once they stopped talking about me—was a little overwhelming, but honestly so much fun.

During dessert, Vito excuses himself to bed. He apologizes that he's got to sleep at odd times due to his shifts at the firehouse, and after kisses to his parents and a sleepy nod at me, he's gone.

Even with one fewer Bianchi at the table, the conversation is no less animated. I listen in and savor the gooey, buttery cake that pairs perfectly with the strong coffee.

As he's shoveling the last bite of cake into his mouth, Benito slaps a hand on the table and leans over to kiss his mother. "Dinner was amazing. Love you all. Got to run. Got to get back to work."

He doesn't bother to clear his plate, and Franco and Grace both sigh and roll their eyes.

Mario gets up to give his son a hug, and Benito waves at me. "Nice to meet you, Chloe," he says. "I'll treat you to some real Italian cooking if you come down to my restaurant."

That elicits an outburst of good-natured insults from the family, and in a flash, Benny is out the door.

Franco jumps up and clears his brother's plate.

I get up to do the same, but again, Grace stops me. "Sit," she says, waving a hand at me. "Relax."

I'm pretty sure if I stay any longer, avoiding Franco's eyes like they are lasers waiting to cut into my soul, I won't be able to relax for days.

I'm ready. It's more than past time to go.

"I'd better head home," I say. "I walked, and it's getting pretty late."

Turns out that is the absolute wrong thing to say.

"You what?" Lucia is abuzz with nervous energy, her pretty face pulled into a strained scowl. "What's wrong with your car? You have a car, don't you, honey? What happened to that little sedan you were driving?"

I shrug. "It's fine. I just... It was a beautiful day, and I thought I'd walk."

That's not true, of course. But the last thing I want to get into is the fact that I'm so broke I don't even have gas money at the moment. I mean, I did... I just chose to put the little money I did have into other things. There's no point in these people getting all worried or worked up about my choices.

Mario shakes his head. "No, no, that's no good. Where do you live? I'll take you home."

That starts the fight of the century—or at least it sounds like it.

Lucia is giving him the area I live in and exclaiming that I must have walked three miles to get here.

Mario pushes back from the table and tugs his glasses over his eyes while he punches my address into his phone. "Is that it? I've been meaning to try this new map app my kids put on my phone. I used it the other day to drive into Cleveland. Worked pretty good."

I bite back a smile and hold up my hands. "Please," I say. "It's okay. I've eaten enough to fuel me for a marathon. I'll be just fine."

"Oh no, you won't." Lucia is acting like I've suggested I swim across Lake Erie nude in January. "And Mario, you've had two glasses of wine. You're not driving anybody anywhere." I follow her finger with my eyes as she points at her son. "Franco, you're driving home anyway. You can take Chloe home on the way."

"Oh no, I... It's okay. I..." The words die on my lips as I meet Franco's stony stare.

He looks annoyed, exhausted, and like he fully expected me to pull a trick like this. He probably thinks his mother and I schemed this up just as a way to get the two of us alone.

All of a sudden, all the food in my stomach isn't sitting so well. "Really, I don't want to be any trouble." I push back from my chair and head to Lucia. The last thing I want is to ruffle anyone's feathers. Especially her son's. "The meal was amazing," I tell her, tentatively opening my arms for a hug.

Lucia pulls me close and holds me tight. "You're never alone, you hear me?" she asked. "You have family here, Chloe." She kisses my cheek and releases me, shouting for her husband to hurry up and make me a plate of leftovers.

"Oh no, I..."

"It's pointless." Franco's grumpy rasp sends chills along my arms. Even under my thick cardigan, I can feel every inch of my skin pebble as though a cool breeze is blowing right through every layer I have on.

I turn slowly and face his searing gaze. "I'm sorry? I..."

He holds up a hand. "You're not going to win this one. Ma will have visions of you dying by serial killer all night, so you're not going to walk home. And Dad won't stop complaining that you didn't like his cooking if you don't take a plate." He crosses his arms over his chest. "You may as well get your boots on. As soon as your leftovers are ready, I'll drive you."

He stalks up to the front door, where his boots are waiting beside mine. I keep my eyes on the floor as he walks past, hoping he won't see I'm embarrassed by every bad choice I've made that's led me to this moment. The outfit I wore, the boots, walking here. I've never felt more wrong or unsettled within myself.

I squeeze my eyes shut and lean against the wall with my back to him as I slip on my boots.

I'll be home soon. Done with this night that I can file away as a wonderful memory of something I never have to go through again.

Once my feet are securely in my boots, I look back over the Bianchi home.

Gracie and Lucia have cleared almost all the dishes, and Mario is coming from the kitchen with a heck of a lot more than a plate. He's packed up a travel bag of some kind. He's easily got several pounds of food in there by the size of it.

"Pops, she's one person." Franco reaches his hand to take the handle of the travel container.

Mario lifts a shoulder. "And now she won't have to cook for herself for a while."

"That's too much," I say, shaking my head. "Too generous."

Mario waves me off with a hand. "Come anytime, sweetheart." He gives me a grin and then turns to his son. "Get her home safe, and then yourself." He claps Franco on the shoulder, and Franco gives his dad a kiss on the cheek.

"Thanks for dinner, Pops. Love you. Love you, Ma. I'm leaving!" Franco bellows through the house, and I hear Gracie come padding into the hallway.

"She's up to her elbows in soap suds. She says bye and she loves you." Gracie kisses her brother's cheek, then smacks him hard on the back. "Don't be a dick," she says, and Franco glares.

"Bye, sweetie," Gracie says to me. "I'll probably see you Tuesday for coffee." She leans in and gives me a kiss on the cheek, and I'm so stunned you could probably knock me over with a feather.

I nod and say nothing, just look back at the dogs on the couch, the table that's almost completely clear of dishes, and I can hear the sounds of water running far off in the kitchen.

I was so anxious to get home, but now that it's time to leave, a part of me feels rooted to the floor.

This is a home.

A real family.

So unlike anything I've ever had, and while it was a lot at first, I'm already sort of adjusting to it.

But then Franco clears his throat and opens the front door.

"Did you bring your bike?" Mario asks, peering past him toward the street.

"Nah," Franco says. "Drove the truck. We'll be fine." He lifts a thick brow at me. "You ready?"

And even though I'm not at all sure that I am, I nod and follow Franco and ten thousand pounds of leftovers out into the night.

The drive is only three miles, but somehow walking it seemed to feel faster than riding beside Franco.

He hasn't said a word since we got inside, other than to ask for my address. He opens his window and then mine just a crack. He leans his elbow out the window, resting it on the door, and drives with one hand. He seems completely at ease with the silence.

For the first few minutes, I am too, but then it just gets weird.

"So, Franco." I force myself to say his name. It feels dangerous and delicious on my lips, and I shake my head to clear away the idiotic thoughts. "Are you a reader?" I ask.

"What?" His question is sharp-edged and defensive.

"Read?" I press. "You know, I own a bookstore now. I was just curious if you, you know...read."

I watch him out of the corner of my eye and see his shoulders relax just a little. "Oh," he says. "Nah. I'm not much for books."

"Ouch," I say, clutching my heart. "I think that brings me actual physical pain."

"Could be heartburn from the coffee and sauce," he says, and something in his voice is a tiny bit lighter.

Is he *teasing* me?

I let myself relax into a full smile. "No, no, I'm pretty sure what I feel is my little bookselling heart breaking. Have you always been that way? Or did you just kind of stop reading after you got out of school?"

He flicks a quick glance at me. "That way?" he echoes. "You make it sound like I'm defective."

Oh boy.

227

The momentary lightness between us has just been obliterated.

Nice one, Chloe.

I slide my hands back into the sleeves of my sweater and wrap my wool-covered fists together. "That came out wrong. Sorry," I say quietly. "Just trying to make conversation. But we don't have to talk. I appreciate you being willing to give me a ride."

I lean a little closer to the passenger side window and stare out into the town that rolls past. I notice plenty of trees in Star Falls, lovely houses, and well-tended lawns. I entertain myself by counting the number of pickup trucks we pass.

I've just counted five when Franco blurts out, "So what's the real reason you walked? Something wrong with your car?"

I definitely can't tell him the truth, but I also don't want him to look at it and realize I'm just about out of gas. He'll either think I'm really stupid, or he'll think I'm pathetic.

"It was stupid of me. I should have driven. I thought the walk would be nice." I'm staring out the window, watching the blocks pass, wishing the longest car ride I've ever been on was almost over.

With every breath I take, the truck seems to be warmer, and a mouth-watering fragrance that has to be Franco competes with the food. A light hint of smoke and oil and...I don't know what it is, but it smells like warm leather and sunshine.

I wish I could lean into his neck and take a deep breath, and yes, that officially makes me creepy.

I can't help it.

He's the kind of man that any woman would want to lean into and smell.

"I don't have anything against books," he says, returning to our previous conversation, thankfully unaware of the deep breaths I'm taking as I pull in his scent. "I do read. I shouldn't have said that before. I mostly read nonfiction and shit online. That's what I meant."

A bloom of heat unfurls in my chest. He's trying to be kind. He's trying to open up a little. I won't read more into it than it means. I'm just super happy that the weird, awkward bubble stealing all the air between us seems to have popped.

"Awesome," I say, a little too brightly. "I wasn't judging you."

"I don't know about that," he says, his voice a sultry purr. "You just about had a full-on heartbreak when I said I didn't read. I think you *were* judging me." But this time, there's nothing defensive or guarded in his words.

I lean back against the seat and smile. "Hmmm, true. I was judging you harshly. In fact, I was secretly planning to pull my aunt's chicken-and-bacon grilled cheese from the café menu just to punish you."

He chuckles a bit and turns on the blinker as he slows to a stop in front of my building. "This you?" he asks.

"Yep." I unfasten my seat belt and pull on the door handle. I open the door just a crack, but I don't step out just yet.

The silence is back between us, the air in the truck thick with tension. I feel like I can't leave without saying something, without addressing it somehow. It's not my fault his mother wants to set us up any more than it is his. And I just don't think I can be friends with Lucia if Franco is constantly...mad like this. Or whatever this is.

"Franco," I say.

He doesn't face me but stares straight ahead. "You're welcome. Have a good night."

He's not even going to look at me. In his mind, he's already left, maybe planning wherever he's off to next.

A woman's place, maybe? Yeah. He's probably got a lot better places to be than with me.

But something inside me doesn't want to be ignored. Dismissed. I pull the door closed and turn fully in my seat to face him.

"Thanks for this." I rest my hand lightly on his arm.

He tenses under my touch and turns toward me.

The engine is idling, and we're parked just below a streetlamp.

He is bathed in artificial light, making shadows fall over the sharp planes of his face. His eyes, even in the darkness, are intense as he just watches me. Waits.

I yank my hand back as if he's burned me, but I don't look away. Something about him makes me want to be bolder. Stronger. I want him to see me. Who I really am, not the needy wannabe date that his mom's made me out to be.

"I just want you to know that I'm not in on whatever plan or scheme your mom has going on. I don't want her to set me up with you. I mean, I had no idea that was on her mind. I just... I mean... You're... You know..." All of a sudden, this definitely feels like high school. I have no clue what to say, and yet words keep coming, spilling past my lips and fighting one another as they come out.

Franco is looking at me with a combination of confusion and something else... Amusement, maybe? I don't like it, and I can already feel the flush burning its way up my chest and leaving a feverish heat in my cheeks.

"I'm what?" he asks quietly.

"Excuse me?" I'm blinking and leaning away from him, but he's leaning toward me. The beam of ugly light from the streetlamp falls over his features as he looks at me.

Really looks at me.

Suddenly, I'm speechless. My body feels warm; my hands shake. With every breath, I smell leather and smoke and pasta sauce, and the truck cab feels suddenly way too small to contain the energy, the whatever this is that I'm feeling. I'm quiet as I fumble behind me for the door handle.

"You said that I'm something, but you didn't finish. So, what is it? What am I?" He shocks the heck out of me by reaching forward and tipping my chin up with two fingers.

His skin is hot and surprisingly rough and soft at the same time, and a bolt of electricity shoots through my limbs. I gasp a little, deep in my throat, and lick my dry lips.

Franco drops his hand and glares again, and I shake the moment off. Whatever that was, that chin-touch thing...it felt good. Too good. Like, I'm hot between my legs, and I'm going to ride my vibrator tonight thinking about those long, strong fingers. His intense blue eyes.

The stubble on his chin rough against my...

Oh hell.

The fact that I'm in a enclosed space with this man thinking about getting myself off to his fingers...

This night has officially gotten out of control.

"I'm going to go in," I blurt out in a rush. "I just wanted to clear the air." I scramble toward the door and practically fall onto the sidewalk.

I smooth down my sweater, trying to fix how I look on the outside in case I look as jumbled up and wild as I feel inside. I fumble for my keys, keeping my chin down.

No matter what, I'm not looking back.

He waits there, idling, until my trembling fingers unlock the dead bolt and the doorknob—two separate locks, and even with just one key, it feels like so many extra steps—and then I open the front door.

I flip on the hall light so he can see I made it inside and there are no killers waiting in the shadows. Once I'm inside, I lock the knob and dead bolt behind me, and then finally the headlights of his truck pull a U-turn in the street, and he drives back in the direction we came.

My heart is beating way too fast, and I've broken into a light sweat. I kick off my boots and head straight for the bathroom.

"That's it," I say. I knot my hair in a bun on the top of my head and dig in the bathroom vanity for my vibrator.

But then I shake my head and put the plastic toy back under the sink.

A bath and a steamy book are the only cure for these feelings.

Because for better or worse, I've got a pickup truck-sized crush on Franco.

CHAPTER FIVE

franco

"You going to Latterature for some food?" When my buddy Jack shouts over the music, my heart stops for a second, like I've been caught stealing.

Which I kind of was.

I still haven't found the damn purchase order Jack lost last week, but instead of digging through yet more piles of paperwork, I'd been staring off into space. Lost in a filthy fantasy about the owner of Latterature.

Ever since last night when I spent, what, ten minutes alone in my truck with the woman, I haven't been able to stop thinking about her.

She's nothing, and I mean *nothing*, like the women I usually go for. And that might be what had me fisting myself in the shower this morning.

"What?" I growl, half pissed that I've been interrupted, half embarrassed.

"I thought you were going to run over there." Jack's still working on the town car, and I've made zero progress on the paperwork. "You said you had to bring her leftovers she forgot?" Jack slides out from under the town car and wipes his hands on his coveralls. "Dude, she forgot it. I call dibs on Mario's cooking."

Normally, I'd agree with Jack. You snooze, you lose. But after Chloe hustled out of my truck last night and left the food my dad had packed behind, I figured bringing it to her would be the right thing to do. At least, that's what I've been telling myself all day.

"I don't know who would be more pissed at me, my mom or my dad," I say. "What's up with Carol? She sick of making you lunch?"

Jack's face darkens, and he gives me a one-armed shrug. "It's weird, man." He looks over his shoulder like his old man is going to walk through the door any second. But he's not.

Jack's dad took a fishing trip two weeks ago when his wife asked for a separation and moved out. The separation shocked me, but Jack has been lost without them.

"What's weird?" I press. "I mean, other than everything going on in your life right now. No offense."

He shakes his head. "None taken." He sighs and yanks off the cap he likes to wear over his wild Irish hair. "I know my parents are separated and shit, doing their own things, but like…my mom didn't come home last night."

My gut tightens, and I'm up out of my chair at the first hint that anything could be wrong with one of my mom's friends. "You hear from her?" I demand. "Is she staying with Sassy or Bev?"

Jack holds up the hand that grips his cap and sighs. "She's all right. I knew she wasn't coming home. She texted me last from…" He curls his mouth into a frown and mutters something under his breath.

"What? What the fuck, you got me worried. What's up with Carol?" I press, not quite ready to drop down into my chair, not quite convinced that my best friend's mom doesn't need us to do something, go someplace.

"She spent the night at Ray Morris's." Jack says the words like he's got a gun to his head, his teeth gritted to hold in the truth against his will.

My shoulders immediately sag in relief. But only for a second.

"Fuck." I swallow back the words I want to say and try to think of a way to be supportive.

Jack's parents have been separated for just a few weeks. If Carol's having sleepovers with other men while his father's out finding himself on the lake...

"Fuck," I say again, and Jack nods.

"Yeah. So, Ma didn't make me lunch, but she's making it for somebody."

Jack looks so heartsick, I can't even chuckle. It sucks. My parents have been together since they were teenagers, and they still seem to feel like the sun rises and sets for their love alone.

"I'm sorry. It's a shit situation all the way around."

Jack nods, slips the cap back over his head, and shakes his head slowly. "I just keep asking myself what's my place here, you know? Should I tell my dad that Mom's out there getting her rocks off? Warn him before he gets home and finds out from someone else?"

I have no clue what to say to that. I mean, he's not wrong. If Carol's banging Ray, it's probably already front-page news. Not a whole lot stays secret in a small town.

"I wish I could help you, man." I feel useless and helpless. I hate that feeling. "If we were twenty years younger, I'd say let's go kick Ray's ass," I say unhelpfully.

It does get Jack to chuckle. "Thanks. I don't think Ma would be too happy about that. She seemed happy last night. When she texted, I mean."

"That's a good thing, right?" I'm grasping at straws here. I mean, Ray Morris has got to be in his mid-sixties. Would I really go kick his ass if Jack asked me to?

Jack nods and sighs again, the long sigh of a man who sees the reality before him but hates that he's powerless to change it. "That's what matters, right? That she's happy? Even if it breaks my dad's heart."

We're both silent then. What else is there to say?

"If Ray hurts your mom, I'll be the first one to go down there and beat the guy's ass. And when your dad gets back, if he's, you know...devastated... He's got you. He's got the shop. He'll be okay.

And you never know. Sometimes the grass is greener, but your mom and pop have been together a long time."

Jack looks sad then. Sadder than I think I've ever seen him. "I know," he says. "That's why I'm pretty sure this is a permanent thing. Neither one of them has been happy for a long time."

He gets back underneath the town car but calls out, "If you change your mind, I'm down for a plateful of Mario's cooking for lunch. No pressure, fucker."

I chuckle and shake my head. "Those are spoken for, but how's about this? I'll treat you to dinner at Benny's place tonight. Go home, change into something respectable, and drop me a text when you're ready. I'll pick you up and drive. Cool?"

"Thanks, man."

He gets back to work, and I'm back to my endless, pointless, meaningless review of Carol's paperwork.

But I think about his parents and how lost Jack will be if they do split up. Will Carol quit her job at the shop? All of a sudden, this project I'm working on seems a lot less meaningless.

All afternoon, I told myself I was waiting to go to Latterature until after work because I had a lot to do. The truth is, I was putting it off.

By the time the sky turns purple and dark gray clouds are skating trails across the horizon, Jack's finished the town car.

"You feel up to a trip to The Body Shop?" Jack calls over his shoulder as he washes his hands in the shop sink.

"You want a tattoo?" I ask, stunned. "I mean, my sister can probably hook you up, but you usually need an appointment. They book out like weeks or more, and it's closed tonight anyway."

Jack shakes his hands dry since we're out of paper towels— another thing that Carol handled when she worked here—and laughs. "No, man. I'm talking the strip club."

Of course the only strip club in the county has the exact same name as the only tattoo shop in the county. Michelle, my brother's

235

ex-wife, met him at the "other" Body Shop. The one Jack's talking about now.

"Nah, I'm not in the mood for a lap dance. We can rain check dinner, though, if you'd rather have some tits in your face." I pull the insulated food bag out of the office fridge, which desperately needs a cleanout.

As we lock up and head to the parking lot, Jack claps me on the back. "Thanks for the offer. Let's grab a nice dinner another time. I think tonight I want some loud music, watered-down drinks, and something soft grinding on my lap."

I nod and wave to him. "Have fun. Be safe out there. If you see Exotic…" I lift my brow at him and try not to burst out laughing.

Michelle, also known as Exotic, was Jack's favorite dancer until she married my brother.

"She's not getting a goddamn thing from me."

"Good man." I laugh.

Jack flips me the finger, but then drives off in his antique truck. I pull out not long after him but find every excuse in the book not to go straight to Latterature.

I stop and fill the truck with gas, carefully cleaning the windows, even though the truck is perfectly clean. I head into the gas station and make small talk with the girl at the counter before finally getting my ass in gear.

I start up the truck and head toward downtown. Worst case, if she's not there, I can drop by her place.

It occurs to me, of course, that maybe that's the real reason I'm stalling going to the shop.

Am I hoping to miss her at the café?

Looking for a reason to go back to her tiny apartment, walk the steps, and show up at her door bearing food?

"Fuck me sideways," I grumble to myself. I'm acting like a damn kid. I smooth my hair in place and angle the truck down nearly deserted Main Street.

It's past six by the time I roll up to the shop. I decide to drive past to make sure she's still there before I bother parking.

I squint as I pass to see if maybe Chloe left a light on, or if she's still back there. Maybe working in the kitchen.

The street is deserted, and something in my gut just feels off. This isn't butterflies or awkwardness about showing up with the forgotten food either.

I don't know what this is.

But in true stalker style, I darken my lights and creep past the café, feeling a mix of concern and shame.

This is normal.

Totally normal.

As I come close enough to the shop to see inside, I spot Chloe standing in the middle of the store. My shoulders relax a little, but then I see her holding her hands up in a weird way—almost like she's at gunpoint.

It can't be.

I slam on the brakes, but the truck doesn't make a sound. I squint to try to make out what's going on, but I can't see anyone else in the café. She can't be standing like that for no reason, and something inside me panics.

Adrenaline fires in my gut, and my pulse starts thundering. Before I even have time to think, I'm turning the wheel of the truck, and I pull over on the opposite side of the street.

I run at full speed across the street, propelled by anxious energy and a suddenly desperate fear that my instincts were right.

I'm a big, strong guy, but if there's somebody armed in there...

Fuck.

I don't have a plan, just a frantic need to get into the store and make sure my mind's just playing tricks on me.

I didn't see what I thought I saw.

But when I get to the front of the store, it becomes obvious I saw exactly what I thought. A dark figure with a mask over his face and his head down comes barreling through the front door.

I see him coming, and I stand with my feet braced, knees bent, ready to fucking tackle his ass.

He seems as shocked to see me as I am to see him.

He stops, pants a little, and grunts in a voice that sounds fake-low, "Get the fuck out of the way before I fuck you up."

"I'm going to fuck you up, you piece of shit." I lunge to tackle him, but the asshole is skinny, and he rolls to one side like he's been dodging the law his whole life.

I grab for a handful of his hoodie and get a decent grip on it. The guy knows he's about to get caught, and he is wiggling and kicking like a trapped wild beast.

For some reason, the dude isn't punching me, isn't doing anything but trying to wrestle away from the fistful of hoodie that's slipping through my fingers.

I'm able to land a couple punches to his head, but they don't slow him down. He's wiry as fuck. He grunts and cusses me out with each blow.

He drops a plain blue zipper bag, the exact same kind that Jack uses to take cash into the bank.

He was fucking robbing the store.

My vision goes red.

I scream, a primal, murderous sound, but the guy knows that I'm big and now very pissed off.

Without a second look at the bag he dropped, he takes off running at full speed.

I debate following him, but it's pretty clear I'm not likely to catch him. He's dressed for escape, and I'm in steel-toe work boots.

My heart is throbbing in my chest as I reach down and grab the blue money bag from the ground so the fucker can't run back and get it.

I yank open the door and start shouting, "Chloe! Chloe!"

I find her exactly where I'd seen her as I crept down the street. But she's not standing. She's lying in a heap on the floor with her eyes closed.

"Chloe!" I yell again and drop to my knees. I fumble in my pocket for my phone and dial the cops, and with my other hand, I reach down and press a hand to her cheek.

She's ice-cold.

By the time I explain to the dispatcher what's happened and give

238

her the pathetic bits of description I can about the thief, Chloe starts to wake.

"Hey, hey," I say softly as a sense of relief washes over me. I've got one hand on my cell phone, and with the other, I stroke her hair away from her face. "Stay with me. An ambulance is on its way."

She blinks very slowly, but within a few seconds, the color returns to her face and she sits up. "Oh my God," she whispers, and before I know it, she's retching on the floor.

"Chloe," I say, keeping my voice as gentle as I can. "Did he hurt you? Are you hurt?"

I can hear the police sirens in the background, and the dispatcher is telling me the police are less than a minute away.

"She's up," I tell dispatch, but she doesn't want me to end the call or disconnect until EMS arrives on the scene.

"Is the door unlocked?" the lady on the other end of the phone asks. "They'll break down the door if they can't get in."

"Yeah, yeah, I'll meet them. Don't let them go busting in the door," I mutter, because now that Chloe is conscious—shaking and crying but conscious—the only thing I give a shit about is making sure she's okay.

"Chloe," I say again quietly. "Are you hurt?"

She doesn't respond.

I hear the squad car slamming its doors out front. I bark into my phone that the police are here and I'm hanging up. I toss my phone on the floor, then run to the front doors to greet the officers.

The squad car has its lights going, and before the officers even reach the store, an ambulance pulls up and parks.

"She was passed out when I came in," I say to the paramedics. "She woke up, puked, and hasn't moved or said a word. I don't know what happened in here. All I know is what happened out on the street."

The officers ask me a few questions about the details, what I saw, what I remember about the clothes, the body size, anything I can tell them about the guy. But unfortunately, it's just not much. With the mask and hoodie, I couldn't tell them if he was pink, purple, or anything else.

"It happened so fast," I say. "I didn't get a look at his hands, but he must have had gloves on. I would have remembered if there was any skin showing. I don't even remember the color of his eyes. I'm sorry. I just... I... Can we do this later?"

My heart is finally starting to slow down, and the only thing I care about is checking on Chloe. The paramedics already walked past me and are talking to Chloe. I am still giving the police my statement when one of the EMS lifts his head and calls over to me.

"Hey, Franco. Can you come back here?"

I recognize the guy as one of my brother Vito's buddies. "Hey, Nick." I look at the cops. "Am I good here? Can I go?"

They let me go back into the store, so I walk over to Nick.

"Is she okay?" I ask. I could ask Chloe herself, but she's shaking so hard that the other paramedic has her sitting on the floor while he asks quiet questions and checks her out.

"Pretty sure it's shock," Nick tells me. "She's going to need a bit, though. I'd be scared out of my ass too. The guy had a knife. From what it sounds like, it was a big one—hunting style. You were both lucky no one was hurt."

Before I know it, I'm stalking past Nick, shoving my way past the other paramedic, and I'm on my knees on the carpet in front of Chloe.

"Hey," I whisper. "You're okay. It's going to be okay now."

She looks up at me and swallows. She blinks, tears streaming down her face, and throws herself into my arms.

CHAPTER SIX

chloe

"Are those mints?" My voice is unnaturally hoarse from all the heaving and crying. "Can I have one?"

I'm in the passenger seat of Franco's truck, and as soon as I see the tin of mints in the center console, I think about my puke breath and my parched throat.

"Yeah. Help yourself." Franco has been quiet on the drive, but to be fair, I have been too.

We spent more than two hours with the police at Latterature. Plenty of time for me to go over what happened.

Again and again.

Too many times, it seemed.

And no matter how many times I explained it, it was never less terrifying.

The guy was quiet and forceful, like he'd done this before and knew exactly how to use my shock against me.

I did as he asked, pulling out the blue zipper envelope that my aunt used to make her bank deposits. I put what little cash we had in the bag.

The guy grabbed the pouch and made me hand over my cell phone. He told me to count to two hundred, and then, he said, I could call the cops. But he said if I followed him or tried anything, that he would *fillet* me.

Those were his words.

I told the police exactly what he'd said, and they traded a look, like maybe it was something they'd heard before.

My worries race through my mind as I crunch mindlessly on a mint. The sweet bite of the candy does nothing to calm my nerves or settle my stomach.

I just can't stop the feelings of panic. I don't think, as long as I live, I'll ever forget that kind of raw fear.

How I'd felt when I'd realized what was happening.

How alone I'd felt.

How terrified.

Even now that I am safe, now that it is truly all over, as the moments tick past, I grow more and more angry.

I just can't stop seeing it. Watching it again and again and going through every little detail.

I must be breathing hard or something, because I feel Franco's hand on my shoulder.

"Chloe?" Franco's voice breaks through the endless loop replaying in my mind.

"Sorry?" I blink and watch his face as he stares at me.

"We're here. Your place."

I realize that we've stopped, and we're parked outside my apartment. That means it is time to go inside alone.

"He has my cell phone," I whisper, a violent shiver shaking my body so hard I can't hide the tremor. "What if he…"

"Come on." Franco leaps out of the truck and comes around to the passenger side. He holds out his hand to me. "I'm going to walk you in, and you're going to pack a bag. You can't stay here tonight. Not by yourself."

I shake my head as the reality of what is happening hits me.

Where am I going to go?

Where can I possibly stay? I can't afford a hotel. I don't have friends in town yet. I've only been in Star Falls a couple of weeks.

All I have is my aunt's apartment and her landline. Maybe one of the ladies would let me crash on her couch, but God, I can't impose.

And even if I could for one night, what then?

Staying here alone while some psychopath has my phone? He didn't get what he wanted from my café. Maybe he'll come back.

The heat of the truck starts to feel stifling, and I break out in a sweat.

"I... I..." I don't know what to do. I can't move. Can't think fast enough.

"Chloe." Franco's voice is raspy, as if he's as worn out as I am. I realize I haven't thanked him. "*Chloe*." He's saying it again, but this time, he's closer. He's staring at me with those summer-sky eyes, and a weary half smile claims his beautiful mouth. "I'm not going to leave you," he promises. "I'm going to go up with you. You're going to pack a bag, and I'm going to bring you someplace safe. Okay?"

I stare at Franco's outstretched hand. If he'd offered his hand to me yesterday, I would have leaped at the chance to touch him.

Today, holding his hand means I have to move. Have to go inside. Face the reality and fears all alone, even if he walks me as far as the door.

I can't do it.

"I have to go home," I say, quietly wringing my hands.

I can't do any of this.

"You *are* home," Franco says, looking puzzled. He rests a hand on my thigh and gives it a gentle squeeze. "Chloe." His voice is a lifeline. Warm, steady, and solid.

Gone is the broody grump who wouldn't look at me over dinner or who glared at me for too long.

This Franco is nothing if not sincere.

"I'm right here. Come on. Let's go inside. I won't let anything hurt you. You got that? I'm right here. And I wish I'd fucking been there at the store five minutes earlier." He squeezes his lips together and flares his nostrils. But then he releases my thigh and clicks open my seat belt. "Take my hand. Let's get a bag packed and get the fuck out of here."

He eases my seat belt away from my body, and now there is

nothing left to do but take his hand and move one leg at a time out of the truck.

The fall air is crisp, and his breath curls in front of his face in soft puffs of steam. My hand shakes as I reach for his. My legs feel weak but also like they are surging with fear, like at any moment, I could break into a run and take myself far, far away from here.

The intensity of the experience is too much. I hit the pavement, and my knees buckle. "Whoa." I reach for the truck door, but Franco is there instead.

His body is warm and firm, and he's got a hand on my waist, but somehow my thighs are plastered against his. I follow my body's momentum and lean all the way into him.

"Whoa," he echoes what I just said, but his word is heavy with something else. His breath fans my ear, and for a moment, I get lost in the reassuring comfort of him. He's like a wall of muscle blocking the rest of the world from getting to me.

It's probably the stupidest thing I've ever done, but I lean my forehead against his chest and close my eyes. Maybe I'm chickenshit, hiding like this behind a man I hardly know. But before I can think better of what I'm doing, I lift up on my toes and wrap my arms around his neck.

"Thank you," I breathe against his neck. The long layers of his hair tickle my face, and I'm a little too short to reach comfortably, but he is already wrapping his arms around my waist and pulling me close. I hug him hard and let the tears burn the backs of my eyelids. "What would have happened if you hadn't come when you did?"

I mean, I know the criminal was already outside when Franco arrived, but the guy took my phone. The store has a landline, but I was so weak and terrified.

Would I have been able to call for help? What if I'd passed out alone?

My entire body trembles, and he holds me even closer. The unbelievable heat of him seeps through my clothes, and, if anything, I hold on even tighter.

He doesn't say anything and doesn't relax his hold on me. "I won't let anything happen to you," he promises. "You're okay. You're going to be okay."

I breathe in the heady scent of his hair, the light fragrance of hair oil, soap, smoke, and I know I have to let go. I'm embarrassing myself further. But my body knows what it wants, and this biker-mechanic-bodyguard is exactly the shield I need right now. I will rally.

I will get past this. But right now? I'm in no state to pretend to be stronger than I am.

"I don't really want to let go," I admit, my words sounding fuzzy against his collar.

I can feel his hands through my sweater, firm but gentle on my waist. "How about we try this?" he says. "Let's walk inside. Let's get you packed. And then, if you need more of this, you just come on back for more."

I nod and loosen my hands and steady my feet beneath me. I wipe my hands on the legs of my pants and shake clear the cobwebs.

One thing at a time.

"Inside. Pack a bag," I repeat, more to myself than to him, feeling suddenly vulnerable again. There is a clear path between me and the exterior stairs that lead to my apartment. No massive man blocking the way. "Where do you plan to take me? I don't want to impose on anyone, and—"

"My place," he says. "You can stay with me tonight."

Something electric dances in my belly when he says that. In the state I'm in, I can't tell whether it's excitement, relief, or fear that I'm feeling. "Your place?" I shake my head. "You don't have to do that. I can just—"

"Do you want to go stay with my mother?" he asks, no sign of impatience in his voice. Unless I'm mistaken, he sounds tired. "Because if you want to put up with Lucia freaking out and fawning over you, I'll take you straight to my mom's."

The idea doesn't sound half bad, but if the alternative is staying with Franco...

"I don't know," I say, sincerely unsure what I want. "Let's just go inside."

I square my shoulders and head for the stairs, and he calls for me to wait up.

I've only taken a couple of steps, and I freeze in place. He holds out his hand. I give him my keys without a word, and then he takes the lead, heading toward the stairs where he'd watched me walk to my unit last night.

"Which one is yours?" he asks when we get to the top.

The exterior lights are all working, so my number is clearly illuminated. The welcome mat is still Aunt Ann's, a faded sunflower pattern with a happy bee dancing above the petals. I point ahead and tell him the unit, and he nods, then grimly storms toward my door as if expecting to see the intruder waiting there for me.

"Franco," I whisper. There's a lot I don't know about technology, and so I know my question is probably foolish. But I can't help my reactions. It's as if everything inside me is hyperalert, ready to descend into full fight-or-flight at the least sign. "He has my phone. Is it possible for him to find out where I live?"

Franco's plush lips flatten into a hard line, and a dark shadow passes over his bright eyes. "We're not taking any chances." He pulls his cell phone from his jacket pocket and unlocks the device. "The passcode is 0131. For my mother's birthday, January 31." He repeats it, so I'm sure I remember it. "I'm going to go in first. If there's any sign of trouble, you call the cops. All right?"

I nod and nervously hold his phone in a trembling hand. I keep the phone at the ready and watch while Franco sifts through the keys on my ring.

"This one?" he asks.

I nod. "The doorknob takes the same key," I whisper, terrified that the criminal is close by.

It's ridiculous, I know. But I've never been the victim of a crime before. And this was such a close call. He'd brought a knife. What might have made him want to use it? And would he have used it on…me? My vision blurs and I feel dizzy again, but I fight through it. I have to be ready to dial. I have to focus and just trust that I'm safe now. I'm not alone. Franco is here, and any minute now…

"It's all clear, babe. Come on." Franco's face softens, and my tummy flips at the casual endearment. He's inside my apartment now, turning on the hall light.

I follow him in and hand him back his phone. "Thank you," I say. "So, so much."

He closes the door behind me and turns the lock, pocketing his phone and breathing a loud sigh. "Look okay in here to you? Nothing out of place?"

I scan the mildly familiar apartment. Aunt Ann's furniture is all still here. But as my eyes adjust to each light Franco turns on, I feel more and more at ease that nothing has been disturbed. Nothing is out of place.

"It looks okay," I say quietly. My aunt's old refrigerator hums loudly, and for a moment, I want to lie down on the couch and just collect my thoughts. Calm my racing heart and weary nerves.

But Franco has other things on his mind. "Have you eaten?" he asks. "Dinner?"

I scoff and shake my head. "I'll probably never eat again," I say. "Unless some miracle settles my nerves, I'll probably just throw everything right back up."

"My father's leftovers beg to differ." His voice is light, and he nods toward the open bedroom door. "You have a suitcase?"

I search his face, confusion and self-doubt at war in my chest. "Are you sure you want to take me home with you? I mean, you hardly know me, and you've done so much for me already. I don't—"

He stops the words by striding across the living room and lifting my chin with two fingers. His touch is gentle, but the friction of his skin against mine brings every nerve ending to attention.

I raise my eyes to meet his.

"You don't want to go home with me?" he asks.

The question lingers between us, something more than the words he actually asked underlying his meaning.

I swallow and blink, not sure what to do.

If I speak, I'll disturb his touch. If I move, I'll break our safe, gentle connection. My body is insistent in its silence, stillness.

"I do," I whisper, closing my eyes. "But…"

"No buts. It's settled." Franco doesn't release my face right away, but he smooths the hair back from my face. "Pack what you need for a couple days. I'll be right here."

Then he's gone, his fingers leave my chin and hair, and I'm frozen in place.

He walks to the kitchen and scans the fridge. There are still aged magnets and notes my aunt scribbled when she was alive on the front. I haven't had the heart to move any of her things. I came from Pennsylvania with a carload of clothes, some books, and personal things, but nothing large like furniture.

I'm living a hand-me-down life if there ever was one. And that thought makes the old inferiority swirl up like a tsunami.

I walk to the bathroom and close the door behind me. I drop onto the toilet and let a few quiet tears fall.

Pull up your big-girl panties, I tell myself.

He's a friend. My aunt's friend's son. He's not judging whether or not he wants to date me. He's helping a woman who's gone through a terrifying experience. I'm just lucky it was him who showed up at the café or I might have to spend tonight completely alone.

I dry my tears and twist my hair into a loose bun, then I wash my face with cold water.

"Franco?"

He's standing in the kitchen but starts at the sound of my voice. "What? Are you okay?" he blurts, then comes toward me like he's genuinely concerned some new danger sprung up in my room.

I'm starting to feel human again, more like myself. I give him a smile. "I just wanted to know if I should pack a pillow and blanket?"

He looks at me with an unreadable expression. His lips are slightly parted, and he seems to notice my hair is up as he trails his eyes from my lips to my hair and back to my face. "No," he finally says. "It's all good. Leave all that, unless you need special things. Ma made sure I have extra of everything."

I shake my head and sling my bags over one shoulder. "I'm getting hungry now, though. I think the shock is wearing off and my survival instincts are kicking in."

248

He nods. "Good thing I brought Dad's leftovers. We'll eat at my place. You want a drink?"

I nod.

"Just wine, or the harder stuff?" he asks. "I think tonight calls for a gin and tonic."

"I usually stick to one beer or one glass of wine, but I'm up for anything."

I click off the lights and am slightly reassured by how homey the place looks now that I'm calming down. Everything is where it should be. This is where my aunt lived. And this is where I'll make a life too. Tonight is just a scary bump in the new path I'm forging. I'll get through it.

And I'll be okay.

At least, that's what I hope.

CHAPTER SEVEN

franco

When I pull up to my place, I leave the truck in the driveway but pop the garage door with the opener.

Chloe spent the entire ride looking at her hands and fidgeting in the seat, to the point where she was making me anxious. But something about seeing the lights go on in my garage, along with the sight of my bike, workbench, and weights restores a little sense of normalcy.

I switch off the truck and turn to her. "I'll carry everything. Let's just get you inside."

She mumbles something under her breath and nods, then shoves open the passenger door.

Once we're inside, I lock the garage and set her bags down at the base of the stairs. She has slid out of her boots and is shifting from foot to foot, looking uncertain.

I check the time, and it's nearly nine. I stifle a yawn at the same time my stomach gurgles. "I'm going to heat these leftovers," I tell her. "I've got to cook some pasta, so it might be twenty minutes. That cool?"

She nods. "Can I help?"

"Let's get your things settled, and we'll cook." I grab her bags and bring them upstairs. "I've got shit everywhere," I say, "but you can leave your stuff up here." I drop her luggage and show her the bathroom. "Towels are here. Feel free to shower or take a bath if you want. Just make yourself at home."

She is looking down at her socks, when I realize she might not feel ready to be alone yet. She might want to make a call to someone, but she doesn't have her phone.

"Hey," I say gently, taking a step closer. "Is there someone you want to call? I don't know what else to do here, but you're safe. You can just relax now."

The saddest expression passes over her face before she carefully composes herself.

In that moment, my heart cracks for her.

She looks so young then, younger than a woman who owns her own business and who moved halfway across the country alone should.

"How old are you?" I ask, the words tumbling out before I can stop them.

She lifts a brow at me, but she answers. "Twenty-nine," she says. "Why? How old are you?"

"I'm thirty-eight," I tell her. "And it's nothing. I just... I'm going to make some food."

I turn and clomp downstairs. There's no point in telling her she looks so young I want to physically stop the world from throwing scary shit at her. I can't. I can't protect her, and I don't understand this almost primal instinct in me to do so.

I have a little sister. I've watched Grace go through hard shit, and yeah, I've always been there to back her play. But this feels so very different. So much more complicated. I don't pity Chloe or feel a duty toward her.

I slam my frustration against the kitchen cabinets and fill a pot of water to boil, heavily salting it. I warm the sauce in a pan, adding a little olive oil and water to thin it without changing the flavor too much.

Just after I dump the box of pasta into the stockpot, Chloe pads downstairs. Her hair is damp and is hanging in smooth, combed locks over her shoulders. Little droplets of water drip from the ends and land on a towel she has wrapped over her shoulders like a shawl.

For the many layers of clothes she wears out there in the world, her sleepwear is surprisingly minimalist. She's wearing a pair of soft sleep shorts, emphasis on short, and a loose V-neck T-shirt. Her feet are bare, and I yank my gaze away from her naked legs to pour myself something strong.

"What're you drinking?" I call from the freezer. I drop a generous serving of ice into a glass and set it on the counter. "I've got beer. I can open some wine…"

"Just whatever you're having is fine," she says. She sits at my kitchen table and picks at her nails. "Can I help?"

I shake my head and fill a second glass with ice. The pasta's got another three or four minutes to cook, so I grab a lime from the fridge and make us each a strong gin and tonic. I hand her a drink, strain the pasta, and then serve up a plate for each of us.

We eat in silence, and it's almost painfully awkward. I can smell the fresh berry scent emanating from her wet hair, and her face is scrubbed clean but has a lot of the color back in it.

"What did you do back in… Where did you move from? I'm sure my ma told me, but I don't remember."

She nods. "Pennsylvania." She takes a long sip of her drink, and her shoulders relax a little more as she chuckles. "I worked in a bookstore," she says. "But the one back home was a major retail chain. You know the kind—we had an in-store café that was owned by another big company. Having books and a café and running it all myself is quite the change."

"Must be." I've eaten every morsel on my plate, and now I'm feeling it. I'm full and tired. I lean back in my chair and sip my drink. "Are books a thing in your family? Like, did you always know you wanted to own your own bookshop one day?"

I'm slowing down her meal by talking to her, but the silence is too painful. I feel like the less we talk, the more we both get lost in the memories of what happened tonight.

She lets out a laugh and sets down her fork. "Not at all," she says. "It was actually a huge shock when I learned my aunt left me Latterature."

"Yeah?" I watch her as she talks, checking out the loose curls that are taking shape as her hair dries.

"Yeah," she echoes. "My family wasn't really close to Aunt Ann. Not as close as my mother and I would've liked. I was really shocked she left the place to me. I wasn't sure I even wanted it, but I knew I had to come here and check it out."

Instead of looking away, I watch, a curious heat rising under my skin as I let myself appreciate this woman.

For the first time, she maintains eye contact. "Can I speak freely?" she finally asks.

"That's the only fucking way to do it," I assure her.

"My dad was a drunk," she says simply. "And I know I should be more considerate. He had a disease. An addiction. Alcoholism is no joke, and it's not his fault that he had a problem. But it's hard to separate the man from the booze when the two have such a close relationship."

Hearing that her dad had issues with alcohol makes me sit up a little straighter in my chair, but I don't interrupt.

"My dad never cooked a meal in his life." She chews another bite of pasta and shakes her head thoughtfully. "He sure knew how to scream at me or my mother to bring him dinner, though." She twirls the curly end of a piece of hair between her fingers and looks at me. "My family life was completely opposite of yours. Dad drank and yelled. Mom hid and enabled. And I just tried to stay out of the way."

"In your own family?" I set my glass back on the table, making a louder thud against the wood than I intend. "That sucks," I tell her. "I'm sorry."

I don't know what else to say.

She shrugs and says almost exactly what I'm thinking. "Everyone has problems," she says. "Well, I used to believe that until I met your family. They might just be as close to perfect as I've met."

I snort at that. "We're not perfect."

"Hmmm?" She's got a twinkle in her clear green eyes. "I don't believe you. Sweet, if a little too involved, mother. A dad who cooks and seems doting. Three gorgeous brothers with good jobs and lives, and a sister who, quite honestly, I'm sure most women wish they could be."

When she puts it like that, yeah. We're blessed. I know this. But that doesn't mean we're anywhere near perfect.

"I wonder about that sometimes," I say, realizing a minute too late that she called me and my brothers gorgeous, so I backtrack. "And for the record, I'm the best-looking of the Bianchis. Benito ain't half bad, but Vito…" I shake my head. "Gorgeous he is not."

She laughs. "I don't know," she says, a teasing, playful note in her voice. I like the way the lightness in her tone sounds. "Firefighters are the stuff of romance novels. I would know, I'm a bookseller."

That makes me snort. "Please do not put the image in my head of Vito on the cover of some book."

"Any one of you could be on the cover—not just him," she says, her face flushing. "Let me do the dishes. You've done enough and have been put out too much already."

I hold my hands up in surrender and let her clear my plate. I have a dishwasher, but she takes the towel from around her shoulders and hangs it over the end of the counter to dry.

I can tell she's not wearing a bra under her sleep shirt, and my cock immediately goes to half-mast in my jeans.

Under all those clothes, Chloe has a *body*. Her nipples are hard, the tips pressing against the soft fabric and distracting me from the fullness of her breasts.

Thank God she turns away to rinse the dishes because I'm twitching like a kid who can't resist popping a sheet of bubble wrap. Those tight peaks are all I can think about touching.

I roughly shove my chair back in and try to think about anything else except her nipples. I start talking too, words spilling out of my mouth. "So, you said you weren't sure you wanted Latterature? What are you thinking? You're going to look the place over, fix it up a bit, and sell?"

She shrugs and glances back over her shoulder at me. "I hadn't made any plans…at least not before tonight."

At the mention of what happened tonight, my belly tightens with a different kind of tension. "And now?" I press.

I shouldn't care what her plans are, but as she stands at my sink in her bare feet, it's impossible not to be curious.

She dries the dishes and turns back toward me. The ends of her hair are hanging over her chest, blocking my view of her more arousing parts.

She smiles, but the gesture doesn't reach her eyes. "I guess I was starting to feel like I could make a life here. Something different from what I had back home. Someplace I might finally belong." A shadow passes over her face, but before I can say anything, she squares her shoulders and puts on a brave smile. "Guess I'm sleeping on the couch?"

"You can take my bed."

She shakes her head. "No. No. I'm not putting you out of your bed. I probably won't sleep much anyway. I'd rather take the couch. Please don't argue with me about this, Franco."

I nod. "I'll grab some clean pillows and blankets." I take the stairs two at a time to burn off some of the electric energy buzzing through my limbs and rummage through my hall closet.

When I'm halfway down the stairs, I see her peering nervously at the sliding glass patio door that leads into the backyard. She moves the curtain aside and checks to make sure it's locked.

"Everything all right?" I ask, and even though she nods, I am not convinced. I start to set out the blankets, a sheet, and two pillows on the couch when she stops me with a hand on my arm.

"It's okay," she says. "You've done enough. Thank you."

I nod and check the front door, garage door, and then the patio slider again so she knows it's all locked up. "Sleep well," I tell her.

I head upstairs but turn back to see her just sitting on the couch, not setting up the bedding. Not moving. She looks up and nods at me, that same artificial bravery plastered on her face.

"Stop," I mutter to myself. "She wants to be alone for a little while."

Post-traumatic stress and my mother's matchmaking ideas are playing tricks with my head.

I stalk up the stairs and into the bathroom. I get ready for bed, then go into my room. But just in case, I climb into bed and leave the bedroom door open.

———————————————

I don't know what time it is when the noise wakes me, but the telltale creak of the middle stair has me bolting upright in bed.

"Chloe?" The upstairs is dark and the sound stops when I call her name, so I lie still and listen, my heart rate waking me up faster than I can believe.

I heard something. I know my house, and when I hear it again, that same creak on the stairs, I'm out of bed and at my bedroom door in seconds.

I flip on the hall light and see Chloe looking sheepish. She's on the staircase, her pillows and blankets bundled in her arms.

"What happened?" I blurt, concern overcoming every other emotion. "Are you okay?"

She's paler than she should be, all bare legs and loose hair. "I couldn't sleep down there. I felt too exposed," she explains. "I thought I'd just make a little bed in your guest room."

"On the floor?" I ask because I never bought another bed since I never had a need.

She nods. "Would you mind? I'll be fine." She trudges up the stairs, and I rake a hand through my hair.

"No, no, no," I say. "You take my bed. I've crashed on that couch more times than I can count." I scratch my bare chest and motion toward my room. "Come on. We'll trade."

She looks down at her bare toes, struggling to hold all the pillows and blankets in her arms. "Franco," she says quietly. "Can I stay on the floor in your room? I can't stop seeing him. I can't stop seeing the knif—"

I don't let her finish the word. I take the pillows and blankets from her arms and motion toward my room with my head. She moves past me without looking me in the eye.

I drop the pillows and blankets on the floor, and she leans over like she's about to join them.

"No," I say, shoving aside the pile of blankets with my foot. "Get in the bed."

She looks at me curiously. She doesn't argue, but she also doesn't move.

"Do you trust me?" I ask her as I pull back the comforter and sheet for her.

I know what I'm about to do, and it could go very, very wrong. But I don't care. Whatever my mom saw in Chloe that made her so desperately want to set me up with this woman, I'm seeing it too.

She hums a yes as she slides onto the bed and slips her toes and then her legs under my blankets. I close the bedroom door, then climb into my side of the bed.

We're side by side as far apart on a small surface as two people can be.

"Come here," I say, rolling onto my right side. I hold up the covers, and she scoots closer to me. "I won't bite."

She giggles, which I take as a good sign, and then pushes closer to me. Close enough that I have to sling an arm over her because there is nowhere else for it to go.

"Goodnight, Franco," she whispers. "Thank you."

I tell myself not to. I try to stop myself. But my mouth has a mind of its damn own, and I press a kiss to her hair and nestle my nose deep in the soft, berry-scented waves. "Sweet dreams," I breathe.

She might trust me, but with her body tucked against mine, the curve of her plush ass fitted against my hips, the length of her hair tickling my bare chest, I sure as hell don't trust myself.

CHAPTER EIGHT

chloe

I wake up cuddled in the most luxurious, comfortable, softest bed I've ever been in. As soon as it hits me that I am not alone in the bed, the fog clears from my mind, and my lids fly open and bug out like a cartoon character's.

The room is dim, the early morning sun still weak behind the blinds. I wiggle my toes, but that's all I dare to move because behind me is a heaping furnace of a shirtless man.

His deep breathing makes me certain he's still sound asleep, but the large palm tucked under my shirt rests against the skin of my belly.

I don't know where his other arm is, but a quick inventory of my body parts confirms it. We're not just spooning. We're nestled like we were made to fit together.

We are tangled up like we've been taking comfort in each other's bodies for years.

We are not just sleeping; we're sleeping *together*.

That we is me...*me*...and Franco Bianchi.

The man who grumped at me the first time we met. Who glared at me across the table through the entirety of my first family dinner.

The weight of Franco's thigh tossed over mine makes me start to sweat. Electric heat sparks beneath my sleep shorts, and I want desperately to rub my thighs together, but I will not budge.

I close my eyes and breathe deeply, but that just makes it worse. The entire bed smells like him. How did I not notice this last night? Yes, I was traumatized and terrified, but I think I could solve all my financial woes if I could just bottle up this scent and put it on the shelves in my aunt's bookstore.

I'd have to call the fragrance Franco, though, because a name like "Italian Working Man" would give off all the wrong vibes.

Okay, it's official. I'm losing my mind.

Last night, I climbed into bed with a man I hardly know, who I thought sort of hated me. Now, I'm lying here wide awake and afraid to move because I don't want to leave the cocoon of comfort and warmth that this man has freely given.

The hard part, and this sobers me up and shoves me halfway out of my sleepy cocoon, is that he's going to wake up and boot me out of his life, probably any minute now.

Deep sigh.

After this morning, I'll cling to this memory for a very long time to come. I hope my vibrator is ready for the floodgates of frustration to open.

I shift a little under the weight of his thigh and scold myself for getting whipped into a lusty frenzy from the smell of his darned sheets, when something happens to correct my thoughts on the matter entirely.

The hard part isn't going to be leaving his bed.

The hard part is actually *in* his bed.

Behind me.

Pressed against my bottom in a way that makes my body do more than just tingle.

My nipples flare to life, tightening into needy, achy peaks. I have to practically bite through my lip to stop myself from thrusting my hips back against him.

How?

How, how, how is this even my life?

I realize in a panic that maybe he isn't asleep, and all the fidgeting, snuggling, and smelling I've been doing have, um, woken him up.

I mean, it's not like he is in this situation because of me. Certainly not *for* me. It's a normal thing that just happens to guys in the morning, but my brazen cuddling is no doubt sending the wrong message.

Or is it the right message?

I don't know, but before I can think myself into a state of absolute distraction, the hand on my belly tightens and a voice caresses my hair. "Mornin'."

I freeze.

The blood in my body slows down, and I stiffen.

He's awake.

Conscious enough to say words. And his hand hasn't moved, but something south of his waistband twitched a little.

I'm sure that wasn't just wishful thinking on my part. "Good… morning," I whisper back, debating whether to play dead, but deciding against it.

I mean, how the hell are we going to pull ourselves apart from each other?

Better question—how long can I stay this way before I *have* to?

If I have any doubts that Franco knows exactly what he's doing, I feel his hand move from my belly to my ribs, and then finally moves to touch my shoulder.

He pushes the hair back from my face, and I feel him lift his head a little while he smooths the length of it under his head. But he doesn't get up.

He just nestles his head right back where it was, nose resting against my hair. I feel the heat of his breaths against my scalp, and all the little hairs on my arms stand at attention. But not as sharply as my traitorous nipples do.

I suck in a ragged breath of air, the strings of attraction that connect my nipples to my core tightening to a blissful ache.

I'm almost painfully aware of his morning hardness pressing against the crack of my bottom, when suddenly he shifts his hips and moves away, putting just enough distance between us that I can no longer feel his arousal.

Damn.

I don't know what I expected him to do when he woke, but moving away from me was the very thing I didn't want.

When he does, though, I quickly remember that he is who he is, and I'm me.

Plain.

Nerdy.

That gift he is sporting in his pajama pants has nothing to do with me.

"We sure got cozy last night. I hope I didn't make you feel uncomfortable."

My body has clearly taken over my brain because before I can stop myself, I blurt out, "It's what you promised, remember? Self-serve hugs? I wouldn't have stayed here if the damsel-in-distress package didn't come with spooning."

He's quiet for a moment and my cheeks burn hot with mortification, but then a miracle happens. Franco rolls back over and tucks his body tighter against mine. "Is that so?" he growls against my ear.

I press my bottom ever so slightly, so the raging erection he's still sporting is back right where I want it. Well, not *right* where I want it. It's lined up with my butt cheeks.

My hands are itching to reach behind me and touch him, take that length in my hands and guide it where I need it most, but I stop them.

Franco groans under his breath and hisses, but he doesn't move away.

"Thank you," I whisper, then make the painful decision to end this agonizing teasing and roll over to face him before I really embarrass myself.

I inch myself away from his hold, not because it's what I want— because I swear on all that's good and holy, all I *want* is to roll him onto his back so I can mount him until I'm screaming his name. But that's not happening.

Not now, not ever.

Instead, I give myself a mental cold shower and curl onto my side facing him. "I don't think I've ever felt safer or slept better."

"Shit day yesterday. Glad I could help."

"I'm glad too," I admit quietly. "Thank you seems like not nearly enough."

I'm suddenly feeling shy as we look at each other under the covers. The sun is starting to come up, and I can see every muscle in his bare shoulders.

His hair is messy, and the stubble on his chin is thick and delicious. Franco is beautiful. The kind of beautiful that I could lie here and stare at for hours.

"Lots to do today," he says, shoving back the covers.

Those words remind me that this is just a friend helping a friend. A guy whose mother would guilt him if he didn't offer help. A courtesy.

Thanks to the still-dark bedroom, I'm hoping Franco can't see me watching every flex and stretch of his body as he gets out of bed.

I try to lower my lids so I don't look like I'm checking out his body, but then I give in and just stare. Why not?

My fantasy is ending, and I want to soak up every last second.

Sigh.

He shakes out his shoulders and stretches his arms above his head, and I close my eyes to stop them from rolling as every muscle of his torso moves like a male model warming up before settling into just the right pose.

Come on.

The guy isn't hot enough in clothes, so I've got to watch him shirtless? What next? Is he going to drop and do some crunches?

"You want to shower first?" he asks, breaking in to my thoughts.

I tuck the blankets up to my chin and shake my head. "No, you go ahead. I'll catch a few more minutes of rest."

If lying here and hoping my flaming arousal cools off a little counts as rest, then yes, I will be resting. I'll be resting for at least as long as it takes him to shower.

He nods and rakes a hand through his hair, leaving it stuck up in the wildest directions, and somehow that's both sexy and cute at the same time.

I consider biting down on the blanket to save my lip from some of the pain, but he closes the bedroom door behind him and I'm alone.

I hear the shower water turn on, and I take one deep breath and savor it. I'm in his bed. My skin still remembers the heat of his hands. This was as close to Franco as I could ever hope to be, and in a few minutes, it will all be over.

I'll be back to my real life, whatever that turns out to be. I'd been so hopeful and open to whatever Star Falls had to offer when I decided to come up here and check out my aunt's café.

But after a night in his arms, the idea of making a life for myself, from scratch, all on my own, no longer feels like such an exciting adventure.

Excitement is what I feel with him, around him. Too bad the only adventure is finding out how many ways a gorgeous, unattainable man can break my heart.

Within the hour, even though I showered last night, I've showered again and joined Franco down in the kitchen. He hands me a mug of hot coffee, and I don't know, but I feel like he's looking at me differently today.

He's got a list written in front of him, and he looks almost excited to share it with me. I notice he's set a spoon and a sugar bowl on the kitchen table.

"I figured I'd let you put in the sugar for yourself," he says, and then he sits down beside me and starts talking.

I'm looking between him and the spoon and wondering how the heck the man knows I take only sugar in my coffee. But then I realize I had coffee at his parents'. Did he actually pay attention to how I preferred it?

I stir in the sugar and only catch up to Franco's voice when he stretches a hand across the table and rests it on my arm.

"You okay?" He's studying my face. "Did I upset you? Too much?"

Wait, what?

"I was a little lost in my thoughts," I admit. "Sorry. Start over?"

He looks concerned but not angry, which is an upgrade from last week, at least. He points to the handwritten list he's put on the table. "So, I called out of work today. I don't know how you're feeling about going back to the store, but I've made a list of things you probably need to do. We can do them together, or..." He pauses. "Were you feeling up to opening the store today? I sort of assumed you'd want to close the store and..."

"You called out of work?" The sweet coffee is strong, and the way it hits my tongue makes me smile. Or at least, I tell myself it's the coffee.

Franco nods. "I'm fired up as hell. You need a cell phone, and you probably need to check in with your mother," he says. "If something like that happened and I didn't tell my mom for a couple days, she'd..." One side of his mouth curls up. "Well, you know my mother. You know how that would go over."

I nod, but the topic of my mother makes me go silent.

"Hey," he says, a question in his voice. "I'm sorry. Did I touch on something there?"

I shrug, though I don't look up at him. But then I do. Darn it. I'm tired of hiding. Of apologizing for who I am and what my family is—or, more accurately, is not.

"My mother isn't someone I can run to when things happen," I explain. "I wish she were. My whole life, I've held my troubles close to my chest and dealt with them myself. Or maybe not at all. My mom always had enough to deal with just having my dad around. It's a lot easier not to involve her." I give him a weak smile. "I'm only sad about it at the moment because I love what you have with your family. It's the dream, you know?"

Franco doesn't seem to miss a beat. "I know," he says somberly. He takes a sip of his coffee, but his eyes never leave my face. "I know how fortunate I am to have the family I do. I complain about them, but..." He's serious for a moment. "My family is a huge presence in my life. No matter how much I give them a hard time, I live my life with my parents on either shoulder. Most of the time, it's a good thing."

I'm not sure what he means by that, and I want to ask, but he's moved on. I don't want to redirect him. I want to know what he wants to share—and more—so I just listen.

"Ma will be more than happy to panic, freak out, and butt into everything you've got going on. And you've got a whole circle of women desperate to mother you until you feel smothered," he says. "And I'm the oldest of four, so it's just my nature. I'm the bossy older brother."

He jumps up from the table and starts assembling some breakfast. He doesn't ask me what I want; he just cuts up some fruit and starts scrambling eggs.

I'm thrilled because I'm starving, and while his back is to me, I can sort out how I'm feeling.

I realize he's handling me, I guess, like he's my bossy older brother. Except when I think of his hand under my sleep tee, hot against my skin. No. There was nothing brotherly about how he held me last night.

I look over the sheet of paper Franco left on the table. "So, um, what's on the to-do list?" I ask.

"Well, I think, first," he says, "we need to get your phone replaced. And then I was thinking…"

Of course, I hear nothing after that because I have no way of paying for a new phone. The one I had was five years old, so not new by any means but still decent as far as smartphone technology goes.

I wonder if Aunt Ann had insurance on the store. I'm sure she did, but the deductible on policies like that is normally very high. And even if I did make a claim, all that will take more time than I have. How long can I reasonably go without a cell phone?

The coffee starts to sour in my stomach, and I push back from the table. "Franco," I start. "I…"

He sets down the fork he's using to whisk the eggs and looks at me. "What?"

I shake my head. "The phone thing is going to be a problem. I..."

This is all just really, really hard to share. I have such shame around the whole situation.

I need capital. A rainy day fund. And with this unexpected setback? I mean, a serious crime would set anyone back. But I didn't even lose the money in the robbery. Just my phone.

At my age, I should have something in savings and far more than a crap car with no gas in it. And yet, here I am.

"Maybe this is a sign from the universe that I should go home," I say quietly. "That I shouldn't be here. That this is not something I can do."

"Wait, what?" He looks confused. He sets the bowl of eggs on the counter and joins me at the table. "I feel like you're not saying what you're thinking."

I'm standing beside my chair, and he comes closer but doesn't touch me.

Just cocks his chin and narrows his eyes. "Talk to me, Chloe. What's really going on in here?" He brings his hand to the side of my face. He taps my temple gently with two fingers to emphasize *in here* and then sort of caresses the side of my cheek before dropping his hand to his side. "Sorry," he mutters. "I can't seem to keep my hands off you." He's shaking his head as if he's scolding himself.

"You have an all-access pass," I assure him, flushing hard and laughing. "I'm the one who invited myself into your bed."

He smiles, and his whole face relaxes. He lowers his chin and stares at me, and in that moment, I feel like I'm seeing a whole new side of Franco. Not a more honest side. Because I think he is always exactly who he is.

The grumpy hot guy thing is not a façade or an act, which somehow makes it so much hotter. He's just always himself. At ease in his body and his life and who he is.

It's reassuring to be around, not only because I like who he is, but because I feel somehow like I have permission to just be me. I want to be more like he is in that way.

Honest.

No apologies.

"It's not comfortable to talk about," I explain, trying on this more honest version of myself. "I know I need to replace my phone, but I walked to dinner at your parents' the other night because I'd used most of the cash I had to buy that stupid television. I know it seems like a weird splurge, but I want to start running events at the store. I thought I could... I don't know."

I sigh.

I lift the list and look over the things he's so thoughtfully penned. "A cell phone, a security system..." I swallow and meet Franco's eyes.

I can do this. I can be brave and honest.

"It's all stuff I need, you're right. But I literally do not have the cash."

Franco is quiet for only a split second. "Okay," he says, nodding. "I get it. Did your aunt leave you anything else? Life insurance?"

I shake my head. "Just a failing bookstore and whatever is in her apartment. I have the place with no lease until the end of the year, but I'm paying the rent and everything."

He seems completely undeterred, nodding again. "All right. So, you need money to replace your phone. Money to do the stuff on this list." He thinks for a second. "Do you want my help, Chloe? If that's not what you want, you need to tell me now to stand down. I'm a lot like my mom in that sense, but at least I know enough to ask before I barge into someone's business."

"What do you have in mind?"

He motions for me to sit. His eyes sparkle and he's got a sexy grin on his face, and since my knees go a little weak at the sight, I have no problem dropping into a chair. "How do you feel about paperwork?" he asks.

CHAPTER NINE

franco

"Chloe, this is Jack Miles."

It's around ten on Tuesday by the time we get through breakfast. I take Chloe over to Easy Start just about the time I know Jack will be taking a break.

He shakes Chloe's hand and lifts his chin at me. "I thought you weren't coming in today, man." He's looking Chloe over and I know his mind is spinning, but he's not saying anything.

Something seems to have shifted in Chloe this morning. She's still wearing her boots and pants that must be two sizes too big, but after spending the night tucked against her ass, I'm actually happy she's hiding what she's got from the world. Under those bulky sweaters, her body is more than what meets the eye. Just like the woman herself.

When I woke this morning with my hand under her shirt, it was all I could do to keep my fingers from wandering to her breasts, ass, thighs…

"Hi, Jack. Nice to meet you." She shakes his hand, and I can tell Jack's confused, but my buddy's nothing if not cool.

They make small talk about Chloe's aunt Ann and the café, until finally, we get down to business.

"Jack," I say, "since your mom's on temporary hiatus, how would you feel about hiring Chloe for a couple days to get that paperwork sorted?"

Chloe and I talked about the idea in the truck, so I know she's down for it. I don't know if Jack's budget at the shop will allow him to pay Chloe for some very part-time work, but I have a list of ideas a mile long. This is just our first stop.

"Listen," I add, "she needs some capital for some improvements to Ann's place. Won't be a long-term thing, but if you and your pops can find some leeway in the payroll, you can help out Chloe, and I'll bet she can find that purchase order you've been wanting me to deal with."

Jack's thinking it over, but he looks dubious. "I've got to call my dad, Frankie," he says, looking sheepish. "Hiring someone's not that easy. There's taxes and paperwork to consider…"

I hold up a hand to stop him. "Look, I get it. If it's too complicated, no worries. Throwing it out there, that's all."

"Dad's still fishing," Jack reminds me. "But I'll give him a quick call. If it's a no, you'll know sooner rather than later."

Chloe's face crumples a little, but I give her a reassuring nod. "Come with me," I say, leading her to Carol's desk. "Let's give Jack some privacy while he calls Earl."

She grabs my sleeve as we're walking away. "Franco." Her voice is tiny again, the fading flower starting to droop. "I don't want to cause any trouble…"

"What trouble? This ain't trouble," I assure her. "It's a phone call. Earl will say yes or no, and then we'll go from there." I turn to her and put my hands on her shoulders.

I meant what I said this morning in my kitchen. I don't know why, but I can't stop myself from touching her.

She doesn't seem to mind, so I squeeze gently and lower my voice. "You asking for what you need doesn't inconvenience anybody," I say. "I mean that. Ask. Speak up. Say what you need. If the answer's no…" I shrug one shoulder. "Then fuck it. Shake it off and keep going. Around me, don't ever apologize for asking for what you want."

She is nibbling on her lower lip and watching my face like I have all the answers there. I don't, but what I do know is that the world helps those who help themselves.

If there's anything I can do for her right now, it's to make her realize that.

"Come on." I motion toward Carol's desk.

I show her the stack of paperwork. Shit that hasn't been paid or organized in weeks since Carol stopped coming into the shop every day.

"You'd think that one purchase order wouldn't be that hard to find," I tell her. "But I looked and couldn't find the damn thing."

In the time it takes Jack to call Earl, Chloe digs into the mountain of papers on the desk. She's organized them by date, which…well fuck, I should have thought to do that.

When Jack comes back to the desk, Chloe's got things looking neat enough for someone to sit down and work.

Jack whistles. "Shit, Chloe. You're hired. When can you start?"

Her mouth falls open, and she looks from him to me.

"I'll butt out," I say, nodding. "Let you two talk details."

I wander around the shop, checking what Jack's working on while they chatter, but I keep one eye on Chloe.

She may have been shy and quiet around my family, but she's looking Jack in the eye and laughing, seemingly totally at ease with him. Seeing her connecting with him like that sets a little ember on fire in my gut. It's threatening to turn into a raging jealous inferno when she catches my eye over Jack's shoulder.

She gives me a saucy smirk and draws her lower lip into her mouth.

Something tight and hot uncoils in my chest at that look.

The pouty lips, the light in her eyes. She even tosses a lock of hair over her shoulder, not that I think she does it on purpose. Her body seems lighter, freer, and she's moving around more. It's fucking hot. And now that I know what she's got under those sweaters, I want more of it. More of her.

"Yo." Jack turns suddenly and calls for me, so I join them back at the desk.

Chloe's cheeks are flushed, and she looks happy.

Jack looks relieved.

"Looks like Chloe's going to fit right in," he says. He extends his hand to shake hers again, and I almost interrupt to tell him he already did that and there's no reason to touch her again, but I stop myself and just watch.

She is practically bouncing as I clap my buddy on the shoulder and let him know I'll see him tomorrow.

Chloe follows me back to the truck, but before I can turn over the engine, she reaches across the seats and squeezes my arm. "Thank you," she says, her voice stronger than I think I've heard it. "With what they are paying me, I'll be able to afford even a top-of-the-line, brand-new, all the bells and whistles phone in about a month." She looks down at her hand on my sleeve, and if she's thinking about moving it, she decides against it. She leaves it there and squeezes. "I may shut down the store for a few weeks while I get things sorted out. We'll see. But Jack said I can make my own hours. I'll find a way to balance it out."

"You'll be able to afford a kick-ass phone in a month?" I repeat. "That's great. That's how long I was planning to extend an interest-free loan for."

She cocks her chin and looks at me. "I'm sorry? What?"

I grin and turn on the engine, then head out toward the mall. "I'm going to buy you a phone today, but it's a loan. Thirty days interest-free. You can start paying me back once you've got some cash flowing."

She starts to complain, but I stop her with a hand. "Chloe, what's the big deal? Are you going to pick the most expensive phone in the place?"

She shakes her head.

"Fine. I'm offering to shell out the cash to get you set up today. It's a safety issue. I won't be able to sleep at night if I think you're going around town without even a way to call the cops. While we're out today, I have a whole list of things to do, remember? So, buckle up and start thinking about what you want in a new phone."

She falls silent again, and I'm sure she's gnawing right through her lower lip.

"Franco," she finally says, breaking through the quiet. "Why? Why are you helping me? I don't think I can do anything to pay you back for all this... I mean, of course I'll pay you back for the phone. Like, no question about it. But giving me a place to stay last night and making me breakfast and now this... It's a lot."

"When I was in my twenties, I was sloppy," I say. "I had a big ego. Big balls. Big head. The whole nine." I laugh and shake my head. "I was a shithead from the word go." I flick a glance at her.

She fully turns in the passenger seat, listening intently as I talk.

"Someone helped me, and now it's my turn to help you. That's what friends do," I explain, but I'm lying to her and myself.

Sure, we're friends...but part of me wants to be so much more. And if I'm being honest, that scares the living shit out me.

CHAPTER TEN

chloe

After Franco took me to get a phone, we stopped by the fire station to talk to one of Vito's buddies who has a business on the side setting up home security systems.

We explain the situation with the store, and the firefighter gives Franco a list of the items they'll need—all of which Franco insists on purchasing himself.

The guy promises to stop by Latterature to install everything after I get wireless internet set up.

"You mind if we make another stop?" he asks. "I'd like to let my sister in on what happened at the café."

I nod, and an immediate feeling of dread clenches my belly. It's nearly dinnertime, and we're headed right back to where everything happened last night.

I don't know what my face looks like, but Franco reaches a hand across the seats and gives my hand a reassuring squeeze.

"You okay?" he asks. "I'll be right there. It's going to be fine."

I look down at his fingers resting lightly on mine. "Yeah," I say. "Of course. I…"

But then I remember. This is not what I want. This is not who I want to be. I'm not going to pretend or lie or make the best of it when what I really feel is scared shitless.

"No," I correct myself. "I'm terrified, honestly. I know it may be childish, and I'll get over it, you know? I will. I'll get over it, through it. It'll get better. But right now, just the thought of going back there makes me feel sick."

He nods, and he laces his fingers through mine rather than pulling his hand away. "I get it," he says. "And it's okay. I don't want to make it worse for you, but I really want to let my sister in on what's going on. I probably should have called her already."

I'm watching our hands and the easy way he holds mine, and I wonder how this is my life.

I'm sure Franco is just *that guy*. He holds hands and flirts with and sleeps with women like it's no big deal. To me, every time he touches me, my body snaps to attention and wants to decode every movement. Every intention. Is he holding my hand to be nice?

I get my answer when he releases my hand quickly and puts both of his hands on the steering wheel as he stares straight ahead.

Right.

He's a good man.

A dutiful son and older brother.

I can be honest with myself about how the man makes me feel, while keeping myself grounded in reality.

This is…friendship, right?

And I need friends, especially here in Star Falls.

We park a few spots away from The Body Shop, and I feel Franco's eyes on me as I stare at my store.

It looks harmless and dark. The handwritten piece of paper I put up inside the door still hangs right where I taped it before we left last night.

I sit motionless as Franco jumps out, comes around, and then opens the passenger door for me.

"Hey," he says, meeting my eyes. "You good?"

I shrug, then nod, then shrug again. "I might need another hug," I mumble, not intending for him to hear.

But he must because he grins, and the sight takes my breath away. His blue eyes flash, and I'm a little embarrassed that he heard me, but hell, this is me trying to be honest. Not hiding.

When we get inside, I'm surprised by the place. I've only been inside one tattoo shop, which is why I've never actually gotten one.

Instead of dingy walls, The Body Shop is decorated in a soothing, cool palette of minimalist, almost midcentury style.

A large gray couch is in the waiting area, covered with pretty pillows that look comfortable and classy. I examine the space in awe, and although I should not be surprised, I am.

"Yo, Echo." Franco drops his keys on the front counter.

The woman behind the counter has hot-pink hair cut short in the front with a sort of curly mullet in back. Her eyes are heavily made-up with dramatic black liner and sharp, glittery pink shadow.

"What's up?" Echo smiles.

"This is Chloe," Franco says, pointing to me.

I take in the chipped black nail polish and torn fishnet top over a ribbed black tank. "So nice to meet you," I say.

"Is Gracie around?" Franco asks.

Echo hooks a thumb toward the back of the shop. "Yeah, your sister's done for the day. She's cleaning up her station. Want me to get her?"

"Please."

Echo heads back through a small door with a peekaboo window. I can already see they have more security than I do.

While Echo leaves, I notice a mount that would hold a tablet or other small device, which is probably what they use in place of a huge, antique cash register.

"Hey, asshole." Gracie comes bursting through the door, her head cocked and her black locks flying. "What are you doing here on a school night?"

She looks from her brother to me and cocks her head in the other direction, doing a sharp double take. "And hey...Chloe," she says, sounding confused. She comes up to me and kisses my cheek, then crosses her arms over her chest.

"You look beautiful," I tell her sincerely, letting myself point to her arms. "I haven't seen all these yet."

She grins, and I swear there's a blush competing with the rest of the colors on her skin. "Thanks, babe," she says, using the endearment like I'm her oldest friend. "So, what the hell are you two doing here and not at work?" She leaves off the word "together," but I am sure, given the look of amused confusion on her face, she's thinking it.

"So, not great news," Franco says. "Chloe was held up at Latterature last night. Asshole with a knife."

"Oh my God. What? Stop. Are you serious?" Gracie looks at me, but the gravity in her voice and the slight shake I hear there have me nodding soberly.

"Yeah," I say. "It was terrifying. Franco happened to come by to drop off the leftovers I'd forgotten in his truck and nearly stopped the guy. Ran into him leaving my shop."

Gracie shocks me, clasping me in a quick, hard hug, and breathes against my hair. "Are you okay?" she asks. "My God, you weren't hurt, I hope?"

I hug her back and shake my head. "I'm fine, thanks to Franco. He's been taking care of me all day."

She releases me, but only so she can hold my shoulders with both hands and stare into my face. "What the hell? People suck." Gracie finally releases me and throws herself against her brother's chest. "Good on you for being there," she says. "Are you okay?"

He nods and rests his chin on top of her head. "Yeah," he assures her. "Totally fine, just fucking pissed off the guy slipped through my fingers."

She strokes her chin thoughtfully as if putting the pieces together. "That's what the sign on the door means?" she asks. "I went over earlier for coffee and to hang out, but the sign says closed temporarily."

I nod. "I didn't want to give a reason or a timeline," I explain. "I have a lot to figure out before I open the store again."

"That's why we stopped by." Franco is looking at Echo. "Wanted you all to know. This happened yesterday when you were closed here, but whoever did this probably has been casing Main Street. The way I figure it, he noticed a new owner, a young woman by herself. Probably had been inside and saw she had no security and no technology, which means a cash business."

Echo points to a tiny sign on the counter that reads, *We love green but don't accept cash.* "We stopped taking cash like two years ago when Gracie raised the shop minimum."

"Brought in a much more serious clientele," Gracie explains, rolling her eyes. "I can't tell you how many weekends I had to turn away drunk kids with a wad of sweaty twenties wanting to get the cheapest tattoo we could do."

"Not much to steal here," I muse, looking around the shop. I notice a tiny green light up in the corner by the ceiling.

"And we have security," Gracie says. "But not all the stores do. It's too goddamn dark on Main Street around closing." She paces the lobby, a scowl on her face. "You know, just because we have cameras...doesn't mean shit. If there's somebody casing Main Street, we need to amp up security. More lights outside, motion sensors, maybe a security guard. The holidays are coming up, and that means more people, more shoppers, and more opportunities for criminals."

I have a hard time believing the building owner will do anything to improve security, but Gracie has a great point.

I make a note to check my aunt's lease and find out about the building owner and any help they might be willing to provide on the security end of things.

Franco and Gracie are talking about how the criminal got my phone when she looks at me and points right at my chest. "Well, you know you can't go home, right?"

I look from Gracie to Franco and back. "I mean... I..."

Gracie turns to her brother. "She stayed with you last night? Are you going to keep her with you? I'm sure Ma and Pops will put her up. Maybe Bev... Bev has that big house..."

I look between them again, feeling like I'm missing something. "You don't think I can go home yet?" I ask naïvely. I mean, let's be real. If Franco wants to offer me another night with him, I won't say no. But that's a far cry from me never being able to go back to Aunt Ann's.

"Do you know how easy it will be for that sicko to find you?" Gracie says, true concern marring her features. "Did you use any GPS apps on your phone?"

My stomach sinks. My entire life is in that phone. Over the weeks I've been getting to know Star Falls, I've used my GPS to find everything.

My new place was saved as "home." The shop is saved.

"You have a passcode on your phone?"

"Um," I mumble as my cheeks heat.

I bypassed the feature because I wanted to save time, and I never thought someone would take my phone and use it against me.

Damn it.

"Franco, you can't let her go home alone. Not until they catch the prick who did this or you can beef up the security at her place." Gracie's arms are flailing wildly as she gestures.

Echo is nodding behind the counter. "I agree."

It's dark outside, and the idea of going back home to Aunt Ann's alone is now the only thing I can think about.

I don't want to, but the real reason isn't just fear. One more night in Franco's bed, in Franco's arms, is a gift I would not turn down if it was offered.

"Promise me," Gracie says. She's so intent on him assuring her I'll be safe, I'm sure there's more going on than meets the eye here. Gracie has some story to tell, and while tonight isn't the time, someday I'll ask her.

"We'll deal with it." Franco nods at his sister and Echo, then puts a hand to my elbow. "We got to roll. Just…" He looks at his sister. "Keep your eyes open, Gracie."

She nods somberly and waves at us. "You need anything, Chloe… Wait." But then she stops. "Oh shit. I was going to give you my number."

"I have a phone now. Your brother helped me get a replacement today." If Gracie is surprised by what I tell her, she doesn't show it. She takes my new phone from me and punches in her contact

278

information, then hands the device back to me. "You text me if you need anything," she says, and she's so sincere, I believe she means it.

"Thank you."

"I mean it," she says, giving me another hug. "Anything."

"Thank you," I repeat before she releases me.

Franco and I are quiet once we're back in his truck.

"You know you don't have to—" I start, but he is talking at the same time, so neither one of us hears what the other tried to say.

"Sorry," I laugh. "You first?"

He nods. "My sister makes a good point." He's looking at me with no hint of a smile on his face. "I don't know if it's the best idea for you go to back to your place just yet."

I nod and look down at my hands. I'm clenching my fists in my lap, at war with fear and vulnerability deep inside. I don't know what to say or do.

"Chloe?" Franco's studying my face when I look up at him. "It's going to be okay," he promises.

I nod, but I need a little time with my thoughts. Rather than pretend I'm okay, I say exactly what I'm feeling. "It makes me feel really vulnerable to rely on you the way I need to right now. Can I just think for a minute?"

"Think? About what?" His eyes darken, and he frowns. "Are you thinking about going back home? To Pennsylvania?"

I shrug. I don't know. Maybe this is a sign I should.

"I just need to sort out my feelings," I say. "I'm scared. I'm stressed. I'm overwhelmed. I feel indebted to you for all you've done…" Tears sting my eyes, but I'm not sad. I'm not sure what I am. "It's all just a lot."

He nods and turns the truck on. We sit in front of The Body Shop for a few minutes, the engine idling, the radio off. Just two people together, each lost in thought. Finally, a loud grumble from my stomach breaks the tension.

"Sounds to me like it's dinnertime," Franco says with a grin. "Can I take you someplace? You mind Italian again?"

I think about how much money I have in my account and desperately wish I could buy him dinner to thank him for all he's done, but before I can protest, he says, "Don't worry. Where we're going, we eat for free."

"Your brother really named his restaurant after himself." It's not really a question, more an observation.

Benito's is this cute little place—surprisingly cute. The exterior looks like a house that's been converted into a restaurant. The parking lot is large, and based on how full it is even on a Tuesday night, he must have a successful business.

Franco laughs as he gets out of the truck. "That's my brother."

When we walk inside, I'm immediately greeted by a feeling just like the one I had at his parents' house.

"Franco." The hostess must be close to eighty.

Franco leans down and lets the hostess kiss his cheek. "Rita, this is Chloe. Ann's niece."

The woman turns her hands to me, holding her palms up like she wants to cup my face. I smile at her, unsure whether I should hug her, shake hands, or wait for her to pinch my cheeks. She gasps and shakes her head. "Chloe, well I'll be damned. You're a stunner." She elbows Franco and lifts a brow suggestively. "Keep her away from your brother," she advises.

Franco laughs, and I instinctively slip my hand into the crook of his elbow.

"Rita is Bev's mother," Franco explains.

"Bev is so nice," I say.

A couple comes in behind us, and Rita knows them, so she shoos us past her so she can seat the folks behind us. "It's their anniversary, so they have a reservation. Go have a drink at the bar, and I'll come get you when I have a table for you." Rita greets the couple with her arms outstretched, wishing them an overly loud happy anniversary.

My hand is still at Franco's elbow, but he angles himself so he can rest his hand at the small of my back. "Go ahead," he says.

I weave through the crowd of diners and find only one empty

stool at the bar. "I can stand," I say, but Franco's hand is already on the wooden seat as he pulls it out for me.

"What are you drinking?" he asks. "Have whatever you want."

The bartender is insanely hot. Like, I mean she could be a model beautiful.

"Holy smokes," I mumble under my breath. "I think I have a whole new respect for your brother."

Franco lifts a brow and leans closer to hear me.

"If I owned this place, I'd sleep with the bartender too," I say.

Franco's eyelids lower, a seductive, sleepy look like he's picturing me in bed with the gorgeous brunette. "There's more to you than meets the eye, Chloe." His voice is a sensual rasp against my ears, and the hairs on the back of my neck stand at attention.

I'm about to try to say something brilliantly witty when the gorgeous girl behind the bar spots Franco.

"Hey, handsome," she calls over the bar noise. "And who's this? I didn't know you had a girlfriend."

I open my mouth to correct her, but Franco leans over the bar and says, "This is Chloe." He introduces me to the girl whose name is Ashley, and without even taking our order, she sets down two glasses of ice water with a slice of lime on the rim.

She starts pouring alcohol into a shaker and then serves up two candy-apple-red drinks in short glasses. "On me," she says. "Enjoy."

Franco takes one of the drinks and hands the other to me. "You don't have to drink it," he says. "It's a negroni. Pure alcohol. Despite its festive color, it'll get you hammered quick."

Right now, that doesn't sound half bad.

We tap the rims of our glasses together, and I taste a small sip. "That is delicious," I tell him. "And strong."

What's more delicious than the negroni is the feel of Franco's thigh wedged against mine. He's standing beside my stool, his large form shoulder to shoulder with me so the people beside us have some elbow room.

We have hardly sipped our drinks when Benito comes running out front. He's dressed like he's cooking, wearing jeans and a white chef's jacket.

"Yo," he greets his brother with a chin lift and claps Franco on the back. "Hi, sweetheart," he says to me as though we've known each other for years and not days. "Ma's going to be over the fucking moon," he says, looking from me to Franco. "Her matchmaking has never worked before."

I can't tell if he's teasing or not because Franco smacks his brother on the back and then grabs my drink before motioning for me to follow him. I wave my thanks to Ashley. Her hands are full shaking another round of negronis, but she gives me a chin lift as I hop down off the stool.

Benito seats us himself, doesn't even give us menus. He just asks me if I have any food allergies or things I don't like. I shake my head, and he disappears, promising a meal I'll never forget.

Sassy is our server, and she keeps us going with an endless stream of conversation as she drops off course after course of food. By dessert, I don't think I can eat another bite, so I refuse the cornmeal cake, but Franco has Sassy pack it to go.

"Don't tell my brother I said this," Franco says under his breath, "but that damned cake is my favorite dessert of all time."

I raise my hand and call out, "Benito." But I say it quietly just to tease Franco like I'm going to give his secret away.

He grabs my hand by the wrist, and the moment changes, shifts from something playful to something very different. We swap a look that's both heated and awkward, and he slides his fingers away from my skin. I immediately miss his strength and heat.

Sassy reminds us the meal is on the house.

Franco hands Sassy her tip in cash and thanks her for the meal. Then he stands and kisses her cheek.

She fusses over me, and I realize she doesn't yet know about what happened at the shop—or at least, she isn't bringing it up.

"Am I taking you home with me?" he murmurs, his lips quirked in a smile.

I must be a little tipsy because I say exactly what's on my mind. "Only if you promise I don't have to sleep on the couch," I say.

I am momentarily horrified.

I mean, the man's opened his home to me, and I've just brazenly demanded what...that he sleep with me?

Share his bed?

Spoon me again until I feel his hard length against my bottom?

I feel the flush light up my cheeks, but that's nothing compared to how I feel when he leans down and whispers in my ear.

"Babe, you're not leaving my side tonight," he says with a sly grin, and for a moment...I'm hopeful for more than a hug.

CHAPTER ELEVEN

franco

We walk through the door of my place together like we're coming home. The feeling is unusual—no, it's more than that. It's fucking weird.

I've had plenty of women back to my place over the years, but never once has the person at my side felt like she belonged there. With me. I'm not sure whether to shake the feeling or embrace it.

I don't have to think long because as soon as we're in the door, we stand side by side taking off our boots. Chloe kicks hers off first and then steps up to me. She's looking me in the face, her sweet lower lip tucked between her teeth.

"Franco, I…"

I have no idea what she's thinking, but she rises on her toes and places a featherlight kiss against my cheek. "Thank you," she whispers, looping her arms around my neck. "For everything today."

I feel like she's moving back, stepping away from me, but I don't want to let her go. I circle my hands around her waist, and that seems to be the invitation she needs to stay right where she is. To come even closer, in fact. "You're…welcome," I manage as she flutters her eyelids shut and sways against me.

I don't know what else to say or how to navigate this. She's going to crash at my place again tonight; I think it's clear we both want that. But what is becoming even clearer is there's more we want from each other than company. More than this chaste thank-you kiss on the cheek.

Do we want more than *that*?

I think so, at least, but I admit I'm not entirely sure. "Are you tipsy?" I ask delicately, not wanting to insult her, but also not wanting to let anything happen when she isn't in a perfectly clear state of mind to make the decision.

Her eyes open, and she releases her hold on my neck. "No," she says.

I hold her tight around the waist. "I'm going to kiss you."

She widens her eyes and licks her lips. Her breath comes in little puffs, nervous and excited. The same as mine. She nods and lifts her face to mine, bringing her nose as close to mine as she can on tiptoe.

I brush my lips against hers, and her sweet, orange-scented breath fills my senses. But just a touch of those plush lips sends my cock into overdrive, and suddenly, my brain is no longer in control.

There is no thinking my way through this. No rational thought that's going to protect me from how complicated I know this is going to get.

For now, though, it's simple.

I want her, and I want her bad.

She tastes divine, and I open my mouth, exploring her depths with my tongue. She mewls against my lips, her hips pressing against my already stiff cock, and I know I'm fucked. Done for. This woman tastes like an angel and is hiding curves that I know were meant to be worshipped. I want to lay her out on my bed and taste every inch of her skin. I want to see her pussy, watch as I touch the trembling flesh. My body is in control now, and I'm just a helpless participant, following the demands of my desire for her.

Her hair is fisted between my fingers and her tits are crushed against my chest. "You want this?" I pant. "It's not too late to say no, and I'll take a cold shower and sleep on the—"

I can't even get the offer out before she's rasping, "I want this. I want you. If you want me, then God, Franco...please..."

While it's nowhere near as picture-perfect as it is in the movies, we kiss and grope and strip out of our clothes the entire stumbling walk up the stairs to my bedroom.

By the time we make it to the bed, Chloe's sweater is gone, and she's fumbling with the button on her cargo pants. I stop her with a hand.

"That's my job," I growl, looking pointedly at her body. "I'm going to take such good care of you."

I can see her entire body tremble under my gaze. Her nipples are so hard I can see the thick peaks just begging to be nibbled through the cups of her bra. She stands with her hands at her sides, looking like she has absolutely no idea what to do.

I shuck off my jeans and socks but leave on my boxer briefs. If I expose my cock just yet, that'll be it. Once my skin touches hers, there'll be no going back. And I want to take my time with this.

She stands there wide-eyed, her lips parted, those erect buds practically shredding through her bra. I close the space between us and lift her chin so our eyes meet, and I just look at her.

"You're beautiful, Chloe," I say, picking up a lock of her hair between two fingers. "And I want to see every inch of you."

She shivers, harder this time, but her eyes never leave mine. "You're unbelievable," she whispers. "Not like I don't believe you. I mean like, you're so gorgeous."

"Thank you, baby." I'm glad she likes what she sees, but right now, all I care about is how hungry I am for her.

I start with the button on her pants, unfastening it easily. Then I work the zipper down and urge the waistband away from her hips.

Chloe's got some curves to her, and I got just a taste of her last night when my dick cuddled up her ass like it was magnetically attracted.

She's wearing boy short-type underwear today, and I shove those down, exposing her trimmed mound. She gasps, a thrilling sound that's heavy with wanting. She clutches my bare shoulders as she steps out of the panties. I toss them aside and look at her. Her hair spills over her shoulders as her cheeks flush. I'm so goddamn hard, I want to get myself off fast so I can savor the experience and get hard again.

But no. I'm not going to blow in ten seconds like a kid. I'm going to take my sweet time, no matter how my dick protests.

She shivers and crosses her arms lightly over her chest.

I shove aside the blankets, and she dives into my bed headfirst, making me laugh. "There's so much more to you than meets the eye," I tell her. "You're serious and quiet, but you're not. You're funny and snarky and playful."

"I'm also really, really turned on," she adds.

I laugh again and climb in bed beside her. I tug the covers over her legs to warm her feet and lie on my side next to her. My raging hard-on knocks into the outside of her thigh as I tuck in closer. "Lie still."

She nods and lies on her back. Waiting. I haven't removed her bra yet, but I really want to take my time getting there.

I support my weight on one arm, so my other hand is free to stroke her collarbone and neck. I kiss her throat and her sternum, warming her body with my breath and heat until she squirms under my touch, and I know she's wanting more.

I trail my fingertips along the top of her bra cup, pressing lightly over the tip of her nipple that's desperately trying to break its way through the fabric to get to me. I pinch her softly, watching for her body's pleasure tell. She gasps and her legs quiver at the gentle pressure, so I try again, harder this time.

"Oh God," she pants.

Fuck. I haven't even touched her yet, and she's crying out to heaven? Chloe is going to be more fun than I've had in a long time.

I ease the cup away from one of her breasts, pushing the fabric down so her nipple peeks out. The rosy tip is dark, hard, and thick, and just seeing it makes me want to bite down and suck deep, but I start slow, licking and flicking the tender skin with the tip of my tongue. She weaves her fingers through my hair and presses my head closer, but I want to take my time. Watch her passion ratchet up until she's explosive.

I lift my head away from her breast and she whimpers in

displeasure, but she's quickly changing her tune as I lock my mouth on to that rosy bud and suck it deep into my mouth.

Her hips jerk and her hands are back in my hair as I work my tongue in leisurely circles around the dark areola, stopping only to nip the erect tip between my teeth and suck it long and hard into my mouth.

Her legs are quivering by the time I get to the other breast. I climb over her body, but instead of coming to rest on her other side, I anchor my weight above her as I straddle her hips. I grind lightly against her, and she rolls her eyes back in her head and slams her lids shut.

Her breasts are full, and I cup one in my hand, feeding her nipple into my mouth. I suck this side harder, leaving a wet mark and a faint pink color when I lift my mouth to check on her.

"This good?" I ask.

She slams her eyes open and grips the blankets between tight fingers. "Don't you dare freaking stop."

I laugh and leave her perfect nipples pointing at the ceiling, her bra cups shoved down near the band, as I move to the foot of the bed. I kneel beside her and run my fingers up and down her thighs, kneading the muscles until her mouth falls open and little purrs of pleasure escape from between her lips.

I gently open her legs. "I want to look at you," I say, warning her. I spread her knees wide and settle between her legs. I can see the tiny hairs on her thighs are pebbled and her fingers are still clenched tight, but she looks blissed out. With her nipples exposed and erect, I could sink myself deep and blow my wad in seconds, but I'm not sure I'm even going to fuck her. I'm having way too much fun exploring.

I palm both of her thighs on my way higher, then I scoot closer between her legs so I can see her pussy. With one hand, I smooth the trimmed hair, getting her used to my touch. She sighs until I take two fingers and stroke her drenched seam. She bucks against the mattress lightly, but I use my other hand on her belly to still her.

When I brush the right spot, she jerks and releases a moan that sends a bolt of electricity to my cock. I'm dripping at the tip now, my cock so fucking hard it's difficult to get comfortable on my belly, but I'm too focused on discovering all her buttons to stop. Her legs open even wider, and I encourage her.

"That's it," I say, the scent of her arousal making my mouth water.

I work my thumb in gentle circles, watching how she writhes beneath me, her thighs tense, her breathing ragged, and I work my fingers inside little by little. She's grinding her hips so hard, trying to draw me deeper inside, that she's practically slamming her body down on my fingers. But I want to be the one to bring her pleasure. I want to control when she comes, how hard, how long, so I can watch her fall apart and come back together.

"Open your legs wider," I tell her.

I don't move my hand from her pussy, but I use the other hand to lift the knee closest to me a little higher. She follows my lead, bending her knees so her feet are on the mattress and then letting her legs fall open.

I lower my face to her inner thigh and lick and kiss her while I stroke her clit with increasingly firm pressure. My fingers are soaked but nowhere near fully inside her yet, and she's jerking her hips rhythmically like she's chasing her own private high.

When I know she's close to spilling over the edge, I slide my fingers deep inside her and piston my arm so I can move in and out without ever fully taking my fingers from her body. My fingers are all the way inside, while my thumb works her clit, and together, my hand cups her sex and strokes and fucks her. I take my time, the only rush the one I'll get when I finally make her scream.

"Oh fuck, Franco."

She's off then, riding the wave, lost to the pleasure my fingers and mouth brought her. I can feel every spasm of her climax against my fingers and in my hair because she's grabbed my head with both hands as she thrashes beneath me.

She slows quietly and comes to a panting rest just as I gently pull my fingers from her pussy. She struggles to open her eyes, but she does, and I stare at her as I slide one finger and then the other into my mouth.

"I want to taste *you*," she says, quiet determination in her voice.

"I'm all yours. Do with me as you please."

I hold her in my arms for what seems like a second before she's up on her knees. She unclasps her bra and tosses it aside. My boxer briefs are off and chasing her bra into a corner of my room while she leans back on her heels.

"Franco," she says quietly, her voice fragile.

"Yeah?"

She swallows hard. "I mean... Everything I want to do with you... It's overwhelming. I want to ride you. I want to suck you. You're so freaking beautiful and sexy, and we hardly even know each other. Is this stupid fast? Or just like two people scratching an itch?"

I shrug one shoulder.

The words die in my throat as I feel her lips close over my shaft. And I'm suddenly not soft anymore.

CHAPTER TWELVE

chloe

Two Weeks Later

Franco is snoring lightly behind me. His body is entangled with mine. One arm is thrown over my naked torso, and our calves and thighs are knitted together in a leg-lock.

This feels so normal. So right.

Being with him like this is like nothing I've ever experienced. He feels like my person now. This feels like falling in love.

Every morning, I wake up convinced that last night was the *last* night. But mornings keep turning into nights, day after day, and here I am. Still sleeping in his bed. Still naked. And yet still feeling the pressure of time passing.

My tummy flips over, knowing it's time for this fairy tale to come to an end. I have to return to my apartment, pay my rent, and go back to my own life.

I slide out from underneath him, carefully moving his limbs off me so I don't wake him. I need coffee. I need to spend some time thinking about the future. For us. For me. For the bookstore...for everything.

I sigh deeply as I'm making us coffee.

"What's wrong?" he asks, walking into the kitchen as he scratches at his chest.

"Nothing."

He raises an eyebrow as his eyes rake over me. "Nothing?" he repeats, sliding an arm around my middle to pull me into a hug. "That sigh means something."

I shrug a shoulder, not wanting to talk about the mix of emotions I'm feeling. I've already overstayed my welcome. One night turned into two, which then turned into a week, and here we are— two weeks later.

"Dinner at my parents' tomorrow?" he asks. The question is casual, but his voice is not.

My heart catches in my chest, and I measure the grounds carefully because there is a slight shake in my hand. "I'd love to go," I say. "But that would be the fourth weekend in a row. The first time your parents invited me and then the last two you brought me with you. Don't you think your family might start to get ideas about…"

I trail off because there is no us. I mean, of course there isn't. But now could be the right time to ask.

"What do you think?" I click on the coffee to brew and join him at the table.

"I think my ma is onto us. She suspects at least." He rubs his forehead just as there's a knock at the door. A loud one. "Fuck," he mutters.

I'm dressed in one of Franco's tank tops, no bra, and wearing just my underwear on the bottom. He's shirtless and in his pajama pants.

"There's only one person who pops by at this hour. You think my ma's going to believe we just had a sleepover?"

I frantically look toward the door. If he didn't seem so unnerved by this, I wouldn't be either. But he's giving off very strong vibes.

He's most definitely not ready for there to be an "us."

I leap up and reassure him. "I'll go get dressed."

Before he says anything, I bound upstairs. I hear the door unlock, and Lucia's voice carries through the house.

"Ma, I already told you. I'm renting. I don't even know if the landlord would allow it."

I quickly make Franco's bed and scan the bedroom for any signs of sex. A wave of deep sadness fills my chest as I realize what I'm up here doing. I'm hiding.

I gather all my things from the bathroom and pack up my bags. I fold the extra blankets and pillows and stack everything.

Then, I wait.

Lucia has to know I'm here.

My car is parked in Franco's driveway.

Damn.

I'm all packed up and sitting on the edge of Franco's bed when he plods upstairs. He notices me just sitting there and cocks his chin.

"What's going on?" he asks, looking around the room, until his eyes land on my bags.

I give him a stiff smile. "I need to get back to my aunt's. The rent is due today. I've spent plenty of time squatting at your place. It's time we get back to normal."

The fairy tale has gone on far too long. Longer than I should've allowed it, because now, I'm afraid my heart can't handle life without him in it.

He scrubs a hand over his chin and nods. "Whatever you want, babe." He looks like he wants to say more, but he just asks, "Are you planning on coming to dinner tomorrow night?"

I stand and shake my head slowly. "You've all hosted me for long enough. I should get back to my place, restock the fridge, and clean. There has to be a thick layer of dust by now."

"What's that mean?"

"It's dirty."

He shakes his head. "About the hosting?"

I glance down at my feet, feeling more uneasy and sadder than I thought possible. "I'm going to skip a week. Let you guys have a family meal without me."

He smiles, but the light doesn't reach his eyes. His lips are tight, and he's got a fist clenched over his chest. "Whatever you want,

Chloe. Will I see you at the install tomorrow? Vito and his buddies were planning on being at your shop around eight."

I nod. "Absolutely. And you'll see me at Easy Start on Monday."

This feels absolutely horrific. Way worse than what I'd imagined. He's not asking me to stay. He's not asking to see me again. He's not saying much of anything.

It was just sex, Chloe, I remind myself. Franco is gorgeous and probably has lots of flings like this.

We hardly know each other. I have to remind myself that this didn't mean to him what it did to me. Just because I've been more real and more open doesn't mean that what's happening in my heart is happening in his.

My legs feel weak, but I stand and give Franco my most sincere smile. "Thank you so, so much for all you've done." I laugh and there are tears behind it, so I can't let it go on too long. "You're..." I trail off because I can't finish without crying.

He knows what he is. I'm the one who doesn't know what she is. Not anymore. He only helped me see a side of myself that I want to develop. And for that, I am truly thankful.

I want to touch him, throw myself against that bare chest and thank him, but I know if I smell him again, the musk and cologne of his skin against mine, I will start sobbing. So I don't. I grab my things in a rush and try to brighten my voice to cover the quivering.

"So, this was fun," I say a little too maniacally as I grab my bags.

I lug my things down the stairs, and Franco stays at the top, just watching me.

"Five-star review. Would highly recommend."

The coffee I made is untouched in the kitchen, which I notice as I'm frantically scouring the counter for my keys.

"Don't forget to turn off the coffee!" I yell, reminding him because his memory is shit when it comes to things like appliances. "Will you be there tomorrow?" I ask. "At the shop." But then I realize that sounds like I'm asking him to see me again, and I don't want to pin him down. Don't want to assume. "No worries either way."

I find my keys, and with Franco still at the top of the stairs looking down, I slide into my boots. "See you soon," I call out awkwardly, hustling out the front door.

And that's all the goodbye I can manage. I tug the door closed behind me, throw my stuff in my trunk, and get into my car. And by some miracle, I am able to keep the tears from flowing until I pull away.

CHAPTER THIRTEEN

franco

I knew letting her go would be a mistake.

But I did nothing to stop her because I'm an idiot and somehow convinced myself she needed space.

I've parked my truck outside Latterature, but it's early. Way too early. It looks like I'm here before Chloe, and anxiety spikes through my chest. I'm worried, first and foremost, because after she left in such a rush yesterday, I didn't hear from her. Not a call, not a text. Not a damn word.

I rake a hand through my hair and check my phone for the millionth time. I hardly slept a wink last night, wondering if she'd made it home safe. If her place was okay. If she was able to sleep. If she missed being with me.

We'd talked plenty about her going back to Ann's to pay the rent in the days before it was due. What we never talked about was what it all meant. What we'd do after she bought herself another month in Ann's place.

Ann's place. Yeah, I say that because it doesn't feel right calling it Chloe's place. The last couple weeks, I've been acting as though Chloe's place is with me.

But is it?

I've got to admit, something in me panicked and shut down hard when my ma showed up yesterday.

She absolutely knows I've been with Chloe. There's no way she *can't* know. And although we've kept things cool around my family, bringing Chloe to two family dinners... That was a first. A first that I assured myself was fine, didn't mean anything. But when Ma showed up, acting like she did, I started freaking out. And my level of freak-out boiled over like a pot filled to the top with water when Ma told me why she'd dropped in yesterday.

As usual, I hadn't been answering my phone—because *sex*—so Ma stopped by my place yesterday to see *Chloe*, not me.

I see the lights go on in the shop, so I get out of the truck and jog up to the store. I knock lightly on the door. I see soft shadows under Chloe's eyes when she looks up at me. She looks like she got as little sleep as I did, but she smiles at me as she unlocks the door and lets me in.

"Hey," I say softly, wanting nothing more than to touch her.

Her face falls completely as she peers over my shoulder.

"Hey, asshole." Vito claps me on the back as he walks up behind me. "Chloe." His voice is so sweet when he says her name. "This is Evan."

She smiles at them both, her eyes never meeting mine. "You're right on time. Thanks for coming," Chloe replies as they get closer.

Right away, Evan gives Chloe a look that makes me want to tear the eyes from his head.

Breathe, Franco.

Chloe asks Evan if they need her for anything because she'd like to go into the kitchen and make us all coffee and some breakfast. She writes down the Wi-Fi password and network name she'd like to use, and my brother gets to work setting up her new router.

Within a few hours, she'll have wireless internet for the store, a tablet for ringing up customers, and a basic security system.

She'll be all set.

She won't need me.

Not anymore.

I wander the stacks while Evan and Vito look at the wiring and drill mounts for the camera heads into the walls and ceiling. Honestly, I don't even know why I'm here. I'm useless at electronic shit.

And other than supervising to make sure my shithead brother and his friend do what, technically, I'm paying them to do, there's no point in me being here.

It's Sunday, and we're all going to Ma's for dinner in a couple hours. I may as well go home, go for a run. Go work out in the garage. I could go anywhere, but here is the only place I want to be.

I pull a book from the shelves and drop into one of the old chairs to skim through it. The words swim in front of my eyes. All I can think about is Chloe. I hear her voice as she chats with Vito and Evan, answering their questions. I'm lost in thought when I feel her hand on my shoulder.

"I made you a coffee." She is smiling at me, no judgment in her voice at all, but the sadness on her face makes me sure she's as confused or hurting as I am.

"Are you charging those assholes for their drinks?" I take the coffee from her with a grin. "No freebies. Not even for family."

She looks a little confused by that, and I realize it was the wrong thing to say. Maybe she thinks I'm suggesting she and I are family? I've got to get my fucking boot dislodged from my mouth before I say something that can't be taken back.

"Shush. I'd better see if Vito and Evan need me," she says softly.

"Wait." I stand and put a hand on her arm. She turns to me, and I set the cup of coffee on the chair. "I've been telling you not to hide from me, and I've been hiding from you. No, maybe from myself." I scrub a hand through my hair and shake my head. "I never should have let you leave yesterday without talking."

"Yo." My brother's voice echoes through the store, and I wince. He's calling out to Evan to hold the ladder, and I realize this is not the time or the place to have this talk.

"Can I see you?" I ask. "We need to talk."

She nods. "Why don't you come to my place after dinner? Or you can call me."

I feel like the tiny voice she's using means she's afraid I'm going to let her down, break her heart. That maybe the phone option was a way to let me off easy—or maybe make it easier on her.

"No phone," I say. "I want to look you in the eye and be real with you. Even if it's not easy. Can we do that?"

She nods again, and a wave of absolute pain washes over me. I don't want sad Chloe. I don't want her braced for the bad news that isn't going to come. I want the spunky, awkward, sweet woman who demanded hugs from my self-serve comfort bar. Maybe she's become the comfort bar for me now.

"Can I kiss you?" I ask. "A hug, anything? I don't like how we left things. I want to make it right."

She parts her lips and grins. "Are you trying to proposition me in my own store? My aunt will turn over in her grave."

"This isn't about sex," I growl and tug her to my chest. I hold her against me and breathe in her hair. She smells different today, like a vanilla candle with something tropical, maybe pineapple. I don't care if she smells like the city dump after a fire. Once my arms are around her, I'm sure I never want to let her go.

"Latterature's got a kick-ass security system—bam!" Vito pounds against the dinner table, making the plates and flatware clank.

"For fuck's sake, V." Benny nearly spills the glass of red wine he was pouring and shoots our brother a dark look.

Ma and Pops glare at Vito, but then my ma nods. "I'm glad. That robbery..." She shakes her head and shivers, then makes the sign of the cross over her forehead and heart. "I've got a daughter who works on that street and a future daughter-in-law, God willing, to be concerned about."

When she says future daughter-in-law, all eyes at the table fly to me.

"Oooooh," Benito teases. "Did Ma's matchmaking finally work on you, Franco? I call dibs on best man."

Vito's about to start his bullshit when Gracie speaks up. "She's talking about me, you dumb fuck. Chloe and I are very happy together, thank you very much."

Pops holds both hands as if surrendering. "I love my children whether they are gay, straight, or whatever."

All four of us kids look at my dad with expressions that range from shock to amusement. He shoves his reading glasses onto his hair and shrugs.

"What's whatever?" Ma asks, looking incredibly concerned, like she's ready to run out and make sure whoever this person is, they are happy and content in their life. That's one thing I can say about Mario and Lucia. They are unwaveringly supportive. When Vito wanted to marry a stripper, all they cared about was if he was happy.

My dad lifts his silver brows and shrugs. "Whatever they want to be, as long as they're happy."

I polish off my pasta and salad as they start to bicker about happiness, then get up to clear my plate. I'm in the kitchen rinsing my dish under the faucet when I feel a hand at my back.

"Son." Ma stands behind me, her eyes worried and her lips drawn. "You've been very quiet tonight. And I notice Chloe didn't join us for family dinner. I've been almost sick all evening thinking I did something to come between you two. I shouldn't have shown up the way I did today. I'm sorry, baby. I…"

I turn and face my mom, but all the fire has gone out of my frustration and anger at her meddling. Now I'm just curious.

"When you first tried to set me up with Chloe…" I say, leaning my ass against the sink. "Why? Why her, Ma? Is she just someone who was there?"

My mom is quiet for a minute. She's wearing a new color lipstick today, which is unusual. I make a note to ask her about it. It's a softer color, and I don't remember her ever wearing light colors. Ma's usually bold and dramatic in everything she does, from nails to hair to lips.

"You know Ann and I were very close," she says, and I nod. "And I don't know how to explain it. I just had a feeling, Franco. When I first met Chloe, I knew she was supposed to be part of our family. I never considered anything but introducing her to you. Not Benny or Vito. I just thought she would be perfect for you. It was like I could see it, and I never questioned it. But I'm sorry if I came on too strong or brought you any trouble."

Ma looks genuinely apologetic, but none of this is really her fault. That falls squarely on me.

"You're a buttinski, and I love you." I lean down to kiss my mother's cheek. "What's up with the lipstick? It's different, but I like it."

She scowls and raises one of those brows at me dramatically. She shakes her head as she sighs. "Carol. That woman. I wish she'd just get over things with Earl and at least go back to work at Easy Start. She's doing everything she can to make some money for herself, including selling this makeup now. She did makeovers on all us girls." Ma cups her belly as she laughs. "Wait till you see Sassy. Carol tried to get all of us to do this dewy, natural look the kids are doing. We all looked like we were sweating. And these stripes on the nose the girls are doing now?" Ma takes two fingers and pretends to draw lines on either side of her nose. "Have you seen that? Like I want to change the shape of this schnoz at my age? What's a little brown stuff gonna do? Anybody within a mile would see me and this thing coming. Why would I spend an hour dab-dab-dabbing all around my nose?"

I laugh. "I think that's called contouring, Ma."

"Contour, schmontour. I bought some of the crap she's selling just to support her, but this—" she points to her lips "—this tiger won't be changing the color of her stripes for very long."

We laugh, but then I grow serious. "So, are you saying you think Carol should get back with Earl? I thought she was off on some new path with Ray?"

"Well, I was talking about her job, specifically," my mom says. "I have opinions about the situation with Earl."

I cross my arms over my chest, bracing myself for Ma's opinions, but she suddenly goes silent. "Ma?" I urge, lifting my brows at her. "You said you have opinions?"

"Son, you know how I feel about divorce."

"Necessary evil." I'm well aware of the fact that Ma takes her wedding vows seriously, and that she feels others should as well. But when the circumstances are harmful, she's fully in support of people doing what they need to be safe. Happiness, though, is another story.

She nods. "I've started to consider other perspectives," she says. "You know I love Earl. He's a good man, and he loves Carol and Jack. Has always been a good provider. As far as I know, and I think I would know—Carol doesn't have a private bone in her body—he's never been unfaithful."

I nod, wondering where this is going. I know Earl is a good man and my mother is a good woman. If she's changing her perspective on marriage, I'm curious to see how. And even more curious to know why.

She looks at me with a strange twist to her lips and a scowl in her brow.

"Ma?" I press. "What is it?"

She looks like she's debating whether or not to say anything, but then she blurts it all out in a rush. "Earl doesn't satisfy Carol sexually. Like, not at all. I don't think she's ever, in all their years of marriage, had an orgasm with him."

"Sweet baby Jesus," I groan. "Ma, the man's my boss. I don't need to know—"

"You asked," she snaps. "And Ray Morris, God bless his little— well, I guess it's not so little, to hear Carol talk."

"Ma, I love you, but can we fast-forward to the point?"

She smiles and shakes her head. "I've been pretty rigid in my beliefs most of my life. But I never had a reason to see things differently. Marriage is forever, and unless someone's drinking or violent or something else…"

Hearing that makes me think of what Chloe told me about her parents. Her father was both, and yet her mother stayed. And it cost her mother close ties with her family.

"When Carol first left Earl, I thought she was being foolish. I called her selfish. To her face." Ma's voice cracks a bit on that admission. "But then Carol opened up. Broke down. You know she had that precancerous polyp removed last year, and…"

I almost tune out because if there is one thing I don't want to hear about right after dinner, it's my mother's friends' polyp stories. "Ma."

"All right, all right, just you wait. You get to my age, and everybody's got stuff, son. Anyway, she realized that if she died, she'd have spent her whole life married to a good man. And there's not a thing in the world wrong with that. But Carol said she wanted a great love. Before it was too late to find it." She blots a tear from her eye with the back of her hand. "And I don't know if she'll have some great romance with Ray, but who the heck am I to judge? I've had it all with your father."

She reaches out and touches my arm. "Anyway, are you all right, son? I shouldn't have just popped over this morning either. It wasn't right of me."

"I'm great," I tell her. "Ma, I wouldn't change anything about you. I want you in my life. Although, maybe in the future, give me a few hours to reply before you show up." I hold her close and tight, pressing down her helmet of hair with a loud kiss. "I love you, Ma. You have nothing to apologize for."

I'm heading out of the kitchen when Ma calls after me.

"Yeah?" I turn back to see Ma standing at the sink looking concerned. "I think Chloe should have Mama Dog. I talked to Bev about letting her adopt if she can get the okay from Ann's landlord. I know she doesn't have a yard at that place, but I'd feel a lot better if she had a security system or a good, strong dog with her in that apartment."

I'm not sure why Ma's telling me this, but I nod. "Sounds like a good suggestion. You should tell her," I say, but I'm not being shitty about it. No matter what happens between Chloe and me, my family has to develop their own relationships with her. Without lodging my ass right between them.

Ma nods as if she understands. Maybe Ma will tone down her meddling a bit, but I wouldn't want her to completely walk away from us kids. Balance. It looks like my mom is actively practicing balance. "I'll give her a call this week," she says. "I was hoping she'd come to dinner tonight, but…" She looks like she's about to launch into a lecture or an apology, so I give her a smile.

"Ma, it's all good. I've got to run."

She nods, a smile on her face, and I stop at the table to give my dad and siblings goodbye kisses. Benny already left without saying goodbye or clearing his plate, I notice, and Vito and Gracie are arguing about something, while my pops shakes his head.

"You want to take one or two of these idiots with you?" Pops asks good-naturedly.

I kiss him goodbye and head out before anyone can drag me into a fight or send me off with leftovers. I've got someplace I want to be.

CHAPTER FOURTEEN

chloe

A knock at the door wakes me from a deep sleep. I squint and check my phone.

Damn.

Three missed texts from Franco.

"I'm coming!" I shout, clearing the sleep from my eyes.

I barely slept a wink my first night back here at Aunt Ann's. I was so terrified of being here alone. Not to mention heartsick at being *anyplace* without Franco.

I doubt I slept for two hours last night. After the excitement of getting the security system installed at my shop, I came back here, changed into something comfy, sat down on my couch to read, and wham.

I check the peephole and see Franco's worried stare through the fisheye.

I quickly open the door to let him in and ignore the butterflies in my stomach.

"Hi," I say. "I'm sorry I missed your texts. I fell asleep on the couch and slept like the dead."

He looks me over, from my sleep-messed hair to what I'm

wearing. His emotions are all over his face—concern, relief, and then amusement.

"I'm just glad you're okay," he says. "I mean, you are okay, right?"

I nod. "Come on in." I'm wearing only shorts and a loose tank top, so the last thing I need is to give the neighbors a show.

He comes in, and I lock the door. "Did you want anything to drink?" I ask. "I'm going to go change."

He grabs my arm and tugs me close. "Don't change," he says, his voice low.

"You like my tank?" I tease. It's one of his. I didn't mean to steal it, but in my rush to gather up my clothes, one of his tanks—no doubt discarded hastily while we were stripping off our clothes—got tangled up with mine. "I was planning to return it. I accidentally packed it, and…well, it smells like you."

If he's not catching the vibe I'm throwing, then I know we're over. I can't be any more obvious without coming out and saying exactly how I feel.

At my admission, he lowers his chin to the top of my head and holds me against his chest. He breathes deeply. "How is it possible to miss someone so much? I just saw you this morning."

Yes.

Everything inside me starts to tingle in excitement.

I wrap my arms around his waist and close my eyes. I can smell the garlic and tomato lingering in his clothes from dinner with his parents. But deeper, on my second intake of air, it's all him.

My legs go weak, and we just hold each other, arms tight, no words needed between us.

I'm the one who finally breaks the hug. In just a thin tank and paper-thin shorts, my body is throwing a fit that all I'm doing is hugging this man.

But he's here to talk.

I need to eliminate my distracted libido from this conversation.

I lace my fingers through his, and we sit on my aunt's couch side by side. Then I grab the crocheted afghan I was sleeping under, my favorite of hers, a soft dusty-pink shell pattern, and cover myself up to my chin.

"No distractions," I explain. "I want to be focused on our talk."

He laughs, and we each scoot to separate ends of the couch. We put our feet together on the middle cushion so at least our legs are close.

"Ma tells me you might want Mama Dog," I say. "Is that your idea or hers?"

Oh God. He starts right in on it, doesn't he? "Well," I say. I nibble my lower lip and try to think how to say this without really saying it. But then I figure, nope. Honesty. For better or worse, I'm putting my truth out there. "I do want the dog. I know it's crazy, but I sort of hoped if there was something here—" I wave between him and me "—that I could use your yard for her sometimes. I mean, that's if I can get the landlord to approve her here."

Even as I say the words, I know they aren't entirely true, so I walk it back.

"God, that's not it either. Not really." I look the man on my couch in the face and decide for real this time, I'm putting myself out there. "Franco, I…" I look down at my hands. "I know it's fast," I say, "but I'm falling for you. And I… I… I'm…I'm gonna shut up now. I think I've said enough."

Chickenshit.

I'm rambling like an absolute teenager, but God, if that's not what this feels like. I bite my lip to stop myself from professing all my needs.

He quietly gets up from the couch. He doesn't say anything. He just paces and clenches his hands into fists. Paces and clenches.

I rush on to fill the silence between us. "I get it, Franco. You're not in the same place as me. And like I said, it's all happening so, so fast. You've done a lot for me the last couple of weeks, and I have been so happy. Really happy. With you. You gave me a reason to stay in Star Falls, you know? But if you don't feel the same, I understand. It's okay. Maybe this isn't where I'm supposed to be after all."

He stops pacing and looks at me. "You can't make that decision because of me, Chloe." His voice is low. "You need to choose the life you want for yourself. Whether or not I'm in it, I don't want you to stay and run your aunt's business if that's not really what you want. And if you're not sure…"

"What do you want?" I ask, tucking the blanket tighter around my body. This is a hard conversation to have without any real clothes on. "Like, really want, Franco? We haven't talked much about your past dating life or if you want to settle down with someone. Have a family…" I swallow against the sudden dryness in my mouth. "You can have anything you want," I remind him.

Please say me. Please.

He sighs and rubs his fingers along his forehead. The hair has flopped down out of its perfect style, and he looks torn. "It's not… It's not that…" He starts pacing again.

I get up off the couch.

Tonight is about our words.

Our heads.

Our hearts.

"I'm falling in love with you," I say simply. "I'm sure of it. I've never felt this way about anyone before. And I know it's too fast. Maybe to you it was an easy fling. Something that was fun while you were helping me out. And that's okay. I'll be okay." I put a hand on his sleeve, trying hard to keep my touch light. As much as I want to be brave, to be strong, standing here in underwear and his tank top pouring out my feelings feels horribly vulnerable. Horribly exposed.

But I think about who I want to be. The life I want to have. I'm not sure if Star Falls is going to be home for me. I'm not sure that I want my aunt's store and apartment and her things. I want my own life. Not a hand-me-down. Franco is the very first thing I've ever chosen for myself. Asked for. I have to be okay if he doesn't want me too. I just have to be.

Franco swallows, and I watch the knob in his throat move. His plush lips, so kissable and soft and full, pinch together. He's still not talking. Still not opening up to me.

That's answer enough for me. I don't just want to own my own truth. I want to be worthy of his.

"Were your parents ever happy?" he asks. He sounds young. Almost meek.

I shake my head. "Not that I ever knew or saw. I mean, I suppose when they were young, right? They had to be for a time. Why?"

He stalks back to the couch and takes his place at the far end. "I've never known anyone like my parents. Anyone who got a happily ever after."

I nod. I understand that. "I want that," I tell him. "But it only works when both people want it and work toward it together."

"What if we don't?" he asks. "What if someday you wake up and think, fuck, why this guy? I want a guy who reads. A guy who knows all the book stuff I love so much. That's never going to be me, Chloe. I read, yeah, but your life is a bookstore. Someday you might think I'm fucking stupid. Beneath you."

I shrug. "I don't know why that would happen. I don't think that now. And as far as I can tell, most of the time, the truth is something we either embrace or ignore. Unless it's hidden from us so we can't really face it. You've been open about what you read, and that hasn't changed how I feel about you. So, if you're not hiding anything and I'm not ignoring what you really are…"

He nods, but he looks unsettled. He's fidgeting on the couch, so I sit up and let the blanket of armor fall away again.

"Tell me," I say gently. "Are you afraid of the future and what might change? Or are you not sure what you feel right now?"

"I know exactly what I feel, and I…" His eyes shimmer, becoming even more intense. "I don't understand it. A month ago, my life was perfect. I had everything I could want. I had my shit together. But then you and those shitkicker boots come to Star Falls, and all of a sudden, everything changes."

"Changes how?" I ask. "I mean, staying with you was a lot. I get that. And I'm sorry."

His expression darkens. "I'm sorry about yesterday, babe. I was freaked out." He shakes his head and sighs, letting out a huge chest full of tension. I can see his shoulders lower. "My mother came to my place looking for you. She thought you'd already moved in and wanted to offer to help you clear out Ann's things."

"She did?" No wonder the poor guy freaked out.

We haven't even had five minutes to talk about what this is, let alone have it on family blast.

He nods. "I'm sorry, though. I shouldn't have let you leave like that. I shouldn't have let you spend the night here last night without even checking in on you. I couldn't even send a fucking text."

"I'm a grown woman, Franco. If anything was wrong, I have options now. A phone. Gas in my car. And the numbers of everyone in your family." I chuckle at that. "I might have ended up on Lucia's couch, but I wouldn't have been alone or in danger."

"I don't want you calling them when you need something," he growls. "I want to be the one you go to. Wake up to. Sleep with. I mean, next to…as well as the other stuff."

We both smile, and the air between us crackles with possibility.

"It's been two weeks, and it's like I don't even know myself anymore," he says, his voice faraway. "But the weird part is, I've never felt more like myself. You make my life feel whole. What did I have before? It's like I was just killing time. Waiting for you."

My mouth falls open because I'm not sure I heard him right. "Really?"

He nods. "Yes, really. I haven't laughed, worried, or had fun in an entire relationship with someone else like I have with you these past two weeks. It's terrifying. Like, what the hell was I doing before?"

"Practicing?" I offer. "Probably mostly practicing sex. You're really good at it now, though. Good enough I think you only need to do it with me from now on."

He laughs. "Two weeks, man, that's nothing. The blink of an eye."

"It is something," I correct him. "It's the start of forever."

310

CHAPTER FIFTEEN

franco

"I like the way that sounds," I admit. "Too much."

Chloe crawls across the couch on her hands and knees. "Can we take 'too much' out of your vocabulary, please? I don't think there's any such thing as too much when it comes to this. To us."

I watch as she settles herself on her heels, the blanket falling down around her hips.

"I don't expect a proposal, Franco," she says. "I need to repay what I owe you. Get the shop back on its feet. If it's even possible. There's still a chance I can't bring in enough to keep the store."

"What will you do if that happens?" I ask.

I am not ready to hear her say she'll leave, but the more I admit to myself that I want this, that I want her, the more I realize I have to accept that none of this is in my control.

She could close Latterature and leave Star Falls. Or ask me to come with her. Things are getting even messier. I hate messy. I hate multitasking.

I've never been good at complexity.

Could I have sorted out the paperwork at the shop myself if I spent enough time and focus? Probably. But that's just not how I'm

311

wired. I'm not good at solving puzzles, finding paperwork, and apparently, I'm not very good at navigating complicated feelings.

I like things simple, direct, honest.

Things with Chloe are anything but that. But a part of me wonders if I'm the one making things so messy.

"What are you thinking?" She reaches across my outstretched legs and cups my chin.

"You renewed the lease here?" I ask.

I'm not good with this many moving parts. My mind feels fuzzy, and my hands curl up in impatience. I don't know what the fuck has gotten into me. Maybe I'm the reason I've never been able to date anyone seriously.

Fucking and fun are simple.

Feelings, especially feelings like this, plans and thoughts about the future, I realize now, are not.

"I paid for the next month," she tells me. "I'll barely be home though."

"What do you mean?" I ask. "You're leaving? Going someplace?"

She nods and releases my chin. "I called my mom last night. She asked me to come home for a bit. She had some really good suggestions about the store, actually. I think I'm going to spend the next few weeks until I leave getting the shop redesigned. I'll have a grand reopening on Black Friday and see if I can start to turn a profit. So, between being at the bookstore and my mom's, I won't be home much."

That's a really smart idea. Main Street does a booming business for the holidays. Even the tattoo shop rolls out specials and giveaways. Foot traffic increases, and a lot of residents buy local to support their neighbors, as opposed to buying gifts online or driving into Cleveland to shop at the big malls.

"Will you be here for Thanksgiving?"

"I get back a few days before," she confirms, crawling over my legs. "But I'll be getting the shop ready for Black Friday. I think it's going to take more work than I even realize."

I spread my legs wide, and she settles between them, leaning her back against my chest.

"So here's what I think," she says. "I think you should help me name my dog." She lifts her face and looks at me over her shoulder. "I'm sure your mom will watch her while I go home for a few days. And since the shop will be closed the next few weeks, I'll be able to move furniture and do some reorganizing with a furry little companion to keep me company. Assuming my landlord says yes."

I like the sound of that. I like the sound of all of it. "If he doesn't, we'll sic my mother on him. Lucia doesn't take no for an answer, in case you hadn't noticed."

She laughs, and the sound is happy again. Free. "Come on. Let's think of dog names."

"Something tells me you've already thought of one," I say.

She nudges me in the ribs with her elbow. "What do you think I picked?"

I don't have the faintest idea, but I'm going to have fun guessing. "Cliterature," I say. "After two of your favorite things."

She gasps in shock but then bursts into hysterical giggles. "Rude," she says. "The clit should be one of your favorite things, not mine."

"Oh," I tell her, "it is. *Yours* is." I kiss the top of her hair and keep guessing. "Captain Saucy Pants McGoo?"

She lifts a brow at me and scowls. "Now you're being ridiculous. Cliterature was better."

I wrap my arms around her waist and rest my chin against the top of her hair. "So," I say, "tell me. What are you thinking about naming Mama Dog?"

"Well." She scoots her bottom even closer to my crotch, sending my dick a message it doesn't want to ignore. "I was thinking Mia."

"Feminine for mine in Italian?" I ask.

She nods slightly, my head bobbing with hers. "Kind of a perfect symbol for what I'm building here. Something that's mine. My choices. My dog. My protection. My new life."

I swallow against the sudden rush of emotion that clogs my

throat worse than a plume of diesel exhaust to the face. It surprises me, but it shouldn't. Everything about Chloe is thoughtful and sweet. I clear my throat and rub at my nose. "That's beautiful. Perfect."

"You're beautiful," she says. "And perfect in my eyes. Well, maybe not perfect. But I like you a whole lot."

"Hey." I lift my chin from the top of her head and angle my neck so I can nuzzle her ear. "I like you a whole lot too," I whisper. "And I missed you last night."

She turns on the couch to face me. "I missed you too," she says. "Did we solve anything?"

"All of it," I tell her, leaning forward to hold her face with a hand. I stroke the plush lower lip with my thumb and look into her clear green eyes. "Welcome to Star Falls, baby," I say. "It looks like you've finally come home."

She blinks fast and grins before physically throwing her body against mine. And God, when we kiss... The feeling is exactly like coming home.

Before I know what she's doing, she's unbuttoning my jeans and urging me to lift my hips. She helps me shake off the denim and my boxer briefs. Once I'm stripped of my clothes, she settles herself between my thighs and caresses my legs with her fingertips while blowing hot kisses against my bare, hard shaft.

I'm so hot for her, I'm nearly shaking with desire. No matter how complicated plans are, these feelings are simple, and I relish them.

Being with Chloe like this is like riding my motorcycle. Easy, free, the flight and the wind and the speed so intoxicating that everything else seems irrelevant.

My pulse thunders as I watch her kneel on the carpet so she can get a better angle on my erection. She flicks the tip of her tongue against the underside of my head, softening and flattening her tongue as she lavishes attention on my dick.

She strokes my sac, fingering the tight seam between them in the way that makes the air fly from my lungs. My legs are tight and loose at the same time, the tension in my sac drawing my balls tight as she finally takes my whole cock into her mouth.

She hums along my length, then uses one hand to add friction and pressure to the licks and kisses.

Sucking me in deep, she pauses to peek up at me, and my heart nearly shatters at how gorgeous she is. Her nipples are so hard, and the one that popped past the fabric of the tank before now knows the escape route, and it slips out again, begging for attention.

I reach down and twist the erect bud between my fingers, saying a silent prayer of thanks that she has such sensitive nipples. When I'm super close to coming, I shift my hips slightly and grab her hands.

"Get on," I demand. "Ride me, baby."

She leaves the tank top on but shimmies out of her panties. She looks at me, her lids heavy, her lips parted, and steps close enough to the couch that with the slightest bend of her knees, she'll be able to line up her pussy directly over my cock.

"Chloe," I growl. "What are you doing?"

"I have ideas," she says thoughtfully.

"You haven't had an idea yet that I didn't love."

She reaches over to my hand and moves it so my fingers are on my dick. "Hold, please," she says playfully. "I'll be right back."

I fist my dick and stroke it lightly to keep it hard, but unless she's gone for several minutes, I'm in no danger of losing my arousal. I watch her bare ass cheeks peek from beneath my tank as she trots into her bedroom. She's back in seconds, holding something behind her back.

"Franco," she says, a glimmer in her eye, "say hello to my now ex-boyfriend. We probably will keep, like, a friends-with-benefits situation, but for the most part, you're his replacement."

What she's holding in her hands sends a thrill of excitement through my body. At the same time, I'm curious and intrigued. "Hello, little man," I say, my voice husky with need. "You can go fuck yourself because Chloe's got me for that now."

She fiddles with the buttons on the matte purple silicone, and it starts to buzz softly as it vibrates on a low setting.

"This is for both of us."

I raise an eyebrow.

She stands in front of me and sticks the tip of the purple dick in her mouth. Okay, fuck. That's hot. Her eyes flutter closed, and she licks the toy, but not in a demonstrative way. This is utilitarian. She wets it with her mouth and then widens her legs and moves the toy beneath the hem of my tank. She holds up the hem so I can see her run the wet tip of the vibrator along her clit. She focuses her efforts and drops the hem so I can't see everything she's doing, but I can tell by the way her lips part and her eyelids struggle to stay open that she's pleasuring herself.

"I thought you said I put that asshole out of business," I grumble, but I'm definitely enjoying the show.

She smiles and pulls the thing away from her body, then kneels above my lap and lowers herself onto my dick. I slide deep in a single, slow, agonizingly blissful thrust. She's drenched and tight, and the pressure is so good, I want to claw at her ass and blast her name from my throat. But her mouth is over mine, and she's kissing and nipping at my lips, so I follow her lead. We kiss while I'm deep inside her, my fingers twisting her erect nipples until she's panting for release.

She's still got the toy in her hand, but now she pulls back from the kiss and centers the tip of the thing as close to her clit as she can get it. She leans forward, all of her weight against my chest, and works her hips so that she's riding my dick while the vibrator works its magic against her clit. It's between us, and I'm literally her fuck chair, which suits me just fine. I can feel the gentle vibrations of her toy through my abdomen, and while it's not exactly adding to my pleasure, it's making my girl so hot and so demanding, she ramps up her thrusts faster and harder. Her stunning thighs are working, every muscle tight as she writhes on my cock, and that makes me greedy for more.

I could fuck her forever. All night. Every day. As many times as she'll have me. But something that feels this good won't last forever. Fuck, it can't even last all night. The way she's moaning and whimpering, horny and hot and working herself into a frenzy on my cock, I'm going to blow before she does if she doesn't come soon.

I add a little fuel to her fire by curving my back so I can draw a nipple into my mouth. She widens her eyes at my interruption to her flow, but once she realizes I'm trying to help, her mouth makes a little O-shape, and she lowers her chest so I can draw a thick nipple all the way into my mouth. I grip her whole breast with a hand, working her bud into my mouth and sucking, slurping, taking out all my passion and fear and need on that poor bit of pink flesh. With my other hand, I smack as much of her ass cheek as I can, the satisfying contact not too hard, but enough to earn another gasp of pleasure from her.

She's ratcheting up the speed on the toy, and then I really feel everything. The way her inner walls tighten as she reaches her pinnacle. The way she floods my cock with her juices as she comes. The way her hands and legs and chest go weak and slump against me as she lets the climax rock her body head to toe. She screams my name, not a ladylike little murmur, but a full-throated, "Fuck, Franco!" and I realize I've never heard my sweet Chloe drop an f-bomb before.

As soon as she's coming, I let myself go, stop holding back my pleasure. Just as she is trembling through her orgasm, I'm coming inside her, hotter and harder than I think I've ever come. Burst after burst of absolute ecstasy comes over me, and my eyes are shut, my mouth open, and I'm grunting my baby's name.

"Fuck," I moan.

Like a rocket blasting through space and then gently drifting back to earth, I come back to myself in a slow, satisfied drift, smelling her, feeling her everywhere. On my lap, against my chest. Loose strands of her hair have caught in my mouth, and I can smell the potent scents of our sex in the air around us. I'm weak and damp and happy and drained.

I don't bother pulling out, and she stays collapsed against me, breathless and with a sheen of sweat coating her skin.

She's still gripping the vibrator in her hands, his dull buzz-buzz sound reminding me we're not entirely alone. I take the toy from her hands and fumble with it until the vibrating ceases. He's sticky with her juices, and as much as I want to taste her, I don't think I'm ready to stick a fake cock in my mouth. Someday. With her, I'd try just about anything.

"I thought that guy was fired," I mumble, almost too boneless to get the words out. "But maybe we should keep him on the bench. You know, for the occasional assist."

"I knew you'd be into kinky threesomes," she murmurs just as weakly against my shoulder.

"Kinky threesome…" I repeat. I stroke the damp hair away from her face and pull her to sitting with me on the couch. "You *are* my dream woman, Chloe."

CHAPTER SIXTEEN

chloe

It's a beautiful, cool morning, and after I left Easy Start, I had three texts from Lucia, asking if she could meet me at Latterature. I said yes, and Mia and I took off in my little sedan, which now has brand-new brakes, thanks to Franco and Jack.

When Lucia meets me outside the store, she has a little gift bag in her hands and a card that reads "Mia." I unlock the store while Lucia coos over Mia and strokes her head.

The dog and I are inseparable now.

Best decision ever.

She follows me through every step of the store, even coming between shelves to find me if I move out of her sight.

"Lucia," I say gently. "I've noticed you look a little different. I like it," I rush on, "but it's different. Not as bright?"

"It's my friend Carol," she says, rolling her eyes. "She's selling this makeup now out of her, well, it's not her home. She's moved in with her boyfriend and is selling makeup since she doesn't feel she can go back to work at Easy Start."

I nod. "Earl's been really generous letting me work in her place."

Lucia nods. "Earl's not a bad man, just, apparently, a terrible lover."

I cough a rough laugh into my hands. "Oh, okay. Wow." I don't think I'll ever be able to look at my boss the same way.

Our small talk is interrupted by a rough knock at the door, followed by Gracie waving at us through the glass.

"Hey, babe." She clasps me in a hug, all rushing and breathless as soon as I open the door. Her black hair is up in a messy bun today, and she's not wearing any makeup. "Do you have any coffee going? I way, way overslept and need a jolt of caffeine. I've got a customer in twenty minutes."

"I'll start some and bring it over," I promise.

She sighs and nods. "You're a lifesaver." Then she looks at Lucia. "Hey Ma, what's going on?"

Lucia flicks a glance at me. "I was just going to try to convince Chloe here to give Carol some work in the shop when she opens. The woman is trying to make a living selling makeup to all her friends. We're going to go broke if she doesn't find a real job soon."

Gracie wrinkles her nose. "Chloe, can you afford an employee? Aren't you working Carol's old job still?"

I nod. "And I don't know for sure that I'm even keeping the store," I admit quietly. It's the first time I've said anything remotely like that to anyone but Franco. "I'm hoping to have a strong showing on Black Friday when I'm back, but if not..." I shrug.

Gracie ponders this quietly for a second, but then she nods. "You know, babe, we cut our costs way down when we cut back inventory. You know the body jewelry we have up front?"

I nod, having no idea what costs a tattoo shop could have. Other than ink and advertising, I couldn't imagine.

"That jewelry is expensive, and if it doesn't sell, we're sitting on money that can't do anybody any good. When Echo started as the piercer and scheduler, we changed our policies. We keep a small supply of basic studs on hand, but if people want specialty stuff, they have to order it from our website. They buy it through us at a markup, and then we notify them when it comes in. The customer gets the jewelry they want, and we get a cut, but we're not out the expensive inventory costs waiting until someone decides they want a pink bedazzled belly ring."

"That makes a ton of sense," I say. "Are you thinking I have too many books?"

She shakes her head. "No. But what if you cut out all the food besides coffee and cookies? I can't imagine how much it costs to have chicken and bacon and all those ingredients on hand all the time. You have to have waste."

My mind starts spinning at the possibility. I love the idea of reducing the food we sell. It won't end the café part of the business. I can still make coffee and offer pastries or even fruit and nuts and other easy to sell nibbles. But cutting back the food service side of the business will reduce labor, energy costs. I'm shocked I didn't think of it myself. But I've been so focused on what I can afford to spend, I wasn't even thinking about what I might be able to save.

"As long as you promise to keep making me those peanut butter crisps," she warns, shaking a finger at me. "Got to run. This is for the coffee." She drops a crisp five on the counter before I can wave her away.

"Gracie, no." I try to stop her, but she's already out the door, her messy bun flopping wildly as she runs.

"Make the coffee. I'll bring it to her when it's done so you can work," Lucia says. "But first, open your gift."

I slide my finger under the flap of the envelope addressed to "Mia." Of course, the card is really for me. It's blank inside, but on the front is a glittery red heart that reminds me of something Lucia would pick out.

She's written a note inside wishing me a happy Thanksgiving and telling me how much she treasures having me in her life.

"Oh, Lucia," I say, tears stinging my eyes.

"There's more," she says, nodding toward the little gift bag.

I pull out the tissue paper, and inside is a gold necklace, just like the one she wears. The necklace has a gold heart with some writing engraved on it. I look closer and make out the words *bella vita* etched in a delicate font.

"What's this?" I ask. "Why are you giving this to me?"

"*Bella vita* means beautiful life," she explains. "I've had such a beautiful life, and I've done my best to give that to my kids." She holds up her hand as if to stop me from refusing or arguing. "I'm not getting ahead of myself, but I am counting on my son not to screw things up with you." She smiles. "No, seriously. When you go home, I imagine it's going to be very hard. Seeing your mom for the first time in so long. Being away from the pressures of the business. I just want you to know, sweetie, that you are loved. No matter where you go or what you do, you deserve a beautiful life."

She looks like she wants to say more but, instead, shuffles me into the kitchen. "Let's make my daughter some coffee, and I'll let you get to work."

"I'm so lucky to have met you, Lucia," I say, wrapping my arms around her. I really mean it.

She's been more of a mother to me than my own flesh and blood. Lucia has done everything in her power to bring me into the fold and make me feel at home in Star Falls.

Glancing around the shop as she hugs me back, I hope I can make it profitable, or else I don't know if Star Falls can stay part of my future.

When Mia and I arrive at Franco's, he's in the garage working on his bike. As soon as I open the car door, Mia bolts into the garage and plasters her paws on Franco's legs.

We've been working with her on basic commands, but jumping up and pawing people when she greets them is something she can't seem to stop doing. I can't blame her much. When I see Franco, I want to do the same thing. But with a lot fewer clothes on.

"Hey, babe," he calls to me. "You want to let her out back to run? I need a couple more minutes here."

"You got it, handsome." I open the door into the house and urge Mia through the living room, and let her out into the yard through the sliding glass doors.

I check to make sure there's nothing unusual out there for her to get hurt on, then I refill her outdoor dish with water.

"Play a little bit," I tell her like she's human. "I'll be back for you in a few."

I head back to the garage and lean against the wall, watching as Franco works. Times like this are when I feel most at peace. I love when we cook or walk the dog or hang with his family.

But when he's lost to his tinkering, grease on his hands, a bandanna holding the hair back from his eyes, he's so peaceful. There's no worry, no stress.

He's just a man whose brain is solving a problem or entertaining some interesting challenge on the bike he's trying to restore. I appreciate his intensity and his focus. Most of the time. I watch him and then grab a lawn chair, pull up a book on my phone and read, or make notes about the store.

But tonight, knowing I'm leaving in the morning and I'll be gone for days, I just want to be close to him. To hold him tight and smell the oil and smoke and salt of his skin.

I watch him for a few minutes until he turns and yanks the bandanna off his hair. The longish layers are flat, but he shakes his head, and they fly around his face, making me laugh. He wipes his hands on the bandanna before pressing the button to close the garage door. "You worried about going home?" he asks, giving me a quick kiss hello.

I shake my head, but in truth, I am a little apprehensive.

"What's this?" He strokes the charm around my neck and squints to read the engraving. "Ma gave you this?" he asks.

I nod. "She's such a sweetheart." I'm starting to get emotional. In a couple hours, I'll leave Mia and Franco and go back to my aunt's apartment alone. Tomorrow night, I'll go to sleep in my childhood bed at my mother's home. I'll be a world away, and yeah, I can't help wondering. Worrying.

"Shit," Franco grumbles. "Way to show me up, Ma. I haven't gotten you a single present yet. Now every time you feel that necklace, you're going to think of Lucia."

I shake my head. "No," is all I can say. "I'll be thinking of you every time. I wouldn't have you without her, remember."

"Let's not give her more credit than she's due," he says. He lifts my chin with a finger. "Can I give you a little something to remember me by?"

"What do you have in mind?" I ask, grinning.

He claims my lips in a tender kiss, soft and gentle. My eyes close and I breathe in the scent of him, feel the scrape of his stubbled chin against mine. He wraps his hands around my waist and holds me close, his tongue sweeping against mine. He tastes of cinnamon and a hint of sugar, like he was munching on mints while he worked. He's delicious and fiery, his kisses hot, and his hands on my hips tugging me close.

"You want me, baby?" he asks, his voice rough against my lips. He lowers his mouth to my neck and leaves scorching kisses from my jawline to my throat.

"God, yes." I lean into his hold, his already-hard cock pressing against the zipper of his jeans.

I move toward the door, but he takes my hand and shakes his head. "I want you here," he says.

"Here?" I echo. "In the garage?"

"I've been dreaming of bending you over my weight bench all day," he growls.

I'm more than willing. I'm so ready for whatever he has in mind. "How are we doing this? Am in your lap, am I…".

He holds up a finger. "You trust me, babe?"

I cock my chin, wondering exactly what he wants to do with me. To me. The uncertainty brings an immediate throb between my legs, and I'm already feeling myself grow wet with arousal. "Of course I trust you," I say. "Tell me where to throw my clothes."

He laughs and takes a seat on the workbench with his knees spread wide. "I'll tell you exactly what I want," he says. "Anything you don't like…"

"I'll tell you," I promise, licking my lips in anticipation. I tighten my legs, needing to rub my thighs together to ease the ache mounting in my core.

He leans back and just watches me. "Strip."

I immediately toe off my boots. As I wriggle out of my pants, I try to be sexy about it, but I end up shaking my bum and almost tripping onto the cushiony mat under my feet. "A little less stage-dive and a little more stripper," I mutter to myself.

He laughs, but he grows quiet as I shove my panties down and toss them away. I'm wearing a thick sweater with a puffer coat over it, which must look hilarious, but he's staring at me like I look good enough to eat. I stand there, bare from the waist down and dressed like a snowman on top.

"All of it," he says, lifting his chin.

I unzip my jacket and shrug out of it before taking off my top and my bra.

"Touch yourself. I want to watch you play with your nipple. Just one."

I do as he says.

I stare at him, swallowing hard as I twist the tip gently between my fingers. "Oh…" A little moan escapes me. When I touch my own breasts, it never feels as good as when he does it. But with him watching me, his hands on his thighs, his lips parted, I've never felt more wanton. My own touch brings me pleasure, and I try to give in to it, squeezing my nipple a little harder, twisting it a little farther.

He wiggles his fingers. "Come here. I want your ass in my face," he says.

I walk toward him, and when I reach the workout bench, I turn around again and face the garage door. My butt is facing him and is almost level with his face.

"Perfect," he whispers. "Now, spread your legs apart and touch your clit. I'm going to watch."

With my bottom facing him, I reach between my legs and slip two fingers through my trimmed hair. I'm already ridiculously wet, so I slide some moisture from my pussy and trace light circles over my clit.

My legs feel a little weak, and I don't know how long I can touch myself like this standing up.

"Did you like being spanked?" he asks.

"Yes." I lick my lips, loving the way it felt.

"Do I have your permission to do it again?"

I nod, not answering with words because I don't trust my voice. I want it. I want him. I want everything.

I swallow hard and cup my pussy. I feel his warm, rough palm stroke my backside, and then his hand is gone, only to return in a quick, firm slap.

The sound of his skin against mine is erotic and dirty, and the actual spank doesn't hurt at all. There's this delicious prickle against my skin.

"Good?" he murmurs, his breath hot against my thighs. I'm so close to him that when he breathes, the sensation of hot air then cool breaths sets every little hair on my body on alert.

My skin is deliciously awake, raw, and desperate for sensation. Any sensation. I whimper and obey when he reminds me, "Clit, baby. I want you to play with yourself while I play with you."

I stroke my clit and gasp as his palm bounces against my backside a second time, then a third.

"I'm not hurting you, am I?" he asks.

"God, no," I breathe. "But I'm not going to be able to stand much longer, Franco. My legs…"

He gets up off the bench then. "Hands on the bench and bend over. Ass up high."

I'm quick to move, eager to have his cock inside me. He moves my legs wider apart, and I nearly squeal in surprise when I feel his tongue sweep across my pussy. But the sound is stolen from my throat when he smacks my bottom again. My butt cheek is tender, the skin quivering, but his tongue at my seam and my fingers at my clit are making waves of intoxicating arousal flood my senses.

I can't think, can't speak words, can only coo and ooh and moan as his tongue softly invades my core while his hand works its magic against my bottom.

I hear the sound of his pants unzipping and feel him stand behind me, his hard thighs lining up with the back of my legs. "Hold on tight, baby."

I grip the workout bench for dear life and lift my hips so he can angle his cock between my legs. I'm so wet and so aroused, I see stars behind my eyelids when he thrusts deep.

He slides inside me, dragging his cock in and then out in such slow, agonizingly good strokes that I am begging, whimpering, and shoving my hips at him, desperate for more.

He cups my exposed left breast with one hand, tugging on the nipple that's already aching and raw. Then he rocks his length inside me, never fully withdrawing, but working his hips so fast that I am overcome with bliss.

I lift up on my toes so he can hit just the right angle, and with a few more pinches at my breast, I'm soaring, flying, screaming his name as a climax fires through my limbs.

Franco starts to come not long after I do, while I'm still bent over the workout bench, my bum in the air, and his hips resting against me.

He roars as he releases, both his hands now on my hips where he can hang on tight while he rides out his pleasure.

He places his mouth next to my ear, his breathing rushed and erratic. "A little something to remember me by while you're gone."

I smile to myself, knowing I'd never be able to forget.

CHAPTER SEVENTEEN

chloe

My eyes fly open to the sound of pounding on the front door. I turn my head, and Franco's still fast asleep at my side with a pillow thrown over his head.

I debate for a second on waking him up, but he more than outdid himself with the naked activities the evening before.

It's probably Lucia. It wouldn't be the first time she dropped by unannounced.

I grab my oversize sweater, covering my upper body and most of my legs. I can barely see, but somehow I make it to the front door without banging my elbows against the walls.

I don't look outside first. My mind is too out of sorts from sleeping. Instead, I pull open the door and come face-to-face with someone I don't know.

I blink, confused, and she does the same. She leans back, staring at me.

"Um," she mumbles before her eyes do a slow trail down my body. "Who are you?" Her voice is snotty, like somehow I don't belong at my boyfriend's house.

"I'm Chloe, Franco's girl." The words sound weird and foreign coming out of my mouth. We've had the talk, but I've never said them to anyone else before, and although it was strange to say, I liked how they sounded.

"His girl?" the woman repeats, her lip curling in disgust. "His girl?"

I nod as I peer over my shoulder and pull my sweater tighter around me, hoping Franco's not far behind. But he's not. There's no motion coming from anywhere. Just me and whoever the woman is who's currently looking at me like I don't belong where I am.

When I turn my head back around to look at the stranger, she's still staring at me, shaking her head and mumbling to herself.

"Can I help you?" I ask, trying to be polite.

She could be anyone. Maybe she's his cleaning woman. His house is impeccably clean, almost too clean for him to do it himself. Or maybe she's a relative because his family is too big for me to even wrap my mind around.

"Uh, yeah. I'm Franco's girl," she informs me as she crosses her arms, looking at me like I'm an intruder.

I blink and jerk my head back. "You're Franco's girl?" I ask, confused and wondering if I've been played.

Wait. There's no way the entire family is in on some grand ruse for Franco to get into my pants. I've been with him for a while, and this woman has never showed up before. Lucia hasn't mentioned anyone else, and there's no way in hell she and Mario would welcome me with open arms if they thought Franco was involved with someone else.

The woman is beautiful. Stunning. Totally someone I could see him with, but the man is mine now. I don't care if I'm not his old type; I'm damn sure his new one.

"I'm sorry," I say to her, my voice saccharine sweet. "What's your name?"

It's not lost on me that I'm barely wearing any clothes as I stand in the doorway on full display for any of his neighbors to get quite a show. In a small town like this, someone's bound to be looking. I have no doubt that by later today, news will have traveled about my public indecency.

The brunette touches her chest. "I'm…"

"Olivia, what the hell are you doing here?" Franco asks from behind me.

I turn and glance at him over my shoulder. He's wearing nothing except a pair of sweatpants, and he's scrubbing his hand through his hair, making the messiness even worse but somehow looking hotter. It's so annoying.

"Franco," she says softly, her face immediately flushing as her eyes travel down his body like she did to me when I opened the door. But this time, it's hungry and less critical. "I was..."

Franco's hand slides around my waist, and he puts the weight of his arm on my hip. He bends his neck, peppering my jawline with a few light kisses. "Morning," he whispers against my skin as Olivia's words die in her throat.

"I was..." she repeats, but again doesn't finish.

"It must be important because you never drop by," he says to her, his entire body pressed against my backside, including his morning wood.

I do my best to seem unaffected, but this girl is trying to start shit with me when I've never done anything to her. "Olivia was just telling me she's your girl," I inform him, wanting to clue him in on our brief conversation before he decided to join us in the doorway.

"Liv," he says, his voice not as pissed as I was hoping. "Why do you have to lie?"

She shrugs with a devilish grin. "Life's too boring sometimes. And the look on her face." Olivia laughs, and it takes everything in me not to lift my hand and help wipe it off her face.

Breathe, Chloe.

"You've always been such an asshole," he tells her, which in the little time I've known her, I can say is totally true.

"I wouldn't be me unless I was stirring up some sort of trouble." She gives Franco the biggest smile before sticking her hand out to me. "I'm Olivia. I'm not Franco's, but the way you're dressed, I know you are. Way to go, girl," she says to me, waiting on me to take her hand.

I'm always cordial. It's one of my flaws. I have the inability to be rude on the outside, even if I'm thinking all the thoughts. "I'm Chloe."

She gives me a genuine smile. "It's nice to finally meet the woman I've heard so much about. You're the talk of the town."

"Olivia is one of Gracie's friends."

"Her oldest friend, and add best to that too," Olivia corrects him.

I can see it now. They have the same fashionable style, and Olivia, much like Gracie, is covered in tattoos.

"What do you want, Liv? You've never shown up at my place unannounced before."

Does that mean she shows up randomly, but calls first? She may be Gracie's oldest and best friend, but if I were a betting woman, I'd say she's more interested in warming Franco's bed than talking to his sister.

"My car's about to shit out on me, and I was driving by and thought I'd come straight to the source instead of trying to make it all the way to the shop." She pitches her thumb toward the sleek sports car parked in Franco's driveway. "Would you look at her? Please," she begs, batting her eyelashes at Franco.

He grunts, but there's no doubt about the way he'll answer. Franco's a good guy. He can't say no to anyone, especially a family friend in need. "Give me a minute to get dressed, and I'll take a look."

"I have to go," I tell him, because I don't want to get on the road late, and I'd rather not be stuck in any type of rush-hour traffic. "Mom's waiting."

Franco presses his hand deeper against my waist. "You sure you can't stay a little longer?" he whispers in my ear. "I'll make it worth your while."

I want to stay and keep an eye on Olivia. I don't trust her, but I trust Franco and the connection we have...the history we've made in such a short amount of time. "I can't, honey. I'm sorry."

"Honey," he murmurs. "I like that."

"Can you move your car to the other side while I grab a shirt, Liv? Chloe needs to head out."

"Mom's house. Sounds like a fun afternoon," she says, fishing for details.

"It will be," I tell her, but I'm lying. I want to have high hopes for the time my mother and I are about to spend together, but I've learned those dreams are often quickly squashed, especially when she's involved.

"Maybe I'll see you around sometime," she says as she takes a step back.

"She owns the bookstore next to Gracie's," Franco tells her.

"Latterature?"

I nod. "That's me."

"Aww. You're related to Ms. Ann?"

I nod again. "She was my aunt."

For the first time, Olivia's face isn't filled with mischief. "I liked her. She was a nice lady. I spent a lot of afternoons after school in there."

I smile at her kind words. "Well, stop in again sometime," I tell her and want to kick myself for uttering those words.

"I may do that." She waves as she hustles back to her car.

"You okay?" Franco asks as I turn around, still caged by his arms and body.

"Fine." I smile, but it's not entirely real. I'm too nervous about heading home and agitated over Olivia's arrival and the way she made my stomach twist.

"Liar," he says with a chuckle.

"I have to go," I remind him as he tries to grope my ass. "And people are watching."

He lifts his head and looks around. "I see no one except Liv."

"That's enough." I push against him lightly, not angry or annoyed with him. "Save this for when I get back."

"This won't save." He presses his cock against me, and it takes all my willpower not to cave.

"It'll have to. I'm sure you'll survive. It's only a few days."

He pouts as he releases me, looking like a sad creature who was just denied something he wanted for Christmas but got a knockoff instead.

"That's like an eternity, baby." He reaches for me, trying to suck me in again.

"Olivia's waiting," I remind him, and her name is sour on my tongue. "But remember—" I reach down and grab his stiff cock "—this is mine and not hers."

His eyebrows rise. "I like this side of you."

I give his dick a squeeze before releasing him. "Don't you dare go outside without a shirt."

Franco laughs. "Because of Olivia?"

I twist my lips, pulling my sweater tighter against my front. "No."

"Lies," he whispers. "She's no one, baby."

"She wants to be someone."

He shakes his head. "What she wants and reality are two very different things."

"Not if she gets her way."

He may like this side of me, but I do not. I've never been the jealous type. I've also never been this deep with a man.

"I have the woman I want," Franco says, pulling me back against him before I make it too far. "Don't forget that either, Chloe. You're mine and only mine."

I melt into his touch, hating that I have to leave. "I'd never be able to forget it even if I wanted to."

Part of me hates the hold he and his family have over me so quickly. I've never met another group of people that make me feel like I belong like the Bianchis. It's terrifying that somehow it'll slip away, but I remind myself that Franco's in just as deep as me. This isn't a one-sided relationship.

I push my ass into him, thrusting myself toward the bedroom. I snag my leggings off the floor and start to shimmy into them before he has a chance to grab me again. Resisting him is damn near impossible for me, and I'm trying to put as many barriers between my body and his cock as I can. Luckily for me, it works this time.

"You sure you can't stay?" he asks, leaning against the doorjamb, watching me.

"I am. It's only a few days. I'll be back."

"Promise?" he asks.

"I'm not moving back to Pennsylvania."

"You sure?" he asks again.

"My life is here."

"With me?"

I nod, stalking toward him slowly. "With you," I say, lifting up on my tiptoes to kiss his lips. "Don't miss me too much while I'm gone."

"Impossible," he murmurs against my lips.

I close my eyes, breathing in his warmth and the scent that's uniquely him. "I'll text you."

"Not the same."

"Okay. I won't, then."

"No. No. Text me."

I laugh, kissing his lips one more time before making a beeline for the front door. I catch myself before opening the door and stick my bare feet into my boots.

"Bye!" I yell out, hoping like hell he's putting on more clothes before he heads out to help *Liv*.

"Bye, love!" he yells back to me.

I throw open the door, ignoring the curvy brunette who's on her phone as she leans against her flashy car, looking like something out of a mechanic porn magazine, if there is even such a thing.

"Bye, Chloe. It was nice to meet you."

"Yeah," I whisper. "Bye, Olivia." I do my best to be pleasant, even though I want to give her my middle finger.

As I'm pulling out, I see Franco stalking out of the house in the same gray sweatpants and a tight-as-hell tank top. It's a shirt, but not the one I'd feel comfortable with him wearing around a very hungry and inappropriate Olivia.

CHAPTER EIGHTEEN

franco

If Chloe is remembering me while she's away, she sure as shit has a funny way of showing it.

All day Sunday, I check my phone for messages or texts. So much so that both Earl, who's back from his fishing seclusion and managing the early stages of amicably filing for divorce from Carol, and Jack give me shit about it.

By Sunday night, I'm looking back at her texts, trying to read any little clue into what she's thinking or feeling.

I got a Saturday night text that said, "I made it." Followed by a "Miss you."

Monday is a repeat of Sunday. But worse.

So, I grump through all of Monday, checking my phone every five minutes and worrying that I'm a shit boyfriend. I've ruined myself being single and fucking free all this time. Yeah, I've had no strings, no drama, but I've also got practice at the long game.

"Franco, you got a minute?" Earl's scratching his neck, a pair of reading glasses on his nose.

I nod and storm from the bay where I'm working over to Chloe's desk. It's hers now that Carol has filed for divorce officially and let Earl know she's not planning to come back to the shop.

"What's up?" I lift my chin at him and quickly take a look at my phone. Nothing. Again. No missed calls, no texts. Not even from my mother. That makes me realize that maybe someone else has heard from her. I'm thinking about asking Ma and Gracie if they've heard from her, but then that's going to start a whole thing that I'm not sure I'm ready to face either. I pocket my phone and look at Earl, who's got a stern look on his face.

"Son," he says, "in all the many years I've known you, I've seen you in a lot of moods. But this is one for the books. Can I ask what's going on? You're stomping around and cursing under your breath and obsessively checking your phone. Are you in some kind of trouble?"

I bark a rough laugh because, yeah, I suspect I probably am. Instead, I sigh again and shrug. "It's Chloe," I say. "Haven't heard much from her since she left for Pennsylvania."

Earl lifts his brows, white and bushy, one of them sprouting a single renegade hair that seems hell-bent on poking the man in his eye. "Oh?" he asks.

I haven't officially told anyone that Chloe and I are seeing each other. Keeping my private life private is such a struggle. I definitely wasn't in any rush to share the fact that I'm seeing her at work.

But now, with Earl looking me over curiously, not saying something feels like a lie. "We've been seeing each other for a while now," I say. "So, not hearing from her while she's back home makes me think of all the shit I've done to make me seem like a real asshole boyfriend."

Earl nods, and I wonder if I've already said too much. "You feel like talking about it any?" he asks.

I don't, but I can't very well say nothing and confirm that I'm an asshole. "She tells me how she feels all the time. She's so affectionate and thoughtful, and my ma got her this beautiful necklace as a gift before she left. I feel like all I've done is..." I swallow the words "fuck her," because I've already said way too much.

He gets it, though, and shakes his head. "So, do you love her, son? Or is this a casual, sexual thing?"

"I...I am falling in love with her," I say. "It may seem to be too soon, I know, but—"

Earl holds up a hand. "Who says it's too soon? Go on. What else?"

"I've never dated anyone, not seriously like this. Never someone I'd see a future of more than a couple months with. We were dating two weeks, and my ma thought she was moving in to my place."

Earl's just nodding. Listening. Waiting.

"It's all just moving fast, and I don't like this feeling I get right here." I touch the middle of my chest, trying to push down the knot under my bones. "Maybe she's having second thoughts about me or about staying in Star Falls."

Earl takes in a deep breath and scratches his neck again. His hair is an ashy gray, the color of dirty snow, and he keeps it short. He's a man I've known all my life, and yet I realize I've never had a serious conversation with him. I've never asked how he's doing, losing his wife. His marriage of however many fucking years is ending, and I've never once given him a hug or asked if he's okay.

I suddenly realize it. That I've been hiding too. I may not wear bulky sweaters to cover my body, but I hide in plain sight. Behind a big personality and a pair of brass balls. If I'm always slick and hard to catch, no one will ever catch up to me. It's a great way to stay safe. Unhurt. Untouched.

I feel the opposite of that now. Raw. Vulnerable. Worried to distraction that Chloe is going to be done with me. I'm terrible at multitasking, and I feel like all I've done is worry since Sunday.

"I think, in relationships, we're each good at some things and not so good at others," Earl finally says. He claps a hand on my shoulder. "Son, when you love someone and you put their happiness before yours, you think about what you're not good at. And you try to be better. You won't always do it right. But if she loves you, she'll see you trying. And that will be more than enough."

I swallow against the knot of dryness in my throat. "That sounds like real good advice, Earl. Thank you."

"Do as I say, not as I've done," he adds. "As you know, Carol and I have split up."

That's far from news, but I let my boss say his piece.

"Carol wanted to work on things for years," he admits, pointing at his son, who's on his back working under a sports car. "Probably since before that one was even born. But I never managed to do anything right. Those aren't Carol's words. Those are mine. I only realize now that I've lost her, that the one person I really needed to be honest with and never was, was myself."

That hits hard.

"If someone really loves you, they're not going to judge you on your results. They'll judge you on your effort. You need to look inside, Franco, and decide what kind of partner you want to be to this girl. Woman, I'm sorry. I'm still old-school that way. Carol keeps telling me that's offensive. She's an adult woman."

I smile and nod. "No offense taken. I'm sure Chloe wouldn't mind."

"If you try and screw up, she can never say you didn't try. Women are smart, Franco. They see through bullshit and lies, but they also see the truth. Even when we pigheaded men can't admit it to ourselves."

He doesn't say anything more, and I truly get his point. He's right. I have been doing what's easy and safe in this relationship.

Sex.

I'm great at it, and it bonds me to her, but is that really all I have to give? That, and a little money to make sure she had a phone. I don't even need to think about the answer to that. I would give her everything.

"Thank you, Earl," I say, and I mean it. I think he can tell. "Are you okay? I haven't even asked, but you've been going through a lot yourself these past couple months."

Earl nods slowly and then gives me a smile. "I am okay," he says. "Thanks for asking. I never imagined I'd be alone at this age, but I think it's been good for me. The soul-searching has been good, but the fishing's even better."

I crack a smile and turn to go back to work.

"Franco." Earl stops me before I get too far. "Why don't you take some time off? We're slow. Jack and I can handle the shop."

I cock my chin at him, wondering what he's getting at. "Are you sending me home?"

"No, not at all. You're welcome to stay, but Pennsylvania's not far away." He nods toward Chloe's desk. "I have her mom's phone number and address. Needed emergency contact information in case of emergency." Earl grabs a folder from inside Chloe's desk and scribbles a phone number and address on a sticky note. "Happy Thanksgiving, son," he says, handing the paper to me. "I'll see you Monday."

I take the address and stare down at it. I freeze for just a second. Am I really going to do this? Am I going to surprise a woman I've been dating for just two months?

"Change your mind?" Earl asks, lowering those bushy brows at me.

"No," I say, throwing my arms around him and giving him a quick, hard hug. "Just wanted to say thanks."

Earl claps me back and nods, then starts shouting at Jack to turn his damn music down. I take off for my truck, a plan already in motion.

By the time I roll up to Chloe's mom's house, I'm a bundle of nerves. My thoughts have been everywhere while I drove here, and I almost turned around twice.

But I keep thinking about what Earl said. The people we love don't tally up our successes and failures. They only care that we try.

I've got Mia on a leash and a bouquet of flowers in my hand when I knock on the door. Chloe answers it, looking more than shocked. She looks like I've caught her, and she doesn't look happy to see me.

"Franco?" She yanks the door open and talks to me through the screen door. She fumbles with the lock on the screen and then shoves that open, nearly hitting me in the chest. "What are you doing here? Are you okay? Is your mom okay?"

This is the moment of truth. She's either going to be happy with my grand gesture, or she's not. I thrust the roses at her. "These are for your mom," I tell her. "I didn't want to show up at her home empty-handed."

"Thank you. Mom's not here right now. She's at work. You're freaking me out. What's wrong?" Mia is wagging her tail like crazy, and Chloe just now seems to realize that the dog is with me. "You brought Mia?" She drops to her knees and scratches the dog's ears.

Even though this isn't the reception I'd hoped for, I ask her if I can come in. "Can we talk?"

She nods and invites me in, and then she locks the doors behind me. Her mother's house is really tidy, decorated with dated but well-maintained tchotchkes and knickknacks on every surface. It reminds me a lot of Ann's apartment.

"Are you hungry?" she asks. "Thirsty? You must be."

I decline anything to eat or drink. My mouth is too dry and my stomach too unsettled. She doesn't seem happy. Definitely doesn't seem to appreciate my grand gesture. Fuck me. Listening to Earl was maybe a mistake? I don't know. I can't go back now, though. I'm here, so I'm going to tell her what I feel.

"Nothing's wrong," I tell her. "Nobody's sick, nothing bad happened back home. In Star Falls."

Her shoulders visibly sag, and I think she's relieved. "Oh, okay. Thank goodness. Then why are you here?"

I am still holding the bouquet of roses for Mrs. Harkin, so I drop them on the coffee table in front of us and just let her have it. "I'm an asshole, Chloe. When I didn't hear much from you after you left, I started panicking. Thinking of everything I've done wrong in the very short time I've been lucky enough to be with you. And I started thinking that maybe I've been treating you more like a fuck buddy than my girlfriend."

She's listening and nodding, her crystal-clear green eyes wide.

"I want that, Chloe. I don't know if I'm ready to live together full time, but I think you're going to have to push me. I'm set in my ways, but that doesn't mean I don't want to change. I want to change if that means I'm going to be better. Better for you."

I pause to take a breath and see if she's going to react at all.

"So, you drove all the way to Pennsylvania to tell me that?"

Mia is sniffing around curiously. I look from the dog to Chloe to my clenched hands. "Yeah," I admit. "I realized that I might lose you. And I couldn't let that happen without trying to show you how much you mean to me. Because you do, Chloe. I should have said it a thousand times a day, so you know. I'm falling in love with you. Fuck, I might be in love with you already." I know I am, but this doesn't feel like the way to tell her. Certainly not the time.

She worries that bottom lip between her teeth. "Franco, I don't know what to say. I can't believe you took off work. You drove all this way?"

I nod. "I couldn't wait another minute without saying those words to your face. I didn't want you sitting in your hometown, thinking about moving away from Star Falls, without knowing exactly how I feel. This shit's never happened to me before. I've never second-guessed shit, but here I am, wondering if you're second-guessing us."

When I say that, she crumples, and tears well up in her eyes. "Oh, Franco." She shakes her head. "You're already everything I want. I wasn't mad about anything. My visit here has just been hard."

"Hard? How? What's going on?" I'm immediately worried that something happened. "I'll take you home if you want to get out of here."

"No, it's not that," she says quietly. She chuckles. "It's so funny. All the years my mom sacrificed to put up with my dad and his bullshit. She's sure making up for lost time. I know she loves me, but she's been so busy with her friends that we haven't spent much time together. It's fine. I mean, I've had a lot of time to think and go through stuff. Mom gave me this." Chloe gets up and walks to her purse, which is sitting on the edge of the coffee table. She pulls out a check and shows me the amount.

"Three thousand dollars? Your mom is giving you three grand? What for?" I ask, folding it back up and handing it to her.

Chloe shrugs. "Mom was never able to have friends or her own money. She's living her best life now, and she wants to share some of what she can with me."

I wonder if this money means that Chloe has been thinking about not coming back to Star Falls. "A little cash must make coming home and leaving the robbery and all that behind you a lot more attractive," I say. I can't even look her in the eye. I don't think my heart can take it if she actually says she's been seriously considering not coming back.

But she shakes her head. "It's the opposite," she says. "I can't wait to get back. I've already spent all this money in my head. I figured I'd pay you back as much as I could first, and then after that…"

I stop her right there. "So, you're definitely coming back to Star Falls? And what about us?"

She shakes her head. "Franco, I've known from the moment I met you that you were the one."

"So, you're not mad that I'm here?" I ask. "Was it stupid to come?"

She shakes her head again. "It wasn't stupid," she giggles. "Babe, I'm in love with you. I want you and have since at least week two when I stole your tank top." She rolls her eyes. "I didn't really steal it, but I might have noticed that I scooped it up with my stuff when I was packing and just decided that tank would be happier with me."

I laugh but don't interrupt her.

"My mom wants to introduce me to her friends. They're all coming over tonight. Everybody is bringing something. I'm supposed to start the turkey in about an hour. Mom plans to work on the actual holiday."

"And I'm crashing the party. Fucking everything up," I fill in.

"You haven't fucked everything up," she teases. "But I'm putting you to work now."

"I'm all yours," I say, and I mean it.

CHAPTER NINETEEN

chloe

Franco left before me, needing to be at his parents' for Thanksgiving dinner. I needed time to prep the store for the big reveal and sale tomorrow.

Franco will be at his parents', and while I have an open invitation to crash their Thanksgiving, I decide to go check on my shop first.

I disarm the alarm as I enter and lock the front door behind me. The store is quiet, and I turn on a few lights. Sheets still cover the front glass so passersby can't see the decorations I've put up. But they look impressive after a few days away. I check the kitchen, and the cider, hot cocoa, and coffee are ready to be brewed. I'll be back here tomorrow at first light to get things started.

I'm just about to shut off the lights when there's a loud knock at the door. I shake my head. Surely none of the Main Street businesses are open on Thanksgiving?

"We're closed," I call out.

But the guy's persistent. "Can I use your bathroom?" he asks. "Sorry to ask, but every place is closed."

I look the guy over, alarm bells ringing every possible way in my head.

No, no, no.

I'm here alone, and he must know as much. I scan his face and don't recognize him, but I don't really know anyone in Star Falls, definitely not a lot of young guys.

He's smiling, but he seems a little flustered and impatient. "You coming?" he yells through the glass.

As I watch him shift from foot to foot in the cold, he jams his hands into his pockets and pulls them back out again. A black mask falls out of his jacket.

My heart catches hard in my chest. It can't be the same guy. It just can't.

He looks down and picks it up, then slides it over his hair.

My shoulders sink as I relax. It's not a black mask. It's a regular old cap.

But no matter what, I know I can't let this guy in. I'm alone. All of Main Street is deserted.

My heart is thundering hard, and I'm thinking fast. "One second," I call out, holding up a finger. "I left my keys in the kitchen. I'll grab them and unlock it."

I'm not sure if he could hear what I was saying over the shaking of my voice, but when I hold up a hand, he grins and nods, moving from shoe to shoe.

My keys are actually in the back pocket of my jeans, but I tug my big sweater over my bottom so he can't see I'm lying. I head calmly back to the kitchen and give him a "just a second" gesture while I disappear into the back.

I grab my cell phone and dial the non-emergency number for the local police. The dispatcher answers on the first ring, and I explain there's a man casing my store and I would like an officer to drive by to make sure I get to my car okay.

The woman confirms there's a squad car nearby. She says to stay put in the store. The officers will knock on the front door when they arrive.

I am freaking out now, though. I've put something in motion that can't be undone. If the guy is just an innocent guy who needs a bathroom... But to be honest, I'm pretty sure that's a line of bullshit.

My nerves are frayed, and the few minutes it takes the cops to arrive feel like three hours. I'm panicked and pacing and don't know what to do when I finally hear a loud knock at the front door.

I peek out from the kitchen and see two uniformed officers standing there. Behind them, the lights are blaring, but there's no siren sound. I feel relief and fear at the same time, but since I don't see any sign of the guy who wanted the bathroom, I come out, cross the store, and unlock the door for the officers.

"Ma'am, are you okay?" the officer asks me.

"Yes, I'm fine," I say. "Is he still out there?"

The officer shakes his head. "We caught him."

My eyebrows rise at their speed. "Thank you."

He gives me a chin lift. "No thanks needed, ma'am. He'll be off to the station in a few. Another car got here before us and were able to chase him down. When they searched him, they found a large knife in his possession."

My stomach twists remembering that night and the knife he had. A knife he could've used on me. "Oh my," I whisper, trying to keep myself upright and the fear out of my mind.

He's been caught.

He'll never hurt you again.

"You saved a lot of businesses a lot of losses by calling," the officer assures me. "If you need anything else, please don't hesitate to call."

As soon as I close the door to the shop, I slide my back down the door, placing my ass on the floor. I give myself five minutes to have a freak-out before I compose myself and head out the door.

It's over. He's gone forever.

I arrive at the Bianchis empty-handed.

Franco's eyes meet mine, and he immediately drops the pan of stuffing on the table and rushes toward me. I'm standing in the front hallway with my coat and boots still on.

"What happened?" he starts, but I shake my head.

"Can we talk for a second in private?" I ask. I love and trust the Bianchis, but this is something I want to share only with him. I don't want the noise and attention. I just need him to know what I've been through. I just need my Franco.

"Absolutely, yes." He watches me with concern on his face. I hand him my coat to hang up while I slip off my boots, and immediately, people descend to greet us. Franco shoots me a quick look before parting the crowd like a champion. I'm so, so surprised and grateful. "We need a moment," he tells them, "alone."

Bev and Gracie groan, and loud laughter ensues as the family urges us to go downstairs for a few moments alone. I try to smile and wave as Franco takes me into the basement kitchen, where food is stacked up waiting to be carried to the table.

"Should we wait?" I ask, motioning to the trays piled high with baked sweet potatoes and toasted dinner rolls. "I don't want to mess up the meal."

"Everything can wait," he tells me. "All that matters is you."

He pulls me close, and for a moment, I just rest my head against his chest. I lock my arms around his waist and hug him hard. He's wearing a soft flannel shirt with a white T-shirt underneath, and his smell is both familiar and comforting. He kisses the top of my hair and rocks me lightly, just waiting.

Doesn't urge me. Doesn't rush me.

Above us, I can hear laughter and heavy footfalls as guests and family walk around. The music is muted, but I hear the occasional barks from the dogs. When my pulse settles a bit and I feel a little calmer, I release him and look into his face, explaining in as few words as possible what happened tonight at the shop. Franco doesn't interrupt until I'm done talking.

"Are you okay?" he asks, his body tense and his expression tight.

I nod. "I'm oddly relieved. They know who the guy is now, so even if he gets out..."

"He's not getting out," Franco says, his voice low and angry. "I'm going to call the station tomorrow and talk to the detective who is handling your case. Maybe I can file assault charges against him.

He did fight me out there on the street. We'll make sure he doesn't get out anytime soon, babe."

I nod against his chest. "I was planning to have time to stop home and throw together some cookies or something. I can't believe I came here empty-handed. I was just so shaken." I wave down at my casual traveling clothes. I'm wearing yoga pants over a loose, comfy sweater.

"None of that matters," he says. He leans back to look me in the face. "You're home. This is a come-as-you-are place. No cookies required. And I love that I can actually feel your ass in those pants," he teases, but he doesn't touch my bottom.

Instead, he kisses my forehead and touches his nose to mine.

"Can I kiss you now, babe? I need to know you're really okay." His intense blue eyes are staring, and I hear the basement door open. "But I missed the shit out of you and have been looking forward to those lips all day."

"Yo, asshole." Before he can bend his face to mine, Vito's voice echoes through the doorway and down into the basement. "You done making kissy faces yet? Pops wants the sweet potatoes."

"Fuckin' V." Franco groans and shakes his head. "Come on down, but you're going to get an eyeful."

He leans down and claims my lips, and I'm giggling as we smooch. Vito storms past dramatically, covering his eyes and making sick sounds.

"Ugh, you two." He grabs the sweet potatoes from the counter, and as he rushes past, he shoves his face close to ours. He makes another gagging sound and sticks out his tongue, then looks at me seriously. "Glad you're back, Chloe. Now get your asses upstairs. I'm fucking starving."

Vito shuffles upstairs wearing his trademark slippers with no socks, but he is wearing real pants and a flannel shirt for the holiday. He doesn't bother closing the basement door, and Franco groans and shouts after him, "Asshole!" Franco releases me and cups my face in his hands. "I'd like Gracie to know the guy was caught, but why don't I leave it to you to tell my family when you're ready to talk about what happened tonight. That okay with you?"

I nod.

That's perfect. I want to share the story, but I don't want it to be the talk of Thanksgiving. Once all the small talk and bickering are over, I'll find the right minute to tell the family.

Before we head upstairs, Franco stops me. "I picked up something for you on the road," he says. "It's nothing big. I actually got it at a truck stop. It's a piece of crap, I'm not going to lie. But I saw it, and I wanted to give you a little something. I'll replace it with something nicer and more sparkly someday soon."

"Franco, you didn't have to…" But he pulls the gift out of his pocket before I can protest. The small item is wrapped in a nearly sheer white plastic bag with the letters THANK YOU printed in red ink. It's tiny enough to fit in his jeans pocket. I can't imagine what he could have picked up on the road between my mom's house and Star Falls, but knowing that he got it at a stop on the road trip he made makes it all the more special. Not to mention, it's the first gift —other than a cell phone, a dog, and a heck of a lot of amazing orgasms—he's given me. I unwrap the bag and inside find a tiny charm attached to a plastic card. The charm is gold toned and is in the shape of a key.

"It's to go with the heart Ma gave you," he says. "I always want to be the man who unlocks your beautiful life. Or some shit," he chuckles. "I'm no poet or whatever. I don't really do words. But I love you, Chloe. I've never been more thankful that my mother is a meddling matchmaker."

I wipe away the tears of laughter and joy that collect around my eyes as I add the very meaningful charm to my necklace. "A few more of these and your mom's going to think I'm copying her style."

"Don't you dare," he teases. He kisses me again, this time longer. His lips linger on mine, soft and insistent, sweet and whispering promises.

"Yo, asshole." This time, the voice that beckons from the top of the stairs is Benny's. "What are you two doin' down there? Pops is ready to carve the bird."

"For fuck's sake," Franco sighs, but there's a smile on his face. "You ready?"

I take his hand and think over all the things that have come together in my life the last few weeks.

Am I ready? Heck, yeah. I've never been more ready. The timing, the place, and the people couldn't be more perfect.

A new love, a new life, a forever home.

"I'm ready," I say, lacing my fingers through his, excited about the future.

CHAPTER TWENTY

franco

Three Weeks Later

"What do you think?" I step back, taking in the new sign on the bookstore as Chloe stands next to me.

She throws her arms around me as she stares at the front window. "It's perfect. Absolutely perfect."

Those are the words I'd use to describe her and the way she's seamlessly fit into my world. "It's not too much?"

"Is there such a thing?"

I've learned that in the eyes of Chloe, Gracie, and my ma, there can never be too much of anything. When I started to design the sign, I gave them a few choices and they always selected the most colorful and loudest option. "It'll grab people's attention."

"That's the point, silly."

I kiss the top of Chloe's head, looking around the busy street. "Are you ready to close up?"

Chloe looks down the street, soaking in the large crowds trying to get their shopping done before they run out of time. "Maybe another hour."

"I'll stay, and then I'm taking you to Benny's for a late dinner."

"Perfect," she says to me before pushing herself away. "I'm starving."

"Me too," I tell her, but I'm not hungry for food.

She moves toward the door, but I grab the handle first, opening it for her. She doesn't say a word, but she looks up at me with a smile that I don't think could ever grow old.

Chloe heads to the register, and I find an empty chair tucked away across the store to relax in. I grab a book off a random shelf that's within arm's reach and crack it open. I pretend to read because sitting in a bookstore without doing anything may seem weird, and I'm not here to creep out the customers.

But when I make it beyond the first page, my phone vibrates, saving me.

Gracie: Do not buy me clothes for Christmas, assholes. Do you hear me?

I laugh as I read her message, remembering all the horrible outfits we've bought her over the years. She's impossible to buy for, and as she's gotten older, it's become worse.

Benito: What the hell do you want, then?

Vito: What's wrong with the clothes we bought for you last year? They were the latest fashion.

Gracie: Do I look like I shop at Mico's?

Benito: All stores have the same shit.

Me: I didn't get you clothes.

Thankfully, I had Chloe to help me find the perfect gifts for Gracie this year. Without her, I would've ended up buying her a new robe or other bullshit she'd probably have no use for. My brothers are easy, but when it comes to Gracie, my mind goes blank.

Vito: You don't count. You have Chloe to help.

Busted.

I glance up from my phone, watching Chloe as she chats with customers. She looks more alive than I've ever seen her. The store is filled with people, and that means money. She no longer seems worried about the future of the store, which is a relief.

Benito: I was going to get you perfume. Cool?

Gracie: What kind?

Benito: If I tell you, it won't be a surprise.

Gracie: If it's aerosol from a chain store, then it's garbage.

Benito: Didn't know you were so fancy.

Gracie: I've known you assholes my entire life, and all you can come up with are robes, pajamas, and crappy perfume.

Vito: You're kind of a picky bitch, sis.

Benito: Too bad she's not as picky with her men.

Gracie: Um, I've seen what you invite into your bed. I wouldn't talk about my choices in lovers, B.

I bite my lip to stop myself from laughing and causing a scene inside the bookstore. Although it's busy, it's still too damn quiet.

Benito: They're all beautiful creatures in their own way.

Vito: How about a Mico's gift card?

Gracie: Don't be a dumbass.

Vito: Me or him?

Gracie: Both of you.

Vito: What about Franco?

Gracie: I know Chloe has my back.

I cringe a little, even though I'm pretty sure Chloe nailed every gift for Gracie.

Benito: Isn't it the thought that counts?

Gracie: Yeah, but I'm pretty sure Mico's and robes require no thought.

She has a point, but we do put thought into her gifts. We have entire threads of text messages, trying to figure out what to get her, but always come up blank. It's hard enough for one of us to come up with a solid idea, but for all three of us…it's impossible.

Vito: I still don't understand what the problem is with Mico's.

Gracie: They have beautiful clothes that never wrinkle, but I'm not ready for the Mico's chapter in my life.

Benito: What did you get me?

Gracie: Condoms.

Benito: Solid idea, but I hate using them.

Me: You're going to hate a screaming baby more.

Benito: I'm pretty damn sure I'm shooting blanks.

Me: You're willing to risk the chance?

Benito: Haven't knocked someone up yet.

That's my brother's dumbass logic. It hasn't happened yet, so he figures it never will. He's bright with some things but so goddamn dense with others.

Me: Well, that's a good way to look at it. You've gotten lucky so far, might as well try to keep the streak alive.

Gracie: Sounds like a beautiful way to become a father. Lord knows, you only bang the best.

Me: By best you mean anyone with breasts, then he does.

Gracie: Someday you're going to have a person show up on your doorstep, and you're going to find out your thoughts that you were sterile were all bullshit.

That sounds like my mother's dream come true. She'd be over the moon if grandkids popped up randomly and the family grew quickly.

Benito: Not happening. No one's told me they were pregnant.

Gracie: I'm sure they'd be more than excited to tell you the news after you discarded them like the half-eaten scraps in your restaurant.

Benito: I treat them all like queens, even if their reign is short.

Gracie: You're all pigs.

Me: Not me. Don't lump me in with those boneheads.

Gracie: You've changed your ways.

Me: I've never been like those two.

Benito: We're not monsters.

Vito: We're lovers.

Gracie: Whatever.

Me: B, I'm bringing Chloe over for dinner in a bit as soon as she closes up the store.

Benito: I'll make something special.

Me: Thanks, bro.

Gracie: I'm starving.

Vito: Me too.

Gracie: Why don't we all go?

I glance up at the ceiling, wanting a nice dinner alone with my girl. But I know Chloe, and she loves to be surrounded by my brothers and sister. It must be an only child thing because every chance she gets, she invites them over.

Me: Meet there at 9:30.

Gracie: Perfect. My last appointment cancelled.

Vito: Solid.

Benito: I'll go save a table.

Gracie: You'll eat with us?

Benito: You just spent five minutes beating me up, and you want me to sit down and have a civilized meal?

Gracie: I took years of your brotherly abuse and still talk to you. I think you can take a few text messages with the reality of your choices.

Vito: Babe, you gave as good as you got. I have some scars to prove it.

Gracie: I learned from the best.

Benito: I have to go prep our dinner.

Gracie: Nothing too greasy.

Benito: Picky.

Vito: See you in an hour.

Me: Bye.

Gracie: Later.

Benito: Peace.

"This is Lexi," Benito says, walking up to the table with his hand against a new women's back.

"New flavor of the month," Gracie mutters under her breath into her glass of wine.

I give her a chin lift. "Hey."

"She's going to join us tonight," Benito informs us, pulling over a spare chair from another table.

This is new. He's never invited anyone to sit with us, not even his close friends.

"Cool," Vito says, barely looking up because he's too busy stuffing his face with the fresh baked bread. "The more, the merrier."

"It's nice to meet you, Lexi," Chloe says to her as she slides into the wood chair as elegantly as I've seen anyone do it before.

Gracie's staring at Lexi like she has two heads. "I'm just…this is different."

"Be nice, Grace," Vito tells her like she's a little kid about to make a scene.

"We're old friends," Lexi says to the table, but she can't take her eyes off my brother. "We haven't seen each other in years."

Surprisingly, Benito's staring at Lexi the exact same way. I never remember him talking about her, but by the look on his face, it was more than a fling. "It's been at least a decade. I can't believe you wandered in here tonight of all nights and to my restaurant."

"When I saw the name, I knew it was you. There's not too many Benito's in this part of the country." Lexi places her hand on his arm, and my brother does nothing to pull away. She turns to glance around the table at each of us. "I hope you don't mind me crashing your family dinner."

"Not at all," Gracie replies. "What brings you back to town, Lexi? I don't remember you from school."

"I didn't go to school here. I moved to Star Falls after college when I started working for a local advertising agency. I stayed a few years and then headed to California to work in Hollywood."

"No shit," Vito whispers. "That's pretty fucking cool. Meet any celebrities?"

Lexi laughs, but she nods. "They're everywhere out there. They blend in after a while, and you stop being so starstruck when you run into them."

"No way. I'd never get used to it," Vito says. "If I ran into a hot actress or two, I guarantee I'd at least get a date out of it. It wouldn't ever get old for me."

I roll my eyes. "They wouldn't want your ass."

He folds his hands together on the table. "They all want a piece of what I have."

"And that would be?" I raise an eyebrow. "They want a guy who lives in his parents' basement? What else do you have except the same bed you've been sleeping on since you were pissing the mattress?"

"You're a real douche," he says to me. "I have a lot to offer."

"You forgot about the stint with the stripper wife," Gracie adds like I could've forgotten that clusterfuck.

"No one gives dick like me." Vito's gaze swings to Lexi. "I don't mean to be so crude. My apologies."

My brother thinks his cock is the greatest thing he can give a woman. He also truly believes no one fucks better. The man is delusional and somehow really confident, honestly believing his own bullshit.

She covers her mouth, hiding her laughter. "No offense taken."

"How's the store? It looked swamped today." Gracie asks Chloe, ignoring Vito's conversation about his abilities.

"Busier than ever. I'm just hoping it stays that way after the holiday shopping season."

"Word will spread about the better selection of books. You've really outdone yourself with all the new changes."

Chloe smiles as she curls her fingers around mine underneath the table. "I'm trying. My aunt had a decent selection, but it was time to bring it into more current times and ride some trends."

"You own the bookstore in town?" Lexi asks Chloe.

"Yeah. It used to be my aunt's, but when she passed, she left it to me."

"She was a kind woman. I had many conversations with her when I lived here. I didn't have many friends, but she was always sweet and a good listener."

"Thank you," Chloe tells Lexi. "It seemed she touched a lot of lives."

Lexi gives Chloe a warm and genuine smile. "And now you're going to touch even more people. An entire new generation here in Star Falls."

I already know Lexi's too nice for my brother. She deserves someone better than him and his womanizing ways.

"They're exactly as you described them," Lexi says to Benito. "He told me so much about you all when we were younger, and when he said you were coming for dinner, I begged for him to allow me to stay."

"Lex, there was no begging involved. At least not this time." He winks at her, and there's a collective groan from everyone around the table.

Chloe leans over, bringing her mouth close to my ear. "I love this."

I turn my head, looking into her eyes. "What?"

"Your family."

"They're your family now too," I remind her. She's one of us now, whether she realizes it or not.

"What are you two whispering about over there?" Gracie asks, never wanting to be left out of a conversation, even a private one.

Chloe straightens again in her seat but keeps her hand in mine. "Nothing."

"She said she loves our family."

Gracie reaches over and touches Chloe's shoulder. "We're your family too."

"Babe," Vito says to Chloe, and the term doesn't bother me at all. "You're one of us now, even if you're too good."

"Too good?" Chloe laughs. "I'm not perfect."

Gracie snorts. "You're pretty damn close to Mother Teresa."

"Am not."

Vito leans forward, invested in this conversation. "Name one bad thing you've done in your life."

Chloe squirms in her chair but doesn't answer right away.

"See," Gracie says, waving her hand at Chloe. "She's a saint. I don't know how Franco got her, but he did."

"Magic cock," I tell her.

"I stole a pack of gum when I was a kid."

All eyes at the table turn toward Chloe.

"Babe, that's normal kid shit. I wouldn't call that bad," I say to my girl, loving that she's so completely innocent.

"Ever steal a car?" Vito asks Chloe.

"No," she says with her eyebrows knitted together. "You?"

Vito shrugs with a guilty look on his face. "I plead the fifth."

"Sweet Jesus," Chloe mutters. "That's so bad."

Vito chuckles.

"Excuse me," Benito says, sliding his chair back. "I better go check on our dinners before it gets too late."

"I'm starving," Gracie says, rubbing her stomach. "I thought the food would be on the table when we got here."

"Is Benito ever in a hurry or on time?" I ask.

"Some things never change," Lexi states with her chin resting on her knuckles as she keeps an eye on the kitchen where my brother disappeared.

"Especially when you're talking about Benito," Gracie mumbles against the rim of her wineglass.

"He's a good guy," Lexi says to Gracie. "He really is. I've known some really shitty ones, and your brother isn't. He can be incredibly sweet and caring."

"I love all my brothers," Gracie replies. "They all have their flaws, but I wouldn't change a thing about them."

I wish I could bottle up this moment forever. Not what's being said, but all of us being together. Time is fleeting and life is precious. I've spent most of my life not putting too much thought into my family and the people who surround me. But as time slowly ticks away, I know there will be fewer and fewer moments like this.

"Are you okay?" Chloe squeezes my hand.

I turn to her and smile. "I'm perfect. This is perfect."

She leans over and offers me her lips. Without hesitation, I take them, kissing her roughly.

"I love you," she whispers against my mouth.

"I love you too."

And I know, if my life ended in this moment, there is nothing more I would've wanted. I have the dream. A good family. A good woman and more love than one person could ever possibly deserve.

epilogue

FRANCO

"Ma." I lift my face toward the ceiling and take a deep breath.

The woman has been relentless lately. Not completely different from how she normally is, but she's been outdoing herself.

"The baby needs all the things," she explains to me.

"I think we have all the things," I tell her, waving my arms around the construction zone that will become the nursery.

Ma shakes her head and hooks her hand in the crook of my arm. "Franco, you have no idea how many things it requires to raise a child."

I peer down at her as she surveys her work, buying everything she can get her hands on—or at least it seems like it. "Did I have seventeen baby blankets?"

She glances up, her lips pursed. "I had more."

I shake my head, not believing a word of what she's saying. "No, you didn't."

"Uh, yeah, I did."

"If I had three baby blankets, I'd be shocked."

Pops walks into the nursery and whistles. "Someone's credit card is screaming," he teases, thinking I bought all this shit.

"Yeah, yours," I snap.

His eyes widen. "Lucia," he says, his voice filled with disbelief and warning. "You didn't do all this."

Her hand tightens on my arm, and her eyes narrow. If I were younger, that look would've had me quaking in my boots. "Mario, don't start with me. This is our first grandchild."

"That you know of," I grumble. We've all assumed Benny has at least one out there in the world since the guy sticks his dick in everything.

"Hush," she tells me in that mom tone. "You want our first grandchild to have the best of everything, right?"

Pops walks around the room, running his finger down the stack of blankets I'd just been complaining about. "Finer things, yes. All the things…no."

"There's still more to get," she tells him, ignoring his concerns, like she often does. "The baby will want for nothing."

"Literally," Pops adds. "But Lucia, darling, you need to stop. Wait until he or she is here. Babies grow. Their needs change as they get older. Save a little buying power for that time."

"I'll get more," she tells him.

We know she isn't going to listen. He's wasting his breath trying to rein in her spending. By the time the baby is born, I'll be shocked if he or she will even be able to fit in the room with all the things my mother drops off every few days.

"Pops, how many baby blankets did I have?"

He looks at me funny. "What do you mean?"

"Did I have five, six, or three? You know, this," I say, holding up a stack of perfectly folded fabric.

His gaze drops to the pile, and his eyebrows knit together. "How many are there?"

"Who the hell knows. It changes daily." I drop the stack back on the dresser from where I grabbed them. "Did I have this many?"

Pops shakes his head. "You had one, and when that wore out, we bought another. Lucia," Pops says, turning his head toward my mother. "Did you buy all those?"

Ma smiles nervously. "It needs to match their outfit," she explains, like somehow it makes sense when it damn well doesn't.

"And which one is baby-puke color? Because everything is going to be covered in it for months," he tells her, shaking his head. "And I mean everything."

"Remember when Franco threw up in your mouth?" Ma asks him, laughing. "I'll never forget the look on your face."

I cringe thinking about it. Puke has never bothered me, but having someone, even a tiny human, throw up in my mouth is a hard pass. "That's awful," I whisper.

Pops covers his mouth like he can still remember the taste. "I'll never forget it. I learned not to hold him over my head after he ate. Some lessons are harder than others."

"I'm putting that away in my memory bank. No holding the baby over my head after eating," I state to myself, hoping I'll make it a lasting impression.

"It's best if you don't hold the baby over your head any time, not just after eating. Babies sleep, eat, poop, and puke, and all of them at the worst times possible."

"You make it sound like a great experience," I tease him.

"Best thing I've ever done. There's nothing like being a father."

My mother clears her throat.

Dad smiles at her as he mindlessly runs his finger across the top of the blankets. "Besides marrying my beautiful bride, of course."

"Smart man," Ma mutters under her breath before reaching up a hand to touch my face. "You're going to be a great dad."

"I had great parents. You two taught me everything I know."

"Then you're doomed," Gracie says, coming into the room with a cup of coffee in her hand. "We're all screwed up."

"Speak for yourself," I tell her. "Name me a normal person."

She moves her head from side to side like she's thinking, but we both know there's no answer. Normalcy is a falsehood. Everyone has issues, but some people have more than others.

"I'm kidding," she adds, bumping my dad with her shoulder. "We had the best parents."

"Had?" Pops asks. "We're still here."

"Yeah, but I'm grown."

"And still need a parent," Ma adds. "Where would Franco be if it weren't for me meddling in his life?"

I sigh. She has a point, but not one I like to give in to. She'll use it as an excuse to keep going on her butting-in, and that's the last thing I want her to do. "You did good, Ma, but it doesn't always work out."

Ma touches her chest with her fingertips, lowering her chin. "I know my children and what's best for them."

"We're not children anymore, Ma," Gracie explains like it will make a damn bit of difference.

"You'll always be my children. I don't care if you're eighty years old and using a cane. Always my babies," she repeats.

Gracie rolls her eyes. "Pops, you need to keep her busy so she doesn't butt into our lives."

Pops raises his hands and lifts his eyebrows. "I can only do so much. I'm just one man."

Gracie grunts into her coffee cup. "Bullshit."

Chloe waddles into the nursery, rubbing her belly. "I'm ready for this to be over," she grumbles. "Soon, my ass won't fit through a doorway."

I move away from my mother's side and slide toward my wife. "Gives me so much more to love," I whisper into her ear and touch her ass, which I've grown to love more than her flatter and less-full version. "We need to keep it."

Chloe looks at me with a horrified expression. "It's going. As soon as I can work out, it'll be disappearing."

"Shit never gets back to where it was," Ma tells her, ruining all Chloe's hopes and dreams of getting her pre-baby body back.

"Great," Chloe groans. "I could do without the extra padding."

I smile down at my girl. "It's the best part."

She slaps my chest with the back of her hand. "Shut up."

"Your tits and ass are primo," Gracie tells Chloe with a wink. "You get stares coming and going."

Chloe's shoulders slump forward. "It's hard to miss me."

I place my fingers under Chloe's chin, raising her eyes to mine. "You're the most beautiful woman I've ever laid eyes on."

She sighs. "Oh, okay."

"Babe, you're stunning."

Chloe grumbles.

"You're growing a life inside you. If we have a little girl, I want her to look like you and not me because let's face it, I'd make one hell of an ugly woman."

"Amen to that," Gracie says with a hint of laughter. "I tried to doll you up when we were kids, but nope, still ugly as hell."

Ma bursts into a fit of laughter. "Your brothers had patience then. They let you practice on them for hours."

Chloe's face brightens. "You put makeup on them all?" she asks Gracie.

"Yep. All of them." Gracie beams with pride, but I feel nothing except annoyance.

I hated when my sister would do our hair, of which we had very little, and makeup. She was so slow, and the shit was hard as hell to get off too. But I did it to make her happy, even if it was only for a little while.

"I want that for our baby."

"Then you better work on another as soon as you have this one," Ma explains with the biggest smile. "You don't want them too far apart in age."

"You know, I did it most of the time just to annoy the shit out of you guys," Gracie tells me.

"It worked," I mumble.

"I'm going to need a little time in between," Chloe says to my mother.

"Don't wait too long. It's better when they're closer together in age."

"More expensive, too," I say.

"It's not cheaper to have kids far apart. They're expensive no matter what, kiddo," Pops says. "I'd be rich if it weren't for you four."

"Rich in the bank, but poor in life and love," Mom tells him.

"Yeah, that too," he says, but I'm not convinced he thinks or feels the same.

"There's no amount of money I'd take to replace my time with you kids," Pops says. "You'll see, son. You'll give that child your last cent to see a smile on their face."

"Speaking of their… Do we know if we're having a boy or a girl?" Ma asks.

"We?" Gracie laughs. "Are you going to be in there pushing too, Ma?"

Ma waves her hand to Gracie to shush. "Do we?"

Chloe looks up at me and raises an eyebrow. We've known for weeks but have been keeping it a secret. Not an easy one to keep either. But we know once they know, the entire town will know. Not that it's a bad thing, but it's been nice to have a secret all to ourselves.

"We do," Chloe says softly as she looks me in the eye, waiting to see if I'll react.

I'm fine with them knowing. "Maybe Ma will stop buying yellow shit if we tell her."

"There's nothing wrong with yellow," Ma informs us like we're monsters. "It's a lovely color. Mint green, too."

"I agree," Chloe says, squeezing my arm. "Maybe we should let it be a surprise."

"No. No. No. No," my mother chants, shaking her head. "I want to know. I *need* to know."

"Don't make her beg any longer, son," Pops pleads with me.

"Fine. Fine," I say, looking down at my wife. "Do you want to tell her, or should I?"

"Jesus," Ma mutters. "Just spit it out. You're killing me here."

"You do it," I tell Chloe.

Chloe's smile widens as she gazes up at me. "Buy all the pink things," she says to me, but she's talking to my parents.

Ma gasps. "A girl? We're having a girl?" She squeals so loud I swear one of my eardrums bursts, and she runs to my father, throwing her arms around him. "Did you hear that, Mario? We're having a baby girl."

I wrap my arms around Chloe, holding her tight while my

mother has her excitement-induced meltdown. I knew she'd be happy. Hell, I was over the moon to be having a little girl.

"Little girls are so special," Pops says to me. "You're in for a world of hurt and happiness."

"Pops, did I hurt you?" Gracie asks him.

"You grew up, sweetheart," he tells her plainly.

Gracie walks up to my father, throwing her arms around him on the opposite side as my mother. "I'll always be your little girl."

"That'll be us someday," Chloe says, clinging to me. "Our own little family."

I lean over, kissing the top of her head. "Just the three of us."

She peers up, placing her hand on my chest over my heart, giving me the sweetest smile. "Maybe four."

I could never break her heart or disappoint her. Family is important to me, but it's always been a dream for Chloe. "However many you want, baby."

She lifts a hopeful eyebrow. "Ten?"

I laugh, shaking my head. "Now you're getting extreme."

"You said however many I want."

"Let's start with one, and we'll see what happens from there."

"Deal," she breathes into my shirt as she holds me tight.

"Now, about the baby shower," Ma says. Thankfully, she didn't hear our conversation or else she'd be giving her input into how many kids she'd want us to have.

"I love you," Chloe whispers to me as my mother goes on and on about the party.

"I love you too," I say back, knowing my life will never be the same and hopeful for everything that's still to come.

Dear Reader,

I love Chloe & Franco so much I had to write a little something extra to their story. If you'd like a little more click the link below to signup for my newsletter and you'll get an **EXCLUSIVE BONUS CHAPTER**!

<u>GET THE BONUS CHAPTER HERE</u>
or visit menofinked.com/ntl_bonus

Gracie's story is coming next and she's about to be swept off her feet by a hot single dad. Preorder your copy of **Never Too Soon** and be ready to swoon!

Do you want to have your very own SIGNED paperbacks on your bookshelf? Tap here to check out Chelle Bliss Romance or visit chelleblissromance.com and stock up on paperbacks, Inked gear, and other book worm merchandise!

never too CLOSE

www.chellebliss.com

CHELLE BLISS

USA TODAY BESTSELLING AUTHOR

CHAPTER ONE

I press print for what must be the hundredth time on my ma's ancient computer.

And nothing happens.

Again.

I hit the on/off button, check the power cables and connections, look for paper, ink, and any other obvious reasons why this goddamn little machine will print recipes and pictures of my mother's rescue animals, but the one day I actually need a physical document, I can't get the thing to show even the slightest sign of life.

"Come on, you little asshole."

I run my hands through my hair before I check the time on my phone.

Almost noon.

Damn it.

One of my mom's foster cats—this one is new, so I'm not sure what her name is—jumps up onto the desk and tries to nuzzle my face.

"Baby, you're adorable, but I don't have time for love right now."

I've showered, but I've still got to get dressed and drive down to the station. My meeting with the chief is in an hour, and I cannot fuck this up.

I scratch her before giving her a gentle nudge away from the desk, and then I check all the printer settings again. When another five attempts at printing still don't work, I give in and run up the stairs, and my sock snags on the wood. I catch myself before I fall flat on my face. "Oh fuck!" I yell out, aggravated beyond belief.

"Vito, language," my mother says, sitting at the dining room table with Sassy, one of her best friends.

Ma has a group of ladies she's tight with, and they keep one another busy. Sassy works as a waitress at my brother Benito's restaurant, Bev runs the local animal shelter where Ma volunteers, and then there is Carol, whose son and ex-husband own the garage here in Star Falls where my older brother Franco works.

Small-town living, but I wouldn't have it any other way.

I get my footing and stifle another mouthful of curses.

Sassy snorts and almost spits coffee onto Ma's tablecloth. "Mornin', sunshine," she says.

I go around the table and kiss Sassy and Carol on the cheeks, greeting them. "Bev workin'?" I ask.

When I get around to my mother, she gives me a fake-angry look but then holds up her hands to cup my face. "She'll be here for brunch in a few minutes. I'm so glad you're here, V. You can meet Sassy's niece."

I shake my head. "Can't stick around, Ma. Sorry. Got to run down to the station."

Ladies' brunch is a new thing they started after my sister Grace had her baby. Gracie is a stepmom to two adorable kiddos and has a one-year-old of her own now, Ethan. The brunches are potlucks where whoever is free can stop by and catch up. And Ma's friends are definitely birds of a feather. Even though only Sassy and Carol are here, at least ten dishes are on the table already.

"This spread could convince me to stick around," I say. "Sassy..." I draw out her name and flash her a flirtatious smile. "Are these your famous raspberry kolacky cookies?" I wink and grab one of the powdered-sugar-covered little bow ties.

"Vito," Ma sighs, swatting at my hand. "We have company coming today."

I shake my head. "Right, right, okay. Ma, can you help me for a sec? The damn printer's acting up again."

My mother crosses her arms over her chest, and the corner of one side of her lips curls up. "Aren't you the one who told me nobody uses paper anymore. Join the digital age?"

I shake my head and crack up at my mother's impersonation of me. "That doesn't sound like me, Ma. Sounds like you're confusing me with Benny."

Ma shakes her head but pushes back from the table. "Sassy, grab the door if anyone comes, will you? And if Eden arrives before I'm back, yell for me. This might take a minute."

I follow my mother down into the basement.

"Oh, kitty." Ma bends down to pet the cat who's still in isolation as soon as we make it to the bottom of the stairs. "How's my beautiful princess today?"

I squeeze my brows and try not to start stressing. "Ma," I say, trying to bring my mother back on task. "I just need these three pages printed. Can you take a look?"

I lean over the print preview panel, relieved that none of the text is readable. It's not that what I'm working on is a big secret or anything, but I just don't really want my family meddling in my business until I actually have news to share.

Ma immediately hits cancel on the print preview and drops into her office chair to get comfy. But then just as suddenly, she whirls to look at me. "Oh my God, son…"

"What? What is it?" My heart starts to race, and sweat instantly coats my palms. "Ma, what happened?" I rest a reassuring hand on her shoulder as my chest tightens.

Ma reaches a hand up to her shoulder and clenches my fingers between her perfectly manicured nails. "Baby," she says, looking sad. "Sassy just told me something upstairs. Something I don't know if you've heard about yet."

I squeeze her hand, all worries about the time evaporating

because Sassy news isn't anything to panic over. "Ma, you're going to give me a heart attack. What is it?"

She stands from the chair and lifts her face to look from her five-foot-nothing frame into my eyes. "Vito, Michelle had dinner in your brother's restaurant last night. Michelle, son. She's moved back to Star Falls."

I'm so surprised by this that I drop Ma's hand and step away from her. "Michelle..." I mutter. "Wow. Well, okay. Is she all right? Her grandpa didn't get worse, did he?"

Michelle fucking Bianchi. My ex-wife. The woman who owned my heart and then literally crushed it under her stiletto heel.

Ma nods. "Looks that way. Sassy said her grandfather needs to move into a memory care place. You know that one on the east side of town."

I do know the one, but I don't say anything. I'm a firefighter, and there have been too many suspicious fires at that place over the last year. That's part of what I want to meet with the chief about. But I hold back what I know and focus on the fact that my ex-wife is back in town.

"I'm sorry to hear that. Michelle's gramps was a great guy," I add.

Ma nods. "But it looks like Michelle is doing very well for herself. She's opened her own business. Teaching at the community college too."

"Teaching?" I shake my head in wonder, but I'm not at all surprised. My ex-wife was always smart. Smart enough to leave my ass behind when it became clear we didn't have the same aspirations in life. Aspirations. Even that word sounds smart. "I'm happy for her, Ma."

"Honey," Ma says, her caring eyes focused so intently on me I don't even have to guess what's coming. I know. My mother is so wonderful but also incredibly predictable. "Do you think you're going to be okay? Maybe you should see her? Sit down for a cup of coffee and just get everything out in the open."

I hold up my hands. "Nah, Ma. Michelle moving back to Star

Falls is none of my business. We've been divorced for five years. I'm over it. I'm over her. All that's old news, ancient history, okay?"

Ma looks at me, an expression of so much worry and love on her face that I pull her in for a hug.

"What I really need right now is to get going, but I can't do that until I get this shit printed."

Her sadness seems to vanish instantly, but I know she won't be convinced so easily. "You got it, sweetie. I'm on it."

Thirty minutes later, I'm dressed in dark gray dress pants, a white shirt with the top few buttons unbuttoned, and I have a tie slung over my shoulder. I dig through my closet for some nicer shoes, but since Ma doesn't like us wearing shoes in the house, I loop my fingers through the laces to carry them to the door.

I look through my room for anything I can use to protect my paperwork and eventually have to settle on an old issue of one of my favorite camping magazines. I tuck the paperwork in, check the time, and haul ass down the stairs.

Just as I skid to a stop at the base of the stairs, my sister Grace raises an eyebrow at me and grins. "This little nugget has been asking for you for the last ten minutes."

"Gracie." I lean down to give my sister a kiss. "And look at you, little man. Got my hands full today, buddy. Hang on." I rush to the front door, drop my dress shoes, and gently set my magazine on top of them. Then I turn and open my arms wide to my nephew.

Gracie sets Ethan on his feet, and he struggles to make it all the way across the hallway. All thoughts about the time rush out of my head as I watch my nephew take shaky steps across the living room. His mouth is open in a thrilled grin, his arms in front of him as he reaches for me. I drop to my knees and inch across the floor just in time to catch him before his little legs buckle.

"What was that?" I ask, picking him up and blowing loud kisses into his belly. "You run better than I do, buddy."

Little Ethan's baby teeth show as he laughs and laughs. He

clamps his mouth against my shoulder and squeezes me tight in a hug.

"So proud of you, little man." I set my nephew down, and when I stand back up, he grabs my leg and tugs to be picked up again. "I got to run," I say reluctantly.

Ma's friends are gathered around the living room table, including Bev, who must have arrived while I was getting dressed.

"Bev." I blow her a kiss and wave. "Got to dash, ladies. Have a good brunch."

The smells of coffee and the sounds of happy chatter are so welcoming, for a minute, I consider texting my chief and canceling our meeting to stay home and hang out with my family and Ma's friends, who, after all these years, are family too. I look down at my nephew and catch a glimpse of the magazine that is protecting my list of accomplishments and my résumé.

I have a moment of self-doubt seize me so hard, I almost drop back onto my knees.

Ever since my divorce, I've been stuck. Lost. Every time I get close to something that matters to me, I lose it, fuck it up, or run away.

I'm thirty-six, live at home with my parents, and haven't been on a real date in three months.

What I'm doing with my life, what I've done... I don't know.

I'm not like Benito, driven and intense in work and deeply committed to sowing my wild oats. My older brother Franco has had the same job for his whole life practically, and he has a woman he loves by his side. Gracie is an accomplished tattoo artist with two stepkids, a great husband, and now her own little nugget, Ethan.

I'm a middle child who's always been the lost kid.-I thought that marrying Michelle was the answer to making the life I wanted, but turns out, I wasn't enough for her.

And I just got passed over for a promotion at work I wanted badly, but I wasn't enough for that either. For a hot second, I consider saying fuck it.

Dreams are for different people.

I could stay and eat brunch and hang with my family, but then what?

When everyone goes home to their lives, I'm going to go back upstairs to my bedroom and feel like shit about myself all over again?

I shake my head and smooth Ethan's hair. "Love you, kiddo, but I got to hustle up."

"Who you looking so sexy for, V?" Sassy gets up and heads over to pick up little Ethan. She lowers her voice. "Speaking of sexy, did your mother tell you who I saw last night?"

I stifle a groan.

The last thing I need is for my mom's friends to get into matchmaking mode.

Michelle is my past. She is most definitely not my future. She made that much clear when she divorced me.

"She did, Sassy, but you know that's old news. Nothing I'm going to get myself worked up over, and none of you need to either."

"What? What'd I miss?" Gracie pours some cream into her coffee and starts cutting up a child's plate full of food. "Who'd Sassy see?"

"Wish I could stay, but I'm late." I slip my feet into my shoes and tie the laces as fast as I can so Ma doesn't yell at me for running around without them tied. "Y'all can talk about me once I'm gone."

I check my pocket for my wallet and phone, then reach for the shelf Pops installed on the wall for my keys. But there's nothing hanging on the hook where my truck keys should be.

"Ma!" I yell. "Where are my keys?"

"Oh, shoot." Ma pushes back from the dining room table and pads over to me. I try not to think about the time. The chief is going to give me hell for this. "I'm sorry, honey. I moved your truck onto the street so the girls could park in the driveway. Your truck is down the street." She fishes the keys out of a pocket in her rhinestone-bedazzled jeans. "Here you go, baby. Have a great day, son."

I grab the keys, grin, and with the magazine in one hand, yank open the front door.

"Oh, uh…hello?" a soft voice says. Standing on the front stoop is

CHELLE BLISS

probably the most stunning woman I've ever seen. And since my ex-wife was a stripper, that's saying something.

"Hello?" I look into her eyes and realize this woman is tall. Like nearly eye level with me, and I'm just shy of six feet. She's not skinny and lean like Michelle was. This woman is full-figured, which I cannot miss since she's holding a wriggling little girl about Ethan's age against her ample chest.

"Oh God. I'm so sorry. Did I knock on the wrong door?" The woman is staring at me, blinking her brown eyes rapidly. She squints and takes a step back, looking for the wrought-iron numbers that correspond to our street address on the front of the house.

"This is the Bianchi residence." I'm gripping the keys in my hand so tightly I feel the metal cut into my palm. I loosen my grip and cock my head. "Who are you looking for?"

"My aunt Shirley," she says, looking dazed. She frowns and pulls a cell phone from the front pocket of a large purse-style diaper bag. "I'm sorry to have bothered you."

She turns and starts to walk back down the walkway when I call out to her. "Shirley... Do you mean Sassy?"

Just then, Sassy bellows from the dining room table. "Eden!" My mom's friend bolts past me to meet the woman—Eden, I assume—at the door. "Oh my God," Sassy cries again. She takes the little girl from Eden's arms and plasters her face with kisses, then turns to me and holds out her arms. "Vito, hold my grandniece for a second. I need a hug from this one."

Before I know what's happening, there is yet another kid in my arms. "Uh, hello there," I say, holding the stranger's child awkwardly in my arms.

The little girl looks like she's about to start crying, and I don't blame her. I'm a strange man, and she was just yanked from her mama's arms. I plaster on a bright smile and sort of jiggle her up and down in my arms the way I do with Ethan. While I try to stall a meltdown, Sassy wraps Eden in her arms and rocks her wildly back and forth, tears literally streaming down her face.

"I'm so glad you're here now, baby. We're going to take good care of you."

378

With keys and my magazine in one hand and this kiddo in the other, I've literally got my arms full.

Sassy finally releases the woman whose cheeks are red even though she's wearing a smile so beautiful my heart cracks a little. She wipes tears from her eyes and leans her head on Sassy's shoulder, which takes some effort since Eden is tall.

"Vito, this is my niece, Eden. Newly landed in Star Falls from the City of Angels." Sassy hasn't released Eden for even a second, and I can't exactly extend a hand to shake hers, so I nod.

"Nice to meet you," I say, my words coming out slow as I look her over. I don't mean to be creepy, but this woman is a fucking knockout. But it hits me all at once that I'm holding her child. Her daughter. Which means a baby daddy or husband can't be far away. I steel my reactions to her and grin down at the little lady in my arms. "And who's this?" I ask.

Eden releases herself from her aunt's choke hold and wipes the last of her tears from her cheeks. "I'm sorry," she says. "You must think I'm a hot mess, just handing my baby to a stranger. This is my daughter, Juniper."

I drag my eyes away from Eden and grin at her child. "Juniper? What a gorgeous name for a gorgeous little lady. You know my nephew Ethan is about your age, and I'll bet you two are going to get along great." I raise my brows at Sassy, hoping she'll get the hint and take the kiddo so I can get going.

But Sassy is in no real rush to do anything but introduce Eden to absolutely everyone. She drags her niece into the living room, and I follow, keeping hold of Juniper while my mom, sister, Bev, and Carol all make their introductions to Eden.

"Ma," I say quietly, hoping I can appeal to her maternal instincts. As much as I hate to break up the party, if I'm late to meet the chief after we both agreed to come in on our day off, I can kiss this opportunity goodbye. "Ma, I've..."

But just as I'm walking up to my mother, hoping she'll take the baby from me, Juniper grabs everyone's attention by ripping out a belch so big that everyone in the room starts cracking up. Everyone but Eden.

"Oh no," she says, her arms out. She's moving toward me, her eyes fixed on her daughter as if she knows what's about to happen.

I'm still laughing in shock at the man-sized belch from the little kid when my shock turns to horror. Little Juniper looks up at me, her little lower lip trembles, and then she projectile vomits all over my dress clothes.

CHAPTER TWO

eden

This is not the reunion I'd imagined when my auntie invited me to her best friend's house. First of all, I was promised a ladies' brunch.

I know Auntie Shirley has a group of friends she's been tight with since high school. But nobody mentioned that any of those friends had hot sons. And the last thing I want anything to do with is a man. Any man. And especially a hot man.

Vito Bianchi is gorgeous. He had this heart-melting, youthful look about him when he was being playful with Juniper, but now, as he shrugs off the shirt that Juniper inconveniently threw up all over, it's like the gods of love and sex are tormenting me. He's got muscles for days. I can almost hear angels singing as he strips off the orange-splattered dress shirt.

I stare, stunned, while Lucia and my aunt grab Juniper and go wash her face in the kitchen. That leaves me with a whole bunch of people I don't know, including him.

"I'm so sorry," I blurt out. "She's not sick, I promise. She gets a little carsick sometimes, and I gave her some cold water with a tiny bit of orange juice in the car, but apparently that did not help."

Once the shock of what's happened wears off, I go immediately into damage-control mode. I rush toward the man and try to help him ease off the shirt so none of my daughter's throw-up touches his skin.

He shakes off the dress shirt and stands before me wearing just a sleeveless white tank and gray dress pants. My mouth opens a little at the sight of his sculpted chest dusted with a tiny hint of dark hair. His arms look so smooth, my fingers itch to touch the well-defined muscles.

"It's all right," he says, his voice sounding sincere. We're almost the same height, so when I lift my chin, our eyes meet. "I, uh… I'll just… I should change."

I'm holding the sticky shirt in my hands like it's yesterday's garbage while my traitorous eyes take in the length of him. "Your pants," I say, biting my lower lip.

He bends his head down to look, and he must see the big wet spot on the front of his pants, right over the zipper.

I want to die.

"I'm so sorry," I say again. "I'll have them cleaned. I'll replace them. I'm so sorry."

For a second, a look that is almost heartbreakingly sad passes over his face. He closes his eyes, then pulls his phone from his pocket. He's got a magazine and a set of keys in one hand, and with the other, he punches in a number on his phone.

"One sec," he tells me, then he turns his attention to the call. "Chief? Yeah, I'm going to be about fifteen minutes late. I got puked on. Thankfully by a child, but I've got to change."

He's quiet for a minute, then ends the call. He faces me with a smile that seems to spread across his whole face. "Could be worse. I could be the one who did the puking. At least I can still make my meeting."

"Oh God." The reality of what's going on hits me. He's dressed up. He was running out the door. And now, we've made him late. "What can I do? Do you have another shirt? Can I iron something?"

Vito looks at me for a second and laughs so hard, I am tempted to join in.

"Iron?" A woman who looks like a female version of Vito is laughing with him. I just met her a minute ago, but I can't for the life of me remember her name. "My brother wears pajamas and house slippers twenty-four seven. He doesn't have another dress shirt."

Vito takes the dirty shirt from me and thrusts it at his sister. "Go stuff this in the laundry. Help your brother out."

She gives Vito a look but then holds out a hand. "Am I washing your pants too?"

For a hot minute, I hold my breath, wondering if he is actually going to strip off his pants right here in front of us all. But he just flicks his sister in the ribs and then takes the stairs two at a time.

While the hottie goes up to change, I head into the kitchen to see how my daughter is.

"Well, don't we make a fine first impression," I say, shaking my head. My aunt Shirley's meeting my daughter for the first time ever, but they seem to be getting along just brilliantly.

Juniper is sitting on the kitchen counter, her own shirt miraculously free of any signs of the mess. Her face is clean, and her hair has been smoothed back from her face. She's got a small bowl of water in front of her and one of those baby washcloths with a soft gray elephant attached to it. She's following my aunt's instructions and gently dabbing at her own cheeks with the cloth.

The sight breaks down a wall I have built around my heart, and I immediately burst into tears.

"Honey, it's okay." My aunt's friend Lucia is comedically short, so she comes over to comfort me but can't reach my shoulder. She rests a comforting hand on my lower back and just pats me. "Throw-ups happen. We have a lot of kids coming through this house. Believe me, we've seen worse."

My aunt has her hands firmly on Junie's waist, so she is secure, even sitting on the counter. "No more tears," my aunt insists. "We're family. Cleaning up messes comes with the territory."

But that's what Auntie Shirley doesn't understand. This is uncharted territory for me. I've had to hide Juniper for so long that having someone love her on sight is foreign to me. I just don't know how to accept this kind of love. This is why I left Los Angeles. I had no idea what I was getting myself into moving here. I had very few options left, though, and if this is how things are going to go, I can't imagine making a better decision.

Lucia wraps her arm around my waist. "You know, honey, how old is Juniper? One? She could be teething too. It might not just be carsickness. Those baby teeth are a real pain."

I wipe away the tears for the second time today and chuckle. "They are awful," I agree.

And she's right. Junie's been chewing and drooling so much lately, I'm sure that red spot I noticed on her gums the other day is another tooth about to break through.

"What do you say, Junebug?" I walk over to my aunt and rest a hand on Shirley's shoulder. I don't want to pull my daughter from her great-aunt before they have a chance to bond. Junie's only had me as a caregiver for most of her life. I'm thrilled she seems so interested in all the new people that she's not clinging to me.

"Mama, elephant." Junie dunks the washcloth into the water, sending a small sprinkle of water onto my aunt's sleeve.

"I see it," I say, grinning at my baby.

"Juniper is gorgeous," Lucia says. "What an angel. You know who's going to love her? My granddaughter. She loves her cousin Ethan, but…" Lucia waves a hand at my daughter's curls. "Look at that hair. She's going to want to play princess and dress-up. I hope you're ready for playdates and lots of willing babysitters."

I cover my mouth with my hand to hold back any words that might come out. There's nothing I can say to this. I can finally see why my aunt was so insistent on my moving here. After everything that happened back in Los Angeles, I believe that I can start over here in Star Falls. When I first found out I was pregnant, I thought my big, exciting life was over. And then, when Juniper's father made his feelings about the matter clear to me, I thought my life itself was over.

My aunt lifts Junie off the counter while I take the bowl of water and dump the contents down the drain. I'm facing the sink and window when a sexy voice calls into the kitchen.

"Ma, I'm going for real now. See you for dinner."

I turn to follow the voice and see Vito Bianchi standing in the doorway. The waves of his brown hair have fallen loose from their careful style, and in place of the perfect dress shirt and pants, he's wearing a pair of dark jeans and a casual cotton button-down.

"Do you really only have one dress shirt?" I blurt out. As soon as I say the words, I shake my head. No freaking filter. I never have had one. "I mean, you look great. I was serious about replacing your shirt and pants. If, you know..." I'm rambling.

Lucia raises up on her tiptoes to kiss her son's cheek, but over his mother's shoulder, his eyes are laser-focused on me. "See you, V," she says. But then Lucia cocks her head as if putting something together in her mind. "Are you going to work? I didn't think you were on today?"

Vito's intense chocolate eyes move from mine to his mom. "Ma, it's something else. I'm meeting with the chief, but it shouldn't take long. See you for dinner."

"Vito, are you in trouble? Honey, is everything all right?" She sounds worried, and right away, I pick up on the smallest details in Vito's reaction.

He visibly winces and kind of pulls away, but then he quickly composes himself and reassures his mom. "Ma, it's nothing." Then he breaks into a grin and lowers his chin to look at Junie. "Bye, Juniper. You sure know how to make an entrance." Then it's my turn. "Nice meeting you, Eden." His voice is softer when he addresses me.

I don't have the energy to apologize again. I'm starting to feel overwhelmed by the emotions of the day, and I've only been here for like twenty minutes.

I nod at him. "Nice meeting you," I say quietly, then I turn away.

Hot guy or not, I can only let so many things get close to my heart right now. Bringing an aunt and a bunch of new friends in is more than enough and maybe even more than I can take.

By the end of brunch, I've laughed so hard and eaten so much, my stomach is turning. My aunt has convinced me to call her Aunt Sassy, because she said every time I say Shirley, no one knows who I'm talking about.

And honestly, the Aunt Shirley I expected is nothing like the aunt I'm seeing. Sassy fits her so, so much better.

It has to be around one thirty when Gracie puts her son down for a nap in her old bedroom upstairs. She yawns and asks her mom to wake her by 2:30 if she isn't up so she can get on the road to pick up her older kids.

Bev hurries back to the shelter, and Carol has a job she's got to get back to as well. Lucia doesn't have a full-time job, and Aunt Sassy doesn't have to be at work where she's a waitress until three. After Grace lies down with Ethan, Lucia and Aunt Sassy put away the leftover food but then retreat to the couches.

"Are you allergic to dogs?" Lucia asks.

"Not at all. I love dogs," I tell her. "I've actually been planning on getting one now that we have a little house."

"Oh, Eden, don't tell Lucia you want a dog. She'll have every rescue from that shelter on your doorstep if you let her." Aunt Sassy leans back on the couch, crosses her legs, and plops her bare feet up on a pretty ottoman.

"Well, my Chihuahua isn't friendly," Lucia warns. "But she loves Gracie. I'm going to send her upstairs. But my Venus is the sweetest. She's been out in the yard plenty for one day." Lucia opens a patio door, and an aged lab-mix-type dog wanders in, wagging her tail so hard it's difficult not to grin. After loving on the lab for a few minutes, Lucia scoops up the Chihuahua and carries it upstairs. "Be right back, girls."

Once my aunt and I are alone, I get down on the floor with Junie and introduce her to the dog. "See, Junie?" I hold my hand out, fingers down, letting the dog sniff me. "Hold Mommy's hand."

I clasp Junie's hand in mine and let the dog sniff her fill. Once she seems satisfied that we're good people, she licks Junie's hand and flops down on her back, legs up.

"I think that means we can pet her," I say, scratching the silvery fur with my nails.

"Venus is an angel," Aunt Sassy says over a yawn. "I never worry about the kids around that one. The Chihuahua, on the other hand..."

Lucia returns and drops onto the couch next to Sassy. "You girls want some more coffee or water?"

"Lucia, I'm stuffed. I'm not going to be able to make it through my shift without a bottle of Tums."

I look at my aunt. "Auntie, are you okay?"

Aunt Sassy pats her belly. "Baby, never better. Don't you worry about me. But just you wait. You hit fifty, and nothing works the same anymore."

Lucia cackles her agreement. "What I wouldn't give to be fifty again," Lucia says. "I'm just grateful I have grandchildren while I'm still young enough to enjoy them."

"Amen." Sassy yawns again. "Lucia, I don't know where you get the energy. One afternoon with the kids has worn me out." She looks at me. "And you. You've been doing this all alone."

An awkward silence fills the room. I don't know what to say to that. I assume my aunt's told her friends about our family. My aunt is my dad's sister, but calling the man my dad would be... Well, let's just say calling him that would be generous.

He left my mom when I was three and didn't bother to parent beyond sending child support—late, and usually less than what he owed—and cards on my birthday and holidays.

If Aunt Shirley hadn't made an effort to stay in touch with me my entire life, I wouldn't know anyone on my dad's side of the family.

And then there's my mom. That's a whole different kind of story, and it's even sadder than being abandoned by my dad.

"How you doing, honey?" Lucia asks warmly. And somehow, even though I've only just met her, I get the sense that she really does care.

"What I want to know," Sassy interrupts, not letting me answer Lucia's question, "is what's up with Juniper's father? What is it with these men who abandon their kids?" Sassy shakes her head and looks at Lucia. "You know I don't condone the kind of father my brother was. But it really pisses me off that my beautiful niece had to go through this not just with her own father, but with the father of this beautiful angel."

Lucia and Sassy look incredibly worked up, and while I appreciate their interest, this is not a conversation I'm comfortable having. No, correction. It's not a conversation I can have. There's a whole legal contract that prevents me from saying just about anything more than the rehearsed line I'm about to repeat.

"We reached an amicable agreement," I say quietly. "I want to raise my daughter on my own. I didn't want to raise her in Los Angeles. It's better for all of us this way."

The answer is close to the truth of the situation. Close enough, but I still get a very sad look from Lucia and a shade of stink-eye from Aunt Sassy.

My aunt frowns. "Well, that asshole doesn't know what he's missing out on."

"Ma, seriously. You going to ground Sassy for that kind of language?"

I look up from my perch on the floor to see Vito leaning against the living room doorway.

And sweet Jesus...somehow, he looks even better than he did earlier.

"V, baby, I didn't even hear you come in. You hungry? We got loads of leftovers. Let me make you a plate." Lucia jumps up before he can accept. She passes by him, and he gives her a kiss as she heads to the kitchen.

Then he strolls past me and takes Lucia's seat next to my aunt on the couch. "You know she wouldn't listen if I told her no," he says, grinning at my aunt. "So, who's the asshole?"

Sassy shakes her head and frowns. "Nobody that matters, that's for sure."

"Fair enough," Vito says. He kicks up his feet and shares the ottoman with my aunt. The gesture is so comfortable, so familiar. I can't believe this is the life my aunt's lived all these years. A pang of longing hits me deep in my chest, and I do what I always do now when the hard feelings close in. I shake them off.

I crawl over to Junie's diaper bag and pull out her favorite toy, a little fabric book with large felt pieces that can be stuck to the pages of the book. I focus on my daughter but address my question to Vito.

"So, uh, how was your meeting?" I settle Junie in my lap and cross my legs to form a chair for her little body. She tears the fabric teddy bear and carrots and cars off the book and then sticks them back on in different places. I avoid making eye contact as I ask the question, but I peek up at him as he answers.

"Good, I guess." He's quiet, his full lips pressed together. He studies my face, and for a moment, I feel like he's going to say more, but then he just says, "Thanks for asking."

I fix my attention on Junie while Lucia comes back in with a plate of food for Vito. "Oh honey, I didn't grab you anything to drink. What do you want?"

Vito takes the plate from his mom and motions to the couch. "Ma, sit. I'll get myself a water. Take a load off, will you? You've been running all day. Hang with your friends."

He takes his plate and wanders off toward the kitchen. I can't even help myself. As he passes by, I check out his ass.

And man, that was the wrong thing to do. It's a really, really nice ass.

I drag my eyes away just as Sassy and Lucia settle in for their next pointed question.

"So, Eden," Lucia asks. She rubs her hands together gleefully while Sassy rolls her eyes and groans. "What kind of dog are you thinking?"

I chuckle and kiss the top of my daughter's head.

Welcome to Star Falls.

I have a feeling I'm going to like living in a small town a lot more than I ever dreamed was possible.

CHAPTER THREE

The one bad thing about living in a small town is sometimes you have to go far outside your comfort zone.

One thing that was never in my comfort zone was school—specifically, college. But ever since our meeting last week, the words of my chief keep echoing in my ears.

I'm a firefighter. Been a firefighter since I was twenty. I toyed around with a bunch of jobs—some I liked and a few I even liked a lot. And I admit there were a few I got fired from, but shit, I was a kid back then.

What I always knew was that I was not cut out for college. Nobody in my family went to college. Gracie is a self-taught artist who started tattooing right out of high school. Franco's a mechanic. Benito did go to culinary school, but that's a totally different type of learning. I mean, there's no math required in culinary school—at least not as far as my brother said. Kitchen math, sure, like measuring, budgets, and shit. But the kind of stuff that put me to sleep in high school? Algebra and whatnot... I just couldn't see spending four years and a load of money to learn stuff I'd never use in my life.

When I met with the chief, I asked him point-blank about my

future. Fourteen years with the department. Excellent reviews and commendations. But I'm the only one who hasn't been promoted. Last month, I applied for two jobs—captain in a city department about an hour away from Star Falls and inspector here in town.

I didn't get either.

I didn't even get an interview.

I had the blessing of the chief to apply for the inspector position, but until the final decision was made, I couldn't really ask him about what I need to do to move up.

When we finally sat down, the answer should have been obvious, but I was still surprised when I heard it.

"There's no question you're a good guy and a great firefighter." Chief shoved the reading glasses off his face and dropped my résumé and list of career accomplishments on his desk. "You know how in-demand these jobs are. Every firefighter in the state would love to move to a place like Star Falls for a six-figure job working investigations. Every time we post an opening, we get more candidates than we can possibly imagine." Chief pointed at me with a single finger. "How many you think applied for the job you wanted? Throw out a number."

I shook my head and sighed. "I don't know, a hundred."

Chief blew air out from between his lips. "V, we had almost two thousand applications come in. Two thousand. We had guys applying from as far as New York and Alaska."

"Two thousand applicants..." I repeated in disbelief.

I knew that the hiring process was often political and came down to who you knew and who knew you, but shit, with that many people, I can understand why I wasn't even interviewed. I couldn't compete with that many guys. A job I'd thought I'd be perfect for, but I was never, ever close to being considered, let alone close to getting it.

"Vito, some of those guys had PhDs. P-h-fucking-Ds." He raised his silver brows and sighed. "Incredible on paper, great references. At this level, the quality of the careers is next level." He met my eyes and shrugged. "It's like anything else. I don't think a piece of paper from a college makes a bit of difference to whether or not I want you in my company. But it's a box the powers that be can check, and it makes the process a lot simpler."

A box they can check.

Four years of somebody's life, maybe more, for the education, not to mention the money, the cost. And for what? After taking some classes on dead poets and basic math, some dickhead with a degree is a more attractive candidate than me after fourteen years on the job?

Even as my gut burned with frustration, I knew Chief was giving it to me straight. There are no undereducated firefighters getting inspector and captain positions. It's the guys who have the time in I do *and* the piece of damn paper to back it up who are edging me out time and time again.

The meeting we had was all the confirmation I needed. I had no path forward in my career.

I'm thirty-four years old, and the one thing holding me back from moving ahead in my career is a damn college degree.

But that's the reason I've spent some of my time on my days off trolling the internet, reading up on local colleges. When I look at the courses that are offered, the application process, the requirements to get in, and then the courses I'd have to take, it sends me off into a funk that has me questioning everything.

I slam the lid of my laptop down a little too hard and check the time. It's almost sunrise, and I've got two hours until my next shift starts.

I tug on a T-shirt and slide into my house shoes before quietly heading down the stairs since Ma and Pops are still asleep.

When Gracie lived here, she didn't start work until after noon, and I had early mornings completely to myself. Now that Pops is retired, he's eased off his sleep schedule. Most of the days I'm on shift, I have coffee with Pops before I head out. It's an oddly comforting routine.

I try not to spend a lot of time thinking about it, but the reality is that every time I get in my truck and go to work, it could be the last time I see my family.

Star Falls is a small town, but there are enough smells and bells to keep our department hopping. Smells being anything from someone thinking they smell gas to smelling actual smoke, and bells meaning everything you could imagine. Falls at nursing homes, home alarms, smoke detectors going off because somebody thought cooking a pizza in a toaster was a thing.

And of course, we see our share of horrific stuff. Accidents. Injuries. Fatalities. Homes destroyed. Precious possessions lost.

Most people spend their lives running from danger and scary shit. When you're a first responder, I don't care what kind, the only way to do the job is to get up close with the stuff that gives other people nightmares.

Staring into the soot that covers the windows of a burning business. Crawling along the floor of a hallway thick with smoke. I've carried kids out of car wrecks with broken bones and injuries that haunted me for months. Wiped the debris off the face of an old lady who couldn't escape her apartment before the floor of her kitchen collapsed beneath her walker. I've smelled things and seen things most people will live their whole lives and never even think about.

After Michelle divorced me, I moved back home. I was heartbroken and never considered living on my own. I don't know why. A lot of guys lose their wives and relationships because of the stresses of the job, but for me, I need the routine of my family. The fact that no matter what I've seen during the shift, no matter how ugly and awful, the world I love and trust keeps spinning.

When I was married to Michelle, I desperately needed that innocence. I needed to know that I could come home to my wife, and she'd be there wanting me to watch some dumb-ass show while we argued over whether to get pepperoni on the whole pizza or only half.

I needed a strong family to anchor me to something that felt stable and real. When that ended, I went back home and never considered living anywhere else. Living under my parents' roof may be a massive strain on my dating life, but I don't think I could keep doing this work without some normal, non-fire-related life to go back to.

There are guys in my company who come from generations of firefighters. Guys whose dads and grandfathers and, in some cases, wives and mothers made careers in the fire service. I think they get a lot out of having people who understand the unpredictable schedule, the wrecked sleep, the hours, and the physical toll of the work.

But not me.

When I leave work, I switch off as much as I can. I'm never not a firefighter, but it's sometimes nice just to be Vito Bianchi, middle child, lost in the noise of my life outside of work.

When I head downstairs, I'm a little disappointed that Pops isn't up. Sometimes he surprises me by sneaking down when I'm in the shower or even before I'm awake. But nobody is sipping coffee or reading the paper at the table. I smell the coffee that I brewed before I jumped in the shower, and I pet the dogs who are so old now, they don't do much more than give me a one-eyed glare before going back to sleep.

I fill a mug and stare into the darkness outside the kitchen window. I can't help but think of Michelle being back in town.

Fuck, it's been a long time since I saw her. A long time since I had sex with anyone. And even longer since I was in a relationship with anyone who I thought could live up to what I had with my ex-wife.

My mom's words come back to me, and I wonder if it would do any good to see her again.

I finish my coffee and get ready to head to the station. I'm not sure why today, of all days, I'm wishing my pops were there to nod at me over his reading glasses, but I feel like I'm literally heading into the fire today.

And I'm not sure I like the feeling.

The call for a structure fire comes in close to midnight. The address is a residence in a neighborhood a short distance from the firehouse, which is good news because we know from dispatch there's a baby on the scene.

We scramble to get into gear and load into the engine, with the lights going but no siren. It's standard operating procedure if we don't need to clear traffic to run without sirens after bedtime.

When we reach the location, a woman is standing in the street in front of her house. She's wrapped in a knee-length bathrobe and is barefoot, cradling a screaming baby against her chest. The minute the crew leaves the engine, the chief greets the homeowner and assesses what he can. Within seconds, he's calling out orders.

The scene is surprisingly calm, all things considered. The company falls into our rhythm, uncoiling the hose and wrenching the nearby hydrant. Chief calls out that the homeowner is unsure of the origin, reported smoke in the bathroom, and the bathroom fan was on maybe thirty minutes.

Chief's calling out that there's no husband, just the woman and baby, who appear upset but unharmed. Everyone's out. That's a good start. Even with no reported people or pets inside, we'll still have to check every room just to make sure.

There have been a few people who've locked an unwanted spouse in a closet and tossed in a match, so we can't just take the homeowner's word for it when they say the place is empty. Chief sends two vets, Miller and Drinan, on a single attack line while we wait for reinforcements to arrive.

Chief is standing at the back of the ambulance where the homeowner and her baby have been checked out for any signs of exposure to smoke or fumes. They're wrapped in blankets against the chilly night made even colder by the fact that they were both barefoot from the quick look I got when we pulled up.

The fire was contained to the bathroom and the hallway, and it looked like the fan was most likely the cause. The bathroom fan had a buildup of dust and dirt. Not uncommon at all, but most people don't realize that the fans should be cleaned.

I feel bad for the woman. Looks like they hadn't moved in all that long ago. Moving boxes were still stacked in the corners of each room. But the house is so small, very few of her possessions will be salvageable between the smoke and the water.

Only once the cleanup is nearly complete and the chief asks me to escort the homeowner inside do I realize I know the lady. And I know her baby.

"Eden?" I've got all my turnout gear in place, so I'm not even sure she can see my face. "It's Vito. Vito Bianchi."

Since I'm on the job, I keep my demeanor professional, but inside, my heart is breaking for her. She just moved to town. She's not even unpacked yet. And now she's lost everything. She's literally wearing a blanket.

Eden's face drops when I say my name. Her lovely face is pale, and she looks like she's both exhausted and in shock. I'm sure she is both. Even worse, little Juniper is quiet, sound asleep against her mom's neck. Eden doesn't look like she wants to move or walk, let alone go into her house.

"Hey," I say, nodding. "I can take you inside. Let's get your purse, your cell phone. You're going to need to stay someplace. Can we call Sassy?"

Eden's eyes are unblinking, staring at me. She shakes her head slowly.

I take a few steps away from Eden and ask what time it is. The captain calls back that it's four in the morning. My shift ends in a couple of hours, but she's not going to be able to sit out here shivering in a blanket until then.

"Eden," I repeat, putting a gloved hand on her shoulder. Through the blanket, I can feel her trembling. "Listen. I'm going to help you. Let's get your purse and your phone. Let's take this one step at a time."

She's staring at the house, soft purple shadows under her brown eyes. "What happened?" she asks. "I didn't...I didn't leave any candles burning."

"I know," I assure her. "This was not your fault at all. We think the bathroom fan overheated. Come on. Let's go inside and get what we can."

This part is going to be hard. Most people don't realize that even a small fire could destroy the contents of the house.

I know from the attack crew that the bathroom had burned, and I mean burned. The flames had been contained to one room, but the smoke, soot, and ash got everywhere. I just hope we can find credit cards, keys, her identification. Hopefully, a pair of shoes that can be salvaged if she's lucky.

The excitement and adrenaline of the night start wearing off, and I stifle a yawn. I haven't slept at all this shift, so pretty soon, I'll have been awake for a full twenty-four. Not ideal, but there are shifts where I can't catch any rest between calls. Then there are some shifts where the most excitement is whether the chief's going to bitch because someone put too much pepper in the chili.

"You ready?" I let my hand fall to where I think the small of Eden's back is beneath the thick protective blanket she's got wrapped around her like a sheet.

"Is it safe?" She suddenly comes to life and shakes her head. "Wait, Vito..." She looks down at Juniper and shakes her head again. "I don't want to take her in there. The smoke, there could be toxins..."

I can't say I blame her. The fire is out, and the smoke has cleared, but with the stench of ash and the particles in the air, I wouldn't let my baby go inside that place either.

She looks down at her bare toes and lets one side of the blanket fall open. "Will you take her?" she asks, her eyes wide and her voice unsteady. "I'll be quick. My purse should be on the counter in the kitchen. I think my phone was on the charger in the kitchen too. I won't be long."

The kitchen is at the front of the little house, and the bathroom is all the way at the back. Not that that means a whole hell of a lot now, but at least she won't have to try to sift through the point of origin.

I reach out my arms, and Eden manages to slip Juniper into my hold without jostling her too much. She sets her in my arms like a baby, not upright against my shoulder like she was sleeping on her mom, which is good because I would rather not have her face against my filthy turnout gear.

Eden tucks the blanket tightly around her daughter, then meets my eyes. "Thank you," she says, then starts to walk away from me toward the wide-open front door.

The captain sees her leaving my side and, taking note of the kid in my arms, nods at me and follows after her to make sure she gets in and out quickly.

"Property owner's been notified." Chief stands beside me and watches as Eden tiptoes past the dark entryway of the house.

"Owner?" I echo. "This place is a rental?"

Chief nods. "Tenant moved in just a couple days ago, sounds like. I told the property owner they didn't need to come out, but Bob Horton owns this place. He panicked and said he's on his way."

"Horton owns this place? The electronics guy? Since when does he own rental property?" As I talk with Chief, I can't help but watch Juniper sleep. She looks so peaceful and so, so beautiful. Like her mom.

Chief laughs, but he softens his voice a bit when the baby squirms. "Yeah, Horton is apparently branching out. I told him he'd need to take a closer look at his cleaning and maintenance protocol before he rents a place again."

I shake my head. "How long did Bob own this place before he rented it? Five minutes?" A low burn of anger builds in my chest. "This is the shit that lights me up," I say, trying hard not to pace in place and wake Juniper. "Bob bought this house, probably on the cheap, did nothing to fix it up, and rented to a single mother with a baby. Horton have insurance? She's going to lose everything."

He nods. "She has renters, and he has insurance on the place. It'll take some time, but she'll be all right."

Little Juniper shivers as though she's having a terrible nightmare.

I rock her lightly in my arms and watch as the captain follows Eden back through the front door. She is wearing a pair of sneakers and the knee-length robe. She has the same diaper bag I saw at my parents' slung over her arm, and she looks far from all right.

I make a vow to myself there and then to make it my business to see that she and Juniper come through this better than just okay.

CHAPTER FOUR

eden

When they say you don't know what you've got till it's gone… Well, I'm living that now.

I know everything I lost in that damn house fire. My clothes, my kid's clothes. Junie's toys, my books. Talk about taking stock of your life. No matter how much stuff I lost, none of that mattered.

Not as long as I have my baby and myself.

We can make it through anything.

Within a few days of the fire, the house was officially taken over by the insurance company, and I had to make an inventory and say goodbye to everything I'd just paid to move across the country.

But the simple fact is, every day I wake up thankful that Junie and I were awake when it started. Thankful that I had renters insurance. Thankful that I had a caring local agent who stood by me when the company grilled me about the claim. That was no fun.

I gave recorded statements about how long I left the bathroom fan on. What I did, where I was, what I was wearing. Even what I had to drink. As if I'd get so plastered as a single mom that I'd burn down a house with my kid in it.

It all happened so fast.

I was going to take a shower before bed, so I turned on the

bathroom light and the exhaust fan so the steam wouldn't fog up the bathroom. Just before I was about to step into the shower, I decided to take a bath instead. I left the bathroom to get a book, heard Junie calling for me from her crib, and I went in and checked on her. I changed her wet diaper, but before I could put her back to sleep, I smelled smoke.

And then, the scariest few hours of my life happened. I thought I'd been through some rough stuff up until then. And while I'm not proud of how I got the money, I have the means to replace what we lost. We have insurance. I have a little nest egg. And pretty darn soon, Junie and I might actually have our own house.

The extended-stay hotel the insurance company put us up in is comfortable, and Aunt Sassy has visited us every day—in fact, she's pestered me to stay with her while we get through this whole mess. But my aunt has a small one-bedroom unit.

She's in her sixties and still working on her feet as a waitress. She has a great life, but she's done a lot already, and just welcoming me and Juniper into her life is generous enough.

Junie is playing on a brand-new playmat on the floor of the bedroom we've been sharing in the hotel while I flip between images of houses on my phone and the local community college catalogue.

Ever since the fire, Vito Bianchi has been texting me every day he's not working to check in on me and Juniper. It's sweet and very chill.

I never get the sense that he's flirting, not that I'd mind if he did. I never really thanked him for being so kind to me the night of the fire. It was all such a shock. I didn't realize he was a firefighter, so I had the hardest time in the moment recognizing who he was.

But since that night, I have to be honest, I think about handsome Vito Bianchi—and I think about him a lot. Too much.

And ever since I moved to Star Falls, I've been thinking about what comes next. I have ten years of guaranteed income and some money set aside for Junie's education, but the reality is, time is going to pass, and I'm going to need a career.

I can't imagine spending ten years out of the workforce to raise my daughter as a single mom is going to make for a really impressive future résumé.

"What should we do today, Junebug?" While my daughter chews on a plastic spatula, I hold up one finger on my right hand. "Junie," I say, trying to get her to follow the numbers. "One means we go to college and check out the campus." Then I hold up two fingers on my left hand. "And two means we go shopping for a new house."

I smile at her and hold up both hands. "One or two, Junie? One or two?" I hold up the corresponding fingers to help reinforce the numbers while I let my sweet girl pick our plan for the day.

Junie climbs up onto her bare feet and reaches one hand toward my right hand and the other toward my left. "One, two," she laughs.

I pick her up and cuddle her close. She smells sweet and fresh, her soft brown curls silky against my cheeks. I smooch her and blow ticklish raspberries against her neck.

"You want it all, huh? One and two."

She laughs hard and kicks her feet, so I put her down and she drops to the playmat to grab a toy.

I check the time. It's only half past nine in the morning. We have no insurance calls to make, no clothes or furniture to replace. We have the whole day ahead of us, and I am hell-bent on making my future in Star Falls a lot better than the first couple of weeks have been.

"So, it's settled," I say. "Let's do both."

I call a local real estate agent and inquire about a few properties. Once I get through to someone and share the properties I saw online, a nice woman named Taylor agrees to call me back as soon as she can set up viewings.

"I might not be able to set them all up today," she warns. "But I believe at least two of the properties have lockboxes, so with some notice, we should be able to get inside."

Taylor takes some information from me, including my name, current address, and my driver's license number. I'm a little hesitant to give that out over the phone, but then she explains it's a safety precaution they put in place for the agent's sake.

"We'd like you to take a picture of your license and text that to this number," she tells me. "Along with the names and ages of all the people who will be attending the walk-through."

"Oh," I say. "Okay. How soon do I need to get you that information?"

"An hour before the first showing, I'll check the system and make sure we have everything we need. So, the sooner you can get that over, the better. But at the latest, one hour before we actually plan to meet. Of course, we don't have firm plans now, so if you can get things to me this morning, we should be good to go as soon as I have time slots confirmed."

"I can do that," I tell her. "The only thing I'm not sure about is the age of one of the people in my party." A slow smile spreads over my face. "I mean, I need to confirm that he's even available. I am new to town, and I only have a few local friends."

"How sweet, Eden. Where did you move here from?"

I give her the standard song and dance. Moved from LA, single mama, one-year-old baby.

She asks me the usual questions—did I ever see anyone famous, is LA traffic as bad as they say, do I miss the weather?

I did, in fact, see many famous people—it was part of my job. But since those so-called celebrities were also my undoing, I give my standard answer to that question too. "I once sat in a booth at a diner behind Keanu Reeves."

That's actually true. I did, so I don't have to embellish too much for that story.

After I answer all Taylor's questions—yes, in person, he looks exactly like he does in movies, and no, I didn't speak to him. Yes, he seemed really, really nice. I confirm that yes, LA traffic is the worst, and yes, I do miss the weather a little.

"But I really love the seasons," I explain. "I'm enjoying having a real fall here in the Midwest."

After we've exhausted her questions, she reminds me to send over my license and the names, and she promises to send over a time as soon as she's set up some showings.

Before I send over my driver's license, I grab my phone and hover a finger over the text messages. I pull up one hunky firefighter's number, and before I can talk myself out of it, I send off a text.

Me: Weird question. Two, actually. How old are you, and are you off work today by any chance?

My heart thumps against my ribs, and I start grinning like an idiot. Is he going to think I'm too forward?

As the minutes pass by and I don't get any answers, I start to spiral into embarrassment.

I'm an idiot. I should text him back and say never mind. Just then, my phone chirps with a text alert.

Vito: I'm thirty-four, and I'm free as a bird. Off until Sunday. Whatcha got?

My palm starts sweating, and my cheeks heat.

Me: I don't want to lure you in under false pretenses, but could I hire you as an informal fire safety inspector? Payment is lunch at the restaurant of your choice as long as it's kid-friendly.

He responds this time in seconds.

Vito: You said my two favorite words. Fire and food. But I am curious why you need my age. I'm not going to pass for under twelve if you're going for a kid's meal discount.

I shake my head and stifle a small giggle while a little tiny spark of excitement blooms in my chest.

Me: I must disclose the names and ages of anyone I want to take on a house showing today. I called a real estate agent. Hence the need for someone who might help me not rent another deathtrap of a house. Maybe this time, I'll buy, but I'd love a hand inspecting things that I never knew existed. Like fan vents...

He sends back a crying laughing emoji and a thumbs-up emoji.

Vito: Let me know where and when. But do me one favor?

I send back just a simple question mark.

Vito: Maybe don't give Juniper OJ in the car...

I full-body laugh at that and send back a long line of cracking up and mind-blown emojis. Then I drop the phone and take a picture of the front and back of my newly minted Ohio license and text it to Taylor along with our names: Eden Byrne, 26, Juniper Byrne, 14 months, and Vito Bianchi, 34.

Seeing our names together like that makes us look like a little family. I shut down the thoughts before they can even take hold.

"No boys, Junebug." I drop down onto the playmat and pretend to cook up an over-easy plastic egg on a little blue skillet. "No boys, no dating. Just friends."

She mouths something that sounds like, "Nahlalaha mends," and I give her a high five.

I can't pretend, though, that I'm not looking forward to meeting my hot new friend later today. Sigh. Maybe my closed-down heart isn't as shut off as I'd thought.

Let's just hope, this time, I don't get burned.

Vito arrives at the hotel where I'm staying a full thirty minutes earlier than I'd asked. He asked if we could go over some stuff before we look at any houses, and I agreed.

When I open the door of my hotel room, he's looking freshly showered and hotter than I remember. He's wearing blue jeans, bright-blue running shoes, and a tight black T-shirt. It's a gorgeous fall day, but both Junie and I are dressed in layers in case it gets too warm or too cool. Vito's got his arms out to hug me, and with his hair slicked back, sunglasses over his eyes, and a sexy grin on his face, it takes everything inside me to stop myself from knocking him over and wrapping my legs around his waist.

He's just a friend, I remind myself.

I lean in for a chaste hug, pat him on the back, and then hurriedly pull away before his cologne or his soap or whatever fucking erotic scent I sniffed in that two-second hug becomes my undoing.

Damn my libido. She's a clueless bitch. She never learns.

"Eden, hey."

"Uh, come on in," I say. I walk away from him and the open door and wave my hand toward the table and chairs in the little kitchenette. "Want to sit?"

"Shit," he says, but then he covers his mouth, points at Junie, and mouths, "Sorry. I mean, oh shoot."

I grin at him and shake my head. "It's all right. As hard as I try to keep the language clean, I wouldn't be surprised if this one can spell the F word before preschool."

"That would be impressive." Vito jerks a hand toward the parking lot. "Ma sent over some food. She will kill me if I let it go bad. Be right back." He dashes away, closing the hotel door behind him.

Once he's gone, I heave a huge sigh. God, he's gorgeous. Adorable. Hot. Sweet. How on earth is this man single?

That's when it hits me.

He lives at home with his mother and father. He's, like, really old not to have his own place. My tummy clenches as I think of all the things that are probably weird and broken about him. Maybe he's bad with money and in debt up to his eyeballs. Maybe he's irresponsible or can't cook. He has one dress shirt, for God's sake.

I square my shoulders and take a deep breath. This isn't a date. This is a new friendship. And anytime my instincts start looking for anything more, I'll just remember that he's probably a mama's boy with terrible habits who would make the world's worst partner, lover, husband. That'll keep me from going into overdrive.

"Knock, knock."

I hear his voice call through the door as he raps lightly. I let him in again, but this time, I step back so there's no chance for a second awkward hug. Besides, there's no room to get close to him. He's carrying a brown cardboard box that looks like it weighs twenty pounds.

"What on earth is all this?" I ask.

Vito laughs and lifts a brow at me. "Lunch, dinner, and a hell of a lot of snacks." He sets the box down on the small kitchen table and points to it. "Leave that here. I need to do something first." He looks around the small living room, squinting dramatically. He seems to make eye contact with Juniper but then looks away. He cups his hands around his eyes and squints, then calls out in a loud voice, "Juniper? Juniper? Are you here?"

He strides into the kitchen and opens the dishwasher, then pretends to call into the racks. "Juniper. Juniper?"

While he wanders the extremely small living space of the hotel suite, Juniper lies with her face on the couch cushion and just blinks at this silly goof of a man.

He's playing a game with her that probably every child knows, but it strikes me in a really deep place. Nathan's never met his daughter. Wanted her gone before she even existed. And this man who's met her once is already playing with her and giving her his time and attention.

I shake my head to clear the confusing feelings and remind myself he's probably a man-child. Don't believe everything you see, I tell myself. He's a gnome. A mama's boy.

"There she is." Vito says, clapping and dropping to his knees. He points to Juniper once he's on her level and waves. "Hiya, kiddo. Remember me? I'm your mama's friend, Vito. Vito," he says again slowly.

"Veeloo," she echoes, a dribble of drool spilling past her lips.

I grab a cloth diaper from her go bag and blot her lips. "Vito, baby," I say, enunciating the T. "Can you say hi?"

She holds out her arms to Vito, and I cock my chin at him. "Is this cool?"

"More than cool," he says. He picks up Juniper, gives her a quick hug, and then sets her on the floor. "I'm going to put some food away, but then maybe we'll have some time to play?"

She waddles after him like one of the children enchanted by the Pied Piper. But I'm no better. I'm in a daze for this man as much as my daughter is. We stand in the kitchen holding hands while we watch Vito get to work.

"It's good you've got all the amenities here," he says as he unloads plastic containers with labels on the lids into the fridge. "Full-sized appliances. So much better than those dorm-sized jobs most hotels give you." Once he's done, he turns the cardboard over, strips the tape from it, and breaks the box down flat. "You got recycling here? I can take this back to my parents' if you don't know."

I watch him make himself at home in my little space and can't quite explain what I'm feeling. In all the time I was with Nathan, he came to my place hundreds of times. We ate out, brought home leftovers, and he never once so much as remembered to bring leftovers in from the car, let alone put anything in my fridge. He wouldn't even help himself to a glass of water.

To be fair, he never stayed more than a couple of hours. Never a whole night. But I don't know how to feel about Vito showing up and just being so at ease.

It's like he's comfortable in my life and with me, and there's nothing new or awkward about this.

But he doesn't give me a lot of time to process or think.

As if he read my thoughts, he opens a cabinet, grabs a drinking glass, and helps himself to a glass of water from the tap. "You want something?" he asks, as though proving he is the opposite of the kind of man I've known before. He might as well be named Not Nathan.

"No. I'm good, thanks," I manage, picking up my daughter and holding her close. I don't like to use her to comfort me, but I could go for a little comfort. But Junie knows what she wants, and she is excited about her new friend.

She wiggles out of my arms and toddles over to Vito before grabbing on to the leg of his jeans.

He sips the water, then sets the glass on the counter. "All right, ladies. What do we got?"

He's looking at me expectantly, and I honestly have no idea what he's talking about. I'm struck speechless by the fact that he's come into my hotel room, made himself at home, and now, he's picked up my daughter and is bouncing her on his hip.

"Eden?" he asks, giving me a confused look. "Everything all right?"

"How are you so good at this?" I ask, not even trying to mask the sound of my confusion.

"Kids?" he asks, sounding equally surprised. "I'm one of four kids, and in the last two years, I've become an uncle to four kids."

I nod. "Yeah, I remember, but a lot of people have siblings and kids in their family. You're, like, really good at this."

"It's in the genes," he says, his voice low. "I come by it naturally. I love kids. Love people, honestly. I'm easygoing. You have to be when you're a Bianchi." He grows quiet for a moment, as if he's thinking. "Have you been around a lot of people who are not good at this?"

I swallow hard and murmur, "Yeah. You could say that."

Vito taps Junie on the nose and grins big at both of us. "Well, ladies, you're in for a treat today."

CHAPTER FIVE

Eden pulls out some toys to keep Juniper entertained while we sit knee-to-knee at her kitchen table poring over the listings on her phone.

"So, the agent sent me six," she says. She's leaning toward me, holding her phone in one hand, but it takes all my concentration to look at the pictures and not at the generous amount of cleavage I can see when she leans closer to me.

Eden Byrne is gorgeous. Her hair is long, and the loose curls practically float over her shoulders. Her eyes are a perfect shade of coffee brown.

Every time she leans closer, I catch a whiff of something light but so elegant. She smells expensive, like the luxury spas Michelle used to treat herself to. What I can't figure out is this girl's story.

"I really like these," she says, flipping the display to reveal a couple of houses that would be way out of my price range. "But then, Taylor sent over this one too. It looks older, but it's the cheapest on the list, so I thought it would be worth seeing."

"Oh fuck," I say before I can stop myself. I look toward Juniper, but she seems engrossed in her magnets. "Sorry about that."

"What is it?" she asks. "Something about this house? Was there a fire or something?"

I shake my head and take the phone from her hands, letting my fingertips just graze hers. Heat flows from her hand through my body, and I'm suddenly feeling about ten degrees hotter.

"No fire," I explain. I zoom into the listing to confirm the address. "I know this house." A little sadness jerks at my chest just looking at the place. "I haven't been there in a while," I say. I hand the phone to her. "My ex-wife's grandfather lives there. I hear he's been moved into a memory care facility across town. They must be selling the house."

I'm quiet for a moment because the thought of Michelle's gramps not being able to live in his house anymore is damn sad. I hope the day never comes when we have to make that decision for our parents. But then I remind myself that Michelle's parents should be the ones dealing with this, not her, but that's a fight I gave up on long ago.

I meet Eden's eyes. "It's a great house," I tell her. "Solid construction. The old man took good care of the place. Real good. But unless the family's done something in the last five years, and I'm guessing by that purchase price they haven't, the interior needs a gut rehab. If you're in the market for a fixer-upper, that'd be a safe investment. But if you want move-in ready…"

Eden is quiet, but then she shocks the shit out of me by resting a hand over mine. Her touch is light and soft. "You're divorced?" she asks. "I had no idea. I'm so sorry."

I can't tell from her tone if she thinks I'm still nursing a broken heart or if she's digging a little for dirt. I hope it's that second one.

"Yeah," I say. "My marriage was like your bathroom fire. Hot, wild, and over almost before it really got going."

Eden yanks her hand away and covers her mouth with a hand as she blurts out a laugh. "Vito." She shakes her head. "You're so unexpected."

I grin at her. "Well, it's true. I'll tell the story. I ain't shy about it." I cross my arms over my chest and kick my legs out in front of me. "I was a twenty-six-year-old hothead," I start out, setting the scene for her. "I'm fighting fires by day, and at night, well, let's just say I'm spending a lot of my nights off at The Body Shop. You know the place?"

She shakes her head. "What is it? A fragrance store? Candles and soaps and stuff?"

I crack a laugh. "Nah. We've got two Body Shops in Star Falls. The one where my sister works is a tattoo shop. Gracie, you met her, is an artist and the owner. My ex danced at the other place, under a stage name Exotic."

I watch as the emotions flicker across Eden's face. Confusion, recognition, and then understanding.

"You married a dancer?" she asks.

I watch the flush creep up her neck. "It's totally fine to say I married a stripper. I knew what she did for work, and I didn't give a damn how she made her living. She didn't do anything more than dance, even though I know she got offers, but she had big dreams. She wasn't about to have a criminal record hold her back." I think back on the good times I had with my ex-wife, and I have to admit that.

She wasn't bad at all until, of course, she decided to dance her way across my heart and out of my life.

"We dated for two years, got married on a whim, and split one year later. And that was that." I look down at my hands. I'm fine talking about it, but it seems weird to tell this woman who I'm just getting to know—and feeling no small amount of attraction to—that I was heartbroken when my marriage split up. "I loved her," I admit. "But I learned pretty fast, love isn't enough. Not to make a marriage work, that is. Funny, isn't it? I guess families are the same too. I love my parents, brothers, and Gracie. And that love is enough. It can be too much sometimes. But that's why I moved back in with my parents after the divorce. The world didn't feel right without people around me who I could trust and count on."

Eden is quiet, and I wonder if I'm bringing her down.

I tap my fingers against the table and motion toward the phone. "So, yeah, you want my ex's grandfather's house, put it on the list."

She reaches across the tiny space that separates us and covers my hands with hers. "I'm so sorry if seeing that house brings back painful memories. There's no way I'd take you there even if I did want it. But I don't. I don't have it in me to rehab a house." She nods toward Juniper. "She's a very easy baby, but no baby is easy enough to raise in a construction zone." She squeezes my hands and then releases them. "Thanks for sharing all that, Vito."

I nod, not sure what else to say. Almost everyone in town knows my history with Michelle. It's been a long time since I talked about it. It almost feels good to. "Thanks for listening," I tell her. "And not judging me. I married for the right reasons. I just picked the wrong person."

My words hang between us, and a slight shift charges the air between us.

"So," she says, swiping at her touchscreen. "What do you think about a ranch versus a two-story?"

I offer to drive so Eden can look over the neighborhoods, the streets, even scanning for parks and things as we drive to each of the houses that have been set up.

"Want to take my car?" she asks, bending down to lift Juniper into her arms.

I look away from the view of her cleavage, but only after I get a nice eyeful. I'm respectful, but hell, Eden's body is something straight out of my fantasies. I never thought of myself as a guy with a type before. I've dated skinny, toned women like my ex, women with a little extra junk in their trunk, tall, thin, dark, light. I don't discriminate. But I also don't ever stick around and get too close. Not since Michelle, at least. But if I did have a type, tall and lush with a rack I could bury my face in would be it, and that's Eden.

Fuck.

I'd better concentrate on inspecting properties for hazards. Not inspecting Eden's smoking-hot curves and dreaming of touching her.

"Vito?" She meets my eyes, and I snap my wandering thoughts back to her.

"Sorry," I say. "Ready to go?"

She follows me out the door, giving me a sexy smile as I wait for the hotel door to close behind us. Then, I turn and test the handle to make sure the electronic safety has engaged, and the door is actually locked.

"You always like this?" she asks, accepting my silent offer to take the diaper bag from her.

"Like what?" I ask.

She is studying my face over the top of Juniper's curly hair. "Attentive," she finally says. "Thoughtful. Maybe safety-conscious?"

I shrug. "I don't think anyone in my line of work can avoid it."

She grows quiet, and I follow her to a brand-new SUV with Ohio plates. "I'm sure," she says softly. "Do you mind driving my car? It's a pain installing the car seat over and over."

I laugh out loud at that and lean maybe a little too close to her. "You realize that's one of the services we offer?"

She looks confused for a second but then bursts out laughing. "Is that true? Do people really come down to the fire station to make sure their car seats are safely installed?"

"All the time." I hold open the rear passenger door while Eden secures Juniper in the seat.

"I don't know why I thought that wasn't really a thing," she chuckles. After Juniper is buckled in, Eden turns to me and extends the hand holding the keys. "You sure you don't mind?"

I take the keys, and I'm damn sure she almost clasps my hands as she passes over an efficient silver ring with just one simple key fob for the car on it. It startles me a little when I realize she doesn't have any other keys. No place to call home that requires keys. The hotel has cards for entry. She just lost her rental home. As far as I know, she has no job, but she does have money. I have so many questions about this woman.

I do my best to shake off the quick brush of her soft skin as I take the fob. I roll my shoulders and hold open the passenger door so she can slide in. Once I'm settled and my seat belt is secured, I look back at Juniper. "Everybody ready?"

Juniper is smashing a plush rabbit against her knees, and of

CHELLE BLISS

course she's securely belted in. Eden is too, so I adjust the mirrors and punch the address of the first house into my phone even though I don't really need it.

"Fancy," I say, grinning as I plug my phone into the loose cable that connects my device to her car. "Your in-dash display is bigger than my parents' television."

It's a joke, and she laughs, which I love. She may have money, but she's not weird about it. Which is great. I don't give a shit if she's got two cents to her name. A woman with a sense of humor and a low-key attitude is worth her weight in gold.

As we drive, I point out the schools and parks and other little points of interest. Star Falls is a great place to live. Great people, beautiful land, big sky. I love it here, and it must show.

"You sound like an official tour guide," she says, but there's a smile in her voice.

"Small-town living," I tell her. "Can't beat it."

She's quiet, staring out the window as we turn onto the street where the first house is. I know the area, but I don't see a for-sale sign in any of the lawns or front windows, so I slow down to a crawl.

"Did you ever live anyplace else? Ever want to live someplace bigger?"

"Like Los Angeles?" I ask but don't give her time to reply. "Nah." I wrinkle my nose. But then I stop and really think about it. Something about her makes me want to dig a little deeper. Give her more of me. "Let me rephrase that. I would absolutely consider moving away from Star Falls for the right reason. I actually applied for a job at a bigger firehouse about a month ago."

"Yeah?" She turns fully in her seat to look at me, but then Juniper starts fussing. "We're almost there, honey." Eden turns in her seat to pick up the bunny that's somehow been slingshotted deep behind the driver's seat. She bends and twists, and I keep my eyes on the damn road, refusing to ogle her while she's picking up her baby's toy.

Once Eden has the bunny, Juniper stops squirming, and I see a for sale sign up ahead about another half block away.

414

"That looks like our stop," I tell her. "Juniper, we're almost there. You ready to look at a new house?

"Yah, yah, yah." In her excitement, she throws the bunny again, and it must land behind me, because Eden shakes her head and blows air through her lips.

"Baby, we're about to get out of the car. I'll get your bunny in a sec," Eden tells her.

Juniper seems fine with that, so as I find a place to park on the street near the property, Eden asks me a gentle question. "But you didn't get the job? Or you did and didn't take it?"

"Didn't get it," I say simply. "I'll tell you what happened on the way to the next house. If you want to hear the boring story."

She nods, and I kill the ignition and offer the key back to her.

"You hang on to it," she says. "As long as you don't mind driving to the next place?"

I nod and jump out of the car. I run around and open the door for her, then stand by while she gets Juniper out of the back.

"Ready?" I ask, locking the car and slipping the fob into the pocket of my jeans. "This could be your new home."

She looks nervous but excited, and she nods vigorously. "I'm so glad you came. Thanks for being here."

A wave of sweet warmth floods my chest at her words, but I just urge her ahead. "Come on," I tell her.

We walk up the drive, but we don't even make it to the front door when a very stressed-looking woman meets us.

"Eden?" She's waving her hand and trotting down the concrete driveway in ridiculously high heels. As she meets us, I can't help noticing that even in heels, she's like six inches shorter than Eden.

"Hi, Taylor." Eden secures Juniper on one hip. Since I have the diaper bag, she's got a free hand to shake the real estate agent's hand.

"So nice to finally meet you," she says to Eden before turning her attention toward me. "You must be Dad." She extends her hand.

I chuckle and Eden's about to say something, but I shake the lady's hand. "What gave me away?"

I'm not trying to horn in on Eden's party or nothing, but if the real estate lady thinks there's a man in the picture, who knows. Maybe the sellers will be more reasonable if they think some happy couples about to buy their dream home.

Taylor steps a little closer to us and lowers her voice. Her bright-pink lipstick has smeared onto her front teeth, and she's got a light sheen of sweat on her forehead. "I hope this won't make you uncomfortable." She tosses a look behind her toward the open front door of the house. "The homeowner was supposed to leave to let you view the place privately. It's something we ask, but this homeowner won't go."

I look at Eden for guidance on this. "You want to pass?"

She bites her lower lip. "It's really cute," she says. "I'd like to see it. Do you think it'll be too awkward?"

"We're fine. Eden wants to see this house, she's going to see the house. It doesn't bother us that the man is home."

I look at Eden. "You good?"

She's looking at me with the cutest expression of shock and something I can't make out. But she nods.

"Excellent," I say. "Ms. Taylor, you good?"

"I'm fantastic," she says, looking relieved.

"Then if this one's ready," I say, lifting a brow at Juniper, "then we're solid. Let's see this house."

The real estate lady turns on her super-high heels and rushes ahead of us toward the house. "Mr. Incandella," she calls. "The family is here."

As I start to follow her up the drive, Eden rests a hand on my elbow. "Vito," she says, those melted-chocolate eyes boring into mine. "I told her you were just a friend. I'm sorry about that. I think she just assumed."

I chuckle. "You think I care that she thought I had something to do with this?" I jerk a thumb at Juniper. "I'm freaking flattered. Now, come on. Let's see this house."

416

CHAPTER SIX

eden

The second we walk into the house, the homeowner appears wearing the world's most aggressive scowl. I'm taken aback, honestly. He looks angry, and unless he's being forced to sell his home for financial reasons, I can't imagine why he'd greet a prospective buyer looking like he's about to go off on us.

"Uh, hi," I say, "I'm Eden. Thank you so much for making time to see us today."

I hold out my hand, but he looks from me to Vito and then back at my hand. Then he reaches out and shakes mine. "Robert," he says.

Vito shakes his hand too, but stays quiet, letting me do the talking. I'm asking how long he's lived here and wondering why Taylor isn't saying anything. Suddenly, I see Vito shift from one foot to the other.

"Do you mind if I take off my shoes?" Vito asks. "My mother would send me to my room without dinner if I wore my shoes in the house."

Taylor looks mortified, but immediately the homeowner's shoulders soften a bit. I look down at his feet and see he's wearing socks with pristine-looking open-toed house slippers just like the ones I saw Vito wearing the day we met.

"Well, if it's all the same to you," Robert says, "I'd appreciate that. My wife…my, uh, late wife felt the same about shoes as your mother."

Taylor tries to get out of her shoes so fast, she nearly tips over. She has to hold on to the wall to wrench her bare feet out of those heels, but she does it, and she finishes just as Vito gets his running shoes off.

He's wearing the most hilarious socks, and I nearly snort. They must have been some kind of gift. I watch him walk up to me, staring at the truly ridiculous sight of a small Chihuahua lifting its leg to pee on a fire hydrant. I'm not sure if they're making some kind of statement, but the socks keep me from being too distracted as the hunky firefighter comes close.

Without saying a word, Vito points at Juniper's super-soft baby slippers. "Come on, kid. This is another one of those no-shoes places. Don't make a scene."

The homeowner, Robert, actually cracks a half smile at that and gives Juniper a wave. "Hello, there."

He seems awkward with her, so maybe not a grandpa himself, but I go through the motions and tug off her shoes and hand them to Vito. He tucks them into his back pocket, and then he holds out his hands for my daughter and, without a word, nods at me.

I hand him my baby and toe out of my shoes. Once we're all out of our shoes, Robert steps aside and lets the real estate agent bring us into the kitchen.

There is a glossy, full-color listing sheet on the marble countertop, and she starts right in, pointing out features of the home and comparing what we can see around us to the stats on the printout.

Vito hands Juniper back to me and stands by quietly with Robert while Taylor shows me the new fridge, the oven, and the double sink.

"The kitchen was rehabbed just two years ago," Taylor says. She's droning on about the appliances being energy efficient, but I stop listening. I'm in love with this kitchen. It's like the designer of my dreams put this place together. You can tell by the layout that the original kitchen was designed for a family. A built-in table with bench-style seats is in a nook on the rear wall of the kitchen and is surrounded by windows that look out onto a fenced backyard.

The counters are white marble with wisps of bronze-gold running through them. The cabinets are a rustic-looking dark wood with matching bronze pulls, and the floors are a lighter wood than the cabinets, likely original but in great shape. The appliances are all stainless steel, which you'd think would clash with the bronze of the hardware, but I don't care. This kitchen has tons of counter space and light. There's even a little window box that could hold plants over the large farmhouse-style sink.

I walk up to the sink and run my hand over the pristine porcelain. "This sink is so big, I could give Juniper a bath in there."

Junie leans out of my arms, trying to turn on the faucet, and I don't try to stop her. I grab the handle to test the water pressure, and to my delight, the fixture has several settings to adjust how much water comes out.

I know better than to act like I'm in love with this place in the very first room, so I look closely at everything I can. I flick the switches and watch the lights come on. I peek inside the fridge and oven... Sadly, they seem brand-new.

"Have these ever been used?" I ask Taylor quietly.

Robert's just asked Vito what he does for a living, so Taylor seems a little more relaxed talking with the homeowner distracted.

She leans in close and says, "I don't think he cooks much."

I nod, wondering why on earth he'd put in such a gorgeous kitchen and not use it, but then I remember he mentioned a late wife, and my stomach tightens.

I don't ask anything more and follow Taylor's lead. She shows us the downstairs powder room, and Vito takes a look under the sink and lifts the lid off the toilet tank. He flushes the toilet once, then looks up at me with a sweet, wide smile.

"Nothing to report, chief," he says. "Carry on."

He and Robert haven't stopped talking about the house and

safety issues since Vito revealed he's a firefighter, so I guess that could be a good thing.

The house has a dining room to the right of the entryway. We passed it to go toward the kitchen, and we head back there after I see the laundry room and the powder room. The dining room is a little empty of furniture and pictures, which seems a bit odd, but the size is fine. We walk past the staircase and front door to the left, coming to a family room that is open to the kitchen. The family room has a fireplace, and it's clear there's been some more renovation here.

"This was originally a Georgian," Taylor explains, "so the living room off the kitchen had that wall to keep it separate. But the family room has been renovated to open up the floor plan a bit. Permits were pulled, of course. The home passed all its inspections, and only licensed contractors were used."

There was a time when I might not have cared at all about that, but after the fire in the rental house, I'm relieved to hear that things were done to code here. I flick a glance at Vito, who looks like he's half listening to me, half listening to Robert. He lifts his eyebrows at me as if to ask how I'm liking it, and I give a short nod, trying not to give too much away.

He slowly nods back, all casual and chill so that it looks like he's just mulling over something Robert has said.

Our little nonverbal exchange prickles the hairs on my arms. The easy intimacy with this man makes me wonder what else could feel easy and right with him.

"There are four bedrooms," Taylor says loudly, dragging my attention away from Vito. "And two full baths. Shall we take a look?"

This is the biggest of the homes that we're looking at today. Four bedrooms, two full baths upstairs and the powder room downstairs. There's a basement, a backyard, and a garage.

As we take the carpeted stairs, I realize that moving to Ohio was a really smart move financially.

The upstairs of this place could be a house of horrors, but based on that kitchen alone, I already know the truth in my heart. I want it. This is a place I could make a home for Junie and me. I can just imagine a dog running in the fenced yard, breakfasts at that eat-in area. I haven't had holidays in the Midwest before, so picturing the leaves changing, snow drifting over the thick limbs of the mature trees…

My heart rate starts to pick up, and I begin to grin uncontrollably. For the first time since I got pregnant, I feel like I can have fun with my life. I have a little money. I have a beautiful baby. I might have a house.

After everything I've been through on my own these last couple of years, I am beginning to see a path to something that feels real. That feels like mine.

I can't stop myself from looking over at Vito and imagining him being here with me. Not just for support. Waking up with him. Washing dishes with him beside me.

A sudden flush creeps up my neck, and I have to wave my hand in front of my face to cool off. That kind of thinking is way too much. We're just friends, and barely that. And with my track record, a new house is more than enough reality to manage.

I clutch Junie tighter and follow Taylor's perfectly pedicured toes up the stairs.

When we hit the landing at the top, Vito rests a light hand against my lower back. "You want me to carry her?" he asks. "You look flushed."

I shake my head and sputter, "I'm good." I've got to put some distance between him and me.

I follow Taylor into the bathroom at the top of the stairs. I'm half tempted to splash cold water on myself, but I don't.

I clear my throat and push past Vito's stupidly sexy arm, which he's using to lean against the bathroom door.

"Master bedroom?" I ask, using every ounce of willpower not to think about the fact that the master bedroom is going to have a nice, big, beautiful bed.

———

By the time we've finished the walk-through, Robert and Vito are talking in the driveway. Robert is pointing up at the roof, and Vito's got a pair of sunglasses covering his face. He's looking up where Robert is gesturing, which I hope means he's trying to point out something about the roof that's positive, like it's been repaired or replaced recently.

"So," Taylor asks, placing her heels back on as I'm setting Junie on the tile foyer floor while I slip my shoes back on. Taylor's grin is huge, and she lowers her voice. "What do you think? Did you like it? Is this a place you could see living with your family?"

My heart catches in my throat at her question. Even though I told her that Vito is just a friend, I'm sure she's not really interested in the specifics. She just wants to know if I'm interested enough to make an offer on the house.

I think through everything I saw. The bathrooms, the basement, the yard. "The upstairs bathrooms have not been renovated," I tell her, "but they have been well maintained. Eventually, they'll need some work."

Taylor nods, a shadow covering her bright expression. "True, but that's why the house is in your price range," she says. "If the upstairs bathrooms had been updated..." She makes a whooshing sound with her lips. "That would up the purchase price by a bunch."

I know she's telling the truth, so I decide to be honest with her as well. "I'd like to see the other houses on the list before I make any decisions."

"Oh my gosh, yes," she says, holding the screen door open for me. "We'll see as many houses as you need. Buying a house is a lot like finding the perfect wedding dress. More often than not, the first one is usually it. But you need to see what else is out there to be sure. This is a big decision, and you need to be certain."

I've never bought a wedding dress. Never even shopped for one. My high school best friend and I had a major falling-out right before her wedding. That was right around the time that everything went down with my mom. I'm ashamed to admit it, but I backed out of being in her wedding, and we haven't spoken since.

"I wouldn't know about the wedding dress," I say quietly. "But I know what you mean."

As we walk down the concrete driveway, my heart rate picks up when Vito lowers his face from looking up at the roof to face me. I'm saying the words before I can even stop them. "I'd like to hear what Vito thought, too."

"Absolutely," Taylor says. But then she looks a little confused. "But it will be just you and the little one? You'll be making the purchase alone, correct?"

I nod in answer to her question, but I pick up the pace when Vito grins and waves me over. When Junie and I reach him, Vito jerks a thumb toward Robert.

"So," Vito says, tugging the sunglasses from his face. "Robert worked at the same mill as my pops. But he was management and Pops was on the floor, so they didn't overlap much." Vito turns to the homeowner and claps his new friend on the shoulder. "Good people," he says warmly. "And this house?" Vito looks me right in the eye and nods. "Passed my inspection. How about yours?"

Just as I'm about to answer, the worst stench wafts up, and I wrinkle my nose. "Oh no," I say. "I think I need to change a diaper." I look from the homeowner to Taylor. "Thank you for showing me the house. If you'll excuse me, I'm going to take this mess to my truck."

Vito fishes my keys out of his pocket. "Want help?" he asks. "I'll be right behind you." He turns and extends a hand to the homeowner, whose face is contorted in a grimace.

"You're going to do that where?" Robert asks. "In the car?"

I nod and shrug. "I have hand sanitizer in my bag, and we'll toss the mess in a trash bin someplace. I'm used to this."

He shakes his head. "But where do you lay the baby?"

"I keep a changing pad in this bag. It's not a problem."

Robert frowns as he looks at Vito. For a second, I feel a little defensive that he's talking to him instead of me, but when I hear what he says, my heart melts a little. "Would it be better to change the baby inside? Any reason she couldn't do it in the upstairs bathroom? I don't mind if you use the towels." He swallows, and a shimmer of tears seems to redden his eyes. "That sink could probably use somebody running the water."

Vito turns to me and lifts his brows. "Eden? Want to use the upstairs bathroom?" He tips his chin a bit and then adds, "I wouldn't mind chatting with Robert a few more minutes."

To be honest, I've changed Junie's diapers on my lap, in the grocery store, on park benches. Taking care of business in the car is no big deal at all, but something about the kind offer from Robert and Vito's encouragement makes it impossible to say no. I'll take a sink and a fluffy bathmat over the changing pad and the back seat any day.

"I'll go with you." Taylor looks like never in all her days of real estate agenting has something like this happened, so I reassure her it'll just take a second.

Junie starts to whine and squirm, so I follow Taylor inside. I kick off my shoes, and Taylor pulls out her phone. "Go on up," she tells me. "I'm going to check my email."

I pad upstairs with Junie and, for a moment, let myself imagine this is my house. We walk into the bathroom, close the door behind us, and make quick work of changing her diaper. I'm a pro at it after thousands of dirty ones.

Since the door is closed, I let Junie crawl on the floor while I wash my hands and dry them on the hand towel.

When we make it back downstairs, Taylor's smile is bright, and she looks surprised. "That was quick. See you at the next house? It's only about a half mile away, so it shouldn't take long to get there."

I nod and head back down the driveway. "All set," I call out. "Robert, I used the hand towel upstairs, but everything else should be exactly as I found it."

The garage is open, and Robert points to a pristine-looking black plastic bin. He grimaces. "Please," he says. "Toss it in there."

I shake my head. "Oh no. You don't want this hanging around until your next trash pickup. We'll dispose of it along the way. No problem."

Robert shakes his head again. "Please. I insist." He looks at Vito and smiles a little. "The garage is very well insulated. I haven't smelled my trash in thirty-two years in this house. I don't expect one little diaper to change that."

Vito lifts his brows. "All due respect, but I've got a nephew about her age. There ain't nothing quite like the smell of baby shit."

The homeowner laughs and actually puts a hand on Vito's shoulders. "I'll take your word for it. But go on. I don't mind."

Vito holds a hand out to me, takes the small bag with the diaper from me, and throws it in the bin, then firmly secures the lid in place. When he turns back around, he holds his other hand out to Robert, and they shake, exchanging a few quiet words.

I wave to the homeowner as I follow Vito to my SUV.

I don't say anything while I buckle Juniper into her seat. I'm quiet as Vito comes around, holds open my door, and waits while I get settled in the passenger seat. But Vito is all smiles and chatter as he twists in his seat and confirms that everybody's ready to go.

"Hey, is that bunny buckled?" He's leaning over the middle console pointing at Juniper's stuffed animal, when I reach for his arm.

He turns in the seat and faces me. "You all good?" he asks. His chin is covered in dusky stubble, like he skipped shaving today. I know I have made terrible decisions when it comes to men, but when I see the curve at the corner of his mouth, the way his cheek dimples ever so slightly…it all just hits me.

The warmth of the SUV, the smell of the new leather, and the richness of his cologne.

"You," I murmur, shaking my head. "What you…"

Whether it's my body talking or my heart or the brain that I can never trust to make the right decisions at times like these, I have to get closer to him. Before I can deny the impulse and talk myself into behaving rationally, I lean forward and cup his chin. His sunglasses are on the top of his perfectly waved hair, his deep brown eyes wide as he scans my face.

His expression changes. He stares without blinking and lowers his chin, almost nuzzling against my palm.

"Eden?" he says, his voice thick and low.

"Vito." And before I can stop myself, I lean in to kiss him.

CHAPTER SEVEN

I don't have time to react before Eden's lips brush across mine. Her mouth is soft as it opens against mine. Her fingers tighten, and a breathy little sigh rumbles in her throat, the sound so fucking hot, it's like someone hit the on switch in my balls. My cock literally jerks in my jeans, but before I even realize it's happening, it's over.

Eden pulls back like she's been shocked and covers her mouth with a hand. "Oh shit. Shit, shit," she mutters. "I am so sorry. I should not have done that."

I reach across the console and tug one of her hands from her face. I lace my fingers through hers and give her a squeeze. "I'm going to stop you right there," I say. "You have nothing to apologize for."

"No, no, I do," she says, her words coming out in a rush. "I don't even know why I did that. I mean...I do know. I just..." She seems to notice that I'm holding her hand, and she lets her other hand drop down to trace my knuckles. "You're not mad?"

I laugh and squeeze her hand. "Babe, I don't know what the guys in LA are like, but if what you're looking for is an invitation or permission or some shit..." I flick a look back at Junie and realize we've both been cussing up a storm. "Or some stuff," I correct, "you got it. You need me to say yes, you got your yes."

"Yeah?" she asks, seeming to calm down a little. She laughs softly as her shoulders relax. "I was more concerned that maybe you weren't…"

I turn in my seat to look at her. "Maybe I wasn't what?"

My eyes travel from her flushed cheeks along the deep vee in the long-sleeved top she's wearing under a light, loose cardigan. Her thighs are painted into the dark jeans she's wearing, and all I can think about is peeling away that fabric and the smooth skin of those thighs clamped around my ears while she rides my face.

"Interested?" I growl. "Attracted?" I shift around in my seat to relieve some of the pressure that's building up from the partial boner that kiss gave me. Fuck, not just the kiss. It's Eden. Her body. Her personality. "If you hadn't ended that kiss so fast, we'd be halfway to making Juniper a sibling right now."

Her laugh is nervous as I turn on the ignition and set the GPS to the next address. I meet Eden's gaze, and we trade grins. Any asshole with eyes can tell Eden is stunning, so I'm guessing she's hesitating because she's been treated like shit in the past. Most women I know have asshole men stories that could fill a library.

Now seems about as good a time as any to ask.

"So," I start. We're just a few minutes from the next house. Not a ton of time to bring up serious shit, but we can at least put a pin in it and continue the conversation later. If it's something she's even up to sharing. "Eden, you know you're smokin' hot, stacked, beautiful. I ain't got the vocabulary to come up with more words, but you're it," I say on a grin. "So, I take it the donor did you dirty?"

"The donor?" she asks, but then she seems to get it. "You mean Juniper's dad?" She flicks a look over her shoulder and smiles at the little girl playing happily with her bunny. "Yeah, that's a story, and thanks, by the way. For the compliments. I don't think I've been called stacked before. At least, not that I ever remember."

"I meant that in the best possible way," I tell her. "And I love stories." We'll be at the next house in like six minutes. "But if it's not

427

a short one, it might have to wait." I nod at the display on her truck that shows the map and that we're almost to the destination.

I see her shift in the passenger seat. "It's kind of a long story, and there are parts of it I…" She sighs. "It's effed up, Vito. Really effed up. I want to share it, but be warned, you might not like what you hear. You might not even like me once you hear it."

"Please," I scoff. "There's nothing you can say that would make me feel any differently about you."

"I haven't made the best decisions in life," she says as she slides out of the car when I park, trying to avoid the conversation. I hope this conversation isn't over because I want to know everything she seems so scared to share.

I go around and grab the diaper bag and sling it over my shoulder. "I know one thing that might help," I offer.

Once she's got Juniper in her arms, I click the fob to lock the car and slip the keys back into my pocket.

She smooths Juniper's hair with a hand but peeks over her baby's head to meet my eyes. "Yeah?" she asks, a small smile playing on those perfect lips. "What's that?"

"When it comes to what you did in the car back there," I say, grinning, "your gut was right on. Maybe before, you trusted your feelings, but you just couldn't trust the person you had the feelings for."

Her lips part, and she looks at me with an expression that's part sad, part thankful. "I think that first house was the one, but I still want to look at a few more to be sure."

Something in her voice gives me the feeling she is talking about more than just the house. "When you know, you know," I assure her, resting my palm lightly against her lower back. "And if it's really the one for you, it'll be there when you're ready. Now, I think I see what looks like some very filthy gutters." I point to the roof of the house ahead of us. "Not liking this one already, but let's take a look. Maybe we'll find some proof that your gut is right and you've already found the one."

By the time we finish looking at every house on the list, it's a lot later than I expected. In the driveway of the last house, Juniper has a full meltdown. She's eaten snacks from the diaper bag, had water and another diaper change, but even Eden looks a little tired and flustered.

"I'm starving," she says. "And you've got to be too." She looks at her watch and bounces Juniper against her hip. "I'd wanted to make one more stop before going back to the hotel, but I don't think Junie's got it in her. Do you mind if we head back?"

My stomach growls. "Can we stop for some food along the way?"

She nods, thanks Taylor for all the work today, and then bustles off toward the SUV.

I click the fob to unlock the vehicle and turn to shake Taylor's hand. "Thanks for letting me tag along," I say. "It was nice meeting you." I'm turning to head out when Taylor calls my name.

"Vito," she says, then looks toward Eden, who is coaxing a very cranky baby into her car seat. "I think Eden really liked that first house. What do you think?"

I nod. "It's her call, but no doubt that house will make a great home. Well maintained, move-in condition. Upstairs bathrooms could use a remodel at some point, but nothing she couldn't live with for a couple years. If she makes a decision, I'm sure she'll let you know."

Taylor nods. "A house like that won't stay on the market long." I'm not sure why she's telling me this, but then, of course, she drops the bomb. "You know, if your credit is an issue, we have programs. I work with a lot of mortgage brokers, and we'll find a way. There's no reason why the two of you can't make this happen."

I bark out a laugh. "Thanks for that," I say. "But my credit's just fine, not that it matters since I won't be buying the house. But I'll pass that along to Eden."

Taylor looks confused, like even though Eden said we were just friends, she doesn't believe I won't be moving in to the house with her. But she just says okay and shoves a handful of business cards at me. I didn't think people used business cards much anymore, but I take them, thank her again, and head over to the truck.

Juniper is in full scream mode, with tears on her red face and her lower lip trembling, coated with drool, she's so worked up.

I've seen epic meltdowns like this before, so I know the best thing to do is let Mom tell me what she wants. I press my hand to Eden's lower back. "Can I help?" I ask. "Jokes? Take her for a walk? We don't need to get in the car right now. Whatever she needs, we do."

Eden looks at me with gratitude all over her face. She looks flustered too. "Thanks," she says, "but I think she's tired. I should have paid closer attention to the time. We missed her nap by about an hour. I'm going to ride in the back with her if you don't mind playing chauffeur."

"Absolutely. Go around. I'll hang with her until you're in."

While Eden runs around the rear bumper to climb into the seat behind the driver, I look down at sad little Juniper. My heart tightens physically in my chest at the misery on her cute face. She's obviously worked up and overtired if she missed her nap, but I can't help wanting to do something.

"Hey, kiddo," I say, reaching a hand out to her. I don't do anything, just reach my fingers toward her, and Juniper surprises me by lifting her arms up and screaming a very easy-to-understand word.

"Up. Up."

I look helplessly at Eden, who is climbing into the back seat. "What do I do?" I ask. "She wants up?"

Eden sighs. "Yeah, I'm sure she does." She looks at Taylor, who's staring at us through the window, and waves. "You know what, get her up. She's had a long day, and she's wrecked. Maybe she'll calm down a bit if we just let her settle."

With Juniper continuing to scream, I reach into the back seat, unbuckle her safety belt, and pick her up from the car seat. She flops against my shoulder, her little mouth biting into my shirt.

"Oh God." When Eden comes around and sees Juniper's basically gone vampire on me, she runs back to the car for the diaper bag.

"Teething," she says. "Poor kiddo. I'll bet she's in pain." She comes back to the passenger side of the car with a little plastic bottle in her hands. "These are organic teething tablets. They'll dissolve against her gums and give her a little relief. Can you hold her while I do this?"

"Yep." I've seen this before, but never up close and personal. It's actually really heartbreaking. She's got to be in some kind of pain, but the second her mom puts her fingers in Junie's mouth, the crying eases. A little white froth bubbles on her lips, but true to Eden's prediction, just having some fingers to bite on seems to calm Juniper down enough to stop the screaming.

"There we go," I say, keeping my voice calm and cheerful. "You got this, kiddo."

Once Juniper seems a little more settled, Eden takes her from me. "I'm going to walk a sec," she says.

She takes off at a nice brisk pace down the sidewalk, patting Juniper's back and letting her grind her mouth against her shoulder like she did to me. I close the doors, lock the car, and catch up to them, walking alongside Eden. We don't say anything; I just keep pace while she coos to her daughter.

"Good way to check out the neighborhood," she says, throwing me a look. "I'm sorry, Vito. I know we're both starving. What a disaster."

I shake my head. "This has been a pretty perfect day in my book," I say. "No fires, no MVAs. I think I can handle running support on a teething meltdown."

"MVA?" she echoes.

"Motor vehicle accident," I explain.

She nods, and as we approach the end of the third block, Juniper has quieted down a lot. We slow our pace, and by the time we get back to the car, Juniper is almost asleep on Eden's shoulder.

She gently sets her daughter back in the car seat, and I watch as her drowsy eyelids blink fast, her thick eyelashes casting shadows on her cheeks.

I always thought I'd have kids someday. I thought I'd end up having them with Michelle. But I could see being somebody's dad like this. What I can't imagine is giving up on a kid that I have, even if shit didn't work out with the baby momma.

My gut clenches when I think about my divorced friends. My sister's husband is a widower, so she didn't have to navigate any issues with an ex-wife, the birth mother of her stepkids. If anybody could do it, Gracie could.

What if Juniper's father is still in the picture? I don't know how cool I'd be sharing a kid with a deadbeat dad. But before I jump to judgment, I've got to remind myself that not everyone has a family like mine. I don't know if Eden even has parents.

"You mind if I ride in back with her?" Eden's got Juniper strapped in.

I don't reply because of course I don't mind. I wait for her to get in, then I close Juniper's door as Eden gets settled in the back seat, climb behind the wheel, belt in, and head back to Eden's hotel.

"So," I say softly as we're pulling away. "I told you my story. Now a good time for yours?"

Eden chuckles softly. She leans back against the clean leather and closes her eyes. "Take me someplace I can buy you a burger and fries, and I'll tell you anything you want to know."

"Deal," I say, then head toward downtown Star Falls.

CHAPTER EIGHT

eden

The burgers from Betta Burger are better than anything I've ever had. The fries are thick, with the skins still on and loads of salt. The patty is perfectly seared but juicy, and the fixings are crisp, fresh, and loaded between a perfectly baked bun.

Vito parked and went inside to order, figuring that the shouting into the drive-through speaker would wake up Junie. He's already finished his burger and fries and is working his way through a peanut butter and chocolate shake while I dip the last of my fries into a tiny dollop of ketchup.

"Come on, you got to taste this." He twists in the driver's seat and holds the cup over the center console. "Just take a sip. I promise I don't have cooties."

I shake my head and think it's already too late for that. I kissed the man just a few minutes ago. It's not a big leap to take a sip from his straw.

I grab the cup and start with a little taste, but I quickly suck down a big mouthful. "Oh my God," I mutter. "What the heck do they put in these? I might have to fight you for the last few sips."

Vito holds his hands up in surrender. "You finish it. I know better than to come between a woman and the best shake in Star Falls."

I take two more long sips and then hand it back to him. "I'm done," I say. "I don't need that much sugar in my life, but that's good."

He slurps the last of the shake then bags up his trash. "I know, right? You need an unofficial tour guide through the best food in Star Falls, I'm your guy."

He holds out a hand, and I give him my burger wrapper and the little waxy bag that has been completely cleaned of any evidence that hand-cut fries were once inside.

Once my belly is full, I lean back against the seat and sigh. "Thank you," I say. "For lunch. For coming with me today. For all of this."

Vito fires up the truck and looks at me in the rearview. "You bought lunch," he reminds me. "Everything else was my pleasure."

He pulls out of the parking lot of the burger place, and I watch little Junie as she sleeps. Her mouth is open, her lips still shiny with a bit of drool. Thank goodness I have teething toys in the freezer back at the hotel. I have a feeling we're going to need them.

"We got enough time for that story you were going to tell me?" Vito's smiling, but the fact that he's bringing it up again has my stomach suddenly doing flips.

I lace my fingers together and squeeze tight. I can give him the sanitized version of the story I gave my aunt, but I have a feeling he's going to want more. More that I just don't know I can offer. But something about the smirk covering that sexy face loosens my defenses.

I can open up.

Nathan can't hurt me or Junie.

Not as long as I don't break the rules.

"Yeah," I sigh. "Okay. So, my daughter's father... The short version is he wanted nothing to do with a child. When he found out I was pregnant, he was happy to help me solve the problem as long as it had nothing to do with him." I can see in the mirror that Vito's lips have gone thin, but he looks straight ahead at the road and just listens.

I appreciate that he's not interrupting me with questions or reactions, but I almost wish he would. I'd rather tell him the things he wants to know than just leave me to share, but he's not interrupting so I rush on to fill the silence.

"I told him I was going to have the baby and I planned on keeping her. After that, lawyers got involved, and we worked out an agreement. It's actually pretty unusual." This is where I stop and bite my lip. I told my aunt some of this, but not nearly all there is to tell.

"Okay," he says slowly. "Does he visit her? Get pictures?"

I shake my head. "No, nothing like that." I rub my forehead and suddenly wish we weren't doing this in the car. I'm sitting behind the driver's seat, and it feels like I'm confessing my sins in one of those boxes like I was forced to do for a while in Catholic grade school.

I can't tell how close we are to the hotel because Vito hasn't punched the address into the GPS, so I figure I might as well keep going. If he doesn't want anything to do with me after this, well, it's probably better I know before I go off and kiss the man again.

"Vito," I say quietly. "Some of the details of what happened are sort of confidential. I haven't even told my aunt everything."

He immediately looks into the rearview and meets my eyes. "What do you need me to do? Spit oath? Blood? I was never a Boy Scout, but if there's something I've got to swear to, I'll swear to it. You can trust me with anything, Eden."

The sparkle in his eye makes me giggle. "A spit oath? Is that a thing?"

He cups his palm like he might actually spit in it, but then he grabs the steering wheel. "Fuck if I know. Point is, you can trust me. I've got no reason to tell anybody your business, Eden. The only reason I want to know is so I know whose knees I've got to crack or if I've got to break some bones for you. Some ex shows up you don't want around, some deadbeat bails on child support..." He lifts a thick brow at me. "We Bianchis take care of our own."

We take care of our own...

Am I theirs? His? I have been going to weekly ladies' brunches and hanging out with the Bianchis more than I used to spend time

435

with my friends in LA—if you could really call the people I worked with and occasionally did dinners and happy hours with my friends.

I decide not to think too long about his choice of words but focus on what he's really asking.

"We signed an agreement," I explain. "It's a confidential agreement, which is why I don't talk about it much. Basically, he gave up all parental rights to Juniper in exchange for money. His lawyers set up a fund that will pay me a modest annual income so I can live off the money until she is older. There's also a small amount put away in a separate trust so she can have a head start on college or culinary school, trade school, or just to travel if she wants when she turns eighteen."

He nods slowly but asks only one question. "No parental rights. What does that mean?"

"He's out of her life for good. And mine too. No visits, no emails, no holiday cards."

"He basically bought you off." Vito sounds disgusted. He grumbles something under his breath, and I start to feel too hot.

This was a mistake.

I told him too much, and this isn't even half of it.

"Vito, I know how it sounds."

"Whoa. I'm not judging you, babe." He looks at me in the mirror, his face severe. "You've got a baby to raise, and you're how old?"

"Twenty-six."

He sighs. "Fuck. You had a job before? You got a degree or student loans and shit?"

I shake my head. "That's part of the problem. I didn't go to college. And Juniper's dad was my boss."

"So, he bought you off on a sexual harassment suit too? I'm sorry, Eden. I don't know if you loved this guy or what, but he sounds like a Grade A douchebag with a capital fucking D."

I lower my head and close my eyes. Did I love Nathan? My answer to that is so easy, but it makes me feel even shittier.

"I never loved him." I almost whisper it. "God, Vito." I tug my fingers through my hair. "Do you know what it's like to be so out of

436

your depth? You probably don't. You have a great family. You're loved. You have people." I think back over the series of stupid decisions that brought me to LA, and maybe it's the fact that I'm in the back seat of the car and I can't look at Vito.

Maybe this is like some kind of confession or therapy session. Or maybe it's just the first time anyone has shown a real interest in what I've gone through, but I just start talking.

And once I start, I'm shocked how good it feels to let some of this go.

"What we had wasn't love," I say. "It was confusion. I was so lost in LA." I look out the window at the green lawns and mature trees, the clean streets and perfect sidewalks. Star Falls is literally a world away from where I'm from. "You've probably heard a little about my childhood from my aunt. My dad left me, and my mom died in prison. She was locked up for attacking a boyfriend with a hammer. And when Mom got sent away, her druggie boyfriend took responsibility for me."

Vito jerks the truck, but he quickly rights us. "Sorry," he growls. And it is a growl. "Did the boyfriend mistreat you?"

"No. Actually, Mom going away seemed to calm Bruce down a bit. He cleaned up his act and left me totally alone. I went to school, cooked for myself, cleaned the apartment. He got himself clean for a little while, but he definitely didn't want to be somebody's stepdad. He worked when he could and actually kept food in the house. Paid the bills." I bite my lip at the memory. Mac and cheese in a box isn't food to some people, but during the eighteen months Bruce lived with me, I never went to sleep hungry.

"That didn't last long," I continue. "Ma passed in prison. She had an appendicitis attack but didn't get medical attention fast enough. And then one day, when I was seventeen, Bruce packed up his shit while I was at school. He left me a hundred dollars in cash and told me the rent was due on the first or I'd have to pay a penalty."

My eyes start to sting when I think about what happened next. How scared I was to be alone. "I'd gotten used to Bruce," I say quietly. "He wasn't family, but he didn't do anything bad. But as soon as he was gone, I needed to figure out how to pay the rent, how to buy groceries. That was when I decided to try to find my dad. Of course, that was impossible, but I did find my aunt, Shirley. She'd never stopped sending me birthday cards and letters over the years. When I told her Mom died and Bruce had left, Shirley came to my apartment. I begged her not to call child services. The last thing I wanted was to be put into foster care at seventeen."

Vito pulls into the parking lot of the hotel and turns off the car. He faces forward, his head lowered. "Go on," he urges.

"Well, the rest is pretty simple," I tell him. "Aunt Shirley paid the rent on my apartment until the day I turned eighteen. After that, I decided I wanted to move someplace that I picked. Someplace that I wanted to be. I had no idea what I wanted to do with my life. But I'd spent so much of my life living with people who didn't want me, in places I didn't want to be, I picked the most glamorous, exciting, fun place I could imagine. The City of Angels."

I smile even now, thinking of my former home. "I worked a ton of random jobs, lived in shitty apartments, and made a really bad choice dating a guy who showered me with attention but who wouldn't be there in the long run. But to answer your question, no. I'm kind of sorry to admit it. I got swept up in the romance of being wanted. But that's all it ever was until Junie. Because of her, I have zero regrets."

I smooth her sweaty curls back from her face and hope I've told him enough but not so much. I mean, I know my story is a lot, and there are still details I haven't shared. But he wanted to know my story and the situation, and that's it.

Most of it, at least. The bits I can share.

"Did you want to come in for a bit?" I ask him. "I think she should sleep for about another hour if I can get her inside without waking her up."

Vito is quiet, but he unfastens his belt and runs around to the rear doors to grab Junie's diaper bag.

I perform a feat of acrobatic wonder, sliding my hands under Junie's butt and setting her on my shoulder in such a smooth movement. She does wake up but then blinks those long lashes and mumbles, "Mama," and falls right back to sleep.

Vito locks the car, and I ask him to grab the keycard to my hotel room from a zipped pocket in the diaper bag. He unlocks the door and holds it open for me. I immediately go into the bedroom, where I have a pack and play set up for Junie. I tuck her in and wait to make sure she is going to stay asleep, then I quietly close the door behind me and head back to the living room.

I half expect to see Vito awkwardly standing by the door, just waiting to bolt after the miserable story I shared in the car. Instead, he's sitting on the couch, and he's spread out all the glossy listing sheets from each house we saw on the coffee table. He's looking over each one, but when I come back into the room, he stands.

"So, I sorted these in price order," he says, pointing to the sheets. "Maybe we go through each one and make a list of pros and cons. A couple of them I'd scratch off the list completely, but I want to know which ones you liked because if I saw red flags in a place you're thinking of buying, I got a buddy who can do a real home inspection for you. Figure out the cost to fix the problem, maybe get some money off the asking price so you can make the repair before you move in."

I'm staring at him, not saying a word, just taking in everything he's saying. I realize I'm staring when he comes around the table with a concerned look on his face. "Are you okay? Am I being too pushy? If you want to make this decision on your own, I'll butt the fuck out, I just…"

I shake my head. "It's not that. I expected you to run after I told you all that shit about Junie's father. About my upbringing."

Vito cocks his chin and lifts one of those perfect, deep brown brows at me. He steps closer, and I can smell the same sensual aroma of his cologne.

"Eden." His voice is low as he reaches for my chin. He cups it in his hand, and his lips curl into a grin. "What you told me only makes me believe even more strongly that you're a fucking amazing woman. From everything I've seen, you're a totally dedicated and loving mom. You've had a hard life, and you're here for your fresh start. Why would I run from the strongest, sexiest, most resilient woman I've ever met?"

He releases my chin and chuckles. "Just don't tell Gracie I said that." He jerks a thumb toward the couch. "Come on, you got a house to buy and a home to make for yourself and that little girl."

He plops down onto the couch like this is something we've done a million times. I pull a pen and some paper from the hotel kitchenette and start making notes about the homes.

"While we're on the subject of this house, are you sure you want to buy?" he asks. "You're thinking you're going to stay in Star Falls?"

I nod. "Aunt Shirley's been after me to move here since my mom died." I toe off my shoes and shrug out of my wrap. It's getting warm in the late afternoon sun, but the windows in this all-suite extended-stay hotel don't open. If I want to cool off, I have to click on the air or lose a layer. "I figure if I buy a house now, I'll have enough equity by the time Juniper is grown to either sell if I need to or pull money out of the house. That's one thing I really want to do with my life," I say, admitting what I want more than anything.

"I never grew up in a house. Never had a savings account. Never knew how to manage money because there was literally never a spare penny. I want to have the life I always wanted. Of course, for my daughter, but not just for her. I want something good that we can share. I want more than what I've had."

As soon as I say the words, I remember that Vito's ex-wife left him because she wanted the finer things in life.

I hope he doesn't think I mean that. I don't know what she wanted, and I sure don't want to judge a woman I don't know.

I don't think having some stability in my life and making sure I don't screw up the chance I've been given to make a normal life for my daughter is hard to understand.

But the smile he gives me washes away all my worries like a sudden storm on a sunny day. "You're going to do it," he says. "I can feel it. I got a good sense about you, Eden. You're a smart cookie."

I point to the listing sheet and think back to Robert's house. "Smart enough to make this work?"

"Is that the one?" he asks. His voice is low, and I'm suddenly aware of his knee gently touching mine.

I don't move away. "Yeah," I say. "I feel like it is." I look into his eyes. "I just hope I'm putting my trust in the right things this time."

"Things?" He scoots closer to me, until he's so close I feel the heat radiating from his arm beside mine. "Things are going to break, Eden. Dishwashers and roofs and sinks."

My heart starts hammering in my chest, and my palm gets sweaty. "I'm talking about the stuff that's harder to fix once it's broken."

His fingertips push my hair away from my neck, and he leans down to murmur against my ear. "Hearts," he guesses. "Broken hearts can be fixed too."

All I can focus on is the pressure of Vito's thigh alongside mine and his sweet, light breath as he whispers against my skin.

"I'm a trained professional, you know. First aid, basic lifesaving. If you're going to put your trust in anyone, it might as well be me."

I shift a little and lift my face so our noses nearly touch. "I'm sure you've stopped plenty of hearts too," I say with a grin.

He snakes a hand behind my neck and slides his fingers into my hair. "You've got my heart and some other parts of me going haywire right now."

He tightens his fingers lightly, the slight tug on my roots sending a wave of arousal from my head all the way to my toes. I close my eyes and shiver, feeling the tiny hairs on my arms stand at attention. "Vito," I breathe.

"Yeah, babe?"

"Remember when you gave me permission to kiss you?"

"Uh-huh." He growls a laugh. "You've got an open invitation with me. You want it, you take it."

"Oh, thank God," I say, then I turn to him, lift one thigh, and straddle his lap.

CHAPTER NINE

The minute Eden settles into my lap, I slide my fingers under her hair, grip her neck, and pull her close.

I kiss her lightly at first, tasting her lips and getting used to the soft feel of her cheeks against my stubble.

Unlike when she kissed me in the car, she's not shy now. She closes her eyes and opens her mouth, nibbling my lips and panting sweet breaths against my mouth.

She opens her lips and flicks her tongue against mine, and that's when I know I'm fucked. A goner.

Her tongue dances against mine, and I swear I see sparks behind my eyes. A feral groan slips out of me. As if my arousal gives her permission to give in to hers, she laces her fingers behind my neck to pull me even closer.

She wiggles her hips against my lap, the denim of my jeans providing so much friction, I'm starting to get uncomfortably hard.

I pull my head back to catch my breath. Her cheeks are flushed, and her lips look swollen and bright red. I lower my face to her neck and nibble kisses along the sharp corner of her jaw.

She tips back, but I tighten my arms around her back and pull her toward me. I want to pick her up and lay her on this couch and do unspeakably dirty things to her, but I'm getting way too close to the point of no return.

She's sweet, she's smart, and she's seen some shit. She's got plans and priorities, and if her thick curves didn't have me hooked, everything else I'm learning about her would seal the deal.

"You're fucking hot, and you're all mine," I say.

"All yours?" she echoes.

I don't care if calling her mine is too much, too soon. She's mine right now. I'm not about to let anything come between us. Definitely not memories of my stripper ex who has no business fucking up our good time.

"At least for this afternoon," I say.

She slips off my lap to sit beside me. I throw an arm over her shoulder and lift her face to meet my eyes.

She grins and, twisting at the waist, grabs my face with both hands. "Yes," she whispers, then runs her nose along the stubble on my jawline.

She moans deep in her throat, and before I can stop it, my hand slides from her hip to her belly. She arches her chest against mine, and even though we are in the world's most awkward position, I feel her full breasts press against me.

I'm trying to figure out how we can get more comfortable while making an even more inappropriate scene on her couch when Eden shoves my chest lightly.

"Lie back a bit," she says, her voice thick and low.

I lean back, and she straddles my hips, but this time, she braces her hands on the back of the couch behind me so we won't tip off the front. She flicks her tongue along my lower lip while tugging the front of her V-neck top down a bit.

I take that as my invitation, and I cup her generous tits in my hands.

A whimper in her throat sends my dick into overdrive. She grinds her hips against mine, and we ravish each other's mouths while I hold her breasts, and she claws the couch behind my shoulders.

"I really want to kiss you here." I grunt the words against her lips, tightening my hold on her breasts.

She doesn't respond, just releases the couch and holds her arms in the air. I grab the hem of her tee and tug it up to reveal her belly. She bends her arms and works them through the sleeves, then sets the shirt beside us on the couch. She's wearing a dusty-pink-colored bra, the cups so thin I can see the sharp outlines of her hard nipples through the lace.

"Jesus fuck, babe," I pant. I swallow and just stare at her, taking in her body. "You are fucking unbelievable."

She looks down at her belly, pointing with a finger. "I've got a few stretch marks. Here…" She uses a finger to work a large circle, motioning over her abdomen. Then she lifts her hands to her breasts. "Here too," she whispers, her voice thick. "No one has seen all this since I had Junie."

"Really?"

I know her kid's only like a year old, but the fact that I'm the first —the only guy to experience this version of her body—gets me.

"Babe," I hiss, thumbing one nipple through the pink lace. "Everything about your body is fucking perfect."

We look into each other's eyes as I shove the fabric away to reveal her hard, copper-colored nipple.

I thumb the peak gently and suck air as she gasps and slams her eyes closed. "Sensitive?" I ask.

"Fuck yes," she breathes. "Don't stop."

I watch her lips part and her hips shimmy as I tweak both nipples between my fingertips. She throws her shoulders back and gasps, leaning into my hands and urging me to work her nipples harder.

"So good," she sighs, opening her eyes slowly. "Vito…"

I lower my face and suck her whole right nipple into my mouth. I hold the weight of her breast in my hand and swirl my tongue over the sensitive skin.

She gasps again and throws her head back, but my eyes are closed.

I'm focused on the pressure she's putting on my erection, the taste of her sweet flesh under my tongue, and the greedy noises that let me know she likes what I'm doing.

Suddenly, I hear a small, muffled song coming from the direction of Eden's bedroom. Juniper's awake. She's not screaming or crying. She's literally singing, "Maaaamaaaa."

"Fuck." I lift my mouth from her nipple and grin. "I'd almost be pissed if she weren't so damn cute."

Eden's grin is even bigger than mine. "Cutest little cockblock in Star Falls." She sighs and leans back to smooth the cups of her bra back into place. "I am so sorry," she says.

I shake my head and rub my face hard. "No apologies needed." I stand while she puts her shirt back on and adjust my cock in my jeans, praying it will go down quickly. "You need me to go?" I ask.

She pulls me close for a hug. We're nearly the same height, so when we're nose to nose, I can plant another kiss on her lips. "No," she whispers against my mouth. "Not until we've gone through the lists of pros and cons."

I slip my hands into the back pockets of her jeans and give her ass a playful squeeze. "One condition," I say. "We pick up where we left off sometime soon."

"Like, very soon," she promises.

She pulls away from me about as reluctantly as I let her go. She smiles at me, her hair mussed and her cheeks flushed as she heads to the bedroom.

"Look who's awake," she says to Juniper.

The hotel suite is starting to get dark, so I keep myself busy while Eden gets Juniper up by turning on the lights and grabbing a glass of water. I hear Eden call out that she's changing a diaper and will be right out, so I pour her a glass of water too and then go back to the listing sheets.

Eden and I spend the next couple of hours playing with Juniper and talking through the list of houses we looked at. There is a clear winner in both of our minds, and of course, it is the very first house we saw.

"So, you think you're going to make an offer?" I ask. I'm putting all the listing sheets into a stack while Juniper smashes a plastic cooking pot against the coffee table. I raise my voice a bit to call over the racket. "No more looking?"

Eden's in the kitchenette prepping some dinner for Juniper. "No," she says, meeting my eyes across the suite. "I think I'm going to trust my gut this time."

I've never been a man to believe in things like *the one* before, but I do believe in trusting my gut. And right now, my gut's telling me if there was ever a *one* for me, I've just found her.

Three weeks later, it's done.

Eden made an offer on the house, Robert accepted it, and the house passed all the inspections with flying colors.

Eden got approved for the mortgage, and since she was anxious to get out of the hotel, she was able to negotiate for a quick closing.

During that time, work was intense.

We had not one, but two unusually serious structure fires. For a small department like ours, one serious fire per quarter is not uncommon, but two in under a month put a strain on the team. Our captain suffered a twisted ankle at the first fire, so there was some shuffling of schedules while the cap healed up.

Eden and I didn't manage to fit in a proper date night, but we've had plenty of dates in, if you call dinner and heavy make-out sessions on the shitty hotel couch dates. By the time the week of the closing rolled around, Ma's friends were taking charge like a well-oiled machine.

"Vito, are you up yet?"

I hear Ma's voice and a noise like she's banging on my door with the heel of a stiletto shoe.

"Ma, fuck." It's not even eight in the morning if my phone's to be believed. Way too early for this shit. "What is it?"

"Can I come in?"

"Ma." I toss aside the covers and stride to the door in my pajama pants. There's a reason I don't sleep naked anymore, and her name is Lucia Bianchi.

I throw open the bedroom door and see the abominable noisemaker Ma was banging against my door. An industrial-sized tape roller that's as big as my mom's head.

"Where the hell did you get this, and why are you banging it on my door?"

Despite the early hour, Ma's fully dressed and made up to the nines. I grab her hand and stare at the glittery-looking hearts attached to her fingertips. "Did you get your nails done this early?"

Ma yanks her hand back and fake slaps me with it. "I got these done two days ago, Vito. I swear I could have little penises put onto my nails, and it would take you and your father a week to notice."

I blast a laugh through my lips and smooth my hair back. "I think Pops would notice dicks on your hands, Ma, but thanks for the visual. I just got a preview of my future nightmares."

I turn from Ma and grab a T-shirt from the floor. Ma shakes her head and snorts.

"Son, what did I tell you about leaving clothes on the floor? Are you going to do that at Eden's house?"

My jaw falls open, and I turn to stare at my mother. "Uh, excuse me?"

My mother rolls her eyes. "Oh please. It's not like we haven't noticed you've been gone a lot. Smiling all the time. And somehow, you seem to always leave the house right before Eden comes over for ladies' brunch. You tell me what all that means. Am I wrong? Are you or are you not seeing her?"

I shake my head and try not to smile. "You and your friends, Ma. You got to stop playing Sherlock Holmes with other people's lives. I thought you agreed to butt out of your kids' love lives after Franco and Chloe?"

Ma's face pinches, and she looks hurt. "Now that's not fair. Chloe and Franco are perfect together. That might not even have happened if I hadn't made sure your brother met the new girl in town. Now, honey, I'm not judging. I just…"

"Ma." I hold a hand up. "You did not wake me up on my day off to quiz me about my love life, did you? What's the tape for? You going to tape me to a chair until I confess I'm dating Eden?"

"You are." My mom looks so happy at that, all I can do is roll my eyes. "Son, ever since Michelle…"

"Don't finish that sentence." This time, my voice has a warning edge to it. Before I can say anything more, Pops comes up the stairs and makes his way down the hallway.

"Son, you're up? I told your mother I was going to head out. I didn't think you'd be vertical this early."

I yawn and shake my head. "I wasn't." My mother opens her mouth to complain, but I hold up a hand. "I'm up now. Where you off to, Pops?"

Mario Bianchi is dressed, showered, and shaved. He's shoved his glasses up on his head, and the silver hair that looks exactly like mine will in about thirty years is perfectly styled. He takes the tape roller from my mom's hand like it's a loaded weapon and shakes his head.

"Your mother's friends are taking Eden's move very seriously. I'm on box duty. Lucia is sending me out to the grocery stores to see if I can get some free cardboard boxes so Eden doesn't have to pay for them."

I shake my head and try not to laugh. "Ma, did you ask Eden about any of this? You realize she'd hardly unpacked when she had to move out of her rental. Most of her stuff is still in the moving boxes they came in from LA."

My mother gives me the most shit-eating grin and crosses her arms over her chest now that her hands are free. "How would you know that?"

I roll my eyes like I'm fifteen again. "I was on the engine that responded the night of the house fire, remember?"

I wave my hands at my parents, both of whom are now crowded into my childhood bedroom. "Okay, look out. Both of you. I need a cup of coffee and a shower. Then I'll run errands with Dad and pick up boxes, body bags, whatever your friends want."

My mother pads across my room and flags me down with those blood-red nails. I lean down, and she kisses my cheek. "Make it a quick shower, honey. The ladies will be here soon."

I snort and meet my dad's eyes, but he just shrugs. He's as whipped by my mother as he was the day they met back in high school. As she brushes past him, he cops a feel of her ass, and I shout, "Pops! It's too early for that shit."

But Pops just looks back at me and waggles his eyebrows, then follows my ma back downstairs, closing my door behind them. I grab a towel and head into the bathroom that I shared with my sister Gracie until she moved in with her husband, Ryder.

While I love the extra space, I have to admit, I miss having my sister around all the time. Things are definitely different being the last kid living at home.

I turn the water to scalding and climb under the spray, grinning about the secret that Eden and I've got going. We agreed to keep the fact that we're seeing each other quiet for now.

Shit's new, and until she's settled in her house, it's not like we're *dating* dating. Dinners at her place or walks with Juniper on my days off aren't exactly hot dates. But it's been more fun than I expected getting to know them while she waits to move into her new place.

It's been nice being excited about something for a change.

The shit at work hasn't changed, and that shit won't change unless I do something about it. I know what I have to do, but I'm just not sure I'm willing to do what it takes.

A fucking college degree.

I wouldn't even know how to do that. Show up with a goddamn backpack? What if the classes I need to take are on days I have to work?

By the time I get off my shift, all I want to do is sleep, do laundry, and catch up with Eden.

If I'd had the energy to think about going back to school before, now, things are changing. I've never dated anyone with a kid, and I can see from just the last month that having a kid is a full-time job.

I don't know how the hell my sister still does tattoos, manages to keep a house clean, cooks, and does everything else that needs to be done with three.

I decide to ask my pops about that when we're alone.

"You ready, son?"

Pops is twisting the lid on a travel mug of coffee when I clomp down the stairs.

"If that's for me, I am." I reach out my hand for the coffee, and Pops nods. "Thank you."

Ma is sitting at the dining room table, a bunch of lists and paperwork spread out. She's taking this move more seriously than Eden is, but I don't say a word. I kiss the top of her hair and realize that Ma's whole life has been about her kids and the people she loves.

She never went to college, never worked outside the home. All the energy and intelligence she has, she gives away. Whether she's volunteering at the animal shelter, babysitting her grandkids, or pounding on my door at an ungodly early hour of the morning, Lucia Bianchi is a force to be reckoned with. Glittery nails and all.

I wrap the arm that's not holding the coffee around her neck and bend down toward her ear. "You're a fucking angel, you know that?"

Ma looks up at me in surprise, her pretty eyes heavy with mascara and liner. My words seem to hit her, and I can see every emotion cross her face. "Vito, language." She playfully swats at me, then blows a kiss at my father. "Don't dillydally," she reminds us.

"Oh, I'm going to dilly, baby." Pops is putting on a pair of work boots by the front door. "But I promise not to let V dally."

He grabs his keys, and I slide my feet into my running shoes and follow Pops out the front door. His truck's parked in the driveway, which means he probably cleaned it and gassed up even earlier this morning. Even though he's retired, he still gets up early, takes care of his truck like it's one of his kids, and never, ever complains, no matter what wild-goose chase Ma sends him on.

I buckle in and drink the scalding-hot coffee with cream and sugar, just the way I like it. "This is good, Pops. Thanks."

My dad nods, but I'm feeling shit today, so I got to say something more.

"How do you know exactly how I like my coffee?" I ask.

Pops shrugs. "Son, don't take this the wrong way, but you've been living under my roof long enough, I'd have to be a dead man not to pick up on some of your habits."

He cracks himself up and I grin, but then he grows serious. "You know how I take my coffee," he reasons. "It's what families do. We pay attention to the small shit."

That gets me thinking.

I didn't notice Ma's new nails. Maybe it's because she's my mother, or maybe it's because she gets her nails done so often I can't keep up. Maybe I take a lot of things for granted. That question's got me feeling hot and uncomfortable.

"Was it hard?" I ask, swallowing a perfect sip of coffee. "Raising four of us? Ma always made it look so easy."

Pops chuckles. "I'm glad you think she did," he says. "But hell yeah, it was hard. But worth every second of the work. And that's what it is, kiddo. Work. But it's the best job on the planet if you've got people you love to do it with."

"What about work? Did Ma ever think about working outside the home? I never felt like we were struggling for money, but raising four kids… That shit ain't cheap."

Pops nods. "I could have moved up into management if I'd just had that stupid piece of paper." He shrugs. "I could have gone to school at night, but your mother and I decided I'd rather make less and be around more." He takes his eyes off the road for a split second to meet my eyes. "I sometimes worry we should have pushed you kids harder on the college thing. I always assumed my kids would go, but I was no help in that department."

"You did more than enough," I tell him, and it's true.

My parents cooked, kept a safe home, and never once let us worry about things that we had no business worrying about.

I grew up totally unlike Eden did, and while I've always appreciated my family and my upbringing, I'm starting to think I never really got how much having these two people as my parents made my life what it is.

It's a life I love, and no matter how lost I feel at times, with Mario and Lucia behind me, my siblings beside me, I can look to the future and know I can handle whatever I set my mind to.

I just have to make up my mind.

"So, Pops," I say, "what do you think about stopping for breakfast after we get Ma's boxes? My treat."

My dad shoots me a look. "Double bacon breakfast sandwiches, and you got a deal."

I lean back in the passenger seat and finish off the coffee my pops made. "You got a deal."

Some decisions in my life have been hard, but I think one just got a lot easier.

CHAPTER TEN

eden

"Eden?"

I bounce Juniper on my knee and look up at the woman who's just called my name. "Hi," I call out, waving my hand so she knows who I am. I secure the diaper bag over my shoulder and follow the nicely dressed woman into an incredibly small office.

"Have a seat," she says, motioning to the chairs on the opposite side of her desk.

"I hope you don't mind I brought my daughter," I say, stating the obvious. "I wasn't able to line up childcare, but that's part of what I'm hoping to learn about today. If doing this is realistic for a single parent."

"Absolutely. Not a problem at all." The woman reaches over her desk to shake my hand. "I'm Catherine Jones, and I'm an admissions counselor. I can answer any questions you have about the programs we offer, tuition costs, things like that. If I need to refer you to one of my colleagues in student life or financial aid, we can probably get everything you need before you leave today."

"Oh, okay. Great. Thank you." I shake her hand and sit down, giving Juniper a teething toy shaped like a little banana with soft plastic bristles at one end. She jams it in her mouth and chews contentedly on my lap.

"My nieces had one of those." Catherine points at the banana. "So cute." She's pulling up a file on her computer while she talks. "Your application materials are complete, and everything looks good. What specific questions can I answer for you today?"

I bite my lower lip and think through the laundry list of worries I have. I start with the easiest question first. "You saw my high school transcripts. I'm a little worried about how much time I'll need to spend on general education requirements before I can apply to a four-year college."

Catherine nods. "Very understandable. You were interested in finance?"

I nod. "I think so. I know I want to learn about money—accounting, bookkeeping, and investments."

"That's what makes the community college model so effective." She goes on to explain that this community college offers a lot of free webinars in different disciplines so that enrolled students can learn a bit about each field of study and the careers that students can pursue.

"We also offer some of our upper-level courses online. Most of the foundations are still offered in person, but you might be able to take up to half the classes you need online from home."

"And if I want to get a degree from a four-year college or university later, those online classes transfer?"

She nods. "Most advisers will help you plan out a curriculum so that you can successfully transfer most if not all of the credits you earn here." She tells me about two colleges in the area that offer transfer incentives to students who have earned associate degrees from area community colleges.

"You know what I might recommend for you?" she says, cocking her head. "Sit in on a class as a guest. We have a new instructor, and she's fantastic. While I can't make any promises, she might be willing to talk with you after class a bit about jobs and her career path." She gives Junie a grin. "You would need to line up a babysitter for that, though."

I nod. "How soon do you think I could sit in?" The back of my SUV is loaded with empty boxes, thanks to Lucia and her friends getting me ready to move. If all goes as planned, I'll be closing on my brand-new house tomorrow. That means weeks of unpacking and getting settled.

I'd like to visit a class as soon as possible so I can spend the coming month thinking about the next big decision—not just where I want to set down roots for my future, but what I want to be when I grow up. And whether getting a degree and going back to school may be part of that plan.

Catherine is tapping away at her keyboard. "Hmm," she says. "Well, this is short notice, but the class I had in mind for you meets tonight on campus at seven and is three hours long. You don't have to stay for the whole class, but if you do, you might catch a few minutes with the instructor." She continues tapping and changing screens. "We have a class taught by a different instructor that might be good for you as well, and that one is tomorrow at noon."

I can't do that one. I know that for sure. I'm supposed to do the final walk-through on the house tomorrow at noon. I've already lined up my aunt Shirley to watch Junie until she has to head into work at three. I can't very well ask her to come over tonight too.

I worry my lip between my teeth. There is someone else who might be willing to watch Juniper. Someone whom I trust with my daughter completely. But this is a big ask. A very big ask.

Then something occurs to me. "Catherine," I say, "do you think I can leave class early without insulting the instructor? I might be able to get a babysitter on short notice, but not for the whole evening."

Catherine smiles. "I'm sure that won't be a problem. Why don't you arrive a few minutes early and see if you can mention it? Then just sit toward the back of the class and slip out quietly. Most three-hour classes break midway through anyway."

"Okay, one second." I grab my phone and stare at it. Vito and I have only known each other about six weeks. Is it way too soon to ask for this kind of help? I don't know, but it's better to find out sooner rather than later how he feels about things like this.

CHELLE BLISS

Me: Is there any chance I could ask you for a huge favor tonight? If you can spare an hour or two to help me with Junie, I promise I will pay you back any way you'd like...

I add some kissy lips emojis, hit send, and then type out one more text.

Me: But seriously, if tonight's not good, it's okay. I can make other...

Before I even finish typing the message, I have a reply. Two thumbs-up emojis.

Vito: Where and when, babe? Just tell me where to be.

My heart flips over in my chest. He didn't ask questions, didn't hesitate.

Something breaks open inside me, and suddenly, I'm feeling excited. Confident, even. Maybe all of this is truly the life I was meant to have.

Supportive people.

A man who cares enough about me to show up without asking questions. Not a man who shows up armed with a team of lawyers and confidentiality agreements.

I look at Catherine and let the first real ray of hope I've felt since I moved to Star Falls brighten my smile. "I have childcare," I say. "What do I need to do?"

"Oh, wonderful." She taps a message into her computer and then prints off a form for me. "I've alerted the instructor through our messaging portal, but take this to class."

I take the form and tuck it into my diaper bag then tap out a message to Vito.

Me: Meet me at my place around 6:15? I can't wait to pay you back for this.

I add a whole line of kiss emojis, and I toss in a couple of eggplants and peaches just for fun. Then I thank Catherine, double-check I have the form I need for tonight, and head to my car with a stupid grin on my face.

Who'd have imagined when I packed up and moved away from the noise and hustle of LA that my dreams weren't where I always thought they were?

If you'd told me four years ago that taking a community college

456

class would get me feeling so hopeful, I would have laughed. But now, I'm about to have the home of my dreams and a plan for a possible career. And that's got me feeling giddy.

The life I've always wanted has never been closer.

"I fed her dinner and changed her diaper." Vito is holding Junie in his arms, following me through the maze of boxes in my hotel room. "If she cries or drools a lot, try a teething ring from the freezer first."

I am moving at warp speed through the instructions, but as the minutes tick away, I'm feeling less and less confident in this plan.

All the excitement of the afternoon comes crashing down as I realize that just because Vito may be willing to do this doesn't mean I'm ready.

"Teething ring first," he repeats, a small smile on his face.

He looks more gorgeous than ever, wearing a soft gray T-shirt under a well-broken-in blue flannel shirt. He's got on distressed dark blue jeans and running shoes, and he smells so good, I seriously rethink my whole plan.

"You know what?" I say, backpedaling so fast I'm feeling dizzy. "This was too much. I'm closing on the house tomorrow, and Junie is teething. I'm not going to go."

Vito slides a hand along my hip and gives me a reassuring squeeze. "First of all, I am trained in lifesaving procedures," he says. "Your daughter will be safe with me. But you still haven't told me what's got you so frazzled. Where are you going? Why do you seem more terrified to leave me alone with your daughter than you did to put in an offer on a house? I've been alone with kids, Eden."

"Oh no. It's not that. I trust you completely." I'd told Vito what time to come by, but I haven't yet explained where I am going and why. "I'm feeling super insecure about this all of a sudden. It's stupid. I was excited all day, but now that it's, like, real..." I sigh.

He sets Juniper down on her playmat and makes sure she grabs a toy before pulling me close. "Babe," he says, his voice low against my ear. "Whatever this is, I'm here for it. Babysitting, moral support."

I peek over at Junie, who is calmly playing by herself. I loop my arms around Vito's waist and rest my head against his chest. "I feel so stupid. So much is changing so fast. We've been living out of boxes forever, Vito. I'm tired. I'm confused."

He holds me firmly, and I let the warmth of his muscled chest support my weight. I duck my chin and hide my face in the spicy cologne that clings to his shirt.

"You wanted me here for something. Whatever it was mattered. If you don't want to share it, you don't have to. But why don't you try to go and just see if you feel better. Sometimes the hardest part is getting out the door. Once you're in the car, you aim for the destination, and don't stop until you get there. I'll be right here with Junie when you get back."

I'm suddenly struck by an idea. It seems foolish, but I'm blurting it out before I can talk myself out of it. "Come with me?" I ask. "I've been looking into taking some classes at the community college. I got a guest pass to sit in on a class tonight. I'm not going to stay the whole time. I'll leave as soon as there's a break—or sooner, if it goes too long. I can't bring Junie into class, but maybe we could bring the stroller and you could walk the campus until I'm done?" I lift my face and look into his gorgeous eyes. There's a thick dusting of stubble on his chin, which he'll shave before he goes back on shift Saturday. I reach a hand to stroke the roughness.

He takes my fingers and brings them to his lips. "I'm not normally one for signs and shit," he says, "but I've been thinking about checking out the community college myself. Been talking myself out of it for months now. This might just be the sign I need to give school a little more thought."

I hold his face with both my hands. "Are you serious? You've been thinking about going back to school?"

He chuckles. "I wouldn't say go back. I haven't spent one second of my life on a college campus." He slides his hands under my hair and sighs. "Not having a degree has held me back in the department. I've been passed over for countless promotions. The last two were just a few months ago," he admits. "It might get me feeling inspired, being on a college campus. You never know. Maybe I'll look around and be like, yeah, this shit's not for me. Either way, I'm down to go, Eden. You got the stroller?"

I nod. "It's in the back seat of the SUV. I took it out of the trunk to make room for all the boxes."

"All right. Do we need to pack anything, or is she good to go?"

He's still holding me, and I feel a strange sense of relief flood my chest. "Vito," I say. I pull back from him and look into his beautiful eyes. "Are you sure about this? Maybe it's all too much, too soon. I'm about to move into a house, and I'm..."

He leans forward and plants a kiss on my lips, a light, teasing one with a gentle sweep of his tongue against mine.

"Eden," he says, "too soon for what? What's too much?" He swallows and looks like he's measuring his words. "I'm in this, babe. Not, like, move into your new house with you in this, but I care about you. I'm falling for you. I'd spend time with you if all you wanted to do was sit on the couch and watch kid shows for hours. Doing something like this? Something that might bring you closer to your dreams?"

He kisses me again. "I respect what you're trying to do with your life. If the only way I can support you is by kicking you in the pants when you're doubting yourself, then I hope your fine behind is ready to meet my toes."

I shake my head, laughing in spite of the tears of gratitude that sting my eyes. "Okay, okay," I say. "I just hope you still feel that way in six months when I've got a leaky sink and a mountain of homework."

He releases me and holds up a finger. "Leaky sink, I got. Homework's all you." He chuckles.

We gather up Junie and head over to the campus. We find the visitor parking lot, and I fish a notebook and the pass that Catherine from Admissions gave me out of the diaper bag.

Vito sets up the stroller and puts Junie in, then fastens the little safety straps. She kicks and laughs, then immediately tosses a toy onto the sidewalk.

Vito picks it up and pretends to kiss the bunny's ears. "It's all right, bunny. Just a scratch." Junie's squealing for it, and he hands it back to her but then motions toward me. "Go on," he says. "We'll be fine. If you have any trouble finding us when you're done, just look for the guy doing wheelies with a stroller."

I shake my head but grab his arm. "Walk me to class?"

A sexy grin spreads across his face. "Lead the way." As we follow the campus map to the building where the math and finance classes are held, Vito lowers his voice. "I like the idea of you being a sexy schoolgirl," he says. "Maybe we can act that out sometime."

Heat pools in my belly, and I rub his back, letting my hand graze his incredibly fine ass. The fall sun is setting and even if anyone saw me grab his behind, I don't think they'd care. The campus looks pretty quiet at this hour, commuter students doing exactly what we are, hustling between the parking lot and night classes.

There are some students hanging around in groups, though. Kids carrying enormous backpacks, talking, laughing. Some running with headphones on. I don't see any babies or children, not that I expected to.

There could be plenty of people enrolled who left their kids at home with sitters or spouses. I'm fortunate to have Junie with me. And to have someone by my side to keep an eye on her while I stick a toe in this scary new pond.

"So, what's the class?" Vito steers the stroller, expertly avoiding a crack in the pavement before we reach the nicely maintained path that leads toward the instructional center.

"It's just an intro course," I explain. "Personal Accounting. I think it covers the basics of money management and bookkeeping."

He nods. "Love it for you. You lost me at accounting."

I slip my hand into the back pocket of his jeans and squeeze. "You know they have all kinds of programs here. Have you ever thought about what kinds of classes you'd take if you wanted to go back for a degree?"

He shakes his head. "And therein lies my problem. I'd probably end up spending more time on the shit that was fun than what I needed to do to actually get a degree."

As we approach the building, I hang back with the stroller. "I won't be long," I tell him. "I'll let the instructor know that I can't stay the whole time. I'll slip out in an hour—or even sooner if it's really boring."

I hold the door open for a couple kids rushing by, but Vito shakes his head. "You stay as long as you want. We'll go exploring."

I clutch the entry pass in my suddenly sweating hand. I hear the buzz of shoes hitting the tile floors, the squeak of the stroller wheeling along beside me.

This is really happening. I've never set foot in a college classroom, and I feel like an impostor. My stomach flips over, and I'm glad I skipped dinner, just eating a banana while I fed Junie her dinner.

"Hey." I hear his voice against my hair. "This you?" He nods toward a closed classroom door. The lights are off, but we're early. Class doesn't start until seven, and it's quarter till.

I nod. "Looks like this isn't a class people come early to. Maybe it sucks?"

He lifts my chin in his hand and kisses me lightly. "Maybe it will. You'll find out," he says lightly.

"Excuse me." A really, really young-looking guy carrying a massive backpack steps around the stroller and yanks open the classroom door. He turns on the light and props the door open. For a minute, I think he might be the instructor, but he takes a seat and plugs in a laptop, so I think maybe he's just a student arriving early.

Vito wheels the stroller out of the path of the door. "You going in?" he asks.

"Yeah." I worry my lower lip between my teeth.

"Maaamaaa." Junie tosses her bunny to the floor, so I release Vito's hand to bend over and get it.

"Juniebug, Mama's going to go into that room right there, and you're going to go for a walk with Vito. Does that sound like fun?" I kneel down to give her back the bunny and kiss her cheek when I hear the clacking of very high heels on the floor.

I hurry to stand, guessing that those are not the shoes of a student. I see an absolutely gorgeous, willowy woman with shoulder-length blond hair striding toward the classroom with a slim leather briefcase in one hand. She's wearing black eyeglasses, but her outfit screams money. She looks elegant, expensive, put together.

I see her look from the stroller to me to Vito, and I clutch the paper in my hand. I'm sure we look totally out of place, but the way she's looking at us makes me feel like maybe Catherine was wrong. Maybe this instructor doesn't allow visitors? She pulls the glasses from her face and cocks her head, and that's when I see Vito's body go stiff.

"Vito?"

The stunning woman knows his name. I look from her to him and back again.

He nods at the woman and releases a sigh so dramatic, I'm sure she hears it. "Wow. There you are. Nice to see you again, Michelle."

CHAPTER ELEVEN

Well, if I'd thought Eden going to college was some kind of sign, I'll be good goddamned if this isn't my sign to run like hell in the opposite direction.

"Vito? Holy shit. Is that you?" Michelle, my ex-wife, glides up to us on heels so high, I can't help but think they are a step down from the stripper shoes she used to wear.

I'm not being petty, though.

I'm stunned and uncomfortable.

Of course, I'd heard she was in town, but running into her here?

No fucking way.

Michelle's brain's got to be running a million miles an hour. She looks from Eden to Juniper to me, and then her whole demeanor softens. "Well, this is a surprise. Can I give you a hug?"

I open my arms and let her give me a hug, but I don't really return the gesture.

As soon as she releases me, she sticks her hand out toward Eden. "I'm Michelle Davis. Vito and I are, uh, old friends."

Shit. This is going to get even weirder if I don't do something fast.

"Babe." I turn to Eden. "This is Michelle, my ex-wife."

I watch as Eden woodenly shakes Michelle's hand. "Hi," she says quietly.

"And is this…" Michelle gives Juniper a huge smile, and she bends down to look into the stroller. "Oh my God, you're adorable. Hi."

Michelle waves at Junie, and I realize it must look like this is my family. But I'm okay with that. I'm not sure how to feel.

Uncomfortable is a fucking given.

But then I remember why I'm here in the first place. I swallow back my feelings and motion toward the classroom door.

"What are you doing here?" I ask Michelle. "You teaching?"

She smiles and looks genuinely happy. "I am," she says. "I moved back to town to take care of my grandfather. You remember Granddad."

I nod, and she continues.

"I opened my own business, and I'm teaching here part time at night." She looks from Vito to me. "What are you doing here?"

I step closer to Eden and put my hand on her lower back. "Eden has a guest pass to sit in on your class." I realize I'm talking for her, and I'm sure that is the last thing she wants. Although when I look at her, Eden still looks shocked speechless. "Babe?" I nod at her.

That seems to break Eden out of her trance. She smiles self-consciously and offers Michelle the sheet of paper that she's nearly crumpled into a ball. "I was hoping to sit in on your class tonight. Catherine from Admissions emailed about me."

Michelle sets her briefcase on the floor and claps her hands. A couple more students have arrived, and they walk past us to get into the classroom. "Hey there," she says, greeting the students. "Go on in. I'll be right there. Hi Lacey, are you prepared for your presentation?"

One of the two women she talks to looks older than we are. She slaps her thigh and laughs loudly. "Ms. D, you know I'm ready for my A."

Michelle grins. "I'm happy to hear it. I'll be right in." She steps to the side and puts a hand on Eden's arm. "Catherine emailed me about you. I'm so glad you decided to visit. Do you have any questions before class starts? If you're able to stay late, I'm happy to chat with you after class too."

Eden looks from Michelle to me, then back again before answering. "No questions. Thank you. I was going to say that I have childcare for a little bit, but I might not stay the whole class. I didn't want to be rude and get up and leave in the middle."

My mind is spinning so fast, I can't think straight.

Michelle shakes her head and takes the pass from Eden. "That's no problem. You leave whenever you need to." She pulls a pen out from her briefcase and scribbles something on the back of the pass, then hands it back to Eden. "This is my work email and phone number. If you have any questions after class, you let me know. I can make an appointment and see you in my office." She looks at Juniper. "And if you need to bring your daughter, please do. I do a lot of work with female clients. I like to help women understand how to make money and how to manage it." She gives me a grin. "No offense to you, Vito."

"None taken," I say, my lips as tight as my gut.

Michelle is being really nice, and I shouldn't be surprised. She's good people. She always was. But after all these years, why couldn't I have just run into her at a gas station or something?

Eden tucks Michelle's contact information into her notebook. "Thank you so much. That's really generous of you."

Michelle pulls the black glasses back over her face. "Not at all. This is literally what I do. Come on in." She looks back at me and Juniper. "V, there's a little playground over by the early childhood center. Your daughter might be able to get some time in the swings while you wait."

I nod stiffly and force a smile on my face. I won't correct her about Juniper. Unless Eden says something, I'm fine with Michelle thinking this is my family.

Eden turns to follow Michelle into the classroom, but then Michelle turns back to me with a stunning smile. "It was great seeing you, V."

I bristle at her familiar nickname. I grip the handles of the stroller, hoping I don't snap the plastic. "You too, Michelle." Then I look at Eden. "Stay as long as you want," I tell her.

Her face is pale and her lips tight, but she follows Michelle into the classroom without looking back.

It's only after the door is shut and I'm alone with Juniper that I realize I should have kissed Eden goodbye.

"So, Juniper, that was freaking awkward." I talk to the little girl the whole walk.

She's surprisingly quiet after leaving her mom, but I'm hoping that she's seen enough of me over the last few weeks that the excitement of being someplace new and being out in the fresh air has her nicely distracted.

I peek over the stroller and make sure Junie is okay. She's tucked under a light blanket, kicking her legs and babbling.

What are the odds that my ex-wife is teaching the class Eden wanted to visit? My gut twists in a knot, and I realize I have to talk to someone, but then the bunny hurtles right out of the stroller.

"Hey," I call out, stepping on the brakes on the stroller. I kneel in front of Junie, a huge smile on my face. "Where is he?"

I tap the blanket on her lap, and she laughs and screeches.

I stand up and look all around and pretend I don't see the bunny. "Is he...here?" I peek inside the sleeve of my flannel.

"Bunny!" Junie shouts, and she suddenly lifts her little hips up and out of the seat like she's going to get up and show me where the bunny is.

"Whoa there." The safety belt is on, so she can't get out, but I don't want her tipping out of the stroller the first time I'm alone with her. "No injuries, no tears," I point a finger at Junie. "I'll get that bunny, but you stay right here, okay? Is that him right there?"

I motion off into the grass, and Junie shouts "bunny" again. I grab it and hand it off to Juniper before we head toward the playground.

I'm expecting it to be locked, but I'm shocked to see that two

466

other kids are playing, with an older lady sitting nearby on a bench looking at her phone.

A security guard in uniform wanders over and waves at me. The guy surprises me by calling my name. "Vito?"

As I get closer, I recognize him, and I reach out a hand and shake his. "Hey, man. You're Martinez, right?"

He nods. "Yeah. Nick Martinez." That's when it hits me. Nick used to be a waiter at my brother's restaurant.

"What've you been up to, man? No more Italian dinners?"

He shakes his head and pats his stomach. "I miss Benito's cooking. I loved that job, but I couldn't hack the hours. I'm enrolled in night school here, trying to get an associate's. It's tough out there without a degree. I'm doing security part-time and doing some training over at the gym."

"I hear that shit," I say. "Good to see you, man. You locking up the playground? We'll get out of your hair if it's closing time."

Nick shakes his head. "Nah, it's fine. If there are families here, I let them stay until class is out. I'll lock up when the classroom buildings close for the night." He looks at me and cocks his head. "I didn't know you had a family, Vito. Congrats, man."

"I wish I could take credit for her," I laugh. "This is Juniper, my uh...girlfriend's daughter." I jerk a thumb behind me even though the instructional center is quite a ways away. "My girl's visiting a class tonight. She's thinking of enrolling." I don't know if Eden considers herself my girlfriend, but I'm a guy alone with a kid who isn't mine, so saying anything else seems like asking for trouble.

If I'm honest, I'd be more than happy with that label for Eden.

Nick takes a few steps closer and then holds up a finger when there's a crackle at the radio on his chest. He reports in to dispatch with his location and then returns to our conversation. "All good," he says. "We had a teacher lose her phone and laptop, but she found it." He grins. "Exciting work when the case solves itself."

I chuckle, but since Nick doesn't seem like he's going anywhere in a hurry, I decide to ask the question on my mind. "Hey, you mind if I ask you how it is? Going to school when you're not, like, eighteen years old?"

Nick nods. "I got to be honest, I was scared shitless. I barely made it through high school. I passed, but I didn't care about learning. Had no clue what I wanted to do with my life." He shrugs. "This is an easy gig, but if I ever want to support a family, buy a house, I got to be okay with a little discomfort. You know?"

"Nah, I get it, man. You doing good now? Classes hard?"

Nick shakes his head. "It all depends on the teacher. Some are great. They really care about helping adult students succeed."

I extend a hand to him and clap him on the shoulder. "You ever want to grab a meal at Benito's, let me know. My treat."

Nick grabs my number and saves it in his phone. "I'll do that. You end up taking some classes, let me know. I'll give you a campus tour." He laughs and points to the playground. "Have fun, little lady. I'll come back after class to lock up."

Nick wanders off, answering yet another crackling call on his radio, so I wheel the stroller through the small fence and park it on the spongy rubberized ground that covers the play area.

"Do you want to go on the swing?" I kneel beside the stroller, and Juniper holds her arms out. But when I don't move fast enough, she starts scrambling out of the stroller.

I grab her hand and swoop her up with a happy shout. She giggles and settles into my arms, and together, we walk over to the baby swing.

She slides into the swing seat without a problem, and I start slowly, giving her a few small pushes.

She delights in the movement, kicking her legs and looking back at me. "Yeah." I cheer. "Is that fun, Junie? You like the swing?"

I have just given her another little push when my phone buzzes in my pocket. Thinking it might be Eden, I grab it and answer without checking who it is.

"How'd it go?"

"No clue what you're talking about, bro." My brother Franco sounds confused.

"Ah, dickhead, I expected somebody else. What's up?" I tuck the phone against my cheek and push Juniper with one hand.

"I thought I'd see if you want to grab a drink at Benito's. You're off tonight, right?"

"Yeah, but I'm babysitting. Eden had a thing, so I'm at a park with Juniper."

"Huh," Franco grunts. "You getting tied down finally?"

It's the word finally that has me shaking my head. "Fuck, man, you'll never guess who we ran into tonight."

I explain everything to Franco and leave nothing out.

"Well, that's freaking fucked up. Did Eden bail?" he asks.

I roll my eyes at the big brotherly support. "She went into class, so she didn't bail on school. Or do you mean bail on me?"

Franco is quiet for a minute, as if he just, for the first time, heard what he said and how it sounded. "Fuck, sorry. That's not what I meant. How did you feel seeing Michelle? Did she look as good as ever?"

I chuckle. "Yeah, of course. Michelle could wear a paper bag, and she'd be hot as hell."

"And?" Franco presses.

"And what?" Junie is twisting back to look at me, so I come to stand in front of the swing and pull her toward me with one hand while I hold my phone in the other.

"You think you want her back? How do you feel, V?"

I don't even have to think about how I feel. I know. "I don't want to go back. There's no doubt about that."

"What about Eden?" he asks. "You think you want to give the whole relationship thing a try again?"

Juniper's grin is enormous, her drooly lips parted to reveal her tiny baby teeth as she swings. "I'm in this. No question in my mind," I say, slowing the swing with one hand. "I don't know what Eden thinks, but for me, this is it. This is what I want."

Franco snorts, and I can just picture him shaking his head. "You going to be cool if she's taking classes with Michelle? I can't fucking believe your stripper ex-wife is teaching college."

"Hey, hey," I say, a warning in my voice. "Michelle was always smart. You know that. Big dreams, big goals. I wouldn't be surprised by anything she set her mind to doing." I do have to consider his question, though.

"About damn time," he says, and I can hear the smile in his voice. "Happy for you, bro. Can I give you two pieces of advice?"

"Sure," I say, but I probably don't want to hear whatever sage advice he's about to give.

"Make sure Eden knows how you feel. Offer to talk to Michelle if that would help. Don't let anything go unsaid, so you never have to question whether you did everything you could to make this work."

His words hit me deep. He knows I did damn near everything I could think of to make things work between Michelle and me, but it wasn't enough.

"What's the other thing?" I ask, pulling a fussy Juniper from the swing. "And make it quick. I got a toddler I got to chase." I set Junie on the rubbery turf and let her run to a seesaw thing that looks like a plastic horse.

"Don't tell Ma that Eden met Michelle. Keep that shit buttoned down."

I bark out a laugh. "Got it, Franco. Thanks for the call. Rain check on drinks." I hang up and slide the phone into my back pocket just in time to help Juniper climb onto the back of a yellow plastic horse.

I haven't been this close to dating someone seriously since Michelle and I broke up.

It may be awkward, but if this is what I want, I need to do everything I can to make it work.

And maybe, just maybe, this time, I'll be enough.

CHAPTER TWELVE

eden

This is going to be the longest three hours of my life.

Okay, no, scratch that. I'm being dramatic.

Going through labor and delivery alone… Those were the longest hours of my life.

But at least I had a gorgeous baby to snuggle at the end of the pain.

Sitting in a classroom being taught by the ex-wife of the guy I'm into? This was definitely not on the list of things I expected to live through in my life.

As soon as I realized that my instructor was Vito's ex-wife, time dragged. Of course, the first thing I fixated on was how goddamn gorgeous Michelle was.

For the most part, I'm comfortable with my body with its stretch marks and many flaws, but come on.

"All right, everybody." Michelle claps her hands together to silence the small talk and chatter right at the stroke of seven. "Thank you all for coming tonight. I know most of you have jobs, families, and a lot of responsibilities outside of this class, so even though this is our sixth week together, I want to thank you for showing up. This is also my not-so-subtle reminder to silence your phones and keep your attention—" she sweeps a hand toward the whiteboard affixed to the wall behind her "—on the work we're here to do."

She turns her back to us for a moment and writes a word on the whiteboard in blue marker. I watch her arms, thin and moving fast in a pristine white shirt, before she faces the classroom, adjusts the black-framed glasses over her eyes, and points to me.

"We have a visitor tonight, someone who is thinking of enrolling in this course. Eden," she says, giving me a warm smile that hits me right in the face like a spotlight. "While you are a guest, you're part of this class, so feel free to raise your hand and ask questions anytime."

I feel the eyes of half the class on me. My cheeks burn, but I manage to smile and mouth thank you, even though my throat is suddenly so dry, I don't think I could speak even if I wanted to.

I must look at the clock on the wall every ten seconds because it gives me something to look at other than Michelle's beautiful ass in that pencil skirt.

It's hard not to wonder how someone lifts themselves up from a job stripping to teaching in less than five years' time. If she could do it, maybe there is hope that I can overcome my circumstances too.

With a good babysitter and a plan, I could easily have a degree under my belt in five years.

Michelle dims the lights a bit and turns on a projector that's attached to her laptop. She's pulled up a financial statement and is talking through the different parts, what information appears, and what each thing means. It's like a puzzle the way she explains it, translating things like fixed assets and long-term liabilities with examples that actually make sense. She relates everything to real-world situations, and I'm so caught up, before I realize it, it's after eight and she's turning on the lights and motioning to the clock.

"Everyone, I'd like five extra minutes to talk with our visitor over the break. Enjoy your break."

Most of the students grab their phones but leave their backpacks on their desks. I'm kind of surprised they're just going to leave their stuff, but then again, this isn't LA. This is Star Falls, so maybe stealing backpacks isn't a problem on this campus?

I'm still in my chair when Michelle rushes up to me, a huge smile on her face.

She pulls the chair of the kid sitting next to me close and sits beside me. "So, Eden." She's literally beaming, and again, I cringe a little at how damned pretty she is. "I am so glad you stayed until the break. I wanted to make sure you didn't have any questions. What did you think of class? Is this what you expected?"

I nod, not sure what I expected. "It was really interesting," I say honestly. "Not confusing at all. To be honest, I didn't really know what to expect. I was trying to keep an open mind, but this was really interesting." I hesitate a second before saying what's on my mind because I don't want to seem like I'm sucking up to her, but then I just say it. "You're actually a really good teacher." I rush on awkwardly, worried I sound like I'm judging her. "Not that I didn't think you would be. I just mean if I'd had teachers like you in high school, I probably would have gone to college."

She nods, presses her lips together, and hums in agreement. "You know, that's exactly why I want to teach." She motions to the whiteboard. "Please don't take this the wrong way, but they pay us next to nothing to teach. I don't do it for the money. I didn't learn from my family how to manage money or build wealth. I learned by getting into debt and nearly killing myself to dig out of it. I want to help save as many people—and frankly, as many women—as I can from going down that path."

She's quiet then, as if expecting me to admit that I'm here to manage debt. I don't have any, but that's not because I learned how to do anything the right way.

I take a deep breath and admit just a little of what I feel safe sharing. "I have a small trust. A structured settlement. It won't last forever, so I'm hoping to learn how to be responsible with money so I can make good choices with the funds I have while they are coming in. And then, I'd like to find a career that I can enjoy once I'm able to work full time. I'm raising my daughter alone at the moment, her father isn't in the picture, and…"

And that's where things start to devolve in my brain. Vito, what he is to me, how long we've been dating… But Michelle reaches out and lightly touches my arm.

"Hey," she says gently. "I get it. And listen, about the elephant in the room. I'm so glad you came to class tonight. I'm sure if you've talked to V about me at all, you know I used to dance." She laughs and shakes her head as if stripping brings up fond memories. "I can't tell you how many clients I have now who six, seven years ago used to stuff singles in my thong." She covers her mouth and full-belly laughs. "Now they hand over their entire portfolio for me to manage." She shrugs like it's not a big deal. "An honest living is an honest living, and I'm not ashamed of my past career. You shouldn't apologize or be ashamed of your circumstances either."

She points up at the clock. "I need to hit the ladies' room before the break is over, but I'm serious. Vito and I were married, but that was a lifetime ago and this is a small town. I knew I'd run across him or one of the Bianchis eventually. I'm just so glad he has you and your daughter. Vito is…" She looks down at the desk, a brief look of sadness on her face. "A good man, through and through," she says. "No matter what happened between us, I, for one, have zero hard feelings."

I gather my things and stand with her. "I'm sorry I can't stay for the whole class," I say. "It's already past my daughter's bedtime."

"No problem. You go ahead." She pushes back her chair and gives me a dazzling smile. "You have my cell and my email. Make an appointment anytime you want some informal advice or guidance. Or if you need help managing the trust you have. This isn't a sales pitch. I'm happy to help you if I can. Give my best to Vito."

She gives me a wave and then heads into the hallway, her high heels clicking until I can't hear them anymore.

I grab my phone and punch in a text to Vito.

Me: I'm ready. Meet me out front of the building?

Then I gather my things and head outside into the cool, dark evening. I need a few minutes to compose my thoughts.

Butterflies of stress flap a thousand little wings in my belly, and my phone buzzes with a response from Vito.

Vito: I can't wait to hear everything. We'll be right there.

Just seeing his words makes me realize how excited I am to share everything with him.

I stare off into the darkness, keeping a look out for a stroller. The butterflies in my belly are flapping their wings, but I feel a lot lighter and more hopeful just seeing Vito's text.

Maybe it's time to stop fighting the story and let my future write itself for once.

Juniper falls sound asleep within minutes of us pulling out of the college parking lot, so Vito and I don't talk much on the drive back to the hotel.

He drives, and I stare out the window, lost in lots of fast-moving thoughts.

When we get back to the hotel, I lift Junie out of the back seat and carry her inside. I put her to bed, then join Vito in the living room. He's standing in the kitchen, tapping a text into his phone when I get back.

"Hey," he says, looking happy to see me. The sight of him fills my chest with a sudden burst of warmth.

I walk up to him, and he pulls me into his arms.

"How's it feel?" he asks. "Tomorrow night at this time, you'll be tucking Junie into bed in her very own room."

I hold him close and nod against his shoulder. "I almost can't believe it. I'm feeling so many things...especially tonight."

He takes my hand and leads me to the couch. "You want to talk about it?"

I look down at our hands and open my mouth, but where do I start? I don't know what I should say first. It was great meeting your stripper ex-wife? Or, your stripper ex-wife is a great teacher?

"Eden, can I start?" Vito's staring me in the face, his lips parted. "I want to hear everything you want to say, but I need to get some shit off my chest."

I nod, relieved that he wants to talk. I still need some time with my feelings before I can even compose a coherent sentence.

475

"I'm sorry you had to meet my ex-wife that way. Super fucking awkward and I hope she didn't put you off that college completely."

I smile and shake my head. "No, she's pretty great, actually," I admit.

Vito nods, but then he takes both my hands in his. "Eden, you're more than pretty great. You have a lot of big shit ahead. I want to be a part of it. I want to be a part of your life."

We both chuckle and lace our fingers tighter.

"I don't know if you need a label, boyfriend, girlfriend, whatever. I'm falling for you, Eden. I think you're the most gorgeous, kindest, amazing woman. And I just wanted to be clear that Michelle is my past. I'd really like for you to be my future. You know what I mean?"

I silence him by leaning forward and kissing him lightly on the lips. "I want that too," I tell him and scoot closer, tucking against his chest.

He rests his chin on the top of my head.

"I want to tell you something," I start. "I'm afraid it might change how you feel about me, and if it does, I'd rather know now before I get in any deeper. Because I'm falling for you too." I pull away then, feeling worried that Vito might reject me for what I'm about to admit. "It shook me a lot, meeting Michelle," I say, looking down into my lap. "But she's beautiful and smart and super fucking nice. I would have rather she be this nasty bitch, but no, she was like someone I could be friends with."

Vito laughs. "Fucking small towns," he says. "Really living up to their reputations."

I sigh. "Yeah. But that's the thing. You and Michelle just didn't work, right? There was no other big secret or anything?"

Vito cups my chin and holds my face so our eyes meet. "No," he says firmly, his voice low and sincere. He releases my chin and shakes his head. "I don't have secrets, Eden. Not one. What you see with me is what you get, for better or worse."

I swallow hard and realize how damning what I'm about to share is. "Well, I have more secrets," I say. "And if you can't forgive me for what I have done, I understand. Just…" Tears sting my eyes, and I clench my hands into fists so I don't cry. "Juniper's father," I say, looking down again. "He was married when I dated him. He was my boss. The owner of the company where I worked. He and his wife owned the business together, but she lives in New York City and handles East Coast development. I never actually met her during the two years I worked there."

I explain that the whole affair only lasted four months. That during that time, my boss insisted his wife was leaving him and that they had an understanding that he could date other people.

They ran a company that provided financing for films, so a divorce would have damaged their reputations and split their assets. He assured me they were married in name only. That was, until I told him I was pregnant.

"That's when I found out the marriage was very much real and not open or anything like that. I met his wife when she showed up at my desk with a team of lawyers and summoned me into a conference room." I choke back sobs, but the tears are flowing down my cheeks.

"Eden." Vito's voice is soft as he strokes the hair back from my face. "I'm sorry if meeting Michelle opened up those old wounds."

I shake my head. "It's inevitable," I explain. "Based on what went down when I got pregnant, I am pretty sure I was not the first executive assistant he played."

Vito's growl vibrates through my chest. "I'm so fucking sorry that happened to you. But I don't understand. Why would this change how I feel about you? If anything, I am fucking furious at what happened to you, and I want to make sure no one ever does anything to screw you over ever again."

"Seriously?" I wipe my face with both hands and face him. "Vito, you come from a huge, close-knit family. Your ex-wife is beautiful and talented, and there's no deep, dark secret there." I bark out a resentful laugh. "I had to sign a contract promising I would not submit my daughter's DNA to any of those genealogy sites until her eighteenth birthday."

"What?" he asks, sounding as shocked as I am pissed. "Why the fuck not?"

I give him a sad look. "I'm sure her father doesn't want her finding all the other siblings he's got running around out there in the world. If the kids start comparing the deals they got…" I shake my head.

I'm quiet then. I'm hoping the details I've shared haven't in any way compromised the confidentiality agreement I signed.

"I'm not supposed to talk about any of this," I explain. "But Vito, I want to talk about this shit to you. I want to trust you with everything. I want you. I just hope after everything I've said, you still want me."

Vito stands from the couch and pulls me to stand beside him. "Babe," he breathes before pressing his lips to mine, "if anything, I want you even more."

CHAPTER THIRTEEN

I slide my hands into the back pockets of Eden's jeans and press her hips firmly against mine. "Babe," I groan, "I want you more than anything."

She whimpers against my lips, opening her mouth so my tongue can tease hers. I feel her lace her hands around my waist as our kiss increases. We're like starving people feasting on our last meal. It's hot, it's furious, it's needy.

With Juniper always around, we haven't been able to do more than this in the weeks we've known each other, but tonight, I want more.

"Eden," I pant, palming her generous ass through the denim. "I want you so bad."

She pulls her face from mine, her cheeks blazing pink. "I bought condoms," she whispers, giving me a grin. "They're in my bathroom."

I groan. That means she has to leave me to go into her bedroom, risking waking Juniper.

She laughs, and I point to the closed bedroom door behind which the sweetest little girl is sound asleep. "Think she'll wake up?"

She nods. "Oh, I'm a mama on a mission. I'll get this done."

CHELLE BLISS

Before I know what she's doing, she's slipped out of my arms and is opening the bedroom door with the stealth of a ninja. I don't even hear the hinges creak as she disappears inside the bedroom and returns in what seems like ten seconds, gripping a box in her hands.

"We don't have to use them all," she says, one corner of her mouth curling up seductively. "But I wasn't going to tear this open in there."

I take the box from her and tear it open, freeing a sleeve of foil-wrapped condoms and dropping them on the coffee table. "We might need them all," I tease, watching as she wiggles her arms out of her sleeves and slips off her top.

She's wearing just her bra, but at the sight of her full tits, the blue veins streaking along the top of her creamy skin, my mouth drops open, and I just watch her.

"Fuck, you're gorgeous." I'm panting now, like someone who's never seen a tit before, but I don't care. Eden is sensual and soft, her curves thick and perfectly proportioned. I could probably come from just watching her undress, but I don't plan on losing control that soon. "Will she be okay?" I ask, jerking a thumb toward Eden's closed bedroom door.

Eden nods. "If she wakes up, we'll hear her. She can't get out of the pack and play, so she won't be able to open the door and surprise us."

I breathe a sigh of relief, then nod at Eden. "In that case, will you please take those fucking jeans off?"

She flashes me a smile and then unbuttons the top button. She works the zipper down and then shoves the fabric over her ample hips. She's wearing boy-cut underwear, a pair that's so sheer, I can see the shadow of her pubic hair through it.

"I want to see every inch of you." I pull her close to me and gently kiss her lips.

"Hmm, please." She closes her eyes, and I reach around her and unfasten the clasp. The flimsy fabric falls away, and I toss it on the end of the couch.

I squeeze my eyes shut as a spear of arousal spikes through my body, my legs going weak. "Fuck," I breathe.

480

Her breasts are large and soft, but when I trail the pads of my thumbs over her nipples, they go stiff and hard as pebbles. I pinch the tender flesh between my fingertips, and her shuddering gasp lets me know she likes how it feels.

She squirms under my touch, and I move her over to the couch. "On your back," I say, fumbling with the zipper of my jeans.

She obeys, lying on the couch as I settle my weight on top of her as best I can. "Am I crushing you?"

"I wouldn't mind if you did," she says, reaching up to stroke my hair away from my forehead.

"Tell me if you can't breathe," I say, then I lower my face to her cleavage. I start with one breast, sucking the entire nipple into my mouth and working the tip of my tongue over her peak until she gasps. She grips the back of my hair with her fingers and pushes my face into her chest.

"More," she whimpers.

I go feral when I hear that, and I clamp her nipple between my teeth and tug.

She goes weak, the pressure of her fingers in my hair slackening while she enjoys every second of my attention.

I suck and lick her nipple until she's writhing beneath me, but then I stop and kiss her, trying to ignore the throb in my balls that's begging for release.

We kiss gently and wildly, tasting each other and savoring the first feel of our bare chests against each other. Eden must have incredibly sensitive nipples because while we're kissing, she's arching her back to press against the hairs on my chest.

"You feel so good," she murmurs against my mouth.

I wish I had words, pretty words to tell her how I feel right now. How seeing her like this beneath me makes me want to look into her eyes and just hold her, naked, for days. But those words will come later.

I move from lying on her to kneeling at her feet, and grab the waistband of her underwear before pulling them off. I spread her legs wide and lean back down so our chests touch.

She tightens her long legs around my waist, pulling our hips

481

closer together, and my cock jumps in my briefs. "I want you, but my body's not…"

I instantly know her run-in with Michelle is toying with her brain.

I silence her with a soft kiss on the lips. "Everything about you is perfect," I tell her. "I'm falling for you, Eden. Flaws and all." I look down at her body and growl. "But everything I'm seeing is perfect. Flawless and perfect."

She nods and blinks self-consciously before pulling my head to her chest.

I rest my face between her breasts and groan. "You're killing me, babe. I mean, in the best way, but…"

She laughs, and we hold each other for a minute. "I'm good," she whispers. "Thank you."

"No, E, thank you." I move back to the end of the couch and tug the panties over her hips, down her thighs, and set them on the coffee table. "For this."

I grip the insides of both her thighs and run my hands from her knees to her pussy. While she gets used to my touch, I lower myself as best I can to fit on the couch, but it's not going to work. "New plan," I say, getting up from the couch and reaching out my hand.

I help her to standing, yank a blanket off a nearby chair, and drop it on the carpeted floor like a picnic blanket. "Now, I'll be able to eat your pussy without wrenching my damn back."

She laughs and lies back on the blanket, opening her legs to me. "You're so safety-conscious," she teases. "At least you're trained if one of us gets hurt."

"The only pain you're going to feel is the kind you want," I promise as I settle between her legs. I hook my hands under her knees and bend her legs so her feet are on the floor, her knees falling open.

Then I lie on my belly and place one hand on her abdomen. With the other hand, I feel my way through her trimmed hair until I feel her drenched lips.

She sucks air as I touch her, and I feel the sound as though she hummed it against my balls. I'm so hard I might just come against the fucking floor. But I quickly distract myself from the demands of my cock by stroking every inch of Eden's middle.

She is gripping the blanket with her hands and tightening her knees, closing her legs around my head, but I push them open again, continuing to work my thumb until she begs me to fill her.

"Vito, I need you inside me. Please." When she finally says the words, I reach for a condom, tear that thing open like there's a winning lottery ticket inside, and shed my briefs so I can sheathe up.

I kneel down on the blanket and settle my weight over her. "You want it like this?"

She nods but then says, "And behind."

"In your ass?" I ask, trying to clarify.

Her eyes widen, and she shakes her head, her gorgeous, soft hair shifting over the blanket. "No, I mean I want you behind me."

I chuckle and she giggles. "That too," I say as I lower my weight and press the tip of my dick to her pussy.

She is wet and sweet, and when I'm fully inside her, she widens her legs, and I swear to fuck I see stars.

I thrust inside her, my hips and thighs burning with the effort, a sheen of sweat gathering on my forehead and chest.

She rolls her hips, lifting to meet my thrusts with her own. My arms burn as I support my weight, thrusting deep inside her while I watch her breasts bounce and her beautiful lips move as she moans.

"I want you to come," I tell her, and her eyes fly open.

"I will," she promises. "But I want this to last."

I shake my head with a grin. "Babe, I promise this won't be the last time, but I can't hold out for long."

She giggles and turns a bit to her side. "Can we flip over?" she asks.

"Fuck yeah." I pull out of her, and her groan matches the disappointed grunt I make at the loss of contact. I check the condom's all good, watching as she gets on all fours.

Once she's kneeling, I settle behind her and grip her thighs. She reaches between her legs to guide my cock inside, but as soon as I'm deep, she lifts her ass in the air, pressing into me. I hold her hips, watching her ass bounce against me as I thrust.

"Vito, oh yes," she moans.

It's the best kind of yes because as soon as she starts, I feel it. I feel her pussy tighten around my cock, and she muffles a shriek into the blanket. "Oh my God!" she yells, shoving her ass against me, writhing and grinding and panting through her orgasm.

The second she's done, I'm done for, and I give in to the climax that shakes my legs and drains me of every ounce of pent-up need.

I collapse against her bare back and plant kisses along her spine until we both crash onto the blanket. I cuddle her close, both of us breathless and sweating and naked and flushed.

"Are you good?" I mutter, tightening my arms around her.

Her face is pressed against my damp pectoral, and she barely moves her face as she mumbles against my skin. "Great."

We hold each other for a few minutes until we both doze off.

I wake up early the next morning in my bed back at home, my morning wood wishing like hell I had Eden by my side. I shoot her a text before I roll out.

Me: I know it's early. Thinking about you. Can't wait to christen your new house.

Ordinarily with a woman, I'd overthink what to do the day after we first hooked up.

But with Eden, I am oddly at ease. Maybe it helps because I'm going to see her today at the closing. I told her I'd be there for the final walk-through of the house and to help with Juniper while she signed all the paperwork.

I'm not nervous at all, but I am oddly excited. The house isn't mine, but I can't help thinking that it's a place where Eden will make a home for herself and her daughter.

And if there's room in that house, in her new life, for me, well... I'm not going to get too far ahead of myself.

But I know what I feel. It's not just the fucking fantastic sex, her killer body, or the fact that she's a sweetheart. Something about Eden feels right. Hanging out with Juniper alone last night never once felt like work. I never once checked the time, counting down the minutes until Eden came back to take her off my hands.

Sometimes, as much as I love my nieces and nephews, they are exhausting. I try to be the patient uncle, but it's hard to play the games they want, to remind them to wash their hands, to break up arguments, and to manage them every single second.

I'd been kind of reconsidering whether I even wanted kids of my own because, while they are amazing at times, the grind of keeping four little humans alive is more than I could fathom. I was settling into a comfortable shell until I met Eden.

Happy alone.

As happy as I could be with my work. Lost in my own little cocoon of safety in my parents' house. Now I'm wondering if, with the right person and the right kid, the worries, fears, and the risk aren't more than worth it.

My phone buzzes with a text and I grab it, expecting to hear from Eden. But the text is from a number I haven't seen in years.

Michelle: Hey V, it's Michelle. I don't know if this is still your number, but if it is, I thought I'd see if you were free for a quick coffee today? If you're working, let me know when you're off.

I look down at the message, dumbfounded.

I haven't heard a word from Michelle in five freaking years. Now she wants to grab coffee? I rub my face and jump out of bed, ignoring the text for now.

I storm into the shower and let the hot water clear my head. It's early, but Michelle no doubt remembers my schedule and my habits. I'm not sure if it's a good or bad thing that I haven't changed.

As I wash my hair, I think about the last five years. How lost I've been. How close I've come time and time again to reaching for what I thought I wanted, only to be passed over for the promotion, if I was even considered at all.

After I'm dressed, I look at my phone with disgust. I don't know what Michelle wants. Maybe nothing. Maybe something. But I don't think I can move forward with Eden until I kick all the ghosts of my past to the curb.

I text Michelle back and head downstairs, hoping I am not making a jackass-stupid move.

Michelle's office is in a nice area of Star Falls. No one is sitting at the reception desk, so I stand there and look around, unsure where to go. After a couple minutes, a man in a suit that probably cost more than my truck payment rushes out to the front.

"Good morning," he says. "Sorry to keep you waiting. Our receptionist is tied up. Do you have an appointment?"

I look the guy over and shrug. "Yeah, I guess. I'm here to see Michelle." I look down at the jeans and flannel shirt I'm wearing and suddenly feel all the old shit come back.

How I was never enough for Michelle. The way she always wanted me to dress better. But I don't have a lot of time to worry about it because Michelle comes through the reception door herself then.

"Vito." She walks right up to me and gives me a very real hug.

I clumsily hug her back, regretting every idiotic thought that brought me here. "Hey," I say, stepping out of the hug as soon as I can.

"John," she says to the guy in the suit, "I'm going to take Vito back to my office. Would you hang out up front until Gennie is back?"

The guy nods, looking me over with a hint of suspicion. I follow Michelle back into her office, looking at the pristine carpet tiles as I follow her. Being here alone with Michelle feels like I'm betraying Eden, even if my intention is to listen to what she has to say and get the fuck out of here as fast as I can.

Eden's final walk-through is at noon, so I have less than an hour before I have to pick her up, and that's about ten times longer than I plan on staying.

Michelle's name is posted on a plaque outside the door, and she scans herself in using a keycard.

"Fancy," I say, following her into the spacious, light-filled room.

She nods. "For client security. I only have a few advisers here, and we keep our private offices locked."

She motions for me to sit down, then pulls up an app on her

phone to order us coffee. "Still the same?" she asks, smiling. "Or do you want something different? I don't want to assume nothing has changed since we last saw each other."

I'm feeling more and more irritated by the second. If she orders coffee, that means I'm stuck here for at least fifteen minutes until it gets here. I'm itching to leave so bad I can't keep my hands still.

"I'm good," I say, waving her off. "I've got someplace to be, so…"

She cocks her chin at me and frowns. "I'm sorry. I thought you…" She firms her lips, punches in an order, then sets her phone down. She sits behind her desk and motions for me to have a seat. I do, figuring the sooner we get through this, the better.

She leans back in her chair and looks at me warmly. "Vito, maybe I was stupid for inviting you here. I thought it could be good to talk a bit."

I nod. "Go ahead and talk."

Even as I say it, I hate that I sound like a moody teenager. I'm a grown fucking man, and this woman loved me once.

"Okay, let me just say this," I tell her. "I heard you were back in town, but I'm seeing someone I really care about now, and I just…" I shrug. "I don't know what there really is to say."

Michelle stuns me by laughing and leaning forward on her desk. "Thank you," she says. "Thanks for being honest. That's literally all I wanted."

She sighs and then leans back. "Maybe it's me who needs to talk. So, can you give me five minutes? If you don't like what I have to say, you can leave and tell me to fuck off, and I won't bother you again."

I nod, feeling a tiny bit less grumpy. "Shoot," I tell her. "Floor's yours."

She gives me a big smile. "Well, you probably heard I came back to Star Falls to help my grandfather. He's in that memory care place up on Devon and Wilson Drive."

I nod. "I heard. I'm sorry things have gotten rough. Your gramps was always good to me."

"You deserved it," she says warmly. "You're a wonderful man, Vito."

Alarm bells like a five-alarm fire sound in my ears. Where the fuck is this going?

"I'll cut to the chase," she says. "You know we didn't work out for reasons. But I have no hard feelings, and I hope you don't either. I'm dating someone now who I've been with for almost four years." She turns a picture frame on her desk to show me a picture of her in a bikini on a beach with some guy wearing orange floral trunks. He looks like a douchebag to me, but Michelle looks happy, so I just nod.

Her voice is soft as she explains. "He's a lawyer. We're doing the long-distance thing for a few months while he's working up a case that should go to trial by the end of the year. Once that's over, he's going to spend half his time here in Star Falls with me."

"That's great, Michelle. I'm happy for you." I rub my hands on my thighs, ready to bolt. "I hope it all works out."

I'm about to jump out of my seat when there is a soft knock at the door. Michelle waves at a woman who I assume is the receptionist. She comes in carrying a cardboard drink caddy with two coffees on it.

"Gennie, thank you." Michelle introduces me to the receptionist, who is enormously pregnant. "I'd like you to meet Vito Bianchi."

I shake her hand and look at her face. "Are you by any chance related to the fire chief?"

Gennie grins. "I'm married to his oldest, Rory." She points to her belly. "His."

Something about the fact that Gennie is related to my chief sets me at ease. I feel a lot less out of place and under the microscope, but the chief's daughter-in-law leaves and I'm again alone with Michelle.

"I got you the usual," Michelle says, shoving a paper cup across her desk at me. "But you don't have to drink it."

I grab the cup and take a sip. I look down at the plastic lid as I mutter, "You remember how I like my coffee after all this time."

Michelle nods. "I loved you, Vito. And I still want the best for you, even if we've both moved on." She sips her drink, then continues. "I like Eden a lot," she says. "The admissions counselor called me this morning to see how the classroom visit went. I think Eden has a bright future."

I shrug, not sure I like the idea of my new girlfriend following in the footsteps of my ex-wife. "Yeah. Eden's great," I say guardedly.

Michelle looks thoughtful as she finally lays it all out on the table. "Eden is actually the reason I wanted to talk to you."

I meet her eyes over my hot coffee and brace myself. I wish I had some antacid. If it's a Michelle idea, I know it's going to burn.

I check the time and sigh. "All right," I say, resigned to listening.

That's all I have to do.

Then, like she said, I can block her and leave the past where it belongs.

CHAPTER FOURTEEN
eden

Today might just be the worst day of my life.

I stagger into the kitchenette of the hotel, feeling like I got hit by a truck. Sharp knocking at the door nearly takes the breath from my lungs as I run to the door to open it before whoever it is brings the two seconds of peace I've had to a miserable end.

I don't even check the peephole, just yank open the door and squint into the sunlight.

"Today's the day." My aunt Shirley is beaming, her arms wide open.

I step outside into the sunlight and let the door close behind me. I wince at the noise and squint, a thousand little needles pricking behind my eyes.

"I know, but it couldn't be off to a worse start." I lean into Aunt Shirley's arms and rest my head against her shoulder.

"Uh-oh." Sassy steps out of our hug and peers into my face like she can read the bad news in my eyes. "Spill it, kiddo. What happened? Isn't today the closing? Did the seller back out?"

I shake my head. "No, thank goodness. No. Everything is happening." I rub my forehead and sigh. "It's Juniper. She's got to be cutting another tooth or something." I tell my aunt about one of the worst nights we've had. "She had a low fever yesterday around lunch, but she didn't seem bothered until about midnight. She woke me up screaming bloody murder. I mean, bloody murder."

I tell her how I couldn't calm Junie down. I was so worried about noise traveling through the thin walls of the hotel and waking every single guest that I put her in the car and tried to calm her while keeping the screaming inside the confines of my vehicle. That didn't work, so I started driving.

"I actually got stopped by a Star Falls officer for sitting on the side of the road with my car idling," I say, shaking my head. "He was pretty sympathetic when I explained what was going on and showed him my hotel key and stuff." I rub my eyes.

Junie finally crashed at four in the morning, but then she woke up at seven super cranky and whiny. I fed her breakfast and just got her back down for what I hope is a decent nap.

Aunt Sassy's right on time, so it's got to be around eleven. "I don't think I slept more than two hours last night." I frown and rub my burning eyes. "I just hope this isn't a sign of things to come."

Sassy crosses her arms over her chest and shakes her head. A soft cloud of her perfume greets me, and it's hard not to smile. She smells like home, like a grandma. "If anything," she says, "this is a clear sign it's long past time you get that baby into your own house." She looks truly undone and starts talking really fast. "Honey, damn it. You should have called me. Even in the middle of the night, I could have come by and helped."

To be honest, I'd thought about that. Aunt Sassy lives in an apartment, so I couldn't just show up with a screaming toddler at midnight and make enemies with all her neighbors.

And then, of course, I thought about Vito. But I know he's back on shift tomorrow, and there was no way I was going to wake up his parents and mess up his sleep schedule.

"I managed," I say quietly.

"Eden. Baby." Sassy grabs my hands and holds them tightly in hers. "I want you to hear me when I say this." She presses her hot-pink lips together, the fine lines around her mouth deepening as she frowns. "You are family, Eden. Flesh and blood. You are not alone. I don't care if it's the middle of the night and I have a hot guy in my bed. You knock on that door, and you ask for help."

She shakes her head and blinks fast, sniffling like she might cry. "I was never able to be there when you were a girl. When you could have used someone close by." She releases my hands and clutches her hands in front of her chest. "I wanted to, Eden. I wanted to be there for you. Please let me do that now. Let me be there for you, sweetheart."

The tears are flowing before she even finishes speaking. I need time to accept that I am not alone anymore. That there are people who don't just want to be part of my life; there are people who would willingly shoulder my burdens.

"Auntie," I say, trying to force a half smile as I wipe my nose with the back of my hand. "A hot guy? Is there something we should talk about?"

My aunt snorts. "That ship's sailed, sweetheart, but you get my point."

I wrap an arm around her shoulder and point toward the door. "Let's get inside. I've got to get presentable before the closing."

I reach for the doorknob and realize the hotel door locked behind us. I pat my back pocket for my keycard, but I don't feel it.

"Oh, sweet baby Jesus," I sigh. I listen for screaming from inside the room, but it's quiet. "I think I left my keycard inside with Juniper."

"Oh, holy mother." Sassy looks terrified and starts tearing through her purse for her phone. "Should I call 9-1-1? Should we break the window?" She starts looking around, and I hope like hell she's not about to pick up a rock.

"Auntie," I say calmly. "After last night, I am sure that if Juniper were awake, we'd hear her. You stay here and keep watch. I'll go to the front desk. I've been staying here long enough that I'm sure they know who I am and will give me another key."

I head over toward the lobby, unable to stop myself from casting a look backward to make sure my aunt isn't about to send a potted plant through a window.

I have to say, though, it brings me a lot of comfort to know I have someone in my life who would destroy public property if my daughter's safety were at risk.

I hustle over to the lobby, smoothing my hair and wiping my cheeks. I have no makeup on and probably look like a swamp troll, but as long as I look like the woman they know is staying in that room, they should let me in.

When I get to the lobby, the girl at the front desk is on the phone. She holds up a hand with a smile and lets me know she'll be right with me.

Maybe the next time Junie has a meltdown, or I have a fire or need anything…maybe I won't force myself to go through it alone.

And then, I hear his voice. "Hey, gorgeous."

I throw myself into Vito's arms and practically smash my lips against his. "I'm a mess," I warn him. "I didn't sleep, I'm not wearing makeup, and I haven't showered since yesterday morning."

He stops my words with a kiss. "You're perfect," he says. "Sassy sent me in here." He holds the extra keycard I gave him a few days ago between his fingers. "Let's get back to your room. I had to wrestle a concrete block out of your aunt's hand, but she made no promises."

The final walk-through and the closing both went off without a hitch. Robert actually hugged Vito and me after handing over the keys. It was a bittersweet moment for him, and I promised him that we'd make some beautiful new memories in the place he's called home.

I'm standing inside the house when I check my phone again, even though my aunt assured me that Juniper is fine. Fussy, but no more freak-outs. That's when the real work starts.

Vito has recruited his brother Franco, his father Mario, and, of course, Lucia to help move over all the essential stuff from the hotel.

The afternoon is a blur of trips back and forth, messages, phone calls, and a hell of a lot of sweating.

By dinnertime, I have furniture in Juniper's room, all my stuff moved out of the hotel, and a couch in the living room to sleep on tonight.

"Hun, what time is the official move tomorrow?" Lucia is wearing the cutest little pair of reading glasses, which she has moved from a beaded chain around her neck onto the end of her nose.

"Around nine," I tell her.

"I'll be there," Franco says. "Text me the address."

"You sure you don't want to stay? I can order pizza," I offer.

Franco shakes his head. "Nah, I'm going to meet Chloe at the bookstore to grab my baby girl. I'm good, sweetheart. We'll see you tomorrow." Franco hugs his brother and calls out a goodbye to his parents, his voice echoing through the mostly empty house.

Lucia and Mario are next to leave.

"We'll bring food tomorrow once you're more settled," Lucia promises. Her eyes grow misty, and she stands up on her tippy toes but I still have to bend down a bit so she can hold my cheeks. "I'm so happy for you, Eden. This is going to make the most beautiful home."

Mario kisses me goodbye and claps Vito on the shoulder. "See you in a couple days, son." Then he turns to kiss my cheek. "And I'll be back tomorrow." He leans down to whisper in my ear. "Lucia already decided you need a dog for that yard. I don't know how long I can hold her off."

Sassy comes into the kitchen with Junie. "Getting dark out there," she calls out. "And I think this little one needs some dinner."

"Do you want to stay, Auntie? Let me buy you dinner."

Shirley shakes her head and holds up a hand. "I got to get these knees in a hot bath. I'm on lunch service tomorrow." She kisses my daughter on both cheeks and blows raspberries against her neck. "You let your mama sleep tonight, you hear?"

Junie giggles and leans her face against Sassy's velvet leggings.

"Thanks, Sassy," Vito says, hugging my aunt goodbye.

"You." She wags a finger at Vito. "I love you, you know that? And you're damn lucky this niece of mine didn't meet Benito first."

Vito waves her off and laughs as he throws an arm around my shoulders, and I melt into his side. We stand at the front door together, watching as the last of our family pulls away.

True happiness always seemed like something other people grabbed so easily. But now, the life I always wanted isn't just close. I'm in it. And I never dreamed it could feel this good.

CHAPTER FIFTEEN

The first month after Eden moves into her house goes by in a blur. I spend almost every night at Eden's place, except the nights when I'm working. It's not that I've moved in; it's just that so much shit comes up with a new house. Furniture to be moved, boxes needing to be unpacked. Eden has rearranged the kitchen pantry so many times, I don't know where anything is from one day to the next. But I don't care. She's over the goddamn moon every day. This home has brought her so much pleasure, and I am just happy to be a part of it.

And it's hard to deny that I'm becoming a bigger part of all of it —not just the house—I'm talking Eden's and Juniper's lives.

Tonight, we agreed that Eden would take the night off from organizing cabinets and we would just sit back and enjoy the place.

I stretch out and rest my head back against the cushions. The TV is on, but the volume is low. I'm not too interested in watching anything. I just want to spend time with Eden when we're not deciding whether heavy canned goods should go on a low shelf or a high shelf. Don't get me wrong. I love the process, but tonight, I don't want to watch her alphabetize soup.

She comes out of the kitchen with two glasses of water. She leaves our drinks on the coffee table and then collapses next to me on the couch. She's quiet for a minute, and I tap her on the thigh with my fingers.

"Go on," I urge.

"What?" Her lips curl into a knowing smile.

"I know what you're thinking. Just say it so we can move on."

She opens her mouth to say it, and I time my words so we both say it at the same time. "Can you believe this is really my house?"

"You're the worst," she says, looping her arms around my neck. She kisses my ear. "I'm not that predictable."

"Eden," I say, tilting my head so our faces are close. "You totally are, and I love seeing you this happy."

She kisses me lightly on the lips, then snuggles against my side. I put an arm around her shoulders and pull her close. "Your mother wants me to get a dog," she says. "She has almost got me convinced."

I shake my head. "I do not get between Lucia and her rescues. That includes you."

"Hey." Eden elbows me. "But I guess I deserve that. You know your mom offered to give me cooking lessons."

"Better you than me," I say. "Ma and Pops are great cooks. I am a great microwaver."

We hold each other tightly and watch the images cross the TV.

"A dog could be good protection," she says quietly. "For when you're not here."

My housewarming gift to Eden was a video security system. She has cameras all around the property, and I set up the text alerts to message both my phone and hers if anything triggers the sensors.

Star Falls is safe, but you can never be too safe. Even if I've mostly been notified that she has an active family of raccoons living out back. Definitely one point in the pro column if she's thinking about getting a dog.

"Do you not feel safe here?" I ask, growing concerned. "When you're by yourself?"

She nods, her soft hair rustling against the fabric of my shirt. "It's not that so much. It's just... I don't know. This place feels different when you're not here, like something's missing."

I lift her chin so I can look her in the eye. "Babe, we talked about this. This is your house. Your first home. You've got to spend time in it. You don't need anyone else claiming a closet or half your bed. Isn't that what you want? Reorganizing everything? Making this the perfect place for you and Junie?"

She shrugs. "Yeah. That makes sense. I know I need to do things for myself."

"No." I shake my head. "That's not what I'm saying. I'm saying this is your house. Your dream. I want you to have a little time to enjoy it. I don't need to have my name on the mailbox to feel at home here."

She's quiet, but then she sniffs hard, and her cheeks grow red. "Is it because you don't want me? Are we too much?"

I move so I'm sitting at the edge of the couch and can see right into Eden's eyes. "Are you serious?" I ask quietly. "What are you saying?"

Eden's voice is shaking. "I know we've only known each other a few months, but would you want to move in here with us?"

The breath catches in my throat at her question. "That's a massive step, babe. Is that what you want?"

Her face is expressionless. "I want to know what you want, Vito. I need you to just tell me the truth." She looks down at her hands. "I feel like ever since I moved into this place, you've pulled away a bit."

I reach for her hands, and we lace our fingers together tightly. "Eden, I'm not just here for the good times. I'm not that guy, the one who bolts the second things get boring or serious or hard." I bite down on my lower lip, trying to find the right words. "I want to be here for you, no matter what you're doing."

It's then I realize that I have completely and totally forgotten about Michelle's offer.

"Shit," I say and slap my forehead. "Babe, I'm a fucking moron. You see what I mean? I forgot to give you a message." I lean back against the couch and sigh. "I've got to take ten steps back. So, on the day of your closing, Michelle asked if we could talk."

Eden's body immediately stiffens, and I know I have only a couple seconds before I shatter her trust in me.

"Now, look, I'll show you my phone, babe. That was the only time I've talked to Michelle in five years since our divorce except, of course, for the day we ran into her at the college." I reach for my phone, which is sitting on the coffee table, but Eden stops me with a hand on my arm.

"I don't need to see. I trust you more than I've ever trusted anyone." The words are coming out of her mouth, but they don't quite match the look in her eyes.

That's not good enough for me.

"Uh-huh," I say, shaking my head. I pick up the phone and swipe the screen. "I want you to trust me completely."

She smiles, a sad, thin thing. "I do trust you completely, but it means everything that you would offer to show me proof."

"How the fuck did we get on this topic?" I ask, crinkling my brow.

"You said you forgot to give me a message," Eden reminds me.

"Right." I scroll to the last text and show it to Eden. "Michelle asked me to give you a message the day the house closed, and I seriously forgot. It left my mind the second I walked out of there, and now I don't even know if the offer still stands."

"Offer?" She sits up straight and now does peer over my shoulder as I text.

Me: I'm a fucking idiot, but that's not news to you. I completely forgot to mention your offer to Eden. She bought a house, and with all the moving and shit, it slipped my mind. I'm with her now. It's been a month, though, so before I tell her, I just want to ask if the offer is still open?

I click send and turn to Eden. "I'm going to tell you anyway," I say, "but I don't know what I'm going to do if shit's changed and I screwed you out of a great thing."

She looks at me, her beautiful eyes squinting, as if she's trying to read the honesty there in my face.

"First of all, I'm so sorry it slipped my mind, and I didn't tell you sooner. I get so focused on work, and then when I'm not on the job, I am all in whatever else I'm doing. And for the last month, that's been you."

She giggles and I nod.

"After you took Michelle's class, she had me out to her office. Said she thought you were really smart and that with some guidance, you could do great things." I shake my head. "Now that I'm saying it out loud, I wonder if part of me wanted to forget the offer. Wanted to put as much distance between Michelle and you as I possibly could." I meet her eyes, and there's no hiding how I'm feeling when I say this. I feel the emotion like a physical pain in my chest. "Her receptionist is pregnant. She's actually married to my chief's son." I grin, but then the seriousness of what I have to say comes back to haunt my words. "Michelle wanted to know if you wanted the job. You can work either part time or full time covering for the receptionist while she's out on maternity leave. It's a paid job, of course, and you can try doing what she does for a few months before you spend the money committing to college and a degree in some financial shit."

The look on Eden's face transforms from playful to stone serious.

Before I can say anything, my phone rings. The caller ID shows it's Michelle. "You mind if I talk to her?" I ask.

She nods, and I click to connect the call.

"Hey," I say.

"Hey." Her voice is loud and bright. I notch down the volume a bit so she doesn't wake Juniper. "I'm good. Is Eden with you?"

I nod at her, and Eden greets her. "Um, yes. Hi, Michelle."

"Hey." She laughs. "You know I gave you my number in class that day, and then I spoke to Vito about the job. When I didn't hear from either of you for a month, I figured that was your way of telling the ex to go fuck herself and mind her own business."

I immediately set the record straight. "Michelle, this was all me. You know my memory and how I get when I'm working."

"Don't worry about it," she says. "I do know, and I wouldn't blame either one of you if you weren't interested in anything that had to do with me."

Eden is leaning forward, looking really conflicted.

"So, no pressure, but I just saw your text. My receptionist is officially going on leave in two weeks. Unless she goes into labor sooner. She's a little flexible on her date, but she wants some time to fix up the nursery a bit more before the baby comes. If Eden is interested, we can try to get her in as soon as possible to do some training with Gennie. I'll handle the rest once Gennie's off."

"Here," I say, picking up my phone and taking it off speaker. "Michelle, I'm going to give my phone to Eden. Let you two talk. I literally just mentioned this two minutes ago, so she may have questions."

I offer the phone to Eden, and she takes it. Then she stands and paces through the living room while she talks.

I get up and wander back to the bathroom, wasting time while they talk.

After a couple of minutes, I head back to the living room. Eden is sitting on the couch, looking down at my phone in her hands.

"You good? All done?" I ask.

She nods, so I come join her on the couch. "You didn't have to leave," she says.

I hold up my hand. "This is between you two now. I was just the messenger."

Eden sets the phone on the coffee table and gives me a confused look. "I don't know what to think," she admits. "It's weird, right? Your ex-wife offering me a job?"

"I'm sure Michelle is excited to meet someone who has an interest in what she does. It would only be weird if you..." I have to stop myself from saying the words.

"If I what?" she presses.

Ah, fuck. I can't get away with not saying it now. I've gone this far. I drag a hand through my hair and tug it at the roots. "I don't want to lose you, Eden. I don't want you to go to work for Michelle and then realize that I'm not good enough for you." I look her in the eye. "I've been through that once, and babe, I don't want to be your rebound guy. I don't want to be the guy you lean on until you find something better."

Eden's face sets into a mask of pure anger. I don't think I've ever seen her like this.

"Something better? You think I would ever find someone better than you?" She stands up and paces the living room, pointing an angry finger at me. "All this time, I've been feeling like a second-class citizen, worried that you're going to get sick of me. I don't have a family and a thousand siblings. I don't cook like your father does or want to stay home and raise kids like your mom did. When are you going to realize how damaged I am and just leave me?"

She's breathing hard, her face is flushed bright red, but I can tell there's sadness right under the surface of the pain.

I stand and cross the living room, taking her in my arms. "I feel like we need to talk. Really talk," I say. I lead her back to the couch, and we sit together, our hands locked. "I don't care if you can't cook. My brother owns a restaurant, and my parents always have way too much food around." I lift her hands to my lips and kiss her knuckles. "What I love about you is that you're real. You're flawed. I am too. You know that. I'd rather wear pajamas than pants. You don't expect me to be anything but what I am. You accept my work schedule, my sleep schedule. What I'm afraid of is that changing."

She squeezes my hands tight. "We're both going to change over time, at least somewhat," she says. "I'm a single mom. I come from a really messed-up family. I don't want to make the same mistakes my parents did. I want to be a different person in five years and maybe even an even more different person five years from that. I want more in life."

Something in my chest breaks open when her voice trembles.

"Listen to me." I cup her entire face in my hands. "You're everything. The way you love your daughter. The way you love me." I lean forward and rest my forehead against hers. "I want you to be happy, Eden, and if you want this job, you've got to take it. I want to support you in everything you want to try. I just don't want you to outgrow me."

We're quiet as the honesty of what we've said fills the space between us. I know too well there are no guarantees in life or love.

I don't know what I need from her. Maybe just for her to understand. Maybe that's all we can promise each other. At least right now.

"I don't know what to say," she admits. Her beautiful eyes well with tears. "I want to grow with you. Not away from you."

"All right. So, let's tackle one thing at a time. Do you want the job?" I finally ask. "You think it's the right thing for you?"

She nods slowly. "It sounds perfect. I can cover for Gennie for a few months. If I don't like the field, I'll find out before I waste money on tuition or student loans. I'm going to need support, though. Babysitting and someone to come home to so I can share stories about my day. I want the job, Vito, but I want you too. I want you to share it all with me. That's the only way we won't grow apart, if we're doing it all together. But I know it's a lot. I'm a work in progress, but I'm a package deal. Me and Juniper. Do you think you can handle us all the time?"

I almost can't say the words. I wish like hell Junie were awake so I could hold both of my girls in my arms. "It feels like something is missing not having this conversation with Junie right here."

I blink fast, and Eden reaches out a hand to stroke my cheek. "That's how I know…" she says, tears streaming down her cheeks. She smiles and says, "See? You're already the man I want and the father figure Junie deserves."

We grab each other then and cling together in a tight hug. I bury my face in the length of her hair and just breathe her in.

She's younger than me, but this woman is smart. She knows herself. She understands that life hands you pain and opportunity, and somehow when it's all bundled together, you've got to make the decision to be happy.

Everything with Eden is an easy decision.

I don't have to decide to be happy with Eden. It's as if just being close to her makes every minute, every day, good.

In a weird way, I already feel like we're family. It's like our circumstances are just catching up to that reality.

"Can I say something?" I ask, pulling away just enough that I can whisper in her ear.

"Only if I can ask you something after."

"I love you, Eden. You are so damn easy to love. And I love your daughter too. I love what we have, and I'm in this, no matter how scared I am." I kiss her lips, a soft kiss wet with our shared tears.

"Move in here?" she asks. "Live with us, Vito."

I'm quiet as I think about it. I know what my answer is. I feel like I have always known this was coming. Is it possible I've known someplace deep down ever since the days she invited me to look at houses?

I moved back in with my parents after Michelle left, and over the years, it's been easier to stay there than it would have been to think about trying something new.

"I have a few conditions," I tell her. "I'm going to pay rent and half of all the costs—groceries, baby shit, and everything else. I'm going to carry my weight. In fact, more than my share of it. I make more than you right now, and I want to help make the money you have last longer so you have more options."

She doesn't say anything, but her face lights up. "Okay. What else?"

"This one I'm serious about," I tell her. "I need my own bedroom. Not for every day, but when I'm off shift and need to crash or when I just need to sleep. I don't want my schedule to fuck up yours. I'll sleep with you every chance I can get, but I need my own room so that we can both get space when we need it."

She's beaming now. "I have extra rooms."

I nuzzle my face against her neck. "So, you taking the job?" I ask.

"So, you moving in?" she asks.

"You going to rearrange everything in the whole house again now that I need a bedroom?" I ask.

"You know me so well," she whispers.

I groan, but then I pull her close. "There are parts of you I still need to know better."

"Which parts?" she asks.

And then I take her upstairs so I can show her.

CHAPTER SIXTEEN

eden

I wake up before sunrise and my mind is spinning, but my first thoughts are of Junie. I squint at the image on the baby monitor on the bedside table.

Juniper is sound asleep, her little foot poking out from under a light blanket.

I roll over, and that's when it hits me. I'm alone in bed. I roll over and touch the cool sheets. Vito slept over last night, but he's not next to me.

My heart speeds up a bit at the thought that maybe he's not sleeping because he's not comfortable here.

Maybe he's having second thoughts about moving in. I take a deep breath and kick back the covers. I'm awake now, so I may as well face whatever this is. I am wearing my favorite paper-thin sleep tee with the wide, loose neck and soft pajama pants. I tiptoe down the stairs and find Vito in the kitchen, sitting in the eat-in nook with a sheet of paper and his phone in front of him.

"Babe." He brightens as soon as he sees me. "You're up early."

I pad over to the table and tuck into the cozy bench seat on the opposite side of where he's sitting. "I could say the same to you." A little bit of tension leaves my belly at the happy look on his face. "Are you okay?"

"Better than okay," he says. He gets up excitedly and scoots next to me on the bench. "Do you want coffee? I made some."

He grabs his empty mug and heads to the coffeepot, but then he shakes his head. "Shit. I drank the whole pot. I'll make more."

I get up from my seat and take the empty pot from him. "I'll do it. You tell me what's got you so excited that you're awake."

As I scoop up the grounds and fill the pot, Vito grabs the sheet of paper off the kitchen table. He sets the paper down on the counter and explains the notes he's made. "I've lived with my parents for the last five years and I'm a little ashamed to admit it now, but I've never paid my parents a penny in rent. I buy groceries every now and then, but..." He rubs the sexy scruff on his chin. "I've been a deadbeat son, but that means I've banked a ton of money." He points to a figure on the piece of paper. "I've been putting my money away and honestly never thought much about what I'd do with it. My truck's paid off. I've got no debt."

He meets my eyes, his bright and full of excitement. "We can use my savings to pay for your college. You don't have to worry about running out of the money in your trust. You can save all that for Juniper."

I shake my head and click the coffeemaker on. "Vito, I would never, ever let you pay my way through college."

He holds up a finger and smirks, his lips a full, sexy smile. "I thought you'd say that. So, I crunched some other numbers." He flips the paper over. "If we use my cash to make some upgrades to the house—new bathrooms upstairs, for example, we can throw some work at my buddies who do contract work on the side, so you know there'll be guys in the house you can trust. Then, when the work is done, you can get your house reappraised and maybe take out a loan against the equity."

I watch him in amazement. I've heard of things like this, but I have no idea how any of this stuff works. This is exactly why I want to learn. "Vito, but then your money is tied up in this house. What if something happens? I'll want to pay you back for the money you put into the house."

Vito drops his sheet of paper on the floor, then bends to pick it up. When he stands, his face looks strained. "Something happens? Eden, what's going to happen?"

I step closer to him and wrap my arms around his waist. "I don't want anything to happen, but I don't know about things like this. I don't ever want you to feel like I screwed you out of your money." I bite my lip, thinking about the vile, horrible things Nathan's wife said at the mediation.

Vito sets his phone and paper on the counter and grips my hips in both hands. "I'm not like Juniper's father. And I'm going to take all the time I need to show you I'm a very, very different man."

"You already have," I say, lowering my head to rest against his shoulder. "You've been up thinking about how to spend your money on me."

"On us," he corrects. He tugs my hips closer, and I can feel the firm lines of his body against mine. "When I wake up in the morning at my parents', I'm in their house. But when I woke up this morning, I was so excited I couldn't sleep. All I could picture was the playset we can put in the back for Juniper. The new bathrooms we can install."

"The dog run for my new puppy..." I say, a pleading note in my voice. "Because one screaming little animal in this house is not enough."

"Hey." Vito pretends to be hurt. "I'm not a little animal. I'm full-sized."

I tuck my forehead against the stubble growing along his neck. "Some things about you are definitely full-sized." I lower my hand to cup his butt cheek through his PJs. "And this too." I slide a hand between us to stroke his growing erection.

He groans, deep and low in his throat. "Baby," he hisses. "You're getting me excited in a whole different kind of way."

"Is that a bad thing?" I ask, pressing my fingertips lightly along the front of the drawstring and lower. His cock responds to my closeness. I press my full breasts against his bare chest and reach back around to grab his ass.

"Fuck," he sighs. "This is reason enough to go back to bed. You with me?"

"First one upstairs has to get the condom," I tell him.

"Has to?" He turns and faces me, then he playfully shoves me away from him, turning and dashing through the house, headed for the stairs.

I laugh and follow after him, keeping my footsteps light so we don't wake the baby. Nothing blocks grown-up time like a toddler awake before dawn.

By the time I get upstairs, Vito is sitting on the bed, his pajama pants off and a foil square tucked between two fingers. He's grinning like he's won a race.

"You're so competitive," I tease, turning so he can see my ass as I shimmy out of my bottoms. He sucks in a breath as I bend deep, step out of the sleepwear, and then turn back to face him.

"I've got three siblings," he says. "It's in my blood."

I smirk as I turn around and let him watch as I ease my super loose top over my shoulders. "I was an only child," I remind him. "I'm okay letting you win."

"Silly woman," he breathes. "You're the prize."

He watches me, his eyes dark and his lips parted as I climb onto the bed. I straddle his legs and climb all the way up his body until I'm just above his cock. I settle lightly against his erection, letting the heat of my pussy press into his length.

He sucks in a deep breath and closes his eyes, but then he drops the condom on the sheet so he can hold my breasts in his hands. "These," he groans. "I could lose myself in them."

He holds the weight of me in his hands and squeezes lightly. The gentle pressure sends waves of desire through my body, my pussy growing even wetter in anticipation.

"More," I tell him, grabbing hold of his shoulders. I reach for the condom and tear it open, but just before I slide the latex over his flesh, I climb off his lap and kneel over his cock. "Touch me," I tell him as I open my mouth and flick my tongue over the head of his dick.

He growls deep in his chest, muttering thankful curses as I take him all the way into my mouth, lapping my tongue against him to make sure he's nice and wet before I roll on the condom.

He caresses my breasts softly as I suck him, until finally he's humming, and I know if I want to keep things going, I'm going to need to sheathe him up.

Once he's wearing the condom, I climb back over him and roll my hips back and forth along his length. He's not even inside me yet, but our pace is frantic and fast. I feel the thick muscles and soft hairs of his thighs between my legs, and I have to grip his shoulders for support.

He pinches my nipples in his fingertips, and I am close to losing it. I nearly cry out, the pleasure is so, so good. But then I lean forward and practically feed him my nipple.

He sucks the tip deep between his lips, the pleasure radiating through my chest and limbs. I am lost to the sweet, golden heat when he removes my nipple from his mouth and rolls his neck in circles while pressing my tender nipple against the stubble of his chin. I chase the ecstasy, rocking my hips against him while I throw my head back and let him work his magic.

I don't know how he does it because my eyes are slammed shut, but I feel him shove a hand between us. I lift my weight a little, but goddamn, my legs are so weak I can hardly support my weight. Then he shifts his erection, and I slide all the way down, crying out for real as his length reaches deep inside me.

"Fuck, I love you. I love this. I love you more, but fuck," he groans.

I can't speak. I'm lost to the colors swirling behind my eyes, to the burn in my thighs as I grind deeper, pressing my weight so every roll of my hips brings wave after wave of bliss through my body.

Once I slow my movements, sweat misting along my hairline, Vito lifts me off his cock and lays me on my back.

He immediately grabs my thighs in his hands and spreads me wide.

I'm boneless, opening to him so he can see, touch, and taste every inch of my most private parts. He drops his mouth to my pussy.

"Fuck, you taste good," he grits out when he stops to suck in a chest full of air. "You have the sweetest pussy."

He pulls his mouth back and trails his fingertips along the insides of my thighs. He nibbles and kisses his way from my pubic bone to my right knee, then turns to pay the same attention to my left leg. I'm completely naked, my tits sagging on either side of my chest, my hair sweaty and matted against the sheets, and yet with his hands on my body, I feel like the most beautiful woman alive.

I curl my toes and try to sit up, but Vito shakes his head and massages the tight muscles in my legs. "I want to devour you," he says, pressing my legs open wider. He situates himself between my open legs and nudges my opening with his cock, murmuring, "You're the most gorgeous fucking woman alive."

I open my eyes a crack and smile at him, but then I immediately slam my lids shut when Vito thrusts inside me.

I try to relax my legs and take the full pressure of every deep thrust inside me, but he's grabbing my legs and closing them together like a clothespin in front of his chest. I try to hold up the weight of my legs, but Vito's cock all the way inside me while my legs are together, my feet in the air, it's more than I can take. I cry out his name as yet another climax steals the strength from my limbs.

He patiently waits until my fingers loosen from the sheets to flip me onto my belly. I lift my butt in the air, but I can't even control my hands and legs. I need Vito to help lift my hips so he can fuck me from behind.

He slaps the side of my ass, the slap so loud I worry it will wake up Juniper, but honestly, it's worth it. When he finishes, he collapses on top of me, our sweaty bodies sticking together.

"That was freaking…" I can't even finish the thought. I squint at the clock and see that we have plenty of time to go back to sleep. The coffeepot has a four-hour safety shut-off, so I don't have to do anything or worry about anything until Juniper is awake.

I think Vito is thinking the same thing because with a numb little grunt, he jerks the sheets up off the bed and tucks them in around us. He settles himself halfway on top of me, his face smashed against my right breast, while his leg is thrown over my right thigh.

"Love you," he says. "Sorry if I drooled on you a little just then."

I laugh as much as I can pinned beneath his weight, and I snake my fingers through his hair. "Love you," I whisper.

My mind is at ease. My heart is happy. If I thought buying this house was a dream come true, I know now that home ownership doesn't even come close to what I feel when I'm with this man.

This competitive, silly, real, firefighting Bianchi. I fall asleep with a smile on my face and the man I love literally on my heart.

"Holy fucking..." Gracie Bianchi—now Cooper—wanders through my new house with her son Ethan on her hip and her mouth wide open. She lifts a perfectly arched black brow at me. "Babe, when you said you bought a house, I was expecting a starter home. This?" She sweeps her hand around the wide-open living room.

My head is spinning right now. Gracie offered to watch Juniper while I go in for my first day of orientation, and I have barely had enough coffee.

Vito has been on the last two nights, so I haven't slept well. That's becoming a real thing now that I know he plans to move in. But since he hasn't told his parents yet, I can't spill the news to Gracie.

"Hey." Gracie's voice is soft as she sets Ethan down on the playmat. He's just about Junie's age, and he immediately waddles, then drops to a crawl to take a toy from Junie's hand.

"Eden?" Gracie waves a heavily tattooed hand in my face. "Hey, girl. You look like you want to start crying. You know Junie's going to be just fine with me and Ethan, right?"

I nod and swallow hard against the emotions. "Yeah, of course. I'm really happy you're here. Thank you for agreeing to watch her."

"It's a lot, though. Going back to work." She nods at Ethan's dark brown ringlets of hair. "You got any coffee going?"

I shake my head. "I was up early and finished a pot. I haven't been sleeping."

Gracie nods, her long black hair grazing her shoulders. Somehow, she looks effortlessly cool in an oversized, shredded concert T-shirt with a tank top underneath it and black jeans. She took her shoes off at the door, of course, and is barefoot. Even her black toenail polish looks perfect.

"How do you do it?" I ask. I drop down onto the floor beside the kids and cross my legs. "I don't think I've painted my toenails since before I got pregnant."

Gracie looks at me, her beautiful eyes rimmed with thick, winged liner. "Girl, I have Ryder. I couldn't do it without him."

I peek at the time on my watch and reassure myself I'm okay. It's only nine, and Michelle said I could stop by this morning for the hiring paperwork and a basic orientation. I figure a few minutes with Gracie is time well spent, because I have no one else in my life I can ask pressing questions. "Was postpartum hard for you?"

Gracie widens her eyes and shakes her head dramatically. "I was still adjusting to being a stepmom to two fully formed humans when this one came along." She jerks a thumb at her son. "I had some infertility issues before I conceived, and I thought the hardest part of all of this was going to be getting pregnant." She plops down on the floor beside me and tucks her feet under her butt.

"It wasn't?" I ask.

"Hell no." She picks at an invisible thread on her tee and shrugs. "I have a big personality." She flicks me a glance as if ready to fight me over the statement, but I just grin. "Ryder gave up his stable job teaching just before Ethan was born. He went to work for a start-up with his best friend, so he was putting in long hours. He cut back once the baby was born, of course, but I fell into a funk for sure. I'm not the kind of person who gets sad, though. I mean, I feel the feelings, but I tend to either go quiet or I get angry. You can probably guess how hard it was to be quiet with a newborn, two children, and a husband who was pulled in twenty directions."

I listen to her experience and can't imagine. I know how hard it was to do everything myself, but to multiply the responsibilities, to have a partner who was out of his routine, and to battle postpartum depression? I reach out a hand and squeeze her shoulder. "Gracie," I say. "How did you manage?"

She chuckles. "I drew a lot. In fact, that's one of the things that got me through. I leaned in to the one thing that has always been there for me. My art. I would swaddle the baby against my chest and sit the older kids down, and we would make art for hours." She waves a hand. "I wish our house was this big because, let me tell you, two kids and a professional tattoo artist can make a big old mess."

It dawns on me then that Gracie has this huge family. Where were they when she was going through all of this? "I'm surprised your mom wasn't constantly helping," I say, hoping I chose the right words.

"Girl, I had to kick my mother to the curb constantly. She'd have raised those kids if I'd let her." She lifts a perfect brow at me and points right at my chest. "You need to set boundaries with Lucia, because I'm telling you. Ma is all heart, and she's eyeballs-deep in good intentions, but she has no filter sometimes. So, if she's showing up day after day, offering to help, you take what you need. I love them to the moon and back. But I've been worried they've been making things too easy on my brother."

She grows quiet and looks at me.

"I'm about to spill some tea, so I sure hope you two are serious."

I smile and nod, but I don't say anything more. I don't want to speak behind Vito's back, but at the same time, I want to get to know Gracie better.

"So, here's the deal about my brother. Ah, crap." Gracie wrinkles her nose and leans in to sniff Juniper's butt. "Not yours," she says. "That means it's mine."

She jumps up and grabs her diaper bag, which looks more like a giant metallic-gray purse than a diaper bag. "You mind if I do this here?" she asks. "Or do you prefer the bathroom?"

"Wherever you want."

She nods and pulls out a changing pad and bribes Ethan to stop playing by giving him a new toy. "I'll just say this," she says. "Divorce does funny things to some people, and Vito's did a number on him. He's spent five years of his adult life living with our parents. Don't get me wrong. After I went through some shit, I moved back in with Lucia and Mario too. But he's been there five years, and if you ask me, he's let himself get too comfortable. Maybe he's comfortable staying in the nest because he has no idea what direction to go if he tries to fly on his own."

Gracie stands Ethan up and lets him go play with Juniper. She's wadded up the diaper and wiped down the changing pad. "Where do you want this?"

I show her the way and then stay with the kids while she heads back into the powder room to wash her hands. When she comes back, she points to her wrist. She doesn't wear a watch, but I do, and I check the time.

"You probably need to get dressed?" she asks.

I nod, reluctant to get up. I could spend the whole day here with Gracie, Ethan, and Juniper.

Maybe Vito and I aren't that different. I'm not sure I want to leave my nest now that it's time to go.

"Nervous?" Gracie asks. "Going back to work after being home with these sweet cheeks all day is tough," she says. "But give Michelle a try. It's bananas thinking that she's now a financial adviser, but..." Gracie shrugs. "She was always good people. Vito is good people." She grins at me, her thick red lipstick perfectly coating her full lips. "You're good people. And it's never too late to try something new, you know?"

I give her a smile and make sure she knows where to find everything. I tell Gracie to make herself completely at home and show her how to turn on the television.

"All I care about is getting out in the yard," she says. "Come on, kiddos. Let's get sweaters. We're going to tire out some toddlers."

I head upstairs to take a quick shower, all thoughts of making another pot of coffee long gone. I'm sure if she wants it, Gracie will help herself. After all, she's practically family. And I intend to start treating her like it.

CHAPTER SEVENTEEN

The last three days of my life have been like so many others over the years. You'd think every one of the horrible accidents or fires might be some of the worst or hardest shit I'd ever been through—until the next one.

I'm fortunate, working in a small town. We have a lot less of this stuff than bigger cities. This stuff being the calls that you feel under your skin. The sounds that lock in your ears and you don't know how you'll ever stop hearing them.

And yet, time passes.

The intensity of whatever the shit was eases. A little. Then a little more. Sometimes I wake up with my heart racing after a nightmare that brings just one small detail back, and that triggers a whole lot of memories. Emotions.

But still, this is the job. I may not like what it does to me, but I love what I do on calls like the ones we had this shift. It takes guts and teamwork to survive the day. It takes training, experience, and maturity to survive the aftermath.

When you get so close to other people's worst moments, worst days, it steals a little of the light from yours.

That's the trade-off.

When you hold the hand of the dying, you willingly give up a little part of the wholeness that makes you alive.

I did that and more today. And I'm fucking ready to go home and let the long, slow process of dealing with it all start.

My shift is over, and I've changed and showered. The mood is intense. The silence among the guys in my engine company is as overpowering and dense as smoke.

I grab my bag and keys and stand on shaky knees, ready to haul ass out of there, when Chief joins us.

His eyes carry the weight of what we're all feeling. I know he's been filling out a ton of paperwork and working on scheduling a critical incident debriefing. That means he's not able to pack what we saw into a tiny box until the intensity fades like the sun hiding behind a cloud. He's had to stare right into that blinding light for longer than any of us.

"Tomorrow," Chief says quietly. No one needs to ask what he means. "Three p.m. sharp. I'm trying to get someone out from Columbus to do a second session for anyone who needs it. This is mandatory."

I nod and brush past the chief, ready to get the fuck out of here. The chief stops me with a hand on my shoulder. "Good work today. Leadership like that made a difference."

"Thanks." The words feel like wool in my mouth. None of what I did today made a bit of difference to the outcome.

I did my best. We all did.

I get out to my truck, and fresh morning air hits my face. I breathe it in, the smells of the call we finished overnight still thick in my nose. I shake my head.

There's no residue. I followed all the protocols. Wore all the gear. Washed away any traces of what happened, but there are some stains that never, ever go away.

This is the part of the job that isn't glamorous. That isn't fun.

These are the things I lock away inside myself when I go home and sleep.

It's just after seven, and I need to sleep. It's only Eden's third day on the job, and as far as I can remember, Sassy's watching Juniper.

My mind goes to shit after a shift like that. It takes some time before I can pull myself from the intensity of the work and get back to the routine of life outside the station.

Once I'm inside my truck, I slam the door hard, images from the night playing like a movie in my mind. I close my eyes against the memories, but that only makes them easier to see.

I check my phone, and there's a photo message from Eden waiting on my phone. It's only a picture of her legs. She's sitting on her bed, her legs crossed. She's wearing a black pencil skirt, black nylons, and sexy high heels.

Eden: Missed u, babe. Missed u bad. This will be waiting for you when you get to my place. Can't wait for you to move in.

I'm supposed to go to Eden's this afternoon after she's off work and after I get some decent sleep. But I can't think that far into the future. I can't reply to her text. I can't do anything but think about what I saw, and I want to stop thinking about it.

I'll be back here tomorrow for the meeting with the therapist, and we'll all go back over it. It's usually the same one, somebody the chief calls in from another county.

It often helps if the person is a total outsider. If the therapist knows the people involved in the traumatic incident, the one that was so bad a whole crew of experienced first responders needed stress debriefing, that makes the whole process a lot tougher.

Some of the therapists are better than others. Most invite us to talk but let us stay silent if that's how we need to deal. Intervening early and giving us the chance to get what happened off our chests is supposed to lead to less PTSD, fewer guys like me having real problems because we can't deal with the stress.

I toss my phone onto the passenger seat and crank the music up full blast. My ears are ringing by the time I pull into the driveway at my parents'.

I walk in the front door, a fucking grimace on my face that's so heavy, my jaw literally hurts. I kick off my shoes and head into the kitchen just in time to see my father with his hand under my mother's robe.

"Jesus Fucking Christ!" I shout and stagger back. Thankfully,

Pops is fully dressed, but he sure as hell was getting a handful of something.

"Vito." Ma clutches her robe closed at the top. Her hair and makeup are not done, and I'm shocked to see her not dressed at this hour. "We thought you were going to text us if you were coming back. We assumed you were going to crash at Eden's."

"Plans changed," I grumble, but then I drop my phone on the counter and brace myself on my palms.

"Oh shit." Pops comes around the counter and claps a hand on my shoulder. "What happened, son? Is it Eden?"

I whip my head up, and my heart practically parkours its way out of my chest. "No." I shake my head. "Multiple fatalities. It was bad."

Ma immediately runs to the sink and starts a kettle for tea. Pops is quiet, but his hand on my shoulder is firm. "When's the debrief?" he asks, his voice low.

"Tomorrow," I say. "Three."

Ma gets a mug and drops a tea bag into it, then scurries around gathering fruit and bread for toast while the kettle boils. "Just something light to eat, baby," she says.

I nod. This is the routine. This is what it's like supporting a guy like me with a job like this. This is the shit my siblings don't see.

They may think I live with our parents because I'm lazy or directionless. I stay because they are my safe place to land. Always have been.

"Ma," I say. "Can you put that tea in a to-go cup? I'm going to grab some fresh clothes and head out."

Ma looks to my pops, tears filling her eyes. "You want me to drive you? You look so tired, son."

I never like this part, but it's always a component of the routine. I lie. Not a big lie, but one that will keep the pain that could tear me apart under control, so that it doesn't shatter the hearts of the people I love.

"Ma," I grumble, trying desperately to find some humor but coming up with very little. "Don't pretend you and Pops won't get right back to what you were doing when I walked in the second I'm out that door." I give her a weak smile. "I'm all right."

She packs up some fruit and hands me the toast on a paper plate. "Eat this before it gets cold. I'll have the rest ready when you come down." She comes around the counter and slips her arms around my waist. She hugs me hard, her soft body going tight. The strength of my tiny mother, the way she's trying to hug the hurt right out of me... It makes my eyes burn and my nose prickle.

"All right," I say, blinking fast and stepping out of her hold. "Thanks, Ma."

I head upstairs and throw clothes and toiletries into a gym bag. I don't think, just grab and shove, until I realize I need socks and underwear, and I grab those too. I head back downstairs, where Ma has a massive casserole carrier waiting for me.

"I'm sending some leftovers, so you just have to heat up lunch." Ma shoves the bag of food at me. "You come home tonight or tomorrow if you need us, baby."

Her eyes are red, but she's not crying. Pops grabs the food from Ma and says, "I'll walk you to your truck."

I don't argue but stop to kiss my mother goodbye before heading to the door, putting on my shoes, and grabbing my keys. Pops is right on my heels, and he goes around the passenger side to put the food on the seat next to my gym bag.

Then he comes around to the driver's side. "This is always your home. You don't need to call."

I nod. "Tell Ma to stock up on bleach," I say, managing a grin. "If I see any more than what I did today, I'm going to need to bleach my eyes."

Pops lightly slaps my chest with the back of his hand, then tugs me close for a hug. He watches from the driveway, and I see Ma standing at the door holding the front of her robe closed, waving as I drive away.

I turn the tunes back on, drown out my thoughts and worries, and focus on driving.

I'm almost home.

When I get to Eden's, Shirley's car is gone, and the house looks empty. I shoot Sassy a text to see what's up, and she replies back with two messages—one text and a picture.

Sassy: Took Junie to the park. Be back later.

I realize as soon as I let myself into the quiet house how much I was hoping to see Juniper. Somehow seeing her innocent, sweet face and dropping down to play with blocks or a playset would do my heart some good.

Since Juniper's at the park and Eden is at work, I shoot a text back to Sassy.

Me: I let myself in, Sass. I'm at Eden's house. Going to catch some sleep till you're back.

I put the leftovers from Ma away in the kitchen and head upstairs to Eden's bedroom and change from my jeans into pajama pants and a T-shirt. I climb under the covers and take a picture of my face against her pillows and shoot off a quick text to Eden.

Me: Rough call at work. I came here instead of my parents'. I needed to be close to you, even if you're not here. Love you. Have a good day, babe.

I click send on both the text and the picture, then I get up and close the door and draw the curtains. It's still really bright in here, so I grab a blanket from the foot of the bed and hang it over the curtain rod to dampen more of the daylight.

Once it's dark and quiet, I climb under the covers and put a pillow over my head. I block out all the light and sound and just breathe. I say a prayer for the people whose lives were lost last night. For the guys on my crew. For everyone I love. I breathe deep and catch the light fragrance of Eden's shampoo. The scent of her hair. The familiar smells comfort me, and I close my eyes. Before I know it, I give in to dreamless sleep.

When I wake up, I know immediately that I'm not in my small bed back at my parents'. The super-soft sheets and comforter remind me that even though I can't see for shit, I'm at Eden's.

I toss back the blankets and stumble into the attached bathroom. When I click on the light, I see how puffy my eyes are. I splash some cold water on my face and brush my teeth because my mouth feels like a wasteland.

I see a pencil skirt, a pair of hose, and a white blouse neatly resting on the side of the bathtub, which means Eden must have come home and changed, and I didn't hear a thing.

I'm still in pajamas, but I don't bother changing.

I check my phone and see that it's after six. I have messages from my parents, two from Franco, and even one from Benito.

Word travels fast through the Bianchi family. Ma must have told them I had a rough day.

I don't, however, have any messages from Eden.

I wiggle my toes into my house slippers and head toward the stairs. When I reach the landing, I see Eden holding Juniper. They are swaying in front of the television, which is on at a very low volume. I can hear Eden and Junie quietly singing along with an animated kids movie.

I just stand there for a minute watching them.

Eden's long, soft hair sweeps her back as she sways. She kisses Junie's cheeks as they watch the show and sing. I can't believe how quiet the volume is, but I'm sure they don't need to hear it to know the words.

Watching them like this, I am overcome by the need to rush down the stairs. To crush them in my arms and keep them close. I want them in my home, in my arms, and in my heart always.

I was right to come here instead of staying at my parents'.

This is where I belong.

This is my family.

My home.

I walk down the stairs, calling out softly so I don't scare the shit out of them. "You didn't have to stay quiet for my sake."

Eden turns, and Juniper squeals out, "Veelo. Veelo."

Eden laughs and repeats after her daughter. "Veelo."

They meet me at the bottom of the stairs. Eden studies my face. She looks so happy to see me.

"You're the most beautiful thing I've ever seen," I tell her.

Her eyes mist, and she grins. "You just want to get some later," she teases.

"Did it work?" I ask.

She waggles her brows at me and moves Junie to one arm, stepping close to fold the three of us together in an awkward family hug. I clutch her tightly and smooch Junie loudly on the cheek.

"You must be starving," she says. "We waited to have dinner."

"You did?" I ask.

She nods. "Come on." She passes Juniper to me, and I cuddle the soft, happy, wiggling thing in my arms.

"How was the park, Juniper? Did Auntie Sassy take you on the swings?"

Juniper starts babbling, and I try to follow her very excited syllables while we walk behind Eden into the kitchen. She pulls Juniper's kiddie seat up to the table, but when I try to put her in her chair, she tightens her arms around my neck. I swap a look with Eden, and she nods, a huge smile on her face.

Since the little nugget seems to want to stay with me, I sit down in the eating nook and settle her on my lap. She's drooling, and a little puddle of spit falls on her chin. I wipe it with my thumb and then wipe the drool on my pajama pants.

The agony of my shift hovers like a shadow behind my back, but my back is strong. Stronger now with my family around me. I'm okay. And I'm going to be okay. Because tonight is just another night.

We're going to eat my parents' leftovers. Put this perfect baby to bed. And then I'm going to ask about Eden's day. Listen to the stories of her new job. I won't share what happened because I want to protect her in every way I can. Even from the demons that chase me down. But that's okay. Because together, we are safe. Together, we are strong enough to weather the job stresses. The money worries. The tears and the laughs. Together, we are home.

CHAPTER EIGHTEEN

eden

I fucked up, and I mean I fucked up bad.

The last month of my new job has been a blur. I have so many passwords for so many systems, I spend half my time searching for my notes and trying to remember how to do the thousand little things that come up in a day. Gennie must have been the world's most patient person because almost every morning, I wake up with a sick feeling in the pit of my stomach just thinking about the notes I've taken to try to remember how to do everything.

It's not getting any easier. In fact, it's getting worse.

Every morning for the last four weeks, I've had to drag myself out of bed and remind myself that it's normal to be completely lost at a new job.

It's completely normal to have to ask a thousand questions.

It's completely normal to feel like a failure from the moment I pull into the parking lot until the moment I pull back out at the end of my workday.

As far as employers go, Michelle has been great. Friendly, positive, patient. She's strict, though, and I can sense her losing patience with me as the days creep by.

The other day, I was technically not on a lunch break but was so desperate not to feel stupid for five minutes, I started reading a book on my phone. Of course, that was the exact time that Michelle walked out and caught me reading. She was not happy, and she asked if I had spare time, if I would please ring her so she could train me on some other aspect of the business.

I felt ashamed. I mean, I've had jobs before. Lots of them. I started working the second I could get a work permit at fifteen. I know better than to slack off while I'm on the clock, but this is nothing like what I expected.

I'm learning nothing about money and finances but a lot about running a small office, how many software systems it takes to run a small business, and how intimate it is working day-to-day with only a handful of people around to ask for help.

When Michelle asks me for something, I feel this intensity, like she's counting the seconds until I get the job done. It's not like she's mean or pressuring me; it's just how she runs her company. She's good at what she does. She talks to a lot of people, makes a lot of calls. Is hands on with everything. Which really sucks when you're the person who seems not to know how to do anything.

And then, I made a mistake.

A big, big mistake.

I know it's only been a month, but the very first day I started, Gennie trained me on the small stuff. Using the calendar system so Michelle always knows when she has in-office appointments. How to take messages so nothing ever gets lost. Don't even ask me how many times I got locked out of my voice mail because I punched in the wrong password.

Yesterday was incredibly busy. A call came in from a very wealthy client. I still think of all the clients as rich people. No matter how many times Michelle tries to tell me to use one of the more delicate phrases—high-net-worth individuals or some such—they are all just rich people to me.

So, a guy in town who owns like three commercial properties wanted to ask Michelle if she could get him a better rate on something than what he was about to get from his current adviser.

He said he hated to rush her, but he was going out of town and wanted to make a quick decision. I honestly didn't understand half of what he said.

All I do know is that he said he hoped Michelle would call him right back. I let him know she was in a meeting in her office with an appointment, took his information, and uploaded the details to the system.

I didn't think about it again until five minutes ago when I got to my desk and found Michelle waiting for me, her lips an unusually angry line.

"Eden," she says. "Do you remember putting Randall Tomlinson into the system yesterday?"

No good morning. No how are you. She hits me with this question, and the only thing I can think of when she says Tomlinson is a guy from a very famous boy band. I put like three new people into the system yesterday, but I don't know which one she's referring to.

"I think so," I say, already starting to sweat. "Did I do something wrong, Michelle?"

She sighs and shakes her head. "You tell me." She nods toward the computer on my desk and stands over me while I rack my brain to try to think of who this guy is and why she's making a big show of asking me about him.

My fingers are shaking as I try to log in, but Michelle groans and waves me away. "Let me," she says.

I literally get up out of my chair and stand over her as she sits at my desk, taps a million miles an hour at the keyboard, and pulls up a screen on the system I swear I've never seen.

"Look here," she says, pointing at the monitor with a finger. "This morning, I ran a report of all the new entries in the database. Three new contacts were entered yesterday." She points to one name and shows me a field where the other financial adviser, Glenn, made contact with the client and made a bunch of notes about the plan of action.

"I see," I say quietly because I do see it, but I don't understand what I'm looking at.

"And this one." Michelle sounds just plain tired now. "See this note here?"

I bend a little closer and see that Michelle herself put in a note this morning disqualifying the person because of a pending bankruptcy.

"Yes, that lead is unqualified," I say, hoping like hell I've used the right words.

"And what's missing here?" she asks. She opens the client data screen for this Tomlinson person.

"Nothing?" I ask. "No adviser assessment or contact was made?"

She slams a hand down on the desk. "Yes. Do you know why that is?" she asks.

I'm starting to get really sick of this game. "Michelle, please don't treat me like I'm stupid," I say. "If I made a mistake, please just say it. Show me what I did, and I'll make notes about what you want so I can try not to do it again."

I can't keep the irritation from my voice. This job sucks. I've been feeling it and thinking it. It's not Michelle. It's the whole business. I want to understand how to manage my money. I don't want to put a million transactions into a million systems and get called on the carpet like I'm an idiot. Maybe I am an idiot. Maybe I just don't care enough. Whatever it is, I'm starting to believe this job —this field, even—is not for me.

"Eden," Michelle says, her voice taking on a cold note that I've never heard before. "I have a history with Vito, and I thought—"

"Oh no." I hold up a finger. "Do not bring Vito into this. He has nothing to do with my performance on this job. If I've fucked up, you make this talk we're having about the work. This has nothing to do with my relationship or your ex."

Michelle is quiet, and she runs her tongue over her teeth, seeming to think for a minute. "This is my place of business, and I'd appreciate if you'd let me finish my statement."

I can't help myself. I cross my arms over my chest and lift my brow. "Please," I say, "finish your thought. What exactly did I do wrong?"

She sighs and waves her hand toward the computer. "You neglected to assign the contact to me, Eden. That means that

Tomlinson is stuck in the system without a contact owner." Everything else she says is a blur of buzzwords and jargon that I don't think I could repeat if my life depended on it. What I guess from her gesturing and tone is that I didn't pass along the message the right way.

"Wait," I say. "So, he's the guy who wanted the call back about the competing rate?"

Michelle's tone is condescending as she says, "You do remember. So, what? Is this all an act, then? I'm so flustered, I can't remember my own password."

My mouth falls open. "Are you mocking me?"

Michelle backpedals immediately. "I'm sorry. That was inappropriate. But you have to understand mistakes like this, carelessness about the tiniest details, those are the kinds of things that cost me money, Eden. Clients at this level expect a certain type of professionalism and service. You're just not meeting the expectations I had for you."

I'm not meeting expectations... I don't need a finance degree to know what that means.

"I'm not working out here," I say, not waiting for her to agree. "You took a chance on me, and I'm not good enough. Say no more."

"Eden, wait." Michelle leans her butt against the side of my desk. "I thought I could do something good for you, make up to Vito all the shit I put him through in the past. I still think you can learn this stuff. You just have to try harder. Pay attention. Care more. You have to act as though every client's business means the difference between making money and losing face."

I shake my head. "No," I say. "Michelle, I don't know why you thought offering me a job was a good idea. If you have shit to work out with Vito, see a shrink. He's moved on, and this..." I wave my hand around. "I don't need these kinds of favors from anyone." Since I haven't even put my purse down, I don't have to do anything but turn and march out of there. I start to, but then I turn back.

"Michelle," I say, "I looked up to you. I looked forward to learning from someone whom I thought saw something in me. But you've treated me just like you treated Vito. You want me to be better, faster, more than I am. You could have been more patient, but that would have just convinced me I should try harder at something that I already know isn't right for me." I clutch my purse and nod at her. "Thank you for the opportunity. I have learned a lot in the time I've worked for you, and I sincerely do appreciate that. I wish you all the best."

I turn on my heel and don't wait for her to fire me before I walk out.

It's still early. Today, Sassy and Lucia took Juniper and Ethan over to a massive sports complex that Gracie's husband Ryder manages.

Before I even realize what's happening, I'm heading to downtown Star Falls. It's not even noon yet, but sometimes Gracie goes to her sister-in-law's bookstore for coffee and peanut butter crisps before she starts work.

I park my car outside the bookstore and head inside. Chloe is at the front desk, tapping away at something on her iPad.

"Eden?" She comes around the counter and gives me a huge hug. I haven't spent a ton of time with Chloe over the last few months. Since she owns the bookstore, she doesn't come to Lucia's brunches, but she is a fixture at Sunday night family dinners.

I'm not as close to her as I am to Gracie, but I hope that can change in time.

"Hey, Chloe." I give her a weak hug and then sigh. "Any chance you have a book that can help me decide what to be when I grow up?"

"Oh God." She motions toward the back of the shop. "This sounds like a coffee and treat situation. You have time?"

I nod. "Nothing but time."

She runs to the back to grab some coffee, and I stroll through the children's book aisle and pick up a book for Junie, and then I wander back to the counter and pay for it.

"So..." Chloe pushes a coffee and a peanut butter crisp toward me.

"Mmm," I purr over the yummy treat. "These are amazing. I'd

love to learn how to bake if you're willing to teach me someday," I tell her. "You don't have to give away your recipe for these, but I'd love to learn to bake anything. I'm pretty basic in the kitchen."

Chloe nods. "Of course. I have some great cookbooks, too, I can loan you if you like to read. I don't keep a huge stock on hand in the store because so many people now are finding their recipe inspirations online. But I'll bring some to Sunday dinner for you."

When she says that, my throat goes a little bit dry and it's not from the cookie. She says it—she'll bring me something when she sees me at the next family dinner, like it's the most normal thing in the world.

Since when did having things like family dinners become so normal to me?

I feel like so much about my life is changing so fast, and instead of being scared or resisting it, I'm just happy. At least, with my home life and family, that is.

"What's this about needing help with what you want to be when you grow up?"

I sigh. "I don't know. I want to have a job that I love. Work that matters, you know? How did you know you wanted to do this?"

An elderly lady wearing a pair of bright-red-framed eyeglasses comes in and goes right up to the counter. She greets me in a very loud voice, and her colorful clothes make me think of Lucia's lady gang. The woman has perfectly styled white hair, and though she's pretty tiny and bent over, she's got a lot of spunk.

"Sorry to barge in." She sets a hand knotted by age on the counter, her nails painted bright red just like her glasses. "Chloe, I'm on the hunt for a book, doll. What do you get for the man who has everything?"

"Rita, is this for another boyfriend?" Chloe covers her mouth. "What happened to Mad Max?"

The older lady, Rita, blows air between her lips. "There's old and there's *old*. And that man was old. I've upgraded to a younger model." She covers her mouth with a hand and stage-whispers, "He's twenty-two years younger."

Chloe cackles and then points to me. "Rita, have you met Eden yet?"

Rita swivels on her heel and gives me her full attention. Her sharp eyes take me in, and she points a finger at me. "I don't know you, doll." She sticks out her hand. "I'd remember a beautiful face like that. And wow, you're tall."

I take her hand in mine and shake it lightly. "Nice to meet you," I say.

Chloe explains that I'm dating Vito, and before she can get out another word, Rita gasps. "Well, of course. No wonder I haven't met you. Vito knows better than to bring a beautiful woman around his brother. Have you met Benito yet?"

I nod. "I have, many times. I see him when he stops by the Sunday family dinners."

Rita looks pissed. "So, you're telling me Vito has brought you to family dinners but not to Benito's restaurant."

"Rita is the hostess at Benito's place," Chloe explains.

I grin. That explains so much. Every woman over fifty connected to the Bianchis must be cut from the same cloth—colorful, loud, and loving.

Rita motions for me to bend closer, and I do. "Come see me over lunch service. I'll make sure you get the best seat in the house."

"It's kid-friendly," Chloe adds. Then she tells Rita, "Eden has a daughter. She's about the same age at Ethan."

Rita practically crows. "Other people's children are my favorite kind. Bring the little one," she says, then she's back to business. "I'm looking for something maybe romantic. A little naughty would be good, very naughty even better. What do you have?" she asks.

Chloe winks at me and leads Rita toward the back of the store just as the front door opens, and a very familiar face makes my heart jump.

"What the heck are you doing here?" I rush through the store to give him a huge hug.

He kisses me lightly on the lips. "Hey, gorgeous. I think the real question is, what are you doing here? Aren't you supposed to work today?"

Crap.

"Well," I say. "Yeah. I mean, I was at work. I think we should maybe talk about it at home."

Vito's gorgeous face looks grim. "Something happen? Did Michelle do something?" He motions around the store. "You done here? You want to take a walk?"

I nod. "Yeah, I paid for my stuff. Let me grab my book." Vito takes my coffee cup, while I slip Junie's book into my purse. "You want the last bite?" I ask, offering him the very tiny bit of peanut butter crisp that's left.

"That's how I know you love me," he says, pointing to his open mouth.

I feed him the last bite and toss the paper wrapper into the trash bin behind the counter. "Should we say bye to Chloe?" I ask.

He cups his mouth and shouts, "Bye, Chloe. We got to run."

I laugh and hear a soft, "Bye, guys," echo from the back of the store.

Outside, we hold hands, lacing our fingers together. We stroll down Main Street past the storefronts, some open, some closed. The Body Shop, where Gracie works, is dark. She'll be here in an hour or so to open. It's wild to me that a place I'd never even visited six months ago is so familiar.

Star Falls has been close to perfect since the moment I drove into town, and it's only gotten better.

Most of it, at least.

I tighten my grip on Vito's hand and slow my steps a little. "Maybe we should talk about this at home. I…" I don't know where to start. I didn't even think about how Vito would react to what happened today.

"Babe." He stops completely in the middle of the sidewalk, stepping aside with a grin to let the people walking behind us pass. Once we're alone, he cups my face. "We can go home, but you've got me worried as fuck. What happened?"

"It's nothing bad," I say.

He relaxes his hold on my cheeks and nods. "Okay. You want to start talking?"

531

I shrug. "I think I got fired today. But I'm not sure because I kind of told Michelle off and left."

Vito's eyes widen, and he's silent for a second. "Okay," he finally says. "You want to back up? What the hell happened?" I can see the wheels beginning to move behind his eyes, and he's starting to look pissed.

I shake my head. "I don't like the job. I thought I would. I thought I'd like finance, but running a small office is the worst. I made a mistake, and Michelle got a little shitty with me—"

He clenches his hands into fists, and I stop him with a hand on his shoulder.

"She threw some weird shit about you at me, and I just lost it. It was polite enough, but I think it's clear that job wasn't going to work out."

"What do you need me to do?" he asks, shoving his hands into his pockets. "I don't know what to feel here, Eden."

"Babe." I touch the scruff on his chin, the beautiful, prickly stubble that sends little ripples of excitement through my body just touching him like this, out on the sidewalk in front of the world. "Can we please go home? I want to think through what to do, and I just…" I check the time on my phone. "Your mom has got Juniper at Ryder's gym thing with Ethan and Sassy."

His expression is grim, and I honestly don't know whether he's mad at me or with me. But it's better I find out now while there may still be time to fix it.

CHAPTER NINETEEN

I'm glad I have the drive home to myself to sort out my feelings. The first thing I feel is rage.

If Michelle made Eden feel any kind of way—bad about herself, bad about me—I'm going to march my ass into that office and tear her a new one. Ex-wife or not, she has no right to talk shit to Eden.

I trusted that Michelle was more mature than that. I trusted that her intentions toward Eden were honest. Maybe I should be a lot less trusting and a lot more protective.

I won't make that mistake again.

"Tell me everything," I demand, pointing to the couch for Eden to sit. "Because if I need to go over there, I won't even take off my shoes."

"Vito," she says. She slips out of her high heels, and together, we walk to sit side by side on the couch. "Are you mad at her or me?"

I can't help the look on my face. I'm sure I'm looking at her like she grew horns, but I can't imagine on what planet she'd think I'm mad at her. "I don't care if you took a shit on her office floor," I tell her. "I'd never be mad at you." I curl the side of my mouth in a grin. "I might offer to rent a carpet cleaner to help with the damage, but be mad at you? Babe, I trust you. I love you. Whatever happened, I'm on your side."

She shakes her head. "I fucked up. I missed a step putting in some data and might have cost Michelle a big client."

I frown. "That sucks, but so what? That's a pretty fragile business if some data-entry error can cost Michelle a client."

She nods, the long layers of her hair falling around her shoulders. "Michelle is pretty intense," she says. "She's great at what she does, but I didn't like it. It was passwords and lame shit that, honestly, I just didn't care about."

I nod. "Do you think it's just the newness of everything, or do you think you really don't like the field?"

She shrugs. "Both. I don't know. It wasn't the right job for me. I'm sure about that. I just have no idea what else I'd want to do."

I blow air through my lips. "Put a pin in that. What the hell did Michelle say about me, and do I need to beat anyone's ass today? I wouldn't hit Michelle, but if I need to blast some eardrums, I'm ready to start yelling."

Eden shakes her head and looks down at her lap. "No, it was fine. It was. She said something about trying to make amends to you by helping me, but I told her I didn't want her bringing you into my job performance."

"Good on you," I tell her. "Anything else?"

"No. It wasn't that big of a deal, it just felt huge. I've never walked out on a job before."

I pull Eden close to me and smooth the hair back from her face. "That takes balls, baby. Not a lot of people would do that, no matter the circumstances." I take in the tightness around her lips and the sad way she's furrowing her brows. "So, you're unemployed? Are you worried?"

She sighs. "Yes, I'm unemployed again, I guess. And no, I'm not worried. I'm just bummed. What the hell do I do with my life now?"

"You try something new, babe. It's that simple. And if you hate it, you move on to the next. Rinse and repeat."

"You make it sound so easy. Like it's no big deal. Did you ever think about doing anything else with your life? Do you ever think about the what-ifs?"

"I think about quitting almost every shift," I admit quietly. "When I see the kind of shit I see, I always wonder if that last call is going to be the one that breaks me. Make it so I can't go back, even if I want to."

She's stroking my thigh with a hand as I talk, and the effect is incredibly distracting but in the best way.

"But then I think about why I do it. And I know I'll never be able to sit back and hear sirens and not respond. It's just who I am. I'm sorry figuring out a career hasn't been that straightforward for you, but can I make a suggestion?"

"Anything," she says.

"Maybe steer clear of my exes. I think we can assume that shit won't end well."

She laughs and says, "Exes? What, do I need a list of names or something?"

"You've already worked for the big one, so I think you're pretty safe. Maybe don't apply for a job at the high school. Or the middle school…"

"Vito."

"I'm teasing," I tell her, although I did ghost a middle school teacher last summer and had to block her number, but that's not something we need to get into today.

"So, I guess I won't need to buy any more suits," she says, looking down at the pencil skirt and tailored blouse.

"Hmm," I mumble. "Or you could just buy them for me. I can think of a lot of ways to make sure your wardrobe doesn't go to waste."

"Like what?" she asks. "We've got some time before Juniper and your mom are due back here."

"Yes," I hiss and grab her hand. "It's like surprise date night in the middle of the day." I tug her up the stairs and close and lock the bedroom door behind us.

"This is like early Christmas," she breathes.

I nod, heat flooding my body. "And you are the sexiest package under the tree."

She rests her rear on the edge of the bed and crosses her legs. "So, you like my business attire?"

"I like it so much, I want to tear it off your body," I say, licking my lips. "I want to take off those hose with my teeth."

Eden giggles and lifts her brows at me. "I'm not sure how easy that's going to be with this skirt on. Maybe I should take that off first?"

I shake my head. "Let me do everything." I stand in front of her and reach for her hands so I can help her up off the bed. "Turn, please," I say, wrapping my hands around her waist and spinning her around so she's facing the bed.

She laughs again, her hair twirling and grazing my face with its luscious, vanilla-coconut scent as she turns. "Now what?"

I reach for the waistband of the skirt and feel for the hook closure at the back. I unfasten it, then grab the zipper, and, inch by slow inch, work my hand along the length of her ass. Once the zipper is undone, I put a hand on either side of her ass and massage her through the fabric of the unzipped skirt.

"Your body," I whisper, dropping to my knees. I reach for the skirt and work it slowly over her hips. I stop when the fabric is just past her butt and suck in a breath. "Do you not wear underwear to work?"

She looks at me over her shoulder, a playful expression on her face. "Maybe?"

"Oh God." In one swift move, I yank the skirt down around her ankles, revealing her long, thick legs wrapped in sheer black nylons. "Not going to lie," I say, running my hands over her ass. "I'm thinking about biting right through these."

Her whole body trembles lightly. "These are cheap drugstore hose."

"Noted." I shove her forward onto the bed. "Get comfortable," I tell her. "I'm going to take my time."

While she's lying facedown, I unbutton my jeans and shed my flannel. When I'm barefoot and in my boxers, I open her legs as wide as they will go while she's still facedown. Then I climb onto the bed behind her and kiss every inch of her left leg, starting at the calf.

I massage the soft fabric of the nylons under my hands as I blow hot kisses along her skin. She wriggles and moans while I work my way up to her thigh, but then I switch and cover her right leg in as much attention as I gave the left.

"Good?" I ask, landing a firm smack against her butt.

"Oh yes." She's resting with her left cheek on the bed, so I can see her eyes are closed and her mouth slightly open. "Babe, that is intense."

"Good." I knead the back of her thighs and calves through the hose until her breathing becomes so even, I'm afraid she's going to fall asleep. That is the opposite of what I want. I move up to her waist and push the hem of her blouse up so the waistband of her hose is exposed. Then I start kissing her lower back, flicking my tongue along her bare skin. She moans and wiggles her hips in response, so I add a little teeth.

I nip at her soft, hot skin and try to grab a bit of the fabric between my teeth, but I end up cracking up and giving in. "All right, I may need to take these off, not bite them off."

Eden lifts her head and says in a soft whisper, "I want them off."

A feral growl works its way from my chest to my lips. "Turn over."

She rolls onto her back and unbuttons her blouse, exposing the modest petal-pink bra underneath.

"Shirt off," I demand, and still lying back, she works her arms out of the sleeves. "Show me your gorgeous breasts."

She nudges the thin satin bra cups past her nipples, the erect peaks stiff and pink. My mouth waters to taste them, but first, I have plans for these hose.

I climb onto the bed and sit between her legs, reaching for the nylons. I make quick work of them and toss them to the floor before I settle my face between her thighs.

I turn my head and kiss her inner thigh, squeezing her thick legs with my hands while working her tender skin with my mouth.

Her breathing is ragged and she's trying to bend her knees, but I use my palms to open her legs as wide as they can go.

I lower my mouth and suck hard, drawing her soft skin into my mouth.

I dip two fingers in my mouth to wet them, then make a V-shape with my fingers and stroke her outer lips.

"V," she breathes, clutching the comforter in her hands. "I need you inside me." And then she's gone before I can protest.

She hustles from the bed to the bathroom, opens and closes a drawer, and then comes back with a condom already out of the foil. She rolls it over my dick, then strokes my balls lightly with her nails.

"Eden…" I pant.

She smiles and straddles my legs and lowers herself onto my cock. We both moan as I enter her, the feeling as perfect and delicious as ever.

Arousal weakens my hands and knees, and I just lie there, my back against the pillows, while Eden grips my shoulders with her hands and grinds on my cock with long, sensual movements of her belly and hips.

I open my eyes to watch her, her chest flushed pink, her nipples still hard and exposed over the bra cups. I feel a tightening deep in my gut, and I can hardly keep my eyes open, the pleasure is so, so good. Eden's movements are sexy and slow until she whimpers and starts working her hips so fast and rhythmically, we're banging the bed frame against the wall.

But then, just as she arches her back and cries out, both of our phones ping at once with the distinctive chime of the home security system.

She clamps her lips closed and rides out her climax, then drops forward and whispers in my ear, "Hurry, babe. Fuck me hard."

She doesn't need to say another word of invitation. I grip her hips to hold her in place and pound into her as fast as I can. Within seconds, I'm falling over the edge and spilling inside the condom, my breathing rapid and my hair falling forward into my eyes.

"We need more of these afternoons," I grunt as she climbs off me, taking the condom with her.

"Let's not tell anyone I got fired. At least until we have one more morning to ourselves. Deal?"

I lean forward and grab her arm, pulling her back toward the bed so I can kiss her. "Deal, baby. Now, get rid of that, and let's get changed before my ma comes up here looking for us."

She giggles and hustles off to the bathroom. I grab my phone and send my ma a text, not at all willing to trust that she won't run up here to say hello since both our cars are outside.

Me: Remember the other day when I walked in on you and Pops in the kitchen? Unless you're in the mood for paybacks, keep Junie downstairs for about five more minutes.

I immediately get a text back with a load of smiley face and mind-blown emojis. I just grin because she's exactly right. That's exactly how I feel. And I have never, ever been happier.

epilogue

EDEN

Six months later

I tighten Juniper's scarf around her neck while I wait for Vito to unlock his parents' house. We're arriving a little later than planned, and I'm afraid we're going to miss seeing Benito before he has to get back to the restaurant.

Vito gives me a bright smile as he holds the door open, and I slosh through the front door in my snow boots. I take off little Junie's boots and jacket and set her on her feet. She's walking like crazy now, and she can't stand to be carried except through the ankle-deep snow.

As soon as she's down, she takes off running and squeals when she almost crashes into Ethan, who is lying on the floor playing with Lucia's older lab mix.

We decided to wait until summer to get a dog, when house-training won't mean constantly mopping up snow and slush from the floor. If the way Junie plays with her grandparents' dogs is any indication, she's going to absolutely adore having a puppy of her own in a few months.

Vito kicks off his boots and hangs both his coat and mine on hooks by the door while I unlace my boots.

"Benny?" Vito cocks his head at the full house ahead of us. "I thought we'd miss you, man. Sorry we're late."

"Baby." Lucia blows me a kiss but stops to loudly smooch Juniper's cheeks. Junie laughs and squirms away, preferring to play with her cousins than be loved on by Gramma Lucia.

We have been living together now for well over six months and dating for almost ten months, so we decided it's simpler to give everyone family names.

As Juniper learns to talk, I thought it would be a lot easier for her to learn to say Gramma than it would be to say Lucia and then later, if Vito and I get married, start calling her by another name.

As much as I love and adore Vito, and I know we're both in this for the long haul, we're in no rush to move any faster than this.

He has his own bedroom at our house with blackout curtains so he can sleep when he needs to. His parents have become like the parents I never had and always wanted.

I'm close with Gracie and Chloe, and I've even become close to Ryder since I started working with him at the children's athletics facility he's opened.

"Hey, hey, there she is." Ryder swoops past Ethan and Juniper to kiss me on the cheek. "How'd it go?"

I grin and punch him in the shoulder. "Take a wild guess."

Ryder shrugs. "I don't know."

I clap my hands together and cross my arms over my chest, preening at what I'm about to tell him. "Prepare to be amazed. Seventy kids from the Star Falls community are now enrolled in a fully funded adapted sports league."

"Whoa, whoa. Hold up." Ryder looks at me with his mouth wide open. "I looked at the numbers on Friday. What the heck happened between then and today?"

Vito comes up alongside me and slings an arm over my shoulder. "My girl went out on some calls."

I nod. For the last three months, I've been working for Ryder's start-up. It turns out that my interest in finance isn't totally going to waste. I have quite the knack for fundraising. He asked me a few months ago if I'd have any interest in seeing what the Star Falls business community's interest would be in sponsoring an adaptive sports league.

Buying specialized equipment like swings and safety gear, not to mention hiring well-trained aides to help run the league, is expensive. Like, made my head swim expensive. But I know there's money out there for good causes, especially for those businesses that want local PR.

You know I went knocking on Michelle's door, and sure enough, she opened the checkbook and donated enough to fund an entire year of sports camps and equipment for one child with special needs.

Ryder had a goal of being able to serve fifty kids, but I wanted to blow that number out of the water.

I spent time while Vito was off on Saturday driving to local businesses and pitching sponsors face-to-face. Turns out, small towns are special places. A bunch of the businesses that hadn't been interested during our phone campaign welcomed me in, listened to my pitch, and opened their checkbooks.

"Holy shit, Eden." Ryder's eyes are wide, and he's yanking his phone from his pocket. "Does Austin know? I have to tell him."

Lucia comes in from the kitchen, a platter loaded high with homemade meatballs in her arms. "I heard that."

Ryder grimaces and calls out, "Sorry, Ma." Grace slips under his arm and tucks a hand in his back pocket.

"Look at you," Gracie says. "Killing it out there. Keep it up, and Ryder's going to give you an office."

"Marry that woman," Ryder says, pointing at Vito. "Don't let this one go."

"I think he's got me pretty locked down," I say, giving Ryder a grin.

Vito leaves us and heads to the dining room table, where Benito is furiously tapping into his phone. "Yo, idiot," he says, smacking the back of his head. "No phones at the table."

Benito gives his brother the stink eye and smooths his hair back. "You're the idiot. I'm dealing with shit."

"Benito." Mario scowls at Benny over his glasses. "Don't make your mother bring out the swear jar." Pops fills the wineglasses and sets the empty bottle on the table, then grabs a second.

We're a big group now, but Sunday dinner is a requirement. Chloe and Franco sit knee-to-knee talking, Benny finishes sending his text, while Gracie corrals all her kids to their seats. Vito picks up Junie and places her in his lap—her favorite place to sit during family meals.

"Why are you here anyway?" Gracie needles, lifting a brow at Benito. "You not working today or something?"

Benito strokes his brow with his fingers and waves a hand at his sister. "Is it a crime that I actually want to take a day off? I've got the kitchen covered. I'm going to spend a whole family dinner with my family for once."

Gracie and Vito trade looks, but they leave the issue be. The Bianchis know how to tease one another, but they also know when too much is too much.

There was a time when a family meal like this might have been too much for me. The noise, the heat, the food, the conversation.

But today, I take my seat at the table beside Vito and feel completely at home.

"So," Vito says, clinking a fork against his water glass. "We have a little announcement. It's little, so Ma, get that look off your face. No babies, no weddings. Nothing like that."

Lucia puts a pout on her lips and waves her matching pink nails at her son. "Is it too much for a mother to want more grandchildren? Is that so wrong?"

"Not wrong at all," Mario says, shaking his head. "Go on, son. What's the news?"

"It's not so much news as just an FYI." He leans down to kiss Juniper's cheek. "You guys know Juniper turned two a couple weeks ago."

Ryder pats his belly. "We're still eating leftover cake out of the freezer."

"That's for the kids," Gracie says, shaking her head and giving him a loving squeeze.

"Yeah, well, Juniper got me a little present for her birthday." He moves aside the unbuttoned flannel shirt to reveal a T-shirt that reads: Best Dad in Star Falls.

"Hey," Mario says, followed by a, "That's what I was going to say," from Ryder.

Lucia alone covers her mouth and cries out with joy. "What does this mean, hun? You're not pregnant, you're not getting married…?"

Vito looks at me, and I explain. "Junie's learning so many new words every day. I figured since she's calling all of you by your family names—Gramma and Papa, Auntie and Uncle—we should teach her to…" I stop, my voice catching on the words. My eyes fill with tears, and my nose stings with the happiest kind of joy. "We should teach her to call Vito Dad."

"Oh my God." Lucia jumps up and kisses me and Vito, then lays a loud, juicy smooch on Juniper's cheek.

Mario raises his glass but says, "To one of the best dads in Star Falls."

"The best." Vito corrects.

"I'll fight you on that. I got one of the best dads in town right here," Gracie says.

As the family devolves into a debate over which of the dads in the room is the best, I reach under the table and lace my fingers through Vito's and squeeze.

He's the best man I've ever known. The only father Juniper has ever had.

He's my family, my partner, my friend. Neither one of us really wants to go back to school.

Vito's stopped applying for promotions at work, figuring that any extra time he has, he'd rather spend with our daughter or on our house.

I may not have it all figured out, but I have everything that I really need. Everything I've always wanted.

No matter what the future brings, jobs will come and go. Money will come and go. But the love I have for these people and this life—that's what's going to stay.

I never dreamed I could have this kind of happiness. And every once in a while, I still get worried that Vito will leave or that Nathan will come back and try to mess up the life I've built for Juniper and myself.

But every time the worries work their way in, I do what I'm doing right now. I reach out and touch the daughter who gives my life meaning. The man who makes me whole.

I have never been happier, and I know Vito and I are going to do everything we can to make this relationship last.

This is what making a life is for me. Imperfect. Loud. Full of people with small-town hearts and open arms.

And as long as I have them, everything else is going to fall into place.

I lift my wineglass and clink it against Vito's, then pass Benito the salad. We eat our meal in the soft glow of the candles on the table, the warmth of the people crammed elbow-to-elbow on more chairs than the table should fit.

We're so close, I can hardly move without bumping into Vito or Benny, but I love it.

As long as I'm part of this extended Bianchi clan, we can never be too close.

never too MUCH

www.chellebliss.com

CHELLE BLISS

USA TODAY BESTSELLING AUTHOR

CHAPTER ONE

benito

"Benito, get inside. You're going to catch your death."

I try to shake the rain from my hair, but it doesn't matter. I'm drenched. I'm pretty sure my raincoat hit its saturation point about two hours ago, but that's what I get for trying to save a few bucks by taking the delivery guys off the schedule.

"I'm all right." I wave my hand at Rita, the hostess who acts like she's the one who owns this restaurant, not me.

She clicks her tongue, and all five-foot-nothing of her huffs to the front door. "You're the hardest working man in Star Falls, but this is too much. You're going to make yourself sick."

There's love under her motherly warning. In fact, Rita prides herself on being an honorary mother to everyone who works at Benito's. Which means I not only have to put up with my own smothering mother, but I have one at my restaurant too.

"I'll take you home tonight," I tell her, wiping the back of my hand over the raindrops dripping down my face. "Lights are out across town, side streets have puddles deep enough to swim in. You're not driving."

Rita wags a highly polished fingernail at me and then points toward the parking lot. "You think I drove myself? With the forecast we had?"

I look through the glass door and see the headlights of the station wagon that belongs to Rita's much-younger boyfriend. And by much younger, I mean seventysomething to her eighty.

"Thanks for the offer, sweetheart, but I have a ride home." Rita rests her bottom against her stool and carefully slips on her rain boots. "And if I'm lucky, I'll have a ride *at* home too." She twists her glossy red lips into a pucker and blows me an air kiss.

I chuckle, trying not to cringe at the image of Rita getting lucky back in the senior community where she lives. "Anybody left inside?" I ask while Rita gathers her purse and umbrella.

"One at the bar," she says, "and there's a couple at table ten." She lifts a hand up to pat my cheek, and I bend down so she can actually reach me. She grips my chin in still-strong fingers. "Now you go dry off and get some rest," she tells me.

I grin at her and hold the door while she opens her umbrella. But before she can protest, I grab the flimsy handle from her and tuck her protectively under my arm. I angle the thin black fabric, pointing the tip of the umbrella into the wind, trying to keep it from flapping the wrong direction and leaving us both exposed to this brutal storm.

I hurry her through the buckets of rain pounding against the paved parking lot until we finally reach the passenger door of the waiting vehicle. I yank open the door and see Samuel, whose big smile glimmers under his bristly white beard.

"Benito," he says, the windshield wipers running on high speed, a measured rhythm that feels predictable and comforting. "Good to see you."

I nod at Samuel, holding the umbrella against the pouring rain while Rita climbs into the car. Once she's in, I close the umbrella, shake it off, and set it beside her boots in the footwell. "Get home safe," I say, then close the door and hoof it back toward the restaurant, trying not to skid and fall on my already-wet ass.

I meet a couple coming out just as I'm going back in. This must be my couple from table ten, so I wish them a safe drive and watch as they duck their heads and hurry toward their car.

I flip the small sign on the front door to Closed, lock the dead bolt, and blow out a hot breath that leaves a tiny mist of fog on the glass. If I have one more customer at the bar, I'll want to make sure he's able to get home safely before I let him out.

I shake my arms, covering the floor with water from my raincoat, and head toward the bar.

"Jesus. You need a towel?" Maggie, my kitchen manager, spots me before I even make it five feet into the restaurant.

I shrug. "I'm all right, Mags. Everybody else go?"

She tosses me a look. "Of course. You told us to close the kitchen early. You think I need to tell those heathens twice?" She chuckles, then gives me a wave. "I'm out too, now that you're back. Jasmine's up front at the bar, but once she sees you, I'm sure she's going to take off. You're good to lock up?"

I nod. "Drive safe."

She nods. "Will do." She jerks a thumb toward the kitchen, and her expression grows serious. "Benny. You remember about tomorrow?"

I tug down my hood and stifle a groan. Truth is, I remember nothing. So much goes into running this place, and Mags is my right hand. She could mean I'm meeting a new bread vendor or that we have a fire system inspection. I don't have a freaking clue.

"Refresh me?" I say, bracing for Maggie's ire. She's been riding me hard the last few months—and with good reason. I've been running like a chicken with my head cut off. If Mags didn't put food in front of me, I'd probably forget to eat most days. Not a good look for the head chef and owner of his own restaurant.

"Jesus, Benito." Her brows, lips, and tone make me feel ten years old again, although my parents would never invoke Jesus when scolding me. Ma still keeps a swear jar in the house even though all her kids have grown up and moved out, and my Italian parents aren't that religious, but we don't take anyone's name in vain if we can help it. Mags doesn't seem to have that same concern, because she's muttering something I can't make out under her breath.

Finally, she frowns, her words sharp as a paring knife. "This is important, Benito. You know we need that grant."

Fuuuuck.

The grant.

"Right, yes. I know, I know, Mags. I got it." I nod, trying to reassure her that I do remember and that I will take this thing seriously. I don't tell her I'll have to dig for the email she sent me weeks ago to remember what *this thing* even is.

Mags and I have a very different opinion about what this business needs. The problem is, I'm a short-term thinker, and she's got vision, which means, in this case, I know she's right. I've got to make more of an effort to see things her way, but before I can say anything, she huffs at me and heads back toward the kitchen.

"Mags," I call out. "Mags, I'll go. I'm going to go."

She stops but doesn't turn back to face me. "Tomorrow. Nine thirty in the morning. You got the address?"

"I got the address." Well, I probably do. Somewhere in my emails or maybe in my texts. I'll find it, and I'm not going to piss off the best employee I have by admitting I only think I know where it is. "Thanks, Mags."

She heads back toward the kitchen to clock out, and I sigh. Without Mags's anger and Rita to worry about, I can finally release some of the tension in my shoulders. The warmth of the restaurant starts drying my damp hair, although my toes are an entirely different story.

Star Falls is a beautiful place to live every day of the year, but when Mother Nature decides to whoop our asses, she doesn't play around.

The rubber soles of my boots squeak on the tile as I pass from the front of the restaurant toward the dining room. I can see there is someone still seated at the bar, but it's not a guy, as I assumed. In fact, from what I can see of her back, the blonde cozied up to my bar looks young. Almost too young.

I toss the bartender, Jasmine, a questioning look, but it's lost on her. She gives me the same shocked frown that Rita and Maggie did. "Did you swim to make all those food deliveries?" she asks.

552

"Just about," I sigh. "You got any coffee made, Jas?"

She shakes her head but offers to make some.

"Nah." I wave my hand. But then I point to the woman on the barstool. "Unless you'd like some for the road?"

At my words, the customer turns slightly on the barstool to face me. I can see right away she's not underage. The crinkles around her eyes when she grins at me assure me she's at least my age. I'm relieved, though I never doubted Jas. She's got a seventeen-year-old son at home who got busted for underage drinking at a lake party this past summer. She grounded his ass for three whole months. I trust her to bring that same mama energy to my business and not serve anyone who isn't legal, even if the whole damn place is empty now.

The woman on the barstool sucks her full lower lip into her mouth and squints at me. "Coffee for the road?" she repeats. "Is that your way of telling me the kitchen's closed?" She softens her words with a grin. "I'm not from around here, so if I'm overstaying your hours…I can take a hint."

Jasmine glares at me and sets two empty mugs on the bar. "You're fine," she says to the woman, giving me a look that I'm sure means something. But right now, I'm too damn wet and cold to interpret my bartender's silent messages. "I'm going to make some coffee. He needs it, even if you don't."

Jas busies herself filling the pot, and I motion to a stool a couple down from the woman. "You mind?" I ask. "No need to entertain me. I've been running deliveries for hours. I'm dying to get off my feet."

My customer waves a hand in silent invitation for me to sit, then she pats the stool beside her. "I wouldn't mind some company."

I shrug out of my wet jacket before laying it over a stool and taking the seat beside her.

I roll my neck and grimace a little when the joints crack as I work out the tightness. I heave a tired sigh, then shove the wet hair back from my face. "New to town, you said?" I ask.

"Here for business," she says, turning a little on her stool.

I look up when Jas sets two steaming mugs of coffee in front of us, along with a condiment caddy containing sugar and creamer.

"Thanks, Jas. You out of here?" I ask, directing the question to my employee.

"You bet your behind I'm out of here." Jasmine motions to the coffeepot. "Be a doll and turn that off before you go? I'll clean it when I open tomorrow."

I nod and then look to the woman beside me. "Jas is about to go. You can stay and finish your coffee. No rush. But if you want anything else…"

"I closed out my bill already," she interrupts, giving me a smile. "But I'll pay cash for the coffee."

Jas already has her purse over her shoulder and her jacket on, tucking her hair under the hood. "Coffee's on the house," she calls, knowing I won't mind. "Everybody get home safe."

After she bustles away, I shake three packets of sugar into my coffee and roll the tiny paper envelopes between my fingers. It suddenly strikes me that I'm famished. I worked through the dinner shift and haven't eaten since lunch. That feels like it was days ago. I reach for one more sugar—even if that only means a couple more calories, I'll take them.

"You know," the woman beside me says, breaking the sudden quiet, "far be it from me to criticize because the meal I ate tonight was absolutely fantastic…"

My gut tightens at her words. I'm braced for the "but." Embedded in that compliment is *something*. A searing critique of my small-town Italian eatery. The outdated carpet. The renovated home with a slightly kitschy vibe that gives Benito's its family atmosphere. I'm a fantastic fucking cook, but I'm a one-man show. I do the orders, the inventory, staffing, training, and, like tonight, I even fill in for deliveries when I have to. And while this woman can't know I'm hanging on by a thread here, I am. She can't know that, but whatever she has to say, I'm sure as hell not in the mood for it.

"Go on," I say, forcing my tight voice to loosen a little. She has no idea who I am. No idea I own the place. That the name on the front sign is me. I could just tell her I'm off the clock, not interested in talking about work. But she's a customer, so I grip my mug a little tighter, take a sip, and wait for whatever critique she has.

She reaches past me and grabs the rolled-up remnants of my sugar packets. "A sugar sifter would be more eco-friendly. Less packaging. Less paper waste."

Huh?

I wasn't expecting that. She could have insulted the decor, the food... But I can't exactly sniff at a sustainability suggestion. To be fair, shit like that—small cost-saving measures that are good for the environment—are on my long list of things to do. They're just so far down the list, I don't know if I'll ever get to them.

"Great idea," I say, trying not to sound like I'm dismissing her. "Although that would mean there would be all these little plastic condiment caddies going to waste. What's worse? Paper in the trash or plastic?"

She opens her mouth to say something but then just looks me over, as if she can't decide whether I'm fucking with her or not.

"I'm kidding," I say lightly, giving her a smile that I hope will distract her from any more comments about how I run my restaurant.

She swivels her stool so it faces me and crosses one slim leg over the other, the tip of her sleek boot slightly grazing the damp leg of my jeans. "I'm Willow," she says, thick brown eyebrows narrowing as she studies my face. "Nice to meet you."

I set down my coffee and rub my hands together to warm them. "I'm Ben," I say, giving her a shortened form of my nickname. If she associates "Ben" with "Benito," as in the name painted on the front door, she doesn't show it.

We shake hands, holding on to each other a little too long at the end.

After our introduction, I realize how quiet the restaurant is. The sound of the rain hitting the roof and splashing against the windows is soothing.

This is my place. My restaurant. The place I've built from the ground up, and while it's a chaotic life, it's mine. This place and the people who work here are everything I care about. Everything that makes me who I am. Well, after my family, that is.

I'm enjoying the quiet and the stillness after the rumble of the furnace kicks off, when the woman beside me lifts the mug to her lips and takes a deep sip. "Can I be honest with you?" she asks.

The low vibration of her sensual, confident voice curls around my ears like a whisper, but it also hits me like a ton of bricks. I'm not sure if she is hitting on me, is lonely, or is just looking for a little conversation. But damn, my body takes notice of every inch of her as she leans toward me.

Her eyes sparkle, the gray almost identical to the stormy skies outside. Her face is free of makeup, but the feature I am most transfixed by is just inches from my face. This woman's top lip has sharply defined peaks, but the lower lip is full and soft. She's nibbling it between her teeth, a playful smirk on her face.

"You want to be honest?" I repeat, warming inside when I meet her eyes. "Star Falls is a small town. If you plan on staying for any length of time, you'll find out trash talk travels faster than this storm did. I'm not much for gossip, so go for it. Speak your mind." I point to the condiment caddy. "Unless you plan on trying to talk me out of putting sugar in my coffee. Then I'd tell you to take your opinions and…"

She's grinning at me like she's known me forever, and she reaches over to touch my arm. "And what?" she presses.

I smile, relaxing into the light touch on my arm. "Let's just promise to keep things honest. Now, lay your truth on me."

She grins again, the flush on her cheeks brightening her whole face. "Have you had the kale ravioli?" she asks. Her voice is so full of quiet enthusiasm, it's like she's asking me if I've got the combination to the safe and she's a bank robber.

I nod, trying my best not to preen. The kale ravioli is my signature dish. It's colorful and rich, nutty and satisfying.

I know it's good.

I know I'm good. But I'm more than happy to sit here and listen to her say it.

"Mm-hm," I mumble. "And?"

She rolls her eyes back and flutters her lids closed. "That," she says dramatically, "was one of the best damn dishes I've ever eaten. I may just have to try to copy the recipe."

I look her over, a swell of pride lifting my chest.

"You liked it?" I ask casually, acting as if I'm bored, even though I know I'm shamelessly baiting her for more. "You had the kale?"

"I loved it," she says. "The perfect balance of comfort food and elevated dining. Totally unexpected."

Her light blond hair is pulled back into a ponytail, the long end resting on the curve of her right shoulder. She's wearing black jeans that barely reach the tops of ankle-high black boots. Her turtleneck is white, and I find myself scanning the front of it to see if she has any droplets of sauce to prove that she actually enjoyed my signature dish. I'm not sure I could eat a great pasta dish—let alone an exceptional one—without spilling at least a few drops on myself.

But as soon as my eyes travel to the front of her body, I realize I look like I'm checking her out. She catches me, her face studying the movement of my eyes over her figure, but she sure doesn't look like she minds.

I have a reputation around Star Falls for being a ladies' man. I've had more than my fair share of bartenders and waitresses walk off the job after spending the night with me and finding out that one night together did not make us *a couple*.

But Willow is hot and seems uninhibited. She hardly knows me and yet is pouring on the charm. I'm either much sexier drenched by the rain, or this woman is hard up for companionship. I'm not sure I care. It's been a long day and a very long time since I've had a night of fun. If I'm reading the signs right, she might leave my restaurant with a lot more than a memory of the best damn meal she's eaten.

"I'm not in town for long," Willow says, resting her palm on her knee when we finally pull our hands away. "What's fun to do in Star Falls?"

The truth is, I don't have a damn clue what's fun anymore. I work, sleep, and occasionally fuck. I'm thinking that very thing when I feel a gentle nudge against my arm.

"Say it," she urges. She's smiling at me, the curve of her upper lip begging to be sucked. I can't resist a beautiful woman, but the more I look at her, the more I can see this woman is not merely attractive. She's confident and assertive. She's a stranger in town, alone at a bar, and she's most definitely flirting with me. I'm sure of it now. And I'm not about to let a torrential rainstorm put a damper on this flame.

"Say what?" I ask, drawing out my words and grinning.

"Whatever you were thinking," she says, a tease in her voice. She runs a fingertip along the lip of her coffee mug and cocks her chin at me. "The look that you had on your face was seriously naughty."

"Naughty," I echo, shaking my head. "Yeah, it was."

"So..." she urges. "Come on, Ben. What were you thinking? What's fun to do in Star Falls?"

I sip the last of my coffee and set the mug back onto the saucer. I chuckle. "Honestly," I tell her, "I was thinking all I do is work, sleep, and occasionally fuck. That's what I do for fun."

"That's perfect," she says, leaning toward me. "Because I was about to ask who I have to fuck to get a copy of that ravioli recipe."

CHAPTER TWO

willow

I don't have a five-year plan.

I have a one-year rule.

And that rule is never, ever stay in one place for too long. There is so much freedom in living with a finite horizon ahead. It's made me fearless in the face of so many things that scared me. Offered me peace when everything around me felt like chaos.

And when it comes to getting what I want, there is no better motivator than the one-year rule.

How would your life change if you knew with every certainty that you would be someplace else, surrounded by a whole new group of people, doing something totally unique, at the end of one year?

You can damn well bet that you wouldn't sit around and wait for anything.

Not for the promotion. Not for a call from some guy. Not for anything.

So much can happen in one short year, but if you sit on your bum and stay in place?

I won't ever let myself get stuck that way.

Never again.

I'm one week into my one-year experiment in Star Falls. This is my last night in the hotel before moving in to the condo my company has rented me for the next twelve months.

I had no intention of hooking up with anyone when I finally made it to the little Italian place everyone in Star Falls raves about. I can't even remember the name of the restaurant now... Bruno's or something. I've been working nonstop and have so many restaurant names in my mind and so many people to meet, it's all a bit of a blur.

What are the odds that I'd meet a hot delivery driver on a cold, rainy night? The only thing waiting for me in my hotel room is a *probably* stale half bottle of Chianti and a vibrator that most definitely needs to be charged.

Our banter is fun.

And when he stands up from the bar to turn off the coffee, he gifts me a glimpse of his ass that has me rethinking my usual safety protocols. He's tall, dark, thick, and funny.

Exactly my type.

But since I am not about to end up the lead story on a true crime podcast, I need to pump the brakes just a little.

While he clears away our mugs and stands to lock up the restaurant, I pull my phone from my purse and text my friend Jessa.

Me: Met a hot guy. May take him back to the hotel. You've got my location?

Two seconds later, I get a row of thumbs-up and celebration emojis.

Jessa: Send me a picture... And be safe.

The little text bubble appears and then a second text.

Jessa: I'll call the cops if you don't text me in two hours. Where are you again?

I message her back, remind her Star Falls, Ohio, and promise to check in. Then I thank my lucky stars that she's on bed rest and staring at her phone with very little to do.

You'd think with a one-year rule, I wouldn't have a lot of friends, but the opposite is true. I've found that the ones who really matter stick around in my life, no matter where the road takes me. New

York, Nashville, Austin, Omaha, Monterey... I've lived everywhere and belong no place. But I have so much love in my life from dozens of friends I've met along the way.

Star Falls may be three time zones away from Jessa, but if she didn't answer, I have two dozen other close girlfriends who'd have my back. Maybe not as immediately as Jess does, but she is sitting three times zones away, cooking a baby who might decide to come months too early if Jessa so much as lifts a finger.

I text back, imagining the stack of paperbacks and adult coloring books I shipped her last week sitting on her bedside table, then turn my attention back to the hometown hottie.

Me: Love you. Feet up and tits out. Cook that baby until well done.

Ben dims the lights in the restaurant and nods at my phone. "You need a ride? Might be tough to get a rideshare at this hour, especially in this weather." His smile is sincere, almost apologetic. "Small-town living."

My car should be arriving along with the rest of my furniture on the truck that's bringing it sometime this week. After I spent nine months in Monterey, a few months shy of the one-year rule, my company decided it would be cheaper to put my car on a flatbed than to have me drive it from California to Ohio in late October. Weather delays and storms like this could have set me back. Time that I would have been stuck in hotels instead of working on-site here in Star Falls.

I reach for the rain jacket that I hung on the purse hook under the bar. "I walked, actually," I tell him. "I'd better bundle up." I set a few dollars on the bar top. "Will you make sure the bartender gets this?" I ask him. "For the coffee."

He nods, looking from me to the dollars and back again.

"You know..." He tugs his rain jacket over his arms and shivers slightly. He must be cold and damp, and I can't help thinking I'd like to warm him up in my walk-in shower. "We don't know each other, but I've got a mother and a sister who would sauté my balls for breakfast if I ever let a woman put herself in harm's way. I'd be happy to drive you so you don't have to walk."

I hop down off my barstool, and he comes to stand beside me. Our height difference is almost comical, and he must see that. He chuckles and shakes his head.

"Scratch that. You wouldn't be walking. That wind would scoop you right up and blow you all the way to your hotel."

I press my lips together and consider his offer. "You delivered dinners tonight? Out in this weather?"

He nods, studying my face. "I did."

"And did the meals all make it safely?"

He looks at me again, a thick, dark brow lifted slightly in question. "I'm extremely good at what I do," he assures me, a confident grin on his face. "Pizzas and pastas all made it to their destinations, toppings intact."

I nod. "If you can be trusted with ravioli, I think you can be trusted with me." But I hold up my phone. "I do have location tracking on my phone and a load of friends who will be expecting to hear from me. So, no serial-killer shit. We clear?"

"No serial-killer shit," he promises, his grin wider now. Then I feel his hand on my lower back. "You *really* liked that ravioli." He says it almost as an afterthought, but I stop in my tracks, my boots silent on the carpeted flooring.

"I never joke about food. I live for it," I tell him.

His smile grows even bigger, the heat of his palm spreading a ripple of warmth through my raincoat. "Then you are most definitely in the right hands."

Holy shit.

Talk about the right hands.

Ben's wet clothes are piled in the corner of my bathroom, the steam from the water fogging the mirror. While he warms up in the shower, I'm in front of the vanity, digging through my overnight bag for a condom. After the things this man did to me with his fingers... I want more. So much more.

Hence the need to strip down, warm up, and move from the lumpy sofa in my hotel room to a more comfortable spot.

I wrap a towel around myself and check the time. It's only been an hour since Ben brought me to my room, helped me finish off that half-bottle of not-stale-after-all Chianti, and we made out like teenagers on a very sad-looking sofa. I have at least another hour before I need to check in with Jessa, and I plan to spend every minute of it wisely.

I grab a foil packet from my toiletry bag and then hang my towel neatly on the hook. Ben is under the hot water, his eyes closed and his dick just beginning to go soft.

We can't have that…

I open the glass door, step carefully inside, set the sealed foil packet on the ledge beside the little bar of soap, and point to the showerhead. "Would you angle that a bit?" I ask.

He nods and reaches over my head. "Like this?"

The hot water hits the back wall of the shower, a little bit of the spray still keeping us warm and wet. I nod, grab a washcloth, drop it to the tile, and then I carefully kneel on it.

"Willow…" He groans as I line up my face with his cock.

My hair is wet and hanging around my shoulders in a waterlogged mess, but I don't care.

Ben is beautiful. His thighs are dense with well-defined muscles, dark hair covering his strong calves, arms, and the divot between his tight pectorals.

He's even got cute guy feet, which is saying something. I can't remember hooking up with many men whose toes I noticed in a good way, but his are actually really, really cute.

I smile as I cup his balls in a hand. "This okay?" I ask, humming the question low in my throat.

"Fuck yeah." His eyes are closed, and he looks like he needs something to hold on to, but the shower stall is huge.

"Shoulders," I say, peeking up past the erection that is slowly coming back to life to catch his eyes. "You can lean on my shoulders if you need to."

His throaty laugh is rich and deep, and it sends shivers along the fine hairs on my arm. "I don't want to crush you," he says. "Not while my balls are in your hand. I'll stand here as long as you need me to, babe."

I grin and lick my lips, then lower my face to his cock. I lick long, wet strokes along his shaft while I gently graze the underside of his balls with my fingertips.

"Fuck... Willow..." My name is silk on his lips as the hot water runs in little rivulets through his chest hair.

I suck him into my mouth, swirling my tongue. When I feel him go completely hard, I point toward the condom.

But Ben's oblivious, his eyes closed, his lips lightly parted. So, I gently slip my mouth away from his dick, and that gets his attention immediately.

"Condom?" I ask.

"Fuck yes. Sorry. Shit, that felt good." He reaches for it, but then he reaches a hand out to me. "Come here," he says. He grabs my hand in the one that isn't gripping the condom and tugs me to standing. He lowers his face to mine and brushes his lips over mine. "Have you ever had good shower sex?"

I breathe in the warmth of his face, nuzzle my nose against his damp skin and slightly stubbled cheeks. "Hmmm... No, actually."

He wraps his hands around my waist, the condom tucked between two fingers. "Move someplace dry?"

I lift my mouth to his and cup his face, pulling him close for a kiss. He flicks my upper lip with his tongue, and I open to a deep, searing kiss. A kiss that brings my hips tight against his, the heat of his erection pressed flat against my belly. I moan low in my throat, a rush of electricity buzzing from my lips to my core. "Dry," I agree, meaning where I want to go—and not me. Because this man has me wet and aching.

He switches off the faucet, and I grab my fluffy towel, then hand him a clean, folded one from under the sink. We dry off quickly, and I'm shocked by how comfortable and easy this is.

He shakes his wet hair like a dog after a rainy walk, and I rub my long, wet strands between the ends of my towel so they don't drip.

We're on top of the bed, towels on the floor, seconds later. I'm on my back, and Ben is on top of me, kissing my collarbone and running his hands along the muscles of my thighs.

"Willow." He breathes my name against my bare, still-damp skin. "What do you like?" He lowers his mouth to my breast and flicks his tongue against my nipple. "This?" he asks, his voice low and raspy, just before he clamps his teeth lightly around my incredibly sensitive peak.

My hips buck slightly, and I suck in a breath as sparks shoot from my breasts through my body. "Oh, that. Yeah. That's good. So, so good," I assure him. "You can be rough with me."

A little whimper slips from his throat at my words. "Like this?" he asks, devouring my breast with his mouth. He sucks hard on my nipple, his tongue finding just the right speed to work me into an aroused haze.

"Yes." I arch my back, straining to bring more of my skin into contact with his heat.

He withdraws his mouth and rests his chin lightly on my chest, then he cups my breasts between his hands and slowly moves his head from left to right. He somehow—and God, I wish this room had a mirror so I could watch him do it—is able to hold my breasts together and rub the stubble of his chin against my nipples until the sensitive skin is nearly raw.

My legs tremble with need, and I open my eyes when he lifts his mouth from my skin. "Do you like being fucked hard, Willow?"

He's staring into my eyes as he asks, and for a second, my heart jumps in my chest. He's so, so beautiful. "Yeah," I say, stroking his stubble with my fingertips. "Fuck yeah. But I'll only come if you're behind me."

"Then I'm going to fuck you that way," he promises. He kneels on the bed, tears into the condom, and sheathes his incredibly rigid cock. Then he motions for me to roll onto my stomach.

Before I'm even comfortable, his hands are on my ass, kneading my cheeks, and he's planting hot kisses along the backs of my thighs. "Ben," I pant, arousal flooding between my legs. "That's so, so good."

I half expect him to plunge into me and go hard, but Ben is not like other hookups. He takes his time, nudging my legs apart, then lifting my hips so I'm kneeling on the bed, my ass in the air.

"Can you breathe?" he asks, and I feel his hand swipe the wet clumps of my hair away from my face.

I peek at him over my shoulder and grin. "I'm good," I tell him. "This is perfect."

I try to stay kneeling as he nudges the tip of his cock against my entrance, but Ben doesn't just drill in and start pounding. He takes his sweet time stroking his head along every wet inch of my pussy. I chirp a little sound when his dick rubs against my clit. He slides his erection through my wetness, teasing every bit of my drenched seam until I drop my face to the comforter and practically smash my ass against his hips, greedy and needy for all of him.

"Ben." I want him inside me. I'm so, so close to coming. He's primed my body to the point that when I feel him grip my ass cheeks and slide inside me, I see stars behind my closed eyelids. "Fuck." I gasp and widen my knees as far as I can, while kneeling to let him go deeper.

"Good?" he asks. "You going to come for me?"

I whimper a yes into the bedding and let my body melt into the pleasure. He thrusts slow and deep, then fast and hard, then back to slow and steady.

My ass is so high in the air, I can feel the moment he hits that spot inside and my body takes over. I move a limp arm between my legs, press back into his thrusts, and hold my fingers over my clit. Between my fingers and his cock, I'm lost, spinning, spinning, crying out, and collapsing against the bed, my legs too weak to hold my body weight up.

He is careful when I lie facedown not to smother me, and he kisses my back and shoulders while I sigh through every second of my postorgasmic bliss.

"The noises you make," he growls against my ear. "Fuck, Willow. I almost came just hearing you."

I swallow against the dryness in my mouth from all the panting and moaning, and I shimmy my hips so he knows I want to roll over.

He moves the massive weight of his body off mine, and I flop onto my back. "I'll scream as loud as you want if it'll make you come," I say. I lift my face to kiss him, then settle onto my back and open my legs. "Come on, gorgeous," I tell him. "Your turn."

My phone buzzes and jolts me from the orgasm haze that has me half asleep. I squint open an eye and feel Ben's arm against my chest. We're under the blankets now, and I have no idea what time it is. I grab my phone and see two texts from Jessa.

Jessa: Bitch, it's been two hours. You have exactly ten minutes to check in before I'm making that call.

And then, two minutes later:

Jessa: Willow, you better be having one hell of a good time. You have eight minutes to let me know you're okay before I call the cops.

The last text came in five minutes ago, so I quickly thumbs-up her message so she knows I'm alive, then quietly try to text without waking Ben.

Me: I'm great. Alive and safe. Having fun. Luv u.

I hit send, and then silence my phone because I know she's going to want all the details. And right now, I have to figure out how to wake my delivery driver and send him on his way.

I set my phone back on the bedside table just as Ben huffs a deep sigh and tucks himself tighter against me. He's sound asleep, like, not just post-orgasm snoozing. His lips are parted, his damp hair curling over his forehead, and he's now got both a leg and an arm thrown over my body. I'm on my back, and I adjust the pillow beneath my head as best I can around the mass of man on top of me.

I consider waking him, thanking him for a good time, and sending him back out into the elements. I don't know if he lives far, has someone waiting for him at home—a wife, a kid, a dog, even. But something tells me that the man who was so attentive, so conscientious about bringing me pleasure, doesn't have a deep, dark secret or loved ones he's abandoned at home.

I could be wrong, but I dismiss those thoughts and close my eyes, letting the last little bits of bliss wash over me. It won't be too long before he probably wakes up and slips out. Right? I just close my eyes for a second because this man feels *good*. I don't believe in long-term plans, but there's nothing long-term about just one night. Won't do any harm to rest like this for a few minutes…

CHAPTER THREE

benito

When I wake up with a desperate need to pee, I realize in shock that I am not in my loft that overlooks a gorgeous view of the river. I'm even more comfortable than I am in my own bed, and that's almost more shocking.

I look down at the naked woman tucked against my bare chest—the reason I'm so damned cozy here.

Somehow, after fucking each other into next week, we're still stuck together. Willow's air-dried hair is splashed across a pillow, her plush ass pressing into my rapidly waking cock.

I drop a kiss to her hair, and she stirs lightly but doesn't wake up, so I climb out from between the covers, trying to disturb her as little as possible. I pad over to the bathroom, shut the door, then turn on the light. My clothes are in a wet heap on the floor, and fuck if I don't wish I could steal a bathrobe and drive home in something dry. The thought of pulling those clammy clothes back on and going back out into the storm... Sigh.

But there's nothing worse than a hookup that overstays his welcome. After I take care of business, I hold my breath and pull on my clothes, stifling the curses that threaten to slip out. Freaking rain.

I manage to wiggle into my freezing-cold clothes, then I click off the light and head back into the room to find my wallet and phone.

As I pass the bed, I notice Willow is awake. She's tucked the blankets up to her chin, and she's watching me move through the dark. We don't say anything, but as I slide into my shoes, something stops me.

I'm suddenly overcome by the desire to stay. To crawl right back into bed with her and go for round two—and then maybe go back to sleep. Through the muted light of the hotel room, I can just make out her eyes following me.

After my boots are on, I walk over to the bed. "Hey," I whisper. "You awake?"

"Mostly," she murmurs. I can make out her smile, even in the dark. "You taking off?"

As tempted as I am to stay, I nod, then lean down and brush the hair back from her face. I plant a light kiss on her lips, then her forehead. "You stay in bed," I tell her, but before I can pull away, she reaches a hand from under the blankets and laces her fingers through mine. Wordlessly, she brings my hand to her lips and kisses the back of it. Then she lets go and turns over, snuggling down into the blanket.

I'm confused by the gesture. It's not an invitation to come back to bed, but it's tender and sweet.

I walk to the door, flip the dead bolt, and then realize once I leave, she'll need to get up and flip the extra locks. "Willow," I whisper, but my voice comes out louder than I intended. "Are you going to get up and lock this behind me?"

She's quiet for a moment, and then I hear the rustling of blankets. She walks completely naked through the room, and as soon as I see the faint light seeping through the curtains from the parking lot and land on her body, my cock does its best to convince me that I don't really have to go home. Her nipples are hard, and the memory of them in my mouth almost has me reaching for her. This was a perfect night, and I can't break the unspoken rule of hookups.

Never let it mean too much.

Never overstay.

Never assume.

Fuck, done, and run.

She runs a hand along my arm and grins at me through the darkness. "Goodnight, Ben," she says gently. It's not a dismissal. In fact, she sounds a little reluctant, like she's thinking about inviting me back to bed.

"You'll lock this?" I ask, reaching for the doorknob.

"I will," she assures me, her fingers tightening on my sleeve. Holding me back. Tempting me to consider staying. That means this is most definitely my sign to go.

My clothes have fully brought my body temperature down, and if I don't get my ass onto my heated seat, I'm going to start shivering. I open the door a crack because, after all, she's totally nude, and quickly step into the hall. Before I walk away, I block the doorway with my body so no one who might happen to pass by at this hour can see in. "You know where to find me," I tell her, giving her a nod.

"Bruno's," she whispers. "Best kale ravioli ever."

I almost choke on my laughter, but instead, I just shake my head, a grin on my face. "Benito's," I correct. "And it's the best *damn* kale ravioli ever."

We trade smiles, and for a moment, neither one of us moves. But then, I hear the ding of the elevator down the hall and figure she'd better shut the door before she flashes an unwitting housekeeper or guest.

I nod, wait for her to close and lock the door, then I head toward the elevator and out into the night.

I'm awakened the next morning by banging and shouting.

"Fuck." I turn over in bed and jam a pillow over my head to muffle the noise. But I can still hear what sounds like giants bowling in the hallway outside my condo. I squint and grab my phone, about ready to call the property manager to send someone up to deal with this shit, when I notice the time. It's after nine.

I have ten text notifications on my phone, but I am sure half of them are from Mags reminding me where to go, so I don't bother reading them. I jump out of bed and bolt into the bathroom, mentally calculating how late I'll be if I skip making coffee.

I fucking hate skipping morning coffee.

I hate rushing.

I hate being late.

All of this because I got home at three in the damned morning after...

The steam is fogging my bathroom mirror when I remember showering last night with Willow. Her body, her lips, her dripping hair. The way she squirmed and moaned as I rammed inside her.

Fuck.

If I had even five more minutes, I'd jerk one out just to ease the pressure building in me at the memory of her.

Willow.

I know she's new in town, but I didn't even get a last name.

I lather up fast, trying to wash the feeling of her from my body. It's weird; it's like my body is still with her. Like I can still feel her limbs tangled with mine. I put my whole head under the spray and try to push away the memories.

Once I'm out and dry, I brush my teeth and throw on a pair of black jeans and a dress shirt, then check the forecast. Cloudy, but no rain. I don't think my rain gear is anywhere close to dry yet. I tuck into a pair of boots, grab a thick zip-up cardigan, and yank open my condo door, only to practically fall over a moving crew.

"Hey." One of the guys nods at me. "You got your new neighbor's number? We're scheduled to do a move-in today at noon, but this was a cross-country move, and we made it ahead of schedule. Any chance you know where she's at?"

I scowl. I didn't even know I was getting a new neighbor. I shake my head. "Sorry, man. I got to run."

The new neighbor explains the noise, but it's barely nine thirty. It'll be a miracle if I make the SBA event before it's over. And I'd rather embarrass myself in front of the entire Star Falls Small Business Administration than face Mags if I blow this off.

I bash on the elevator button, but it must be jammed with shit from the movers because I wait a whole minute before turning and bolting toward the stairs. I take them two at a time, tucking my phone into my sweater pocket so I don't drop it.

I literally run to my truck and pray the traffic light gods look favorably on me.

"I've been a good boy," I mutter. "I could use a little positive mojo right now."

As I navigate through our small town, my phone rings. I see who it is on the caller ID and smash the button on my SUV's display screen.

"Ma, I'm in the car, and you're on speaker."

"Benny?" Ma's voice sounds concerned. "Honey, why am I on speaker?"

I roll my eyes. "Ma, I'm not just sitting in the car. I'm driving. I'm talking hands-free because it's the law now. You know this. What's up with you?"

Ma launches into an update on her morning—she's good, my father's in Cleveland at a doctor's appointment. "He wouldn't let me go with him, Benny," she finishes.

I partially tuned Ma out while she was chatting me up. She often calls me on Monday mornings, while my brothers and sister are working or off taking care of their kids. I'm the youngest of four, and all of my siblings have partners and kids, so I'm the only one around during the weekday mornings when Ma wants to catch up.

"Wait, wait." I can't tell what time it is since my phone and my display are showing me the time I've been on this call, but it's got to be quarter to ten as I pull into the very full parking lot of the Star Falls Community Center. I park in a spot at the far end of the lot and grab my phone. "Ma, what'd you say about Pops? He wouldn't let you go with him to the doctor?"

I turn off the engine and slide out of the car, tucking my phone between my shoulder and my ear. My parents do everything together. They have slept apart only a handful of times since they got married, and they met when they were fifteen. Pops doesn't buy a slice of cake without Ma approving the flavor and amount of frosting. I can't believe he'd drive into Cleveland for even a routine doctor's appointment and not take Ma with him.

"He told me not to worry, Benny, but you know that means I'm going to worry. Are you still in the car? You sound funny."

"Ma, I'm… Do you know what kind of doctor it is?"

We have great primary care here in Star Falls, but for surgeries and more serious stuff, most people go to one of the major hospitals in Cleveland.

A sick feeling creeps up the back of my neck. Fear, maybe. Anxiety? My parents are still young, but hell, youth doesn't guarantee good health.

Our family has been spoiled in that department.

My mother's explaining that she has no idea and that she's even considered snooping on my father's phone to find out, but they've never had that kind of marriage. I listen as much as I can, but when the doors of the community center open and a dozen people head out into the gloomy morning toward their cars, the dread in the pit of my stomach deepens.

"Ma, Ma…I hate to interrupt, but I—"

I'm trying to talk over her, but I'd have to shout over her, and right now, there is nothing more important than this. There is nothing more important than my family. So, I shut my lips and listen to Ma talk. No matter how pissed off Mags is going to be at me for blowing this meeting. I made my bed last night when I fell asleep in the arms of a gorgeous woman instead of going home early and setting my alarm. Looks like I'm going to have to lie in it.

By the time Ma and I end the call, I'm back behind the steering wheel. I turn over the engine and head into downtown Star Falls. If I'm going to be on Mags's shit list, I might as well bring a peace offering. I park in front of the bookstore café and squint to see if Ma's there yet. Of course she is. And she's not alone.

I yank open the front door and shout, "Yo-yo, Ethan."

My sister's son immediately jumps up from a toddler chair and runs to greet me.

"Uncle Benny."

I pick up the little rat and smooch my lips against his soft ear. "You reading already? You're way too little to be reading, E. You're like a teeny tiny baby."

Ethan curls his upper lip, playing along with the game he never gets tired of. "Not a baby," he growls. "I'm a big boy."

"Yes, you are." I set him on his feet, and he takes my hand and pulls me toward the counter, where my mother looks worried.

"Benny." She opens her arms, but instead, I open mine and fold my mother against my chest. In her stacked heels, she's still ridiculously short, but her highly sprayed dome of auburn hair just tickles my chin when I lean down close to kiss the top of her head.

"Ma." I give her a squeeze, then nod at the front counter. "Where's Chloe?"

My eldest brother Franco's wife Chloe owns the bookstore café and normally runs the place with some part-time help. Especially unpaid part-time help like my ma. We all love it. Lucia never worked outside the home, but now she helps care for her grandbabies or her kids' businesses. She's so involved in our day-to-day lives, she doesn't have time for anything that's just hers. Except for my dad. And he's the reason I'm meeting her here for coffee.

"I told Chloe you were on your way. She ran back to grab some peanut butter crisps to go with your coffee." Ma blots under her eyes with her fingertips, careful not to poke her eyeballs with her long, perfectly manicured nails. The color of the day is navy, and little glittery gems are glued to the polish, which perfectly matches Ma's gem-studded jeans, silver boots, and navy top.

I scan the bookstore, looking for anyone else who may be listening. Ethan's back in the children's reading nook, plastic trucks and board books scattered on the colorful braided rug.

"Gracie working?" I ask, nodding at my nephew.

"Not yet." Ma points at her watch. "I've got Ethan until we pick up the big kids from school."

Gracie works at the tattoo shop just a couple of storefronts down from the bookstore. She's probably enjoying a few minutes of alone time while her husband's kids from his first marriage are in school and her toddler Ethan is here with my mother. My brother-in-law is an early bird, so he's probably been at work since seven.

I rub my face, realizing the hell I'm going to pay when I get to the restaurant. But this is where I need to be.

"Benny." Chloe comes bustling from the back room, a white paper bag and two large coffees in her hands. She drops everything on the counter, then comes around to give me a kiss hello. We're a touchy-feely family, and even though Chloe's one of the newest members, she's taken to our smooches and hugs like she was born to be a Bianchi.

"Hey, kiddo." I give her a quick squeeze. "How's my dickhead brother?"

A sudden slap against my bicep reminds me Ma is standing right there. "Benny. Language."

I chuckle and shake my head in apology. "Sorry, Ma." Then to Chloe, I say, "How is my d-head brother?"

Ma snorts and gives me another good whack while Chloe just flushes pink. She's used to the way we play in this family. I grab the white paper bag of peanut butter crisps, and she slides one of the coffees across the counter toward me. "So, should I mention any of this to Franco?" she asks, sounding concerned.

I look to Ma. "What do you think? Is this family-meeting material, or are you just venting until Pops gets home?"

My mom sniffles and blinks her heavily made-up eyes. "Let's just keep this between the three of us for now," she says. "I'm hoping your father tells me everything when he's home, and then we can all put this worry behind us."

My mouth goes dry as I think about the alternative. I'm so used to my parents being there whenever I need them—and even more often when I don't need them. We used to do weekly Sunday dinners, but now that all of my siblings have kids and spouses of their own, Sunday dinners have become monthly events, not weekly.

I miss the old days when we ate together every week, just me, Ma, Pops, Gracie, Franco, and Vito around the table. But things change. Families expand. Kids are born, and our parents…well, they grow older. Whether we're ready for it or not.

I clear my throat, pushing away the emotions before I start blubbering like one of the kids. I grab the coffee and the bag, lean down to kiss Ma goodbye, and nod at Chloe. "Text or call me, Ma," I say before I leave.

She nods at me, the sadness in her eyes and the dragging down of the corners of her lips nearly breaking my heart into pieces.

After I leave the bookstore, I walk up to The Body Shop and peek in the window. I know it's closed. It's too early for them to be open, but there's something about knowing that my sister will be here in a couple hours that brings me comfort. Everywhere I go in town, there are reminders of my family. The garage where Franco works. The fire station that's Vito's second home.

Some people grow up wanting to leave the place they were born, but not me. Star Falls is my home. Always has been. Always will be.

That's why I opened my own restaurant, even though I had plenty of offers after culinary school. This is what I want to do, where I want to be.

It's just a shame that things change.

It's not enough anymore to make the best kale ravioli in town. I need to up my game at the restaurant.

I'm drowning in paperwork, but who has time to get organized when we're open seven days a week?

The building I rent for the restaurant needs a new roof, but under the deal I signed, I'm responsible for improvements and maintenance to the place. It seemed like a great deal six years ago when I opened the doors.

Now, with a roof that won't likely make it another winter, life is piling on, and I'm not sure I can handle one more stress.

I pull into the empty lot of my place and thank God that Mags's car is not already there. I'm going to have to eat some serious humble pie.

She's going to be pissed I missed that meeting. I get an idea and pull out my phone. I pick out a small bouquet of flowers from the local florist. I don't have Mags's home address on me, so I think the better of it. I can't exactly send her flowers to the restaurant, or people will think something's going on between us.

Shit.

But there is someone I wouldn't mind seeing again. Someone whose last name I don't even know. I delete the order I started for Mags and pick out a bigger bouquet of tasteful flowers instead—nothing that screams "I'm a stalker in love." More like, "I'm a classy dude who had fun fucking you last night and would love to know your last name." I fill out the delivery instructions, including the room number and her first name. That should be enough for them to reach her. On the card, I type out:

Not as good as the kale, but… Thinking of you. B

I include my cell phone number, pay for the order, and slip my phone into my pocket. Then I peek inside the bag and count the peanut butter crisps. I'm going to need every one of them to stay on Mags's good side.

CHAPTER FOUR

willow

When I check my phone after my presentation, I see a dozen missed calls from a number I don't recognize. I grimace and am just about to check my voice mail, when a young woman from the audience confidently approaches me.

"Excuse me? Ms. Watkins?" The woman's smile is friendly, so I slip my phone back into my purse and give her my full attention.

"Hi." I hold out my hand, and we shake. "I'm Willow Watkins, but please, call me Willow."

She nods. "I'm Maggie Tempestini." She motions to the rows of folding chairs behind us. "I, uh, was hoping my boss would be here today, but he must have gotten—" she frowns "—distracted."

I nod, sensing tension there but choosing not to comment on it. "Well, I'm glad you made it. Are you interested in the SBA grant?"

She nods again. "I manage a local restaurant with strong ties to the community. We're family-owned, not corporate, and the owner trains and employs a lot of people with nontraditional backgrounds for careers in food service. Our oldest employee is in her eighties, and we have two bussers with developmental disabilities," she says with no small amount of pride. "We make great food, and our people are treated very well, but the owner…" She bites her lower lip, the only glitch in her well-practiced speech. "His heart is bigger than his head."

I've heard that so, so many times before. I conjure a vision of the countless restaurants like the one where Maggie works—the owner pulled in a thousand directions, things falling through the cracks. "Let me guess," I say softly, leaning a little closer. "You badly need kitchen upgrades? You're behind on vendor payments or rent?"

She shakes her head, and a hand flies to her throat. "No, thank God. No. It's our roof. We're renting the space, and we're responsible under the lease for replacing the roof. I know Benito thinks we can make it another couple of winters, but the grant you're offering would get us there so much faster."

I break out into a grin when she says Benito's. "Do you work at the local Italian place? Killer kale ravioli?"

Maggie's mouth drops open, and she raises her brows. "You know about us?"

"I ate there last night," I tell her. "It's one of the few places people won't stop telling me about." I think back to the faded carpeting and Mom's basement vibes that passed for the place's decor. Benito's was homey and inviting, not unlike dozens of restaurants like it across the country.

Maggie claps her hands. "So, maybe since I know you loved the kale… You did love it?"

I nod, a vision of a very naked busboy's bare ass pressed against the glass wall of my hotel shower clouding my memories of the meal. I choke down a cough. "I did. I absolutely loved it," I assure her.

"Well then, maybe—" Maggie clasps her hands together "—you can let me know what we need to do to have the very best chance of winning the grant?"

This, too, happens every year. The company I work for, Culinary Capital Partners, goes into cities and small towns after running the numbers. We evaluate a region's demographics, infrastructure, socioeconomics, and lots of other variables. Then we select a market that appears ripe for a new restaurant or chain expansion opportunity. I've worked for the last eight years on the development side. After our numbers team makes the internal assessments and recommendations, we determine the type of restaurant most likely to be viable in that space.

We then lease or buy property, complete the renovations, do all the hiring, and open the doors with a very aggressive goal for the establishment breaking even within the first two years after opening. By year three, a majority of Culinary Capital restaurants are profitable. I get involved in the very critical period before the doors are open. Once we establish a site and a plan for the restaurant, I move in to the town for six months to a year to oversee the on-the-ground operations. My job is part general contractor, part bookkeeping, part HR, and all about the food. It's why I love doing what I do.

Culinary Capital does a lot to give back to the communities. We're a for-profit venture, and we do know how to make money. We're selective about everything, and I have to be a bulldog on the ground, making sure construction or renovation costs stay on deadline and within budget. I recruit chefs and court discounts with vendors that ensure every project is a winner for the company's bottom line.

But inevitably when we move into a town, the restaurants already in place suffer. A glossy new eatery will inevitably drive away customers, and sometimes struggling restaurants aren't able to compete with the new, shiny place in town. Businesses have closed; people have lost their jobs. It's the hard reality of doing what we do. In order for us to make money, sometimes, others lose it.

To offset the very bad blood that would otherwise exist between us and the food community in the cities we go into, I started a grant program, normally administered by the local small business association.

The grant varies in amount by region and location, but any restaurant that might be impacted by our move into the market is eligible to apply for a no-strings-attached grant. Some of the grant recipients take the money and send their head chef to a special training program, so they can expand their menu or modernize their food handling practices.

In some communities, restaurant owners have hired chefs with no formal training other than basic state-mandated sanitation and food safety. I know of at least three chefs who were able to attend culinary programs paid for in part by a Culinary Capital grant.

The amount of money we're making available to the food service community in Star Falls is not small, so I'm not surprised that Maggie is here, trying to figure out what she can do to make Benito's application more competitive.

I give her a smile. "I won't play favorites," I tell her, "and I don't make the final decisions myself anyway. As I shared in the presentation, we work with the local SBA so the community that will be impacted by the grant has a say in who receives it." I lean close to her and give her a smile. "But how about I come into Benito's again this week and have a chat with you and the owners. I'd love to hear more about the place, and maybe I can give you some tips on how to write a strong proposal."

She grins so wide, she looks about ready to bounce on her heels. "Thank you," she breathes. "Thank you so much, Ms. Watkins."

"Please, call me Willow." I pull a business card from my portfolio, hand it to her, and jot her name and cell number down in my contacts. I confirm when she's on shift and try not to feel guilty for having some ulterior motives behind my offer. It'd be nice to see the sexy delivery driver again, assuming he'd be anywhere I might find him. I lucked out on a rainy night to catch him at the end of his shift, inside the restaurant.

It occurs to me then…

"Maggie," I ask, curiosity getting the better of me. "Is Benito's just the name of the restaurant? Or is there a Benito who runs the place?"

I hope my cheeks aren't flushing. This is ridiculous. I'm a grown woman who has every right to hook up with a man I find attractive. I only hope he was a busboy and not a man whose restaurant might apply for a Culinary Capital community development grant.

"Oh yes," she says, rolling her eyes. "You'd have met him if he'd have shown up like I asked him to." She seems to catch herself midsentence, stopping the next words from running out of her mouth while she blushes hard. "Benito is... Well, he's an amazing chef. And a larger-than-life ego. He's just—"

I hold up a hand, cutting her off. "No need to explain. I've worked with hundreds of restaurant owners in my career. You don't get to be in that position without having a lot of...let's call them quirks."

She looks relieved, and I want to reassure her that she hasn't said anything that's going to damage Benito's shot at the grant. I'm only one of the people on the committee who will review the applications. I'm not in charge of the final decision, but still.

As Maggie bounces through the now-empty meeting room toward the parking lot, I hope against hope that I don't have to recuse myself from the committee entirely because I fucked a hot restaurant owner my first week in Star Falls.

I smother a grin and pull out my phone to check my messages. That would be a first, and I don't know how I'd explain to my boss my reasons for pulling out. But as I think back to Ben's mouth on my breasts, his cock slamming deep inside me, I hope against hope that Ben isn't *the* Benito.

I tuck my phone beneath my ear and head toward the parking lot to wait for a rideshare, listening to the voice mail from the strange number.

"Ms. Watkins, this is Cal from Advanced Long Distance Movers. We're a couple hours early, so we're already at your building..."

I punch the number back into my phone. The call is picked up on the first ring. "This is Willow Watkins," I say. "I'm about fifteen minutes away."

Looks like my furniture is here, which means my car should be here as well. I checked out of the hotel, knowing the movers were scheduled to arrive this afternoon. I look over the empty conference room to the two large suitcases of the things I'd packed for my first week in Star Falls.

A new deal in the works. A hot new hookup. And a new home. I can never get enough of the excitement for new, new, new. I have a huge grin on my face and an unstoppable feeling in my chest as I grab my roller bags and secure my messenger bag over my shoulder.

The adventure of the next year starts now.

———————

By the time the movers had unloaded my furniture, I'd already corrected a small parking snafu with the condo's management office. Turned out they hadn't secured paid parking with my long-term rental, but a few firm smiles and well-placed calls from my assistant back in Chicago sorted that out.

It's nearly six by the time the movers clear out. My new condo is on the top floor of a luxury building with a view overlooking the river. After yesterday's storm, the sky is still gray, angry clouds drifting past like lazy kittens stretching and rolling across the horizon. The river has a running path, and as twilight settles over Star Falls, I can see strollers and joggers, couples and dogs, filling up the blacktop path.

I look over the boxes and plastic-wrapped furniture with excitement. Setting up a new place and settling into a new home never fails to excite me. I'll be busy all week with site inspections and meeting the contractors we've hired for the renovation of the soon-to-be hottest family eatery in Star Falls. But I'll spend the majority of the week unpacking, finding just the right shelves for my mug collection, the perfect way to display my copper pots and spices. I practically live in the kitchen, and this condo's open floorplan with a massive island was what sold me on making this my home for the next twelve months.

I'm still wearing the pencil skirt and tailored blouse I wore to this morning's SBA meeting, but my feet are bare, and my hair has long fallen loose from the tight bun I'd worn for the presentation.

I'm debating ordering a pizza, changing into sweats, putting on some music, and going deep into unpacking mode, when I'm hit by a sudden craving for kale ravioli.

I bite my lower lip and grab my phone. Jessa answers on the first ring.

"Please tell me you're calling to tell me all about your hot hookup." Her voice sounds shaky, like she's been crying.

"Hey, hey," I say, tempted to switch to video so I can see her. My heart tightens in my chest, and my worries kick into overdrive. "Jess, are you crying? Am I calling at a bad time?"

Her laughter is sad, not bitter, but not funny either. "I'm not even a mom yet, and all I do is worry about keeping this baby safe," she says. "I'm a wreck today. Some days, I'm happy to binge an entire season of *Gossip Girl* while I still can uninterrupted and with a lap full of snacks…"

"Like a lady," I interject.

"Like a damn lady," she corrects, her sniffles louder now. "Okay, I know you called me, but Willow, can we video for a sec?"

I lean against the white marble countertop and prop my phone against a small box labeled "Flatware."

"Jess, I'm here for you, babe. Do it."

I hear static on Jess's end, and she does what I was hoping to. She initiates the video call, and I practically squeal when her beautiful, puffy face comes into frame.

"Oh my God. Look at you. Your new place." Jess wipes her face, and I can see her looking around at my new surroundings.

I shake my head. "Eyes on me, bitch. Tell me who made you cry so I know whose balls I need to squeeze. Or ovaries. I'm an equal opportunity vigilante. Tell me who made you cry."

She shakes her head and points at her belly. "Balls it is, then. This baby boy… I'm just worried, Willow. Today, I felt some things, and I just spiraled."

I nod and listen to Jessa describe the twinges and pains, the aches and waves of nausea and heartburn that she's been dealing with throughout the time she's been on bed rest. I know as well as she does that the condition she has is serious. This will possibly be the only pregnancy she carries herself. But the doctors have told her she'll have plenty of notice before something goes wrong. She'll have time to get to the hospital. She just needs to rest.

"But how the hell am I supposed to rest when all I want to do is cry?" Her tears flood her face again, and I am hit with an unfamiliar pang of guilt. I wish I could hug her. Wish I could be there to wash her face and bring her tea. To sit beside her as she watches *Gossip*

Girl and log her farts and everything, it seems, are important signs that her body is working and the baby is still okay.

A tear slips down my cheek. "I know, Jess. I wish I were there."

That seems to sober her up. She shakes her head and wipes her face with one hand. "Fuck that," she says. "You're living the dream. Now I want to hear everything. Especially about your hookup last night."

I peek at the time on my phone. Jess and I have been talking for a half hour already. I know her mother is staying with her while she's on bed rest, but Jess is single. She decided when she turned forty that she wasn't going to wait around for the right man to have a family. I'm two years older than Jess and filled her ears with reasons why I won't ever have kids and what I truly think men are good for— moving heavy things and giving better orgasms than the vast collection of toys I have. But in the end, Jess decided to go through sperm donation. She knew it would be a tough road, but this tough, this way? Nope.

I ignore the growling of my stomach and decide kale ravioli and chatting with Maggie at Benito's will have to wait until another night. I may not be in hugging reach of Jess, but what I have to give her is what makes our friendship tighter than sisters. Tighter than friends. I have time.

"All right," I tell her totally unironically, flicking on the lights as the sun sets over Star Falls. "But before I tell you about the guy, I have to tell you about the ravioli."

CHAPTER FIVE

benito

"Benito. Benito. Some delivery guy is up front for you, honey. He says he needs to talk to you?"

My heart freezes in my chest. I'm plating a delicate dish, three spinach and ricotta-stuffed rotolo on a bed of marinara, when my hostess Rita's voice echoes through the kitchen.

"Want me to take it?" Mags's voice is like ice. I can hear the f-bomb she is holding back.

She knows as well as I do there should be no deliveries made from the front of the house, and certainly not at this hour of the day.

She probably expects it's someone making a personal call to demand I get current on a bill or something. Hell, that's what I'm afraid of too.

In my mind, I race through the bills and emails and calls I haven't answered, trying to calculate who might be out front looking for me, but I don't have a damn clue. No matter what it is, I sure as shit can't let Mags handle it.

All day, she's been avoiding me, giving one-word answers to questions and very obviously stepping as far away from me as possible in the cramped kitchen as we work through the dinner rush. She gave the peanut butter crisps I brought from Chloe's to Jasmine, so I know she's *pissed* at me for missing the small business association meeting today. I didn't even try to explain why.

If whatever is going on with Pops is serious—and I can't fucking let my head go there—I'll have to share it eventually. Maybe. Probably. Fuck. One worry at a time.

I plate the rotolo and eyeball Mags. "Take over here?" I ask, wiping my hands on a towel.

She nods but doesn't say anything, stepping into the practiced rhythm of working alongside me. She plates the rest of the dish while I walk through the restaurant toward the front entrance. I have to stop and shake a few hands and clap a few shoulders of the diners who call to greet me, so it takes about ten minutes before I actually make it to the front.

It's well after seven, but the lobby is still full of families waiting for tables to free up for dinner. I don't see anyone who looks official or who looks like they are looking for me, so I step beside Rita behind the hostess desk.

"Sweetheart!" she shouts over the low chatter of my waiting customers. "Benny's here."

I lift my head and follow her hand, which is waving at a fidgety kid who's staring out over the parking lot. He's wearing a blue windbreaker, and his hands are jammed into his pockets.

I squint at him as he approaches, immediately relieved. He is one of the kids I hired over the summer while he was on break from college. If I remember right, I didn't offer Nico a part-time job when school started back up because he was nice enough but a little slow. I feel like I remember a few too many messed-up orders and forgotten side dishes. Mags was the one to tell him we only needed full-time help, essentially letting him go for me. She's always there to take the hard jobs off my hands. The thought of it stresses me out now, but whatever Nico wants, this is something I have to handle alone.

Rita said he had a delivery for me, but maybe that was just a ruse? A way to lure me out front to talk. There's no way this college student is a bill collector now. At least, I sincerely fucking hope not. "Nico? Is that you?"

Nico breaks into a grin and gives me a wave. "Hey, man. Great to see you. Great to be back in the old place." He sniffs the air. "Smells amazing, as usual. You been good?"

I feel my blood start to boil, but I calm my anxiety. This is fine. Everything is fine. "Yeah, man," I say. "Busy as usual." I motion back toward the dining room full of guests. "Dinner rush, you know how it is," I say, trying not to sound like a dick. "Rita said you had a delivery for me?"

The kid's face brightens, and he says, "Yeah. I'm working for Gloria's Floral Fantasies now." At the name of the florist, I hold up a hand. I know the place. That's where I ordered Willow's flowers from this morning. A sinking feeling hits my gut as I wonder what the fuck could have happened. "Let's talk outside." The last thing I want is everyone in my restaurant hearing my private business.

We step out front, and I cock a brow at Nico. "So, you're delivering flowers now?"

He grins. "Yeah, man. It's part time, and it's very cool. I make my own hours, as long as I get the deliveries done within the business day. I can work around my class schedule. It's pretty sweet, actually."

"Good for you." I hear myself saying it, but my foot starts nervously tapping against the pavement. "I hate to rush you, Nic, but I've got to get back to the kitchen."

"Right." Nico slaps his face with a hand and then holds a finger up to me. "One sec, man."

He jogs off toward a large panel van painted with Gloria's distinctive logo on the side in purple. He comes back about a minute later with a beautiful bouquet wrapped in clear cellophane.

"What's this?" I ask, squinting at the bouquet. "Somebody send me flowers?"

Nico chuckles. "Nah, but that'd be sweet, huh?" He holds the bouquet out to me. "You ordered these earlier? The person you sent them to had checked out of the hotel by the time I got there. When I saw the name on the receipt, I figured I'd drop them off here. Or, if you know where the person went, I can try to deliver it there. It's not really protocol. But you know, I worked for you and you're such a great guy, I thought…"

My mind is spinning. These are the flowers I bought for Willow. She's gone? Checked out of the hotel already? A stinging sensation travels through my belly. She's gone. She never even told me her last name.

"Wait," I say. "Did the hotel have any forwarding information for her? Can you try to redeliver if they have an address?"

Nico shakes his head. "Sorry, man. I asked, but they said they don't release that stuff. Privacy and all." He shrugs. "You want me to take the flowers back? You can always call Gloria and ask for a refund. She doesn't normally do that, but seeing as it's you, maybe…"

"Nah." I take the flowers from him and squint through the cellophane. I'm honestly kind of shocked how surprised I am. Deep down, I'd been hoping that by sending my number to Willow, she'd reach out. Want to see me again. My body immediately goes back to last night. To her hotel room. The hot shower, my clammy clothes. Her luscious body tucked beneath mine.

I shake my head to clear the memories. "Look, man," I say. "I've got to get back, and I don't have any cash on me, or I'd tip you. You want to come in for a minute so I can hit the petty cash? Or you can come back with your girlfriend some night for dinner. On the house."

Nico gives me a huge grin. "Free date night? That'd be awesome, Benito. I'll totally take you up on that. Thank you." He claps me on the arm and turns to head back to the van.

I stare down at the massive bundle of flowers in my arms. I see the little plastic fork thing that should hold the card with my message to Willow and my number on it. There's nothing there.

"Nic!" I shout after him. I point to the plastic-covered flowers. "There was supposed to be a card. You got any idea where it is?"

Nico shrugs. "Sorry, man. Must have fallen out. This is my last delivery of the day, so if it's not there, I don't know where it went."

I nod and head back into the restaurant. I'm needed in the kitchen, and I need a way to explain why I've got an armful of white, pink, and red flowers delivered to the front door of my restaurant.

Something deep in my gut twists as I think about Willow. She did say she was new in town, but she didn't say she was staying. I shake my head slowly, rushing back through the restaurant and ducking into my office. I set the bouquet on my desk, completely pissed at myself.

"It was just a hookup," I remind myself. Like dozens of others I've had. No reason to feel disappointed. This is just one hookup that I didn't have to end first. I'm not usually on the receiving end of a diss like this, and I don't love the feeling. But is it really a rejection? How would she even know that I'd follow up? She probably assumed she was just another random hookup. A one-and-done good time.

That's what she is, so whatever this is I'm feeling is just stress from other shit getting under my skin. It has nothing to do with the woman herself.

But even as I'm thinking it, I know I'm lying to myself. Willow was gorgeous. Easy to talk to. Not the first woman who's loved my kale, but... I don't know. I'm, like, deeply pissed that she didn't get my message. Pissed she'll never know I tried to find her after our one amazing night together.

I sigh and think about what to do with the flowers. I originally thought about getting flowers for Mags, and she *is* really mad. They won't go to waste, and maybe the gesture will earn me a little goodwill with her. God knows the peanut butter crisps weren't enough. She couldn't even be bothered to eat them.

I pick up the house phone and dial the kitchen. Mags answers.

"Hey, can you come back to my office for a sec?" I ask.

"Benito." She sounds pissed, and she should be. It's still the dinner rush.

"Mags, for fuck's sake. Give me five minutes. Please?"

She sighs deep and hard, like an exasperated older sister and not my restaurant's right hand. "On my way," she says, then hangs up without a word.

I grab my cell phone to check my messages while I wait for Mags. I only have one, and it's the one I'm hoping for.

Mom: Benito, it's your mother.

I chuckle to myself. My parents know how texting works, yet they can't manage to stop themselves from identifying who they are in voice mails, emails, and texts. I read on.

Mom: Your father is home, but he won't say anything. He's acting funny. Let's talk when you can. Love you, son. Thank you for letting me lean on you today. You're my heart, Benny. My sweet littlest boy and such a good, good man. Love, Ma

It's a lot to read, and I can hardly process the parts of it. Ma loves all four of us. Franco, Grace, Vito, and then me. But she's always had a special bond with me. Her last baby. Her youngest son.

It's nothing I don't know deep in my soul, but seeing it written out like that, in an awkwardly formal text that's so like Ma, brings a burn of worry and love for my family to my eyes.

I'm blinking fast when my door flies open, and Mags stands in the doorway, arms crossed.

I hold up my hands in surrender. "Come in and shut the door a sec?"

She motions toward the kitchen. "Benny, we're fucking swamped—"

"I know. This'll only take a sec." I nod at the flowers. "I'm sorry I let you down today. Some shit came up, but I want you to know I appreciate you. And I really respect what you do to keep this place— and me—in line."

She squints at the flowers, her face immediately softening. "Wait. This shit's for me? You got me flowers?"

I swallow hard, feeling just the tiniest bit shitty that I didn't actually buy these for Mags. I try telling myself that it's what I had intended to do, that my heart was in the right place, but Mags is already pulling off the clear plastic wrap and sticking her face deep in the blossoms.

"Oh my God," she whispers, drawing in huge breaths from the roses, gardenias, and greens. "These smell amazing. I didn't expect this from you. Fuck, Benito."

She reaches down to pull the empty plastic fork from the center of the bouquet. The flowers are planted in a really pretty white dish, and there must be some kind of foam thing at the bottom, because the plastic fork takes a little work to get out. She tosses that in the trash bin beside my desk and uses both hands to peel back the plastic wrap that protects the whole bouquet.

"I seriously was pissed," she says as she unwraps the flowers. "You know how important that grant is to this place, and you knew how much that meeting meant to me…"

She trails off and I nod, slipping my phone back into the pocket of my jeans. "You can leave those in here until we close," I say, getting up from my desk. "I just wanted you to know I'm sorry I let you down and I appreciate you."

I head past Mags, making my way toward the closed door to get back to the kitchen, when I hear Mags suck in a breath.

"Are you fucking kidding me?"

I turn on my heel and stare. "What?" I ask. "What's the matter?"

Mags is holding a tiny white envelope and a standard florist card between her fingers. Right then and there, my stomach plummets into my toes.

"These flowers were for me, Benito?" She gestures accusingly with the little white card. *Not as good as the ravioli, but… Thinking of you. B.*" She reads the message I'd intended for Willow in a mocking voice. "Nice, Benito. Fucking classy. I'm sorry if this comes off as disrespect, because no matter what, it's your name out front. This is your place and all that shit. But this?" She drops the flowers on my desk so hard, I'm shocked the planter dish doesn't shatter. "You really can be a major dick sometimes."

She throws the white card on the floor and storms past me. Then she marches out of my office and slams the door in my face.

Shame floods my cheeks, and I head back to my desk to drop into my chair. The dinner rush is not going to wind down anytime soon, but something tells me I'll be managing the kitchen on my own the rest of the night.

And despite my best intentions, like everything else in my life lately, I can't help but feel I'm getting exactly what I deserve.

I haven't said much other than what was required since I came back to the kitchen. After the last customer clears out, I send the kitchen staff home. I want to be alone in my kitchen, and I can't stand the silent questioning, the accusing looks. I can't stand having all the ways I suck at everything being rubbed in my face by the people I'm supposed to lead.

My employees. My kitchen. My team.

After the bussers have the floor done and prepped, a couple of the servers pop in to say goodnight, looking like they want to try to figure out what happened between Mags and me tonight by reading it off the kitchen walls or something.

But I stay silent, angry at myself. Angry at Nico for not delivering the flowers before Willow checked out. Angry at my dad for making my mom worry. I'm just fucking angry, and I'm taking my feelings out on a dirty stockpot and a scouring sponge when one of my mom's best friends, Sassy, fake knocks on the kitchen door.

"Hey there, boss." She cocks a painted-on brow at me and unties her apron. She yawns and checks the time. "It's awfully late to find you here rage-cleaning. You want to talk about it?"

The look I give her must answer for me because Sassy crosses her thick arms over her generous chest. "Well, all right, then," she says, sounding put out. "You want to sulk about whatever shit you pulled on Mags tonight, that's your business."

She turns to leave as if the threat of her leaving will convince me to change my mind, but I don't say shit. I turn the hot water tap hotter and scour until I think I'll rub a hole in the stainless steel.

Sassy hesitates, and then I know I'm in trouble. My mother's close-knit friends treat me like family, but tonight, I'm not in the mood. I'm just not interested in sharing all the ways I've fucked up with Sassy. Not tonight.

"Benito," she starts, but I stiffen and don't look up. She knows me well enough to know that when I go silent, it takes an act of God or threats from my ma to get me talking. She sighs softly. "Get some rest, sweetheart. See you tomorrow." Her voice is gentle, a lot less probing, and I hear the care buried under the sass.

I wait until I hear the solid clack of her sturdy shoes before I go back to scrubbing as though I could clean the shit feelings away if I just worked the pot hard enough.

A second later, another voice breaks me from washing. And I'm just about to lose my shit when I see it's Rita.

"Benito?" she calls. "You in here, honey?"

I drop the scouring pad in resignation. "By the sinks, Rita." My voice is flat, and I know I sound like a damn child. But I can't help it. I just want five minutes alone with my thoughts in my kitchen. Alone with my failures and fuckups. I'm still responsible for this place, no matter how out of control I feel. It should be fucking obvious that I need to be left alone. But for Rita, I pull back my temper and draw in a breath.

Rita walks up to me, and I feel her small hand on my back. "Honey, could I ask a favor?"

I crane my neck to look back at her. I'm immediately concerned that something's up with her. Rita never asks me for anything. Hell, she didn't even want me walking her to the car last night in a torrential downpour.

"What do you need?" I ask, turning off the faucet and giving her my full attention.

She motions toward me with both hands, gesturing for me to bend down. Puzzled, I do what I think she wants. She takes my face in her hands the same way my ma does. She closes her eyes and squeezes my face lightly in her veined, knobby hands.

She draws in a deep breath and then sighs. "Benito, I'm not your mother. But if Lucia were here, she'd want someone to be honest with you." She presses her neon-pink lips together—a bold and dramatic shade for a woman of any age. "Take a goddamn day off, would you? You look like you're about to blow. Go for a run, go get laid. Whatever you young people do these days. Play some of those violent video games I hear so much about." She frees my face and nods. "I'm worried about you. And a lot of other people are too. Even if we don't all know how to show it."

I scrub a wet hand across my eyebrows, the tenderness and her lack of prying freeing me up a little. "I...I fucked up, Rita," I admit quietly. "With Mags. With a lot of things."

She shrugs, pushing heavily bejeweled glasses onto her forehead. "Who doesn't? So what?" She taps her chest. "We all know your heart, Benito. Say you're sorry and get back to doing what you do so well."

What is that? I wonder. I'm not sure I even know anymore.

Instead, I say, "We need a new fucking roof before winter, Rita. You got a rich boyfriend we could hit up for some cash?"

She barks a laugh. "Baby, I'm good. But I'm not *that* good."

I wink at her. "You'd school me, Rita. You'd teach me things a man could only dream of."

She shakes her head and points a neon-pink nail at me. She must paint her nails every day to match her lipstick. "If I were thirty years younger, Benito..."

"Thirty!" I exclaim. "Rita, I'm thirty-one. You'd still be, what? Fortysomething?"

"Fortysomething," she confirms coyly, not willing to reveal her real age, even though she knows I've got that information on her employment paperwork. "Nothing wrong with a little age gap."

I wave her away. "Goodnight, Rita. Samuel picking you up?"

She nods and blows me a kiss. "I locked the front doors. I'll go out the employee entrance."

I dry my hands and pat my pocket for my keys. "It's dark out back. I'll let you out the front." I walk her out the front, waving a hand at Samuel, who's idling in the lot with his brights on. Then I lock up and head to the kitchen.

I take a long, deep breath. I'm finally alone. The restaurant is quiet. Even the heat has turned off due to the automatic timers Mags set up last year.

She said we'd save a shit-ton on utilities with the smart controls set to heat and cool on a schedule, and of course, as always, she was right. But that means not even the old furnace is knocking as I get back to work. It's peaceful, being here alone. The place I've built at thirty-one years old. My dreams, my sweat. Even my tears.

After a little more listless scrubbing, I finally give the old stockpot a break. It's nearly ten before I head into my office, throw the card Mags tossed onto the floor into the trash, grab the damn flowers, and head out to my SUV.

I make the drive home, thinking about how the hell I'm going to apologize to Mags. Maybe I can reach out to the SBA and ask for a meeting. See what I missed in the presentation about the community development grant thing that Mags wants me to apply for. Maybe I should call out sick for a couple days. As long as Mags is there, the kitchen will run fine. I spend every waking minute there. It might do everybody some good if I took the damn break everyone seems to think I need. I don't know. If I stay home, I'll check my email. I'll worry. No, fuck that. I'll obsess. Over the roof, the bills, the paperwork.

I love being in the kitchen. I love cooking. Maybe I could take a day off and test out some new recipes at home. Call up my pops and see if he wants to head into Cleveland for a trip to the specialty markets. Pops. I didn't reply to my mom's text earlier, so that's something I can do if I take a day off. Go visit my parents. See if I can get to the bottom of what's up with Mario and Lucia.

I pull into my assigned underground parking space and juggle the flowers in my arms. I ride the elevator to the top floor of the building before I realize that I don't want these damn things. I should have known the card would have fallen someplace inside the plastic. I wasn't thinking. I shouldn't have tried to regift them to Mags. So many should haves and shouldn'ts.

When the door opens on my floor, I don't even head toward my unit. I turn the opposite way and head for the utility closet where the trash chute is located. I'm going to chuck this entire bouquet down the chute and put this whole damn day behind me.

I yank open the utility closet door, but the light is on and someone's in there, struggling to open the trash chute and fit a very full bag of trash inside.

"Hey, uh, you need a hand?" I ask. I know almost everyone in this building, but I don't recognize the woman in front of me.

She turns at the sound of my voice and says, "Thanks, I just moved in. Is there some trick to keeping this thing open while you put your trash…"

Her words die on her lips as we blink at each other in shock.

The woman throwing her trash out in my building is none other than my hot hookup from last night. The woman standing in front of me in black yoga pants, a loose top that's falling over one shoulder, and a messy bun is Willow.

CHAPTER SIX

willow

I lean forward and stroke the rich, velvety petals of a dark red rose. "You did *not*," I gasp. "Please tell me you did not regift flowers from one woman to another."

Ben leans across my white marble counter and grabs the bouquet. "This little fucker has caused me more trouble…"

"I blame the man," I say playfully, yanking the bouquet out of his hands and setting it protectively by the sink. "Not the flowers. And since these were meant for me, I think I'll keep them, thank you very much. They've come full circle. Finally made it home."

Something about saying that, finally coming home, sends a cold shiver skating down my spine, and the hairs on my arms lift in warning. *Homes are temporary*, I remind myself. Everything is temporary. These cut flowers won't last more than a couple days, maybe a week, if I water and feed them. Nothing is meant to stay in one place forever. Not people, not flowers.

I turn back to Ben, who is unwrapping thick moving paper from my barstools. They are really heavy, and the movers offered to unwrap them. But by the time everything else was inside, the bed set up, and most of the furniture reassembled, I didn't have the energy to have strangers spend another minute in my place. I'll gladly accept a little help from Ben though.

"While you literally find yourself a chair," I say, opening my completely empty fridge, "can I offer you some tap water? You might have to drink it from your hand, though. I haven't unpacked the glasses yet."

Ben crinkles up a load of brown moving paper and sets a vintage bronze barstool in front of the kitchen island. "Here okay?"

I nod. "Perfect. Although now that you saved my behind in the trash room, you're going to have to show me where to recycle all my moving boxes and the packing paper."

A slow grin spreads over his face. "Should we also toss out the evidence that you cheated on the best restaurant in Star Falls by ordering from—" he squints at a small pizza box resting on the counter near the flowers "—Papa Gino's pizza? A chain, Willow? How could you order mass-produced pizza when you claimed just last night that food is your life?"

"Food *is* my life," I insist. "But there are times when cheap food is nostalgic. Some of my best memories were made over a gas station taquito or hot dog."

"And some of your worst memories probably happened after eating that crap too." He's smirking, but I'm not going to join in on the joke.

The memories of road trips with friends, of the many things I've chosen to do in my adulthood with people who choose to spend their time with me, are running through my memory. Maybe he's always lived in Star Falls and had gourmet meals. I sure as hell didn't. But I don't want my issues to ruin what might otherwise turn into a really fun night.

I arch a brow and come around the island to lean against the cool marble beside him. "So," I say, looking him over. "I'm not exactly great at math, but I put two and two together. You're Benito, king of Italian cuisine. Am I right?"

He sucks his lower lip into his mouth like he's biting back a laugh. "Well, I am Benito Bianchi," he confirms, stretching out a hand to me. "Creator of Italian delicacies, regifter of flowers, and savior of ladies who can't figure out trash chutes."

I take his hand and hold it in mine, and almost without meaning to, I trace my fingers across the back of his knuckles. His hands are strong and warm, the kind of hands that could shape dough or tug my hair with equal intensity. I know because I've already experienced one of those. Despite what seems like a giant ego on this man, I can't say that I'd mind experiencing him again.

As I stroke his hand with my fingers, the air between us sizzles with the memories of last night. The unspoken question of whether we're headed in that direction again sparks between us like fireflies on a summer night, suddenly playful and unexpected.

Hooking up with Ben might be more complicated now. I know a little about who he is. I know about his business, his roof, his kitchen manager, and her none-too-subtle frustration at Benito's business practices. As if that wasn't enough, we're next-door neighbors. For a woman who never likes to dig too deep or stay too long, this situation already feels like far too much.

"Do you prefer Ben?" I ask, switching the topic to something neutral. "Or was that just your bar name? You know, the one you give hookups if you want to stay anonymous."

He chuckles. "I'm never anonymous. Not in a town like Star Falls."

I resist the urge to roll my eyes, because he doesn't even sound like he's boasting. In a town this small and quaint, I'm sure it's true.

When he turns to face me, his stare is intense. I feel like I'm under a spotlight, and yet, it's not uncomfortable.

I feel my body come awake under his gaze, like my limbs are flowers starving for the kind of light only he can produce. I no longer feel the sore feet and tired hands from moving and standing all day.

What are the odds that Ben would have tried to send me flowers? That we'd end up being neighbors?

Despite all the reasons why I should thank him for the tour of the trash room and send him home, my resolve to stay professional and keep my distance from this confusing and charismatic man crumples with just one flick of his tongue across his plump lower lip.

"My family calls me Benny," he says, his voice rumbling with something that sounds like pride. "Benito when my ma's mad. I answer to just about anything, but I'd really prefer if you called me something more descriptive."

I can't even stop myself. The flirtation comes out of me, despite whatever warnings my logical brain is trying to send to stop this. "What would you like me to call you?" I ask. "Sex god? Ravioli-making rake? Deliveryman of dinner and orgasms?"

He grins. "I resemble those remarks."

I lace my fingers through his. "You do. You were sexy in a freezing rainstorm, Benny," I say, trying out the cute version of his name. "I think you should be very, very flattered. I meant those things as a compliment."

He turns quickly and slides a hand under my hair, his fingers brushing the tender skin of my neck. "I am flattered," he says, bending low and whispering hot against my ear. "And excited. I thought I'd never see you again."

"And here *we* are." My eyes flutter shut, and I breathe him in deep. On the surface, I pick up notes of garlic and olive oil. But deeper, I smell a hint of cologne and mint, and another hot, delicious scent that my body immediately remembers from last night. From when he was naked, his limbs thrown over mine, his bare skin smooth and hot beneath me and around me.

"So," I rasp, my voice thick in my throat, "aren't you going to ask me my last name? You might decide you want to have flowers delivered again in the future."

He lowers his lips to my ear and kisses my earlobe, his fingers still firm behind my neck. "Nah," he murmurs, snaking his fingers through the hair at the base of my loose bun. "I'll make sure all my deliveries are made in person from here on out. More personal that way. I wouldn't want the card to get lost and have you think that Papa Gino was trying to get in your pants."

I chuckle and give in to whatever this is. Benito is a man of contradictions. He's a little cocky, but I kind of prefer him hot and full of himself, actually.

It's easier to focus on his body and the obvious chemistry we share than to think about the man himself. His business. His staff. His heart. This is just about the connection, and connections can be light and easy.

"I like the sound of you getting in my pants, Benito." I turn my face toward his, my eyes still closed. The heat of him warms me from my fingertips to my bare toes, and the slight tug of his fingers in my hair sends a tremor through my body. A low moan slips from my lips.

"Willow." He says my name like it's his favorite food. I can feel his lips shape every letter as he speaks. "I want to put you on this counter and have my way with your pussy. But I don't think the marble is going to feel as good for you as I want it to."

Another shiver claims my flesh, and I feel my knees buckle slightly. "My bed is unpacked," I say, the words slow, my limbs drowsy with arousal. I lean forward, pressing myself against his hips, and feel the erection straining against the front of his jeans. "But I have no idea where the condoms are in this mess."

"My place?" he asks. "I'll drive."

I pull my face back and grin at him. "I have a car now, you know. No more rideshares."

He scoops me up in his arms, and I wrap my legs around his waist. "I'll insist on giving you a ride. Where are your house keys?"

I point to a lanyard inside a small brushed-bronze bowl on a sideboard near the front door. "You don't think it will be awkward carrying me over the threshold of your place? It might give the neighbors the wrong impression."

His mouth is on mine, crushing my lips, his strong hands cupping my ass as he stumbles toward my front door with my legs still wrapped tight around his hips. "Fuck the neighbors," he rasps, staggering across the condo until he's pressing my ass against my door.

He pulls his lips from mine, and I gasp. "I'm a neighbor now, so, yes, please."

"Keys," he barks. I reach for the bowl and grab my keys, clutching them in one hand. Then he leans into me, and my vision goes dark as he kisses me until I can't breathe.

When we're both gasping for air, he sets me gently on my feet, yanks open my door, then grabs my hand.

I walk the twenty or so steps down the hallway carpet in my bare feet and watch while Benny digs into his pocket for a set of keys. He curses quietly to himself as his trembling hands fumble with the lock. When the door finally swings open, he reaches for me and tugs me inside. I realize I haven't even stopped for my phone. I'm going inside the place of a guy I hardly know. My new neighbor. I don't have a way to call or text, no alarm to set if we fall asleep like we did last night.

I don't know what's come over me, but I don't care. Benny flips on a light, and a warm yellow glow brings his place to life. I feel oddly safe here, comfortable. Like I can already see a future spending a lot of time going between his place and mine.

He's not a serial killer, I tell myself. Serial killers don't bring women home to their place when they live next door. Serial killers don't send women flowers after a one-night stand. Serial killers don't make gorgeous ravioli and own businesses in small towns.

"Willow?" My name on his lips has me looking up at him. He's watching me, the deep brown stare intense. His cheeks are flushed, a light stubble on his face revealing the tiny cleft at the tip of his chin that I remember from last night.

He's backlit by the soft glow of a large light fixture that hangs over his island. The marble is different, the place much more lived-in than mine, of course. But it's warm and masculine. His kitchen is dark, the marble a sleek black sparkling with swirls of gold. I feel oddly happy to be here, and something deep inside wants to name it. Wants to think about why, but I won't go there. Not tonight.

"I was promised some personal attention," I remind him.

He growls, an animalistic sound, and his eyes flutter shut for a moment. "Come on." He takes my hand and leads me to the room that must be his bedroom. His unit is actually bigger than mine. He has two bedrooms, and I'm assuming another partially open door leads to a second bath.

Suddenly, the rush of getting to his place slows down. Something about going into his bedroom… This feels different from a sexy, anonymous hookup in a hotel. This is his home. Where he sleeps. Where people he's dated have stayed.

I look over the dark room while he turns on a small bedside light using an app on his phone. The curtains on the window are open, and the moonlight that's reflected off the river outside casts a white glow over the room.

"Willow." His voice is quiet.

I step into his arms and lift my face. He kisses me lightly, probingly, as if he's tasting a brand-new dish for the first time. His lips are light on mine as he presses and licks, explores my tongue and the depths of my open mouth. His breath is so natural, so sweet. It's like our bodies perfectly balance each other. I close my eyes and reach for his ass, pulling our hips close.

"Willow," he says again.

I hum my response against his lips.

"I do want to know your last name," he whispers. "I don't want to have to stalk your discarded junk mail to figure it out."

I giggle and pull my face back from his. "Watkins," I say. "Willow Watkins. Nice to meet you."

"It's so fucking good to meet you," he says, wrapping his hands around my hips and picking me up again.

He sets me down on the edge of his bed. It's made, but hardly. The white down comforter has been tossed across the king-sized mattress but not really smoothed, and I can see the edge of his dark-green sheets because he hasn't bothered to cover the entire surface of the massive bed. His pillows are all wonky, like he rolled out of bed after clutching them in his arms and bunching them under his head and they've patiently been waiting there in the same position for his return. I can understand the feeling.

When he leans me back against the soft covers, I look up at the ceiling and lift my hips, letting him strip off my yoga pants. The cool air meets my bare flesh and raises goose bumps on my thighs, but

I'm not moving. Not covering up. I feel exposed but not vulnerable. Sharing pleasure, showing him my body... That's easy. And I love it when relationships are easy.

Benny kneels next to the bed, and he's pulling off my panties and setting them someplace out of my sight. I flutter my eyes closed and give in to the feeling of his warm palms skating up the length of my thighs. I moan, a soft but greedy sound. He's just barely touching my skin, but already, I am starving for more of him.

He tugs gently at my hips, urging me toward the end of the bed so he can kneel on the floor and reach my pussy with his mouth. I feel kisses following his fingers, first along the tops of my thighs and then between my legs and along my inner thighs.

His breathing is ragged against my skin, and my nipples tighten deliciously, a thrill radiating from my breasts, through my belly, until the pulse pounds in my core.

He widens my legs, pressing my knees open. "Willow," he gasps, "you smell like fucking cherry syrup. Sweet and..." I feel his lips against my seam, and my hips buck. "I'm not going to be able to hold back," he mutters, turning his head and cursing against the tender skin of my thigh. "You got to talk to me, babe," he says. "Smack me in the back of the head if you have to. I don't want to do too much, but fuck, you're beautiful."

I reach down and slide my fingers through his thick, soft hair. The waves of it are smooth, like he doesn't even use styling product, and the heat from his skin radiates into my tightening grasp. "You won't be too much," I tell him. "But I might be too much for you. I know what I need to come," I warn him.

"Take it," he begs. "Take it from me, babe. Don't hold anything back from me."

His words do something funny to me. He sounds sincere. This isn't just dirty talk he's trying on to see what it does to me. He doesn't sound like he's trying to impress me now, the cocky bravado totally replaced by intensity.

When he lowers his mouth to my pussy and I feel the lightest touch of a fingertip, I gasp, and he praises me.

"Yeah, baby. Help me learn what you like. You like this?" He strokes me in long, smooth touches, the pressure so delicate, I want to thrust my hips against him to speed him up.

"Fuck, yes." Part of me wants to pull back a little. Communicating like this is rare for me.

I force my body to relax, my legs to open. I try hard to get the hell out of my head and let him lead our pace. This is different from last night. More intimate, if that's possible. It feels good but also scary.

"Is there anything you don't like?" he murmurs, and I feel the light rasp of his breath on my trimmed hairs. His hands don't stop kneading me. It's like his palms are massaging me while his fingers stroke me. I can't keep track of everything I feel, but it's all so, so good.

I'm lost in a haze of bliss and warmth, all of it coming from his voice, his touch.

"I'll tell you," I promise. "You won't break me."

With that, he lowers his lips to my clit and flicks the hot tip of his tongue against me. He slides one finger inside me while he sucks my clit into his mouth.

The pleasure is immediately intense, but perfect. He matches every movement of my hips, every gasp and groan with more pressure, faster movements, or by slowing down agonizingly. I grip the sheets in my hands and lift my knees, propping my feet on his shoulders.

"Fuck, yes, Willow. You're so goddamn perfect. You're beautiful. Fuck," he grates out, lifting his mouth only for a second from my clit. "Fuck my face, babe. Take what you want." As soon as he gets the words out, he goes right back to sucking me while he maintains the slow, relentless strokes of his fingers inside me.

By the time I feel the intensity building, I'm holding his head and rocking my hips hard against his mouth.

"More," I beg him. "Your fingers… Fuck me, Benny. Oh God, fuck me harder."

He pistons two fingers inside me, his mouth keeping a steady pressure on my clit, and even though I can't make out the words, he's muttering, whispering against my pussy, urging me, praising me as I grind and grind.

I lift my hips and work my hands in his hair, chasing the climax that's just out of reach, every nerve ending in my nipples and core liquid and melted, aching and desperate.

With every groan I feel against my flesh, the rumble of his curses, his breaths, his kisses, he adds just the right friction to send me skyward.

When I finally come, it hits me like a blast of wind, pushing, pushing, pushing me through wave after wave of pleasure. The sensation is harder, more intense than any I can remember.

As my body releases, my legs collapse against the bed, and he turns his face to rest his head against my thigh. He's panting, and I'm completely out of breath, the pounding of my heart so fierce in my chest, I'm sure he can hear it.

"I'm so fucking glad I found you," he says.

I pull my weak fingers from his hair, and we just lie there together for what seems like minutes, neither one of us speaking, neither one of us breaking the erotic spell. This feels right. Like I could crawl up the down comforter, tuck myself under, and cuddle into his pillows. As long as his body was spooned right there behind me.

I could imagine never leaving.

Never getting enough of this.

As my body cools and I come down from a place so lust-drenched and delicious, I feel like I can hardly think straight, his words echo in my mind. I hear what he said with stark and sudden clarity.

I'm so fucking glad I found you.

And that's why I jump out of bed, throw on my yoga pants, and run.

CHAPTER SEVEN

benito

Between having a gorgeous woman literally run from my bed to the bullshit I've been dealing with in the kitchen with Mags all week, I practically collapse when I finally make it over to my parents' house.

I arrive at my parents' early, hoping to score a few minutes alone with Ma before the chaos of my three siblings, their spouses, and the many kids. But my hopes are pretty much dashed when my sister Grace opens the door.

"What the hell, shithead," she says, leaning forward to kiss me on the cheek. "You're early."

"What'd I do now?" I ask, kissing her back. Gracie's long black hair is up in a sleek ponytail, and at my question, she lifts a perfectly shaped black brow at me.

"Nothing, Benny. Absolutely nothing. Ryder's parents took the kids to the city for a sleepover for the weekend, so I'm kid-free. I'm cursing and drinking while I've got the chance. As long as Ma doesn't hear me. I have no spare change for the swear jar." She nudges me in the ribs. "For reals. You're never here before the food is on the table. What happened? Restaurant burn down?"

I say a silent prayer and look for some wood to knock. "Don't even joke about that," I tell her. But the fact that Grace is swearing and sassy makes things feel a little more normal. I need some normal today. I need my family today. This is home, and I'm so grateful I have this place to come to.

I flick Gracie in the ribs like she nudged me, but harder, little-brother style.

"Hey!" she yells. "Stop."

"What's the yelling about?" Ma pads into the hallway, her brows furrowed in full mama mode, until she sees me. Her face immediately shifts into a look of concern. "Benito? Baby, what's wrong?"

She practically pushes past Grace to get to me.

"Thanks, Ma," Grace says, plopping down on the couch with my parents' dogs. The little Chihuahua tucks down into Gracie's lap, and Grace swaddles her in a blanket. "I'm just the one who got flicked in the rib cage. I'm totally fine. Don't worry about me."

"You hush," Ma says, nodding severely at Grace. "Let me discipline your brother."

I shake my head. I am thirty-one years old, I own a business, and I haven't lived at home for nearly ten years. But you're never too old to be disciplined by Lucia Bianchi—not if you deserve it.

Ma glares at me as she reaches for my face, and I bend down to kiss her. She grips me tight, pushing up on her bare toes to hug me. "My heart," she whispers in my ear. "Is everything okay?"

"I can hear you," Gracie says, sounding bored. "You want me to leave? You guys need some mother-son privacy? I'll go find Pops and tell him some secrets of my own."

Ma and I look at each other, and I nod at my sister. "Would you?" I ask in a low voice. "I'm not shitting you, Gracie."

Grace gets up off the couch, carrying the Chihuahua bundle in her arms. She stares at me, her heavy wings of eyeliner missing for the more casual family dinner. "What the shit is going on?" she asks.

"Gracie." Ma doesn't even have to get it out. My sister holds up a hand and stops her.

"Sorry, Ma, sorry. Why do I feel like you two really are telling secrets? What's up?" She looks from me to our mother, a sincerely worried look on her face.

"I got into some hot water with Mags." I think fast and then explain. "It's nothing. Ma and I talked about it the other day. I was going to update her."

Grace has a bold personality and takes no shit from anyone. But the one thing my sister has is a seriously generous heart. She juggles Ma's dog in her arms and nods. "You need another ear, you can bend mine. You two talk. I'll go find Pops."

"He's in the basement, Gracie," Ma calls, which cracks me up because unless my pops is in the kitchen, the only other place he'd be before a Sunday dinner is the basement, where we have a whole second kitchen. Smaller, but when you raise four kids under one roof in a modest home, a second kitchen is a necessity, not a luxury.

Once Gracie goes downstairs, I lean close to ask Ma about the latest with Pops. She shakes her head. "He won't say a word, Benny. I asked him what it was all about, why he's so secretive about going to the doctor, but he just said it was routine and not to worry."

I'd ask Ma if she's tried that, but "not worry" and my ma are two things that never have gotten along together. I nod. "Well, sooner or later, you're going to get a doctor's bill or a co-pay statement from your insurance, right? That should have the name of the doctor on it, and then you just ask him. You show him the paperwork, and you demand he give you the news."

Ma looks elated at first and then just as quickly deflates. "I never even thought of that," she says. "You're right. But how can I go all private detective on your father? I don't even want to. Things between us have never been like that, Benito. We've been together since we were fifteen years old. How many secrets do you think we've kept from each other?" She holds up a hand, her fingers circling together to form an O. "Zero. No secrets. We tell each other everything. I want him to tell me what's going on of his own free will. I'm not going to go all Sherlock Holmes on Mario."

I don't blame her. I'd want to know too. I can't imagine why Pops would be holding out on Ma, unless it's serious. "You want me to say something?" I ask. "I'll tell him right now that I know he had a doctor's appointment last week and—"

The sound of Gracie bellowing as she stomps up the basement steps stops me cold.

"So, Pops, you made two pans of lasagna?" She's practically screaming.

I groan and shake my head at Ma. "She needs fucking acting lessons, that one."

Ma grimaces, and I hold up a hand. "Sorry, sorry. Freaking. Freaking acting lessons."

Pops throws open the door, carrying a steaming hot pan of lasagna between two well-worn, red-checkered oven mitts. "Benny," he cries out, looking over his shoulder at my sister. "Gracie, why didn't you say your brother was here?"

She doesn't answer and gives me a death glare, her eyebrows bouncing up and down on her expressive face. "Well, Pops, you're on your way up. I didn't think Benny getting here was exactly front-page news." She sounds grumpy, but her attitude is directed at me.

I step away from Ma, knowing our conversation is finished. She reaches for my arm, though, and gives it a squeeze. "Benito…" she says.

"I got it, Ma. I'll help Pops with the other tray."

I can hear her huff a sigh of relief. She knows I won't confront my pops until she says she's ready. But I'm uncomfortable as I follow Pops into the kitchen. He sets the lasagna down on a dish towel and then turns to hug me.

"Benito." He holds me tight. This isn't just a quick welcome, a routine peck, or a slap on the back. Pops is holding me. "Great to see you, son. I didn't expect you so early. You need to take off right away? You're staying for dinner, aren't you?"

I nod slowly, releasing my dad even more slowly. I try to look him over for signs that something's different. Same thick, graying hair that stands in waves like mine. Same reading glasses Ma forced him to get not that long ago. He even smells the same, the faint whiff of his cologne hitting my nose as I clap him on the back of his flannel shirt.

He gives me a huge smile, then gestures excitedly to the lasagna. "Make a plate, son. I don't want to hold you up. Eat, eat."

I shake my head. "It's all right, Pops. Mags is covering dinner tonight. I'm not going in to work."

That may have been the worst possible thing I could have said. Now my dad's looking at me like I said I wanted to put ketchup on his lasagna. "Mags? Running the kitchen? Benny, what's going on? Is everything okay at the restaurant?"

I nod and wave a hand at him. I don't know what to tell him. Part of me wants to share the shit going on. The roof, the SBA grant that Mags wants me to apply for, the mix-up with the flowers that Mags still hasn't forgiven me for. But then I think about my dad, his heart, his who knows what. How can I stress him out with my shit when I don't know how stress will affect him?

I rub my face and head to the fridge for the pitcher of water. My throat is suddenly dry. I've never, literally never, been in this situation with my parents before. I've hidden shit from them all my life, but nothing serious. Getting drunk at prom and throwing up on the rented shoes. Crashing Pops's truck the first time I used it alone because my girlfriend at the time was trying to jerk me off while I was behind the wheel. Sneaking a whole unopened bottle of wine to drink in the basement with my brothers on a hot summer night.

All that shit, though… It's kid shit. Normal growing-up stuff. Not secrets. Not like whatever it is Pops is hiding from Ma.

"You make the salad yet?" I ask.

My dad's face breaks into a massive grin. "It's been years since we cooked together. You got the tomatoes?"

I grab a couple of tomatoes and groan. "Pops, you need me to go shopping for you? These look like something the dog shit out."

My dad cackles, but then he comes over to inspect them over my shoulder. "Are they that bad? I just bought them this week. I was up in—" He stops himself suddenly. "Well, if you think they're bad, son, just toss them."

My heart shudders in my chest.

Total lockdown.

He bought these earlier this week when he was in the city. These aren't from the local market. But this is clearly something he doesn't want to talk about.

I debate whether I should press him on the issue, ask him where he got them from, but I let it go. Pops was about to say it, and then he stopped.

Whatever it is he's got going on, he's not ready to share it. And no matter how much it's killing me, I'm not going to push.

At least, not yet.

The four of us are just about to sit down to eat when Vito lets himself into the house.

"Dumbass," Gracie and I both call out at the same time.

My mother scolds us as Vito shakes his head. "You know, that never gets old." He slips off his boots.

Ma gets up from the table to hug him. "Vito," she says, leaving a big maroon smear on his cheek. "Where's my grandbaby? Where's Eden?"

Vito goes right to Pops, leans over his chair, and smooches his cheek loudly, then smacks me on the back in greeting. "Asshole," he mutters warmly. "What the hell you doing here so early?"

The question is actually starting to grate on my nerves. I run a business. I'm sorry I haven't been able to make family dinners for the last ten years. I've slipped out of my own family eatery almost every Sunday to at least sit down with my family for an hour. They're making it sound like an act of God that I'm here and not rushing to get back to Benito's. I guess, in a way, it is, but I'm starting to feel like the asshole they keep saying I am.

I lift my wineglass and ignore my brother's question.

"Franco and Chloe coming?" he asks.

Ma shakes her head. "What do I know? Nobody tells me anything. I still don't know where my grandbaby is."

Vito nods. "Junie's cutting a molar. She's running a low-grade fever, been napping all afternoon. Eden stayed behind."

Ma immediately starts making suggestions, offering to make soup and things for the little girl Vito shares with his longtime girlfriend, Eden. Juniper's biological dad gave up all parental rights, and Vito and Eden are in the process of both planning a wedding and having Vito legally adopt Juniper as his own.

Vito serves himself some salad, not even noticing that no one else has food on their plates when Ma starts yelling at him as the door opens again. This time, it's Franco, the eldest.

"Yo, yo," Franco says in the way only he can. He yanks off his motorcycle boots and holds up his hands. "Got to wash up. Just helped a lady on the side of the road with a flat tire."

My brother is a mechanic, so it's not surprising he'd help a lady in distress, even on a Sunday. He comes back to the table after he washes up in the powder room and, starting with Ma, gives everyone kisses or hugs hello. "Chloe couldn't make it," he explains, taking the chair next to me. "You're here early," he says, nodding. "Good to see you here, man. You staying?"

I nod. "Where's Chloe?"

Franco points to his nose. "She feels like she's coming down with a cold or something. Doesn't want to spread the germs. You'll have to put up with just me tonight."

I reach for the bottle of Chianti and fill Franco's glass. He looks around the table. "Looks like I'm right on time." He lifts his glass in the air. "The OG Bianchis."

"This is really something." My pops sounds emotional. He lifts up his wineglass. "All my kids together at one time." We all raise our glasses and then drink. "I love the spouses and the partners and the grandkids, but this is special." Dad's quiet for a moment, then he gets up from the table. "I forgot something. Excuse me." He pushes back from his chair and heads into the kitchen.

Gracie and Franco start talking about work, while Vito immediately starts eating his salad.

Ma and I are the only ones who exchange worried looks.

"Should I help him?" I ask the question quietly, hoping only Ma will hear, but Gracie, with her damned bat ears, points across the table at me.

"What the fuck, Benny? What's with all the whispers?"

"Language, Gracie." I say it in my best impersonation of Ma, and both Franco and Vito burst out laughing.

Gracie looks pissed, and Ma's got a deeply worried look on her face, but we all shut up pretty quick when Pops returns. He's holding a brick of cheese and a grater. We're all silent, Gracie glaring at me, Franco and Vito looking at Gracie, and Ma and me eyeballing Pops.

Mario looks over the table, then holds up the brick of cheese, a perfect forest-green wax sealing one side of the triangle. "Parmigiano-Reggiano," Pops says. "Who wants cheese on their lasagna?"

Ma and I visibly relax, while Vito holds up his plate. "Where's the grater I got you for Christmas, Pops?"

My father thinks for a moment, then sets down the flat old-school stainless-steel grater. "Let me find it."

"Nah, forget it. I'm yanking your chain, Pops. Top me off." Vito holds out his plate, and our dad grates a healthy mound of the rich, aged cheese over V's lasagna.

I'm just about to take a bite when I hear the harsh buzzing of somebody's phone.

Everybody starts hollering about whose phone it is, but I can tell from the vibrating tone it's mine. I thought I left my phone in my glove box, but I must have had it in my pocket and set it down near the couch when I said hello to Gracie. I grab it from the coffee table and swipe to silence the alert. I have two texts from Mags, one after the other.

Mags: B, sorry, I know you're taking tonight for family dinner, but this is a 911. How soon can you get here?

And then, just a few minutes later:

Mags: No one's hurt. But this is IMPORTANT.

These messages are more civil than anything Mags has said since I tried to regift Willow's flowers to her.

I rub my forehead and sigh. Fuck. The timing.

I hate having to choose, but Mags said 911. I've got to go.

I head back to my seat and shovel a bite of food into my mouth. "Sorry," I say, holding up my phone. "It's Mags. I got to go in."

Ma wordlessly gets up from the table and grabs my plate. I know she's going to try to send me home with my food, so I stop her. "Ma, I'll eat at the restaurant. Save those for me, though. I'll stop this week for lunch."

I blow a kiss to my pops, who waves at me while he listens to Vito telling him about Eden's new job. She started working for Gracie's husband's business and seems to be thriving there. Pops is engrossed, so I take an extra minute to look back over the table before I leave.

Ma is passing Vito more salad. Franco and Gracie are laughing about God only knows what. Pops had parked his glasses oddly on his forehead, not on top of his hair or on his nose—probably because he can't see his food with them on, but he can't see the end of the table with them off, so the forehead is a convenient place to stash them until he actually needs them.

My family is my everything, but my restaurant is my life's work.

I throw a last look back at my family, wave a quiet goodbye, and head out the front door.

I can only hope whatever's going on at the restaurant is worth leaving Sunday dinner for.

CHAPTER EIGHT

willow

The last week has flown by. I've been on the jobsite by sunrise nearly every day, meeting with the general contractor and supervising the last-minute decisions and approvals. I've been working out of my car, taking meetings and calls with my colleagues at Culinary Capital, and lining up final in-person talent interviews for the chefs I plan to hire for the new restaurant we're opening in Star Falls.

By the time I get back to the condo every night, unpack a few boxes, and cram some takeout into my mouth, it's a miracle I have enough energy to text my friends and brush my teeth.

Some nights, I can't even do both.

I would be lying if I said I hadn't also spent many of those precious few moments of free time regretting that I ran out on Benito. For a couple of days, I was acting like a safecracker, resting my head against the wall and listening to see if sound traveled between our units before I left my place. I've been living like a covert operative.

If I heard the faintest echo of the TV, I'd rush to the trash chute or the elevator, hoping against hope that I wouldn't run into him. When I heard the door of his unit slam in the late evenings, I knew he was home.

And I've never felt so stupid.

By Sunday, I resolve to do something about how I'm feeling.

I put on my most flattering black jeans, boots with a kitten heel, and an ultra-soft white sweater. I add delicate gold earrings, a necklace, and a casual, loose bun that I hope have me looking professional but not like I'm running into an office. I check over the notes I took from when I met Mags. She works every Sunday night. So, after a very small battle with my nerves, I check the time and call Jessa from the car.

"Still pregnant," she says, answering on the second ring. "Or did you call to talk about you?"

I chuckle. "Both."

The drive to Benito's is short, so after Jessa updates me on the adult coloring books, crying, and streaming shows she's been watching, I update her on Benito.

"I don't get it," I tell her, checking my lipstick in the mirror at a ridiculously long stoplight. "I don't get spooked by men. I don't know what the hell happened."

"That's not true," she says, and I can practically hear her shaking her head, the long, dark waves moving over her shoulders where she's propped up in bed. "You don't get serious. There's a difference. Maybe this guy hit a nerve, babe. Do you like him? Like, *like him*, like him?"

I sigh. "I don't know, Jess. We hooked up twice. I mean, I don't know enough about him to like him or not."

Jessa snorts. "I'd say any guy who can make you orgasm multiple times is more than a stranger, babe. You're starting to get to know him, at least."

I check my teeth for lipstick and then realize I'm obsessing over the stupidest little details and slam the mirror on my visor closed. "Well, I'll keep you posted. Things might get a little complicated. I think he may apply for the small business development grant Culinary Capital is sponsoring."

She sucks in a breath. "Oh, conflict can be juicy, but conflicts of interest? Never sexy."

I sigh. "Pros before bros," I chuckle. "It's kind of my thing."

"You're a pro through and through," Jessa assures me. "Maybe it's time you let one of those bros come at least as close to you as your job."

I know she means well, but I'm pulling into the restaurant parking lot. "I got to go," I tell her. "Love you. Hydrate and rest," I remind her.

"If I hydrate any more, my baby won't be the only one in diapers," she says wryly. "Love you. Call me soon. I'm almost through season three, so you know what that means..."

I shake my head and cut her off. "Jessa, you know how it ends."

"I still can't even." She blows me loud kisses over my car's speakers, and I end the call.

The parking lot of Benito's is full. I scan the lot, but I don't see Benito's SUV anywhere. Maybe he takes Sundays off? That could be why Mags works every Sunday. My shoulders sag a bit. This could be good, or this could be a sign from the universe that I should not have made this spontaneous trip on a Sunday. On the one hand, if Benny is off, I won't have to face him. But if he's not working, Mags may be too busy in the kitchen to talk to me about the grant.

Either way, I'm here. And I'm in the mood for a great meal. I gather up my purse and my courage, and I head inside.

The elderly hostess is holding court at the front of a very busy waiting area. She's sitting on a stool but hops up every few minutes to point long, painted nails or the ends of her glittery plastic glasses at someone whose table is ready.

"Darling!" she shouts over the low conversations. "Yes, I'm talking to you, Ed and Nina. Table for five is ready. Come on, now. Let's get you seated."

She motions to the people whom she obviously knows by name, jumps off her stool, and grabs an armful of menus. She notices me and nods. "Hello there, gorgeous. I'll be right back with you." But then she cocks her head at me and seems to look behind me for the rest of my party. "How many, love?" she asks. "Here for dinner?"

Nina and Ed and their kids are still gathering up toys and tying shoelaces, so I hold up one finger and nod. "Just me," I say. "Table for one or a spot at the bar. Whatever works."

She nods and grabs another menu, motioning for me to follow. I step aside to make room for the family who I assume will sit at one of the many tables between the lobby and the bar.

As I walk through Benito's, I see table after table full. Not an empty seat in the house. This is exactly the type of crowd I would expect at a place like this on Sunday evening. Families and couples are here for Sunday dinner. Kids crying in high chairs. Teenagers slunk down in their seats, peeking at phones hidden in their laps. A table with two older women is rowdy with laughter, and the hostess points at them as we pass.

"Bev, Carol, keep it civil," she shouts, laughably louder than the women at the table. "This is a family joint."

One of the women barks a laugh and points at the hostess. "Rita, come join us when things slow down."

The hostess, whose name must be Rita, shakes her head. "No rest for us working girls, ladies." She turns to Ed and Nina before she sets the menus down on the table and gestures for them to take their seats. Then she jerks a thumb at me.

"Bar's wide open, sweetheart. Take your pick." She turns and walks back to the hostess station, so I head over to the bar and sit on the same tall stool where I was the other night.

A second later, I feel a hand at my elbow. "Excuse me." The dad from the family who was just seated hands me a menu. "I think Rita gave us one extra. This one must be yours."

"Oh wow. Thank you," I say.

He nods and heads back to his table. I'm acutely aware of the fact that I'm alone, and I'm used to it, but the sense of being out of place hits me hard. Maybe it's because everyone seems to know one another. I've worked in a few small towns before, but I've never been any place like Star Falls.

I turn back to the menu and try to focus on what I'm going to eat. I've had the dish I'm probably going to love the most, so I decide to try something new. The last thing I want to do is fall into a pattern. Some people find predictable comforting, but not me. Spinach rotolo with meatballs, it is.

The bartender I had the other night points at me and looks as if she's trying to place me. "You were here the other night?" she asks. "Restaurant lady?"

I have to laugh. After the very little small talk I'd made with the bartender, the one thing she remembered about me was that I work in restaurants. I nod. "Also known as Willow. You're Jasmine?"

She nods. "Good memory. Don't feel bad if I ask you your name the next hundred times I see you. Some days I can't keep my own kids straight."

She pours me some water, then I order an iced tea and the rotolo. "Jasmine," I add, deciding that even if now is not a good time, I should send word to Mags that I've arrived. "Could I ask you to let Mags know I'm here? I know she's probably swamped, but we met earlier this week, and I told her I'd stop back in."

"Mags?" Jasmine lifts her brows. "Yeah, sure. Happy to." But then Jasmine frowns and leans forward on the bar. "She's not looking to leave, is she? Are you here to talk to her about a job?" Jasmine looks worried and smooths down her plain black button-down shirt. "She and Benito are going through a rough patch," she says. "But he's a good man. Despite his giant you-know-what."

I almost choke on a sip of iced tea. "His giant what?" I ask.

Jasmine shakes her head. "That man's ego... He's something else." But then her eyes grow soft, and she smiles. The sounds of clinking silverware and conversation seem louder as I lean closer to hear her. "He's got an even bigger heart. I don't care what anyone says. He's a good one."

She nods at me and points to a house phone. "I'll let Mags know you're here. What's your name again?"

I remind her, giving her both my first and last name. Then I settle into my iced tea and try for the first time in a long time not to feel like such a stranger.

Mags rushes out, her hair tied back behind a bandanna and her cheeks flushed pink. She's reaching out a hand to shake mine and grinning. "Willow," she says. "I'm so glad you made it." She motions down to the empty space in front of me. "Your dinner will be right up, but I wanted to see how long you can stay. I've got—"

I hold up a hand. "It's no problem," I say. "I knew you'd be busy. I felt like a fantastic dinner and some time with my book. I'll hang around until you have a few minutes to talk."

"Are you sure?" She looks worried. "It might be a while. Sundays can get…"

I hold up my phone. "I've got a whole library of stuff to catch up on. Take your time."

She nods and hustles back to the kitchen, and I decide to take my own advice. I flip open my e-reader and scan the dozens of titles in my library. Cookbooks and books about food science. Business books. And, of course, a couple of romance novels. I settle on a book that is high on spice and low on drama. That's what I want in my life; that's why I've got this bad boy on my bookshelf.

I sip my tea and scan the pages, growing more and more engrossed in the story of a biker who goes to prison for a stitch, but when he gets out, he meets a woman whose daughter is in distress, and I love it. Found-family vibes—my favorite kind. I'm deep into the action when a server sets a plate in front of me.

"Spinach rotolo with meatballs?" The older lady looks me over. "You need anything else, hun?"

"Sassy." The bartender waves at the woman who's brought out my dinner. "Did you meet Willow? She's a restaurant person."

My waitress, whose name I now know is Sassy, gives me a long, approving look, then grins. "You look too skinny to be a foodie." She taps a hand over her ample chest. "This is the body of a woman who knows her food."

I grin and nod at her. "I'm on the operations side," I explain. "Restaurant financing and investments. But I adore cooking and especially eating."

She nods at me. "You're in the right place. Benito's the best chef in Star Falls, but that's not saying much. Probably the best chef even in the city. You let Jasmine know if you need anything, and I'll hustle over. You want cheese?" she asks.

I nod. "Who turns down cheese?"

Sassy crows, a long, happy sound. "There's my girl. I'll be back in a second."

She rushes off, leaving a faint cloud of cigarette smoke and hair spray behind her. I haven't even looked down at my meal when I feel a light hand at my elbow.

"Willow, I'm sorry to come just as your food has arrived, but I wanted you to meet someone."

I turn at the sound of Mags's voice and crash eyes with the man I've spent all week avoiding.

Benito Bianchi.

His chocolate-brown eyes go cold, the soft stubble on his face highlighting both the dimple in his chin and his slight frown. He cocks an eyebrow at Mags.

"Mags, I don't understand…" he says, and I can tell he's struggling here.

I jump from my stool and extend a hand to him. "Mags, it turns out Benito and I have met." I hold out my hand, hoping he will shake it. "I didn't realize he was the owner when I ate here last weekend."

Benito's frown doesn't soften, but he does take my hand. He holds it carefully, like he's afraid I'm going to pull away, but it's he who pulls away first.

"I'm Willow Watkins," I say, but his touch is already gone. The heat that seared my skin leaves a chill in its path. My stomach flips, and I can feel the steady beat of my pulse hammering in my throat.

Damn. This was a bad idea. Such a bad idea.

I add a new rule to my playbook. Never sleep with a man in a too-small town. It doesn't have the same ring to it, but it's a policy I think I'm going to have to stick with. Especially if I'm going to make it through the next year.

"Nice to meet you," Benny says distractedly, but then he turns to walk away.

"Benito," Mags says pointedly, "Willow is with Culinary Capital."

He gives her a pointed glare, and I can almost see the unspoken question written all over his face. *What the fuck does that matter to me?*

Mags rushes to explain. "Willow's company is sponsoring the SBA grant. The one we're planning to apply for." She sounds so hopeful, so earnest. Like she's not only hoping that Benny remembers what she's referring to, but by putting Benny and me in the same room, we'll work some kind of finance miracle and make all the restaurant's problems go away.

I've seen it before. No matter the size of the restaurant, how well they're doing, almost every owner needs a crew that has their heart and soul in the work.

I see that in Mags. She may come off a little rough around the edges, but she cares. That's what this place needs. Whether Benito realizes it or not, Mags is an asset to his operation.

"Mags was able to attend the talk I gave at the SBA meeting earlier this week," I explain quickly. "She mentioned the restaurant's interest in applying for the grant my organization is sponsoring, and I told her I'd be happy to stop by sometime and chat a bit about writing a strong application."

"Writing a strong application," he echoes, his voice as stormy and cold as the rain that fell on us the night we met. "Let me make sure I'm following," he says, pointing to me. "Your company is in town to do what, exactly? Give away cash? What's the catch?"

Mags looks horrified and rushes in to explain. "Benito, they are opening a new restaurant in town. But they are also sponsoring a grant so the restaurants in town that will have new competition can benefit from the—"

"Whoa, whoa, whoa." Benito holds up a hand and cuts her off. "Let me get this straight. This lady here is going to open a brand-new restaurant here in town. Poach my customers, probably my staff, and who knows, maybe even my recipes." He looks down at my untouched plate of rotolo with a scowl. "But she's going to throw a little cash at my roof as a consolation prize? What is that, guilt money? So, you don't feel as bad when you put the little guys like me out of business?"

Mags's mouth has dropped open, and I'm fully standing now. "That's not exactly how we operate," I say, my voice tight.

"I know all I need to know, and I'm not interested." Benito nods

625

at me, then he calls for Jasmine. "Jas, wrap Ms. Watkins's dinner to go. It's on the house." He turns to me and squares his shoulders. "We'd prefer if you kept your grant and your snooping as far from my restaurant as possible."

Leaving Mags, Jasmine, and me all stunned speechless, Benito turns and storms away.

CHAPTER NINE

benito

Well, if Mags was pissed at me before, the scales have sure as hell tilted now.

What the hell was she thinking, bringing Willow into the restaurant?

What the hell was I thinking, bringing that woman into my bed?

I've never shifted from regret to rage so fast in my life.

I pace the floors of my condo, trying to reason with myself. My mind swings from worry to worse.

Willow had said that her life was food. She actually said that she was going to try to copy my kale ravioli recipe.

My temper is about to bubble over when there is a harsh knock at my door. I can hear Willow's voice calling my name.

"Please?" She knocks again. "Benito, I just need a minute. Would you please open up?"

I ignore her. The way she's been doing to me the last week since she ran out of here and left me with the taste of her on my lips and nothing but confusion in my chest.

Just when I think she's given up, she starts in again.

"Benito, would you please let me explain? Please. If not for my sake, for Mags's."

Hearing her say Mags's name sets my teeth on edge. I don't know what this woman's intentions are—not with me, my recipes, or my staff—but I yank open the door so I can tell her once and for all to her face to keep the hell out of my business.

When I see her standing there, she looks happy. Happy to see me. The momentary warmth on her face does a number on my anger, but only for a second.

I turn away from the soft waves falling from her bun, the light blue eyes searing into my brain.

"Come in," I tell her. "But don't get comfortable. You've got five minutes." I cross my arms over my chest, but suddenly, I can't control the rush of anxiety through my limbs.

At the sight of her, my body starts a war with my mind. I'm furious, and I should be, but the moment she closes the door, lowers her chin, and walks across the condo, it takes everything inside me to stop myself from going to her.

I've never had a hookup sink her claws into me so deep. And I've got to free myself before some real damage is done. "Five minutes," I remind her. "Then it's my turn."

She nods and looks around as if she wants to sit. I think about being a dick and just standing there, but she looks vulnerable.

I hate it, but I motion toward my L-shaped leather sectional. "Sit," I tell her.

She nods wordlessly, then sinks down on the edge of the sofa.

I wait until she chooses a spot, then I walk to the farthest possible spot from her and sit in my recliner.

Plenty of distance between us.

No way for us to get close.

It's dark out now, and the park lights reflecting off the river cast a warm yellow glow over my place. I tap my phone and use an app to turn on a couple of lamps so we're not sitting in total darkness.

Her face is cast in shadow, the rise and fall of her breasts in the soft white sweater she's wearing seeming more and more uneven. She leans forward and wrings her hands. "I owe you an apology," she says, meeting my eyes. "I'm honestly not even sure where to start."

"Start at the beginning," I say curtly. "Or just cut to the part where you admit you're trying to steal my recipes and my business."

She shakes her head, looking confused. "What are you talking about, Benny?" She pauses after she says my name, as if it sounds as intimate to her as it does to me.

I can't make her take back the way her voice curls around every syllable.

My cock tightens behind my jeans as I remember her crying my name against my ear the first night we meet.

The way her fingers tightened in my hair as I ate her pussy.

"Just…" I stammer. "Say what you came here to say."

"Ben…Benito, I'm not what you think I am."

I can't stop baiting her. I know it's my shittiest quality. I fucking told her to talk, but I'm furious, and my body won't stop reacting to her. With every blink of her sweet blue eyes, every time she bites her lip, I want to go to her. I have to physically grab the arms of my chair to stop myself from getting up.

"So, tell me who you are, Willow. I don't know a damn thing about you. Why you're here, what you do for work. Who your family is. Are you married? What's next? You have a husband and two point three fucking kids out there someplace?"

Her expression changes then, like she's retreating inside herself. It's a look I've seen thousands of times before. On Mags's face when I push too far. On the faces of countless women I have pushed away. Something about seeing the shutters close on Willow breaks a little something inside me. I start to backtrack before I can even stop myself.

"That was out of line," I admit. "I'm sorry. I'm…" I rub my face. "I'm really fucked over here. I'm angry and a whole bunch of shit. I'm going to shut my mouth and let you speak."

She nods and then leans back a little bit into the couch. "Thank you," she says softly, her gaze never leaving mine. "I understand that you're pissed. So, thank you for letting me get a few things off my chest."

She swallows and I almost say something, but I hold the words inside and take a deep breath.

Then I wait.

"I am the chief operations officer of a restaurant investment group. About six years ago, one of our scouts ate at a restaurant in Florida. Single location, family-owned. The menu was unique, but the branding was even more unusual. We approached the family with a franchise proposal, but they didn't want to expand. Then, about two years ago, one of the grandchildren from that same family graduated from culinary school. The granddaughter wanted to open a second location, but the family didn't have the capital or the know-how. So, they came back to us."

She swallows and clears her throat, and I curse myself for not offering her water, coffee, anything. I can be furious, but I don't have to be a shit host. "You want a glass of water?" I ask.

"You said I only have five minutes," she says, a small smile on her lips.

"It doesn't take long to drink a glass of water," I say coldly, still not willing to budge.

She nods, looking a little stunned, but holds up a hand. "I'm good, thanks. I'll get this out and be on my way."

When she says that, I have to stifle the urge to tell her no, she can stay. An annoyingly persistent part of me doesn't really want her to leave.

My fucking betrayer of a body.

My brain is furious at her.

I want to know what fucking game she's playing. But then, I don't know what I want. Her, maybe? I don't like it. I don't get it. But I get up and grab a kettle just so my hands have something to do. "You drink tea?" I ask without looking up.

"I do."

I fill the kettle to the max fill line and start the burner. Then I storm back to my chair because she's clearly going to wait until I sit down to keep talking.

"So," she says gently. "The granddaughter wanted help opening a second location. We danced around different options for ownership and viable locations to expand into." She pauses then, and I can feel her eyes on my face. I look up at her, trying to be unmoved by anything she says, anything she does. "For a lot of reasons that are proprietary, so I can't share the specifics, Star Falls was determined to be the perfect location for a second restaurant. I spent a year negotiating the deal with the family, the county, and the city. I'm here to break ground and supervise the build-out. Then when the new place is done, the granddaughter will move here to Star Falls and possess her own small part of her family's legacy."

"While Culinary Capital takes a massive cut of the profits, for what—the life of the restaurant?" I ask. I can't help myself. This doesn't sound like a good deal for anyone but Willow's business.

Willow sighs. "We signed a profit-sharing agreement that should make us whole on our investment in under thirty-six months. Our contracts have standard clauses with mutual audits and full transparency. We relinquish our investment twelve months after we're made whole. If our data and analysis are correct, the granddaughter will own the restaurant outright in as little as three years. We're not in this to screw over the little guy. My company is owned by two sisters whose father was one of the original franchisees of Papa Gino's."

She stops and meets my eyes when she shares that little fact. No wonder she ordered from them the other day and was so defensive of the mass-produced product.

She goes on. "We believe in helping communities create sustainable and profitable food industries. Sometimes that means we open franchises, and sometimes we work with people who have a gift for food but need a little support when it comes to all the other things that go into running a successful restaurant."

That fucking stings like lemon juice to the eyes. "Like me?" I demand, defensive again.

It's shockingly noble—if what she's saying is true. I've heard so many horror stories. Buddies who got taken advantage of by vendors, by real estate agents, by anyone and everyone who saw dollar signs at the first hint of their restaurants being successful. I've never heard of a finance company helping small business owners keep their businesses.

Not like this, and I don't trust it. I don't trust her.

I leap out of my chair and turn off the kettle that's just starting to steam.

Willow gets up and follows me into the kitchen. She reaches for my arm. "Benny, what I'm saying has nothing to do with you. Please, will you let me finish?"

I yank open a cabinet, pull out two mugs, and grab the honey. "How do you take your tea?" I demand, refusing to look at her.

"Just a little honey is fine, thanks." I hear the hint of a smile in her voice, like she's laughing at what a pouty bitch I'm being. I don't give a fuck.

This woman is bad news, and I need to listen to what she's saying so I know enough to keep her the hell out of my life.

She talks while I fix our tea. "We started the SBA grant program about five years ago. It was after…" She pauses and seems to consider what she's about to say. She walks to the purse she dropped on the floor by my front door and grabs her cell phone. She swipes the touchscreen and shows me an app. "This is what we used to do."

I glare at her hand, but I finally take the teabags out of the mugs, dump them in the sink, and grab her phone. "What am I looking at?" I ask.

"In every community where we open a restaurant, we know we're going to affect the local economy. In some places, the trade-off is worth it. We create new jobs in a place that needs them. We provide opportunities for people who wouldn't have had them otherwise. For several years, when I was on the ground supervising the build of a new restaurant, I would also coordinate with the local community to give back in some very tangible way."

The social media feed she's showing me has dozens of pictures going back years. Willow is shown hugging people in community centers, test kitchens, and even in backyard fundraisers.

"We stopped the year we worked with children of incarcerated parents," she says quietly. "After that, I couldn't manage it all. The community events, the work, the people."

I see a glimmer of something real in her eyes, and it's brutal. As if, for just a second, she dropped the mask, dropped the facade, and the real Willow was laid bare. I look away from her and back at the

632

phone. The more recent pictures show Willow at ribbon-cuttings and pig roasts.

"So, what, you give away money now? The grant is supposed to replace the community service stuff?" I ask.

She nods. "Yes. It's a newer program, but we estimate that for the additional expenditure of funds, the success of the new restaurant happens even faster. It's inevitable that some businesses will suffer and some jobs will be lost, but the goodwill and publicity the grants give us have actually helped the restaurants we open get profitable more quickly."

"Got to spend money to make money," I say acidly.

At that, Willow grabs her phone away from me, her fingers brushing mine. "You know what, Benito? I've had about enough of this pouty bullshit act. You want to know about the restaurant that you think I'm stealing recipes for? You want to know how much damage I've done to Benito's?"

She says my name a little mockingly, and for a hot second, I'm ashamed that I named my restaurant after myself. It sounds pompous as hell, especially after seeing all the good she seems to try to do. But I shove that away.

My work is my life.

I am that restaurant.

There is no me without it, and no restaurant without me. We may as well share the same name. We share the same heart, soul, and identity.

"Tell me," I say, baiting her. "Go on. You have three more minutes."

"Nice of you to keep track, but I only need one," she seethes, her anger catching up to my own. "One year from now, a Pancake Circus is going to open up. It's a family-friendly themed breakfast and brunch place. The original location in Florida is open for dinner, but our analysis led us to decide what would thrive best in Star Falls is a place that fills the need for large seasonal breakfast crowds and a consistently high-quality breakfast and brunch experience."

"Breakfast and brunch experience?" I repeat numbly. "Pancake fucking Circus?" I can't believe what I'm hearing. First of all, the place she's opening has nothing to do with Italian food, let alone dinner. So, she couldn't have been serious about stealing my recipes…could she? And second, she has a point. I've always thought Star Falls needed something better than the hole-in-the-wall strip-mall breakfast diners. I see the vision, and even worse, I don't hate it.

"It's fantastic," she says defensively. "But the good news is that in twelve months, another family will have their dreams come true, someone in Star Falls will be the recipient of a ten-thousand-dollar grant, and I will be on to the next project."

My stomach sinks.

Not just at what she's said about dreams coming true, but the grant amount. I had no idea it was that much. A chunk of cash like that would allow me to do a massive roof repair without spending a penny out of pocket. The roof could last another couple of years with a major repair job like that. The grant really could be the answer to my prayers.

But even worse, she's only here to supervise the build. She'll be gone in a year.

Two hours ago, I would have thought that was the best damn news I'd heard all week. But now, it sinks in my gut like a lead balloon.

"I'm not here to poach anything, steal anything, or cause you any grief, Benny," she says, her cheeks flushed with anger. Her blue eyes pop against the rage staining her cheeks, and I come around the counter to confront her, my anger dissipating like the steam over my mug of tea.

"So why did you run, then?" I ask, my hand on her arm. "Willow, why the fuck did you leave the other night?"

My business aside, this is what I really want to know. This is what's gutted me and eaten away at me the last week. The anger drains out of me in a rush as soon as I say the words, and I release her arm, my hands and knees feeling weak, like I've opened myself up and admitted something so big that the sheer effort has worn me down.

Willow reaches for my hand and slowly laces her fingers through mine. "I was surprised myself," she says quietly. "I think it just hit me all at once. Who you are. That your employee had come to me for help. I felt trapped, in a way. I don't know how to be honest. I just ran. I'm sorry. I have been looking for a way to apologize all week."

I tighten my fingers around hers. "Showing up at my restaurant was probably the worst way to do it."

She nods. "I know. You've got me in knots, Benito Bianchi. I'm…" She pulls her hand away from me. "I never stay in one place for too long. I never get too attached, but I was feeling attached. You sounded attached. You said…"

I remember what I said. I have been replaying the moment in my head on a loop all week. "I know what I said," I rasp out. "I'm so glad I found you."

We're both quiet, nothing but the hushed sounds of our breaths as we consider what we've just said.

"You were just supposed to be a hookup," she says quietly. "That's all this can be."

"I don't do relationships," I tell her. "You don't have to worry about getting attached to me. It's not going to be a problem."

"What you said about finding me…"

"Forget it," I tell her. "Your pussy was in my mouth, babe. Have you tasted yourself? Of course I was fucking glad I found you."

"Are you still?" she asks, lifting her face toward mine.

"Are *you* glad?" I ask. "Do you want to be found by me?"

"For now," she says. "While I'm here in Star Falls."

"I can handle an expiration date," I tell her. "I'm actually really good with keeping things fresh."

She rolls her eyes and purses her lips. "You got any more puns I need to brace myself for?"

"Why don't you Willow Walk-er your hot ass over here?"

"No," she says, shaking her head. "Nope, nope. Never use that one again."

"All the blood's rushed to my dick," I say. "I might not be thinking straight."

I know I'm not going to regret this. My body is all in, and if there is one thing I'm great at, it's keeping my brain and my heart separate from my hookups.

I can have fun with Willow and not let it get complicated. In fact, if she's wired as much like me as I think, this may be exactly the situation I need. No strings, no long-term. Just the fun. Just the good parts.

I step forward and curl a hand around the back of her neck. "Willow," I murmur, lowering my face to her neck.

As I plant soft kisses along the column of her throat, I drink in the scent of her, the feel of her soft hair tumbling from its bun against my fingers.

"Benito," she breathes, her hands circling low to cup my ass.

I groan and press against her, my body taking over and shutting my mind down.

She may be a woman who doesn't plan to stay in Star Falls for too long, but I'll take every moment she's willing to give.

CHAPTER TEN

willow

Three weeks later...

"Benito, you have to go." I wrap my legs around Benny's waist as he slides deep inside me. "Benny, fuck..."

"Shh." He leans forward and claims my lips with his. "Are you kicking me out again?"

I nibble his lower lip between my teeth and breathe him in. "Yes, again. I have a conference call in thirty minutes, and I do not need to show up looking like I just..."

A lightning bolt flashes behind my eyes as he rolls his hips, putting pressure on that sensitive spot that has me arching with need. Benny makes me greedy. He's more delicious than tiramisu, more decadent than a meal cooked by a Michelin-starred chef.

For the last few weeks, we've spent every evening together and quite a few entire nights. We fuck, we laugh, we eat, we sleep. Rinse and repeat. He's the most fun I've ever had, and yet...

A horrific series of siren sounds blare from my phone.

I flop a weak hand toward my bedside table, trying to silence my alarm.

"I have to get moving," I force out the words between his thrusts, my eyes rolling back in my head. I see darkness behind my closed lids. It's as if every inch of me is consumed by Benny. I feel him, smell him, taste him as he supports his weight on top of me and gently grinds his cock deep. My breasts are smashed under his chest, and he whispers the words against my lips between kisses.

"Come to my place after work?"

I groan, drawing in a deep breath. Even first thing in the morning, the scent of his soap, cologne, and the faintest hint of herbs from the kitchen cling to his warm skin. It's ridiculous, the effect this man has on me. I try to talk through the growing excitement that has my clit pulsing and my hips working slow circles against his. "Not tonight. I've got a video date with one of my best friends."

"After?" he asks, pulling out excruciatingly slowly and then, with a jerk of his hips, seats himself deep.

"Fuck yes, after," I pant. "After…"

I lift my hips and widen my legs, wriggling my hips and grinding up against his body until I am trembling, coming, my hands gripping his face as I kiss him.

"Fuck," I gasp into his mouth, and I feel his body tighten as my climax brings on his.

We writhe and curse, praise the heavens and moan, until he collapses against my chest, shuddering and sweating.

Far too quickly, he covers my bare chest with kisses. "Have a great call," he says, then he starts to roll away, but I grab him and hold him tight.

"Stay a second," I tell him. I don't like shoving him off me while his heart is still thudding against mine. I stroke his hair and kiss the top of his head, thanking the gods of video conferencing that my team won't be able to smell me. A sleek bun and a black top and I can be on that call in five minutes. That leaves me five more minutes with him.

We're silent as the sweat cools between us, and Benny's limbs grow heavy on mine. "I'm stopping by my parents' today," he says. "And Mags is closing the kitchen, so I'll probably be home by eight. You want to eat together after your call, or will that be too late?"

"Depends," I murmur into the thick waves of his hair. "Who's cooking?"

He chuckles. "Your choice. I've been working on a new recipe, and I'd love a guinea pig."

"Deal," I say. "Your place, my palate."

"Your mouth," he growls, kissing me again. Then he rolls off the bed, slides the condom off, and wanders into my bathroom to toss it out. I watch his bare ass as he goes, his cock still hard. His thighs are thick and hairy, and I feel a grin cross my face as I watch him. He dresses in a miraculously short amount of time and then holds out his hand to me. "Come on, gorgeous. Unless you're planning on takin' that call from bed?"

I grab his hand, and he kisses the tip of my nose after I climb out of bed.

"Lock the door behind me," he calls out, releasing me and heading for the front door.

I grab the sheet, which is halfway on the floor anyway, wrap it around myself, then stand behind the door while Benny lets himself out and walks to his condo next door. He looks back at me, gives me a feral grin, and then goes inside his place.

As soon as he shuts his door, I lock mine, drop the sheet, and run for the bathroom. I check the time. I have like five minutes to make myself look like I didn't just have two orgasms. Easy peasy.

I throw on a work top and fix my hair, then while I brush my teeth, I pull up the agenda for the call. Odd, but there is no agenda. Just a "status chat" with the strategic team back in Chicago. I shrug. I can provide status reports without any prep, so I hope this is a short but sweet call.

I'd really like to shower sooner rather than later. Not that I'm anxious to get the scent of Benny's sweat off my skin, but if tonight goes like the last few nights have, I won't have to wait long to taste and smell him again.

I grab my laptop and set up at the kitchen counter with the morning light over the river illuminating my face. I look happy. And I'm sure it's more than just the orgasms from Benny. Everything in my life right now is going perfectly. I have a man in my bed who gets me, people in my life who love me, and work that thrills me.

Things are perfect.

I fire up the laptop with a grin on my face, but it dies as soon as I see Alexandra's face.

"What's going on?" I ask, without even saying good morning. "You all look like someone shit in your coffee. What's happened?"

"How are things in Star Falls, Willow?" Alexandra, my administrative assistant, is the only one who isn't muted. "I'm giving everyone a moment to get oriented before I open the meeting to Theresa."

"Theresa?" I ask.

Theresa Ginetti and her sister Rosemarie are the founders of Culinary Capital, the daughters of the Papa Gino's pizza franchise. They are hands-on owners, but having one of them attend a routine status call is *not* normal.

Something is going on.

Something big.

"Yes. Theresa," Alexandra says softly. "She'll be joining us today."

Before I ping Alex with a private chat message and ask her what the hell is up, the Zoom room comes into view as all the attendees are let in. In total, there are seven people on camera, including me.

"Good morning, Willow." Theresa addresses me by name first, then checks in with each of the staff members on the call.

It takes a moment or two for her to greet each of us, but it's a habit she's gotten into, and it's one I appreciate. We're a small company in terms of staff, and having the founders know each of us by name, know exactly what we're doing, is the kind of business that sets us apart from our competitors. Even though I'm itching to know why we're all here—an all-hands meeting with no agenda, by the looks of it—I'm not sensing any bad-bad vibes.

I think about texting Alex, but her eyes look glued to the camera, like she has no idea what's up either. She looks even more scared than I feel.

Theresa quickly puts the questions in the air to rest. "So," she says, her face strained by a tense smile. "I have some news that I wanted to deliver myself."

My stomach sinks.

I don't know what kind of not-good news Theresa would deliver herself, but I rest my hands on the cool marble counter and brace myself.

An image of Benny flashes in my mind. I wonder if he'll be free after this call. I'm going to want to talk to someone, work through whatever this is, and even though this thing between us is new and has an expiration date, I already feel like he's someone I can talk to.

But thoughts of Benny fade away the moment I hear Theresa's announcement. "The Pancake Circus franchise deal has hit a wrinkle. More than a wrinkle. A wall."

Theresa's eyes seem to be looking right into the camera. I feel like she's staring directly at me. She shakes her head. "It's not the first time this has happened with a deal, but it is the first time this has come up on one of your deals, Willow."

My stomach sinks even lower, like a stale biscuit dropping to the bottom of an empty trash bin. I swallow against the sour taste in my mouth and nod. "Okay," I say. "What happened? What can I do?"

Theresa explains that the granddaughter who'd wanted to open the Ohio location wants out.

"Out?" I shake my head. "The deal has been signed. We've broken ground on the renovation. We're three weeks into the build-out. There's no getting out of this deal."

Theresa sighs. "I know. Our lawyers are swapping letters, so for now, no changes. Business as usual. But I wanted you to have a heads-up." She runs a hand down her cheek, her expression a little sad. "I'm trying to get to the bottom of this amicably, but their lawyers have told me that whatever is going on in Florida is serious enough that the family is considering filing suit."

"A lawsuit? Against us?" I shake my head. "They can't do that. On what basis? What about the mediation provision?"

Our contracts take years to conclude, and every single one includes a long dispute resolution provision. Before anyone can sue anyone, everyone who is party to the agreement is bound to first try mediating the issues, which is basically a much less expensive process that would avoid the hundreds of thousands in legal fees and years of delays that a lawsuit would involve.

"I know that, Willow." Theresa sounds tired. "They must be incredibly upset to already be talking litigation."

"I can't believe this," I say, the reality of the situation sinking in. "I was involved in every phone call, every Zoom meeting, every on-site visit with the family. They wanted this second location. We didn't put pressure on them. For God's sake, they came to us."

"Willow." Theresa shakes her head and rubs a weary hand across her brow. "I know that. You didn't do anything wrong. Something has happened, and..." She sighs. "Rather than calling us, they ran to their lawyers."

"Have you called them?" I ask. "Voice to voice, to ask what's going on?" I already know the answer to this question, but I want to know if Theresa even tried.

"I can't call them now. You know that I can't." Theresa again shakes her head.

If the family has already retained a lawyer, it would be unethical for someone from Culinary Capital to speak to them directly.

If Theresa wants to contact them, the only thing she can do now is go through their attorneys.

"And we have no idea what changed? Why, all of a sudden, they just want out?" Acid is burning in my stomach, and I am half tempted to take myself off camera and go find some antacids.

If a lawsuit is filed, the first thing that will happen is the Pancake Circus family, the Kincades, will file an emergency injunction. That will stop us from building or spending any money or moving forward in any way on the second location. I know that because it's happened to Culinary Creations exactly two times in the years I've worked here. Just never on a project that I was responsible for.

"I'll share more when I know more," she says, nodding. "I'm going to excuse myself for my next meeting, but Willow, I've asked their attorney to provide a formal demand letter explaining exactly what they want within two weeks. I'll keep you posted."

"And what should I do in the meantime?" I ask. "Business as usual?"

Theresa sighs, and she sounds as frustrated as I feel. "I wish I could say yes, but until we know what the problem is, I'd like you to slow down what you can. If they haven't provided a written demand in two weeks, we'll regroup and I'll loop in counsel so we know we're doing what we can to protect ourselves. Thanks, everyone."

Theresa disappears from the call, leaving the six of us staff members quiet and looking lost. My assistant, Alex, immediately asks, "What can I do, Willow? Should I contact some of the contractors?"

"I'll do it," I tell her. I'm tremendously grateful for her, and the offer is so sweet, so generous. But this is something I have to handle personally. "It's better that it come from me."

Suddenly, something else hits me. "Alex," I say, "I just thought of something I should have asked Theresa. I've already announced through the local SBA that the community development grant is open for applications. Should I shut that down? I need to know if she's going to honor the grant if we pull out of Star Falls."

Alex nods. "On it," she says.

The rest of the team gives their condolences to me, letting me know they feel terrible and they're happy to help with anything they can do. I love my team. We're like family in so many ways. But there is nothing they can do. This is something I have to face myself.

After the Zoom is over, I chomp down three antacids and make some tea, then take the world's hottest shower while I try not to panic.

This is just business.

I angle the rainfall showerhead so it envelops my face and hair with hot water. I hold my breath, then let it out slowly, letting the delicious steam soften the tightness in my shoulders. I lather my hair, trying to work out what could have happened.

I can't understand what went wrong. I truly can't believe this deal might end. A lawsuit could tie up the company for years in expensive litigation. All that time wasted. Money wasted.

By the time I've shaved my legs and rinsed my hair, I'm fuming mad.

I know business is business, but I've never had a deal go south. And I'm not going to stand by and let this one fizzle away, costing my company hundreds of thousands of dollars in lost profits and legal expenses. All the contracts we've signed. But this deal falling apart won't just cost hundreds of thousands. At the end of the day, this could be a seven-figure catastrophe for my company—with my name all over it.

I wrap myself in a towel and rage-dry my hair. As I'm brushing my teeth, I grab my phone and think about texting Benny. My gut wants to vent to him. Tell him what's going on. But if this deal falls apart, I'll be leaving Star Falls.

The longer I think about it, the more enraged I am. I have to stop myself from stomping all over the condo because I might have downstairs neighbors still at home.

I'm dressed in jeans and eating some yogurt in front of my laptop when I get an instant message on our corporate messaging system from Alex.

Alex: Theresa says yes, keep the grant open. If we go to litigation, we'll include the grant as damages.

Damages.

Fuck.

I message her back, but my heart's not feeling very thankful.

Me: Thanks so much, A.

Enraged, I sort through my emails for the contact number I have for the granddaughter of the founder of Pancake Circus. The woman who wanted this deal to go through and who now wants out.

I find not only her email but her personal cell phone. I grab my phone, punch in the number, and without hesitating, hit call.

Theresa may not be able to call her as long as she has an attorney, but I'm the one who met with this woman countless times. I'm the one who listened to her—in our offices back in Chicago—when she changed her mind and decided she wanted to pursue her dreams of owning her own place. I'm the one who championed this deal with Culinary Capital. If she wants out, I'm the one she should be explaining herself to.

It rings once, twice, and then a third time.

"Hello?" A hurried-sounding voice that most definitely does not belong to Audrina Kincade answers.

"Hello, may I speak with Audrina, please?" I try not to sound pissed. I try to sound professional. Pleasant, even.

"She can't come to the phone right now," the voice on the other end says. "Can I tell her who's calling?"

I hesitate, but instead of saying the company, I just give her my name. "This is Willow Watkins."

"Just a moment, please." The woman must not even set the phone down because I hear a muffled sound, and then she calls to Audrina.

I can hear the conversation almost as clearly as if I'm on speaker.

"It's who?"

That's Audrina. I recognize her voice.

"Willow? Do you have a friend Willow, honey? I don't know who that is…"

Whoever answered Audrina's phone is not her mother, and she doesn't sound old enough to be her grandmother. Where the hell is she, and who is answering her phone?

"Come on," I beg, whispering my prayer to the heavens. "Just talk to me, Audrina. Just come to the phone."

But then I hear Audrina's voice as if she's right there in the same room with me.

"Willow is the restaurant woman," she hisses. "From Culinary Capital. Hang up. Just hang up on her."

And the next thing I know, after a flurry of sounds, the call goes silent.

So much for talking to Audrina.

Just as I'm about to accept defeat, I see an email pop up from Theresa marked confidential and proprietary. I open it immediately and read it out loud.

Kincade family attorney has agreed to give me a demand letter within two weeks. Stand down until then. Slow as much work as you can without alarming the contractors. If we can resolve this, I don't want to fall too far behind. Stall the grant, but we'll honor it. Just sit tight. We'll know more in two weeks.

Thank you, team.

Theresa

I drop my head into my hands. Two weeks. We'll know more in two weeks. Which probably means Audrina will tell her attorney that I tried calling her, and that, no doubt, will get back to Theresa. But I don't care. This is all I've worked for over the last two years. There is no reason for this deal to fall apart.

I may be stalled, but I'm damn well not going on vacation. I'm going to do everything in my power to make Pancake Circus happen.

CHAPTER ELEVEN

benito

I'm parking on the street in front of my parents' house when my pops comes out the front door. He's carrying Grace's son in his arms and manages to juggle the toddler in one hand so he can wave.

I climb out of the SUV and point at little Ethan. "Little man. Got a hug for your favorite uncle?"

My dad blows air through his lips, laughing at my boast. "Don't tell Vito and Franco that this one's your favorite." He sets Ethan down on the driveway, and the little guy toddles up to me so fast, he stumbles over a pair of ridiculously cute shoes. I swoop in fast and scoop him up before his knees hit the ground.

"Whoa. Look at those reflexes, huh? Uncle Franco is too old for that kind of action, and Vito..." I shake my head and then tap the end of Ethan's nose. "Vito's just not that sharp." I point to myself. "Say it with me—Benny is the best."

My pops shakes his head while I blow raspberries into the little guy's neck. Ethan screams with laughter and kicks his little feet, then wriggles out of my arms and army-crawls up the driveway toward his grandpop.

"Where's Ma?" I ask, leaning over to kiss my dad's cheek.

"Inside," he says. "She's sewing something for Eden and Juniper."

"They're here too?" I ask, a little irritated.

My parents' place is like an open house almost every day of the week, but sometimes I wish I could have a few minutes alone with them. There's never enough of Mario and Lucia to go around, and I'd really like to have some time to talk to my ma alone. Maybe even both of them.

Pops nods. "Everybody's in V's room."

Vito moved out of my parents' house and into a house he shares with Eden almost a year ago, but my parents still call his bedroom Vito's room. Even though it's now a dedicated craft room for my mom. Hell, my parents have converted every one of our bedrooms to serve some new purpose, and yet they still refer to them as our rooms. It's just one of the ways they let us know that we still have a place under their roof. It's about more than being family. It's about always knowing we can go home. I pray I never need to, but there's something really comforting about knowing I have a place to land no matter how life pulls the rug out from under me.

While Pops and Ethan head to the backyard to play catch, I kick off my shoes and head to see Ma. As I walk into the house, I smell something delicious and unusually sweet. I make a stop in the kitchen and see a cooling rack covered in un-iced cinnamon rolls on the counter.

I give them an appreciative sniff, pour myself a cup of coffee, and take a few sips before heading upstairs.

No matter how long it's been since I lived here, I respect the house rules. Shoes off. No cursing—which none of us can manage to do, no matter how old we get, but we try—and no food or drinks in the bedrooms.

I set my coffee cup on the counter and am about to head up the stairs when I get a text.

Mags: Did you sign off on the application?

No greeting, no good morning, just a question. I sigh and tap out a quick reply.

Me: It's on my list for this week. Will get to it.

The truth is, the application for the Culinary Capital community development grant has been done for two weeks. Mags met with Willow at some point—I don't know when and, to be honest, didn't want to know—and filled out all the paperwork for me. All I have to do is complete the financials, because I don't give anyone access to my books but me, and sign.

But I've been dragging my feet. Willow has assured me that she has nothing to do with making the final decision about the grant. She has never been anything other than a goodwill ambassador, basically talking up the grant and spreading the word, trying to soften the blow to the community when a new restaurant opens up and creates competition for the rest of the businesses out there.

But something inside me feels weird about asking for charity. Especially from someone I'm sleeping with. Yeah, we could use the cash and I definitely need the new roof, but the grant application isn't due for another week. I don't know why getting it in early means so much to Mags, but she's been riding me like she's personally expecting to get the cash if we're awarded the grant.

I check my phone. There's no response to my text, although I see the little text bubble like she's about to send me back a message, but nothing comes. Mags is either pissed or has accepted my answer.

I head up the stairs and hear Ma baby-talking to Junie.

"Who looks like a little princess?" she asks. "Look at you. You're such a big girl."

I peek my head in the door of Vito's old room. Eden is sitting on his bed, and Ma is sitting at her sewing machine. Juniper, who is about the same age as Ethan, is twirling in a very brightly colored mini-cheerleader costume.

"Yo, yo," I say, winking at Eden.

"Hey, Benny," she says, smiling. She gets up from the bed and clasps me in a quick hug.

I bend down to kiss my ma's head and then kneel down to meet Junie at eye level. "What's this?" I ask. "Halloween costume?"

Eden laughs. "Worse. Junie is obsessed with the cheerleaders at my work. Your mom decided she needed her own cheerleading uniform."

My sister Grace's husband runs a kids' athletic facility, but I had no idea they had cheerleaders. "We talking kiddie cheerleaders or grown-ups?"

"Benny." My mother smacks my arm and pushes sparkly red reading glasses up off her nose. "The *kids* are the cheerleaders."

Eden snorts. "Running out of prospects?"

I almost curse, but then look from my mom to June and say, "No, and I'm not looking either."

Eden lifts her brows, and even my ma looks intrigued.

"Son, you have someone special?" Ma jumps out of her chair just as Juniper tries to do a handstand on the floor by herself. "Whoa, whoa, sweetheart. Wait for Nonna."

Ma kneels down on the floor by Junie while I wave a hand. "It's casual," I say, searching for the right words.

I don't have to explain because Eden answers for me. "You only do casual, right?" There's no judgment in Eden's question, and unlike my siblings, she isn't teasing me. She sounds genuinely interested.

"Ah." I wave a hand, brushing the question away. No point in analyzing my love life with my brother's girlfriend. Or anyone, for that matter. I know I'm the last in the family to settle down, and what's the rush? "I'm married to a sexy beast of a restaurant. That's more than enough commitment in my life."

"If there is someone," my ma says gently, "even if it is casual, you know you can always bring her to Sunday dinner. We'd love to be more involved in that part of your life. You need someone to care for you. To be there for you, Benny. You work so much, and…"

I look my ma over. She looks concerned, like maybe she's overstepping by asking about that part of my life. I love her for it.

There's never been a girl I've brought home—not since high school, and that doesn't exactly count.

I know I have a reputation in my family for fucking anything that moves and never staying with one woman for too long. And I know my parents worry. I certainly don't want them worrying about or even thinking about my love life.

"Ma, don't worry, okay? I'm fine. I've got plenty of people to care about me. And I'm in no rush for one of these of my own," I say, holding out my arms to Junie. She lifts her arms and demands that I pick her up, so I do then spin around with her in my arms, making the pleats of her tiny cheerleader skirt whirl. She cackles and drools on my arm, and then I catch a whiff of what's happening in her diaper, which is my cue to hand her to her mom.

"When do they learn to use the bathroom?" I ask, wrinkling my nose.

"Not soon enough." Eden grabs her backpack and heads toward the bathroom with Junie while I chuckle.

I'm still waving a hand in front of my assaulted nose when Ma sits back down at the sewing machine.

Since it looks like we have a minute alone, I lower my voice. "So, Ma, what's the latest with the old man?" I ask.

She blinks her deep brown eyes, loaded with sparkly silver eyeshadow, at me and shakes her head. "He hasn't said anything. Maybe I should stop worrying, I don't…"

Just then, we hear Pops on the stairs. "Lucia!" he yells. "I've got a grandson who is dying for one of these cinnamon rolls. We got plans to frost these any time soon?"

I extend a hand to my mother and help her up. She gives me a hug and murmurs, "My boy. My heart." Then she looks up at me, her lashes blinking fast. "Maybe no news is good news. Let's go eat."

I hear Eden running water in the bathroom, so it's time to put this conversation on pause anyway. I'm about to follow my ma down the stairs when my phone rings. The caller ID reads *Benito's*.

"This is Benny," I say, not sure who from the restaurant would be calling, but I check the time on my watch.

"Benny, it's Jasmine."

"Hey, Jas. Everything all right?" I stomp downstairs, hoping Ma's whipping up some cream cheese frosting for those rolls. If not, I may have to do that myself.

The entire family gathers in the kitchen, and I'm trying to hear what Jasmine's saying.

"Mags…" I barely make out over the chatter of my parents and the babbling of the kids. "So, what do you want me to do?"

"Hold up, Jas. I can't hear you." I give up on trying to take this call with my family around, so I head to the living room and drop down on a couch. "Sorry. I'm at my folks'. Hit me with that again?"

Jas huffs a sigh. "I know you're supposed to be off today, but Mags called out. What do you want to do?"

"Wait, wait." The blood starts to boil in my veins. Mags *just* texted me, and now she's calling out on the night she's supposed to close? "Did you talk to Mags? What do you mean, she called out?"

Jas hesitates a minute. "I don't know, Benny. I don't want to get in the middle of anything. She just called and said she couldn't come in tonight and she'd work it out with you later."

"Why the fuck didn't she just call me?" I ask, my voice rising along with my temperature. Thankfully, Ma didn't hear the f-bomb I just dropped or the one I was about to.

"Who's covering lunch?" I ask. "Who's there right now?"

I check the time on my phone. It's only eleven, so we're about to hit the lunch rush. Mags was scheduled to work from noon to nine today.

"Carla and Duncan are covering lunch. Mags just called me about ten minutes ago."

"She called you?" I'm barely able to control my temper.

"Well, the restaurant, Benny. The kitchen's swamped, so I answered the call."

I tighten my grip on my phone. There's only one conclusion I can jump to, and I know it's a dangerous one. Did Mags text me before the start of her shift to see if I'd signed that application? Did she intentionally call out to punish me for not doing it? And to not call me like a chickenshit, when she knows the kitchen can't run through both a lunch service and a dinner with the same crew? I'd be stuck paying overtime for one, and that's assuming Carla and Duncan would be willing to work through close.

This means Mags knew today was my day off, and she decided not to let me know I'd need to come in. She's fucking with me. That's the only explanation.

What doesn't make sense is why. Benito's is my fucking restaurant. If she needs reminding, I'll march her right out front to the parking lot and show her exactly whose name is on the fucking sign.

"I'm on my way," I tell her. "If you hear back from Mags, you tell her to call me. No. Forget that, Jasmine. I'll tell her my fucking self."

Thank God I showered after the fuckfest I had with Willow this morning. I have more clothes in my office, so there's nothing stopping me from heading right into work. I open up my contacts and pull up my last text to Willow.

Me: Day went to shit, babe. I've got to close the kitchen tonight. Late late dinner or rain check?

I have a reply back in seconds.

Willow: Day went to shit here today too. I'll cook for you tonight. My place? As soon as you can?

I send her back a thumbs-up emoji, then head into the kitchen. I reach past Pops and pull the only frosted cinnamon roll off the display plate. "Can I grab and go? I'm sorry, but Mags called out. I got to go in."

My pops waves at me to eat, while Ma starts scurrying, trying to make me a plate of the food she's cooked Eden and the kids for lunch.

"Ma, I'm a chef. I'm going to the restaurant. I'll eat, I promise." I jam a bite of the treat into my mouth and talk around a mouthful of food, mostly because I know it'll rile my mother up. "Duhlishush, Ma."

"Oh, get out of here," she says, smirking and waving me off.

Pops walks me to the door and rests a hand on my shoulder. "I'm so proud of you, Benny," he says.

There's something quiet in his voice, and I'm again hit with the realization that I don't really know what's going on with my parents. Just because Pops hasn't been back to the doctor, or at least he hasn't brought it up, doesn't mean that he's okay. That there isn't something simmering that could make the precious little time we have together even more precious.

I can't think that way. Not now.

I nod and swallow a wave of tough emotions. "Later, Pops," I say, wishing I could say more, but not knowing what or even how to say it.

I climb behind the wheel of my SUV. When Pops goes back inside, I dial Mags's number.

Ring.

Ring.

No answer.

The voice mail picks up, and I hang up before I can start cussing into the phone. I don't need to have that kind of unprofessional evidence out there. I take a few deep breaths and start up the truck. What should I do? Call? Text?

My head is starting to throb. This is the kind of shit Mags normally helps me with. When we have asshole college kids who blow off work, or when a new line chef decides to get a little sloppy with the time clock, Mags intervenes, playing good cop so I can play bad. I hardly ever have to deal with the messy personal shit because Mags is so good at it. I squint my eyes closed and curse the fact that I've relied on someone else for so much.

What would Mags do? Would she call and leave a scathing message, swearing and blowing off steam?

No. She'd pick up the phone and leave a professional and clear message.

So, I dial her number again. This time, it goes straight to voice mail.

She's probably screening my call, but I'm going to handle this like the owner of a business. Like a man who can handle shit and get it done right.

I think about what I know Mags would say and then what I want to say. So what comes out of my mouth when the voice mail invites me to leave a message is somewhere in the middle.

"Mags, it's Benito. Jas just told me you called out. You texted me this morning, so I had no reason to think my day off would get fucked up, but now I'm going in to cover for you. I'm not going to lie. I'm pissed. Whatever's going on, not calling me is just plain shitty. You know it and I know it. But I'll get over it. What I really want to tell you is that I need to know what's really going on. If you're mad at me or trying to punish me for something, let's get it out in the open. I'm your boss and your backup, and I deserved better. But I'm going to handle it. I'd just like to know if this is the new normal I should expect, or if there's some other conversation we need to have."

Before I hang up, I see the curtains part. Ma is looking at me, and even at this distance, I can see the concern on her face. It occurs to me that maybe something is going on with Mags that I don't know about. That she's not ready to talk about, even to me.

"And shit, Mags," I say, softening my tone. "We've worked together a long time. I'm pissed, but I'm also worried. We're friends, right? So, whatever is going on, call me direct. Let's sort it out."

I hesitate, and before the silence of the dead air on the voice mail system cuts me off, I end the call.

It wasn't pretty, but it was honest. And that's the best I can offer. I guess I'll see if it's good enough.

CHAPTER TWELVE

willow

I am tucked between Benny's legs, leaning my bare back against his naked chest. He's got his arms around me, my breasts cupped in his hands. As we talk, he lazily squeezes and strokes my boobs.

I can feel his hard cock behind me, but I'm trying to focus on what he's saying and not on what our bodies have spent the last few hours doing and should already be tired of but are not.

"This whole Mags thing," he mutters. "I don't get it. She's always been my right hand. I don't understand why she's pissed all the time." He's quiet for a moment, and I try to focus on his words and not the heat of his palms on my sensitive flesh. "I hate this feeling," he rumbles. I can feel the truth of his words, the vulnerability he's exposing radiating from his chest.

Something about not looking me in the face, but talking to the top of my head, has Benny opening up. As much as my body is in delicious agony, I can't turn off my brain. Not when he's talking about real stuff like this.

"What feeling?" I press. "What do you hate?"

He's quiet, and his hold on my breasts tightens. "I feel like nothing I do is good enough."

He falls silent, and I follow his lead. I want to ask more, want him to say more, but I feel his dick soften behind me, so I know he's lost in thought.

"I am not the easiest person to work with," he admits. "And I haven't always made the best decisions for the business. But I'm always straight with my people. I tell it like it is. No means no, yes means yes. I don't play games. At least, I don't think I do."

He's quiet, and I lace my hands through his so I can touch him. His arms are heavy and warm around me, and I lean my head back against his chest. We sit there quietly, our clasped hands resting together on my belly.

"What do you think Mags needs?" I ask. "Most of the time when people are angry at work, there's a really simple explanation. They want more money, more respect. Do you think she's feeling unappreciated?"

Benny sighs, and the soft heat of his breath ruffles my hair. "Maybe. Probably. I don't know."

I nod and give what I know of the situation some thought. "Have you asked her? I know you need to address the fact that she called out tonight without even contacting you, but what if you set that aside for a minute. Just ask her what she needs from you as a boss. As a leader in the place where she spends a lot of time and gives a ton of her energy. Have you ever done that?"

Benny is quiet, and I pull one of my hands away so I can stroke the long, tight muscles of his thigh. Beside mine, his body looks so hairy and thick. Strong where I'm slight. We look beautiful together, and it's hard to sit here and see the lines of his perfect body without touching it.

He gives a slight groan, but I'm not sure if it's because of my massage or my question. "I do annual evaluations and shit, if that's what you mean. I don't have an HR department or anything, but I give raises and reviews. Mags has to know how much she means to me."

"Maybe it's more than that." My mind drifts to the Pancake Circus family. I've been giving the whole situation a ton of thought. I should say I've been spiraling about this all damn day.

I just cannot imagine why they would back out, but the longer I think about it, the more I realize there are things that I need to know, need to do. I cannot let this go into litigation. There has to be a way to work out whatever it is that's happening. I wish, more than anything, that Audrina would have picked up the phone, and taken my call. I tried to do exactly what I'm telling Benny to do. I'm sure it'll work since it's not like Mags won't speak to him. She just didn't answer his call today.

"You never really know what's going on with someone," I remind him. "Sometimes you have to ask. But if you do ask, you have to be ready to deal with whatever the answer is."

He kisses the top of my head and doesn't say anything.

I shift slightly so I can meet his eyes. "Is it money?" I ask. "Do you think this has anything to do with the grant?" I feel a little sick at the question.

I believe the grant is important to Mags. Important enough that she came to the SBA meeting. She met with me separately at the restaurant to talk about it. I haven't done a lot of talking with Benny, despite all the fucking we've done, but I don't get the sense he's even half as interested in the grant as Mags seems to be.

Benny shrugs. "I wish I knew what she wants. I don't have a fucking clue." His handsome face grows dark, and he nods at me. "What about you? How's Pancake Circus treating you?"

Now, it's my turn to sigh. "Not a whole lot better than you're doing."

Benny wraps his arms around me and holds me tight against his chest. "Want to talk about it?"

His voice purrs against my ear, and I think about it. I really do. But if I tell him there's a chance this deal won't go through, that I'll get pulled out of Star Falls... I know this is a no-strings situation. I know we've only been hooking up for three weeks. I know all of that. But that doesn't mean I'm willing to give him up. I want him for as long as I can have this. And when I can't, well, then it will be time to deal with goodbyes. But nothing puts a damper on short-term fun like long-term realities.

"You know what I'd like more?" I ask, turning around and

kneeling between his legs. "I'd like you to fuck me until I forget I even have a job."

His brown eyes sparkle, and the corner of his mouth curls up in a seductive grin. "I never knew that was an option. New achievement unlocked."

"It's not an achievement until you do it," I remind him.

He puts his hands on either side of my face and leans forward. When his lips touch mine, I let myself go, lose myself in the heat and delicious sweetness of his full lips, the scrape of the stubble on his chin against mine. I open my mouth to kiss him, and his tongue sweeps against mine.

"Willow," he groans against my mouth. "I want to fuck you so many ways I can't decide where to start."

I pull back from the kiss and settle on my belly between his legs. "Think about it," I tease, pressing my lips to the head of his cock. "I'll keep myself busy until you decide."

I grip the base of his cock in one hand and suck his head into my mouth. I swirl my tongue around every tender inch of skin, paying special attention to the underside of his shaft. I suck him in deeper, licking and sucking, my hand sliding up and down his shaft. I pull my mouth back to take a deep breath of air and lick my palm so it slides against his erection without any friction. He gasps, his hips bucking, and I take him deep into my mouth again until he laces his hands through my hair and gently tugs.

"Up here," he demands. "I want you to fuck me."

He rests his head back against my headboard, and I straddle his hips. Bracing my hands on his shoulders, I don't slide onto him, but sit on his thighs. I reach for the bedside table and open a drawer, only to come up with a completely empty box of condoms.

"Uh-oh," I say, shaking the empty box. "Small problem."

Benny groans. "I have some at my place..."

I think for a moment. This is the worst possible time to have this conversation, or maybe it's the best?

"Should we talk about going without?" I ask him. "I have been on the birth control pill for two years to help with my fluctuating hormones. Aging is a bitch. I get tested every year when I have my annual physical, and I haven't gone without a condom in a long-ass time. Is it something we should consider?"

"I'm good with the birth control pills, but babe, why are you testing your hormones?"

I shake my head. "Benny, I'm forty-two. Will be forty-three this summer and it's not uncommon to start menopause at my age."

His eyes widen, and then a slow grin covers his face. "You're forty-two?" he asks, sounding incredulous. "Forty-two? As in forty-two whole-ass years old?"

I climb off his lap and give him a look. "Why? Does it matter? How old did you think I was?"

He reaches for me and pulls me closer. "Willow, you look…I don't know, mid-thirties."

"Forty-two isn't young, but it isn't old," I insist.

He holds up his hands. "It isn't. I get it, but you're older than me by a lot."

My stomach sinks. I honestly never thought about whether Benny would care how old I am. What does an age difference matter if this is just a casual fling? But then I start to panic. How young is he?

"What's a lot?" I ask. "Are you over forty?"

He shakes his head. "Thirty-one, sweetheart."

My shoulders sag. "You're a baby." What I mean, though, is he's young enough to have never been married. To never have had kids. Most of my friends are through their first marriages. Some are on their second divorces. A couple have young kids, but a lot more have kids who are already in middle school. All of that is ahead for Benny. There's no reason why he should spend the next however much time with someone he could definitely not have any of those things with.

"I'm hardly a baby," Benny says. "But you're probably not going to have kids, then?"

A cold chill creeps up the back of my neck. This is why I keep things casual. This is why I don't stay with one guy or in one place for too long.

"I don't want children," I tell him, unable to keep the edge from my voice. "I never have. My age has nothing to do with that."

He's quiet, studying my face in a way that makes me feel exposed. I reach for the sheets and wrap myself up. He doesn't say anything, just waiting, I guess, for me to explain myself. I shouldn't have to explain myself. Not having kids, not wanting to be a mother, shouldn't be something I have to defend. Not to anyone. And yet, it feels like I owe this to him. I hate that feeling.

Benny must read the look on my face, or maybe it's the way I've pulled back and wrapped myself up. Because the next thing I know, he's kneeling on the bed and taking me in his arms.

"Hey," he says. "Come here."

He sits back against the headboard and holds me, still wrapped in the sheet, in his arms.

"I had an amazing childhood," he offers. "Two amazing parents. Three older siblings who adore the shit out of me. They can be assholes, but they're my assholes." He chuckles. "Truth be told, there's so much chaos in my life with my business, I don't know if I have enough energy for a relationship, let alone parenthood."

I listen, not sure what he's getting at.

"I don't know if I ever want kids," he says. "I love my family and they mean everything to me, but…" He shrugs. "Willow, I don't care how old you are. I don't care if you're past your childbearing years." He releases me only to make air quotes around childbearing. Then he wraps me up in his heat again. "I fucking love whatever this is we're doing. And I'm okay to keep doing it, without condoms, as long as you feel safe to."

I turn to look at him, his seductive grin turning my insides to hot jelly.

"Is it weird that I kind of love the fact that I'm banging a cougar?"

"How about we not call it anything?" I ask, my shoulders softening. "We're two grown adults, two consenting adults, and…"

I stop when he takes my face in his hands. "Yes, we are. Enough about the age gap, the kids shit… Now, can we get back to doing what we do best? Just being us?"

"Just being us," I echo. That is what I want. Easy. Fun. Light. "I think I can do that."

"So, are we being us with condoms or without?" he asks. "Because I'll walk down the hall naked and grab some from my place if that's what it takes."

I stifle a laugh. "I'm not about to let any of the other women in this building see what they're missing out on. All of this is mine for now."

For now.

The words rise between us like a wall, but Benny doesn't seem to notice or care.

"I'm all yours, babe," he agrees, then grabs my face and pulls me close.

Now our kisses are frenzied, his tongue hot and searching. The sheet falls away from my shoulders, and I don't know if he's yanked it away or if I've shrugged it off, and I don't care. I'm so hot for Benny. Hot for younger-than-me, impulsive, hothead Benny. This is all mine, and even if *for now* means weeks and not the months to one year that I'd planned, I'd rather have what I can get of him than let any of this go.

We kiss, kneeling on the bed until we collapse, Benny lying on his back and me straddling him. But he seems to have other ideas.

"Lie back," he says. "I want a taste."

I close my eyes and lose myself in the gentle kisses, until I feel his palms open my thighs wider.

I arch my hips, aching to feel any part of him inside me. He kisses my pussy, licking and stroking my clit, bringing me agonizing, beautiful pleasure but never entering me.

I roll my hips, I tear my fingers through his thick hair, but he never moves his mouth from my pussy. I'm ready to explode when I feel a rush of cold air as he moves away.

"No," I grunt, not wanting him to stop, but praying that he's moving because he has something even better in store. "More, please, babe."

Without a word, I feel the tip of his cock at my entrance. He's over me, supporting his weight with his arms while he rocks his erection against my pussy. Without the condom, the feel of his bare skin against me is more than I can take.

I suck in air and cry out, the need for him so deep, so consuming, that I slam my palms against his ass cheeks and practically drive him into me.

"You're so greedy, baby," he pants. "Tell me how bad you want me."

"Fuck," I hiss when he slips the tip of his cock just barely inside me. "Benny, please. Oh my God, please."

Instead of giving me what I want, he teases me, rocking his hips back and pulling his cock from my body, then nudging oh-so slightly forward.

"Benny," I cry, thrashing against the sheets, my knees open wide and my eyes slammed shut. "Benny, fuck me."

But he doesn't. Instead, he flips me onto my stomach and yanks my hips into the air. Then he kneels behind me and spreads my ass cheeks with his hands.

"I never want this to be over," he breathes, and I can't stop and analyze what he means.

I just need to feel it.

The mind-shattering bliss when his erection finally slides between my legs and into my body.

"Oh God." My face smashes into the mattress, my ass as high in the air as it can reach. "Deeper, deeper."

He obliges, but this isn't a hard fuck. This is a slow, deep coupling, his strokes long, his sighs that end in my name breathless and heady. He grips my hips like he's holding on to me for dear life, just like I'm gripping the blankets. I press back to meet his gentle thrusts, my need for release so intense that I'm bouncing, rocking, thrusting back against him, practically forcing him to fuck me harder.

This union, his bare skin against mine, this intimacy, is more than I've shared with anyone in a long, long time. It's so good. His length inside me, the pace of his thrusts, the pressure of his fingers.

The pleasure as he hits deep is so intense, I feel tears gather at the corners of my eyes.

"Touch yourself," he pants. "I want to feel you make yourself come."

Even though my face is down and my ass is up, I practically drag a weak hand between my legs. I don't need to touch myself, but I do, pressing two fingers against my clit while Benny picks up speed, thrusting harder, spurred on my throaty, desperate moans. My fingers slip along the front of my body, Benny fucking me harder from behind until, finally, I feel his cock get even larger and he slows, croaking out a helpless "Willow…" as he starts to come, and that sets me off.

I see nothing but darkness behind my lids, my face off the side so I can gasp in chestfuls of air as I come, wave after wave of pleasure flooding my body until I'm so weak, so done, my knees give out, and I collapse onto the bed.

Benny uses his arms to brace himself, lowering his body, his cock still inside me, until he's lying on top of me. I can feel the erratic pounding of his heartbeat against my back. My pussy throbs and my chest is squished under his weight. It's all so good. It's so much. His heat, his size, his perfection.

I giggle, forgetting that we didn't have the condom to hold back the mess.

But Benny doesn't seem to care. In fact, he pulls me closer, cuddling my face against his chest and tightening his arms around me.

I lie there quietly, my body cooling, my breaths perfectly in time with his. It's so much. The way he feels. The way I feel when I'm with him. It's amazing and arousing and exciting, but it's a lot. More than I've felt with anyone. Not just the sex, but this part. The way he holds me after. The way he dozes but still kisses me, my name a whisper on his lips, even when I think he's asleep.

This man is a lot. He might even be too much.

He's snoring lightly, his arms locked around me. But I can't sleep. I'm thinking, my mind whirling. "I'm going to get a sip of water," I whisper, kissing him lightly on the cheek.

He rolls over, tucking himself deep in the bedding.

I grab his T-shirt from the floor and toss it over my head, then head into the bathroom to clean up. Benny is still sleeping, so I head out to the kitchen and pour myself a glass of water. It's quiet, and the water of the river sparkles under the light of the moon.

I like it here. I've liked a lot of places I've lived. I've had some gorgeous homes, condos, yards, but I never expected to find a condo in a small town overlooking the river that would feel like home. Home isn't something I've had much of in my life. It's a strange feeling and not entirely unwelcome.

I check my phone for messages. I have three texts from Jessa, all venting about bloating and where exactly her newest show went off the rails.

I check my work email and have about twenty. Nothing pressing. I snooze them all until morning, until I reach one from a name I recognize.

Maggie Tempestini.

I click open the email and read it twice. I'm not sure I'm believing what I'm seeing, but I can only read it so many times before I know it's true.

Mags has sent me her résumé and a cover letter. She's applying for a job.

She wants to leave Benito.

CHAPTER THIRTEEN

benito

A lot has changed over the last few weeks, and it's all Willow's fault. I can't get enough of the woman. She consumes my thoughts. When she sends me a text message during the day, my palms get sweaty, my heart starts racing, and a stupid grin eats up my face like I'm fourteen freaking years old.

The fact that I've been with her now for six weeks, almost seven, and I still feel as excited to see her every night as I did when we first met is surprising.

Things have changed slowly. We still fuck like horny teenagers, but we talk about everything. Her childhood, mine. The restaurant. Her business. Our friends and family. I know this thing, whatever it is we're doing, has an expiration date. She's leaving in a year, and I know that. But fuck if I don't want to stop time and stay here.

I've never felt this way about another woman before. I'm the short-time guy. Hook up and move on. That's what I've always done. And this should be the same thing.

But I can feel everything changing.

The only thing that hasn't changed is the shit with Mags. She's still avoiding me. After she called out of work without speaking to me, I took Willow's advice.

I asked Mags if we could talk, and we did. That went over like a week-old loaf of Italian bread. She stared at me, arms crossed, frowning while she said nothing was going on. She's fine. Everything's fine. She wasn't feeling well, apparently. She didn't apologize, didn't explain. Just listened, nodded, and repeated that line, "There's nothing to talk about. Everything's fine."

So, I've tried to act like everything is fine. Meanwhile, the application has been sitting on my desk staring me in the face. Although I can also feel the daggers as Mags glares into my back when we're in the kitchen together. I still need a roof. My office is a mess and worse than it's ever been. Because now, instead of working late or spending mornings in the office, I spend every spare moment I can with Willow.

I've been wanting to introduce her to my family, but I don't know. She's important to me. In ways I don't think I even fully understand. But how? What would I say? Hey, Ma, Pops, this is Willow...the woman I'm hooking up with until she moves away in a couple months.

The idea depresses me so much, I try to put it out of my head. But it's always there, like the scent of herbs in my kitchen, the pull of the heat and the drama and the pace of my business.

I am looking down at the SBA grant application that's due today. I sigh deeply. I know Willow has told me she's not the final decision-maker, but it doesn't make it any easier. Something about submitting this and asking for money that comes from her company.

None of it sits right with me.

I check the time. It's three in the afternoon. Mags is in the dining room, working on the schedule for next month. We've been hired to cater a rehearsal dinner at a venue off-site, so we are going to need to hire temporary staff to keep the restaurant functioning while we handle the event.

I wander out to the bar where Sassy is sitting at a table drinking a Coke that's mostly ice while she chatters with Mags. I nod at the few customers we have, then motion to an empty chair at the table.

"Mind if I crash the party?"

Sassy shakes her head, but Mags doesn't look up or even answer. I take a seat, and Sassy jumps up. "You want something, Benny?"

I shake my head but give my mom's friend and one of my best servers a smile. "Thanks, Sassy. I'm good."

She presses her lips together, then says, "My break's over. Later, Mags."

I frown and watch Sassy grab her glass and scurry off. I'm not one of those bosses who makes my employees punch a clock for every break. If it's slow and Sassy needs to have a seat, she knows I'm not going to care. Based on the way she hustled off, I have to assume that she and Mags were probably talking about me.

I motion toward the papers in front of Mags. "How's it look?" I ask.

She doesn't look up. "You know."

I rub my hands over my face. "No, actually. I don't. Care to go into a little more detail than that?"

She huffs a sigh, and my temper starts to flare. "The bride wants a three-course dinner with dessert and a salad course," she explains. "Appetizers during the cocktail hour, and then she does not want a buffet, but plated meals for three hundred guests. We are going to need a staff of at least six chefs. And the venue won't give us access because there is another event that morning until like four hours before service is scheduled to start. We're going to need staff here and at the venue to do prep, and then it's going to be tight."

I shake my head. I don't even need to look at the books to know we can't spare that kind of staffing. For a Saturday night, I'm going to need to hire and train people, but I may need a catering van to move food from here to the venue. I rub my eyes.

"What did we quote them per plate?"

She glares at me. "You gave them a discount. Remember?"

We don't cater a lot of off-site events, but this wedding is for one of my brother Franco's friends. I tried to cut him a good deal. I can see I cut deep into my profits in the process.

"Right," I sigh. "Okay, so what are our options? I can't hire six chefs, and unless I close Benito's for the night…"

She tosses her pencil on the table dramatically. Thankfully, there are no customers close to us, but Jas is behind the bar and she's staring at Mags with her mouth open.

"What's the problem?" I ask.

"You want me to work a fucking miracle, Benny, but I can't do this." She looks up, and her cheeks are red, her eyes glassy like she's near tears. "I know you don't like letting anyone near your books, but I don't know what we can afford or what we can't. We need six people minimum to manage this wedding, or we need to close the restaurant. I don't know what else you want me to do."

I stand up from the table, nearly tempted to grab the papers from her and throw them right in her face. But I'm the boss. It's my name on the front of the restaurant. Instead, I point to the papers and jerk a thumb toward my office.

"My office," I seethe. "Now."

I turn and storm away, Mags close on my heels.

Once we're in my office, I can't help myself. I slam the door and start yelling. "What the fuck, Mags?"

She yells right back at me. "Fuck what, Benny?"

I take a moment, compose my thoughts, and stomp toward my desk. "Mags," I say. "I don't know what's gotten under your skin. But I'm not going to accept 'It's fine' for an answer. What is wrong, and what can I do to get us back on track?"

Mags paces the far side of my office, looking stressed and angry. "I haven't been happy here for a long time, Benny."

This is news to me.

But I don't interrupt. I listen.

"When you hired me, I was so proud to work here. So proud. Benito Bianchi, king of Italian cuisine, saw something in me." The way she's saying it, it does not sound like a compliment.

Though my blood is boiling, I stay silent.

"But no matter what I do, you never take me seriously. There's no room to grow, Benny. You don't grow. You don't change." She waves a hand around accusingly. "This place has the same shitty carpeting you had when you hired me. Six years, Benny. Do you know how many times the carpet should be changed in a business like this? With the traffic we get, we should be doing updates constantly. Improvements, repairs."

Now that she's started, she's on a roll. "We have the same menu, the same vendors. The same servers." She gestures angrily toward the door. "Do you realize Rita is like eight hundred years old? Half the time, she can't hear the customers when they ask for a high chair or to be seated on the patio. And Sassy—"

I hold up a hand, trying hard as fuck to keep my hand from shaking. She has no right to talk about my staff, their age, or their performance. None. "Maggie, this is not about Sassy or Rita. I need to ask you to leave the team out of this. Just tell me about *you*."

She points at the grant application on the desk. "We need a new roof. You won't let me help with the books. You don't take any of my ideas seriously, so I don't even know why I'm here."

I draw in a deep breath through my nose. This conversation is going to be real fucking hard to come back from. I've broken up with a lot of women and have been dumped by many more. I can see the writing on the wall. So, I know I need to tread carefully. "So why are you still here, Mags." It's not a question, and I say it as calmly as I can.

Her lower lip trembles as she admits, "Because you're the best. Everybody knows it. I can't apply to work anywhere else because everyone in town is going to ask why the hell I would leave Benito's. I'm stuck." Her voice rises, but then she seems to realize she's close to shouting and calms down. "I'm stuck here with you, and you don't give two shits about the things that are important to me. You don't give two shits about me. So, what? I'm supposed to rot here until I'm Rita's age because there's no place else to go?"

I take a few deep breaths and remind myself that this is not a lover's quarrel. Mags and I have never so much as hugged a little too long. This is about work, and I need to keep my cool. No matter how my ego and my anger are firing at a rolling boil.

"Mags, I'm going to say a few things, and I'd like you to sit so I can say them to your face, not your back." I motion to a chair in front of my desk. "But if you don't want to sit, I'm not going to beg."

She crosses her arms over her chest and looks at me, a sad, hurt frown on her face. But then, as if she realizes she's backed me into a corner, she nods and drops into a chair. "Yeah," she says, brushing the hair back from her face. "Okay. Go ahead."

I choose my words very, very carefully. "Mags, you and I have worked together a long time. And I understand that you feel some attachment to this place. I rely on you like a business partner even though you're not. I'm sorry for that. I'm sorry if I created an expectation in you that you would have more authority over this place. I don't know how we got here, but here's where we're going."

I meet her eyes, my stare cold but kind. At least, I hope it is. "Hear me on this, because I'm not fucking around. This is my business. My place. Everything from the shit carpeting to the employees you may think you're better than."

She opens her mouth to interrupt me, but I hold up a hand. "Please," I say firmly. "Let me finish. I'll let you have your say, but I need to get this out."

She swallows hard and leans back in the chair, arms still tight over her chest.

"You are a tremendous asset in the kitchen, and that's what you're paid to be. Nothing more, nothing less. You do work for the best fucking restaurant in Star Falls, and that means not only me but that means everyone else I choose to have as part of this operation. I will not—do you understand me on this?—will not stand by while you insult the team that stands by me day after day."

What I don't say is that these people are family to me. I'd sooner shoot off my own foot than fire Rita. The day I tell Sassy she has to go because she's old is the day I shut the doors on this place for good.

I may not be the best businessman, but I know my values. Food, people, and customers.

Those are what matter and in that order.

"Now," I tell her, "I appreciate that you've taken the initiative to complete this application, but I'm not going to submit it." Her eyes widen, but I push on. "I'm not going to apply for the SBA grant.

You don't have to like it, you don't have to agree with it, but it's my decision. End of discussion."

Mags looks down at her clogs, her lips pinched in a tight frown.

"We've had our differences, and I'm going to say one more thing, and then I'm going to let you speak." I take a deep breath and lean over my desk toward her. "Mags, as much as you've meant to me all these years, I can't have the attitude you've shown around here. Not toward me, and certainly not toward your team. Now, I'd like you to tell me what you plan to do. I need to be surrounded by people who have my back. Not the other way around. I'm not going to watch my back in my own restaurant. If you can't stay, then I'll give you a great reference. It's that simple."

I clamp my lips together, congratulating myself on keeping my fucking cool.

Mags meets my eyes. "I've been applying," she says quietly. "I wanted you to send in that grant because I applied for a job with Culinary Creations. I sent Willow my résumé a couple weeks ago. I was hoping if she saw the application, she'd know what a great job I did pulling it together and would interview me."

I congratulated myself way too soon. "Excuse me?" I seethe. "You did what?"

She lifts her chin. "I sent Willow my résumé. I was hoping to get in on the ground of the new place. Make a name for myself."

I feel my guts stir around in my belly, and a sour flavor coats my tongue. "What'd she say? Was she happy to poach my best employee right out from under me?"

Mags shakes her head. "She was kind of weird about it. That's why I've been so stressed out. If I fucked up by reaching out to her and I fucked over things with you…" She laughs, a bitter, grating sound.

"What do you mean, she was weird about it?" I ask. I can't deny that I'm curious. "What did she say?"

Mags lifts a shoulder and shrugs. "She just talked about what a great guy you are, such a good cook and a good man." She flicks a look at me. "She talks about you like she knows you. Like she's in love with you or something. But she said she's not interviewing now and that I should communicate with you. Give you a chance to work through any issues we're having."

My heart swells at Mags's words.

We're both quiet for a second. The reality of what we've said, what's left unsaid, and what can't be unsaid hangs between us.

"Where does that leave things?" I finally ask her. "I'd like to resolve this so I know whether I need to replace you."

"I'd like to take some time off," Mags says. "I have a couple vacation days left. A week, I think."

I nod. "Okay."

"Can you cover the kitchen?" Mags looks worried, sucking her lower lip between her teeth.

"Absolutely. You take the time you need. I'll handle the rest," I assure her.

Mags stands and walks toward the door. I don't know what the right thing to do now is. Do I thank her? Give her a stern warning? I've never fired anyone. This is as close as I've gotten. I've always had Mags to do the tough stuff for me.

"Hey, Mags," I say, stopping her before she can leave.

She looks back at me, the expression on her face as uncertain as I feel.

"I appreciate everything you've done over the years. Don't think a day goes by that I'm not crystal fucking clear how much weight you carry here. Thank you. No matter what happens from here, thank you."

She blinks fast, nods once, then leaves.

I look over the grant application on my desk, then crumple it in my hands, tear it in two, and toss it in the trash bin. Then I grab my phone.

Me: You got some time? I'd like to talk to you about some things.

Willow replies a minute later.

Willow: I'm in the city for a last-minute meeting with a contractor. I might not be home until late. Tomorrow? We could spend the morning together...

Me: Morning, yes. Will I see you tonight when you're back?

There's a long pause before Willow responds. I hold the phone in my hands, shocked at the way my heartbeat picks up and my breath tightens in my chest as I wait. We've spent every night together for almost two months now. Why would tonight be any different?

But then the message comes.

Willow: B, I need to handle some stuff tonight. Text me in the morning?

I'm stunned at how disappointed I am.

Is Willow seeing someone else?

Why else would she need a night to herself?

I consider asking her, but look where that got me with Mags. Demanding answers and confrontation might just lead to shit I'm not ready to handle.

I thumbs-up the text and don't say more. I put the phone in my desk drawer and drop my face into my hands. I'm probably losing Mags. I may be losing Willow even sooner than I expected.

Somehow with just two conversations, this shitshow that is my life got even shittier.

CHAPTER FOURTEEN

willow

I make the drive back to Star Falls after dark, listening to nothing but the sounds of the road under my tires and the racing of my own thoughts.

The season has changed in the time I've been here. Early fall has shifted from colorful and brilliant, the bright green grass softening to a sleepy color, the bold red and orange leaves long swept into piles, the trees having dropped most of their leaves.

All day, I've felt hollow, and I can't figure out why.

The Kincade family's attorney sent the demand letter as promised. The people who came to my company wanting to open a second location are now completely done. They essentially are insisting that if we don't release them from the contract, they will file an injunction to stop the progress on the new location. They intend to file a lawsuit to try to terminate the contract altogether.

There was no demand made. No explanation that they want more money or more creative control. Nothing. They didn't even explain what the basis of the lawsuit would be.

Theresa hasn't said anything yet, but I know what this means— I'll be pulled back from Star Falls. Right now, there is no other deal

675

ready for me to move to, so I'll likely live here or from a suitcase while I hit the road, looking for another destination.

Normally, the idea of getting back on the road excites me. After a year on a project, the thrill of a new place makes me feel alive. I love adventure. I'm curious and, to be honest, a little restless. I am usually the one chomping at the bit to say goodbye to the old and a hearty hello to the new.

But today, none of my typical enthusiasm is anywhere to be found. I think about the cities I might explore, the cuisines just waiting to develop into viable businesses. Instead of curious or even just ready, I feel deflated.

I sigh as my eyes adjust to the familiar streets that lead to my condo. The place I've called home—if only temporarily. The place where I've cooked and laughed, taken calls for work, and video-chatted with Jessa.

The place where I first received flowers from Benny.

The place where I look forward to seeing him every single night.

Benito Bianchi.

It's really him, I think, that I will miss the most. What started out as just a hookup, a short-term whatever this is… I don't know.

I'm starting to think that what bothers me most about leaving Star Falls is the thought of leaving Benny.

Which, honestly, doesn't make any sense.

This will be the first project I've been pulled off prematurely. I have no condo back in Chicago. No storage unit full of memories where I can wander through the past, no aunt or cousins to crash with while I figure out my next move.

My childhood was a nightmare. Parents who were more enamored with alcohol than they were with me. My mom stayed with my dad much longer than she should have until, finally, he left her in the worst way possible. He died in a car accident. The irony of it was that my dad wasn't even intoxicated at the time. He swerved to avoid hitting a deer, blew a tire, and hit a tree.

Once my mother lost my dad, she descended quickly into more drinking. By the time I was in high school, Mom was in active kidney failure, on dialysis, and battling late-stage lung cancer. There was no extended family to take me in, so I spent the last year of high school in a foster home. The people who cared for me were nice enough. I was fed. I had an allowance and decent clothes. I wasn't mistreated. But I was basically a stranger living under a roof with people I didn't know. Who didn't really want me there. They were not bad to me. And that's the best I can say about them.

At least they were an improvement in some ways over my own parents.

During that year in foster care is when I developed the one-year rule. I promised myself that I could survive anything for just one year. And if I did, I'd never have another bad year in my life. I'd travel, meet amazing people, do cool things. And I have.

I've been on my own ever since I turned eighteen, and I have lived every day the way I wanted to. Making great money. Eating great food. I travel. I have a gorgeous wardrobe. I have enough of what I want to feel happy, but not so much that I can't pick up and move when the spirit and timing move me. I am a pro at adulthood. I know how to keep people I love close and leave anything that doesn't make me happy behind.

By every definition that I've ever cared about, I should be blissfully happy.

But now, facing the disruption of what should have been another easy year, I'm feeling conflicted.

No, worse than that—I'm miserable.

When I reach home, I see that Benny's parking spot is empty. He must still be at the restaurant. I'm suddenly gripped by an idea. I should go there. Get my ass back in the car and go there now just to see him. I don't know what I was thinking, telling him I needed a night to myself. I met with a roofing contractor in Cleveland this afternoon, and I didn't want Benny to know the whole truth yet.

The fact that I'm leaving. I don't see how I'm going to see Benny and not tell him the truth. I know what's coming, and I don't know that once I see him, I'll be able to keep it from him.

I lock my car and grab my purse, stopping myself from running to him. I go into my unit, call Jessa, and then take a long, hot bath. I put on my comfiest pajamas. I climb onto the couch and look out through the windows at the view of the river. Something tightens in my chest. I've grown so attached to this place and to the fact that he's just on the other side of that wall.

I get up and grab my phone from the counter to check the time. It's almost ten, which means Benny should be home any time now if he's closing up the restaurant. If he didn't, he's probably already next door.

I type in a text and hit send before I can talk myself out of it.

Me: I'm home, and I would love to see you if you're up for it. Rough day. Fair warning, I might not be good company.

I climb on the couch and turn on the TV. I flip through the channels but can't settle on anything that will hold my interest. All I can think about is the fact that I might be leaving. I am leaving. The words vibrate in my head until my temples throb. I want to clutch the arms of my couch and slow down time, but I can't.

I don't hear back from Benny, and after thirty minutes, my stomach starts to hurt. I'm such a fool. When I told him I was busy, he probably called someone else. He had a whole life before we started hooking up. He's probably with someone else right now.

Earlier today when I said I needed space, I practically gave him my blessing to go there. I told him I needed alone time, and now I'm telling him I want him. What a freaking mess.

I turn off the TV and decide to try to sleep, when there is a soft knock at my door. My head jerks up, and my pulse starts racing. I rush to the door, check the peephole, and when I see the familiar dark stubble and dimpled chin, I throw open the lock.

I don't say anything, just stand there staring. Benny looks like he's been hit by a truck. There are bags under his eyes, and the corners of his lips pull down into a slight frown.

"Rough day?" he asks, pointing to me. Then he points to himself. "Total shit day."

He opens his arms, and I go to him, resting my head against his chest and holding him so tight, I can't believe he can breathe.

"Come on," he says. "Let's go to bed."

He comes inside, and I lock the door. He strips off his shoes and coat, then follows me wordlessly to my room. He peels off all his clothes except his boxer briefs, and we climb under the covers. For the first time ever, we don't fuck like bunnies. We don't laugh, kiss, or even grind against each other. He rolls onto his side, tucks me close against him, and strokes my hair. We stay awake like that for what feels like hours. No talking. Only him holding me and breathing into my hair.

When my arms start to fall asleep, we roll over, again without a word, and this time, I spoon him. I press my cheek against the hot muscles of his back, an arm thrown over his body. I bury my face against his skin and just breathe him in. It's so quiet, so still. I hear the soft sounds of his breathing, the steady beat of his heart in time with mine, and tears inexplicably burn my eyes.

This is so good. It's so good in so many ways. I don't know if he feels it too, but it's the most poignant and painful goodbye.

———

The somber mood follows us into the next morning. I wake before Benny and get up to use the bathroom. When I come back to bed, he's lying on his back, his eyes open.

"You still want to spend the day together?" His voice is thick with emotion.

"Yes," I tell him. "I'll start some coffee."

"Come back to bed first?" He sits up, and I climb in beside him. He opens his arms, and I slip under the blankets.

The sheets are warm and wrinkled, and I just want to snuggle down with him and never, ever leave.

The thought hits me, and I realize it's true.

I don't want to leave. Not Star Falls. Not this condo. Even more than that, I don't want to leave him.

I close my eyes as he strokes my hair and murmurs a question. "Were you going to tell me that Mags sent you her résumé?" he asks.

My eyes fly open, and I look up at him. "No," I say sincerely. "Benny, I would not have told you. Her career goals and job search are her private business. I wouldn't have gotten involved in whatever business you two need to sort out. But I also had no intention of hiring her. I wouldn't steal your most valuable employee from you."

"Not stealing." He wraps his arms around me, and I reluctantly settle back against his chest. "It's not stealing if she wants to leave, Willow." He doesn't sound angry, only resigned. "I'm hurt. Angry, maybe. She told me she sent her résumé over to you. I guess she even filled out the grant application partly to impress you with her skills."

I sigh. "So, she talked to you? Was that yesterday? Your shit day?"

"We talked, all right." He sounds so subdued. Defeated. Sort of like how I feel. "I wouldn't blame you if you did want to hire her," he tells me. "She's been amazing for the last six years. But lately, things have been rough. I wouldn't hold that against her, though. Things end, and not usually great things. I'd give her a good reference. I'll do it right now if you want."

I again pull out of his hold and shake my head. "Benny, I don't want to hire Mags."

I don't want to admit to him that I can't. I won't have a restaurant at all—no staff, no kitchen, no contractors. Everything I have worked for is about to go up in smoke. But I am not ready to talk about it. Not until it's official. Maybe there's a tiny part of me holding out some hope that there is some other way.

"But," I tell him, "if I did have an interest in hiring her, I would talk to you about it before I made a move."

I meet his eyes, and I know he believes me. His shoulders soften and he nods. "Come on," he says. "Let's shower. I have a plan for us."

"A plan?" We didn't make plans, other than to spend the day together. "What kind of plan?"

He kisses me softly. "You'll see. You up for a little adventure today?"

I sigh into his kiss and nod. "Yeah, I am."

While I make coffee and shower, Benny goes home, showers, and gets dressed. I email Alex and Theresa that I'm going to be out of the office handling some personal business until early afternoon, but that I'll be available this afternoon. I assume Benny has to work later, and thankfully, I don't have any meetings or emails that can't wait until later.

Once he's back, we eat a quiet breakfast, the strain of our separate stresses keeping us both quiet. After we eat, he tells me to wear comfy shoes and a warm coat, so I dress for the late November weather, and we head out.

"So," I ask as he pulls out of the parking garage. "What are we doing?"

He reaches across the center console and takes my hand. "A little tour of Star Falls. You've mostly seen the inside of my bedroom, but I'd like to show you some more of the fine small town you're going to call home for at least the next few months."

My stomach churns, the delicious breakfast and coffee not at all happy with this plan. "Benny, I…" But I don't know what to say. If I tell him that I'm leaving, that Star Falls won't be my home, then what? We go back to my place and break up now?

I don't want that. In fact, I don't want that even more than I don't want to take a tour of Star Falls. So instead, I lace my fingers tightly through his. "I'd like that," I say.

At least what I'm saying is the truth, even if it's not the whole truth.

We drive through a lovely-looking neighborhood. The houses are on the small side, a mixture of brick and siding. But they are, for the most part, comfortable and well-maintained, only a few here and there showing signs of neglect and wear. Even though fall has blown the leaves from the trees and most of the flowering plants have gone dormant, the neighborhood feels safe and homey.

There are minivans and pickup trucks parked on the street, and most of the homes don't have fences. I see plenty of swing sets and above-ground backyard pools. This is definitely a place where people raise families. Host holidays. I wonder how crowded the streets are with bikes and baby strollers in the summer.

Finally, Benny pulls to a stop and parks the SUV on the street.

"Where are we?" I ask.

He turns to me, the hint of a smile finally warming his face. "This is my childhood home. Where I grew up."

I cock my chin at him in confusion. "Your childhood home? Your parents' house? Are they home?"

He shrugs. "Possibly. I don't know. Maybe. It's early, so probably."

I narrow my eyes at him. "Benny, are you trying to introduce me to your parents? Is that…"

I stop myself because it can't be.

First of all, I'm wearing yoga pants and running shoes. My hair is in a bun. I don't have cookies or wine or flowers. I mean, it's been years since I met anyone's parents in a dating-type situation. I don't date like most people. I don't stick around long enough for most guys I hook up with to want this.

I'm not sure how I feel about it.

"Benny, I don't think this is a good idea."

He nods, looking immediately hurt. Something sharp flashes across his face. "Yeah, I'm sorry. I thought maybe it'd be a bad idea. Never mind. It's okay." He looks away from me, suddenly withdrawing. I feel like he's pulled into himself and disappeared, and the feeling fucking guts me. He puts both hands on the wheel and turns on the ignition.

"No," I say. "That's not what I mean."

I reach out and hold his arm firmly.

"Turn off the truck. I want to meet your parents. I would have liked to dress a little nicer, and I would have brought them something. Flowers, cookies, I don't know."

He turns his head slightly, his warm brown eyes searching my face. "It's okay. I probably fucked this up. I should have asked you. I should have…" He groans. "Willow, I've been fucking up everything in my life lately."

I don't know what Benny's been going through. The stress with Mags might just be a part of it. We've spent so much time having fun, having sex, and talking about surface-issue stuff that I can see there are ways he might need something more than that. He needs a girlfriend. A relationship. I can't be that for him. I won't be staying, but I can do this. I can meet his parents. If it brings him one ounce of peace today, I can get through it.

"Come on," I say, opening the door and jumping to the curb. "You promised me a tour. There's no better place to start than here."

He climbs out of the SUV, clicks the locks, then holds my hand as we walk up to the front door. The air around us is heavy. This feels important. I'm meeting his parents. The guy I've been hooking up with for two months.

Am I his girlfriend?

What will he say to them?

I don't have a ton of time to wonder because he unlocks the door with a key and holds open the screen for me.

"Shoes off, if you don't mind," he says, removing his boots once we're in the front hallway.

I slip out of my runners and hand him my jacket, which he hangs on a hook by the door. Then, we walk inside.

The Bianchi family home is dark, like maybe his parents are still asleep, but Benny doesn't seem too worried.

"Ma. Pops," he calls out, motioning for me to follow him. The second we walk into the living room, I see Benny's demeanor change completely.

He's smiling, and his whole body seems to relax. The gorgeous brooding brown eyes go soft, crinkling at the corners. He runs a hand through his hair and smiles at me. Beaming. He's happy, and he seems very happy that I'm here too.

This is what it looks like to go home. This is what home feels like.

A wave of longing, disappointment, and regret washes over me. I'm suddenly certain this is a terrible idea.

My knees buckle, and I brace myself. Benny knows that I lost my parents and spent a year in foster care. But we've only talked about the easy stuff. The fact that my foster family was used to younger kids, so my bedroom for my entire senior year of high school was Barbie-pink and filled with dolls. He knows I taught myself to cook that year because my foster parents both worked and hated cooking.

My parents had never been great at consistency, so I had always had an interest in cooking. But spending hours alone after school in my foster parents' kitchen is where I fell in love with food. I could chop, read recipes, and tweak them based on things I knew I preferred. That year was life-changing in good ways, but what I never shared was how lonely it was. How I felt closer to YouTube cooking show hosts and social media chefs than I did anyone in my life.

Food has always meant home to me, not any one place. Family has been the friends I choose, not any one person or group of people.

But walking through Benny's parents' house, I can see into the life that formed this man. Framed pictures of Benito and his siblings hang on the walls and cover end tables. Artwork scribbled by the Bianchis' grandkids wallpapers the entire fridge. Benny walks through the first floor, petting two dogs who both look too old to bark at me, a stranger who no doubt smells like Benny.

He heads toward the back of the house and flips on the kitchen lights. "You want something to drink?" he asks. "Glass of water?"

I shake my head. It's surreal walking through the quiet space. The dining room table is exactly what I'd expect. A long table has a couple of leaves that extend the length to fit the twelve chairs that surround it. A table runner goes down the middle, and a basket of fresh oranges and apples sits in the center.

Benny fills a glass of water and motions for me to sit at the table. I take a seat, and immediately, my mind fills with images of the many years that he has eaten meals here. Spent time with his parents, his sister and brothers. A longing and a sense of loss hit me so hard, it's as if someone has stolen the air from my lungs.

"This okay?" he asks, smoothing my hair back from my face. He's standing beside me, sipping a glass of water.

I'm not okay, but I nod. "Are they home?" I ask. Maybe they're out. Maybe this is just a tiny little baby step into Benny's world. Maybe we'll leave and I'll never have to put all the pieces together. I'll never have to see all that I've missed out on in my life right here in front of my eyes. I won't actually have to meet the people who make this house a home.

Benny nods. "Ma's probably sewing upstairs. I'll go check if they don't come down in a minute."

As if they're summoned by Benny's words, we hear feet on the stairs.

"I'll be right back, honey." A man's voice, gravelly and warm and sounding a lot like Benny's, echoes through the house.

We both turn toward the voice, and I feel Benny's hand tighten on my shoulder. "That's my pops," he says softly, his voice brimming with love and pride.

I stand from the chair, and Benny tucks me under his arm. For a moment, I feel like a kid again, like we're going to prom or something and he's excited to show off his date to his parents. I plaster a grin on my face, hoping I don't look terrified. But that grin melts into a mask of horror when I set eyes on the man coming toward the dining room.

The man has a full head of thick gray hair, its waves long like Benny's but disheveled. His chest is completely bare, and as my eyes roam down his body, I realize he's not just shirtless. He's butt-ass naked. Nude. I'm talking not a stitch of clothes from his head to his bare feet. And he's sporting a massive erection that bobs ominously with every step he takes toward us.

"Jesus fucking Christ!" Benny shouts and turns me toward him, clamping a hand over my eyes. "Pops, what the fuck?"

"Benny?" Benny's dad says slowly, his voice disbelieving and low. But then, as if it hits him all at once, he starts cursing. "Oh shit. I'm sorry. Oh shit."

"Pops, for fuck's sake. Don't apologize. Go put on some goddamn pants."

"What's going on, Mario?" And that must be Benny's mom. I cover my eyes tight with my hands, lower my face into Benny's warm plaid shirt, and do my almighty best not to laugh.

Then, Benny's hand still clamped over my eyes, I hear a rush of footsteps, a lot of very loud voices talking over each other, and doors slamming. Only when Benny releases me do we look at each other, our eyes wide with shock.

Then we double over, breathless with agonizing, uncontrolled, gut-wrenching laughter.

CHAPTER FIFTEEN

benito

My parents sit beside each other at the dining room table, holding hands. My mother's face is beaming, her cheeks flaming red. Thank the sweet Lord almighty Ma is dressed, and Pops is not only covered from head to toe in clothing, but he's also wearing his glasses. I wouldn't mind a hood, a bucket, or an eye mask for myself. Anything to protect my eyes from any more unexpected *sights*.

"This is new for us, you see," Ma's explaining. She seems a little embarrassed but mostly happy. Wish I could say the same for myself. "We didn't know what to expect, and since I have the no-drinks-upstairs rule, your father had to come downstairs to get some water. And well…we thought we were alone."

I hold up a hand, feeling simultaneously queasy and like I might burst into nervous laughter all over again. "Ma, I don't want to know the details of whatever the hell that was that I walked in on. Could we just move past it and never, ever speak of it again? Except maybe in therapy. Because I'm scarred. Literally traumatized. All the good work you guys did raising me? Undone with one…" I wave my hand at Pops. "Just one look and decades of solid parenting down the drain."

"Now, son." Pops is looking at me over the rims of his glasses.

"You know you're always welcome here, but when you stop in at eight o'clock in the morning…"

"Pops." I shake my head. "You have grandkids coming in and out all day. What if one of them were here?"

I'm not that mad, but I'm still weirded out. Reality-check time. My parents still have sex. Whoopee. Great for them. Am I okay with the idea that they still get it on? Yes, sure. But does that mean I want to see it happen? Did I ever, and I do mean literally ever, need to see my dad's dick let alone my dad sporting wood for my ma?

Abso-friggin-lutely not.

I think I'm going to be sick.

Ma gets up from the table and clasps my hand. "Honey," she says in a low voice. "This is what's been going on with your father."

"Just tell him, Lucia." Pops is shaking his head. "It's not like it's going to stay a secret." He points into his lap. "I don't know how long it'll be till this stuff wears off, but I'm not getting up from the table until it does."

"Stuff? Wears off? What the hell did you two do?" I grimace, trying to block out visions of sex lubes and toys and massage oils out of my mind.

I might actually vomit. I cough into my hand.

"Benny," Ma says, her voice soothing and sweet like she's talking to a toddler and not her adult son. "Now that your father and I are empty nesters, we have been enjoying each other's company. We're like newlyweds again."

I hear the tiniest little huff of a giggle from Willow, and I groan, a full-body sound that comes with a massive grimace. Willow seems to be taking her unwilling role in my parents' sex life a little too well.

Talk about a memory that will last a lifetime. I can't believe she hasn't run screaming from the house already. I flick a glance her way, and her eyes are wide, her lips pressed together tight, either to hold back laughter or—if she's feeling like me—the puke that threatens to spew out if I don't get a grip.

"Ma, for fuck's sake, please…"

"Benny. Language." Ma's face, bare of makeup for once, looks stern. She looks over to Willow. "I'm sorry. You must think Benny was raised in a barn."

Willow shakes her head, those perfect lips still clamped shut. She manages to squeak out, "No, uh, not at all."

Ma looks back to me, her face brightening with happiness. "Benny, your father went to the *doctor* a while back," she puts such a strong emphasis on the word doctor that I immediately understand what she means. "He had some tests done to make sure he was in good health…"

"I got Viagra," he says bluntly, pointing down to his lap. "You just happened to walk in during our maiden voyage."

"Pops." I nearly scream it. I don't know how much more of this I can take, but then it hits me.

Ma's trying to tell me that Pops is okay. I look to her for assurance. "So, that was all about this?" I put my hand out palm up, and then I raise just my index finger nice and slow, to imitate a growing erection. "Everything is okay?"

"Everything is great," Ma assures me.

"I'm not so sure it's great." Pops frowns and fidgets in his seat. "Does anyone know how to turn this thing off?"

"Pops." I rub my face so hard I hope my eyes get ripped out of my head so I can't see my dad squirming around because his dick won't get soft.

I hear Willow giggle beside me. "Honestly," she says, "if having your son walk in on you doesn't do the job, I don't know what would."

I turn to Willow, and both my parents stare at her. Then, like someone clicked a switch, all four of us burst out into laughter. Ma slaps the table to hold up her weight, and my father looks like he's actually in pain, which he probably is.

Willow wipes tears from her red cheeks, she's laughing so hard, and I have to get up and pace the room because I give myself the hiccups from lack of air.

Finally, when we all calm down, Ma comes around the table and hugs Willow's shoulders. "Well, welcome to the family, Willow. After all this, I think you're officially a Bianchi."

By the time Pops's hard-on decides to make a graceful exit, it's nearly ten o'clock. Willow and Ma are upstairs looking at something Ma's sewing. I'm in the kitchen with my pops alone, thankful that he can stand and walk without having to follow his erection around.

"So, Pops," I say. "You had Ma worried as hell. Everything check out with the doctor?"

Mario nods. "Because of my age, my local doctor wanted some special heart tests. Then those people sent me to urology, and it just went on from there. Anybody and everybody got a look at my junk before they'd put me on any medicine to help in that department." Pops shrugs. "I guess it's a good thing, but I had more people with their hands down my pants than I did when I was single."

I groan, but Pops continues.

"Clean bill of health. A starter dose of some meds to help me in the bedroom, and we'll see if things improve. Although..." he looks at me, lifting a thick silver brow. "Nothing kills the mood quite like your son and his new girlfriend walking in on the fun. I may have to take a double dose next time."

"Please, God. Pops, can you not? I'm thrilled you're okay, but I never, ever want to get this close to your sex life again."

"You know, son, if it weren't for your mother and I having such a great time in the bedroom, we wouldn't have made four kids."

"Pops, I don't think *my* heart is healthy enough for this kind of stress." I shake my head and breathe a deep sigh of relief when he changes the subject.

"So, Willow..." he says. "It's been a long time since you brought a woman home to your parents. Is it serious? I didn't even know you were seeing anyone."

I don't know how to answer his questions, but I do what I always do with my folks. I tell the truth. "She's amazing," I say, not able to stop a grin from covering my face. "She's brilliant and funny. I learned today she's incredibly resilient."

I glare at Pops, and he chuckles.

"We've known each other a couple months, but she's only in Star Falls a short time."

Pops's smile fades away. "How short?"

I shrug. "A year, tops."

Mario claps a hand on my shoulder. "I'm sorry. Where does she live full time?" he asks. "Would long-distance be an option?"

I shrug again. "There's a little more," I tell him. I explain the age gap. The fact that she doesn't want to have kids. That her business might put mine out of business.

"And yet, you brought her here," Pops says. "To meet us. She means something to you, Benny."

I nod. "I think so."

That's not the whole truth. I know so. I'm sure of it, actually. The more I talk about the reality of Willow leaving eventually, the more I know I can't let her go. I don't want her to leave me. Don't want her to leave Star Falls. I don't know what I need to do, but maybe, just maybe... I have under a year, but who knows. By that time, maybe I'll be able to convince her to stay.

My pops hugs me and holds me tight. "You deserve happiness, Benny. And nothing really good ever comes without complications. You'll work it out."

He releases me, and I search my dad's face. "How can you be sure?" I ask. "There are so many things stacked against us. How can I be sure it's not all going to be too much?"

"Too much?" My pops echoes my words. "It's never too much. Not when you love someone," he assures me. "Just trust that, Benny. No obstacle you two might face will be too much. Not if you don't let it."

The front door opens, and my sister Gracie breezes in, her toddler on her hip. "Ma! Pops!" she shouts. "You guys busy?"

"Oh, they were," I mutter under my breath. "Sorry, but I had to say it."

Mario groans and sniffs in indignation. "Well, if a man can't make love to his wife in his own house..."

"Hold the phone." One of Gracie's thick brows is sky-high in her forehead, her lips pulled into a grossed-out grimace. "Did Pops just say he was *making love to his wife?*"

"Don't even get me started," I tell her, shaking my head. "I saw it, Gracie. Saw things no man should ever see."

Gracie puts the baby down, and he toddles over to me. I open my arms for a hug and murmur against his neck. "Make it go away, Ethan. Make the memory go away."

Grace looks horrified as she hugs Pops and holds up a hand. "Stop. I have already heard more than enough."

"Pops got himself on Viagra," I offer. I use my finger to again simulate a hard-on, and Gracie makes a puking sound.

"Oh my God, I told you to stop." She smacks me on the arm. "That's sick."

"It's nature. It's natural, I mean…" Pops holds his hands in the air. "I give up. I'm sorry your brother had to see my morning wood, Gracie, but…"

"Pops. Oh my God, stop." Gracie covers her mouth like she might actually puke when Ma and Willow come down the stairs. Gracie turns to our mom and kisses her cheek. "Don't tell me," she says. "Ma, I don't have the stomach to hear about your sex life."

"Gracie, please, it's bad enough that Willow had to meet your father for the first time in the nude, but in front of the baby." My mother scowls. "Let's leave the bedroom talk to the grown-ups, please."

Gracie is covering her entire face with her hands. She's squeezing her eyes, heavily winged with eyeliner, closed, and she's making a fake-retching sound behind her hands. "Oh my fucking God, I'm leaving. I'm done."

"Language." Ma never misses even one curse.

Willow is standing behind my mom, grinning at me and watching the scene unfold. When Gracie finally uncovers her mouth, she looks from Willow to me and then back at Willow. "Please tell me you're with my brother and you have nothing to do with the apparent sex den my parents have turned this place into."

Willow extends a hand to Gracie. "I am with your brother. Willow Watkins."

Gracie looks at her hand but then says, "Are you not a hugger?"

Willow grins, a large smile that lights up her whole face. "No, no. Hugs are great."

Gracie clasps her in her arms, the neck of her very loose

boatneck top falling over one shoulder, revealing both a bright-red bra strap and an arm loaded with ink. "Nice to meet you. I'm the smart one in the family, and this is my kid, Ethan. I have two more in school."

Willow nods and bends down to greet my nephew. While she's kneeling, Gracie spins and throws a look at me. "What's with all the secrets in this house? Ma and Pops have set up a sex dungeon, and you have a girlfriend? Do Vito and Franco know?"

"There is no sex dungeon," my father says on a long sigh. "And I don't know if your brothers know about Benny's girlfriend, but this is the first we're meeting her."

"And she is wonderful." Ma is beaming.

She hasn't even put on makeup yet, which means she's really feeling comfortable around Willow. Not that she has had any time since Willow and I interrupted her and Pops.

"She is wonderful, and Pops and Ma are healthy and *active*." I grimace as I emphasize active. "And Willow and I were just leaving." I nod at Willow, who is looking at my sister like she's about to burst out laughing.

"So soon? Can't you stay for lunch?" Ma picks up Ethan and smooches him loudly on the cheek.

"Ma, I might never get my appetite back." I lean down and kiss her goodbye, then give Ethan a loud raspberry on his chubby little neck. "I'm kidding. Love you, but we got places to be."

I give Pops a hug and am about to make a joke, when it hits me. My father's okay. He isn't hiding a health scare. He's not sick. He's doing pretty fucking great, actually. The reality fills my chest with relief, and I hold him for a long time. "I'm so grateful you're all right, Pops," I say, my voice low. "I just wish I didn't learn you were okay by seeing your dick out."

I pound Pops on the back, and he laughs again, seemingly unfazed by how scarred I am. He puts a hand on my shoulder and meets my eyes. "I will never leave my bedroom naked and aroused again, son."

"Oh my God, Pops." Gracie fake-retches again, and now I know Pops is enjoying this.

Ma brings Willow into a three-way hug, balancing Ethan on one hip and squeezing her tight. "You come back Sunday for dinner," she tells Willow. "Even if Benny is working and can't be here. Our home is always open to you. And if you don't have plans for Thanksgiving, you're invited. And Christmas. We don't usually do a big meal for New Year's Eve because the kids like to go out or do their own thing, but you are always welcome."

I swoop in and tug on Willow's hand. "Let's say goodbye to Pops before Ma gives you a house key and invites you to little Ethan's high school graduation in about sixteen years."

"Would that be such a bad thing?" Ma asks.

My pops gives Willow a quick hug, and I hear him apologize again. Whatever he says has her flushing with real laughter.

"I won't, I promise," she says.

We walk hand in hand toward the front door, put on our shoes, and then stop because Gracie meets us at the door.

"Bye, asshole," she says, giving me a "what the fuck are you doing" voice. "What am I? Chopped liver? No goodbye for your sister?"

I kiss my sister's cheek, and Willow gives Gracie another hug. As we're walking out the door, I call behind me, "Ma, Pops, make sure y'all are careful. We don't need any more siblings."

Willow and I run to my car as they assault us with laughs and the sounds of Grace's fake retching.

CHAPTER SIXTEEN

willow

"Soooo," I say as Benny navigates the SUV away from the curb. "Your parents seem nice."

Benny looks at me and then widens his eyes. He's got both hands gripping the wheel, and I can tell he's seriously shaken by what we just saw. "Lemme tell you," he says. "They are the best people ever. But that…" He clears his throat. "That was way too much for a first meeting."

Way too much.

A first meeting.

It was a lot, but Benny's parents are everything I would have expected. And more than anyone could ever ask for. Warm, loving, and welcoming. I felt immediately at home in their house, and worse, I didn't want to leave.

"If this is what your parents pull out on a first meeting, I'm not sure I can handle Thanksgiving and Christmas," I tell him, something low in my belly gnawing at me. A part of me desperately wishes I'd still be here for either of those holidays. Was there a part of me that had already picked out the corner of the condo right near the windows where I'd set up a tree?

I feel like the last two months have been a fever dream of sex and pretty lies. But I'm sure now that the pretty lies had nothing to do with Benny and everything to do with me. How I feel about never staying in one place for very long. How I feel about fresh starts and new adventures. How can I love something so much and grow tired of it at the same time?

I try to add a smile after my words because the truth is unfolding inside my heart faster than I can stop it, and I feel like I might cry. As we pull away from his parents' house, I'm really conflicted about leaving.

"Where to now?" I ask, trying to sound bright. If Benny has to work this afternoon, we only have a couple more hours together. I want to enjoy every last minute.

"You'll see." He tightens his fingers through mine but doesn't meet my eyes. He stares straight ahead at the road as he tells me about his family.

By the time I realize where we are, Benny has run through his entire family tree. He pulls the SUV to a stop in an empty parking lot and cocks his chin at me.

"I must have the wrong place," he says, sounding confused.

My heart swells to nearly bursting, and the words lodge in my throat. "No," I say. "This is it. The future home of Pancake Circus. How did you find it?"

Benny shifts in his seat and faces me. "It's important to you," he says quietly. "And even if I hated the idea at first, I want to be supportive. This is what you do. Why you're here."

He's quiet then, as if he's thinking what I'm thinking. It's why I'm only here for a short time.

"Looks pretty quiet. I expected contractors and construction and shit."

I nod. Yeah. Me too. Instead, I ask, "Want a tour?"

He kills the engine, and we cross the gravel lot. There used to be a restaurant here years ago. A place with a large parking lot and a drive-through, but it's long since been abandoned. Permits are taped to the dark front windows, but Benny is right. Other than that, there's no sign that a new business is well on its way to being born. It's a sad symbol of my life in a way—so much potential, so much hope. And now it's stuck, not quite what it was and nothing like what it could be.

I push all the conflicting thoughts away.

"Come on," I tell him. "Let's go inside."

He follows me to the front door, and I use the access code to unlock the lockbox, then I take the keys from it and unlock the front door.

Inside, the electricity is off, but we still have power running to the building, so I lead him back into the big kitchen and flip on all the lights.

Benny sucks in a deep breath. The place smells a little funky, like ammonia, mildew, and mice droppings. But the kitchen is huge, easily three times the size of Benito's. He runs his hand along the stainless-steel counters. They are in disrepair—banged-up from boxes and other items being put on the counters over the years when the place was not functional. Before Culinary Capital bought it at auction, in part because of its distressed condition.

"You know," he says, "this place has been closed as long as I can remember."

"It was open until a few years ago as a private event space," I tell him, explaining what I know. "It used to be a…"

"A Papa Gino's Pizza." He snaps his fingers. "No freaking way. I remember now. Back when I was really little, I came to a few pizza parties here."

I nod. "The sisters who own the company I work for are the Ginetti sisters. When the franchise opened, their father envisioned a few locations that could have games and play areas like some of the big chains. This place started out as that." I smile. "Theresa still has one of the original arcade games in the office in Chicago. It doesn't work, but it's a symbol. A symbol of so many things. Dreams. Fun. Family."

Benny watches me as I talk, his eyes dark with something that I can't interpret. He is so, so pretty. His chin is lifted, that dimple winking at me as he listens. I've never felt bonded to a man this way before. It's as though he was made to be mine, and the invisible threads that connect us throb as I talk.

697

I know he wants to come closer to me. To touch me. To hold me tight while we share these memories, these very real parts of our lives. And yet, he just stands there, the electric tension between us sparking with lust and maybe so much more.

"So, then," I say, brightening my voice to try to shatter the stillness, "in its second life, Papa Gino's here was a drive-through hot dog and burger joint. That didn't last long, but the owners decided to hold on to it and keep it as private event space until about nine years ago. The place has been mostly abandoned since then."

Benny looks confused. "It's a wild coincidence that a Papa Gino's used to be here. Did the fact that their dad once owned this place factor into the decision to build here?"

I nod. "I think so. Maybe there was a little nostalgia behind the final decision, sure. Papa Gino, the real Papa Gino, was from Chicago, and he liked to bring his family to Michigan, Indiana, and Ohio for vacations. The owners of my company have been to Star Falls many times over the years. It's a special place, and when Pancake Circus came to us, we primarily looked for locations just like this in the Midwest."

"Locations like this," he says quietly, his voice simmering with heat. "Small towns with untapped potential?"

"Exactly," I say. I suck my lower lip into my mouth. Untapped potential. Like him, like me. Like us together. I don't say it, but it's like Benny feels it.

He finally crosses the kitchen and stands in front of me. He smooths a loose hair behind my ear, his fingers grazing my cheek. "Lucky me. You ended up here." The words hang heavy between us, like he wants to say more and is weighing exactly how to word it. But the raw emotion is clouded over, and his lips twist into a smirk. "Just think. You could be making out with some sandwich-maker in South Bend instead."

The laugh hits me hard. "Well, then I think I'm the lucky one." I lace my arms around his waist and rest my head against his chest. Then I sigh and close my eyes.

He holds me close to him, rocking slightly to the hum of the electric lights overhead.

"So, why's it so quiet here?" he asks, his voice echoing in the silence.

I lift my chin and look up at him. "There have been some delays," I say cryptically.

My heart is pounding hard in my chest. I don't want to admit that everything is falling apart. That the project is about to get canceled. That I'm probably just days away from being pulled out of Star Falls.

"I'm sorry," he says. "I understand delays, all right." He rests his chin on the top of my head and holds me tighter. "Shit that doesn't get done but needs to—bills, repairs, and HR issues. Sometimes I feel like the longer I'm in business, the worse it gets. Things don't get easier over time, unless I'm just a major fucking moron who can't learn."

He pulls away from me and walks slowly through the kitchen, running his hands along the abandoned surfaces. I wonder if he, like me, can almost hear the ghosts of chefs who worked here, meals made and served. The smells and tastes of what this place could be are so real to me, I almost can't stand the silence.

Benny fills the space with his honesty. "I wish I'd known before I opened the restaurant what kind of shit I'd face." His brown eyes look sad, the dimple in his chin really pronounced as he frowns. "I just wanted to cook, you know? Make great meals. There's nothing better than the feeling of feeding people something they love. But even more than that, I love food. I love the weight and texture of pasta dough in my hands. I love the precision of dicing a shallot for a glaze and seasoning something until it's just right."

He laughs, sounding bitter but not angry. More like, resigned.

"I'm so good at what I love, and everything else..." He groans and then leans his butt back against the counter and runs a hand through his hair. He's wearing a lightweight forest-green puffer coat, and the sleeves make a swishing sound as he moves his arm. "Can I be brutally fucking honest?" he asks. "Real talk?"

"Yes," I whisper. I want him to be. I'm hoping he'll say something that will make it easier for me to open up to him. Because I have to, and the sooner I do, the better.

"Willow." When he says my name, he sounds pained. "I suck at running my business. My books are a mess. The only thing that stops me from getting the utilities shut off is the friends I have who work for the city. They know I'll pay when they remind me. I always do. But I just can't even get ahead of the thousand things there are to do."

He tugs on the ends of his hair and paces long strides through the empty kitchen. "I want to be as good as I am at food with everything, but I'm not. I can't be. I fucking suck at everything that is not food." His voice rises, and he sounds like he's unburdening himself as he vents. He points at me. "That community development grant? The one Mags is pissed at me about? I desperately need the money. No lie. I don't have the cash for a new roof. And if that roof makes it through the winter, it'll be a fucking miracle. If it doesn't, then what? Health inspector shuts me down?"

As I watch him pace in increasingly frantic circles through the massive kitchen, my heart catches in my chest. I have heard this same complaint time after time, year after year. People who love the passion of the work but not the drudgery of it. I get it. I understand it. All that other stuff is actually stuff I'm great at. My entire career has been filled with chefs like Benny.

What my entire career hasn't been filled with is men like him. Men who make my heart tighten in my chest with a look. Men who would bring me home to their parents, walk in on those parents having sex, and stick around for coffee and conversation. Men who make kale ravioli so delicious, I knew from the first bite I would never taste anything like it and I would never tire of it.

Benny leans back against the counter, dropping his shoulders in defeat. "I'm in so deep, Willow. Not debt, thank God. I don't overspend, but I'm right there, right on the edge. I make enough to cover my people, my rent, and my costs. But extras? What restaurant owner has the time to take off to spend with their families, friends? I don't have that kind of flexibility, let alone the money to go on vacation, take a real break. But I'm missing out. Life is passing me by. I know I'm only thirty-one, but when I thought for real my pops could be sick..." He rubs his eyes hard, like he's holding back tears.

"I haven't spent enough time with him. I don't want to lose my family even though I'm right fucking here. And I don't want to lose my restaurant."

I join him, wrapping my arms around his waist and leaning my face against his warm chest. The heat of him radiates through his flannel shirt and puffer coat, and I breathe it in. He's talented—more so than me, I'm sure of that. I was never a great cook. I just loved doing it. That's why I found my place around food and not in a kitchen of my own.

None of this should ever work, but a small part of me sparks with an idea. But first, I need to tell him the truth.

"I went to Cleveland yesterday to meet with a roofing contractor," I say, my voice low, my cheek pressed to his chest. "I wanted to see if I could use any of my connections to negotiate a lower price on a roof for you."

Benny puts his hands on my shoulders and moves me away from him, not in a rough way, but so he can look into my eyes. "You did what? Why? Why would you do that?"

I give him a small smile. "Because I knew you weren't going to apply for the grant, and I know you need the roof." I shrug. "I didn't get very far. I was able to get one of the contractors working here to pull the last permit on the roof you have now." I sigh, because what I have to tell him, I'm sure he already knows. "Your landlord kind of screwed you. The roof that you're supposed to replace should have been replaced eight years ago. When you signed your lease, he probably knew you'd need to replace the roof before the lease was up."

Benny's mouth drops open. "I had a lawyer look it over," he says. "I even had an inspection..."

I nod. "I'm sure it's all aboveboard. There's a lot of wiggle room in this stuff. A couple of warm winters and maybe that roof would last five years longer than expected. But with the last couple of years you've had here in Ohio..."

I press my hips to his and cup his face in my hands. "The contractor I met with yesterday is booked solid through July. He said with how bad the last few winters have been, he can give you a discount and get you on the schedule, but if anything happens this winter, you'll be looking at a patchwork job. Maybe closing the restaurant until it's up to code. Hard to say, but with how wet the fall has been, he didn't want to commit to getting a job that big done as a rush. And definitely not cheap."

I lean forward and place a light kiss on his lips. "I'm sorry. I tried."

Benny's eyes darken, and he lowers his brows. "You did that for me?"

I nod. "Well, I didn't do much but look into the options. I didn't solve anything."

Benny then takes my face in his hands and strokes my lower lip with his thumb. "You went out of your way to help me. You got your contacts involved. You put yourself out there for me."

I lower my chin so I can kiss his thumb lightly. "It's what all of us who care about you would do," I tell him. "Mags, me, Jasmine, Sassy, Rita, your parents. You're surrounded by a lot of love, Benny. Sometimes it might just be hard to see it for what it is."

He smirks that sexy, confident smile that sends my heart into my stomach, and heat floods through my body. "You think Mags and Rita love me? I mean, I know I'm the sexiest single man in Star Falls, but..." He strokes my cheek. "I have the only woman I want."

I look up into his face. "I don't know what to say, Benny," I whisper. "I love spending time with you, but I'm a short-timer. I'm leaving soon. And I'm more than ten years older than you. You really think this could work out? I mean, like, long-term? What about kids? You mean you don't want to give your parents more little Bianchis to look after?"

I feel tears burning the backs of my eyes now. I don't regret any of my decisions. I never wanted kids. Not after the childhood I had. And I never believed I could want a man who wanted anything different from what I wanted.

But now, I don't know.

Maybe I could want the man. I just don't know where that leaves the things that he might want.

"Willow, family is about so much more than kids." He holds my face so our eyes meet. "Don't get me wrong. If the right woman came along and she wanted a ton of babies, that'd be a decision that we'd make together. Time, money, all that shit would go into it. But if the right woman came along and kids were not on the table, you think I'd throw away the woman I love for something I don't even know if I want?"

I back away. Whoa. Love. Love… He said it, and it's far too soon for that.

"Slow down," he says, stepping close to me. "You look like I probably did when I saw my dad's dick."

I am trying to relax. Trying to let my brain work this out.

He leans down and kisses me on the lips, a light, sweet kiss. "Baby, I've known you were special since the moment I met you. I am falling in love with you."

"Benny, it's been…"

"I know," he says. "But tell me something. How did you feel when you ate my ravioli?"

I curve my lips into a frown. "That's not the same as——"

"Willow," he presses. "Say it. What did you feel?"

"I loved it," I admit. "It was unlike anything I've ever had. I knew from the moment I tasted it, I could eat it a thousand times and never get sick of it."

He nods. "I'm a simple man. I know what I like. I know what I feel. I'm not asking you for forever, but I'm asking you to consider dating me. Fuck the one-year rule or whatever. Who knows how you'll feel by the time this project is over." He waves a hand around the kitchen and smirks. "Shit, at this rate, you'll be in Star Falls for the next three years. Who knows? A couple more construction delays, and you might end up staying a lifetime."

His grin is so warm, so genuine, tears fill my eyes. "I'm not that simple," I tell him. "Nothing about me is that easy. My past, my present."

He nods. "I know we're different. I know that you're classy and I'm all ego. I'm not good with numbers, and look at you." He motions his hands around the kitchen again. "You do this. This is your job."

He's not wrong. We're so different, and yet, every comfortable moment of the last two months I've spent with him.

Every night, I've fallen asleep in his arms. Every morning, I've woken up beside him. We've talked about surface things, but he's a man I can go to with anything. I know that I can, and worse, I know that I want to. Deep down, maybe everything I tell myself about why this can't work are just bullshit excuses. A way for me to run from something more real than anything else I've known.

"What are you saying?" I ask, because I don't know what else to say. That I love him? That I'm falling in love with him? Hell yeah, I probably am.

But the timing couldn't be worse. This could never work. Just like Pancake Circus, one major snag and the whole thing would fall apart in my hands.

"Willow, all I'm saying is that I'm falling for you. I think about you constantly. I used to spend every waking minute thinking about my restaurant and food, and now I spend every waking minute thinking about my restaurant and food and you. I want it all. I want you as part of my life, and I want to think about a future that lasts longer than a project. Will you at least consider it? I'm not asking you to marry me. Hell, I'm not even asking you to stay here in Star Falls or to give up your job."

He pulls me close and crushes me against his chest.

"I never want you to choose between something you love and someone you love. Just tell me you're in this with me. Whatever that means. Is that asking too much?"

That's the question.

I can't face the reality that this project is going to fail and I'm going to be on a plane in a few days or a few weeks, and then I'll be the one to have to make the choice.

I know he says he's not asking me to make a choice, but he's not going to give up his business, and I wouldn't ask him to.

But I'm not ready to give up everything that I've worked my entire life for because of love.

His hold on me loosens, and he looks guarded. He searches my face for his answer. "Willow? Whatever this means, are you in this with me? Not just hooking up, no fuck buddies. I want to know you're mine for as long as you'll have me. If that means after this project is over, you leave the state, we'll find a way if we still want that. I'm not asking for then. I'm asking you for right now. Are we doing this, you and I?"

Tears wet my eyelashes. "Do you mean dinners with your family? Dates? The whole nine?"

He nods. "Everything except surprise visits with my parents. I might have to start calling first."

I laugh and step into his arms. I rest my face against his chest and listen to the beating of his heart. It's fast and steady, like mine. I close my eyes and let my fears roar through my ears.

This will never work! the fears shout.

Though this time, with Benny's arms around me, a tiny voice inside me asks back, *But what if it does?*

But I'm leaving. My rational brain insists on seeing the facts.

You have long-distance relationships with everyone you love, my heart reminds me.

But I'm so, so scared, my head finally admits.

I look up at Benny and reveal the truth. "I'm scared. Scared this could work. Scared how much I want you. Scared that it's all too much, too soon. Scared it can't last."

"Be scared with me, then, Willow. Not of me. Not of this. I'll never hold you back, but I don't want to let you go."

I close my eyes and lift up on my toes. Every ounce of my heart, body, and strength is pulling me—not away from him, but toward. Is this too much? Too soon? Probably all of it. But maybe for the first time in my life, I've met someone who's worth trying for.

"Okay," I whisper. "I'd rather be afraid with you than let you go. I'm in it, Benny. I'm in this—whatever it is, for however long it lasts."

CHAPTER SEVENTEEN

benito

"We have twenty minutes before I have to leave for the restaurant." As soon as I close the door to my condo behind us, I have Willow pressed against the door.

"Plenty of time," she breathes, already tugging at the bottom of her sweatshirt.

I unzip my jeans and kick off my shoes, then throw myself against her, pressing my chest against hers. Her top is off, only a paper-thin bra separating us.

"Mine," I growl, shoving aside the fabric of her cup and sucking her nipple deep into my mouth. "This is mine, and this…" With my mouth occupied on her breast, I bend down and grab her ass with both hands. "Willow, you're fucking perfect. Your body, your…"

"Less talking, more sucking," she begs, arching her back.

I swirl the tip of my tongue over her hard nipple, scraping the peak with my top teeth in my frenzy to taste her, claim her. I've fucked her almost every day since I met her, but every time I kiss her, it's like a hunger inside me demanding more, more, more. I'll never get sick of this. I'll never get enough of her.

She whimpers my name as I graze my teeth lightly across her flesh. "Benny…"

I move my mouth from her tits to her lips, and she grabs my head, fisting my hair with greedy hands. We feast on each other's mouths, tasting and prodding, our tongues clashing like two people who've been starved for each other.

This is just part of why I know I'm falling in love with Willow Watkins. I can't imagine being with a woman who doesn't ignite my body and stimulate my brain. She's everything. Not just a snack. She's sustenance. And I want to devour her, consume her.

My cock is throbbing inside my briefs, and I pant kisses into Willow's mouth while she strokes me through the soft fabric. "My bed," I groan. "Now."

She starts to move, but I stop her by sweeping her into my arms.

"Benny." She laughs, but she wraps her arms around my neck and buries her face against my cheek. We try to kiss as I stumble toward my room with her in my arms, but I can't see, and I smack her knee into the door frame.

"Oh my God." My eyes fly open at the sound. "I'm so sorry. Are you okay?"

She's laughing and waves me forward. "I'm fine, keep going. I'm fine."

Both of us laughing, I set her gently down on the bed, and she lies back, watching as I shed the last of my clothes.

"You have like fifteen minutes," she says, her eyes wide. There is a flush across her chest that I want to lick, shoulder to shoulder, neck to navel. For a minute, I seriously consider calling in to work. I've never done it. Never blown off work for anyone. And I can't start now. That would be a very dangerous habit. Knowing how I feel about Willow, Benito's would be closed by Christmas.

"More than enough time," I say.

I run my hands up her thighs, grip the waistband of her yoga pants, and tug them and her panties off in one pull. One of her breasts is poking out from her bra cup, and her pussy is bare for me, her legs open and waiting.

She's the most delicious sight I've ever seen.

I drop onto the bed and lie on top of her, positioning my throbbing cock between her legs. "I want you in every way possible.

I want this forever," I grunt, nudging my cock against her drenched entrance. "Tell me you want this, Willow. I want to hear you say you want me."

"Fuck yes, I want you," she says, her hands clawing at my ass. "Fuck me, Benny. God, I need this. I need you."

That's all I need to hear. I piston my hips and drive all the way inside her so fast and so deep, we both cry out. The pleasure is so exquisite, so complete, I have to slow myself down or I'll pound her until I come. And I want more than that for her.

"Fuck me," I tell her. "Move, baby."

She's underneath me, but she widens her legs and I hold her knees open with my palms. She thrusts her hips up while I roll mine in time with hers, our movements so frantic, so rushed, my balls slap against her ass. She wriggles and moans, gasps and begs me for more, harder, and I give her everything I have.

Everything I know she wants.

In and out, in and out, I press her knees wider, opening her more, my cock driving deep until finally she screams my name. "Benny. Oh fuck."

I feel the walls of her pussy tighten around me, milking my cock. She's so wet, I have to grit my teeth and curl my toes to hold back just a little longer. She's crying, tears on her cheeks, moaning my name as she jerks her hips harder against mine. "So good," she murmurs. "You feel so fucking good."

Her breathing is ragged, her beautiful lips dry from panting, and a sheen of sweat breaks out across her hairline. I lean down and claim her mouth, kissing her and releasing her knees. I support my weight with my arms, but as soon as she claws at my back, pulling me closer, rubbing her tits against my chest, I lose it, lose every ounce of control. I fall off the cliff, coming hard and hot deep inside her.

"Fuck," I roar, banging into her so hard the bed rocks back and forth on the hardwood floor.

I ride my orgasm, the climax so powerful my toes cramp and my hair is drenched with sweat. The come-down is slow, and before I know it, I feel Willow's nails scratching through my hair.

"Babe." I can hear her whisper to me, but fuck, I'm wrecked.

"Mm-hm," I grumble, my face smashed between her tits. This is heaven. I'm sure of it. I'm dead, and this is the eternal happiness I've somehow earned. I'm never, ever moving.

"Benny, you have to get to the restaurant, babe." She scratches my scalp in long, relaxing strokes. If she thinks that's going to get my heavy-ass legs moving, she's so wrong.

"Five minutes," I mumble, drooling on her, but my cock is still inside her. I'm warm with her underneath me. God, this feels like bliss. All I could ever want. More than I've ever had before.

As I'm lying there, her nails bringing my head a new level of happy, I can't stop the words. They echo in my thoughts, coming from a place deep in my chest.

I love this. I love you.

I love you.

The thought has my eyes flying open. Did I say it out loud?

I look up at her, her flushed face pink and smiling. "Hey there, gorgeous."

She doesn't look spooked, so I take a long, slow breath.

"You are amazing," she says, tapping a finger on the tip of my nose. "And you're going to be late."

"Worth it," I say, reluctantly pulling my semihard cock from inside her and rolling over. "Fuck, I hate leaving you."

"I hate that you have to go," she says, a satisfied smile on her face.

"Stay here as long as you want," I tell her. "In fact, please promise me you'll be here when I get home."

She grins. "I have to go home and shower. I have work emails I have to…"

I hold up a hand. "I'm going to leave a spare key on the counter. Just promise me you'll be back here in my bed waiting for me when I get home from work."

I lean down to kiss her smiling face. She is perfect. Sweet, sexy, smart. Mine. "I'll be here," she promises.

Then I take the world's fastest shower and run off to what is now the second love of my life—my business.

I arrive in record time to find the place unusually busy. Rita offers me a quick wave as she seats a handful of late lunch diners, and when I check in with Jas at the bar, she gives me a weird look.

"You look happy," she says. "What's the big smile about?"

There is warmth in her words, and I smile even bigger.

"Nothing," I tell her, although that's a fucking lie.

I'm in love.

I'm happy.

The world has never seemed brighter. Now, if I could just block out all the shit that causes me stress.

Well, that ain't happening, as I can already tell from the look on Jas's face. She leans forward on the bar and motions me to come close with a hand.

"Well, you might want to hold on to that smile," she says. "Mags is waiting for you in your office."

The warmth and satisfaction of my morning with Willow fade away like someone splashed me in the face with a bucket of stinky mop water.

"Thanks, Jas." I nod, then head into the kitchen to check on the staff.

Carla and Duncan are managing the lunch orders just fine. The controlled chaos calms me, and it's hard not to think back to the kitchen at the old Papa Gino's place. What I wouldn't do to expand my business. Make it bigger, better. I love this crusty old location, but after six years here, the lure of something new does have some appeal.

But I watch my kitchen run like a tiny but tight machine, and I say a little prayer of thanks for what I do have. I have so much. Someday I'll get my shit together and can maybe dream about more. But until I've earned it, this is Benito's. This is me.

I make my way down the back hallway toward my office, where I find the door open, Mags sitting in the same chair in front of my desk where she was before. She jumps to her feet when I walk in.

"Mags," I say, not able to stop the scowl from covering my face. "I thought you wanted some time off."

She nods, and her face looks pale, her eyes puffy. "I did. But I didn't want to leave things where they were yesterday. Benny, I don't want you to fire me. And I don't want to leave."

I throw my hands in the air. "Mags, I'm not the one who started all this shit. You're the one who's unhappy. What do you want from me? You want a job? You got it. But I'm not going back to—"

She holds up a hand. "I'm sorry to interrupt. I know. I've been out of line. It's not anything you've done or anything you've done differently. It's just..." She looks at me through her lashes, lowering her head. "A couple weeks ago, a city guy came out to read the gas meter and made a really shitty comment about you. About you not paying your bills."

A flood of anger flows through my limbs. "Who was it?" I ask. "Did you talk to the guy? Get his name?"

She shakes her head. "He was new. I've never seen him before, and I was so stunned, I didn't know what to say."

I think about this for a second. "Where did this happen? Where were you when he said this?"

Mags looks down at her hands. "He was at the bar. After he read the meter, he ordered lunch to go. I threw some extra focaccia in for him and thought I'd do something nice, you know, his being a city worker and all. I brought it out to him, and as I was handing it over, he made that shitty comment."

My blood is boiling. "Who else heard him? He said this in front of customers?"

Mags's face goes pale. "Yeah. Lunch rush. Jas heard, and Sassy for sure. I don't know how many diners, but it was pretty awkward."

I slam my ass into my seat, wondering how long I'd get locked up for beating the shit out of a city worker. There's probably an extra penalty for crimes like that, but maybe in my defense, I could claim he was damaging my business's reputation.

"Fuck," I sigh, the anger suddenly draining out of me.

As I think back on the last few weeks, I start piecing it all together. I let the delivery guys go and have been doing a lot more work myself. Sassy and Jas whispering on their breaks. A new restaurant coming to town, even if it's not open yet. Mags probably saw the writing on the wall. Benito's is in trouble, even I refused to see the signs.

"So, that is what all this has been about?" I ask. "You're afraid I'm about to go under?"

Mags shrugs. "I didn't know, not for sure. But you're so goddamn stubborn, Benny. You don't let anyone in. I've been here with you for years now, years of my life. Day in, day out. You call me your right hand, yet I don't know anything about the business. Nothing real. If we were in trouble, I'd probably be the last one to know." She meets my eyes, a challenge in her look. "If something was going on here, something serious, would you tell me first? Or would I be the last to know because you'd need me more than everybody else?"

I rub my eyes, and it hits me. She's right. I've been an arrogant, selfish bastard to the people who most deserve my trust. And it's all because I'm scared. Scared they will leave me once they know the truth. That one crack in the facade and the whole goddamn place will fall down around my feet.

"You're right about so many things, Mags," I tell her. "I need help. Benito's is not in trouble. I'm in trouble. I'm overwhelmed. I'm shit at paperwork and staying organized and creating a budget." I shake my head. "I don't want to ask for help because I don't want to admit that I'm a failure. This place is my life. It's all I ever wanted. What kind of man am I if I can't run this place myself?"

Mags laughs. "You're a typical man," she scoffs. Then she leans forward in her chair. "Benny, it's not a sin to ask for help. Look at you and all the people you help. Rita, for one." She presses her lips together and looks pained. "I shouldn't have said what I did about Rita yesterday. I've been feeling like an asshole about it. She's a great lady, and the customers love her. But you're the person who gave a very old lady the only job in town she could get. Why? Because she's good for the business? No. Because you can help her. That's the kind of man you are, Benny. Yes, you're arrogant and cocky and all the rest, but you're also a truly good, good person. I wouldn't want to work for anyone else."

She leans back in her chair. "I'm sorry I haven't dealt with any of this well. But I'd like to stay. I'd like to take on more responsibility. I'll do the books, or I'll just set up your bills on autopay. Whatever you want. I don't need to make more money, not at first. Can you try giving me more responsibility, and if it works out, can we talk about a bigger role for me here?"

I sigh. "I'm not going to make it easy on you," I admit. "I'm stubborn, and I hate being told what to do."

"Don't I fucking know it," she chuckles. "And yet, I'm here. And it's technically my day off."

I think about Willow. About the fact that she's only here for a year. How I have a ticking clock and want to spend every minute of the time we have together. Making whatever we have work so that she is sure what we have is real. Because even now, with Mags in my office, a restaurant full of customers, and a kitchen I really need to get into, my thoughts are of Willow. My body misses her. Wants her. Can't wait to get home to her.

And then, of course, there's my family. More help with my work means more time with them too. It's a win-win. That just means that I actually have to do it. Open up to someone. Admit the things I suck at. I have to be okay with failing. Because if I let Mags take over or even just pitch in with parts of my business, I have to accept that it's because I can't do it all.

I know it's true.

It's about time I get honest about it.

"All right," I tell her. "You want a title and a pay raise; you'll need to show me we have the money for that. And I'm going to let you write up the job description, figure out the schedule, all that shit. There's a lot I'm terrible at, Mags. And you're going to see the real mess I've made. That scare you?"

She beams like I just promised her a partnership. "No. I was scared not knowing what was going on. I'm up for the challenge of cleaning shit up."

I hold up my hand in warning. "But look, you're going to get mad. You're going to get frustrated. You're going to think, this is so fucking easy, why doesn't he just do this or that. And that's going to shut me down and piss me off."

She nods solemnly. "But you know I can't lie to you, Benito. I have to call you out on your stupid shit."

I arch a brow at her. "This ain't going to be easy. I'm just warning you. My ego's on the line here."

"I know." She's quiet then. "It would be a blow for anyone's ego to have to own up to stuff they can't handle and ask for help. I'll do my best not to make it too personal. And I won't take it personally if things get heated."

I slap my hands on the desk and stand from my chair. I hold out a hand to her. "If I didn't trust you, Mags, this wouldn't be happening. Thanks for having my back even when I didn't see it or acknowledge it."

She shakes my hand and turns to leave. "Oh," she says. "Since I'm here, you want me to stay?"

I'm tempted. If she stays, I can go home to Willow. Home to tell her everything that I'm going to fix. Everything that I'm determined to make work. But then I look at Mags. Every choice I make from here on out, I'm going to try to do the right thing. Not going with what's easy or what pleases me.

As much as I want to let her close so I can spend time with Willow, I need to give Mags some time off. I need to make a little progress in my office so I'm ready for her help tomorrow. I know what I need to do, and for once, I'm going to say yes to the shit I hate doing. I'm going to face it and do it.

"No," I tell her, shaking my head. "You get out of here. Take the day off. You want to work tomorrow, I'll see you when we're both fresh."

She nods and gives me a smile as she leaves. Then, since Carla and Duncan are covering the kitchen, I open my desk drawer and pull out the laptop that I use so rarely, it's not even charged, and I get to work.

CHAPTER EIGHTEEN

willow

After Benny leaves for work, I make his bed and grab the spare key from the kitchen counter. I lock his unit behind me and head home, braced for what's coming.

I check my email and see I have close to fifty new messages and an invitation to a meeting with Theresa for tomorrow morning. I send Alex an instant message and ask if Theresa is free now.

Alex: Let me check with her assistant. One sec.

While I wait for Alex to reply, I wander over to the huge glass windows that overlook the river. I stare out into space until the pinging of the IM system brings me back to the moment.

Alex: She wants to talk now. Just to you. Can you jump on?

I confirm that I can, quickly smoothing my hair back into a bun and peeking at my reflection in the camera on my phone. I look fine. From the neck up, there will be no signs that I just got fucked within an inch of my life by the most amazing man. The most amazing chef. The reason I might consider something very different for my life.

I click on the meeting invite that Alex sent, and within seconds, Theresa's furious face fills the screen.

"It's fucking done," she says quietly. "Pardon my language, but all this work, all the time they spent pursuing us. I'm pissed off. So much waste. The Kincades filed an injunction to stop work on the property in Star Falls," she tells me without preamble. Without so much as even a hello. "It's over, Willow. Pancake Circus is dead. I'll announce the news to the team in the meeting tomorrow, but since you reached out, I figured I'd give you a heads-up."

I knew this outcome was inevitable, but hearing it from Theresa's mouth sours my stomach. "Thank you," I say. "And I'm sorry."

I have nothing to be sorry about, of course. None of this has anything to do with me, and yet the only word to describe how I feel is sorry. Sorry that my company will lose valuable time and an enormous amount of money while we fight this out with the Kincades in the legal system. Sorry that this means my time in Star Falls is officially coming to an end.

"No point in having Alex make your travel plans back to Chicago," Theresa says, her voice frustrated. "I don't have another site set up for you yet, so you might as well stay in Star Falls while we have the lease on that condo you're staying in. Unless you have someplace else you'd like to stay. I'd love to have you back in the office to strategize and meet with our attorneys. Are you all right staying there until we figure out our next steps?"

I nod. "Of course. But I'd like to take a little time off, if you're okay with it."

Theresa nods. "How much time are you thinking?" she asks.

I calculate the distance in my head, the idea starting to take shape. "Two weeks, tops." I rush on to explain, so she doesn't jump to any incorrect conclusions. "One of my best friends is on bed rest, about to have her first baby as a single mom. I'd like to visit her while things are settling down."

She nods. "All right. Make sure Alex knows your schedule. You may have to take calls with our attorneys while you're away, but I'll do what I can to accommodate your time off."

"Theresa," I say, before she's able to end the meeting. It's just me and her, my boss. The woman I've worked for and whose company has given me purpose for...well, maybe for too long. "Thank you," I tell her. "I love what I do. I believe in what we do as a company. And I am just sorry that things have turned out this way."

Theresa nods, but I can tell she's stressed, angry, and probably scared. This deal going south is going to cost the company millions. There's just no putting a positive spin on that. "Enjoy your time off, Willow."

Then, without a goodbye, she ends the meeting. I immediately pick up the phone and call Jessa. She answers on the first ring.

"Do you have a radar for tears or something now?" she asks, sounding weepy and miserable. "Or maybe I just cry all the time and only notice it when you call?"

We're not on video, but my heart clenches at her sniffles. "Jessa," I say gently. "Would now be a good time to come visit you? I can stay in a hotel if I'll be in the way."

"Oh my God," she wails, literally wails into the phone. "How soon can you get here?"

I grin, and tears wet my lashes. "Okay, calm down. I haven't booked anything, and I can't stay long. I need to take a trip for work, but I'm thinking by the end of the week. Possibly sooner."

We hash out the details, and I even talk to Jessa's mom, who sounds grateful to have someone coming by to help. After I end the call, I send an email to Theresa confirming I'll attend the meeting with the team in the morning, but that I'll be out of the office for one to two weeks after. I add a line at the end of my email with a request.

Theresa, I know we're going to have to communicate to the contractors that the work will stop. Is it possible you'd let me handle that personally? I've been working with these companies and would like to preserve the relationships if I can. You never know what might happen. If we settle, etc., we'll want to keep the same team in place. And I'd like to be the one to soften the blow if I can.

She replies back with one sentence. *As long as the lawyers say it's okay, yes.*

That's good enough for me. I start to get excited, quickly checking airfare and booking a flight out of Cleveland tomorrow night. I'm not sure that I can fix any of this. But I have a plan to try.

I spend the rest of the afternoon packing my bags and cleaning my place. On my counter is the white flower dish that came with the bouquet Benny gave me the day after we met. What a long time ago that seems like now, but really, it's only been a matter of months. But during that time, I've changed. I've opened up to things that I never thought I wanted. I only hope that this is what I truly want. This is a lot to think about...too much, really.

But for the first time in my life, I'm curious what might happen, what new adventures and exciting firsts I can experience if I ditch the one-year plan. If I stop chasing new dreams. If I set down roots and let myself finally find a place I can call home.

Now I just have to break it to Benny that I'm leaving.

———————

I spend the afternoon running around Star Falls. I make a stop at the very small mall to pick up the sexiest lingerie I can find. I buy a bottle of champagne and two flutes, then stop at the florist to buy two red roses. I want tonight to be special. It will be our last night together for a while, and I don't know what will happen when I talk to Benny about my plans. Will he still want to date, knowing that I'm leaving? Knowing that my plan might not work?

I want to be prepared to make it special. Especially if this is really, truly the end for us. I don't want to think that it could be, not after everything he said. But something like this could be too much for a new relationship to manage. I have to brace myself for whatever happens.

When Benny arrives home, it's well after ten. As promised, I'm in his bed. There is a bottle of champagne chilling by the bedside, along with the flutes. I plucked the red petals from the roses and sprinkled them in a path from the front door to the bedroom, which was dark except for the warm, flickering orange glow of a bunch of candles.

I'm lying on top of the bed, my entire body covered head to toe in comfy pajamas and socks. Underneath, I'm wearing the very naughty items I bought at the mall, but I want to leave that little tidbit as a surprise.

"Babe?" I hear him call as he locks the front door.

He follows the rose petals to the bed and leans down to kiss me. "What's all this?" He takes in the candles and the roses, a grin on his gorgeous face.

My heart seizes in my chest. He looks tired but happy. A lock of hair flops over his forehead, and I reach up and push it back.

"I smell like I just took a swim in garlic sauce," he says, sniffing. "Give me two minutes to shower."

I pop the cork on the champagne and fill two glasses, then when I hear the water turn on, I slide under the covers and take off the warm socks that cover the thigh-high red stockings I'm wearing under my pajama pants. I lean back and listen to the water running through the pipes. I think about what I'm going to tell Benny. Where to start. It's not going to be easy, but if he is half the man I believe he is, things will be okay.

He comes out of the bathroom a few minutes later, his hair damp and a loose pair of pajama pants riding low on his waist. He is stunning. Beautiful. His face lights up with a cocky smile, and he takes a running start and then dives into the bed on top of me.

He lands with a crash, shifting the bed on the floor, and we both burst out laughing. He nods at the champagne. "You've been busy today," he says, kissing me once, twice, then three times on the lips. "Mm, fucking delicious. So, what are we celebrating?"

I lean over and grab a flute, then hand him one and take the other. I hold mine up and offer a toast. "Well, to both of us failing and then rising like phoenixes."

He looks confused. "I don't get it, but I'll drink to it."

We clink glasses, take a sip, and then I set both flutes on the bedside table beside us.

"So," I say, leaning back against the pillows. "Pancake Circus is dead. But I have a plan to bring it back to life."

"What?" He widens his eyes, and his mouth drops open. "Willow, what does that mean? What happened?"

I explain about the Kincade family backing out for reasons that they haven't shared. How the injunction will possibly stop construction and tie up any progress on the project until the long legal battle is sorted out.

"But," I say, "I've lived and breathed this project for two years. I know this will work. We just have to get the place open." That's when I look at him. "I booked a flight down to Florida. I leave tomorrow. I'm going to the original location, and I'm going to stay there until the owners agree to talk to me."

"Can you do that?" he asks. "What about the lawyers?"

"Technically, my company can't communicate with the family except through their lawyers, but I'm not personally named in anything that I've seen yet. As far as I know, it's a loophole. I need to know, Benny. I need to know why they want out and what I can do to make this happen."

Benny lowers his brows and reaches past me for another sip of champagne. "What if you can't change their minds?" he asks. "Holy fuck, Willow. I'm just getting it now. You'll leave, won't you? You'll have no reason to stay in Star Falls."

"I do have many reasons to stay in Star Falls," I say. "I just need to work out why this is happening. I need to understand so I can make a good decision about what I want to do next."

His face darkens, and he rolls onto his side to face me. "What does that mean?" he asks. "What you want to do next. That means where you'll go next. What city, what project. You're leaving me."

He looks so sad, so broken. And my own heart cracks open just a bit at the realization. It's one thing to know that I might leave. It's another to face that it's happening right now.

"I have some ideas," I say. "But I can't make any decisions until I have the work stuff sorted out." I reach for his face, smooth his damp hair back. "Benny, I've never been a relationship person. I'm a short-timer. One year here, another there." I meet his dark eyes. "But you've made me rethink what kind of person I really am. What kind of person I could be."

I pull my hand away from him, a sudden flush of vulnerability making me feel very, very exposed.

"I'm afraid to admit how much I think I want this," I whisper. "You make me want to experience new adventures. The kind I can have by staying in one place. By staying with one person. But I'm scared."

He scoots closer to me and rests his head on my thigh. I lean back against the pillow and stroke his hair, and we're quiet for a minute. The candles flicker and burn, filling the room with the light fragrances of vanilla and something heavier, like sandalwood.

"I did something terrifying today," he says. "I told Mags she could help me with more work at the restaurant. I need help, and I fucking admitted it."

His damp hair feels soft between my fingers, and I lightly scratch his scalp as I touch him. "And?" I ask. "Was that the right decision? How do you feel now?"

He absently runs a hand along my thigh and closes his eyes under my soft touch. He sighs. "I still feel terrified. But something's got to give, and I'll never know if I don't try."

He stops suddenly, his fingers tracing along the leg of my pajamas. "Wait a second," he says. "What's this?"

I grin. He's felt the seam of the thigh-highs I'm wearing under my pajamas. "This is my attempt at admitting the truth, no matter how scary it is."

We rearrange ourselves on the bed. Benny sits with his back against the pillows, and I straddle his lap. His eyes immediately go to the bright red fabric on my toes. Before I even touch him, before I even take off a single stitch of clothing, I see his dick start to tent the front of his pajamas.

"We're very different, Benny," I tell him, slowly unbuttoning the front of my pajama shirt. "In some ways. But in other ways, we're so very much alike."

I watch his face as he stares at my fingers as the first button opens.

"I've never been in love. Not really. Never had a family. I have, of course, but not really. I've never had a home—not a permanent one. But being with you makes me want all those things. It's terrifying. It's stressful. It's confusing." I unbutton the rest of the buttons and let the soft gray pajama top fall open. "But I can't think of anyone else I'd want to do all of that with."

"What else do you want to do with me?" he asks, his voice thick and raw. His eyes follow my movements as I wiggle out of my top. And then, he asks, "What is all this?"

"A little goodbye present," I say. "I'm going to be gone at least a week, and I wanted to make sure you had something to remember me by."

"Take off those pants," he growls. "I want to burn the image of all of you in all of that onto my brain forever."

I climb off the bed and let the pajama pants fall to the floor, then I turn around and give him a view of the outfit I bought today. A sheer black bustier encases my breasts in lace, delicate red roses embroidered over my nipples. A matching thong and garters barely cover my lower half, and since the tiny Star Falls mall was sold out of black thigh-high hose, I'm wearing bright-red fishnets.

"It's the best I could do on short notice," I tell him, spinning in a circle to show off the backside and the front.

"For fuck's sake, Willow." Benny practically lunges out of bed and pounces on me. His mouth, hot and breathless, immediately clamps down on my hip. "I want to taste every inch of you in this getup."

His fingers trail over the teeny-tiny fabric of the thong. Then his hands are everywhere, stroking my thighs, touching the fishnets, kissing and nibbling, grazing and licking until my knees go weak and I have to lie down on the bed.

"Ass to me," he demands.

He doesn't have to ask twice. I lift my ass in the air, and he reaches around my waist to tug the thong off. "We don't need this. Everything else is fucking perfect."

Somehow, after a lot of maneuvering and laughter, he gets the thong past the garters, and I'm bare to him, kneeling with my ass in the air while he licks my pussy from behind. He licks me in long, slow strokes, sucking my lips lightly into his mouth. My arms go weak, and my eyes flutter shut as I give in to the pleasure, the all-consuming bliss that is his mouth on my most sensitive parts.

But I don't want this to end too soon, so I turn around and motion for him to lose the pajama pants. He does and then sits back on the bed, his back to the pillows. I kneel with my legs wide open over his ankles and slowly inch my way up his body. I sit in his lap, carefully positioning his massive hard-on between us but far away from my needy pussy. I want to ride him, want him deep inside me. But not yet.

With my ass high in the air so he can see it, I dip my head low and take his cock into my mouth. I hum against his heat, working my hand around his shaft in time with my deep, slow sucking.

He whimpers, grunts, his hands fisting my hair and urging me up and back, up and down. I love the feel of him. The scratch of his soft hairs against my skin as I offer him all the pleasure I can bring.

I'm flooded with need, clenching with every pass. I want to share this pleasure with him. Give it and take my own. I lift my face and am about to climb onto his lap when he holds my face in his hands.

"I fucking love you, Willow Watkins," he grits out. "I love you."

I don't say anything. I don't feel like I have to. He knows how I feel. He knew how I felt long before I knew. And I do know. I know that whatever happens in the future, I've never wanted anyone more. I've never wanted a man's body, his business, his companionship, and his comfort more than I want all that with Benito Bianchi.

I climb on top of him, letting him enter me inch by agonizingly slow inch. He slams his head back against the headboard, and then, once he's fully inside me, he holds my breasts in his hand and pinches my nipples through the lace.

I gasp, the breath stolen from my lungs, but the intensity of the pleasure flooding my body. I'm weak with him, weak for him. My eyes clench shut, I throw my head back, giving in to everything this can be, everything this always has been. Everything it will be.

I move the cups down and thrust my chest forward, and he sucks my nipple into his mouth. The heat and wetness, the clamp of his teeth over my tender skin, sends me sailing, riding a wave of pleasure.

I rock hard against his cock, riding him, working my hips back and forth so hard I can hear the scrape of the thigh-highs against his legs.

If it bothers him, he's going with it, because he's sucking my tits like a meal and bouncing his hips up and down to match the pace of my grinding. I wrap my fingers behind his neck and pull his face closer, harder, riding and riding, chasing the bliss of release until I feel the tremble, the tightening.

"Fuck." I gasp, and then I stiffen, every muscle in my body tight in anticipation of the crash that takes over. I shudder and shake, and I can't stop the moans of absolute bliss that rocket past my lips. "Fuck, I'm coming. Oh God."

I scream through it, trembling all over. As soon as I still, dropping my head against Benny's shoulder, he puts his hands on my waist and fucks me while I'm boneless on top of him.

He writhes beneath me, lifting me up and slamming me back down on his cock. It feels so good. I feel myself losing control again, the tension building, the pleasure so overwhelming that another orgasm hits me, draining me of every ounce of strength. I'm floppy now, my face against Benny's bare chest, his cock pumping hard as he, too, comes with reckless moans and a fierceness that takes his breath away.

We collapse beside each other on the bed, panting, sweaty, our hair wild. He rolls onto his side, and I settle between his arms. I chuckle when he lifts a thigh and locks it over mine, covering me in heavy limbs.

"Is this your way of keeping me from leaving?" I tease.

"Is it working?" he asks.

I draw in a deep breath and close my eyes. "You don't have to keep me to have me," I say, my words blurry with sleep. "I love you, Benny. I love you too."

And saying it doesn't feel like too much.

It doesn't feel like too soon.

It feels right because I know it's true.

CHAPTER NINETEEN

willow

Florida is a lot warmer than Ohio in November. I shrug out of the wool pea coat I wore on the plane and drag a roller bag behind me. I'm going to need cooler clothes where I'm going, but I don't want to confront the Kincades sweating like I ran a marathon to get here.

Since Audrina wouldn't answer my calls, I figured the only way to get some answers was to do what any stalker in pursuit of information would do. I show up at Pancake Circus. The original location. After checking in to a hotel for my one-night stay, I call a rideshare and text Benny.

Me: Wish me luck.

He sends back three thumbs-up emojis within seconds.

The rideshare picks me up at the front of the hotel, and I watch the landscape roll by on the short drive. The driver doesn't say much until we pull into the parking lot.

"Great place," he grumbles, not sounding at all happy. "Best eats in town."

I smile and thank him for the ride. If there's one thing that unites people, it's good food.

The parking lot of Pancake Circus is packed. The faded neon sign and the obvious signs of disrepair just add to the charm of the place. I'm again reminded why we picked this restaurant. An amazing menu. A bit of a gimmicky concept, but memorable. I just hope they don't kick me out or call the police. I've got Jessa on standby in case I need someone to wire bail money.

When I get to the door, I see a hand-lettered sign taped to it. "Closed for private event. Tickets required."

I pull open the door and am greeted by a handsome young guy. "Hi," he says brightly. "Thanks so much for coming. Are you here for the fundraiser or the restaurant?" He gives me a warm smile. "In case you missed the sign, we're closed for the day. But we'll open back up tomorrow for regular business."

"Uh…" I scramble to figure out the right thing to say. I want to get to the bottom of this, but I don't know if I should be here if there's a private event. "I was hoping to talk to Audrina Kincade," I say, looking around as though I might see her just standing around. "Do you know if she's here?"

"Of course," he says. "She's running the event. Are you a friend?" he asks. "I have a short list of people who have complimentary tickets. I can just check…"

Two other people have come up from behind me, so I step aside. "Why don't you go ahead," I say, waving them past. "I need to get out my debit card."

I listen while the people behind me pay for entry to the fundraiser. I luck out because while the younger woman pays, the older woman nods to me. "Do you know John Kincade?" she asks.

I nod, because I do. That's Audrina's grandfather. The man who opened Pancake Circus. "Not very well personally," I admit. "But professionally, yes."

The woman shakes her head slowly. "It's such a shame. They're such wonderful people." She leans in close to me. "I can't imagine losing everything like that. And you know how hard it is to deal with insurance companies these days."

I have no idea what she's talking about, but I nod and then step back into line. I hand the young man at the hostess stand my debit card and pay for a ticket. "Can you tell me how the family is doing?" I ask, not sure what I should say. I want to know what happened, but

I'm afraid if I just come out and ask it, he won't sell me the ticket, won't let me in. That seems ridiculous, though. This is a fundraiser, so they should let in anyone willing to pay for a ticket. "And what really happened?" I add.

The young man runs my card and hands me a paper wristband. I peel the sticky backing and put the thing around my wrist while he explains.

"It's so sad, but they are so lucky nothing worse happened," he says, his voice sincerely distraught. "Mr. Kincade's wife accidentally started a kitchen fire in their home. She was able to get out safely, but they lost everything." He shakes his head. "They have insurance, but there's an investigation and a lot of delays and paperwork. And just the emotional side. Jeanine just turned eighty, and John is, I think, eighty-four now. They've lived in their home for over fifty years. And everything is gone overnight."

"Oh my gosh," I say. "But they are okay? No one was hurt."

He shakes his head. "No, thank goodness. Jeanine was in the hospital for a day or two being treated for minor burns and to make sure her diabetes was under control, but she's fine. Their church asked if they would close the restaurant for just one day to let people come and make donations to help the family with small expenses until the insurance money comes in."

I nod and thank him, then let him get on to checking in other people. Once I get inside the restaurant, the mood is a lot lighter. Food is out on long buffet tables, and people are talking and laughing, sharing memories and snacking on staples from the Pancake Circus menu. I make my way through the crowd and see Jeanine and John Kincade. They are sitting together at a booth, holding hands. They are smiling, but it's obvious the strain they are under.

People are coming up to them, chatting and leaving cards and envelopes on the table. The whole scene is surreal, and I feel like an intruder in a place I don't belong. I didn't bring my checkbook, and I don't know if there's another way to make donations, but I don't have to wait long before the sound of a microphone coming on draws all eyes to the center of the room.

"Hey, everyone." A young man holds the mic, and his smile lights up the Kincades' faces. "As most of you here know, I'm Nathan Kincade, John and Jeanine's great-nephew. I just wanted to thank you all for coming. As you know, my uncle John and aunt Jeanine have been staples of this community for over fifty years. In this time of personal struggle, our family has come together, but I think I speak for all of us when I say the show of support from the community has been overwhelming."

There are some claps and cheers from the crowd at that.

Nathan continues. "All the food and drinks have been donated for today's event, and my uncle's kitchen staff and servers have donated their time off the clock to serve and clean, so every penny of whatever you donate today will go right to John and Jeanine to help them cover any expenses they have until they have help from the insurance company." Nathan points to a man in the crowd. "No pressure, Don. But, yes, I'm looking at you."

Don holds his hands over his heart, and the crowd laughs.

"Don's my uncle's insurance agent. But we know, Don. You're not the one who writes the checks."

"But I would." Don, much quieter than Nathan without a microphone, still manages to be heard as he says, "I would if I could."

By the time the laughter dies down, Nathan is pointing to a bunch of unusual artwork that's hanging on the walls. "And for those of you who don't know her, talented textile artist Annie Hancock has donated some amazing pieces to be auctioned off. If you want to bid on a piece, just put your name down and the amount you want to bid on the sheet by the artwork itself." Nathan puts a hand over his heart. "Annie is a longtime customer of Pancake Circus and is just one of the hundreds of people like you all here today who have stepped up and contributed in a show of support for John and Jeanine."

When the applause dies down, Nathan again encourages everyone to eat and drink and expresses thanks on behalf of the family. As soon as he sets the microphone down, I make my way through the crowd and put a hand on his elbow. He turns to me with a warm smile.

"Hi," he says. "Thank you so much for coming."

"I'm so, so sorry that this has happened," I say. "I wonder if you could tell me if Audrina is here. I was hoping to just say a few words to her and then be on my way."

"Of course," he says. "Last I saw her, she was in the kitchen supervising. Let me get her for you."

To my shock, he doesn't ask who I am or what I want. I wouldn't be surprised, though, if this has been happening all day. People showing up wanting to express support and share condolences.

Nathan returns a few minutes later with Audrina close on his heels. The moment she sees me, her nostrils flare and her eyes narrow. "What are you doing here?" she demands.

Nathan looks from her to me, and for a second, I'm afraid she's going to make a scene. "I'm so sorry about this," I say. "Can I please have two minutes of your time? Then I promise, I'll leave, and you'll never see me again."

Nathan looks at his cousin, but she just points back toward the kitchen. "Cover for me?" she asks. Then she glares at me. "This won't take long."

I feel like an absolute asshole as I follow a storming Audrina through the crowded restaurant to a small door marked with a sign that reads *Office*. She yanks open the door and waits until I'm inside. She closes the door behind us but then stands by the door, her arms crossed over her chest.

"You shouldn't be here," she says, her voice accusing. "How dare you show up like this? What the hell do you want?"

I wish I could hug her, tell her I'm so sorry for what they are going through, but I only have a few seconds to get this out before she's no doubt going to send me packing. I say what I came to say quickly.

"Audrina, I had no idea this was happening today, or I never would have shown up. Since you wouldn't take my calls, I took a chance and flew down here. All I want is to talk to you. I think I have a solution that can get you out of the Star Falls situation and all of us out of an expensive legal mess. Can you give me five minutes, please?"

She looks stunned but then peeks at her watch. "Okay," she relents. "Five minutes."

She takes a seat at an old metal desk that is covered with papers and envelopes. She motions for me to sit, so I pull out a very old, well-worn wooden chair and perch on the edge of it.

"I don't want to assume, but it looks like you maybe wanted out of the Star Falls location because of the fire?" I phrase it as a question.

She lowers her chin and nods. "Yeah," she says. "But my grandparents don't know about that yet. After they lost everything, they moved temporarily into my parents' house. We thought after Grandma got checked out by the doctor that she was okay, but..." She blinks fast. "Physically, they're okay. Emotionally?" She shakes her head. "Have you ever experienced a house fire?"

"No," I say, silently thankful that I have not. "But I imagine it's absolutely devastating."

Audrina nods. "Fifty years of treasured heirlooms. Clothes and pictures, toys and letters." Her voice breaks. "I know it's just stuff, but some stuff can't be replaced. Some stuff carries meaning. And for my grandma..." She sighs. "She blames herself. She feels like she destroyed our family's history. Our legacy." She meets my eyes. "I can't leave them, Willow. Two years ago, I thought striking out on my own and doing my own thing would be an amazing adventure. Now?"

She leans back in her chair, opens a desk drawer, and pulls out a box of tissues. She dabs at her eyes. "My grams could have been hurt or worse in that fire. I can't leave them. Can't spend the remaining years we have together so many miles away."

"Changing your mind is not a basis for getting out of a contract," I say, nodding. "I'm so sorry. You probably feel trapped."

She looks at me suspiciously. "I did, still do." She wrinkles up the tissue in her hand. "My lawyer told me there is no way out of the Culinary Capital contract. Everything is legit, which is why they signed off on it in the first place. I told them they had to find a way out, so we filed the injunction. I know I can't get out of the deal for good, but my lawyers said they can delay things for at least one year."

She tosses the shredded tissue into a small trash bin by the desk and stares at me. "So, if you're here to get to me to change my mind, it won't happen. I'll give you the money you spent on the ticket to get in here, and you can go."

She stands up and looks like she's going to storm out when I hold up a hand. "Please, Audrina. Wait. I told you I thought I had a solution. Can you hear me out? Please?"

She looks me over skeptically but eventually nods. "All right."

We talk for the next forty-five minutes. I feel terrible taking her away from the event, but if we can sort this out now, it will be the solution to both of our problems. To the problems of a whole lot of people.

I answer all of her questions and ask a bunch of my own. We disagree about a lot, and at times, we raise our voices so loud, I'm worried that someone from the event will hear. But by the time I have the information I need, we're on calm, if not friendly, ground.

Now, I just need to convince my boss that this will work.

I make my way through the noisy crowd at Pancake Circus, nodding to Nathan as I show myself out. My first instinct is to text Benny, so while I wait for the rideshare to take me back to my hotel, I send him a message.

Me: What do you think about me sticking around in Star Falls? Like for good?

Instead of a text back, my phone rings.

"Are you serious?" he asks. "What's going on? How'd it go in Florida?"

"Well, I'm still here," I tell him. "I'm headed up to see Jessa tomorrow morning. But so far, so good. I'm cautiously optimistic that I can make this work."

"Who do I have to bribe?" he asks. "Because if it means you staying in Star Falls…"

I grin. "Hopefully it won't come to under-the-table deals," I laugh. "There are going to be so many lawyers looking this deal over..." I sigh. "It's scary, Benny."

"What part?" he asks. "The lawyers? Talking to your boss?"

All of it, I think. Commitment. Giving up the familiar. Putting myself out there in such a big way that I realistically don't know if I can ever come back from this decision.

As if reading my silence, Benny says, "All of it?"

I laugh. "Yeah, honestly. All of it. How's Mags?"

"Good," he says. "She's a fucking genius with spreadsheets and shit. Honestly, babe, I should have asked for help years ago. I feel like an asshole, seeing how much she got done in only one morning. One fucking morning."

"Old dogs can learn new tricks," I say, stepping off the curb as my rideshare shows up.

"Yeah, but this old dog is younger than you, babe," he reminds me.

"We going there?" I ask him.

"I am completely, totally, head over heels excited about having you in every way possible," he croons, his voice curling around my ears like a song. "When you coming home, babe? I miss you already."

"A week," I tell him. "I don't think I'll need much longer."

"Send me nudes every night to hold me over?" he asks.

I burst out laughing and wave at the rideshare driver who looks up at me in the rearview mirror. "I have to go," I tell Benny. "But I will send what you asked for."

"Yesss," he hisses. "I knew I loved you. Bye, babe."

"Bye, Benny."

As I end the call, I look behind us at the enormous faded sign for Pancake Circus as it grows smaller the farther away we drive. Then I look out the window, settling back in my seat. This driver is a lot chattier than the last.

"Did you go to the Kincades' fundraiser?" the woman asks. "Terrible tragedy. Such a good family."

I nod. "It is, and yes," I say. "They are a good family. The very best."

I stare out the window the rest of the way to my hotel. Unlike most trips I take, I'm not chatting up the driver. Not anxious to learn about the local food scene, the cuisine, the weather. My mind is on other places. Like the place I'm going to start calling home.

Five days later, I hug Jessa goodbye from the ottoman where I've been sitting with her since I arrived. I place a hand on her belly and wish the little guy a long and happy stay in his mama's belly.

"I'm so glad you visited," Jessa says, tears already falling down her cheeks. "God, I wish you could stay. I'll give you half this kid. We can be like those friends who adopt a baby and raise it together. Co-parents."

I wipe the tears from my cheeks and then hand her a tissue. "I would," I tell her. "In fact, if you'd asked me six months ago, I might have even said yes."

"Damn that sexy chef who stole your heart. Platonic co-parent homewrecker, that's what he is." Jessa rubs a hand over her belly. "You could have all this," she says wistfully. "Diaper blowouts and spit-up. Instead, you chose orgasms and great food. I just don't get it."

"Come visit me?" I ask her. "I know it will be hard with the baby, but I don't want to lose touch."

I'm getting emotional now. So much is changing so fast, not only in my life, but in Jessa's.

"How the hell would we lose touch? Our whole friendship, except for the one year you lived here, has happened over video. You think I'm going to forget how to video chat once I have a kid?" She pushes her long, dark hair back from her face. I've been washing it in a basin every day since I arrived because she really struggles to get up and stand in the shower. I've done so much to take care of her while I've been visiting, but now that I'm leaving, I realize how much she won't have and will have to do without when I'm gone. I think about all the millions of moments I've lost not being physically present with the people I love, always on the road, always moving on to the next adventure.

"I'll come visit you too," I tell her. "You're a priority, and I want this baby to know who his other mother is."

"Oh no." Jessa shakes her head. "Your co-parental rights have already been terminated. You get to be the cool aunt, though."

"I can handle that."

Jessa's mom comes in to let me know the car is here to take me to the airport. I kneel on the carpet and wrap my arms around Jessa. "I love you," I tell her through tears. "And I'm so happy for you. You're the best mom and the best friend."

"I'm so proud of you," Jessa whispers through her tears. "You are settling down, but you're not settling, Willow. I think you're finally making your own happy ending." She releases me and pats her belly. "I made mine. Now go on and get yours. And video chat me when you get to Chicago."

I kiss her, hug her two more times, and make Jessa's mom promise to call me the minute she goes into labor. Then I climb into another car and head to yet another airport. I'm off to try to convince Theresa and Rosemarie Ginetti to let me take the biggest risk of my career yet.

CHAPTER TWENTY

benito

One year later...

"Pops. Ma. Would you hurry up?" I nervously check my phone for the time. Today is the grand opening, and I need to be in two places at once. "Ma!" I holler again, but this time, I stop, images of my parents getting it on flashing through my mind. "Oh, for fuck's sake. I'm leaving," I call. "Don't you dare come down here unless you're fully dressed."

The door to the basement opens, and my pops comes up into the dining room, chuckling. "I really scarred you for life, eh, son?" He's wearing dress pants and a nice shirt, his glasses low on his nose. "I was trying to print out the receipt you sent me just in case your contractor needs it."

I soften the edges of my voice, relieved that I did not, once again, interrupt my parents' coitus. "Thank God," I tell him. "But don't worry. Mags handled all that yesterday. We've got this under control. I just need you guys to come with me."

Ma comes practically tumbling down the stairs, a pair of heels in her hand. "What's all the hollering about?" she asks. "Are we late? Benny, I thought we had tons of time?"

I kiss Ma and take the heels from her so she can grab her phone

CHELLE BLISS

and purse. "We do, but I want to get there early for Willow. Come on. I need you guys to get moving."

My parents trade looks but don't argue. We head out to my SUV, and I hear Ma asking my dad, "Why again do we have to drive with Benny? Why can't we take our truck?"

"It's a surprise, Ma," I holler, unlocking the SUV.

On the drive over, my parents talk, but my mind is racing. Pancake Circus died a year ago. The dream of it and the reality. Willow went to Chicago to try to convince her bosses to let the Kincade family out of the deal. Willow offered to take Audrina's place. To stay in Star Falls and run the restaurant, while Audrina stayed on as a consultant, allowing her to stay in Florida with her family.

But between the lawyers and the Ginetti sisters, that deal was a no-go. But Willow wouldn't give up.

She went full throttle into the problem, arguing why it would be better for the Ginettis to terminate the deal and let the Kincades out than to litigate and waste a lot of money and time. After a lot of legal wrangling and after the Kincades agreed to pay a crapload of money to repay a portion of the expenses it would require for Culinary Capital to start over, the old deal was canceled. No more Pancake Circus in Star Falls. But a new deal was signed in its place.

Willow Watkins quit her position as COO of Culinary Creations. And she entered into an agreement with Culinary Creations as a client. Willow is now the proud owner of her very own breakfast and brunch restaurant here in Star Falls. Her consulting executive chef, yours truly, was paid a handsome sum to help create an original menu since the Kincades did not want to license any of their recipes as part of the termination agreement.

Thanks to the generous consulting fee I received, I was able to give Mags a nice raise, pay for a new roof over at Benito's, and buy a couple of extras. Both of which I'm hoping to unveil today.

We pull into the pristine blacktop of the Pancake Paradise parking lot. Willow's car is already there, along with a dozen others. She picked a weekday to host a friends and family only soft open of the restaurant, so the crowd is small. But I see a familiar face pushing a stroller in circles in the parking lot, so I tell my parents to join me as soon as they can.

I run across the lot and give a big hug to Willow's best friend, Jessa.

"I'm so glad you could make it," I tell her, hugging her tight.

"You promised me ravioli," she says, hugging me hard. "What woman could resist that?"

I bend down to little Walker, who is red-faced and squirming in his seat. "Have you seen Auntie Willow yet, little man?"

"Oh yes," Jessa says. "We came out here because I need a break. I'm looking at those two bonus grandparents for some relief."

Jessa points to Ma and Pops, who already have their arms out to pick up Walker.

"Good," I say. "I'll see you inside."

I turn to head inside the restaurant, patting my phone as it vibrates with a text.

Mags: It's all ready. And it's covered, but I saw it, Benny. Fuck, it's beautiful.

Just seeing the words, I know my life is about to change even more.

Me: Love it, thank you. C u soon.

Inside Pancake Paradise, I'm shocked to see my whole family is already here. I'm amazed to see everyone not only present and on time but looking as excited as I feel.

I make the rounds of the room, hugging Franco and Chloe, who stand together holding hands, Chloe beaming like today is her grand opening and not Willow's. That's what I love so much about Chloe. She's so, so sweet and so loving. Her peanut butter crisps are on display on the front counter—another way we were able to pay forward the good fortune as part of the deal with Culinary Creations. Chloe licensed her recipe to Willow to include the amazing cookies on the menu.

"Happy for you, bro," Franco says, clapping me on the back. "It's a great day for our family."

I shush him because God knows my fucking brother and his big mouth will blab before Ma and Pops see the surprise. "Thanks, man," I say, and then I point to Chloe. "Don't let him fuck this up, okay?"

She laughs and loops her arm through Franco's, then silences him with a kiss.

"That'll work," I say, heading over to Gracie next.

"Not bad," Gracie says, a huge smile on her face. "Not bad at all."

"Not bad," I mock her, repeating her words. I point to the walls vibrantly painted with murals in each section of the huge restaurant. Incredibly detailed palm trees and flowers cover the walls, and in the kid-friendly play area, life-sized monkeys, zebras, parrots, and elephants come to life, thanks to Gracie's art. "Couldn't have done this without you, sis."

I hug Gracie and hold her tight. Ryder, Gracie's husband, is sitting next to his buddy, Austin. We chat about Gracie's artwork until I feel a slap on the back of my head.

"Hey, dumbass." I turn to face Vito, who's looking at me with a goofy grin plastered on his face. "When's breakfast?"

"Oh my God, man." I give him a punch to the ribs, then a brotherly hug. Eden and Junie are over in the kids' area, playing with Gracie's three kids. I wave and blow them kisses, relieved when I see Ma and Pops wandering over with little Walker. When I turn back, Gracie is introducing Jessa to Austin.

We're all here.

Everybody but one.

I walk back into the kitchen and find her. Willow's silky blond hair is up in a bun, and she's wearing a chef's coat over a dress as she talks with her staff.

"Remember, everyone," she says, clasping her hands in front of her chest, "I am so, so happy to have you all on my team. Let's have some fun and make some great food."

When she turns to leave and she sees me, her face lights up. She practically runs for me and throws herself against my chest.

"Nervous?" I ask, kissing the top of her head. Even though we already had this talk when we woke up this morning, I know how different it is to have hungry stomachs waiting and a crew at the ovens ready to go.

"Happy," she says. "Surprisingly un-nervous." She rises on her toes and whispers in my ear. "A morning of orgasms definitely helped chill me out."

I kiss her lightly. "Just doing my part."

The lease on Willow's condo is up in two weeks, and she's decided to move in with me. We both love the building, and Jessa and Walker are going to crash in her place while they're here to celebrate the soft open. The last year has flown by, but if one thing hasn't changed, it's how I feel about Willow. If anything, I love her and want her as much, if not more, than I did a year ago.

So much so, in fact, that I've made a few changes of my own.

Our family and friends order off the menu, give Willow feedback on the dishes, and congratulate the chefs on the opening. Everything is delicious, and while there are a few minor delays, some cold toast and warm milk that need addressing, Pancake Paradise is ready for business.

By the time we're done eating, my family all heads out, pretending they have to get to work and other places. My folks stay back since they are riding with me to our next destination. But before we go, I need a minute alone with Willow.

I see Mags walk in, and I wave her over.

"I know you want to get to cleaning and debriefing with your staff, but I asked Mags to come by to supervise and train." Willow looks confused, but she's nodding. "Can I talk to you in your office for a second?"

She gives me a look but agrees and heads back to the small, perfectly orderly space that is her new office. As soon as she shuts the door, I pull her into my arms.

"Baby," I say. "I don't want to take away from your big day, but I have two surprises for you." I chuckle. "Well, I guess depending on how the first one goes, there may only be one surprise, but we'll see."

She looks at me, puzzled, but as soon as I get down on one knee, her mouth drops open.

"Willow, you're the love of my life, and you know how much I love my restaurant." I laugh, and she covers her mouth, her eyes glossy with tears. "The day I met you was the day I knew you were different. No other woman sucked my dick in the shower like you did."

"Benny." She's crying now, a smile on her face, and pulls me to standing. "What are you doing?"

"I want you to marry me, babe. Spend your life with me. Make amazing food, amazing memories, and even better orgasms." I lean down to kiss her. "If you tell people about this later…"

She is full-body cry-laughing now. "After what I've seen of your parents' sex life, I hardly think they'd be shocked."

"Oh," I tell her, then reach into the pocket of my jacket to pull out a small velvet box. "Also, I got you a ring."

She's doubled over now with laughter. "At least you didn't propose with a plate of ravioli."

"Would that have worked?" I ask. "Because it would've been a whole lot cheaper."

"Give me that," she says, taking the box from me. She opens it to reveal an oval-shaped diamond with two star-shaped diamond clusters on either side. "Oh, Benny."

I take the box from her and slide the ring over her finger. "I hope this means you're saying yes, because if not, the next part of the surprise is going to really suck."

"Yes," she says, throwing herself into my arms. "Yes, yes."

I pick her up and swing her around, then set her on her feet and take her hand.

"Okay, we can celebrate later. Next surprise."

I pull her from the office into the restaurant, where my parents are waiting for us. "Ma, Pops," I say as we approach them. "I have two more surprises for you…" I hold out Willow's hand, where her ring sparkles on her finger. "First, you're getting another daughter."

My ma squeals—I'm talking shrieks—and grabs Willow in the tightest hug ever. Pops has to break in between the tears and the rocking to congratulate Willow, but I'm already headed for the door. "Come on, come on. Next surprise. Let's go."

Ma, Pops, and Willow look confused, but they follow me to the

SUV. They chatter among themselves, all three of them together in the backseat while I make the quick drive over to my restaurant. Well, it was my restaurant. I find my own eyes stinging as I pull into the parking lot. My entire family and all our friends have made the trip here for the second surprise. My whole staff, Sassy, Jasmine, Rita, Carla, Duncan—everybody but Mags, who agreed to hold down the fort at Pancake Paradise for a couple of hours so I could orchestrate this whole day. She'll celebrate with us later. She knows I couldn't have done any of this without her.

In addition to our family, I invited my ma's friends, Carol and Bev, so we could all be together for this special announcement.

Once we're all together, gathered in the parking lot of my restaurant, I take Willow's hand and drag her to the front of the crowd. I don't have a mic, but I don't need one. Everyone's fallen silent, waiting and watching.

"Everybody. Thanks for being willing to go along with the surprise. I have excellent news." I hold up Willow's hand. "She said yes."

Jessa screams from beside Ryder's friend Austin, and I have to wait until the hugs and tears and congratulations die down before I can get to the next part.

I wipe a tear from my own eye, my emotions really getting to me now that everyone is here and the moment has finally come.

"First of all," I say, "I want to thank you all, my family and friends, who have supported me throughout the years I've owned Benito's. I've missed a lot of time with a demanding mistress—" I motion toward the restaurant "—but it only prepared me, I hope, to be the best possible husband to this angel."

I kiss the back of Willow's hand and have to pause to collect myself. I wipe yet another tear from my cheek as I turn to face the cord keeping the tarp covering the Benito's sign in place. When I give the cord a yank, the tarp falls away, revealing a brand-new sign. The name on the sign is no longer Benito's. The sign reads Bianchi's Family Eatery.

My ma immediately bursts into tears, and Willow gasps.

My voice cracks a little as I continue. "Over the last year, I've

741

had a lot of help making my business better than it has ever been. And it's more than I ever thought it could be. Thanks to all of you, for all the work you've done, the love you've shown me, and the time you've spent even just eating my food, Benito's is better than ever. And this seemed like the perfect time to make a change that reflects what I believe is Benito's future. A future more focused on family. On the beauty and love that we share. Of every blessing and good thing we have because we have one another."

There's not a sound as my family and friends look at me, their expressions ranging from shocked to proud.

I clap my hands. "Well, that's it, people. A new sign. And I'm engaged. Let's celebrate."

Willow laces her fingers through mine and lifts up on her toes to kiss me. The next hour passes in a blur of congratulations, well-wishes, expressions of love, and a hell of a lot of teasing about what I did with the old sign, the one with my name on it.

Truth be told, I threw it out. Because if I've learned anything over the past few years, it's that there is no me without the people I love. Without my siblings and their spouses and kids, who bring my life such richness. Without my parents, whose unfailing love for their family is the foundation of every value I have. Without my friends and all the people in the Star Falls community who make the life I have and the work I do so joyful.

And last but not least, Willow.

She may have taken a long road to find me, but nothing we each had to go through was too much to bear, too much to experience. Because now that we have each other, our work, and so much love in our lives, this is not the end of our story.

It's just the beginning.

become a member of the family...

Want a place to talk romance books, meet other bookworms, and all things Men of Inked? Join Chelle Bliss Books on Facebook to get sneak peeks, exclusive news, and special giveaways.

Want to be the first to hear about the next Men of Inked book or everything Chelle Bliss? Join my newsletter by visiting _menofinked.com/inked-news_ or scan the QR code below.

What to read next...

LOOKING FOR A NEW FAMILY SAGA?

Start the Original Men of Inked Series

Learn more at ***menofinked.com/inked-v1***
or visit ***chelleblissromance.com*** to purchase a
signed copy to add to your personal collection.

LOVE AUDIOBOOKS?

ABOUT THE AUTHOR

I'm a full-time writer, time-waster extraordinaire, social media addict, coffee fiend, and ex-history teacher. *To learn more about my books, please visit menofinked.com.*

Want to stay up-to-date on the newest Men of Inked release and more? Tap here to join my newsletter or visit *menofinked.com/inked-news*

Join over 10,000 readers on Facebook in Chelle Bliss Books private reader group and talk books and all things reading. Tap here to become part of the family or visit at *facebook.com/groups/blisshangout*

Tap here to see the Gallo Family Tree or visit *menofinked.com/gallo-family-tree*

Where to Follow Me:

- facebook.com/authorchellebliss1
- instagram.com/authorchellebliss
- bookbub.com/authors/chelle-bliss
- goodreads.com/chellebliss
- amazon.com/author/chellebliss
- tiktok.com/@chelleblissauthor
- pinterest.com/chellebliss10

www.ingramcontent.com/pod-product-compliance
Lightning Source LLC
Chambersburg PA
CBHW010738130726
47899CB00015B/3466